THE BIG KIDS

Robert Hennemuth

Llumina Press

Cover Design by Kaye Veazey

ISBN: 1-59526-125-7
        1-59526-124-9
Printed in the United States of America by Llumina Press

Library of Congress Cataloging-in-Publication Data

Hennemuth, Robert.
The big kids / Robert Hennemuth. p. cm.
ISBN 1-59526-124-9 (alk. paper) -- ISBN 1-59526-125-7
(pbk. : alk. paper) 1. College students--Fiction. 2.
Ithaca (N.Y.)--Fiction. I. Title.
PS3608.E56B54 2004
813'.6--dc22   2004025218

AUTHOR'S NOTE

I could not have written this book without the extraordinary freedom and unflagging support provided by my wife, Paula. Similarly, my children offered their encouragements and left me alone to write when there was always so much else to do. I am indebted to Emilie Barmashi, Laura Ritz, Dick Baker, and Randy Robinson, whose early reactions and thoughtful reading gave me new insights and ideas. Numerous family and friends also helped me with open-minded feedback and genuine succor. I am especially grateful to Anne (and, in particular, for some wonderful line edits), Kaye, G.I., Fred, Laurie, Swuftie, Frank and Al. In the end, this story is intended as a fond remembrance to my brothers, and a love song to my wife. I will have succeeded if it is received as such.

RH

CHAPTER ONE

October, 1973

At five-feet, ten-inches, with waist-length auburn hair and deeply freckled skin, Caitlin Fossburgher was hard to miss as she strode purposefully through the Arts Quad on her way to the Women's Gymnasium on North Campus. Wednesday was her favorite day of the week because she could take her time getting to her next class, warm up, and watch George come flying into the room late and breathless from having run there from the engineering quad. Caitlin had only known George for a month but she loved him, although neither of them had used that word yet. They had met at the callback board for the major play try-outs in September, when neither of them had been chosen for second auditions.

She also loved their teacher for Dance & Movement For Theater, a class she had switched into after the first week of classes, when George told her about it. When Caitlin got to class the room was already filling, primarily with the graduate theater students for whom the class was a requirement. Caitlin stripped down to her tights and began stretching on the bright wooden floor in front of the floor-to-ceiling mirrors.

Across campus, George raced across the Arts Quad, between the theatre building and the stately, domed Architecture building with *Happy Birthday Goodluck* scrawled in black paint across the dome. He had thirteen minutes to go from Ancient Civ to Dance & Movement, pull off his pants, stretch into his tights and slip on the ballet slippers. He hated how he would be sweating by the time he got to class, but if he didn't jog most of the way he'd be late, and Peggy Verne frowned when he was late.

Peggy Verne, modern dancer and teacher, clapped her hands to quiet her students and then gave them a moment more to stretch. It was late October, and beyond the windows of the Women's Gymnasium on North Campus, the upstate sky was a fetid grey shadow streaked with a slight mist. The dance studio was made bright by the lighting and the mirrors and the energy of her students straining in their limited ways to impress her with their work.

It was not a serious dance instruction class. Her students were mostly graduate theater students and a few undergrads trying to improve their stage movement skills and fulfill their phys-ed requirement for graduation. Some were earnest, some just biding time, and it was incredibly hard to tell who was who.

At forty-two, her body was not as taut but her figure was every inch as graceful as when she flew across the stage of the New York Ballet. When she taught the dance majors in the other classes she was strict, disciplined and short tempered, but this class allowed her to laugh and nurture her students with a number of improvisational modern dance assignments. She threw in plies and leaps more for exercise than skill.

Peggy loved the rich subtext within this class, too. Theater students spent all of their waking and many of their sleeping moments together, which made for wonderful interplay between them when they were deprived of their voices on the dance floor. They were also extroverted, inventive and fragile. The older students - mostly professional actors coming to hide in a graduate program and hone their skills and resumes - had impassively weary and rubbery faces, except perhaps the graduate student she now asked to perform. His hard, narrow face underneath his mop of deep red hair left Peggy with the distinct impression that he would be a bastard to live with.

The graduate student moved to the center of the shiny wooden floor to dance, as George Muirfield slid through the door and sat quickly on the floor. A slight veil of perspiration was evident on his forehead. Peggy smiled at George and raised her finger to her mouth, then nodded to Alex to continue. Even his dance made Alec seem hard and narrow to her, but Peggy appreciated how cleverly he invented his routine.

The student finished and the class applauded. He had leapt across the floor, turning razor-sharp corners and switching his frame from rigid to limp with beautiful fluidity. Peggy smiled, cooed to him how wonderful his performance was, and asked him to do it again. A scowl washed across his complexion but he shrugged and moved back to his starting position. Peggy leaned forward with her chin on her fist, her pale blue eyes slightly hooded. The student began again, tightened his body for his first leap and did a beautiful rendition of his first jump, followed by a swift glide to his left and a relaxed stutter step backwards toward the class. He twirled, stopped, looked left and from there began to plie, but then abruptly stopped. There was a silence as the students watched Peggy smile and admonish him. Dance assignments must be practiced and repeatable, not improvisational, she said firmly. The student shrugged, and returned to his spot on the floor.

She asked a few others to go, and then asked George if he was ready. She knew he would be, and appreciated his earnest resolve to improve his modest skills. George took a position near a corner of the room, crouched into a ball with his hands flat on the floor and paused. Peggy liked his sense of imagery and his use of the room, and sat attentively as he moved (too slowly she thought) as if he were a mime finding himself in a box. George then changed the image completely, moving like an animal hiding from something into the middle of the floor. Turning face forward to her for the first time, he stood motionless at an angle to the floor and moved his lips in circles, eyes closed, to the laughter of all in the room. Then he fell backwards in a careful flip and back into the ball he had started from, except on the other side of the room.

The class clapped lightly, and Peggy nodded as she urged George to think about adding more dance steps to his routine. There was time for one more, so she chose Caitlin, knowing as they all did that Caitlin and George were seeing each other. Caitlin was working much more on her classical dance skills, and for her assignment, she leapt and plied in a lithe, pleasing rhythm across the floor again and again, her hair pulled back in a makeshift braid. She became completely unconscious as she danced, swirling on a stage in her mind far away from the Women's Gymnasium on North Campus. When she finished Peggy clapped and said, I was right there with you Caitlin. Good job! The class was already pulling clothing on over their tights.

After Dance, Caitlin and George always walked back to the Green Dragon, the coffeehouse in the basement of the Architecture building, to sip Darjeeling tea (with honey for their throats) and share a fresh bagel with thick cream cheese for lunch. On their way, Caitlin talked about an exciting new version of *Oedipus Rex* that Derek Steele had announced he would direct in the spring. A three credit course was going to be offered for students to be in the chorus. As they walked, they held hands without looking often at each other, in the way that couples do who share a comfortable secret between them.

As they neared the Green Dragon, George told Caitlin about his fraternity visits the weekend before, making her laugh at his mimicry of the people he had met. Caitlin did not understand George's recent interest in fraternities, and she didn't take his preoccupation seriously. Along with her, he was clearly becoming part of the theater crowd, and would no doubt quickly lose interest in this frat stuff. No one in theater would dare admit some curiosity about the fraternity system, let alone a genuine interest in joining.

Inside the coffeehouse, Caitlin saw an open table as they entered and headed for it without a word. George went to stand in line asking over his shoulder if she wanted their usual. She took off her quilted jacket and put it over the back of her chair, and looked around the room to see if other actors were there.

On the Arts Quad there were two coffeehouses. The Temple of Zeus in the basement of Goldwyn Smith Hall was filled with full-sized replicas of famous Greek sculptures and was the favorite of English, art history and government majors. The Green Dragon was more bohemian and run-down, and attracted architects and theater and music students.

George was joining her with their cups of tea and a huge, fresh poppy seed bagel, as three graduate students from their dance class entered and took a table along side of theirs. Everyone spoke excitedly about Derek Steele's plans for *Oedipus*, and wondered who might be right for the roles of Oedipus and his father, both of which would clearly go to graduate students.

Catherine Marsden, a slender, pale-skinned twenty-three year old graduate student leaned back in her chair, laid her head against George's shoulder and bemoaned the lack of strong female parts in the play. George knew that Catherine spent a lot of time with Derek Steele but was unsure if they were romantically involved. He wondered whether she would want to be directed by Derek. He tried to picture Caitlin directing him, and thought they would fight.

Caitlin leaned across Christopher Haskins, the dark, bearded actor who would be chosen to play the father, to talk with his best friend Alec. It was always this way with actors, George thought, with Catherine's head nestled against him and Caitlin's hand planted firmly on Christopher's leg. There was a natural ambiguity to the physical boundaries between them, and George was not yet fully comfortable with it all. In the class-room and in rehearsals, actors serious about their craft spent their waking moments being parts of each other. Teachers asked them to do improvisational exercises lying in piles on the floor, or wrapped around each other, in order to create tension or lust or whatever emotion might be called for.

To play a character in method acting required each of them to break down their egos and their bodies into dozens of parts and then reconstruct them around a new character. The older students thought nothing of nudity – it was simply there, and being naked with each other, even in a bed, often did not mean anything except that they were naked, and in bed.

George was fascinated with this apparent numbness of being. He pursued it intensely in the belief that it would help him to be a better actor, but he was still confused and misled by its trappings. When Catherine put her head on his shoulder, he could not help but feel the familiar whirl of flirtation and curiosity. When Caitlin left her hand on Christopher's leg, George's territorial anger made his shoulders hunch. And practiced actors such as the man Caitlin leaned upon immediately sensed George's possessive jealousy, and smiled benignly toward him, which only confused him more.

Still, George was thrilled by the camaraderie he and Caitlin shared with the graduate students. They had both landed parts in one-act plays directed by graduate students for course credits. Because they were taking the dance class and acting in the plays they felt connected to the small circle of theater people. Caitlin had secured a non-singing role in an unusual one-act play that was part opera, and the graduate student she spoke with now was her director. For a moment, George watched the director's hands moving emphatically in circles while the two spoke, his eyes pulling Caitlin's into his, and he couldn't stand it. So he looked away to watch the people behind the counter pour coffee and put muffins in wax paper bags.

It was Wednesday, he was already five-hundred pages behind in his other subjects for the week, and he had rehearsals every day from five to nine at night. Catherine, whose head felt so good on his shoulder, was the bride he was unhappy to be giving away in his one-act play, though they shared no scenes, or even lines together. It was a cold and distant story about narrow minded characters living in Stalin's Russia, and George was having trouble understanding how to become his character, who never moved from his dining room chair on the stage, except to stand rigidly to address a family who did not listen to him.

Come on G, Caitlin said, we've got to go. She stood up, pulling on her coat. Caitlin liked to call George, "G" because she didn't care much for his name. "G" had a cheekier ring to it. George eased Catherine off his shoulder, rose to follow Caitlin, and told Catherine he'd see her tonight. Catherine smiled, said, See ya dad, and turned to the others. When George and Caitlin climbed the little concrete steps outside the coffeehouse, they were greeted by a bleak sunshine in the warmest part of the day.

Cornell University, founded in 1865 by Ezra Cornell, sprawls across an enormous acreage on the highest hill in Ithaca, New York. From numerous vantage points, Cayuga Lake can be viewed stretching to the northwest, but the profound, natural beauty of the university stems from two deep gorges that cut dramatic swaths east to west through the campus. On the north side, water rushes from Beebe Lake down Fall Creek Gorge, hundreds of feet below the bridge that unites North Campus with the Arts Quad. Not far from the edge of Fall Creek Gorge, at the original northern edge of campus, large, private properties were developed in the late 1800s and early 1900s as a result of Ithaca's brief period as the Hollywood of the East. Silent film stars, directors and producers built homes, and the transcontinental railroad was routed through Ithaca from New York on its way west, to serve the film industry as well as the agricultural basin of upstate New York. This was all before talkies and Hollywood eclipsed the town's celluloid sun.

By the time the movie industry began to migrate west to Hollywood, Ezra Cornell's dream of an institution where any person could find instruction in any course of study had been planted on land grants from the state of New York, taken hold, and sprouted. The first Ivy League school to grant admission to women quickly outgrew its buildings and as the film stars headed west to Hollywood, fraternities and sororities moved into their now vacant homes, and offered new housing alternatives to the swelling classrooms of students.

George Muirfield knew none of this when his roommate first convinced him to spend an afternoon looking at fraternities during informal rush. He had no expectations whatsoever, and was therefore taken aback at the ornate grandeur of the houses. There were tall, dramatic houses perched on the edges of gorges, and stately homes with pillared porches and large, wainscoted rooms. But inside these homes, the fraternity brothers rarely matched their surroundings. Gawky, awkward boys with slide rules in their pockets stammered when asked the simplest of questions. Jocular, athletic boys talked endlessly of sports. Rich young men swirled about wearing sweater vests and laughing loudly. Serious intellectuals spoke sarcastically about life, college, and existentialism.

So when his roommate asked George to go with him for the second informal rush tea to see more houses, he almost said no. The first time had been a lark, and it was true that fraternities fit George's notion of what college should be. But George put far more stock in what came to him than what he might go seek. To this point in his life, his future always seemed to find and guide him. When his peers declared that they were going to be this or that, George simply shrugged. He had not chosen his parents, his upbringing, his life. His path was unknown to him, but it was already laid out in time. He had no more control over it than the rain. And knowing this was not only comforting, it was freeing. Surety replaced doubt. Fate would reveal itself to George, and his obligation was simply to give himself to it.

George highly doubted that fraternities would make the cut. Caitlin and the theater cooed to him and tugged at his soul; the confluence of his life stream was rolling elsewhere. Otherwise, the fraternities would have resonated more for him. They would have *beckoned* him.

And yet, when his roommate persisted, George decided to give it one more try. A small corner of him found fraternities intriguing. The houses had rhythms and subtexts that George could sense but not parse. There was a knowingness, a richness, in the glances exchanged between the brothers as they spoke to the freshmen that rang true somewhere deep inside George. Something was at work; he just wasn't sure it was for him. Years later, he would not remember and even stoutly deny his ambivalence; yet it is precisely these seemingly innocuous choices that enable fate to lead us to unforgettable places.

In life, the glorious pastiche of one's memories is inevitably marked by certain people whose character or appearance or words penetrate through to the soul. They are the people we remember vividly decades after they have left our lives, whose faces and antics, once recalled from some crevice in the brain, elicit an unexpected gush of fondness and melancholy. It is, of course, as much who we were when we knew them that made them so special, but it is them we remember.

When George Muirfield accompanied his roommate to the second informal rush teas in November, he had no idea that the boy standing at the door to Eta Chi would etch in his memory. Will Houghton, known as "Huff" to his brothers in Eta Chi fraternity, watched the two roommates approach him and grinned widely as he went to shake George's hand. When George was still three steps away, the senior lifted his hand, palm straight up and arm outstretched, until it came between their two faces. George being taller, Will Houghton's hand hovered above his own head. To meet his grip, George brought his own hand even higher, palm down, which Huff vigorously grasped and shook first forward and backward on the same plane, before firmly guiding their hands down on a slight angle to the level of their chests where he continued the thrusting motion with vigor.

Huff was standing in the doorway because, as rush chairman of the fraternity, he was responsible for the orchestration and execution of the fraternity's recruitment process. It was an honor he had looked forward to for months, and one he took with total seriousness. So as he gripped George's hand, he stated his full name warmly and enthusiastically, and looked intensely into George's eyes, searching. Although potential pledges would be thoroughly vetted by the entire brotherhood, Huff believed that the weight of the house rested on his shoulders. It was his obligation to look below the surface, into the very core of each freshman, to find the distinctive glint of character needed to become an Eta Chi.

Competition for freshmen grew intense between the top ten to fifteen houses, and he was well aware that in the past two years, Eta Chi had not lost a single pledge to another house. The house had made twenty-six bids two years ago, and twenty-six students had chosen Eta Chi over competing bids from other strong houses. The following year, only twenty-three students out of the hundreds who came through the rush process had made it through the brothers' vetting process and been offered bids, and twenty-three had accepted. So Huff felt obligated to not only find the right freshmen, but also to win over every single one of them.

At this point in the process, Huff ruled people out, not in, and his initial read on George Muirfield was acceptable, so he abruptly turned to Stephen Dawn and lifted his hand up to Stephen's nose. George watched with fascination as Huff took Stephen's measure at the same time he thrust their hands back and forth with equal vigor. They had been to a number of other fraternities, but there was something markedly different at work here. Handshakes finally completed, Huff gestured stiffly toward the house, introducing them immediately to a tall, broad-shouldered student who was a little heavy in the waist. Bob Woodbridge wore a brown hunting vest and his large, muscular arms moved loosely and expressively as he spoke. His face was strong and ruddy, and he had a deep, raspy voice that was oddly pleasing.

What houses have you seen so far? Bob asked the two freshmen. They told him and he nodded vigorously, looking carefully at each of them. Those are great houses, Bob told them. You should give them serious consideration. You might also want to look at Phi Psi or Alpha

Omega, Bob Woodbridge continued. Those are both houses we compete with.

But let me introduce you to our house, he went on, and with that he pointed into an enormous, rectangular great room with a large fire burning in a walk-in stone fireplace against the front wall. Opposite the fireplace, where seven or eight people stood conversing, there were three groups of people standing by French doors that looked out on a slate terrace. He took pains to note which of Cornell's seven colleges various brothers were in and the extra curricular activities they pursued. Stephen asked about the history of the house, and Bob Woodbridge told them about Desdemona Bishop, the famous silent film star who built the house and insisted on having a salt water pool. As Bob spoke, he guided the two boys through the French doors to the terrace.

There, as they gazed downward at the empty pool and out into the valley beyond, Scotty approached them, already shivering from the cold air, and introduced himself. George was focused on Bob Woodbridge, listening to the words flow out of him in a resonant and confident rhythm, and it took him a moment to take in Scotty who seemed almost frail standing next to his fraternity brother. For every careful, precise breath Scotty took, Bob breathed vigorously through his nose, and yet the two bantered lightly in an almost practiced way about their house and themselves. Bob was going to be a writer and Scotty an engineer, they explained, as they moved Stephen and George through the house into the dining area and introduced them to four brothers standing together near the kitchen door. Then they thanked Stephen and George for coming, shook hands and walked back toward the foyer.

The four new brothers quickly divided into pairs, and the first two escorted Stephen upstairs to see the sleeping rooms, while George remained in the dining room with a short, gruff senior in the Agriculture College, and a blond, fresh-faced sophomore in the Arts & Sciences College. They asked George what he had been doing at school so far and he told them about acting in a one-act play, which neither seemed interested in, and how he had almost tried out for crew. The senior smiled and told George about 150s football that he had played for the last four years, and how much he loved it. The sophomore excused himself quietly and returned in a minute with L.E.O. Pennington, a tall, slender boy with long hair, who waited politely for Art to finish a story about football before telling George he had heard he was interested in theater.

Unlike most of the people George had met so far, L.E.O. Pennington's eyes did not glisten or glow intensely. They were hazel, and deep, and tended to scan rather than pierce. George could not tell if theater was the best or worst thing he could have mentioned. But he looked intently at L.E.O. Pennington and told him with pride about his current work playing the father in Chekhov's one act play, *The Wedding*. L.E.O. listened quietly and the two drifted apart from the others, back to the great hall where the fire still roared, and L.E.O. told him about his love of theater and the performing arts.

George brought the conversation back to the fraternity, asking whether L.E.O. liked this house. L.E.O.smiled, saying, This is a very interesting place, George, and it's worthy of your consideration, but I always tell freshmen to ask themselves a question. Where do you see yourself in your life? What adjectives describe the kind of place that calls you? He looked up at the rafters that held the massive ceiling above the great hall, before he went on. He was still staring over his head as he said, Many people are drawn to this house, but only a small number are destined to join. Every year lots of freshmen think they want to join Eta Chi, but most have paid no attention to which house is really calling them.

You mean, George asked, that more people want to join than you have room for? Yeah, L.E.O. replied, that's true too. George considered L.E.O. for a moment, smiling. He didn't know what to make of L.E.O. Pennington, and hoped it was time to leave.

It was cold and rainy as George and Stephen made their way back to campus, and they stopped halfway across the suspension bridge to watch the water rush below their feet. Autumn in Ithaca begins in August and last until November, when the freezing rains foretell the coming snows. October is lustrous; chilly winds and the dramatic colors of dying leaves make the continually gray skies bright with contrast.

Both boys were struck by how unusual their visit to Eta Chi had been. Eta Chi seemed forbidding, almost taunting. Why, for example, did the writer guy on the terrace tell them that they should look seriously at other houses? They agreed that it was less comfortable than the other places they had visited, and more formal. Stephen said he felt like he had been interrogated. By contrast, they thought the brothers at Phi Delta – the house they had seen just prior to Eta Chi – had been warm, welcoming, without pretense. Still, Eta Chi was a majestic structure. Stephen assured George it would be an incredibly cool place to live.

The suspension bridge, they had been told, was the project of an architecture student in 1957 whose professor told him that a suspension bridge could not be constructed over the gorge. The student set out to prove the professor wrong, and the suspension bridge was now a walkway across the gorge that united Cayuga Heights with the campus. It was where freshmen were supposed to get their first kiss at college, and it was flanked on both sides by netting to prevent people from "gorging" themselves.

Cornell was known as a pressure school, and legend had it that, next to some school in Texas, more students committed suicide by jumping into the gorge than any other school. George assumed this was why the school felt compelled to put netting on either side of the suspension bridge, although he thought it incongruous that this constant reminder of suicide would be the spot where you were supposed to get your first kiss.

In any event, he didn't understand why people seriously intent on jumping to their death wouldn't first jump into the netting and then roll out of it to accomplish their objective. But when he pointed this out to people, they looked at him oddly, so he stopped making a point he found obvious and slightly comical.

The water looks the same to me, George said from under the brim of his hood. He wore a bright yellow Sperry brand foul weather jacket, and felt warm except for his hands that dangled freely. Stephen had on a long overcoat and carried a brown striped umbrella that almost touched his head.

I think there is something special about Eta Chi, Stephen said after a moment. It had been cold and rainy all day, which had made each house they visited feel warmer. But now the day had turned dark, and the wind whistled through the gorge, chilling them. George shrugged, stamped his feet, and suggested they get going.

The cold wet damp worked its way under their jackets and George and Stephen walked in silence the entire way. Stephen was reliving the informal rush teas in his mind. He was excited to think that a fraternity could be more than a party house. He liked the image of finding people who wanted both to be serious about their academics *and* get drunk. After all, he said to himself, getting drunk seemed to be one thing he and George really had in common. Walking along beside Stephen, George was thinking about his history prelim, and what Caitlin was doing, and the upcoming play.

Caitlin Fossburgher lived in a single room in an experimental coed dormitory across West Campus from Boldt Hall. The dormitory was coed by room rather than floor, and there was precious little privacy there, which drove George crazy. A boy two doors down from Caitlin was constantly at her, and Caitlin just put up with him. He was an engineering student not ready for college who followed Caitlin up and down the hall, and even into the bathroom, talking to her while she sat in a stall or took a shower. Boys were supposed to use the bathroom on the other floor but no one followed the rules except first thing in the morning.

Whenever George pictured the boy in Caitlin's room it made him furious, but he tried not to let it show in front of her. When he came to see her, the boy would inevitably be sitting on her floor, and after an awkward few moments would leave with a pouty smirk on his puffy round face, and tell her he'd be back after George left. Caitlin just said he was harmless, and told George not to bother about him.

When George and Stephen got back to their room, George headed off to see if Caitlin was in her room and Stephen decided to get an early dinner in the West Campus cafeteria. George made an effort to walk around the edges of the dust bowl on West Campus that filled with mud every time it rained, but he still managed to cake his hiking boots with mud. He stomped his feet at the dorm entrance but still left a trail of brown crud up the two flights of linoleum stairs to her floor. He cursed and removed his boots before he walked onto the floor.

Caitlin's door was open and her lamp was on, but the room was empty. He asked her neighbor, who was always pretending she was British, if she knew where Caitlin was. The girl replied that she might be in the loo. So he walked down the corridor to the lavatory and knocked and called out her name.

She's in here with me! replied the boy whom George could not stand. George gingerly poked his head around the edge of the door and looked in at the boy who sat on a stool facing the sinks and mirrors. The boy's back was against the wall that separated the sinks from a row of individual showers. He looked drunk. His face was flushed red and he grinned stupidly.

What the hell are you doing in here, George asked him. It occurred to him that he was holding his boots that needed to be washed off, but he was not about to walk in and condone the other boy's presence in the girls' bathroom.

I am having a wonderful conversation with my Caitlin while she stands naked under the steaming hot water of the girls' shower room, he replied jovially.

Shut up Clive, Caitlin yelled.

Another girl's voice, this one from the bathroom stalls around the corner, yelled, Would someone please tell Clive to get the fuck out of the girls' bathroom? Please?!?

The moist, warm air from the shower floated everywhere. George told Clive he was going upstairs to wash his boots, and when he returned Clive had better not still be in the bathroom.

But by then the girl from the toilet stall brushed past him, saying, Oh just do it here. I'm done. As she walked away down the corridor, she called back, Clive, you are an asshole!

George moved into the bathroom and at the sink nearest the door began to wash his boots. He felt more comfortable being in there with the two of them. Clive stood up, staggered slightly, and giggled. He said, I am going to dinner Caitlin, do you want me to wait for you?

No, Clive, I do not. Clive acknowledged her answer with a grin, and walked out the door, holding it wide open for a minute. He stood there in the hallway smiling at George who glared at him until he finally let the door swing closed. The shower went quiet and George shook the excess water off his boots and was trying to wipe up the mess in the sink when Caitlin appeared wrapped in her towel and leaned against him briefly. He smiled at her and she asked him what he was doing washing his boots in her sink.

I got mud on them.

I can see that, Caitlin said. Her face smelled like lilacs to George, and he felt the dampness of her towel where it had pressed against his shirt. For a long, long time, George would remember this moment as the first time he got lost in the identity of someone else. Caitlin made him forget himself, and this sensation made him feel almost weightless when he was near her. It also made him dependent on her, in ways that he would not grasp until long after his life had led him elsewhere.

There are people who always seem to know what they want, and Caitlin Fossburgher was one of those people. From the age of six, she had wanted to be a stage actor, or somehow involved in live theater. By age thirteen, she had developed a young girl's compassion for children and volunteered at a local theater program that helped disadvantaged children through exposure to drama. This led her to believe that if she did not become a famous stage actor, she could live a fulfilled life through using her drama skills in other ways.

But Caitlin's first goal was to learn the acting craft, and she arrived at Cornell ready to be a theater arts major. The second of five children, Caitlin grew up in a rambunctious, but conservative and privileged home in Bucks County, Pennsylvania. Her father, a devout Roman Catholic, may have doted on her, but her mother, a Christian Scientist, raised her. It was her mother who insisted that she, like her older brother and younger siblings, be both responsibly independent and passionately spiritual.

Caitlin thought little about the ambivalence with which many in the theater viewed the world. She knew that actors liked to explore the edges of morality by playing people much different from themselves, but Caitlin saw the portrayal of even the most evil or unchaste of characters as the power of theater to teach about goodness. And so while keeping her own spirituality intact, she felt free to explore and engage with her fellow actors in ways that her father would no doubt have disapproved.

Theater was redemptive, she always told George. It informed the audience, even through immorality, about the redemptive quality of goodness. This was, in fact, what made theater such a wonderful medium through which to help unfortunate children. But as for her relationship with George, which Caitlin saw clearly as outside of the realm of theater, there could be no ambivalence as to convention.

However it may have looked to those around them, the foundation of their relationship was a conservative and moral one from its beginning. And so while they might be bold and unconventional in public, they were the opposite in private. Caitlin wanted a serious, meaningful and consuming commitment and George was quick to consent. Had he thought deeply about it, he would have understood that his commitment was born more of compliance than conviction. But George had Caitlin and others did not, and he could trust this.

December brought final rehearsals and three nights of performance, the third and final weekend of informal rush, and final exams. George's and Caitlin's plays were performed in the basement of the Theater Arts building, in a small, square performance room with black walls and dusty floors.

Playing Catherine's father in *The Wedding*, George sat rigidly at the dining room table that centered the little stage. His character was quite old and emotionally distant. He wanted to *feel* like his character, to inhabit the character's world, but received little guidance from the director who was focused more on the main characters. So George called to mind his own grandfather and a maintenance man whom he often saw in the building late in the afternoon, and tried to copy the hesitation and care with which they moved.

The father was not a central figure in the drama, but he did stand at one point late in the play to make a speech. George loved being part of it all, although he was unsure where he actually fit within the cast. The other actors had more experience and bigger roles than he.

It was not until the first night of performance that George realized who actually came to see the one-act plays. A scattering of curious students were overwhelmed by the entire theater arts department faculty and theater arts majors. This had the unintended effect of introducing George, personally and on stage as an actor, to the professors who directed the university performances. To George's delight, they liked what they saw.

After the third and final performance, the audience filed out, leaving the actors to break down the simple set. Derek Steele and Stephen Hurowitz were still sitting in the front row of the seats holding court with the graduate students who had directed the play and played the major parts.

Derek critiqued the direction of the play and asked the student director why he had blocked, or staged, the scenes as he had. Why, for example, did Eric place the bride down stage from the groom at one critical juncture? Why had he allowed the actors to stand in place for so long during the third scene? And why was he able to get so much more control of the flow of the scenes out of the kid playing the father than he did from Alec and Catherine?

George felt his face redden slightly, and stopped breathing as he listened. He didn't get what Derek Steele was talking about, but there could be no mistaking what he heard. He looked to Caitlin who sat behind Derek Steele, and she smiled broadly as their eyes met. Derek then said, Look it's time to eat, let's all go and get pizza and we can talk it through. Eric, the director reached for his coat and gazed at George. He looked angry, but in truth he looked angry a lot of the time. Come on, he said, You're coming too.

And with that, George knew he had broken through to the other side of the invisible ring that encircles all cliques. It did not matter that Derek made no more mention of his performance. Something he had done on-stage had improved the production. George now believed himself to be an actor. He was sitting with others whom he knew were talented. A new order and meaning centered his universe. And Caitlin sat next to him, with her hand resting comfortably on his thigh.

CHAPTER TWO

January, 1974

On the Tuesday following New Year's day, Will Houghton was on the road at seven a.m., leaving his parents' brownstone in downtown Philadelphia, to get back to school. To say that he was excited would not do his mood justice; this was his time to shine, and he believed that everything was in place for formal rush. The four seniors he had asked to lead power rush teams had agreed to arrive by two p.m., to make final preparations for the rush meeting to be held that night. They had to make final assignments for the teas, and more importantly, finalize the power teams.

Huff never drank coffee as he drove, but he loved to stop off at a little diner he had discovered about halfway to Ithaca. It was a tired, old place with round, cushioned stools lined up at a counter in front of the cook. He watched the man break eggs with his right hand as his left hand listlessly pushed hash browns back and forth with a spatula. The same waitress he remembered from prior trips poured very hot black coffee into a small, thick porcelain cup in front of him, and Huff thanked her with a formal smile. She mustered half a grin and moved down the line of her well-worn path.

Huff could feel the butterflies in his stomach, and the acidic edge to the steaming coffee should have been unappealing, but he blew on it and sipped and it tasted good. Chairing rush made him feel grown up, responsible, proud. He alone had the burden and the glory of making history; it excited him in ways he barely understood. Eta Chi was an apotheosis, a magnet for the strongest personalities and most fascinating men he had ever met. As rush chairman, he had puzzled mightily about Eta Chi's core – what it was that made it so special. If he could not define its essence, how could he ensure its perpetuity by selecting freshmen with the right…whatever?

From his jacket pocket he withdrew a small notepad that he always kept with him and opened it up to the page from the night before. He had tried to list things that defined his brotherhood and he read it over:

Ambition, Service, Moral, Diverse, Individualistic, Independent, Dependent, Sassy, High Expectations, Savvy

He added "Formal" after the last word and closed the cover. Were any of the freshmen he had seen even worthy of consideration? What did all those words add up to? The waitress refilled his coffee cup and he looked up and smiled.

Lost in thought, Hon? she asked.

I am lost in the pursuit of glory, he responded.

Four hundred miles away, George Muirfield awoke in his bed. He lay still, feeling the pulse of his heart in his eyelids. Then he sprang from bed and shook his head and smiled. It was his ritualistic way of rising, a moment of self affirmation. Alone, refreshed, pleased with himself, ready. The only thing necessary to kick him into gear was coffee.

Before going downstairs, George Muirfield surveyed his room, and quickly packed his suitcase. Christmas break had been fine, and part of him wanted to spend a few more days at home, but he couldn't. Before the fall term had ended, when George had accompanied Stephen to the last informal rush tea, his roommate had made him promise to return early for formal rush. The sweaters his mother had given him for Christmas he laid in his suitcase last, hoping they wouldn't wrinkle too much. He wondered if he would wear sweaters to formal rush, or whether "formal" meant jackets and ties, but the only house he could imagine being so formal was Eta Chi. He guessed he'd be wearing his sweaters. He carried his things downstairs with him to the kitchen where his mother sat at the kitchen table by a window.

Do you really have to go back to school so early? she asked her son. Most people would have taken her question as plaintive, but George knew she was just making conversation. His mother tended toward melancholy, but she was not plaintive.

I do, he said softly. He poured himself coffee from an electric pot that had yellow flowers painted in a ring around its middle, and sat down with his mother. The Boston Globe was spread out in front of her, and she asked if he wanted the sports section, but George shook his head no. His mother smiled toward him affectionately. He wanted to go, but took his time, sitting quietly with his mother. Outside the window the winter air seemed to clarify the trees.

George Muirfield took enormous pleasure in small moments, when he could feel time slow down to a point of flux. It happened when he was already ahead of himself, already on to the next moment in his mind. As he sat with his mother, he had already left home and was driving his car. He loved to drive his car. But resisting his impulsiveness was itself a delicious pleasure – a teasing, secret suspension of time sitting in his mother's kitchen, holding himself back. He let it build up as he sat there, and had two more cups of coffee before he finally kissed his mother on the cheek and said his goodbyes.

Then his things were in his car, a maroon Camaro with a four on the floor and the custom grip he had put on the stick shift that allowed him to wrap his fingers individually around its grooves, and he was pulling out of his parents' driveway. The grey January world beyond his windshield was a liquid, urgent, beckoning fantasy. His car maneuvered effortlessly through the little streets of his hometown, as the image of the long, open highway west made George's stomach whir.

Driving his car, George always felt pulled forward by the world in front of him, as if he need not really steer. Secretly he bet he could close his eyes and drive safely just by letting himself be led. He even connected this sensation to the subconscious way he performed onstage. Then the heavily wooded borders to the Massachusetts Turnpike, dark green conifers stretching endlessly out of sight, wrapped around George like the arms of a protector, and he charged west, lost in unconscious pleasure.

❧

Huff arrived at Eta Chi by noon, and soon his lieutenants began to arrive in great humor. They greeted each other loudly, and Huff shook their hands forcefully as he peered into their eyes. This was their moment, and he couldn't be prouder. The four brothers he had chosen to be his support were as excited as he was. All of them were seniors except for Bob Woodbridge, whom Huff found a refreshing counterbalance, as well as a terrific recruiter. Bob reached people that Huff couldn't, and that was important.

They met without delay, established the teams, and then set about preparing the house for the next day. The rest of the brothers arrived throughout the day, and by seven at night when Huff stood before the brothers in the great hall, all but four of the sixty-three brothers were present. The energy in the room was electric.

He called the meeting to order by saying "Gentlemen!" in a dramatic voice. The brothers instantly began to snap their fingers and emit a quiet, guttural whistle. Within the culture of the house, this was a symbol of approval and excitement. Some of the brothers hooted softly and smiled to each other as they snapped their fingers with exaggerated gestures, until Will quieted them down with a wave of his hand.

The goal, he said quietly, is not to lose a pledge to another house. With this, the brothers erupted in applause and hooted with abandon. Then Huff got them to quiet down again and made assignments for the first day of formal rush. Sophomores who had never been through formal rush before listened intently, and whispered to each other about what they recalled from their freshman year.

There were three rules Huff reemphasized for the benefit of the sophomores. First, there were to be absolutely no negative remarks about any other house. If a freshman asks your opinion about another house, you are to tell them that it is a very good house and they should consider joining it. We will not be dragged into a comparison of our house versus others. That, he explained, is a sign of weakness and pettiness. He could see some of the sophomores exchanging surprised looks at this notion.

Second, when you like a freshman it is incumbent on you to get them around to brothers who have not yet met them, and then leave them there, so that both the brother you are leaving the person with and you can form an unbiased opinion.

Third, be discriminating! We want people who will add to the luster of this house and not just people who are easy to get along with. A bid from this house is more special than any other house, and you must think this way without acting arrogant or superior with the freshmen. Think about yourselves, and about what attracted you to Eta Chi.

It is not arrogant of us to insist on being the most discriminating house on the hill! It is incumbent on us! Each and every freshman we bid must distinguish himself, and we must distinguish ourselves if we are to win him over. Any questions?

There was an hour's worth of questions, thoughts, and ideas from the group. Brothers took the time to relate the experiences they had found most compelling when they rushed. And finally Jackson Miles, the house president, spoke about his four years at the university and the incredible difference this house had made on his college days. He talked about learning and being challenged to excel by his brothers. He praised the efforts of Will Houghton in preparing them for formal rush and reminded everyone that Huff was in charge for the next three days. When Jackson finished, the brothers clapped loudly and whistled, and the meeting was adjourned.

The next morning at ten minutes to nine, Will Houghton was in place at the front door. Brothers carried tables from the dining room into the great hall and set up coffee and bug juice, cookies and peach cobbler which the fraternity chef had arrived early to make from scratch. And at five after nine, the first freshmen rounded the corner into the semi-circular driveway of Eta Chi fraternity toward Will Houghton with his arm outstretched above his head, the palm of his hand faced flat up to the sky. It was game time.

On the first morning of formal rush, George and Stephen walked across the suspension bridge and down Thurston Avenue until they reached the little side street that led to Phi Delta. It was a tall house with pleasant views of wooded hills on either side, made somewhat somber by the shadiness provided by the trees and its rather drab brown siding. Inside there was an inviting coziness to the rooms which moved front to back from the front hall. It was the kind of home you felt comfortable in during a rainstorm, of which there was no shortage in Ithaca.

The fraternity brothers at Phi Delta welcomed the two boys enthusiastically. Of all the houses, Phi Delta gave off the most relaxed and inviting vibe. The brothers were pleasant and informal, and they made it clear how disdainful they were of pretense. George felt comfortable at Phi Delta to same degree he felt ill at ease at Eta Chi. As he chatted with some of the brothers in the dining room, he wondered why they should even keep Eta Chi on their list. It would make more sense to focus here. Then one of the brothers inquired which other houses George and Stephen were looking at. Stephen answered and George watched them recoil.

Eta Chi! one of the Phi Deltas said in a raised voice. The others laughed derisively. I can't picture either one of you fitting in with that crowd! Stephen's face reddened as he tried to agree with them. George was impassive. What could cause the Phi Deltas to react so strongly? It was true that Eta Chi was odd, even uncomfortable. And George felt genuine warmth and realness in the Phi Deltas. But this notion of "real-ness" only confused George. What was more real than the majestic, overwhelming union he shared with Caitlin? Or the purity of emotional exchange he witnessed and envied between the theater students in the re-hearsal rooms? The more he thought, the less he understood.

Halfway through the tea, George and Stephen sidled their way outside and headed down Cayuga Heights Road to Eta Chi. The enormous stone chimney centered the one story wing to the left, and the stone front of the main house emanated a sense of permanence. Will Houghton stood in the doorway, beaming as they approached, and led them energetically through his ritualistic handshakes. Another brother escorted them inside, to the library where *They Reap Rich Harvests Who Wisely Sow* was carved into the ornate cherry mantle of a second fireplace.

As they met more brothers, George studied the Eta Chis intensely, hoping to solve their puzzle by close inspection. He noted the same bristling edginess between the brothers he had seen before. Primed from their conversations with the Phi Deltas, Stephen asked why Eta Chi had a dress code.

The Eta Chis laughed. One brother acknowledged that their dress code was an issue of great debate in the house. Then Bob Woodbridge's large voice enveloped them. Eta Chis believe in respecting each other, and elevating the dynamics of our lives by insisting on excellence. This is not a frivolous place, and we don't treat each other casually. Don't mis-understand me, he went on. We know how to let our hair down, and our politics range from Republican to Communist, but we choose to honor each other through standards of decorum other houses no longer have.

Bob Woodbridge breathed through his nose for emphasis. George eyed Stephen and the two roommates raised their eyebrows simultane-ously. This was certainly different, and George could tell that Stephen was excited. George said he'd be back in a minute, and pretended to head off to the bathroom. He moved quickly through the house to avoid being asked to join a conversation. He headed up the front stairs in the main foyer, and then the next flight to the third floor where there was no one around. He looked carefully at each of the rooms on the third floor, noting the messiness or the order of a particular person and the kinds of posters they put on their walls. It was fun to poke around above the din of conversation on the floors below him, and it made him look at the house differently. It gave him the sensation of being at home in his parents' house, where there was usually nothing but empty rooms when he walked around.

Bob Woodbridge's words rang clear. He felt it, more than thought about it, but remained unconvinced. It sounded like bullshit. Didn't it? He found the back staircase and was surprised at the dinginess of the walls and stairs. They were marked and cracked, and completely uncared for. When he found himself in the kitchen he walked out into the dining room and saw Bob Woodbridge and a crowd of about ten others, one of whom he recognized to be Scotty.

He walked up and nodded to Scotty, who was on the outer perimeter of a group that listened to L.E.O. Pennington. L.E.O. wore thick, squareish eyeglasses and looked bohemian. He was trying to convince the crowd that aliens existed on earth and that the mysteries of the Bermuda triangle were attributable to their presence.

Why do you think, he asked the group, that there are so many disappearances of aircraft in that region? The ocean is so deep there that they could have a base too far down for us to know about and then come up to the surface to conduct experiments on us!

George scanned the group, trying to gauge peoples' reactions. Bob Woodbridge seemed to indulge L.E.O., nodding his head occasionally and murmuring. Scotty looked embarrassed. Then Stephen walked up with someone George had not met before, who announced that the tea was over. Everyone was welcome back this afternoon. As the group broke up, Stephen tugged George on the sleeve and whispered, Come on, and the two headed out and back to the campus.

Over lunch, Huff reviewed his lists with each of his lieutenants. When he reached George's name and asked for comments, the reviews were mixed. George was fascinating. He was too full of himself. He was an oddball. He was a perfect fit. It was Bob Woodbridge who liked him the most. Huff, taking notes, raised his eyebrows repeatedly. He suggested that George Muirfield had certainly made an impression, and everyone laughed. Huff decided he wanted to get to know this freshman himself. When he asked about Stephen Dawn, the comments were more positive. Stephen was intense, intellectual, a good guy.

In the afternoon, Stephen headed straight back to Eta Chi to "test" it further. George had decided to look at a third house, so he walked up the hill to Chi Psi, and stood outside for a minute by himself. It was a grand looking house, situated on a small bluff at the top of the hill on the edge of the main campus. From where he stood, near the oversized windows to the south, he could faintly hear the water running through the gorge. He could hear the buzz of lively conversation inside, and smoke curled pleasantly out of an enormous chimney. It was everything a fraternity house should be. But George turned and walked away. Something was making him head to Phi Delta. As he crossed the suspension bridge, he stopped and let the clean winter wind chill him. It rolled through the gorge and penetrated his parka to the point where he felt the warm air layer between his parka and shirt dissipate.

Phi Delta is the obvious choice, he thought. It's got the most plusses and the fewest minuses. Maybe it's the place that's calling me after all. He imagined himself walking to Phi Delta at the end of a full day of classes, and liked the notion. It felt right. Actually, he knew it didn't matter how it felt. In the back of his mind, going to Phi Delta was a better way to resist returning to Eta Chi. All this would unfold as it was meant to. He nodded to convince himself, and breathed through his nose the way Bob Woodbridge had. He left the suspension bridge to go to Phi Delta. It was time to secure a bid.

At Eta Chi, the brothers met in the Great Hall shortly after four p.m. and began their first vetting session of formal rush. During the fall, the brothers had made oral bids to four freshmen. The first few bids in any year are the easiest, Huff knew, since there had to be near unanimous support in order to make a bid during the fall. The difficult time came from this point on, when there would be controversy over some good candidates. So he wanted to set the stage right at the beginning, and he noted as he called the group to order that the energy of the night before had been replaced with the lethargy that follows a day of high socializing.

He asked if anyone had noticed the freshman who had somehow broken his pants zipper in the mailroom that afternoon and walked around socializing for over an hour *with his hand on his crotch!* Laughing, the brothers regrouped and the meeting started.

Huff did not really know how many bids to expect from this first meeting, but it was important that they begin to focus everyone on the process. So he led lightly with two boys whom he did not know much about. Only a few brothers knew them, and though L.E.O. Pennington spoke highly of one of them, he could not offer enough insights for any decisions to be made, so he proposed "Bring Back" and asked others to get to know him tomorrow.

Huff next asked if there were any freshmen who should be dissuaded from looking further at the house and a half dozen brothers raised names. Each name was considered individually, and the brother who raised the name was required to state a reason. Peter Harris, who always got laughs on this agenda item, spoke through his unmoving lips about a freshman he had talked to for two minutes before realizing HE WAS A DORK!

Huff smiled until the laughter subsided, and asked for confirmation. He counted twelve hands, and put that particular name on a separate list. Next to the name he wrote "dork."

After all of the other names had been reviewed and ended up on the same list with notations including "too false," "clueless" and "manic depressive," Will presented the first serious candidate for a bid.

Harold Wise? He said in a loud voice. He lifted his chin and looked out across the sea of faces. The skin on his face tingled. It made a tremor run down his spine. He knew he was on a precipice, one he would occupy for only a few days, one that would secure him in his own firmament, even if no one else understood. He was adding to his life, somehow. If he could just make a difference here and now, if he could bring just the right slate of freshmen into Eta Chi, he would have earned the right to look back with pride. Years from now, he could stretch his arms behind his head, and recall how he continued the magic. And he was going to start with Harold Wise.

Half a dozen brothers raised hands to be heard. He recognized L.E.O. Pennington first, and L.E.O. stood up from where he was sitting on the floor and told the group that he had spent time with Harold at the request of Art Woodhall. He is outgoing, friendly and has a great sense of humor. But there is a lot of depth to the guy as well, although I am not sure I can say why. He seems to get the big picture about things and still not take things too seriously. He is an Eta Chi.

L.E.O. sat down as brothers snapped their fingers. The five brothers to follow spoke highly of Harold as well, each relating what they knew about him, what the substance of their conversations had been, and five out of the six wanted to put him to a vote. The sixth, Scotty, said he liked him a lot but wasn't sure enough people had gotten to know him yet and therefore would propose "Bring Back."

Huff asked how many brothers had met Harold, and most of the boys raised their hands. We need more commentary then folks, Huff said. More brothers raised their hands, and for the next thirty minutes, a profile of Harold was created that would have shocked him had he been able to listen. When Harold Wise graduated from high school on Long Island, he thought he would someday be a gym teacher, but only after he had proven himself in other ways. His father had died when he was in the seventh grade and he had shouldered the burden of caring for his mother and younger sister. He laughed hard. He was sharp, high-energy, no bullshit. He loved sports. He was politically conservative. He was very, very funny. All this and much more came tumbling out of the mouths of brothers.

Huff was about to put Harold up for a vote when Mike O'Hare and Tim Truesdale, spoke against Harold. Mike stated that he found Harold to be too superficial. Tim then followed with comments to the effect that he had seen Harold in classes at the hotel school and he was a little too rambunctious. These comments elicited questions from others who had not spent much time with Harold. How gregarious was he? Did that mean that he was annoying? What kind of contributions would he make on campus while he was at Cornell? Did he make fun at the expense of others?

When all the questions had been answered, Huff asked if there were any further comments. L.E.O. Pennington motioned for a bid. There was a snapping of fingers that began across the room and soon all of the brothers, and even Scotty, were snapping their fingers, and after a show of hands, Eta Chi had its first formal rush bid candidate.

On the heels of this first success, Huff then raised three additional names of the freshmen whom he knew would have the best chance of receiving enough support around the house. And by seven p.m., Eta Chi had four formal bids to give.

Winter had clearly settled into Ithaca, and the air was cold and unforgiving for the dorm visits. Brothers wore parkas to get from their house to the dorms, and traipsed snow and dirt into the dorms. Most fraternities sent teams of three or four brothers, so it was common to see four boys walk into a freshmen dorm on West Campus, stamp their wet feet, remove their parkas and knock on the door of a standard double room.

The first evening of formal rush in 1974, Huff sent Power Team C to Harold Wise's room, led by Bob Woodbridge. As team captain, Bob would normally be the one to actually make the bid, although he could let someone else on the team have the fun. Huff thought that Bob's outgoing nature and pronounced bearing would be a good match for Harold.

Harold welcomed the brothers into his room in Fields Hall. Bob entered first, followed by Scotty, Max Burdoin, a quiet and genteel hotel student from Georgia, and a sophomore pre-med student from New York City. The four brothers sat on the parallel beds with their parkas under their arms, happy to be out of the cold.

The sophomore was assigned to speak first, and he took charge right away, asking Harold how his first taste of formal rush had been. Before Harold could respond, the sophomore pressed on, telling him how much he himself enjoyed the day, and how important he regarded the rush process. Social and outgoing, Harold immediately agreed with the sophomore. He took in the four brothers with a quick but studied glance. He had an athlete's instinctive awareness of people around him, and the sophomore's behavior made him pause and slowly clench and unclench his fists.

Harold Wise's tensile physicality matched his restless and impatient mind. There was something in him that reminded you of every balding, paunchy, forty-something gym teacher you've ever known, except he was nineteen, in great physical condition and brimming over in testosterone. He was, paradoxically, a keenly sensitive boy with an abiding and innate sensitivity for people who had experienced significant loss. . He thought his compassion and insight came when he lost his father. He would never understand that he had been born this way. In any event, these qualities would make him an endearing and wise adult.

The sophomore resumed speaking, and Harold, suppressing his tendency to banter, listened intently. He assumed that Barry was leading up to something, but he could not be certain of where this was going. Then Max Burdoin began to speak in deliberate tones about the hotel school and how he had struggled to find the right fraternity that fit his expectations. From what Harold could tell, Max could be telling him that he was in or out.

Where are we going with this, fellas? Harold finally blurted out. Bob's deep voice immediately enveloped the room, and everyone looked at him.

This afternoon after you left the tea, the fraternity held a meeting about which freshmen had impressed us the most as being ready to be a part of the unique experience that we call Eta Chi, Bob began. If Barry and Max seem a bit formal or serious tonight, it is because they take extremely serious the privilege and honor they feel in extending to you a formal invitation to become one of their brothers.

Harold whooped and laughed as Bob handed him the small, formal envelope with his name written in calligraphy. Inside the bid card read:

Beta Tau of Eta Chi extends to you its sincere wish that you accept the enclosed formal bid to pledge and join its fraternity of brothers

Bob extended his hand and Harold grasped it hard, smiling widely.

You guys scared me silly there! Harold said chuckling. Then he shook each of their hands in turn, and thanked them and told them he was thrilled to accept their offer.

Bob explained that if he did indeed wish to accept, he should sign the pledge card and turn it in to them or to the IFC on Monday. Harold withdrew the card, signed it and handed it to Bob saying, Let's get this over with right now. I'm in!

Bob invited Harold to come over to the house the next day at his leisure, so that all of the brothers could welcome him into the pledge class. He also told him to save the following Sunday evening for a party he would not soon forget, and with another round of handshaking, the brothers left Harold for their next assignment. Harold called his mother and gave her the good news, and then headed out to the pub in the West Campus dining hall, whistling.

Bob Woodbridge next led his team over to Boldt Hall to see Stephen Dawn. They had a list of twelve freshmen to see, and they were in Bob's descending order of importance. Power Team C may have been thrilled at Harold Wise's reaction, but Bob was personally disgusted that they had performed so officiously. He leaned closer to Scotty who walked next to him and said, You are going to have to play a bigger role, Scotty, or the two chuckleheads behind us will screw this whole night up!

Scotty whistled softly under his breath, and smiled. I'm glad I'm not the only one, he replied.

This was Bob's first time leading a power team, but he had been the junior man on a power team last year, so he knew what worked well. He craned his neck to speak to Barry and Max who walked a few steps behind him and told them they needed to relax a little. Max, a senior and the elected pledge captain, had never liked Bob much, but he respected his insights.

You think we were a little awkward back there? When he said "there" it sounded like "thayyah."

Bob stopped and they gathered in a little circle. Scotty stomped his feet to stay warm.

Let's be as real and as passionate and honest as we can be when we speak with these kids tonight, Bob said. This is our opportunity to see them in their own environment, and to share with them what is special about our house. We don't need to be forced, and we don't need to impress anybody.

Barry said he was sorry.

God, man, don't be sorry! Bob barked. Come on, let's go look at some potential brothers! When they knocked at Stephen and George's door, a Phi Delta answered the door and smiled to Bob. The Phi Delta had unsuccessfully rushed Eta Chi last year, but he had befriended Bob and they ate lunch together sometimes at Willard Straight Hall.

Give us about fifteen, would you; we just got here, Chuck said.

You have both of them with you? Bob asked.

Yeah, we don't stand on formality at Phi Delta, Bob, you know that. As he spoke, he raised his voice to make sure the boys in the room could hear.

Bob laughed, and led his team off to the adjoining dorm to see their next candidate.

Stephen and George had not known what to expect the first night of formal rush, and they were sitting quietly in their room when a group of four Phi Deltas first knocked on their door at seven forty-five p.m. The brothers piled into their narrow little room. Stephen sat on his bed, and George at his desk. Three of the brothers sat on the beds, and one dropped to the floor in between.

George told them that neither he nor Stephen knew much about this part of the process, and the Phi Deltas laughed and told them to relax. They wanted to spend a few minutes with them on their own turf, and answer any questions they might have about Phi Delta or fraternities in general.

Stephen asked when he and George could expect the fraternities to be making up their minds about who would be invited to join. The four brothers looked at each other and a moment of silence filled the room.

Actually, the lead Phi Delta said, you don't need to wait any more. We are here tonight to offer each of you the chance to become Phi Delts! All four brothers then began to speak at once, and there was laughter and congratulations as he handed the two boys small envelopes.

Now, the Phi Delta said, as the room became quiet again, this was not exactly how we wanted to tell you, so let me begin by sharing with you how Phi Delt came to this decision, and why we feel it is so important for you to join our house. We voted on each of you separately today, and the mood in the room when each of your names came up was absolutely incredible. Everyone in our house is comfortable with you and sees you as bringing a lot to our house.

Another boy broke in, saying, And we also believe we are the right place for the two of you! His voice was pitched a little high, and rushed as he said, I am sure you have looked at a number of houses during rush, but I am willing to bet that the feeling you get when you walk into Phi Delta is special. It was for me, when I rushed, and it is for me today. It's comfortable, and welcoming and respectful of who you are as a person.

George looked at the boy talking and could not remember if he had met him before. Stephen's face seemed slightly flushed behind his glasses, and he was smiling and nodding.

This is fantastic, Stephen said. And at least speaking for myself, I am really happy to hear that we have the opportunity to join Phi Delta. His face wrinkled slightly and his lips moved carefully as he talked. Now, since this is the first night of formal rush, what are we supposed to do? I mean, George, don't you think that we at least want to speak with the other houses? The four Phi Delts nodded seriously.

George said, Yeah, well, help us to understand what this means. When are we supposed to give you an answer?

The Phi Deltas told them there was no hurry whatsoever. The house would be excited to have Stephen and George spend as much time at the house during the next two days to help them decide, if they were not ready this evening to make the commitment. One of the other boys said that it had taken him a day to make his response last year.

Stephen felt tension in the room and didn't know what to say. He was excited to get the Phi Delta bid, but was really consumed with the idea of Eta Chi. And he knew that they were outside waiting to see him. He looked at George who seemed unfazed by it all. Then George said, Guys, I want you to know that both Stephen and I are very serious about your house. I know when I walk in there I feel like I am welcome, and it seems like a terrific house. So, let us think about it overnight and we will be certain to see you tomorrow.

The Phi Deltas rose and shook their hands. Chuck stopped on his way out the door, and said, Fellas, I think I should tell you if you don't know, that we have only extended this offer to ten other freshmen out of the hundreds who have come through the house and hoped to get a bid. We see you as key members of this year's pledge class, and want you to take this offer as a serious and high honor. I will be excited to call each of you my brothers.

The door closed behind him, and Stephen and George slapped each other's hands high in the air. Neither said a word, until Stephen said, I wonder where Eta Chi went! which made them both laugh. Then Bob Woodbridge poked his head through the door, asking if the enemy was gone yet. Once in the room, Bob asked if they could have some time with Stephen alone, and George looked at Stephen curiously, and then said he would be down the hall in the common room. Bob thanked George and said that another group of Eta Chis would be by to see him before the evening was over.

Scotty spoke first when George left, pressing his glasses to the bridge of his nose, and asking Stephen whether the first day of rush had been fun. Stephen said yes, he had enjoyed Eta Chi a lot that day, and he was glad to see them here tonight. He then told them how he had just received a bid from Phi Delta, and all four brothers congratulated him and shook his hand.

We often compete against Phi Delt for freshmen, Bob said. It is a wonderful house. You rushed there last year didn't you, Scotty?

Yeah, Scotty said, and I still think their parties are better than ours! The others laughed. But, Scotty went on, before you accept Phi Delt's bid, why don't we spend a moment talking about Eta Chi. Okay?

Stephen nodded, and the Eta Chis spoke in turn. Stephen told them he was excited by what he heard, and that he was looking for a house where he could not only have fun and make friends, but also be connected to something important.

From where Scotty sat, Stephen appeared gaunt, and pale. He certainly said the right things, but there was not any sort of buzz to him. He was likeable, earnest, and smart. He was the perfect picture of how Scotty felt about Phi Delts. As they talked, Scotty thought back again and wondered if he had joined the right house, because he thought of himself as more like Stephen than the majority of the brothers in his house. No you're not, he said to himself, stop dreaming.

Bob concluded the session by asking Stephen to come by the house tomorrow for a closer look. Now that he had the bid from Phi Delt, Stephen owed it to himself to take this opportunity to compare and contrast. You will not be disappointed, even if you end up joining Phi Delt, he promised.

The Eta Chis left, and Stephen found George and recounted what their visit had been like. They spent the next 30 minutes uninterrupted, before another house knocked on the door. Stephen volunteered to step out, and they said they didn't care, but he left anyway. A short, jumpy boy introduced everyone and then nervously asked George what other houses he was considering. George told him, and the boy said "*Nooo* contest!" in an elevated voice.

George immediately wanted to imitate the boy, but resisted. He couldn't get it out of his mind, though, and as the boys continued to speak to him, he kept imagining himself responding "*Nooo* kidding!" or, "*Nooo* way!" When he managed to listen to the last boy to speak, he refocused just in time to hear him say, You know George, we are a diverse house, and while we are well represented on the varsity squads, the way to think about us is that, regardless of whether you are into sports or not, our house is a *varsity* house. When he said the word varsity, he lowered his voice an octave for emphasis.

George could not stop himself from smiling. He pictured Caitlin watching this and wanting to puke. It made the entire rush experience seem juvenile, and a waste of time. These fraternities were nothing more than a lark, and he, consumed by Caitlin, did not belong. So why was he even sitting here?

Stephen came in and scowled. What are you doing? he asked sarcastically. George looked around their room. His side was more cluttered than Stephen's. The chest of drawers they shared between their narrow little closets was old and dusty. He couldn't tell his roommate that he was trying to contemplate his future. That an image was developing in his mind like an impressionist painting. That he was just too close to the canvas to see the future right in front of him.

This is a *varsity* room, George said as he lay still with his hands folded on his stomach. He lowered his voice just as the fraternity brother had.

You're a moron, Stephen replied. Then four Eta Chis, led by L.E.O. Pennington, rapped on the door to see George.

The energy in the room seemed to bump up. The fraternity brothers were funny and edgy. Throughout the conversation, George found himself in a wordless interplay with L.E.O. L.E.O. would barely change his expression as one of his brothers made a point, and George would smile. Or George would nod vigorously at something, and L.E.O. would stare off, so as not to smile. George found more substance in L.E.O.'s subordinated gestures than in all the words he had heard that day.

L.E.O. could tell from listening that his brothers were positive about George, so he quietly suggested that George come to the house tomorrow morning. George said he would definitely come by at some point.

I will make a deal with you, L.E.O. offered. Come tomorrow morning at nine a.m. I will personally get you out the door at nine thirty so you can see the other houses. Deal?

And because L.E.O. was the first Eta Chi he felt he could trust, George said Deal.

George went down the hall after the Eta Chis had left, and was happy to find the common room empty. He moved to the pay phone on the wall, and dialed Caitlin's number in Philadelphia. When her mother answered, George could sense her smile into the phone and then yell upstairs for her daughter. After a moment, Caitlin's voice poured thought the earpiece. Her voice was soft, lush, warm.

I miss you terribly, G. My sister says I'm pathetic. But it's only a few more days. Do you miss me?

I miss you something awful, George answered in a husky voice. It was true. He hadn't realized it.

The operator broke in to ask for a $1.35 for an additional three minutes, and George was ready with change that he plunked into the silver slot.

Every extra minute gives me hours! Caitlin said, laughing. George thought he could feel his girlfriend through the phone line, and told her so. Then the three extra minutes were gone, and George hung up and looked around the tired room. He pictured Caitlin coming back to school, and wondered what he would tell her of rush. Then his mind returned to L.E.O. Pennington. Something had happened between them, something that gave George a new, unarticulated notion. All he knew was that he was headed to Eta Chi the next morning, and now that felt right.

CHAPTER THREE

Day two of formal rush was even longer at Eta Chi than Day One. Huff gathered the brothers for forty-five minutes before the tea began. All four bids had been accepted on the spot, Huff was glad to hear. He reminded everyone that formal rush was far from over. Brothers needed to continue to recruit the freshmen who had accepted, lest another

house lure them away. Then he asked for updates.

L.E.O. spoke for his team when the time came, and reported favorably on three freshmen, recommending that three be "No bid." At the end, he asked everyone to spend time with George Muirfield, who had impressed his team the most. He said he knew that some people had reservations about him, but his team all agreed that he was a distinctive character who brought something to the party.

Huff wrote "distinctive?" next to George's name on his clipboard, then asked for a show of hands of people who had not met him, and pointed to four of those who had raised their hand and asked them to get with L.E.O. before the tea started.

Bob Woodbridge was in the kitchen when his team report came up, so Scotty spoke in his stead. When he got to Stephen Dawn, he paused for a moment, and said, We liked this guy last night. He's definitely interested in our house. He also got a bid from Phi Delt last night, and they seem to be rushing him hard.

After the meeting broke, L.E.O. found Bob Woodbridge and asked him to help with George. Help me think who should see him first, because I think we will lose him if we aren't careful. Bob looked at L.E.O. and nodded several times fast. Let's nail him, he replied. Let's do Jackson, then Peter Harris, then Bill Dunn!

Bill Dunn! L.E.O. shot back, a little too loudly. Then he lowered his voice. Are you crazy, Bob? Bill Dunn's a pint short of a gallon!

Bob smiled. Bill Dunn was a lost soul, an eccentric who fumbled his way through every day. But he was passionate, broad-minded, curious. Perfect, Bob guessed, for a freshman theater-arts type.

Look, Bob said, George Moosefart or whatever his name is is about as far to the left as Max Burdoin is to the right. If he is a theater arts guy, he's creative, and open, right? So give him Jackson and Peter to blow his doors off, and then let Dunn take him on one of his magic carpet rides!

When the tea started, George was the third freshman in the door. On the way to the house, he had actually looked forward to Will Houghton's bizarre way of shaking hands, and Huff did not disappoint him. Their thrusting handshake continued even longer than before. Then L.E.O. walked up and asked if he still had only 30 minutes. George returned L.E.O.'s mirthful gaze, and said, Whatever it takes!

L.E.O. nodded, and ushered him right over to Jackson Miles and left. On the way, L.E.O. told him that Jackson was the house president, a varsity athlete, a part-time preacher at a local church, and had a grade point average over 4.0 in the engineering school. George looked attentive as L.E.O. introduced him and Jackson walked him around the house, but inside George was a thousand miles away. He was back in high school, remembering the first Renaissance man he ever met.

Prescott Humphries had a head of ringlets, a full and strong face and an adult bearing. He looked like a Roman statue. He was also undeniably the most accomplished academic student. He was the preternatural Renaissance Man, an icon of success that would form a permanent line of demarcation in George's psyche.

As Jackson spoke earnestly about Eta Chi, George heard the roar of his eighth grade classmates. They were roaring because Prescott Humphries, at age thirteen, had just leaped so far in the standing long jump competition that he had landed well beyond the end of the measuring tape. His feat, which had the masters scratching their heads to figure out a point total to award the boy, only added to his legendary status among his classmates.

Standing in Eta Chi, Jackson Miles had no idea what impression he was making on George Muirfield, except that the freshman looked rapt. So he thoughtfully inquired about the only thing he knew about George -- he had heard that George was an actor. George zoomed back to the present and responded shyly. At last he had met another Prescott Humphries, a man among men, a symbol. Two things happened simultaneously in him – he began to speak excitedly about the theater, to prove himself to Jackson Miles, and as the words poured out of him, he recalled his arrival at Cornell, his first experience as an Ivy Leaguer.

Smiling, Jackson looked intensely at George and saw the same robust enthusiasm pouring out of his eyes that he appreciated in Bob Woodbridge. George was describing the dizzying sensation of transforming yourself into another character and demonstrating the impact even the slightest shift in a wave of the hand could have on stage.

He doubted that George was a serious person, but he liked him. He raised his arm to shake George's hand, and startled George with the restrained power in his grip. Then L.E.O. Pennington was at his side, asking him to sit down with him in the dining room.

George considered L.E.O. as they sat down opposite each other. He was gaunt in appearance, lean and sort of rubbery. His straggly hair draped below his chin, at the bottom of a long face.

The two regarded each other silently. It made George feel as if he were doing improv in the theater, only he knew this was real.

I know how confusing this process is, George. L.E.O. finally said. It's false, it's forced, and it's stupid.

George wasn't sure whether to agree, so he just listened.

But it's the process we must follow. So while I can see the distance in your eyes, I want you to give the whole thing a chance. I am pleased that I found my way to Eta Chi, and my intuition is screaming that I would be pleased if you did, as well.

George found L.E.O.'s use of the word "pleased" at once odd and heartwarming. L.E.O., George asked, I understand your point about rush, but why is this place so…forbidding?

L.E.O. said nothing, so George plowed on. I trust you, and believe what you say. But there is an aura to this house, a kind of superior formality. Isn't there?

What you sense, L.E.O. said, is a ferocity that lies just below the surface of our formality. It's what enthralls and repulses me, to be honest.

George absorbed L.E.O's words slowly. Finally, he said, So my choice, assuming I have one, is between houses that feel comfortable but shallow, and one that will enthrall and repulse me?

L.E.O. picked at the edge of his fingernail. I don't actually think you have a choice, he said finally. But if you do, then yes, that's right.

Bob Woodbridge and another boy approached, and Bob introduced George to Bill Dunn. George saw L.E.O. glance at Bill, and then Bob, before he suggested that George spend a little time with Bill. As Bob and L.E.O. walked away, George looked curiously at Bill Dunn. Bill stood five-foot eight, with long, stringy hair that went in a number of different directions across his head. His head was what you noticed most about Bill, because it moved constantly. Sometimes his head rocked gently back and forth, and other times it jerked in a sort of stutter step as if Bill had a tic. He didn't though. It was just his mannerism.

Anyway, the point is we are all here to get along, Bill said. What are you majoring in?

George didn't know what he would major in but he loved theater.

Right, right, right, Bill nodded approvingly. Has anyone shown you the chapter room? No, of course not, we lock that up. We get all locked up in that room. Chapter meetings are good for your health!

George was getting lost, but he tried to listen. He had been intrigued with his visit so far. After a time the two boys found some common ground and they laughed with each other over Bill's continuing indecision about what to major in. George finally asked him why other houses said such negative things about Eta Chi. Bill Dunn's head moved around nervously as he explained that Eta Chi always won.

I guess it's plain old insecurity, you see? We always get our men, just like in the old westerns. Or is that the FBI? Anyway, these other houses, they don't like losing out to us.

Do you know why Eta Chi always gets its men, as you say?

Nope, Bill answered matter-of-factly. I don't know. We just do.

L.E.O. Pennington returned, and told George it was eleven twenty a.m. Was George aware of the time? In truth, L.E.O. worried that Bill was turning George off. George looked at L.E.O. uncertainly, and said, no, this is fine, and then he rose and told L.E.O. he was truly enjoying his time here. As he said this, Bob Woodbridge walked past with three people, including Harold Wise. He grunted approvingly, and introduced George to one of Eta Chi's newest members.

Harold thought George must be a brother, but then realized he was a freshman, so he asked if he had accepted his bid yet. George told him he didn't have one to accept, and Bob offered that they were still working on George.

There are few salesmen more zealous than those newly converted, and Harold immediately launched into an impromptu testimonial about his new fraternity. He asked George where else he was rushing, and when George told him, he chuckled and said that he could understand that. And then Harold's chuckle progressed into a sustained, guttural belly laugh that George would remember, and imitate, for the rest of his life. It was a knowing, deep, staccato laugh that started under Harold's breath and then built slowly and convincingly into the most pronounced and joyful appreciation for life's foibles that George would ever hear.

When George walked out the door at noon, Harold's belly laugh still resonated through him, putting him in an upbeat, spirited mood. He met Stephen for lunch as planned, and the two shared their experiences over hamburgers at the Ledge. Stephen had gone to Phi Delta, and the roar of approval he received when he walked in the door made him blush for twenty minutes. Phi Delts swarmed around him, congratulating him, welcoming him and listening attentively to him. He told George he felt huge.

George got excited about the prospect of going to Phi Delta that afternoon. He walked Stephen through his morning, especially his time with the extraordinary Jackson Miles, which Stephen listened to with his eyes getting wider and wider behind his glasses. Jeeesus, he said, when George told him about Jackson Miles' G.P.A. In truth he felt slightly jealous of George. The adrenaline rush of his morning faded.

The day went fast from then until the dorm room visits that night. Although George wouldn't have called it a roar, he was welcomed warmly and profusely at Phi Delt. A number of brothers engaged him in serious conversations, and he left there pleased to have been accepted by their fraternity. When a Phi Delt inquired, George continued to maintain that he was looking at Eta Chi. It occurred to him that Eta Chis rarely asked him about other houses.

⌘

On the second night of formal rush, eleven candidates were voted upon favorably at Eta Chi making the total number of bids 19. Huff was comfortable that the pledge class would end up at around 24 boys.

There was no magic number. For years house treasurers had kept records demonstrating that upperclassmen always moved back into the house when they opted to take fewer freshmen. Based on the available records, prior year pledge classes had ranged from as low as 17 boys up to as many as 31.

During the same meeting, which began at four forty and lasted three hours, the brothers also chose to no-bid thirty-five boys who had rushed the house hard. And unlike any other house to their knowledge, Eta Chi sent brothers to visit the rooms of boys who were no-bid, to tell them. Other houses let freshmen reach the conclusion that they had been rejected by simply not making a room visit during formal rush.

Both George and Stephen had been hotly debated. Huff raised George's name in the middle of a run of favorable bid decisions, although he didn't offer up his name with much forcefulness or particular favor. In fact, when he said, "George Muirfield?" he did so with his eyebrows raised and his voice a little soft, as if to indicate that he wasn't sure what the reaction might be. In fact, he knew that the house was divided. Max Burdoin had decided George was too flighty, too much of a smart aleck, too...too.

Before George had left the tea that morning, Max and two other seniors had spoken with him at some length. Elevated from meeting Jackson Miles and his conversations with L.E.O. and Bill Dunn, George had gone out of his way to impress and entertain the seniors. He spoke rapidly and excitedly about acting, and music, and the incredible way rain fell on the Arts Quad. He was full if himself, and Max didn't care for it. So, in preparation for the bid discussion, Max had gone to work on his classmates, including Huff, and shared his dim view of George.

Why would we want someone of such dubious merit? was how Max ended each entreaty. Like most days, Max wore a maroon cardigan sweater over a turtleneck and wool slacks. As he spoke with his brothers, hands in his pockets, he never oversold his position. He just commented, and nodded his head slowly as he talked. George's flash is superficial, don't you think? he asked Jackson Miles.

Jackson Miles liked George, but he valued the views of his classmates about what it meant to be an Eta Chi. He did not personally see George as a threat to the house, but if his brothers did, why take a risk? Max asked Jackson to help him articulate this point.

L.E.O. Pennington was the first to be heard after Huff called George's name. He talked about the diversity and intensity of the house, and how he saw George as a real addition. Bob Woodbridge spoke next, and related a conversation he had with George during informal rush. He believed that George, already involved in campus activities, would continue to represent the house favorably on the hill. Then Huff, smiling, introduced Bill Dunn. Bill Dunn said he had looked into George's eyes and seen true character.

In every bid discussion there is a moment when the sentiment of the brothers begins to either solidify or splinter, and Max Burdoin knew that this was a good time to raise his hand. Bill Dunn was considered kooky and inconsistent. The effect of his endorsement was bound to be tepid. So he stood up, walked to the front of the meeting where Huff stood and apologized to his brothers for taking an alternate view. In a steady drawl, he talked about his responsibility as pledge captain to see that the pledge class inculcated the integrity, honor and service that made a young man an Eta Chi.

He then questioned whether George really had demonstrated these values to anyone. In fact, he was of the opinion that George did not, and would not, at least to the high standards we all must expect. He then looked to Jackson Miles, hoping that he might follow him, but Huff next recognized Art Woodhall. Art said he was glad someone else had raised doubts about George, because he himself wondered about the guy. He was simply not that comfortable with George, who struck him as a bit of a whack job.

Huff saw Jackson Miles raise his hand and if the room had been quiet to this point it now went silent. Jackson spoke in soft but measured tones, and the eyes of entire room were focused on him. He said he was concerned about the future of Eta Chi, and felt it his responsibility to protect the unique character of the house by erring on the side of caution when extending membership to someone who was this controversial.

The room swayed as soon as Jackson spoke, but Scotty waved his hand emphatically, so Huff acknowledged him. Scotty pressed his glasses to his nose, and girded his otherwise thin voice with a passion that everyone noticed. He stood next to Bob Woodbridge, who was clearly addled as well. Listen, he began, I am not one to become overly excited about situations like this, but I believe that we would be doing a disservice to ourselves if we did not vote "bring back" at this point. One more day will give brothers who have thus far remained silent the chance to form an opinion. If the house does not want him after tomorrow, so be it.

Bob motioned for a vote on bring back, and although this was not technically a chapter meeting in which the brothers followed Robert's Rules of Order, L.E.O. immediately seconded, and Huff suggested that he would be all right if such a vote was made. More than half the room raised their hands in favor, while a strong number of brothers, and every senior, except for Peter Harris, voted against. Huff looked across the room for a moment, and decided not to become entangled in what number of votes would be required. George Muirfield would be brought back.

After a number of other candidates names had been raised and voted on, Huff offered up Stephen Dawn for a vote. While he had known that George was controversial, he was relatively confident that Stephen was a strong candidate across the house.

Sandy Hitchens, Bob Neff and Jerry Wells, all seniors who had been influenced by Max Burdoin to vote against George (without really having formed an opinion on him), stood and spoke in favor of Stephen. All three boys were polite, well groomed, and articulate. And they were popular in the house. In fact, Jerry Wells had been elected Consul for the Spring semester, following Jackson Miles, whose term ended at Christmas break. Although they would not have acknowledged it, everything about Stephen reminded them of themselves.

Stephen was earnest, and well intended, and he would no doubt acquit himself admirably, they attested. He was a serious student. He was principled. Some of the younger brothers began to snap their fingers, sensing victory, but they were not followed by the rest of the room.

Scotty had listened carefully to each of the three speakers, trying to think through what it was about Stephen that made him hesitate. Stephen was all the things that were being said of him, but Scotty couldn't get out of his mind the feeling that had struck him in Stephen's dorm room the night before. For all of his good qualities, Stephen didn't have the zip in his step that made Eta Chi different.

So he raised his hand to be heard, and said simply, I like Stephen, so please don't get me wrong. I think he would make a great Phi Delt, but he doesn't have enough zip to get a bid at Eta Chi. Then he sat down.

Bob Woodbridge smiled widely and asked to speak. He was relishing the opportunity to challenge what he called the Old Guard – those seniors who were clinging to what he viewed as an outdated set of values. In his mind, Max Burdoin was the Imperial Wizard of the Old Guard, and this was the perfect opportunity to spear Max's balloon.

First of all, he said in his loud, sonorous voice, I want to echo Brother Scotty's sentiment that Stephen Dawn is a fine young man. I have spent time with him and I would be pleased to call Stephen a friend. But friendship is not a significant criterion for membership in this house, and when we look at what the critical success factors really are, I am afraid I second Scotty's viewpoint.

We must remain vigilant in the selection of our brothers! When each of us walks into this house at night after a day of classes on the hill, we do not expect to be coddled. We expect to be challenged and enlightened, and the pledge class we are assembling for Brother Max (as he said "Brother Max," Bob waved in his direction, signifying his importance) is so far filled with people with the energy and the character called for.

The brothers erupted in applause, because Bob's speech had been so clever. Other brothers then came forward to express their reservations, finding some slight impression of Stephen that now loomed large before them. One boy even said that the honor of their house required vigilance against candidates like Stephen who would cause the house to fall off the hill into the extended mediocrity of other fraternities. The worm had turned.

Huff brought the vitriol down a notch, noting with a laugh that the two boys in Boldt Hall were creating quite a stir. He recommended that no vote be taken on Stephen for the moment. It would be better, he said, for both Stephen and George to be resolved on the same day, so we don't have to give one of them bad news without informing the other of his fate. And so the brothers quieted down and discussed other candidates. But, Huff told himself, lines were being drawn here that he had not expected, and he had better position tomorrow's discussion carefully to avoid dissension.

That evening, an Eta Chi delegation knocked on George's door, and Power Team B, led by Jerry Wells, asked Stephen if they could spend some time alone with George. Jerry had volunteered to see George when Huff confided in him that he was troubled by what had happened at the afternoon meeting. He led a power team with only one other senior, Isaac Simon, a government major on his way to law school whom Jerry liked because he was so humble.

Surprisingly, Jerry's team also included two sophomores, Charles Lord and Buzz Delaney. Eyebrows had been raised when two sophomores were named to a power team, but no one doubted their ability. Charles was an imposing, loquacious, six-foot-six boy with a deep voice and wickedly sardonic attitude. In a coup, he would succeed Huff as rush chairman in his junior year.

One look at Buzz Delaney and you knew the type. He looked like a model, and had the disdainful smile and knowing shrug of a cool, popular kid that made girls forget the boy they were dating. He was also the perfect foil for Charles' cutting wit, acting sheepish and apologetic for him.

Jerry gripped George's hand firmly and smiled genuinely after Stephen left the room. He told George he specifically asked to be on this visit tonight because he had heard so many good things about him. George sat in his chair facing the door, and the four brothers took places opposite each other on the two beds in front of him. The power team had clearly been having a good time together and their energy carried into the room. They laughed as Charles imitated one of the girls that had been calling Buzz relentlessly. Then Jerry asked them to be serious for a moment.

George thought they must be about to make him a bid, and he started to prepare how he would respond. Then Jerry Wells looked straight at him and said, George, we are not here tonight to offer you a bid. The room got a little warmer.

Don't you think that's a little over-dramatic? Buzz asked. He looked at George and said, We haven't made a decision either way, George, but you will be up for bid tomorrow, so this is the time for…As Buzz paused, Charles broke in.

For you to tell us whether you're a cross dresser! Charles' big head bounced as the room laughed. Come on, Charles went on, we're going to make the guy pee in his pants.

Jerry Wells looked exactly the same as he did when they entered the room, but inside he was fuming. He enjoyed having fun as much as the next guy, but he also had spent the last three years practicing the fine art of formal rush, and he saw no place for the high irreverence on display here. So he regained control of the conversation, politely observing to Charles and Buzz that they needed to be more efficient with the limited time they had. Buzz put on his sheepish look and apologized. Charles just squinted.

When George first heard they were not giving him a bid, his mind's eye zoomed up to the corner of his room, and he watched the interchange dispassionately. Inwardly, he noted that nothing ever seemed to be easy with these people. Then Jerry turned to face him directly. George zoomed back to his body, composed and ready.

Jerry Wells had fine, rosy skin and an appealing, oval face. When he spoke, he lifted his face slightly, which made his cheeks seem to puff out. He made a cheery impression, and yet there was nothing at all soft about him. He would, in fact, go on to be an astute and competitive business executive for Hilton International.

I apologize for the uneven start we have made here, he said. It's my fault. So let me go first, and share with you what I call the magic of Eta Chi. Jerry spoke for five minutes while the others listened, and George relaxed. Isaac Simon followed, talking about the different ways to be a brother in their fraternity. Lord and Delaney chimed in too, telling George how much fun they thought the house was.

As the boys talked, George pushed his hair behind his right ear, and leaned forward. When it was time for him to speak, he told the boys about Fred Wineberger, the first person he had met at college.

So here I am, bursting at the seams, and I walk into the infirmary. Do you guys know where the infirmary is? It's halfway to downtown, for chrissakes! Anyway, I walk in and I think the room is empty, and then I see this kid lying on one of the beds. So I go over, and start talking to him, and it turns out the guy is only sixteen years old and all he can say is – *My parents abandoned me!*

The Eta Chis laughed. George imitated the way Fred had lain so limply on his infirmary bed and then did a perfect rendition of the boy's clipped New York accent. But then he told the Eta Chis about Fred's ambition to be the editor of the Cornell Daily Sun. I admire that in Fred, he explained, because there are about two dozen things I want to accomplish at college. George never knew quite what he was going to say, but when the words tumbled out, his eyes glowed.

So my point is, when I met Jackson Miles today, it made me think of Fred Wineberger, and then of all the things I want to do while I am at Cornell...

Jerry Wells was studying George intently. He had expected to dislike him, but he was impressed. And sitting next to him, Lord and Delaney had loved his imitation of Fred Wineberger. They all agreed afterwards that George was not shallow. Isaac was still not sure, but Jerry was convinced. Now George had a second senior on his side.

Huff had sent Power Team A to see Stephen Dawn, and they arrived about five minutes after the first Eta Chis had left George. Jackson Miles, Sandy Hitchens ("Hitch" to his brothers), Bob Neff and Art Woodhall moved through dorm visits like synchronized swimmers through a pool. Jackson was always the centerpiece, but each of the boys was passionate and quick-witted.

Stephen had learned that George had not received a bid, and secretly hoped he would get one before his roommate. When they settled down in the room, Stephen told them he was seriously interested in Eta Chi. In fact, although he liked Phi Delta, Eta Chi struck a deep chord in him. He thought that Eta Chi's focus on academic excellence really set it apart. As he said this, he looked directly at Jackson Miles.

Hitch replied that he was very excited by Stephen's enthusiasm. He identified with Stephen strongly, since he had been bid by both Phi Delta and Eta Chi as a freshman. Hitch adjusted his glasses and wiped his fingers across his moustache as he said, You can't go wrong with either house.

Bob Neff and Art Woodhall offered comments about how Stephen should think about the fraternity experience, and then Jackson Miles told Stephen that the house was seriously considering Stephen. He hoped that Stephen would help his own cause by spending some time at the house the next day. Stephen readily agreed to do so, and thanked them as they rose to leave.

❦

The Phi Delts did not arrive until nine thirty p.m., and again wanted to see both Stephen and George together. It was a fun, light discussion. The Phi Delts told them about the other boys who would be in their pledge class, how excited the fraternity was about the group that had already accepted their bids, and insisted that the class would not be complete without both of them. The only uneasy moment occurred halfway through the visit, when one of the brothers asked if they were both still rushing Eta Chi, and the boys responded affirmatively.

The Phi Delt who had asked scowled at the floor, and then looked at each of them and said, I don't see what either of you could see in that house. Stephen looked sideways quickly at George, but George did not look back. The boy continued, Eta Chi just doesn't fit either one of you. It's all about being flashy and cool, and it's not a place you will ever be able to call home. When he finished saying this, another brother took the conversation back to Phi Delta and asked them if they knew about the Eternal Keg. Stephen said no, and the boy explained that there was always a keg of beer tapped in the basement of the house, and beers were a nickel apiece. He smiled at them, and they smiled back, and the conversation resumed until they left at ten fifteen p.m.

That night, Stephen and George went to the bar in the West Campus dining hall and drank beer until one thirty in the morning, and then waited in line at Johnny's hot truck for "hot suicides." Johnny's hot truck served hot submarine sandwiches and sodas from ten p.m. until two a.m. every night on the sidewalk just below West Campus. George looked up through the side take-away window of the big truck and asked Johnny if he was in the mood to make him a roast beef sui. Johnny was temperamental, and roast beef suis were not on the menu, but sometimes he'd make them. A roast beef sui was a kitchen sink sub with every other ingredient Johnny had in the truck with roast beef on top. It came with melted cheese and pepperonis and lettuce and pastrami falling out of its sides. Its name fit.

The boys brought the subs back to their room, and inhaled them. The day had exhausted them, and the beers had made them ravenous. George was licking oil off of his fingers contentedly when he asked Stephen if he could picture them at Phi Delt. Stephen said yes. Then George asked him if he could picture them at Eta Chi. Fuck you, Stephen replied. George said he felt like he could throw up, and cursed Johnny's hot truck as he climbed into bed.

The last day of formal rush, fraternities usually have most of their pledges sewn up. It makes the day different, and George and Stephen, who had decided to visit Phi Delta first, could feel it from the time they got to the house. Brothers were more relaxed, and the freshmen who had already accepted bids were hanging around, getting used to their future home. The fact that classes had not yet started made it feel free.

George left at about ten thirty a.m. and walked slowly to Eta Chi. The day was cold, and after a minute he pulled the fur-ringed hood on his winter parka up over his head. He wished he had brought his gloves. He pictured the fire roaring at Eta Chi, and picked up his pace. As he walked along Cayuga Heights Road, he looked at the cemented stone walls bordering his path, but his mind was on Phi Delta. He could easily picture himself there.

Will Houghton greeted him cheerfully when he arrived, and Jerry Wells ushered him inside in front of the fireplace. The two stood talking for a while, and before long, George was amusing Jerry with demonstrations of acting techniques. Jerry beamed as George spoke, and when he finished, Jerry ushered him into the small room they called the Darling room, with nicely upholstered sofas and wallpapered walls. Jerry became businesslike and outlined for George the brothers he needed to see before the day was over.

George took the mission seriously, and ended up staying at the house right through lunch, until he realized it was three p.m. The tea was winding down, and George found Jerry Wells sitting in front of the fireplace on a wooden bench. They agreed that George had met everyone Jerry wanted him to, and Jerry asked what George thought. Jerry's cheeks puffed slightly as George told him how confused he had become. I honestly don't know what I want to do, Jerry, but I think I will wait to see if I even get a bid here before I obsess over it. Jerry nodded and told him they'd be by to see him tonight. Then they stood and shook hands, and George headed back to Phi Delt for a last look before dinner.

❧

When the brothers gathered for the final meeting of formal rush, they had received acceptances to all but one bid they had extended, and they were confident that the one holdout, Fritz Hublein, would accept as well. Huff offered up eight more boys for bid consideration. The first three had impressed the brothers and were voted in with roars of approval.

After considerable thought, Huff had decided to put forth George next, followed by Stephen. George made Huff think hard about what was really important for his legacy. He liked the fire that Bob Woodbridge and others had for him, he liked the zeal in George's eyes when they shook hands, but he was mindful of the seniors' distrust. The seniors were relying on him to fulfill the tradition, to discriminate in favor of what Eta Chi stood for. But George was a bridge candidate, someone who might be essential or disastrous. How was he really to know?

Twenty hands went up at once in response to George's name, and Huff scanned the group. He recognized a senior first, and the boy took a breath and waited for the room to grow still before he spoke. I know that George is a controversial candidate, but I would like to speak in favor of a bid, he began. A scattering of fingers snapped briefly, but Peter held up his hand for silence. I tend to have strong opinions about people, which some of you like and others may not, but let me say this: of all the people who have walked through our door this year, I believe George Muirfield has the greatest potential to become Consul of this house.

The senior knew what he was doing when he said this, but even he was surprised at the visible reaction he received. There were quiet gasps, a whistle, and two, softly-whispered, "No way!"'s. He thought he saw Max Burdoin actually turn red in the face for a moment.

Huff quieted the group down, let the senior conclude his statement, and then pointed to another senior. The boy stood up off the floor and disagreed, stating that he had spent time with George both during informal rush and this week, and he did not see any such promise in George. In fact, George struck him as all style and no substance; he did not believe the house would benefit from making him a bid.

Max Burdoin spoke next, followed by Hitch (who really did not have much to add, but wanted to support Max). Max chose his words carefully, but was emphatic about the significance of an Eta Chi bid, and the need to uphold standards. He told the group that they were speaking about a candidate who would not represent the house with the appropriate measure of polish or maturity. He never once used George's name, but simply referred to him as the candidate.

Seeing no other seniors' hands, Huff went to L.E.O. Pennington, who moved to the front of the room, and talked for close to five minutes about the value of having diverse, independent personalities in the house and the importance of the brothers focusing on what was important. George Muirfield, he concluded, has strength of character and intellect and it really doesn't matter whether everybody likes him or not.

Scotty and his roommate followed L.E.O., describing George as an exciting and unusual person who would undoubtedly entertain and challenge his brothers. This caused three seniors to immediately ask to be heard and Huff knew what had awakened them. This process is not to identify people who can entertain us, one senior sniveled. There are lots of Phi Delts and DU's we find entertaining, but we would never offer a bid to.

Tim Truesdale, a senior known among the sophomores as The White Elephant because of his enormous ears and chalky-colored skin, complained that the group was going far astray on certain points: namely that "this candidate" had shown no love for the house, no aptitude for brotherhood, no compelling reason for admittance.

Huff cringed. He knew that the brothers didn't take Tim seriously, and that his antiquated view on membership would rile the others. Then Mike O'Hare spoke. Mike was the most emotional brother in the house. He was quick tempered, excitable, and neurotically defensive of their fraternity. When Tim Truesdale spoke of love for the house, something snapped in his head, and he started to rant about the love they all showed the house, and that the house deserved.

Mike did not really know how he felt about George, but he was hot about what George was doing to this meeting of his brothers. He saw the house splitting apart over a candidate (something that Huff, in fact, also saw, but more objectively), and his anger spilled out. He paced back and forth in front of the brothers, exhorting them to come together and love this house as he did.

One of the sophomores called out and asked him which way he was going.

Mike screamed, I love this house! Do you love this house?

It was all Charles Lord could take. He cracked up and told Mike O'Hare to take a Quaalude, for god's sake. Everyone laughed. Charles went on, though he had not been prepared to.

Come on, fellas, we are not advancing any cause here at the moment. We look and sound ridiculous. I happen to like this guy. I don't love him, I have no idea whether he will be consul or not. But I don't think the house will fall off the hill if he joins the house. How much can one person do?

One person is the start of the end, Bob Neff replied, and that is what Max and Tim are trying to say. The group considered him carefully. Let's be clear here, he went on, we all know what can happen to fraternities over time. Look at DU. Four years ago when I joined this house, DU was a reputable, leading house. And now it has fallen into chaos. A friend of mine joined DU and he is sickened by what he sees. There are no standards there anymore. The brothers do whatever they want. They destroy property, get in trouble with the university, get arrested for drugs. I am warning all of you right now, that we must beware of and vigilantly defend against creeping DUism.

Every senior applauded Bob's comment. The rest of the house looked on. Jerry Wells, who had clapped along with the rest of the seniors, then spoke.

I want to say, although I am in full agreement with Brother Bob, that I do not view George Muirfield as a threat to DUism. In fact, and I know that he's kind of wired about this theater stuff, I actually find him conservative overall. And I think he has the right stuff to be an Eta Chi. So with apologies to my fellow seniors, I will vote to offer George a bid.

Bob Woodbridge seized this moment to weigh in, announcing that in his view, George was an outstanding candidate, who might become an acting legend or consul or something else altogether. He asked the group to look around the room and think about what distinguished the brothers in this fraternity. It is not values, although those are part of it. It is not entertainment, though that is part of it too, even if people don't want to admit it. It is passion. And George Muirfield not only has passion. He evokes passion in others. Look at this conversation, and look inside yourselves. Be honest. And don't assume that George will simply take our bid when we offer it to him. He is serious about Phi Delt and we will have to win him over to us.

Fingers started to snap across the room. Huff called for a vote if there were no further comments. Thirty-four brothers voted in favor. Twenty-eight brothers voted against. Will Houghton was momentarily unsure what to do. A simple majority was unacceptable in normal circumstances, and in this case was out of the question. He asked for further comment.

More brothers spoke, some couching their remarks in terms of defending the values of the house, others in light of their personal interactions with George. Then Jackson Miles decided to speak. We have all met people whose presence commands respect, but the reverence with which his brothers considered Jackson Miles exceeded simple respect. Jackson was their leader.

I have deeply considered the comments everyone has made here today, and I am more proud than ever to be a part of this house. Most of the brothers snapped their fingers loudly. Jackson went on. I agree with Bob Woodbridge that we must think first about what we are trying to do, and the qualities of character we are obligated to pursue as a legacy to our years here. I have heard many brothers whom I respect raise serious concerns about George Muirfield, but I have yet to hear one specific fact to substantiate what they are trying to convey. And Jerry Wells, your new consul, has spoken strongly in favor. I abstained from voting the first time, but I am now going to vote in favor of bidding George Muirfield unless brothers can come forward and offer some concrete details of his shortcomings.

The house erupted in hoots and cheers from the sophomores and juniors. Bob Woodbridge and L.E.O. Pennington high-fived each other. Scotty clapped loudly and others began to join him, but Huff yelled until they were quiet. He asked for comments, but none of George's previous dissenters raised their hands. Max Burdoin stuck his hands in his pockets and looked away impassively. All in favor? Huff asked. Five seconds later, George Muirfield had a unanimous bid.

We have a lot more work to do, Huff reminded the boys, and they settled down. Huff would later conclude that he should not have offered up Stephen Dawn next, but it had been his plan before, so that is what he did.

Jackson Miles spoke first, stating that he thought Stephen was a fine young man, with a sharp mind and a dry, ironic wit who would make a great brother.

Jerry Wells seconded Jackson's comments, saying that he enjoyed Stephen immensely. He found him thoughtful, and insightful, and committed to being a contributing brother to the house.

Art Woodhall, Mike O'Hare and Sandy Hitchens spoke next, talking about their conversations with Stephen, why they liked him, and how they thought he would be a true friend and ardent supporter of the fraternity.

Throughout these comments by many of the leading brothers in the house, there was an unfamiliar reticence in the brothers listening intently. Huff could not put his finger on it, and maybe it was the aftermath of the battle just concluded, but he could tell the group was not yet prepared to vote on Stephen. Personally, he liked Stephen, and he also thought of him as a safe candidate. He recognized L.E.O. Pennington, who also spoke in favor of a bid, but with little of the passion evident in his prior remarks. Then Scotty raised his hand and asked Huff if he felt the same thing in the room that he did.

Scotty was sitting on the floor and he did not get up to speak, but his voice was clear and thin in the air. Look at us. We are trying to like this guy because…why exactly? Because he will be an ardent supporter of the house? That doesn't do it for me. I told everybody last night I liked Stephen and I do. But that shouldn't be the only reason we offer him a bid. Let's hear someone offer more than that!

Huff pointed out that the brothers who had already spoken had already pointed out a number of his good qualities, then recognized a senior he thought was in favor of Stephen.

I have to admit to being lukewarm about this guy, he started. And we have never been a house that just tries to fill the beds. But when I compare him to some of the other pledges we have voted on, he is as good as some of them in my opinion. The one question I have about him is this –

will he do anything other than sit around here and be a good fraternity brother? Has anybody spoken with him about that?

No one answered immediately. Max Burdoin then shuffled to his feet and said he thought that this was too narrow a way to look at people like Stephen. We need people who will also focus on this house, and hold leadership positions right here. Stephen could end up being a valuable addition for that alone. And we all know that we compete heavily with Phi Delt for freshmen and he is clearly one of their top bid candidates.

Buzz Delaney booed, and Charles Lord joined him. Since when do we look at Phi Delta as the right profile of people we want in this house, Buzz yelled. I am only a sophomore, and this is my first time going through formal rush, but I have already heard so much about how distinctive we are I was beginning to wonder where I was. Now you tell me that we should take this guy because Phi Delt likes him.

If Max Burdoin had intended the Phi Delt comment to be a challenge, he did not see what a challenge it would become. Four brothers stood up and picked at something they knew about Stephen and then said, Let him go to Phi Delt! Or, I think he's good Phi Delt material!

Jackson Miles whispered to Huff to bring this to a vote, but before he could, Mike O'Hare stood up again and said that he was thinking of changing his mind about Stephen. He said he had been thinking about what Bob Woodbridge had said about passion, and he didn't feel that in Stephen. He smiled, and said when I want someone to love this house, I want them love this house! Everybody laughed.

Huff said, All right. We are out of time. We have to get the teams ready for the dorm visits. All in favor?

Wait a minute, Bob Woodbridge interrupted. I have a question. I think we are all kind of flat here because of the George Muirfield debate. I don't care if we are late going to the dorms, this is more important that being punctual. So if it's all right, Huff, I would like to ask everybody if they are excited enough about Stephen Dawn to make him one of our brothers. Or, if people just don't want to piss off Max Burdoin again!

Max Burdoin looked startled, but said quickly I am not pissed off. I was heard on George, and the brotherhood voted. I want everybody to vote their conscience now. He looked pale, and could have strangled Bob Woodbridge, but no one could have guessed that.

Huff said, Okay, everyone ready to vote clap your hands! And everyone did, and growled their readiness. All in favor? he asked. Fifteen hands were raised.

All opposed?

I am voting in favor of Eta Chi and against Stephen Dawn, Bob said loudly as his hand shot up. And more and more hands followed, until the entire room stood quietly with their hands raised, save four seniors (including Jackson Miles who watched the room intensely with his arms folded on his chest.)

That night, Jackson Miles asked Huff if his team could be the one to tell both George Muirfield and Stephen Dawn the news. Huff started to say no, but then hesitated. Bob Woodbridge had already pitched the idea of putting together a special team to bid Muirfield, which included Jackson. So he suggested that Jackson, Bob, Jerry Wells and Scotty do the Muirfield bid first, and then Jackson's regular team could do Stephen later.

The special team assembled and went to visit George first. It was snowing and the roads and walkways were slippery, and as they walked along they talked about how excited they were to get to do this bid. Each of the boys knew that something had happened at the house that day, and they were very curious about Jackson's thoughts on it. But Jackson acted enthusiastic and undaunted by the day, and he cautioned the team against too much optimism until they had George's signed bid in their hands.

George and Stephen both greeted the boys warmly. When they asked to speak to George, Stephen wished George good luck, and they all laughed as he left the room.

Before Jackson could start, Bob extended his hand and said to George, Welcome to Eta Chi, my friend. Jackson Miles solemnly told him that at an electric meeting of the brothers this afternoon, George received the most rousing endorsement he had ever seen at Eta Chi. He handed George the bid envelope, and told him the entire brotherhood stood behind this bid, and shook his hand.

Bob knew that Jackson was critically important to this presentation, and he loved the way Jackson took pains to express his personal enthusiasm over the opportunity to take George as one of his brothers.

Scotty spoke next, and in a slightly halting voice, told George that he spoke for all of the brothers in hoping that George would make Eta Chi his home for the rest of his Cornell experience. He told him how George was viewed as a key pledge in this class, in fact the missing link that they had been looking for all during rush.

Then Jerry Wells puffed his cheeks a little, and George and he exchanged huge smiles as he talked about the difference character makes in life, and the choices that stand out as turning points in a career. Eta Chi is one of those choices, he told George, and I am supremely confident that it is the right decision for you.

Bob said, It looks like we want you to join. The two boys regarded each other openly for an instant. Then George asked whether Stephen was going to get a bid.

Jackson told George that they were not going to offer Stephen a bid, but asked him not to say anything. Jackson assured him that he himself would come back later tonight to give him the news. It was very close, but Stephen had fallen short of unanimity.

Jerry asked him how he felt about that news, and George said, I just wanted to know. I don't know what I think.

They nodded their heads. This happens more than you might think, Bob explained. We know that Stephen has Phi Delt, and your friendship can be just as strong without sharing a room in the same house.

George told them he was okay with that, thanked them, told them he was very excited about their bid, and wanted to sleep on it. They left shortly.

When Stephen came back in, George told him about the bid, but said they would not reveal anything about Stephen. Later, after Jackson and his other team had spoken with Stephen and George returned to the room, Stephen laughed it off and told George that if he was George, he would join Eta Chi. I would, I'm serious. I'd leave you in a heartbeat.

George said it was going to be a tough decision for him. It was the truth. What did his life have in store for him? He could stick with Stephen and join Phi Delta. He could pick Eta Chi. Or he could just come to his senses and focus on Caitlin. His crystal ball offered up only clouds.

CHAPTER FOUR

The theater arts and music departments at Cornell shared Ridley Hall on the arts quad, in the northeast corner between Goldwyn Smith Hall and the gold-domed architecture school anchoring the north end of the Quad. Ridley was an unassuming, dusty old place. Tired, dark wainscoting separated the doorways to rehearsal and practice rooms and professors' offices. At the north end of the building two department administrators sat outside the Dean's office and cajoled and reassured the fragile egos and personalities of actors, directors and professors.

Derek Steele entered through the main door, strode past the large cork bulletin board filled with announcements, schedules, and callback lists, and greeted the administrators in a loud voice. He had come back from Christmas break with his head almost exploding with ideas for *Oedipus*. It was Monday morning, and the first class of Oedipus chorus was scheduled at 11:08 a.m. Twenty-seven students had signed up for the course, and the thought of having so many people to work with thrilled him. They had no idea what they were getting themselves into; he would have to slowly introduce them to his vision, in order not to scare them away.

He walked into Practice Room One and looked intensely around the room. The group buzzed with energy. Derek had convinced some of the better freshmen and sophomores to be in the chorus, rather than try out for any plays this spring, and they followed his gaze around the room as he sized up the kids he didn't know. George and Caitlin sat on the floor, quietly stretching, watching him. Derek noticed them without acknowledgement.

George was excited to be in the class. But he was positively thrilled to be reunited with Caitlin, who had rushed into his arms on one of the slippery paths that crisscrossed the hill below Uris Library making them both fall, laughing, into the foot of white snow that bordered the path. The forcefulness of Caitlin's presence consumed and confused him after his week of the all-male formal rush. She was affectionate, lively and effusive with him. She kissed him repeatedly. She had missed him terribly during break, but she assured him it was all right now. They were back with each other. George found it hard to think about the fraternity bids that had seemed such a high priority for the last five days.

He and Caitlin did not know what to expect in the *Oedipus* chorus, but they knew that Derek was the most progressive and abstract theater professor in the department. The graduate students had said that this was going to be a groundbreaking work. When they arrived at the class, they were surprised at the number of students they didn't recognize, but went immediately to a corner of the room to stretch in preparation for whatever Derek asked them to do.

Derek called the group to order, and sat in a folding chair in the middle of the room. The students sat on the floor against the long, inside padded wall. The room was lined on two sides by tall, old windows, and the floor was covered with rubber mats.

Derek talked about the play for awhile, about the differences between the Greek and Roman versions of <u>Oedipus,</u> and the need for this class to commit to this project from the beginning. This was a three credit course, but there would be an enormously demanding rehearsal schedule in addition to the three classroom sessions a week. If anyone wanted to get out because of competing demands on their schedule, they needed to do so by Wednesday.

But for their commitment, Derek promised them an experience they would never forget. They would learn Tai Chi. They would develop such a bond as a chorus that when they spoke, the audience would hear one, distinct and haunting voice. They would be part of a cutting edge experimental theater performance. George and Caitlin glanced at each other as Derek spoke, grinning excitedly.

In the afternoon, after they had finished classes, George and Caitlin met outside the Straight and walked, arm-in-arm, into the enormous, high-ceilinged common room behind the main lobby. The Straight, or Willard Straight Hall, was the main student union and administration building. It centered the main campus, separating the arts quad from the engineering quad. In the main lobby, there was a large, central administration section that looked like a wall of tellers at a bank. Student workers sat behind grates on a high counter, and sold tickets, gave directions and coordinated events. Above the main lobby were university and dining offices, and a large gaming room where students could play pinball, foosball and ping pong.

One floor below, an enormous dining hall with seventy rows of long, wooden stationary benches and two cafeterias fed the campus on weekdays. Two floors below the dining hall was the Willard Straight Theater which people normally entered through a separate door in the back of the building. It was a 700 seat theater, with a large main stage with trap doors, extensive lighting capability and reasonable backstage access.

In the room where George and Caitlin sat, areas were sectioned off by groupings of furniture where people sat and talked quietly, read or gazed out the windows that sat atop twenty-foot paneled walls on three sides. The high windows offered a sensation of grandeur. George tried to explain his fraternity dilemma to Caitlin, describing what formal rush had been like, and how he could not decide which house to join. Caitlin tried to picture what George was telling her, but in the end, she told him it all sounded silly.

So when George walked upstairs shortly before five to turn in his bid, he wasn't sure why he was doing this at all, let alone which house made the most sense. And then he saw Bob Woodbridge at a desk in the brightly-lit room that was the headquarters of the Interfraternity Council.

Hello, George. Bob's resonant voice made others look up from where they sat, sorting pledge cards. George zoomed back to the preceding Saturday, when he had walked over to Eta Chi and found Bob Woodbridge sitting alone in the music room.

I didn't expect to see you here, Bob. In his pockets, George fiddled with both the Eta Chi and Phi Delta bids, but he didn't tell Bob Woodbridge that. It seemed so crazy to say he was unsure of whether he was going to submit either one of them. He had walked upstairs to force himself to make a decision.

Bob was smiling, explaining that he helped out at the IFC, and casually asked George if he had come to his decision yet.

George fingered the Eta Chi bid in his pocket, and then pulled it out and handed it to Bob. The Eta Chi looked quickly at the bid, grinned, and extended his hand warmly.

You're making the right decision, George. What got you to finally make up your mind?

It was our conversation on Saturday…about the lights.

Bob nodded solemnly. When George had found him in the music room, they had sat and talked for a long time before George finally returned to the issue of how uncomfortable he felt in the house.

It is less comfortable, George, Bob had responded firmly. Because almost every brother who walks into this room makes the lights come up a little brighter. *You* make the lights come up, George. But it makes our house edgier, and even uncomfortable. So what you have to ask yourself is: do you want to live with men who make the lights grow brighter or not?

It was your explanation about the lights, George said again, lost in thought as he fingered the Phi Delta bid still in his pocket. Bob asked him if he could make dinner tonight, and then said the house is going to be ecstatic. They shook hands again, and George left, feeling relieved. Bob picked up the telephone and dialed the house. Mike O'Hare answered the phone and Bob told him to go tell Huff that Muirfield had accepted. Mike ran through the house, yelling for Huff. Eta Chi was 24 for 24.

George swung past his room, put on a tan corduroy sport coat and wide wool blue tie and zippered up his parka over the sport coat. It was bulky this way, but it was cold outside. Stephen arrived as George left their room and George said he had made his decision: he was going to be an Eta Chi, and he was headed there for dinner. Stephen congratulated him, and the two boys stood in the hallway for a moment considering each other. Well, Stephen finally said. George smiled, and said, This will work out, Stephen. We will make it work. Stephen smiled and said that he had always known that.

When George stepped outside the dorm, Stephen swung open the leaded window in their room and craned his head through to see him. Did you really just realize that? You are a bigger moron than I thought! Stephen cackled as he started to close the window and George packed a snowball and threw it at the window as it closed. Fifteen minutes later, as George entered Eta Chi, the boys were filing down the stairs and heading into the dining room for dinner. He saw Huff in the group, and Huff immediately stopped, walked over and wrapped his arm around George and said, You scared the hell out of me, young man!

Other brothers shook George's hand and welcomed him to the house, and Scotty swooped over and patted him heavily on his back. Before dinner the brothers stood solemnly behind their chairs and Jerry Wells said the fraternity meal prayer.

O Lord, Bless this table
As the guiding light of Eta Chi
Reveals truth and honor
In our lives together and
Forevermore.
Amen

Many of the brothers said amen at the same time, and then all sat down while brothers who were on kitchen duty served each table family style. Conversation resumed and George was introduced to Wally Stimpson, another freshmen pledge, who sat at his table.

All of the brothers wore jackets and ties, which were required Monday through Thursday, and Saturday evenings. Friday evenings, and at all lunches and breakfasts brothers wore casual clothing, although athletic wear was forbidden. Brothers prepared the dinner on Friday evenings, and no dinner was served on Sunday evenings, so that Andy, their chef, could have Friday and Sunday evenings off.

George watched and listened to the brothers' banter, and felt comfortable enough sitting there at dinner. The dress code gave dinner a purposeful and ceremonial feel that reminded George of high school. But the luster and excitement of formal rush had been replaced with the normal dynamics of school life, and a distant disappointment hovered within him. Where was all the invigorating drama of the preceding week? After dinner he went with Scotty upstairs to his room. Scotty explained what would happen during the pledge period, and told him he was welcome to visit whenever he liked. There would be an account set up for him, and meals he ate at the house would be billed to him, or to his parents, or whatever.

Scotty suggested he walk with George back to campus, and they walked in darkness along Cayuga Heights Road, up Thurston Avenue past Phi Delta, and across the suspension bridge. On the bridge, the wind blew hard down through the gorge and made them both shudder.

On the campus side of the gorge, a set of concrete steps rose steeply in a zigzag to the top of the hill. When they reached the top, George wished Scotty well, and headed to his dorm on West Campus. Stephen was at his desk studying, and nodded to him when he walked in. *Goodbye Yellow Brick Road* played softly on George's stereo, and Stephen asked if it bothered George. George shook his head no as he sat on his bed. He propped himself against the wall with his feet sticking over the edge, and tried unsuccessfully to read one of his textbooks. He spent most of the night doodling in the margins and went to sleep early.

The following Sunday, George reported as instructed to Eta Chi at five p.m. All of the pledges had been asked to be punctual, and as they arrived, they were told to leave their sleeping bags in the library and gather in the dining room. It was the first time that each of them had met everyone else in their pledge class, and they introduced themselves to people they did not recognize and talked about their impressions of the house. It was awkward at moments, but within thirty minutes, they had grouped off at tables and were laughing about what had happened to them at formal rush. Max Burdoin had come in just after five p.m., and told them to get to know each other until five thirty.

After a while, Jerry Wells, Will Houghton and Max Burdoin entered the room, and Jerry raised his voice to quiet the room. He stood near the kitchen entrance and welcomed them again to Eta Chi. Jerry told them how excited he was to greet them all, and that the brothers felt that this was a special class which would distinguish the house in years to come. He recognized Huff and explained that Huff had served as rush chairman, and was largely responsible for shaping this pledge class. He also explained that once again Eta Chi had succeeded in pledging every single freshman they bid, and led the group in applauding Huff's accomplishment.

Huff smiled, waved them quiet, and said, My job is now done and I look forward to welcoming you officially into the house tonight once your formal pledge meeting is done. My last official duty is to ensure that you all get to the Stables and get back here safely before morning.

Cullen Hastings raised his hand and asked about people who didn't have sleeping bags, and Huff said that many of the brothers had sleeping bags and would gladly loan them out.

Jerry Wells next introduced Max Burdoin, explaining that Max was the house's elected pledge captain. It was his responsibility to shepherd the pledge class through the pledging period and initiation. He is your lifeline for the next three months, Jerry told them, so call him with your questions and above all follow his instructions and guidance.

With that he told them that it was Max's meeting, and the brothers would be gathering at about eight p.m. for the party.

Max handed out a thickly-bound book entitled *The Benjamin Trident* that had the Eta Chi emblem embossed on the cover. Max explained that the pledges would be required to take a closed book examination on the weekend prior to initiation weekend. A passing score was required to participate in Initiation. The examination was based on the contents of the book, which told the history of Eta Chi, and set forth the expectations for brotherhood.

Fritz Hublein looked across the table to George and raised his eyebrows twice with a slight smile on his face. George widened his eyes in return. Max looked a little too serious for either of them.

You will also complete a number of pledge projects over the next three months, Max went on. When he said "number" it sounded like nuuuuuhmba. Then he instructed them to remove the index cards from the books he had handed out, and told them to write their name on one side of the first card, and then on the reverse side to list in order of preference the brothers they would like to have as a big brother.

Edward Stamer, one of the two Architecture students in the pledge class, asked for an explanation of what a big brother did. Edward was tall and blond, but he had a round, soft face and a voice that was light and raspy.

Max explained that all pledges were assigned a big brother as a personal guide and mentor through the pledging process, but the relationship often extended through college. You should pick someone whom you feel a connection with and you want to be able to confide in. We ask you to give us three names because we ask brothers the same question and try to match you together. If none of the brothers you select ends up being available, I will work with you to find a suitable match.

George puzzled over all of this. He leaned to the person next to him, a short, wiry boy named Ronny Trillo and whispered that joining a fraternity was becoming awfully complicated. Ronny had watched all of this with a smirk, and he nodded to George as he wrote "Ben Trident" as one of his three names, and then showed George. They both laughed. Max looked over and asked if they had any questions, and George shook his head no.

George sat looking out the window for a bit and wrote Scotty Willingham, Bob Woodbridge, Jerry Wells on his card, and walked up and handed it to Max as others were doing. Max thanked him formally, and stopped to read George's selections before looking up at him and smiling. No suh-pra-sis here, he said. George shrugged and returned to his table.

On the next index card, they were asked to write on one side all of the important dates for the next three months. George's card looked like this:

Feb 7	Valentine formal
Feb 20	Sketch – pledge paddle due to BB
Mar 1	Campus party – all frats
Mar 6	Required pledge meeting (Sat night)
Mar 22	Required pledge meeting

Mar	30 Pledge paddles(?) due
Apr	8 Initiation weekend
May	13 Darling formal

There were other dates that George didn't write down because they sounded more optional. Then the pledges were told to write on the other side of the same index card the dimensions and rules for the pledge paddles.

It took Max a long time to finish his introductions, partly because he liked to speak slowly, partly because he approached his task solemnly and partly because he had a lot to cover. When he finally let them go, brothers were already gathering in the library behind the glass doors which were closed to allow them some privacy.

By nine p.m., the brothers had worked the freshmen up into a lather about how much fun they were going to have. Then the sixty-odd brothers and the twenty-four new pledges drove thirty-five minutes outside of Ithaca to the Stables, a bar converted from an old horse barn. In the middle of the floor, a circular wrought iron staircase wound to a second floor that had long since been closed off. The bar itself ran along one wall, and there were only a few windows on the front wall, and off to one side. It was an Eta Chi tradition to rent out the Stables once a year on the Sunday following formal rush. The owner was happy to oblige since Sundays were normally quiet, and the amount of liquor consumed made his budget for almost a week.

Scotty handed George a beer, shook his hand, and said, Hey little brother! George laughed, and said, that was fast! For the next hour, the boys drank a lot of beer, and the upperclassmen told stories in informal groups about the rush process. The room grew loud and hot. Then Huff stepped up the circular staircase until his head was near the ceiling, put his fingers to his mouth, and whistled loudly to get the room's attention.

Ladies and Gentlemen, he began, as brothers hooted at him, it is my pleasure to introduce to you the pledge class of 1974! The room exploded in cheers, and Huff grinned wildly. His face was flushed red, and he took a sip from the beer in his hand before he continued.

He then asked Art Woodhall and Tim Truesdale to take his place on the stairs and lead the room in the brothers' traditional salute to the new pledges.

Art called out for Walt Stimpson to join them on the stairs, announcing to the crowd that he had invited Wally, who was a pledge in case anybody didn't know, because Wally impressed him as being a good limericker.

A good what? Someone yelled.

A good Lim – er – rick – er!! yelled Art.

And with that, Art offered up a limerick at the top of his voice:

Pardon me, ladies and gentlemen
I seem to have lost my condoms!
I put them right here
In my darling's brassiere
But obviously someone else found them!

There was laughter for an instant, and then the room erupted in song. The brothers stood, their glasses and bottles raised defiantly in the air, and belted out a refrain that would be repeated between every limerick recited that night.

Aye, Aye, Aye, Aye
Ee – Tah – Cheez never eat pussy
Bullshit!!
So let's have another verse
That's worse than the other verse
And waltz me around by my woolies!

If any of the pledges were as surprised as George, he could not tell. The brothers sang with gusto and exclamation, punctuating the end of each chorus with a sip or gulp or chug of beer. It seemed to George that the serious boys who had spoken so solemnly to him during rush had been released from prison. Even the softest-spoken seniors whom George thought boring and stilted wandered about the bar raucously. By midnight, Max Burdoin was hugging anyone within his reach, his face softer, somehow, and blotchy. In a corner, Wally Stimpson and Fritz Hublein conspired and then climbed the circular staircase, and sang their own version of the chorus over the hoarse voices of the brothers.

Aye, Aye, Aye, Aye
Your mother does squat thrusts on tree stumps
That's right!!
So let's have a verse
That's worser than this verse
And waltz me around by my woolies!

The brothers roared their approval, and then Bob Woodbridge stood on a bar stool, raised his bottle of Molson Ale, and called out another limerick –

There once was a pledge from Phi Delt

The room booed so loudly, Bob had to stop and raise his hand to quiet them down. He waited until the booing waned, and began again -

There once was a pledge from Phi Delt
Whose girlfriend before me knelt
She said open wide
And give me your pride
Because this is bigger than anything I've felt!!

And the brothers cheered even louder. George slapped Bob Wood-bridge on the back, laughing. Bob was shaking his head up and down in exaggerated swagger. After a bit, Bob draped his arms around George and Scotty and asked Scotty hoarsely if he thought George was ready to go streaking through Kappa Psi. Scotty leaned close to George and explained that some of the juniors and sophomores liked to streak through the so-rorities.

The room was swaying and the smell of beer mingled with perspira-tion. George was not sure he heard Scotty clearly but he smiled and laughed. Before long the party was beginning to dissipate and three car-loads of boys, including Bob Woodbridge, George, Harold Wise, Fritz Hublein and a number of juniors and sophomores left the dirt parking lot in a gust of dust.

It was one twenty in the morning when the cars pulled up in front of Kappa Psi. The boys giggled as they quietly moved from their cars to the front door. The sorority was silent and dark, with a lone light on in the living room that ran across the front of the house. The door was locked but one of the boys whispered, Come over here near the side door! He lifted a window, put his foot in the cradled hands of a brother and crawled inside. The back door opened a moment later, and the boys walked softly into the kitchen. There was a small night light in the corner, but the house was still. The group moved into a small, darker pantry between the kitchen and the dining room. They were laughing so hard that one of them shushed the rest.

The older boys started taking off their pants and the freshmen asked them what the hell they were doing, and the laughter started all over again. Take off your pants, they instructed, and carry them! The freshmen looked at each other in the darkened pantry with a mixture of alarm and humor, but did as they were told. And then one of the boys said Let's go! He raced out of the pantry naked from the waist down, holding his pants and shoes above his head, and started whooping as he led the rest of them up the stairs at one end of the living room to the second floor.

Once at the top of the stairs, he paused and waited to be sure that the boys were on the stairs behind him, and then he walked slowly down the long corridor singing "Whoo, whoo, whoo, whoo" in a loud voice. As George and Harold Wise passed through the middle of the floor, two bed-room doors opened slightly and girls with flashlights looked outside and giggled. One of them whistled.

Harold Wise let out an enormous, gleeful laugh and began to prance down the hall holding his arms high in the air. George, quite intoxicated, followed his lead, and was laughing so hard that he dropped his underwear without noticing. Once they got to the end of the hallway, the boys descended another stairway, and ran noisily out the front door. By now lights were turning on upstairs and some girls leaned out the window yelling at them.

The boys hooted as they climbed into their cars and sped away down Thurston Avenue. The vinyl seat in the car felt cold on George's bare skin, and his head was starting to hurt. When they got to the fraternity, they were still laughing, and they piled out of the car and walked across the ice-covered driveway barefoot, and still half-naked. George was sure that if he looked up he would see bright stars, but it helped the feeling in his head to look down.

Inside, the boys pulled their pants back on. The house was awake and boys were running around, mostly upstairs. Scotty told George to get his sleeping bag and come up to his room, and George headed into the library to collect it. He could smell the beer on his own breath, and felt woozy. A brother whose name George could not recall was softly playing versions of Pachebel's Canon on the piano, and he smiled as George waved to him. The two had not spoken much, and the brother asked George how he felt now that he was really an Eta Chi. George put his hand on the piano to steady himself, and said, Man you guys are different from what I expected.

The brother kept playing, but he nodded and grinned. Don't worry, he finally said. You'll do fine. George nodded and said good night, and lurched toward the foyer. When he got to Scotty's room, both he and his roommate were already asleep, so George threw his sleeping bag on the floor, climbed into it and closed his eyes. His head thumped when he lay down, and he knew tomorrow was not going to be kind.

When Caitlin saw George walk in to *Oedipus* class at 11:08, he looked haggard and rumpled. He waved to her with a bleak smile, and sat down next to her on the floor, yawned, and sat very still. Caitlin asked if he was okay. Yeah, of course, he replied, just beat. He had not mentioned to her that he was going to a party the night before, and he was not sure he was ready to describe the event to her. He also felt uncomfortable without his underpants on, and could not figure out why he had been unable to find them in Scotty's room that morning.

After class, they went to the Green Dragon for lunch and Caitlin pressed him about what was wrong with him. George told her he went to Eta Chi and ended up drinking a lot and staying up late.

On a Sunday night? Caitlin asked, disapprovingly. George gazed silently at his girlfriend, noticing for the hundredth time the oddly free feeling of denim against his naked skin. Caitlin did not drink, and privately she wished George didn't. She wondered if fraternities were just organized barrooms, as her father had told her. She hoped this wasn't the start of a different side to George.

George grimaced when he saw Caitlin's disapproval, and changed the subject. He was beginning to feel better. The fresh salt bagel he had bought for himself, layered thick with cream cheese, tasted wonderful with his coffee. He had loaded the coffee with sugar and light cream, and sipped it carefully between bites.

There are, of course, innumerable moments in one's life that seem to stop and swivel. The confluence of George's hangover (which made his salt bagel and sweet coffee taste so incredibly good), Caitlin sitting next to him in a simple plaid shirt and blue jeans and smelling of lilacs again, his somewhat blurred recollection of the night before, and Derek Steele's technicolor vision of the play which he had just shared with the class washed over him. George sensed a great clarity about himself, and an enormous excitement surrounding him. He was on the eve of something; he just wished he knew what.

Caitlin looked around the Green Dragon, hoping that Derek Steele would come in. She and George were clearly hooked on Oedipus, and Caitlin was infatuated with their professor. She thought he was brilliant and his brooding passion about the theater gave him depth and sensitivity. She also liked how ruggedly he spoke to her. Well, he spoke to the whole class, really, but she imagined he spoke to her.

The Roman version of *Oedipus* was set in the declining wasteland of the end of an age. There was no glory left, only poverty and corruption and discord. And Derek Steele envisioned the chorus of Oedipus as a living backdrop to the play – a moving, disheveled depiction of the masses surrounding the conflict Oedipus faced. But before they could bring any of this to life on a stage, the class had to first learn how to move, not only as a unit, but also on iron beams which would be suspended across the stage. They also had to learn how to speak in one voice.

To accomplish the first objective, Derek brought in a Tai Chi teacher named Quinn, and announced that before any actor would be permitted to climb onto a beam, they would have to meet Quinn's approval. Quinn was a short, wiry man in his early thirties who talked in a soft but clipped way. No one ever learned where he had come from, but he stayed with the class through the play, and, in fact, became the director of the chorus during the final stage of rehearsals when Derek worked with the main cast.

As weeks fell away into February, *Oedipus* became an obsession with the chorus. They worked long hours outside of class, and Caitlin and George became inseparable. They ate every meal but breakfast together, studied together, learned Tai Chi together, and spent Monday through Thursday evenings in Ridley Hall, often until ten p.m. From there they would walk across the Arts Quad and down the hill to West campus to

Caitlin's room and study for an hour or two before George left for his room.

On weekends, they spent all day, both days, in the library, catching up on their other classes. In *Oedipus* class, Caitlin and George tended to separate and focus, but outside of that, they were within touching distance of each other, and usually touching. Caitlin lavished attention on George in spare moments. When they took study breaks in the library, she would stroll with him and stop and wrap her arms around his neck and hug him tightly. He could not decide whether this made him excited or embarrassed, but he hugged her back. They stood for minutes like that as students walked past them.

It was not obvious to George how engrossed he had become with either *Oedipus* or Caitlin until the Friday night before the Eta Chi Valentine formal. Stephen was complaining to him that he never saw George anymore as they sat at their desks in their room with their backs to each other. Tapping his foot against the rung on his chair, Stephen reminded George that he had blown him off three times in the past week, and George looked up from his book and stared at the index card propped against his typewriter.

Oh shit! I completely forgot about that formal party!

What? Stephen answered, irritated. It was clear that George wasn't even listening to him now.

George explained about the formal, and Stephen asked him whether he had even gone to Eta Chi in the past month, and George said, I must have! but then laughed. In truth, he had not been back to the house since the night he had gotten so drunk.

Stephen said he was glad that George had not joined Phi Delt, because he would be wasting his time explaining to everyone where his wayward roommate was.

George protested, but it jarred him awake for a moment, and for the briefest of moments he felt bad that he had totally ignored Eta Chi. He wondered how Scotty was and made a mental note to ask Caitlin if she would come with him to the party. Then the regret was gone, and he told Stephen about Tai Chi and how he had found his center. Stephen smirked and told him the only center he cared about was the student center, where he was heading now if George wanted a beer. George replied that he would meet him there in half an hour, and Stephen said, Whatever.

After Stephen left the room, George sat in a meditation position on the floor between the two beds and began to contemplate his center. The floor was much harder than the rubber mats in Ridley, which made it harder to concentrate, but he was determined.

He closed his eyes and pictured himself in *Oedipus* class, listening to Quinn explain the life force that was available to anyone who took the time to find and harness it. His center, Quinn told him, was somewhere in the middle part of his body, but only George could know exactly where.

One of the first steps to understanding was to look inward with your mind's eye and discover this place.

It might be up high in your chest, or down low, it might be to one side or the other, but it was where the center of your being resided, and it had a shape and a color and a weight all its own. Most people live their lives unaware of their centers, but it was where you must begin in order to learn how to gain control over your body.

George had tried unsuccessfully to find his center in his first several attempts. He had closed his eyes, but ended up listening to the room around him, to the shuffle or movements of people on either side of him. He had felt his arms and legs grow weary of the sitting position, and struggled against the impulse to move and fidget, and ended up opening his eyes to look for Caitlin.

Then, in one class, Quinn had wished to demonstrate the difference between muscular energy and life energy, and all of the students took turns lying on the floor and going through a series of relaxation exercises. Before the exercises, a student would cup one of the prone students' heads in his hands and gently lift the head off the mat and simply hold it carefully a few inches in the air. Quinn would ask the students holding the heads to note the weight of the heads in their grip.

After the prone students had gone through the relaxation exercises, the other students lifted their heads again. When George lifted the head of the student he worked with for the second time, he was shocked by how much heavier it was. Quinn smiled and spoke softly, explaining that there are muscles in the neck which usually do not relax, even during sleep, in order to protect the head and brain from injury. Our muscles unconsciously are at work, independent of our conscious effort, he told them.

When it was his turn, George gave himself completely to the relaxation exercises and let his head float freely in the hands of the boy holding it. And when the exercise was completed, he went to lift his head but found that his body did not automatically respond. He had to concentrate, with his head still on the floor, to will himself to lift his head, and when he did, his head and neck felt suspended in the air. A giddiness overcame him. Quinn was standing over him, smiling. I have been waiting for you, George, he said simply.

After class, George told Quinn he felt like his head was still free-floating above him, as if it were not really connected to his body. Quinn nodded, telling him that the feeling could last quite a while. It lasted two days for George. He began to take Quinn more seriously.

Three classes later, during different relaxation and meditation exercises, George felt his skin tingle and then his head soared inward toward a large, very heavy copper-colored orb with a small tip protruding from its bottom. The orb was suspended by a means he could not see in the low middle section of his body. It swung freely but imperceptibly, in a gyroscopic pattern. George had found his center, and after examining it for a time, he came back outside himself, and opened his eyes to tell Quinn. But Quinn spoke before George could, saying, I know. I can tell from the way your body moved.

For George, and for about two-thirds of the class, the revelations of Tai Chi proved a powerful elixir. Awakened to new understandings about themselves, they moved quickly to learn more. In subsequent classes, Quinn showed them how energy could be directed to flow from the center to any part of their body they wished. In this way, they learned that they could acquire far greater balance and control of the way that they moved. And unlike muscles that grew tired from exertion, the power that flowed from their centers grew stronger over time.

To demonstrate the supremacy of this life energy over physical strength, Quinn asked the students to first attempt a task by relying on their muscular strength, and next by directing energy from their centers without any muscular effort. Quinn had George stand against the interior padded wall and put his hands on the arms of Arthur Conde. He instructed Arthur to use his full effort to keep George pinned against the wall. Arthur, who was smaller, but quite a bit stronger than George, put his hands on George's shoulders and leaned into him with one foot extended behind the other.

George was told to push Arthur off of him without allowing his back to come away from the wall, so George placed his hands on Arthur's forearms and pushed. Arthur did not budge, so George strained as hard as he could, but Arthur barely flinched. Then Quinn told George to center himself, and to direct energy to his fingers to push Arthur. Not your hands, George, and not your arms, but simply your fingers, he instructed.

George placed his hands again on Arthur's forearms, and closed his eyes. By now he found it easy to return to his center, but he had never been asked to direct energy so precisely. The class waited, and a few giggled softly, whispering. Quinn hushed them, and urged Arthur to exert his full strength. Then George was inside himself again, at his center where things seemed curiously silent and in slow motion. He pictured his fingers, and then his center, and then he willed a flow of light to bolt from his center to the tips of his fingers.

Arthur flew across the room, tumbling into the opposite wall with his feet in the air. George opened his eyes slowly, unsure if anything had happened. Arthur pulled himself up and George asked if that had been real. Quinn spoke to the students who watched, telling them that George was the first student whom he found acceptable to work on the beams. Arthur rubbed his neck and asked Quinn if he could work with another student. Quinn laughed, told him he should want to work with George, but he didn't care.

On stage, there are actors who become their characters and interact with other actors genuinely. These actors are usually referred to as "giv-

ing actors," or "actors' actors." They are not always commercially successful, but they are appreciated for their craft, and can almost always
find work. And then there are other actors who see the theater as more of
a presentation to an audience. They do not really incorporate a character,
and barely notice the dynamics going on around them on a stage. They are
sometimes successful, but they are obsessed with their own image. Arthur
was one of the latter.

Caitlin had watched George grow quickly into one of the former, and
she was scared and jealous of his progress. When he threw Arthur across
the room like a tennis ball, she shook her head and turned away to look
out the window. He had been telling her about his center, what it looked
like, how powerful it made him feel, but she had thought he was just getting carried away in the moment. And now this.

She could tell that the directors increasingly took notice of him. He
seemed to grasp things so quickly, even when he started from nowhere.
She was still leaning on the window sill when Derek Steele came up behind her, gently touched her shoulder, and looked at her inquisitively. She
turned to him, smiled and said, I'm okay. Good, he replied, because we
need you to focus no matter what. Then he turned and barked out the next
assignment. She looked at the back of his curly brown hair as he spoke,
and wondered if Derek had just come on to her. She hoped not, but Derek
was one of those professors who lived quite the full life with his students
outside of class.

It may have been the thought of Derek Steele in the back of her mind
that led her to say Great! when George asked her the next morning to accompany him to the Valentine formal. Somehow, even though she could
not picture herself going to a fraternity house with a bunch of sorority
girls in make up and Lilly Pulitzer dresses, going with George was a way
for her to confirm her relationship with him. Even if it was only confirming it to herself.

So she put on one of the dresses that had not made it out of her closet
since arriving at school, and put her hair up. She never wore make up except for eyeliner, but she even had fun applying that in the mirror in her
bathroom over the sink where George had washed off his boots. Then
George came to pick her up, and she inhaled sharply at the sight of him.
He had told her he would be wearing a tuxedo that he had rented, but she
had not been prepared to see him in formal clothes. He looked gorgeous.
She asked him to wait a minute, and ran down the hall to borrow some
lipstick from a friend before they left. Even Clive whistled when he saw
them leave.

Eta Chi was not what Caitlin had expected, and the girls weren't either. All of the boys wore tuxedos, and while some of the girls dressed
like prom queens, others looked positively frumpy. George introduced her
to Will Houghton and Jerry Wells in the foyer, and they were gracious,
articulate and fun. The Darling Room had been converted to a bar, and

George got her a coke and himself a screwdriver while she spoke with Will Houghton's date. She was a very down to earth type from the University of Pennsylvania, who had come to the Valentine formal for the last three years.

The lights flickered and the boys escorted their dates through the library into the dining room. The ceiling of the dining room was decorated with paper hearts, and there were candles lit on each table. Polite boys in waiter uniforms served pumpkin soup, followed by chicken cordon bleu with roasted potatoes and assorted vegetables. Coffee was served with dessert – a banana cream pie that brothers at the table explained was one of Andy's signature recipes.

Then the brothers rose and stood solemnly behind their chairs. Most of them put their hands behind their backs as they sang The Darling Song with harmonious reserve. Jerry Wells addressed the group, asking them to join him in thanking Andy for such an incredible dinner, and everyone stood and applauded loudly as Andy came out in a chef's hat and took a bow. Wells next asked for a similar tribute to the brothers who gave up the opportunity to invite their Darlings in order to serve the meal, and the room applauded again.

Caitlin watched George curiously throughout these moments. He did not know the words to the song they sang, but he joined in as best he could, standing stiffly behind his chair. He conversed excitedly with a boy named L.E.O. and several other boys at their table. They were in a place far, far away from the rehearsal rooms in Ridley Hall, and while she was by no means uncomfortable, it seemed false and unnatural. George, however, looked so at ease, so enthusiastic, that she had a hard time picturing him in the way she really knew him – in their theater classes and in the personal cocoon they had made for themselves. George left her for a moment to speak with someone at another table, and then returned to lead her into the Great Hall where a jazz trio played dance music. The boys had hired a small trio to play dance tunes. The massive rug that normally covered the entire, shiny, hardwood floor of the Great Hall was rolled to the far end, and they danced until the room was hot. Next to them, Scotty was dancing cheek to cheek with a girl named Marilyn who had invited Caitlin to come over to see her sorority sometime.

George seemed preoccupied as they danced, but Caitlin ignored it and let herself listen to the soft, rhythmic jazz standards with her eyes closed while they danced. She could feel George's breathing, and rested her head softly on his shoulder. His right hand stayed lightly but reassuringly on her back. After awhile, but before she was really ready, George suggested they leave. He went and collected their coats, and they were out the door before the song ended.

On the way back to her dorm, Caitlin thanked George for the night, and she said how impressed she was with his fraternity. It certainly is not what I expected, and now I understand why you wanted to join it. George said little in reply, but agreed with her quietly.

Privately, George kept reliving his conversation with Max Burdoin during dinner. Max had looked at him with the wisp of a smug smile curling above his prominent chin and told him he was shirking his responsibilities as a pledge. George was a standout in the pledge class, the rest of who were coming over to the house regularly, and getting to know their brothers.

George asked what kind of commitment was exactly required, and Max smirked before replying that George was proving to the brothers that it had been a mistake to offer him a bid.

I have been busy, was all that George could think to say as he looked hard at Max.

Too busy? Max had replied lightly before excusing himself to return to his date.

George pulled the car into a parking space below his dormitory before he decided to forget Max's remarks. Caitlin was talking, and the car had finally warmed up, so he kept it running for them. The hot air felt good on their feet.

Well, George said, I am glad we went, and I clearly had the prettiest date in the whole house! Caitlin punched him playfully on the arm.

You looked pretty good yourself, she told him. Then they sat in the car for awhile and kissed, stretching across their seats awkwardly. The familiar pattern of their relationship had returned by the time they got out of the car.

The following Monday, Derek Steele introduced new exercises in *Oedipus* class. He wanted every member of the chorus to develop their own character, and stay in character throughout the play. Although they said all of their lines together, and would be heard as one voice, their characters should be fully developed.

Once they had chosen what and who their characters would be, the next step was for them to build the bodies of their chosen characters. Derek was standing in the middle of Rehearsal Room One. He wore a heavy tartan plaid shirt, blue jeans and black basketball sneakers. It was March first, and the play was two months away, but he felt behind schedule.

There are three basic bodies in this world, he said in a loud voice, and they are head, heart and hip. You can break down every body you see into components that belong to one of these three styles. So I first want you to express yourself in each of these three body types. First the head people. This college is filled with head people, so it will be very easy for you to identify them around you. They are the ones that walk with their foreheads in front of the rest of their bodies.

The class laughed.

That's right. You know the ones I mean. They are thinking so hard that their thoughts pull the rest of their body along. They don't notice anything around them, and they often have skinny arms because they can't get out of their own heads long enough to work out.

The students laughed more as Derek demonstrated head people and they followed his example.

Good! He yelled. Okay, next are heart people. I don't see many heart people on this campus, but I do see some on the first warm day of spring. All the female architecture students wander out of the building across the quad to feel the sun. Have you seen them? Their heads don't lead their bodies, because they are not head people! In fact their heads lag their bodies slightly. Their arms swing loosely along their bodies and their palms face out in front of them. They swing their chests back and forth, because their hearts are pulling their bodies along. Can you see it?

The class tried to reenact what he described, and he picked Caitlin as a perfect example. She held her face at an angle as if to catch the sun, and strolled across the room, swaying her chest and moving her hands and shoulders in little round motions.

That's a heart person! yelled Derek.

Now you all know about hip people, right?

Silence followed as he looked around the room.

Come on, he said, exasperated. Hip people are the most obvious! Think of football players with their helmet in one hand and their other hand where...? On their hip! Watch them swagger across the field. Their hip is the motor that takes them across a field!

The students imitated hip people easily. They strutted and sashayed around the room. Then Derek sat down and they all followed his lead. This only begins the inquiry into your body, he said. Sometimes a head person plays football, and sometimes a heart person thinks first. Your assignment is to find your character's body, with whatever mixture of those three body types he or she is, and then move consistent with that throughout the play.

But first you have to unlearn your own body type. You have to prepare your body to accept a new one, and the only way I know how to do that is to teach you how to put your body into its natural neutral position. So that's where we will pick up next class.

George and Caitlin were laughing so hard, they almost ran out of the building after class. They immediately began to pick out the head, heart and hip people who passed them on the quad. A professor walked by, and his head leaned way out in front of him as if he were fighting a strong headwind.

Head, they said simultaneously to each other.

A girl passed them going the other way, so they only saw the back of her, but she moved slowly and sensuously along the walkway, looking up at the gold dome on the Architecture building.

Heart, said George.

No way, Caitlin shot back, clearly a hip person. She's too cold, too oblivious to be a heart person. And so on.

On Wednesday, Derek taught them how to find neutral. Your body has developed habits and patterns you are not aware of, he began, and they are contrary to the natural structure of your body. Your muscles and your brains and your attitudes all influence the way you walk, the way you bend over to pick something up, the way you sneeze.

Did you know that there is a position in which your body can stand upright without using your muscles? Your body has a natural, "neutral" position. It looks nothing like all of you look at the moment. It is geometric and angular, and it allows the body to truly rest, even when standing. So what we need you all to do is unlearn everything you have told your body to do since you were a baby, so that you can then build a new body – the body of your character – for you to assume while you are in character.

Derek showed them how to assemble themselves from the bottom up, angling their feet and their legs and hips and torso in accordion fashion so that by the end the class looked somewhat like puppets suspended by strings from the ceiling. And once they found their own, unique neutral position, he asked each of them to incorporate one, tiny attribute at a time and to let their bodies feel the attribute and then connect it to the next one.

Within a week or two, students who walked into the class as heads or hearts would find neutral and slowly emerge as different body styles, and find it increasingly easier to stay in that body style than if they simply tried to copy someone they had seen. Homework included submitting minute details of the characters and body styles they had developed for themselves within the chorus, so that Derek could observe and comment on areas where they were inconsistent or just bad. He was a harsh judge, and his students responded with countless preparations in the evenings until his criticisms were replaced by smiles.

In order to prepare the chorus to speak as one, Derek told them he had never heard a chorus on any stage, in any performance, that anyone could understand. But *Oedipus* was going to be different. By now he did not need to ask this class if they were willing to put in the work to accomplish this goal. But he did, and they started clapping wildly.

There are seven, distinct harmonal resonance parts of your body, Derek taught them. Your first task is to learn how to separate and focus each of those parts so that each of you can start to control where the noise you make is coming from. He had the class hold their stomachs and emit

a low, deep "Ohhh" sound. When they all could feel their stomachs resonating, he had them move their hands to their chests, and in a slightly
higher pitch say "Ahhh."

From here they moved to their necks ("Eeeeh"), and then their nasal
passages ("Nnnnnh"), their foreheads ("Mmmmmh") and the tops of
their heads (a very high "Eeeeeeeeh"). The class looked around at each
other and smiled as they practiced. Then they had to isolate each resonant
area, so that there was no spillage from the stomach region to the chest
region, and so forth.

In addition to knowing how to recognize and control their own
sounds, Derek also insisted that they learn to listen to each other with far
bigger ears than they usually used. They started down this path by sitting
in a tight circle in the middle of Rehearsal Room One and making a sound
song. But they were not allowed to make any sounds that were inconsistent with the group's intent.

This proved difficult indeed. Actors by nature like to perform, and
unscripted sounds or songs or whatever seemed like just another improvisational exercise. Derek sat off to one side, and every time one of the
students made a sound, whether it was a voice or a thud, or even a slight
movement, he called time out and told them to begin again. He did this
until he could sense the frustration building in them, and then he stopped
the class early and told them to come prepared next time.

To begin the next class, Derek told them to wait for a full two minutes
before anyone made the first sound. Arthur Conde lasted 48 seconds.
Derek admonished him, and reset the clock. Twenty-seven boys and girls
sat, eyes closed, in a tight circle waiting for time to pass, fearful of making a sound until, after awhile, someone built a long, slow breathing into a
light whistle. The whistle stopped, and there was silence again for a moment, and then two sounds broke loose, one a growl and the other a sort
of whoosh. Pitter pats followed, and before long there was an acute, sen-
sory cacophony of sounds, some long and repeated, others momentary
and aching. And finally silence again.

The students slowly opened their eyes, but almost no one moved, and
Derek smiled broadly. After a while, he said, Now you get the basic idea.
All we have to do now is combine your characters and your bodies and
your speeches and choreograph the play with all of you moving on pipes
thirty feet above the main stage in Willard Straight Theater!

The class gasped.

Did you say thirty feet? Arthur asked incredulously.

Thirty feet for some of you. We won't make anyone go up who
doesn't want to. Derek replied.

Caitlin looked at George with her eyes enormously wide. George
rocked back and forth, grinning wildly at Derek. He didn't notice Caitlin
looking at him until she tugged at his sleeve.

CHAPTER FIVE

A few days after the March 6 pledge meeting, Scotty walked to campus early and swung by Boldt Hall. He hoped to catch George before he went to class, but the door was shut and locked, so he left a note on the door, asking George to call him at the house.

They had lunch together the next day at the Straight. George loped down the wide staircase to the cafeteria level and ran up to Scotty who was waiting at the turnstile. They were genuinely glad to see each other, and for most of lunch George told Scotty about head, heart and hip people, and they spotted the different types moving around the room. Scotty told him about his engineering classes, and described the computer programming class he was taking.

In order to write computer code, Scotty had to create and order thousands of punched-through cardboard tickets. It was not uncommon to see engineering students carry shoe boxes of cards around with them. Scotty described how one of the kids in his class dropped his shoe box upside down on his way into class, spilling all of the cards out of their order. They laughed and chatted some more, until George asked why he had wanted to have lunch.

Scotty sat up on the long, hard bench opposite George and leaned forward. Don't shoot the messenger, okay? he began, but you need to show a little more interest in the house.

George nodded and said, Okay. Scotty said that the house expects pledges to spend some time there to get to know it before initiation, and initiation is only a few weeks away. So why don't you come over once in a while the next few weeks? Hang out in my room, wander around and let everybody see you, he told his little brother.

George explained how busy he was with *Oedipus*, but agreed he would find the time to show up occasionally.

Did Max Burdoin send you? he asked Scotty.

Yeah, Scotty answered. It was true. Max had told Scotty that George was not demonstrating enough commitment to become a brother. So Scotty wanted to help his little brother, but somehow George made him feel embarrassed.

That's cool, George replied. That's what big brothers are for.

The two boys laughed. Scotty asked when the play was, and George gave him the dates in late April. Then they headed their separate ways to class.

❧

Sometime during the last week in March, George looked at his class schedules and began to panic. *Oedipus* consumed him, with rehearsals now scheduled five nights a week and Saturdays. Preliminary examinations were coming the first week in April, and he knew biology and philosophy were going to be bears. He had managed to get to Eta Chi twice in the few weeks after lunch with Scotty, but the first time the house was empty, save for a couple of sophomores sitting on the rug in the Great Room with a couple of girls. The second time he caught dinner on a Friday night, when everyone he ran into was on their way somewhere.

On Wednesday, *Oedipus* rehearsals moved from Ridley Hall to the Straight Theater, and the class got their first look at Derek's vision. The stage was barren of any set or props, except for three inch round metal pipes that rose from enormous iron stanchions on the stage floor. Connected to the vertical piping were pipes that ran horizontally in an arc from one end of the stage to the other.

The first horizontal pipes were about ten feet off the floor, and there was about eight feet between levels. Each of the horizontal pipes was ten feet in length, so that the image one had from the orchestra was of a connecting series of frames. At each end of the framework, there were additional lattices, which allowed actors to climb to each level.

Quinn told the class to sit on the stage and watch as he climbed around above them and demonstrated the rules that would be required for all actors above floor level. There would be no guy wires or other supports or netting for the performances, so the safety of the chorus was paramount. George and Caitlin looked at each other with raised eyebrows. It was intimidating to see the height of the top bars.

Quinn had made the class work on bars in rehearsal room two, but they had spotted each other and the bars were only a few feet off the floor. Around him, George could hear some of the class whisper that they were not going to go up there. This actually made him relax, since he had assumed he would have to compete for the top section. There was no way he was going to stay on the floor!

That weekend, rehearsals went well on Saturday and Derek invited the entire class over to his house for a party to blow off steam before the really grueling work came in the final weeks. George had a required pledge meeting at Eta Chi on the same night, so he and Caitlin agreed that she would go without him, and he would arrive later, after his meeting was over. They smiled excitedly as they made their plans. It was thrilling to think that they would be seeing Derek's home. Caitlin couldn't wait to understand more about him.

George was as excited as Caitlin to be included in the party, and he kept thinking about what it might be like as he drove to Eta Chi at seven p.m.. He walked through the foyer to the dining room with its chairs so handsomely carved in the shape of "EX," and found the meeting just beginning. Max Burdoin spoke to the group to quiet them down, and talked about Initiation the following weekend. They were to arrive at five sharp on Friday night, and be prepared to commit themselves fully to the weekend until noon on Sunday.

Then Max spoke with some disenchantment about the pledges' progress on their pledge paddles, and George looked around the room carefully. Apparently he was not the only wayward pledge, which made him feel better. He let his mind drift off to picture Caitlin arriving at Derek's and what it must be like, before he saw Max start to hand out papers.

This is a closed book examination, Max said. You must receive a passing grade on the test before next weekend. George looked around the room again and pledges were flipping through *The Benjamin Trident* in anticipation. Scotty had forewarned George about the test, and he had looked through the book before driving over that night, but he was not prepared.

Max told the pledges he would return in an hour, and left them alone in the dining room. After a few minutes of silence, Fritz began to laugh, and asked quietly if anyone had a clue to the answers. Some laughed and said no, while two pledges shushed them to stay quiet.

Let's be real, fellas, Harold said in a loud voice. The pledge class of 1974 had their first moment of truth.

Yeah, come on, guys, Fritz rejoined. If they really wanted us to be serious about this, why would they leave us alone in here with our books on our laps?

A solemn boy responded, If we are going to join this fraternity, what's wrong with following their rules? All you have to do is read the book, for god's sake.

Silence hung in the air. By George's guess, there were about eight to ten boys who were prepared for the test.

All right, George finally spoke up, why don't we do both?

The boys looked to him doubtfully.

I mean, we can try to do the test without the book and see how far we get. Those who are satisfied with their tests can finish and leave the rest of us behind to work longer together. So that is what they did.

Boys who had prepared for the test finished in about forty-five minutes, but instead of leaving, they offered help to boys who were never going to finish unaided. The solemn boy said he had thought about this as he took the test. Max only said it was to be a closed book examination. The books could remain closed but the brothers could assist one another, couldn't they? The boys laughed softly.

Some of these boys would point back to this night as the genesis of a unity in their class, while others would frown at the suggestion. But the boys who had prepared for the test quietly helped those who had not, and when Max walked back into the room, they were all done and he felt a new camaraderie in the group as they joked with each other.

It was nine fifteen when George begged off going out with the boys he would soon be calling his brothers and headed impatiently for Derek's house. The house was about another ten minute drive away from the campus, and he saw a number of cars parked in the driveway and along the edge of the property when he drove up. It was a lovely place built of stone, with a stone fireplace rising dramatically up the middle of the house. Smoke billowed from the top.

Inside, the air was thick with the sweet smell of marijuana, and people were in various states of undress. The house was very warm, especially in the main room where a fire roared in front of a bearskin rug, complete with the stuffed head of the bear staring off into the dining room. The warmth, Caitlin told George later, had made Arthur take his shirt off, and before long that seemed like a good idea to everybody.

Derek sat on the bear rug in front of the fireplace with his back against Caitlin's. Both of them looked sideways at the flames as they talked softly. George stifled the impulse to approach them, and was beginning to speak with Arthur when Caitlin waved him over.

Hey, she said, come sit by the fire! George swung himself onto the floor, off to one side so he could put his back against the wall and look out at the room.

George, Derek said, Caitlin makes a great backrest and fire-talker.

They laughed. Derek's face was mellow, and it was obvious to George that he was stoned. It was strange for him to see Caitlin with Derek this way. Had he seen Caitlin against Arthur's back, for example, he would have been engulfed with jealousy. But Derek was their swami, and everyone knew he was basically living with Catherine whom George had seen when he walked in. So George stayed cool and after a while he got up and wandered into the kitchen to see what kind of drink he could find. Catherine, his daughter from *The Wedding* who still called him Dad, or Pops, leaned against the refrigerator, talking seriously with Alec and Christopher about *Oedipus*. Catherine was playing Oedipus' sister, although it was a small part in the play. Christopher and Alec were in tee shirts and Catherine had unbuttoned her shirt so that it hung open to the waist. Her bra, George noted, was pink.

George nodded to her as he opened the door to the fridge and she moved out and then in with the door. She liked George and smiled to him as he grabbed a Rolling Rock.

Take your clothes off, daddy, she said impishly.

Yes, please, George. Alec said. We all want you to disrobe. Christopher giggled. George smiled and walked off into another part of the house with an "I don't think so" trailing off his tongue. The house looked out on woods beyond an enormous, wrap-around screened porch. The woods were lit by spotlights, and George stood at the window for a moment. He wasn't sure what to do. It seemed strange to hang around near Caitlin. There hadn't been much beer in the fridge. So he wandered into another room, darker than the others, where he could hear music playing.

The room had high ceilings and large, old windows that looked out at another side of the porch. Tall, worn, Victorian couches faced each other across the room. Between the couches three couples danced to music that came from little speakers high up on one wall. George sat down on one of the couches to watch the dancers. The men had removed their shirts. Two women were shirtless and a third was in her leotard.

All of the dancers were from *Oedipus* Chorus class, and despite the appearances, George knew that only one couple was actually seeing each other. Then Louise walked in and got a big smile on her face when she saw George. She walked over and stood swaying to the music in front of him and told him he was her savior.

Hello, Louise, George said. Louise always flirted with George, and although she had one of most extraordinary figures George had ever seen, she grated on him. She had huge teeth, and a prominent nose, and shoulder length black, curly hair.

Come on, George, I have been waiting all night to dance with you. Louise was wearing a tight leotard that was almost invisible in the darkened room. As she swayed, she moved her hips in a round, rhythmic way that made George grin.

Not tonight, Louise, he said softly. Louise promptly sat on his lap and put her arms around his neck. I am high and I want to dance with you. George felt her body still moving slightly to the music. All he could think of was Caitlin walking in and seeing this. Louise's leotard felt soft and slippery in his hands, and he was becoming aroused in spite of himself.

Okay, you convinced me, Louise. Let's dance. Louise stood up and took his hand as he followed her to the middle of the room. *Country Girl* by Crosby, Stills, Nash and Young had been playing, but the record ended, and the next record slipped down onto the turntable. Simon & Garfunkel's *Bridge Over Troubled Water* warbled through the speakers. And the dancers, who had free-flowed separately to the faster music all moved together to dance slowly.

Louise continued to pull George across the room until they entered a little study. She wrapped her arm around George's waist and said come over here, giggling. She pulled him to a little table where there were bottles of liquor and glasses. She took two glasses, poured Jose Cuervo Gold Tequila into each, and handed him a lemon wedge with a glass. She did all this one-handed so that her arm never left his waist, and George took the glass, drank it in a gulp and put the lemon into his mouth. It burned in his throat, and made his nostrils flare.

Louise did the same, and then re-poured one glass. Drink up, she said, I'm way ahead of you. Here, wait! Louise took a salt shaker, told George to open wide, and then shook salt onto his tongue. The second swallow tasted strong, and the lemon made George squint. He wrapped an arm around Louise and told her she was a bad influence and they both laughed.

Louise started to drag George back to the dancing space, but changed her mind. One more, she said, but this time tequila tongues! George looked at her questioningly, but she pulled him back to the table, took the bottle and moved him onto a nearby chair and told him to sit and close his eyes. George did as she instructed, although he felt pangs of guilt, knowing that this was going in the wrong direction. But by now the tequila ran around his head and he could smell Louise's skin and feel her body leaning against him.

The next thing he felt was her lips on his and he opened his eyes for an instant, just as Louise opened her mouth and the tequila flowed from her mouth into his. Her tongue met his. Then she was on his lap and they were kissing while her hands moved across his chest and touched his face.

After a few minutes, George was so intoxicated with both the tequila and Louise, he had completely forgotten about the party going on around him. Then lots of voices started calling people together, and George looked at Louise, his conscience returned, and he told her to come along. They moved toward the voices, holding hands, until they saw people gathering around Derek who was still lying on the bearskin rug. Arthur explained as they approached that they were going to do a sound song on Derek!

George saw Caitlin smiling, telling others to take different parts of Derek's body and resonate one of their areas on his skin. Derek was in his underwear, and his eyes were closed, and two students were already humming through their foreheads onto his arms. Caitlin threw her long, dark red hair across Derek's chest, put her nose against his side and began resonating through her nasal passages. Louise laughed and George dragged her toward his legs, and they got down on their knees together and started humming through their foreheads on Derek's bare legs.

The sound of fifteen or twenty people huddled around his body on the floor, humming onto his skin made the onlookers laugh in disbelief, but then even the people who just watched started humming in resonance too, and the sound song was joined by all.

When the song began to fade, George stood up and walked outside to clear his head. The fire was so hot that he felt lightheaded. He looked up at the night sky and said aloud, What am I doing? Then he laughed at himself, muttered "Only time will tell..." at the doorbell, and returned inside. He intended to find Caitlin and suggest they head home. But Caitlin was nowhere to be seen. Derek still lay front of the fire, and George wondered if he had passed out.

Louise sneaked up behind him as he stood looking at Derek and put her arms around his waist. She said nothing, so he turned to her and she put her lips up to his. He could see that she must have more tequila in her mouth, so he leaned down and kissed her and let the tequila flow into his mouth. Then he took Louise's hand and moved her into the dancing room, and after he had swallowed and breathed for a moment, he said, Let's slow down, Louise. But John Mayall's *Room To Move* started playing and George exclaimed, This must be fate! I love this song! And the two started dancing.

As they moved to the fast beat of Mayall's harmonica, Louise reached down and unbuttoned the snaps to her leotard. Her leotard rode up as she danced, and the next time George looked, Louise was naked from the hips down, and he knew then he was too far into this to stop. She was dancing suggestively, the room was empty, and when Mayall started singing "Chicka Chicka, Chicka, Chicka," Louise moved to George and wrapped her arms around his shoulders and they started dancing slowly, ignoring the frenetic pace of the song. He felt every part of her rub against him, and then they were kissing again. They were on the couch by the time the song ended.

After the sound song, the party had pretty much broken up, and the house emptied out quickly. It was one in the morning, and the only people left in the house were George and Louise on the couch, Catherine in the kitchen washing dishes, and Caitlin, who had found a bedroom and drifted off to sleep. As people left, Derek had struggled up off the floor and wandered upstairs, seen Caitlin lying on his bed, and thrown himself next to her and fallen back asleep.

After a while Derek turned over in his sleep, and his arm draped across Caitlin's chest. When Catherine walked upstairs, she found them and stood there uncertainly. She couldn't imagine who Derek was lying with, and then her hand went to her mouth when she recognized Caitlin's long, red hair. She moved out of the room, angry and confused. She thought she knew Caitlin and did not believe she would do this to her. Then she wondered what had happened to George. She walked back downstairs and sat in front of the dying fire to think. From the living room, she heard muffled sighs and voices, and grew alarmed.

She had finished the dishes as everyone left, and had turned off the lights before going upstairs. But there were clearly sounds coming from the sitting room, so she got to her feet, and craned her neck around the wall to see who was in the other room. That's when she saw George and Louise making love on the couch and screamed.

Jesus Christ! What the hell is going on here? My boyfriend is upstairs sleeping with Caitlin while her boyfriend is screwing someone on the couch downstairs!

Catherine's yelling had the desired effect. George and Louise yelped in surprise, stopped moving and stared at Catherine with their eyes wide. Catherine moved back into the other room, and told the two of them to get out of there now! George and Louise appeared a moment later, half dressed, buttoning their clothes, mumbling apologies. George looked around the room like a scared animal. What had Catherine just said about Caitlin?

Out! Catherine said in a deep, anguished voice. *Now*. George and Louise moved uncertainly toward the front door. George turned and whispered to Catherine, Where is Caitlin?

She's upstairs in my bed asleep, Catherine said. I think you better get the hell out of here. George hesitated, but Louise tugged on his arm, saying, Come on, George, let's go. We'll sort this out tomorrow.

Outside, George noticed Louise's nose when she took her hand and swept back her disheveled hair. He asked her if she had a ride, and she said, Yes, with you. So he drove them back to campus, and Louise showed him where she lived on North Campus. Park here and come in with me, she said matter-of-factly.

George looked at her closely. He really didn't want to come with her, but he had just lost his virginity to Louise, and it seemed ridiculous to say no. So he parked the car and the two of them went into her dormitory. He didn't realize that she had a single until they reached her door. She unlocked the door, and looped her arm through his as she opened the door, and said, Now... where were we?

I think I better go, Louise. George said. He kept thinking about what Catherine had yelled at them on the couch. What in the world had happened tonight?

Louise pulled him close as if to kiss him goodbye, but as she did, she turned him inwards into the room and pushed. In truth, George did not fight very hard. Then their bodies met again, the door swung closed and he felt her breasts against him. He forgot about everything else until morning came.

Caitlin walked downstairs in Derek's house at six thirty p.m., and looked around with a yawn. She saw Catherine sleeping on the floor on the bear rug, and was tiptoeing into the kitchen when Catherine opened her eyes.

Hi, said Caitlin. Catherine tried to remember whether she had seen any clothes on Caitlin when she was in bed with Derek, but couldn't. Catherine finally directed a question into the awkward air between the two girls.

What happened last night?

Oh my god! Caitlin said as she took in the look on Catherine's face. Nothing happened, Catherine! I went upstairs and the bed looked so inviting I decided to lay down for a minute, and the next thing I knew it was morning, and Derek was lying next to me!

The fury and misery that had kept her awake most of the night drained away instantly. This made total sense given who Caitlin was, and Catherine laughed at herself for thinking otherwise. I believe you, Caitlin, she said. You are too innocent for words!

The two made coffee and sat down in the kitchen to talk. When Caitlin asked what had happened to George, Catherine was prepared. She told Caitlin that she told George to go home and let Caitlin sleep.

But did he think I was, you know, with Derek?

Well, I may have contributed to that but I'll help clear that up today. She did not tell Caitlin exactly how she had found George and Louise, but did tell her that George gave Louise a ride home. Caitlin shrugged her shoulders. She knew that Louise was after George but she trusted him.

Plus, she *had* awakened next to Derek, and though she would not let on to Catherine, she had gotten a secret thrill feeling him next to her, breathing restfully in his sleep. It was about seven thirty when Catherine gave Caitlin a ride back to campus and told her she'd see her Monday at rehearsal.

About the time Caitlin started showering in her dorm, George woke up. His body was tangled up in Louise's and it made him think of *Tangled Up In Blue*. He could feel her breathing in her sleep, and her hair was near his nose and tickled. When he stirred, Louise snuggled up against him and fell back asleep. He laid on his side, looking at her desk, and felt his head pound slightly. Equal doses of guilt and elation coursed through him from the night before. Curiously, he did not feel much guilt at all about Caitlin, although he knew he had been unfaithful to her. The guilt washing over him flowed from inside, from his parents, who raised him to think that premarital sex was sinful and empty. He grinned to himself, and thought there wasn't anything empty at all about it. Then he thought about Louise, and began to fret.

The reality of lying next to Louise, who was in his *Oedipus* class, began to loom large. It was warm in her room and he stared wearily at the wrangled yellow sheet that lay over them. He could feel her naked breasts stuck to his back, and her long legs cradling his own. He could not picture going to class and dealing with her and Caitlin. And Derek! Even if Caitlin had not really slept with Derek, which he doubted, Catherine had seen him and Louise on the couch, and Derek would know that by today.

He began to inventory everything he didn't like about Louise. It wasn't that he didn't find her attractive, even though her teeth and her nose were huge. But it was the way she chittered to him. It was like a squirrel, he thought miserably. And now that they had had sex, what would she be like!

Louise awoke just as he thought this, and smiled at George's back. Thank god for tequila, she said to herself, and then her head began to throb, and she whispered softly, How's your head?

George craned his neck around to see her, and said, Thick! and they laughed lightly. He turned and moved his hand across her abdomen and Louise purred. Her skin felt soft and taut, and for the next hour, they explored each other again, this time gently and deliberately. Then they rose and Louise went off to the shower while George dressed. Alone, he looked around her room like a little boy, and wondered how they would approach the subject of what next.

When Louise returned from the bathroom, she was wearing a white terry cloth robe, and wringing the water out of her hair, that lay twisted and matted down one shoulder.

So, she began, smiling largely at George. George looked at her big teeth and tried to put them out of his mind. Are we going to declare our alliance to the world and eat brunch together, or do we need to talk?

George tilted his head back and said simply, Both. He couldn't believe he said it; it just seemed to come out of his mouth naturally. Louise smiled, and said, Fair enough. Go wait while I get dressed. George left the room and stood against the wall in the hallway. At least they were on North Campus, and not West Campus, where eating brunch would undeniably be noticed by everyone he knew.

Louise opened the door a moment later. She wore tight blue jeans that showed off her figure, and a red collared blouse underneath a fur-lined brown coat. She had put red lipstick on and it glistened. George thought he could taste her lips still.

They walked in silence for a bit, but before they arrived at the North Campus Union, George spoke. Listen, Louise, let's get the talking part over so we can have a nice brunch together. Louise looked at George dubiously.

I am not about to deny what has happened here, but I am, as you know, in a relationship with Caitlin.

Who's just slept with our professor, Louise rejoined quietly. She was looking at the pavement as she walked, and George could sense her anger and it confused him. They walked along for a moment.

Maybe, George said. But I need to understand that situation, and I think it is fair to say that, well….last night was…improvisational, if you know what I mean.

He looked quickly toward Louise, and then away.

And this morning, Louise said confidently, looking at him in earnest. What was that?

That, George replied, was something else again! They both laughed. Louise slipped her hand into his. I'll say, she said.

All right, enough said, George went on. Let me sort out my situation with Caitlin before we "talk." Does that work for you?

Louise nodded and said, Fine. In truth, she wasn't at all sure what she wanted anyway, and this gave her some time to pull back as well. She would never know that George had been a virgin when she unsnapped her leotard and taken him on the couch, and she did not attach the significance to it that George assumed she did. But it *had* been fun.

On Sundays, Caitlin and George usually studied in the Rockefeller Room of Uris Library, and she thought that the best way to approach George would be to spend the day there until he showed up. She knew he would. So she walked up the West Campus hill at about ten in the morning and started studying at a table where she could see the entrance to the library.

George walked in about twelve thirty p.m. and waved to her. Inside he was shaking, but he put a cocky smile on his face as he came to her table. The sun shone in through the windows and the room was mostly empty. Caitlin's face looked freshly scrubbed. She is so appealing, George thought. So? He asked her.

Shame on you for even thinking something, George, she said. I fell asleep upstairs by myself. I did not sleep with Derek or anyone else. She watched his eyes carefully to gauge his reaction. He sighed and shook his head as if he wasn't sure, but he could tell she was telling him the truth. It just fit her.

Okay, he whispered, I believe you. How did you get back this morning?

No thanks to you, Mr. Chauffeur! Catherine dropped me off this morning, and I understand you drove Louise back last night?

Yep, George answered. It appeared that she did not know what he had been doing, and he wondered what to say.

Did she make any passes at you? Caitlin asked.

Yep, George repeated. Louise's flirtations had been the subject of their conversations before. He moved across to the opposite side of the table, and said, Louise tried her best! He opened a book and smiled at his girlfriend and raised his eyebrows twice jokingly. Inside, he was panicking. This was not going to be simple, no matter what happened.

Caitlin smiled at George across the table, and turned her head inquisitively. George shook his head negatively as if to say it was nothing, and the two focused on their work for some time. George stared blankly at the page, furiously contemplating what he should do. The risk of saying nothing was too great. For all he knew, Derek would announce it laughing in class the next day, or Catherine would tell her, or Louise would do something.

So George decided to tell at least part of the truth. He rose, and motioned for Caitlin to follow. They walked into the lobby area, and he sat her down where two chairs faced each other.

I have to tell you the truth, he started. Caitlin narrowed her eyes and grew nervous.

You know how you went up and fell asleep last night? Well, I thought you were with Derek.

George let that sink in for a moment. It was the truth, sort of.

So, he continued. When I drove Louise home, we ended up fooling around a little.

Caitlin looked away and tried to calm down. Under the circumstances, she saw the ambiguity of the situation, but Louise! God, how she hated that.

What do you mean, a little? She asked her boyfriend. George puzzled for a moment. He had not really thought through anything more than what he had already said. Describing any part of this would make this mess bigger, he guessed.

And, where exactly did this happen? In your car? Caitlin pressed him.

George looked at Caitlin reproachfully. Well it wasn't upstairs in Derek's bedroom! he retorted, buying time.

You can sleep in Derek's bedroom anytime you want, sweetie, Caitlin said smiling. Now tell me so we can put this behind us. Did you kiss her?

George thought about the tequila tongues for an instant, recovered, and told Caitlin that, yes they had kissed and "fondled around some" outside his car. They were quiet, and George started thinking about their own relationship, which in the preceding months had not progressed far beyond what he had just described. Still, if someone had told him that he and Caitlin would never make love, he wouldn't have believed it. Especially now. But Caitlin would be a virgin on her wedding night, and until last night, if he had been honest with himself, he would not have had a hard time believing that.

Maybe because she felt guilty herself about how it felt to wake up with Derek's heavy arm wrapped over her, or perhaps out of relief that George hadn't done very much with Louise, Caitlin decided to let the whole thing drop for awhile. She sat closer to him and said, Well I don't think either of us expected this to happen when we went to Derek's!

They stood, and hugged each other hard. Caitlin started to kiss him, but he pulled away and frowned a little as if to say they were in public. But Caitlin pulled his head to hers and kissed him again, for a long time. George felt people walking past them, and his discomfort grew. Then he opened his eyes and saw Louise walk in through the main doors and pulled himself apart and whispered, Here comes Louise.

For a moment he wasn't sure if he had said it to Caitlin or just in his head. Then Caitlin wrapped her arms tightly around his head and whispered back, All the more reason! and started to kiss him passionately. George looked over Caitlin's shoulder toward Louise, but Louise walked downstairs without reacting, and George guessed that somehow she had not seen them.

Then Max Burdoin shuffled through the lobby from behind George, and said "George..." as he passed by. Caitlin pulled away this time and said hello back to Max, with a big smile on her face. After he had moved on, Caitlin whooped with laughter, and told George she'd see him back at their table after she went to the restroom.

George stood still in the lobby, looking dazed. He told himself that this was only the beginning of something that would no doubt end in disaster, but he could not help himself. Seeing Louise had made him want to talk to her, so he went to his books, wrote " Back in a while..." on paper which he put on Caitlin's chair, and headed out another door that he knew led to a stairwell.

On the basement level, the ceilings were low, and the stacks of books dense. There were shiny wooden cubicles every so often, and having padded lightly down the stairs, George meandered through the stacks, thinking that Louise must be sitting at one of them. He saw only two other people on the entire floor. Louise sat in a cubicle at the very end of the stacks in the corner. She had her feet up on the desk and a book in her lap. As he approached, Louise made no comment or reaction. The silence was palpable.

Hey. George whispered as lightly as he could. Every word seemed to disturb the ambience of the place. Louise gave him a childlike wave, and smiled.

Do you study down here a lot? He asked her. She brought her finger to her lips to tell him to be quiet and pointed to a pad of paper.

George noticed the dark red polish on her fingernails, and wrote down the same question he had whispered.

It keeps me from being distracted, she wrote back.

From what?? He wrote.

People kissing in the upstairs rooms…Louise responded below his question. For the first time, George saw hurt in her eyes, but it was fleeting, and Louise penned, Why are you here now?

George sighed and looked around him.

I don't know, he wrote in reply. Louise looked at him and pulled her mouth to one side in a frown. Why are boys like this, she wondered.

Wrong answer, darling. She finally wrote back. She regretted using "darling" but she thought it sounded cool, and she liked being pursued by George.

Want to go drink tequila? George scribbled. Louise considered George for a minute. She knew they would have a great time, but she couldn't get the image of Caitlin out of her mind. Why don't you ask Caitlin instead, Louise wrote back. She seems interested.

George snorted softly. Because I am asking you, he said out loud.

Louise reached out and ran her hand through his hair, and said, Then, let's go. George told her to meet him outside, and he went to get his books. He found Caitlin studying and whispered that he was tired and was going to his room to sleep, and she made a pout on her face for a moment, but blew him a kiss and returned to her work.

George and Louise walked back to his dorm to get his car, and they drove into College Town to The Palms, a seedy hangout up the hill from the square, where they drank beer in between shots of tequila. They both knew they were going to go back to Louise's room and make love, and the anticipation, enhanced by the drinking, made their eye contact delicious. Later, on the way to the car, they stopped and Louise kissed George hard and their hands roamed freely over each other. The air was chilly and their lips were slightly chapped, but they were beginning to get the sense of each other and it inflamed them both.

Much later, in the middle of the night, George lay awake, peering in the darkness across Louise's room. She slept soundly cuddled up next to him, but sleep avoided him. For some reason, the heaviness of his actions began to weigh on him. Their sex had been wonderful -- crude and wanton and prolonged – but now George regretted it all. This time his guilt came for Caitlin, and strangely, somehow, for himself, and he knew he could not continue with Louise. But what really haunted him was that making love with Louise was something that could not be undone. He could force it from his thoughts, or pretend it had only been a dream, but the passage itself was irreversible. Wasn't it? He dreaded the morning, and when sleep did come, it was fitful.

CHAPTER SIX

March in Ithaca is the cruelest month. It remains blustery-cold, with at least two major snows, and no sign of spring. April is not much better, as the thaw arrives and turns the earth to mud, but the air is still cool, and the first growth of spring is pending for weeks, until it pops open all at once. There is no gradual, occasional flutter or harbinger of new life. And it is overcast with a bleak, gray light that has no smell.

The first week of April was in keeping with the season, and by mid-day on Monday, George had reawakened to the fact that this would be a week from hell. At *Oedipus* class, Derek worked the class hard, telling them that rehearsals would begin to lengthen, starting that night. He said nothing about the party over the weekend, and never even looked mischievously at George.

After class, he headed to the Straight to meet Scotty for lunch again, and the light drizzle made his feet feel frozen. In his mind, he reviewed the work ahead of him. He had prelims on Thursday and Friday, and his philosophy paper was due Friday too. Derek told the class to expect rehearsals to run from seven until ten thirty or eleven. George shook his head, disgusted with himself. What had he been thinking this weekend?

Over watery chicken soup and grilled cheese sandwiches, Scotty told George that he had heard he was making quite a commotion in the library. It took George a moment to figure out which commotion Scotty was talking about, and then he groaned.

Doesn't Max have anything better to do with his time than worry about what I am doing in the library? He asked his big brother.

Maybe he secretly wishes he was you, Scotty answered. Actually, Scotty thought George had a lifestyle he, Scotty, wouldn't mind. He found Caitlin incredibly attractive.

Anyway, that's not why I wanted to see you, he went on. (Thank god, George interjected.) I wanted to be sure you're ready for this weekend, and see if you wanted to come for date night this Wednesday.

George said he would try to make it Wednesday, and asked what was needed for the weekend. Scotty reminded him about his pledge paddle, and told him to just do something, even if it wasn't much. To show up without it would not be looked on favorably, he explained. George asked Scotty if Max had sent him again, and they smiled at each other. Scotty said he had come on his own this time. As they headed off in different directions after lunch George told his big brother he wouldn't let him down.

By nightfall, when George walked up the hill to the Straight Theater for their first practice on the big stage, he had organized himself for the week. In his room he had stared at Stephen's lacquered, lovingly carved Phi Delta paddle, and given himself Wednesday, from four to five thirty to do something for his own. He laid out the entire week, hour by hour, on a piece of paper, listing the items he had to review for his prelims. He figured that he would write and type his philosophy paper first.

Rehearsal that week was exhausting, personally and professionally. Louise took opportunities during breaks to sidle up next to George and chitter about things. Caitlin eyed Louise every time she walked near George, and widened her eyes at him if she saw the two of them talking. Derek worked with the main cast while Quinn worked the chorus, and he was a demanding instructor.

George was one of ten students who worked on the highest piping throughout most of the play, and it required all of his concentration to keep his balance as he moved in the steady, slow motion Derek wanted from them, while remaining in character, and following the patterns he had choreographed for his character. On Tuesday, Derek became incensed at the poor showing of the chorus in delivering one of their main speeches, so he kept them there late reciting it twelve times in a row until they had reestablished their rhythm.

On Wednesday, George took the scrap piece of wood left over from Stephen's paddle and fashioned one as best he could. He carved "Eta Chi" into it with his pocket knife, looked at it and shrugged, and headed off for date night. He had invited Caitlin but she had shaken her head no. She was behind in her work too. So he went alone, and enjoyed the break from the week that the walk to the house gave him.

Date night was a Wednesday tradition. Anywhere from three to twenty girls typically accompanied brothers for a brief, but nice meal. The Darling of Eta Chi, who was elected by the brotherhood each spring for the coming year, always received an invitation from one or another of the brothers and almost always came. This was true even if the Darling happened to be dating one of the brothers seriously. It was understood that she was the fraternity's darling and proper decorum dictated that she always be invited, and shared, in a polite way, by all of the brothers.

George ended up at a table with the current Darling, Maria Kitsouk-jas, and one other girl. Will Houghton, who had invited Maria that particular night, introduced George to Maria, explaining that George was an actor. Maria had glossy, straight black hair, and brilliant blue eyes that flashed while she asked him questions. George liked her immediately, and the conversation at the table was light and animated.

After dinner, the brothers stood behind their chairs and sang the Darling Song to Maria. At Date Night, the brothers sang directly to Maria unless they were accompanied by a date, and she sat there with a warm smile on her face. She had been elected the preceding year by a senior whom she had been dating, but she was not currently seeing anyone in the house. After dinner, she thanked Will and wandered off for a moment with George to ask him more about acting. George told her he had to leave for rehearsal, and the two agreed to walk back to campus together.

On their walk, Maria told him about how much she loved being Darling, and how adorable she thought all of the brothers were with her. She was tall, confident, and strode with solid purpose as she talked. George couldn't help but appreciate the generous roundness of her figure, especially from the waist down. She was so comfortable with herself that George found himself captivated. He did not view her in any sexual way, although he recognized her appeal. She was like an instant friend. Years later, George would be struck by the significance that small details of his life, like walking Maria to campus, would have on later events. But for now, he simply enjoyed her company on the way to rehearsal, and told her he hoped to see her soon as he left her at the entrance to the library and hurried to the theater.

Rehearsal was slow, and long, and the chorus stood around more than usual as Derek worked out the blocking with the main characters. Louise waited until Caitlin had gone off for a bathroom break and wrapped her arm familiarly around George and asked him what the story with Caitlin was. George could felt her body pressing against his, and twisted away slightly even though it felt good.

I don't know what we are doing, Louise, but I need for you to not do this while I sort it out. George whispered plaintively.

A girl gets lonely, you know, Louise said playfully. Inside, she felt sick to her stomach at the look on his face. It was not a look of intimacy. It was not even a caring look. She could have kicked herself for going out with him the second time, and she moved off quickly. You're a dick, she said as she left.

After rehearsal, George walked Caitlin back to her room, and they hugged and kissed for a minute outside her dorm. She felt so warm, so genuine, in his arms that George cursed himself for having fooled around with Louise. If he could have undone it, he would have. Or would he? Caitlin tousled his hair and said good night, and he headed back to his room. It was twenty after eleven when he started in on Biology for Non-Majors. He hated this class. He finished at four in the morning, and caught a couple hours of sleep before getting up and typing the first half of his Philosophy paper. He had yet to write the second half, and the first half made about as much sense to him as the class did.

By six p.m. that night, he had taken his Bio test, which he knew had not gone well, and he was trying to bring his paper on *The Meaning of Self In Solipsism* to some kind of graceful close. Stephen came into their room as he headed off for rehearsal and they talked for a minute.

What is that miserable piece of wood on your bed? he asked George with a wicked sneer on his face. George shrugged. It's my pledge paddle, he finally said. He started to laugh desperately, and the two egged each other on until tears rolled down both their faces. I've got to go, he finally said as their laughter died off.

That night, George worked from ten until one in the morning finishing and typing the second half of the paper, and then began to study for Ancient Civilization. Around six a.m., he fell asleep at his desk for thirty-five minutes and woke up in a panic. The panic was immediately replaced by exhaustion, and he went to shower. At least, he told himself, it was the last day.

Friday evening, George dragged himself down the hill toward Eta Chi, carrying in both arms his bright blue sleeping bag in its shiny, plastic sac, a small bag with a change of clothes and toiletries, and his pledge paddle. On his way he saw four other boys similarly equipped, and one of them was Harold Wise. Harold chuckled when he saw him, and called to him in a big voice – Hey George, are you ready?

He laughed harder, and George joined in with him. As they walked together, George asked Harold if he knew what the weekend would be like. Harold made his eyes wide, and said, Well you know what they use these pledge paddles for, don't you? He guffawed rapidly, his eyes widening. They make you stand in a row and bend over and spank each other with your pants pulled down! And with that, Harold started laughing hilariously, nodding his head vigorously for emphasis.

George started coughing, he laughed so hard. Oh, come on, he finally said, I saw my sister's pledge paddle – she made a lamp out of it, for chrissake.

Harold grunted dismissively. Haven't you ever heard of the turkey trot? he asked George. A sly grin prefaced another deep belly laugh. *Ohhh, baby*, Harold yelled to no one in particular as they approached the house. *Here we go!*

Max Burdoin greeted them at the door, solemnly. Harold entered first, and after Max shook Harold's hand, he turned to George and said, Welcome to my world, as he reached for George's hand. They joined the other pledges in the dining room as brothers wandered about, speaking quietly, and acting serious. Their faces had an angry cast.

Harold went to sit with Fritz and Edward Stamer. George grabbed a chair at another table next to Cullen Hastings. The pledges were quietly nervous for this initiation to begin and end. Not one of them had any idea what would come, and the image of fraternity initiations, of hazing, and silly or ridiculous proofs of allegiance to the brotherhood plagued their imaginations. The torturous expressions of the brothers circulating around them did not assuage their insecurities.

After all pledges had arrived and been accounted for, Max asked for their attention, and gave them instructions that would need to be followed throughout the weekend. He explained the interfraternity council's rules on initiations – no leaving the premises, no physical hazing. He stressed safety, telling them that this weekend was intended to be a serious, meaningful experience in which the bonds of brotherhood would be consummated.

George leaned over to Cullen and whispered that this seemed quite religious to him, and he wondered if they would have to go to confession? But Cullen barely acknowledged him, so George faced forward to listen again.

Secretly, Cullen thrilled to the prospect of the weekend, and he did not want to miss anything Max said. He knew his excitement would seem strange to most of the pledges, but he saw great potential in the symbolism he anticipated in the event. It was symbolism that he thought brought unity to communities, whether it was a fraternity or a city or rural town. It was why he had enrolled to become an architect – to create symbolism through structures that he envisioned as unifying.

Across the room, Harold was excited for an almost opposite reason. Impatient, bristling and aware, he loved the complete unknown of what was to come. He let his imagination soar with thoughts of degrading or bizarre rituals that could become the fodder for stories and connections with his brothers that heightened an environment the way that alcohol fuels rashness and candor.

There were boys in the middle, like Edward Stamer, who saw this weekend as merely an annoyance to be suffered for greater gain. Edward was political, and thought he would like the workings of the fraternity once he was through what he called the Looking Glass of initiation. George was simply ambivalent and tired.

There were a few boys on the far fringes. Wally and Steve and another boy believed they were doing something important, almost sacred. Their participation would be earnest and introspective, while Fritz Hublein and Ronny saw it clearly as a sham, an artifice to be manipulated by the brothers as a whim, and by each of them as pledges, if they were clever enough.

Once finished with introductions, Max led them through the first of many secret oaths to protect and hold inviolate the rites of initiation they were about to begin. They read, signed and repeated aloud this first oath. Cullen repeated his solemnly. George assumed his character from Oedipus as he read his. Ronny winked to Fritz during his recitation.

Then the brothers filed into the room, and according to the instructions they had received, each pledge followed a particular brother out of the dining room. Each pledge was assigned a room that was darkened by blankets or black trash bags covering the windows. And so the weekend, and the secret ceremonies, began.

George awoke Sunday morning from his first real sleep in days with the dulled ache that always follows too little sleep. He could tell it was morning from the light around the edges of the blanket covering the window in the room, and he relaxed in the knowledge that it would soon be over. With rest, he could see more objectively the parameters and intent of the weekend, and this soothed him. It also embarrassed him for having made such a scene the preceding night. He had threatened to leave, and demanded to see Scotty, who had been rushed back from a quick visit to his girlfriend at her sorority on orders from Max Burdoin.

When Scotty walked into the fraternity Max was waiting anxiously for him at the front door. Scotty thought Max would scold him for leaving the house during initiation, but Max immediately said, Your little brother says he wants to quit the house. Max didn't care much for George or Scotty, but he was the pledge captain. His job was to get the pledges through initiation, and he needed Scotty's help. So Scotty nodded and walked up to the room that George had been assigned on the third floor. He rapped on the door, and as he entered, he said in a quiet voice, Pledge, stand and face away from the door.

George was not quite turned around but Scotty told him to forget it and sit down. George, his eyes bleary and red, squinted at him briefly and then slumped to the floor. Scotty sat cross-legged opposite him, and considered his little brother for a moment. George and Scotty gave very different impressions. Scotty's freckled skin and fine features fit perfectly his wire-rimmed glasses, wiry frame and carefully combed red hair. George's slightly tan, smooth face sported a roman nose and full lips in a kind of nonchalant disarray. His brown hair usually swished across the middle of his forehead above intense blue eyes. But the George Scotty was looking at now was exhausted, almost incoherently so.

You look like hell, George. George's head wavered like someone about to fall asleep sitting up, but his voice was strong when he replied.

I haven't slept in three days, but no one told me we wouldn't be sleeping this weekend. These people are not what I thought they were, Scotty, and I don't know what you see in them.

What do you mean? Scotty asked.

Look, George said, if one more asshole comes up to me in a robe acting like he's Julius Caesar and asks me to think about the lights, I am walking out of here. I don't want to join a fraternity to run around in rainbow-colored togas whispering crap in Latin. Give me one good reason to stay. I dare you to give me one good reason to stay. And what the hell is so funny? Scotty was laughing softly and George's voice was slightly raspy now. His indignation waned, and he looked more defeated than righteous.

Scotty knew that he was supposed to stay in character and tell George to think about the lights, but he couldn't bring himself to do it. Besides, George was clearly over the edge and probably wouldn't make it, unless he managed to sleep through the rest of the weekend. So he decided to break the rules and tell his little brother the truth.

You're right, he said. Some of the brothers take this stuff too seriously. And I find the whole thing kind of weird myself. But this only happens one weekend a year. Nobody does this stuff the rest of the time. And believe it or not, if you have the right attitude about it, it can actually be fun.

George looked incredulous. Scotty told his little brother not to take it all so seriously. You're probably over emotional about it because you haven't slept in so long. Have you really been up for three straight days? George nodded and tried to describe his week.

Look, Scotty said, all of your instincts up until this weekend are not wrong about this place, so just go to sleep. I'll try to get you uninterrupted sleep till morning.

What time is it? George asked.

It's late on Saturday night, Scotty said. Look, if you want to leave the house afterwards, you can. But if you leave it now you can't get back in so easily, and I think your lack of sleep is making this harder on you than it really is.

George told his big brother that he doubted he would ever connect with the fraternity thing, but agreed that his head would explode if he didn't go to sleep. So he asked if they could talk in the morning, and started to climb onto the bed. He was asleep before Scotty closed the door. It would be years before George realized that he had been allowed to sleep through the most memorable part of initiation.

On Sunday morning initiation concluded close to noon, and the upperclassmen and all of the newly initiated brothers shook hands and enjoyed a sumptuous brunch in the dining room. Bloody Mary's and screwdrivers flowed liberally. Each of the boys who had just been initiated viewed their brothers and their house differently. Cullen went around the room slapping his new brothers on the chest with the flat of his hand, or hugging them exuberantly. He was reverential and passionate about his experience. The ceremonial rites of initiation had filled his soul with feelings he had never known before. He did not simply embrace this newfound brotherhood; he luxuriated in the warm bath of its meaning, unaware that his reaction was extreme.

George remained leery. All of the brothers, including Max, welcomed him to the brotherhood as if nothing had happened the night before. L.E.O. Pennington wrapped his arm around George's shoulder and told him he had made the right decision. Still, George saw a large chasm between himself and Eta Chi. He thought sequentially about Caitlin, Louise, putting his resonating forehead on Derek's leg, and the play. This place seemed a distant and fundamentally different world. And he felt quite certain about which of the two he would choose, should the paths continue to diverge. Somehow, he could not stop picturing himself on the couch in Derek's house with Louise, in the throes of sex, and Catherine surprising them with her screams.

Most of the new brothers walked as a group back to campus in the middle of the afternoon. Away from the upperclassmen, they laughed and shared their thoughts about the weekend with more candor. Fritz told about sneaking out of his room and pretending to be one of the brothers.

I did, really! I went up to Stilton's room and knocked on the door and yelled, Pledge, get on your knees and pray to Eta Chi!

That was you? Steve Stilton asked hotly. The boys roared laughing.

I knelt for about an hour thinking I'd be in trouble if they came in and found me sleeping!

Harold snickered, and confessed that he had not understood until Sunday brunch that the boys were permitted to ask to go to the bathroom.

So what did you do? the boys asked him.

Well, the room they put me in had this long line of beer goblets lined up on a shelf, so I filled every one of them by the time the weekend was over!

The group roared. Someone asked him if he had done anything about it at the end, and Harold started laughing from his belly and said he hoped whoever lived in the room didn't think there was beer in those goblets!

George walked along quietly, but he couldn't stop grinning at the thought of Harold standing in the middle of one of the sleeping rooms urinating into beer goblets. He felt embarrassed again that he had not approached the whole thing more lightheartedly, and wished he had a funny story to tell. The sun shone with a hint of warmth in it, and the day was glorious.

Another boy turned the conversation to a serious note, and told his new brothers he was proud to be an Eta Chi. This caused the boys to start exchanging the secret handshakes they had learned at the conclusion of initiation. The ritual that would become woven into the fabric of their college days still felt new and awkward. Invisible to anyone unaware of it, the simple handshake (for there were a number of different ones, depending on the circumstances) involved a simple movement of the left hand. It was instantly recognizable to anyone who knew to look for it.

George wondered aloud how someone whose right hand was crippled and thus had to shake hands with their left hand would be able to demonstrate that they were an Eta Chi. But the boys puzzled over his comment, and did not reply.

Upon reaching campus it was Harold who set forth a challenge to the group as they began to break up and go their separate ways.

Okay, gentlemen, he began. We are now brothers and we have a choice: do we make this a memorable experience or not?

The boys looked uncertainly at each other. Wally said, Hell yes we do, and the rest joined in agreeably. George nodded his head as he looked at Harold and wished there were more Harolds in the world. When he left them, he headed straight for Caitlin's room, without even dropping off his baggage. She had told him she might study there on Sunday for a test she had Monday. But as he walked onto her floor he came in behind the girl down the hall who liked to act British. She had on blue jeans with the Union Jack sewn onto the fanny, ripped slightly and held together with a huge safety pin. She told him Caitlin had "gone to library."

Where did you grow up? he asked her.

Indianapolis, she responded brightly. But it just as well could have been York!

He left there and went back to his room to drop off his things. He hoped he wouldn't run into Stephen, whose initiation into Phi Delta had taken place at the same time. He wasn't supposed to reveal anything about his, and he was sure that Phi Delt was the same. But he just wanted to get away from the whole topic, and he knew Stephen would want to talk about it. Luckily, their room was empty and silent, and George went to sleep on his bed until dinner.

George walked up to the library to see if Caitlin wanted to go to the Straight for dinner. She sat in their normal room, at a table by a big window. She wore a navy blue turtleneck and tight jeans that made her legs look as long as they were. Her dark red hair was pulled straight back with a shiny brown barrette, and the skin on her freckled face shone.

She was excited to see him, and they went to dinner and she asked him a million questions which he did his best to answer without really telling her anything. It made her mad. Silly little boys with games, she said, irked. You probably even have secret handshakes! she scoffed.

We do, George replied, smiling. After a while they stopped talking about it and Caitlin told him about the rehearsal he had missed on Saturday. She described the costumes they would be wearing, which they would be fitted for on Monday. It felt so good to be back in his world. George felt whole for the first time in days.

The next day, the chorus was fitted for their outfits, which for the boys were jock straps and breast plates made to look like metal. The girls would be wearing short, torn skirts and loose, greenish-brown tops that resembled rags. They would be required to body paint their entire bodies with the same colors as the huge, cloth backdrop that hung behind the pipe structure bending across the stage, so they could blend in against the backdrop.

Derek wanted their slow motions to make the entire stage look like it moved in distress and disarray - to reflect the crumbling society in which the play was set. Their first dress rehearsals were the next weekend, five days before the play opened.

Derek was taxing the resources of the Straight Theater to the maximum. The chorus had one large dressing room. The main characters dressed in the room used to store props, costumes, and stage paraphernalia. The chorus dressing room was covered on two walls by full length mirrors. Obviously, the room had once been used for dance rehearsals.

By now the chorus was so closely knit, they thought nothing of nudity. Even modest girls like Caitlin simply turned away from the crowd when she stripped to her underwear and applied her body paint, and then disrobed to don the bra and underwear that had been dyed the colors of the backdrop.

Louise loved getting ready, and always took longer to dress once she had stripped. She would look at herself in the mirror and look to see if George or one of the other boys might be glancing at her full breasts and sensuous hips and backside. During the final dress rehearsal she was next to George who was applying his body paint and looking in the mirror to make sure he had not missed any spots on his legs. He was in his jock strap and she was naked.

Hey, she whispered, flashing her big teeth toward him, doesn't this make you horny?

George looked at her reflection in the mirror and smiled.

Please don't tempt me, Louise, I'm, trying to get into character, he whispered back. He was serious. It took him a long time to transition his body and thinking into Heraldus – the mythical name he had given his character. But she wasn't willing to concede.

I hear first night jitters are easier if a little recreation takes place the night before...so what do you say Heraldus? George looked at her in the mirror. He knew it was wrong, he heard his inner voice telling himself to do the right thing, but was tempted nonetheless.

I'll talk to you *after* rehearsal, he said, although he and she both knew he had succumbed right then. His regret, while genuine, was overcome by a more primal urge. Or so he tried to tell himself. It didn't sound true to him, but he didn't change his mind either.

The play ran for two weeks, with four performances the first weekend, and three on the first weekend in May. It was a powerful, fascinating production that received distinctive reviews in the Daily Sun and the local Ithaca papers. On Saturday of the first weekend, Max Burdoin, L.E.O. Pennington and Bob Woodbridge went to the show together. Max was curious in spite of himself to see George on stage. L.E.O. and Bob often went to performances together. None of them knew much about what they were going to see. Max assumed George would have one of the principal roles.

When they entered the theater, the starkness of the stage set was the first of many affronts to their senses. Huge, interconnected pipes rose from the stage floor. Behind the pipes, a dirty green, tan and brown sheet hung in tatters. The stage floor looked dusty. One actor sat at the edge of the stage, his legs draped over into the orchestra pit, strumming discordant chords on a guitar. He was colored from head to toe in the same colors of the dirty sheet that hung behind the piping. The three brothers took seats in the fifth row. They talked about what they saw. Bob thought it was brilliant already. L.E.O. said he wished he had done this kind of acting. Max just stared.

The play opened with a wailing, sonorous gasp that seemed to fill the theater with a chilling whistle. There was no one on the stage, but the chorus was directly behind the backdrop, and as they began the opening lines, they moved in such slow motion it was hard to see what was happening through slits in the sheet.

Behold the story of Oedipus
In War-ravaged Rome, littered with the remains
Of rotting carcasses and broken spirits

The chorus chanted, assuming their positions on the scaffolding and pointing to Alec and Christopher who emerged in fog, speaking heatedly to each other but only mouthing their words, so that the only words heard by the audience were those of the chorus.

The glory of the gods thrice ignored
Hath loosed Zeus from his mountaintop to this distant shore
To wreak new havoc on poor Oedipus and his father
Forsooth...

The chorus still moved to their positions, so slow and deliberate were their motions, and their voice, cold and whispery and utterly one to the human ear, floated above the audience like a silken cloud.

By now George was in position high above Oedipus and his father, and Heraldus was dreaming of his homeland as he reached out toward the audience in a silent, fluid arc. George was deep in his character, and his body moved through his choreography as if he were on solid ground. He was centered, secure, and in another world.

After the play, the audience roared and applauded boisterously. Max was speechless. It had taken him until the third act to find George on the stage, dressed in almost nothing from what he could tell. At least he had been able to recognize Caitlin quickly. She had hovered on the stage just behind the main characters. Bob and L.E.O. were ecstatic about the production and gibbered excitedly with each other about the staging. Max asked if they should go backstage to congratulate George and they enthusiastically agreed.

In the dressing room, the actors reacted to the thunderous reception by the audience with hoots and hand slapping. Even Derek suggested their performance tonight merited a party so they immediately began to undress so they could go out and celebrate. Caitlin was talking excitedly to Derek in the corner and Louise was making fun of George when Max led his brothers into the room.

Max stood at a railing on a stair landing three steps above the floor of the room and dropped his jaw.

Louise was next to George stark naked, pulling on her tight jeans without any underwear. Before George saw his brothers, he had pulled his jock strap off and was pulling underwear up his legs. All over the room, girls and boys were in various states of nakedness. Arthur, who liked to strut as much as Louise, flexed his biceps and pretended to be Atlas in his jock strap. Caitlin was pulling her bra off in the corner against the mirror, and Max spied her just in time to see her breasts dangling in the mirror.

George looked up and froze when he saw Max, mouth agape, furtively scouting the room. Behind him, Bob stood smiling widely, and L.E.O. looked like he was trying not to look into the room. He looked around the room to see what they saw, and a vicious smile came to his face. He approached the landing where they stood, extended his hand to Max, and as Max gripped his hand in return, George said, Max, welcome to *my* world!

Bob's curly-haired head came over Max's shoulder, and he said in a loud voice, That was the best play I have ever seen. The room went silent for an instant, and the chorus noticed the fraternity brothers for the first time. Then they erupted in cheers. Caitlin looked over and rushed to pull her shirt on. Somehow, she felt suddenly naked, and irritated. The rest of the chorus couldn't have cared less. Then Max said, Well, we better be going. And they did.

⌘

Over the next few weeks, the academic year neared its end, and the student body zoomed in on final exams. On the last Saturday before examinations, Eta Chi held its final chapter meeting of the year, and all the new brothers were told not to miss it. In addition to being their first chapter meeting experience, it was also the seniors' final one, and traditionally the seniors gave speeches about their days as Eta Chis. At the same meeting, the room assignments for the following year were made. George had agreed to room with a boy from Seattle named Jason Conner, so they drew a number together, and got a room on the sophomore hall.

Chapter meetings were held in secret, in the chapter roomin the basement of the house. The room remained locked, except for the monthly meetings. George was with his new roommate when they descended the stairs, and they talked softly as they rounded the corner and were admitted. Inside, rows of chairs lined the walls and filled the body of the room. On one wall, there were three large, wooden chairs and a podium, where Jerry Wells, Art Woodhall and Stuart Castle sat looking out at the rest of the room.

The last part of the meeting was when the seniors each stood up and addressed their brothers. Jerry Wells, as the consul, acknowledged them as they raised their hands to speak. Some told funny stories about events that had happened while they had lived there. Others spoke seriously about the impact that one or more brothers had on them, thanking them publicly as a goodbye. At the conclusion of each speech, the brothers snapped their fingers as applause.

When Bob Neff rose to speak, about two thirds of the seniors had already finished their remarks. In retrospect, George found Bob's decision to wait until that moment quite a curious choice. In fact, it was something that stayed with him for a long time, because as an actor George was beginning to understand dramatic moments. The timing of a speech could be more important than its content.

Did Bob wait because he was unsure of what he wanted to say? Had he been afraid to speak? Was he, perhaps, simply unaware? George would never know. But his words, captured as faithfully as possible hereafter, were the only ones that George, and his new brothers, would be able to recall clearly –

My brothers, I stand before you with both some humility and a fierce pride in the house that has been my home for the past three and a half years...(a scattered collection of fingers snapped across the room). *I remember when I rushed this house, and how it stood out in my mind from every other house that I visited. Only the seniors will remember, but Billy Harrelson was my big brother when I was a freshman. Billy was captain of the basketball team on the hill, and he was about a foot taller than me.*

Anyway, Billy taught me certain things about this house that I believe I have tried to carry on, and I know that the other seniors have kept evermost in the front of their minds as we have lived here. We have an obligation to uphold the important traditions in this house, and as we leave the house to the juniors and sophomores and new brothers, I will say to you that I am truly worried.

What separates Eta Chi from the other houses? What led each of you here? I know it is many things, and I realize my time is limited, so let me tell you what I believe should be considered the core of this house – a core to be cherished and protected.

George listened intently. It was a great speech so far, one that he would have been proud to perform. When Bob spoke of the core, George thought of his center. The room was achingly silent as Bob went on.

We are a collection of strong-minded individuals who have embraced a set of standards. Standards of decency, of honor, and brotherhood. Standards that, in my opinion, are becoming non-existent in the other fraternities on the hill. I went to dinner at Delta Upsilon this spring. I had been invited by a friend of mine, and I was excited to see his house, because I had not been there since I had rushed it as a freshman.

I can tell you that I was shocked by what I saw. A house once proud, once considered a top house in our system, was little more than a locker room. There were no standards of dress at dinner. Brothers came to dinner in sweat pants and tee shirts, sweaty and unshowered. They grabbed things off the table and ate without waiting for each other. Some of the boys there had girls with them, and the girls were whistled at and treated immaturely.

When I asked my friend what had happened to his house, he shrugged. HE SHRUGGED! All he would say is: things change.

By now, Bob paced back and forth in front of the brothers, who followed him with their eyes. George looked around the room, gauging peoples' reactions. Charles Lord was raising his eyebrows at Buzz Delaney, looking like someone trying unsuccessfully to be serious.

Now I will say this for all of you to hear – THINGS DO NOT CHANGE! People change things! The future of this house is not pre-ordained. It is...

He paused, unable to finish his sentence. Then he took a breath and continued.

I see some disturbing things happening in this house. There is a little less care being exerted to care for the house, there is an acceptance of people not giving this house the respect and focus it deserves, and there is the start of talk that brothers want to change the dress code. None of these things taken alone mean that much. And I know that some of you probably think I am overreacting. But just as we took a stand against communism in South Vietnam, we here, in this house, must take a stand against Creeping DU-ism!

The seniors began to clap, and stood up and clapped harder once the clapping had started. Bob raised his hands for them to be quiet, and they sat back down.

I see some of the sophomores and freshmen looking at me strangely, and that is okay. I do not expect you to do anything differently tonight, or tomorrow, or next week. All I ask is that you think about this house and make whatever changes you make with due consideration for yourselves, and for the decades of brothers who have come before you and delivered into your hands the best, most distinctive, most principled institution I have ever been associated with. There is only a short slide into mediocrity, and I ask you to beware of Creeping DU-ism as you build upon the traditions of this house that led each of you to join in the first place.

Bob sat down in his chair and the seniors erupted in applause again. They started chanting "Eta Chi, Eta Chi," and were joined by a number of the juniors who seemed to gain courage with the seniors' enthusiasm. The sophomores sat and snapped their fingers politely. The freshmen followed the sophomores' cues, except for Jim Steuben and Cullen Hastings, who stood and clapped with the seniors.

Afterwards, George sat with Scotty in his room and asked him questions about Bob's speech. What was behind it? Why did the seniors and juniors seem to split with the sophomores? What did Scotty think?

Scotty looked carefully at George. He wondered what George found so interesting in a speech that he thought came out of the last century. But he told his little brother as best he could how the seniors were called the Old Guard, and that there were a number of juniors who also fell into that camp, and how the sophomores thought that they were too old fashioned.

He explained that there had been a push to eliminate the coats and ties at dinner, but it had been voted down in a heated debate at the last chapter meeting.

It's one of reasons I am moving out of the house, he told George. I don't want to spend five nights a week getting dressed up for dinner. I love this house, but I can come over when I want and see everybody, and get the best of both worlds. George stared at Scotty as he spoke. He liked the dress code, and wanted it to continue. He was not entirely sure why, but the formality of Eta Chi – its proud adherence to convention and tradition - struck him as essential. And Bob Neff's exhortations rang in his ears. There was a deeper meaning to all this. The dress code was merely a manifestation of some greater truth.

On Monday of exam week, George sat in the Straight dining hall having lunch with Caitlin. He was eating a hamburger with onions and catsup. Caitlin sipped soup and reached over occasionally to take one of his French fries. They were both drinking sodas in big, waxy cups. She had arranged to rent an apartment in College Town with a girl she had met in Spanish class, and after describing the apartment to George, she returned to the topic that she could not get out of her mind.

Ever since she had seen George and Louise in the dressing room of the play, she had fretted over the way that they were with each other. Have you seen Louise lately? she asked her boyfriend. George grimaced, because he knew it was not a real question. It was simply an opening to the same discussion they had had half a dozen times since the play ended.

No, Caitlin, I have not seen Louise since the last night of the play.

Caitlin raised her eyebrows a little and shook her head slightly at an angle. She wanted desperately to put this behind them, but it would not go away. Their conversations always went the same route. She was suspicious of George's fraternization with Louise, and wanted to be sure that he was hers. George would admit to a kind of odd, touchy friendship with Louise, but then promise that it was not romantic, and had no bearing on the two of them.

It was not an easy sell. Caitlin knew that there was something in the way that George and Louise looked and spoke to one another that was...disturbing. But they saw Louise less and less following the end of the play, and Caitlin's suspicions had begun to subside. She and George were so close and so comfortable that she felt crazy to keep thinking about it.

Nonetheless, she finally decided to ask George straight out if he had slept with Louise. So she did, just as he was taking a big bite of his hamburger.

George said Mmmph! and then chewed slowly looking at his girlfriend. He had thought that this was all getting put behind him, and he had not expected the question. He knew if he told her the truth, she would break up with him, and if he didn't tell her, they would be living a lie.

Right then, before George could actually reply, Charles Lord and a girl George had seen with Charles lately sat down with the two of them. Charles said "Georgie!" in a big voice and introduced them to Holly Menard. George looked quickly at Caitlin, and smiled weakly, and said, we'll talk, but…no.

Holly Menard looked like the quintessential co-ed. She reminded boys of Cybil Shepard, because of her straight, white-blond, shoulder length hair, and smooth, clear skin. She had a genuine smile with straight, glossy teeth and narrow lips which she always covered with a frosty pink lipstick. Pastel sweaters and simple, collared white blouses completed the look. Today she wore a navy blue blouse and white khaki pants and tan sandals

When Charles introduced Holly to George and Caitlin, Holly looked at George strangely for an instant and then the four of them chatted lightly as Charles and Holly began to eat their lunches. After a few minutes, Holly looked at George and said, George, what did you say your last name was?

Muirfield, he replied.

Oh my god! She exclaimed, I know where I've seen that name before! I have your underwear in my room!

Charles choked on his sandwich and started laughing heartily.

Georgie, you dog you, I didn't know you knew Holly!

George looked at Holly bewildered, and said, What?

You know, she replied, your underpants! When you were running naked through my sorority, you dropped them and I was the lucky girl who picked them up! Holly smiled broadly. She thought it was funny.

George relaxed a little, and said, Oh, right. George pictured his mother insisting on using that indelible marker to write his name on his underwear before he left for college. He doubted that she had anything like this in mind when she marked his clothing.

Charles said " Georgie!" again.

Caitlin looked at George carefully, and when he turned to look at her, a bit sheepishly, only he could see what was going through her mind. And he could see it wasn't good.

CHAPTER SEVEN

October, 1974

To say that Charles Lord was unwitting would be to miss the point entirely. And yet, Charles was not anything in particular. He wasn't zealous. He was not indifferent. Raised a Jew, he was conventionally religious, but not to the point of inconvenience. At six-feet-six inches tall, Charles was a large, rugged-looking boy with a big head of black curls and a thick moustache. But he was a bit of a nudge and not very athletic (a point his peers never considered, given his imposing size).

Growing up in a liberal, politically charged household, Charles had never found himself drawn to a liberal agenda. But he certainly wasn't politically conservative; he liked to think of himself as a centrist. When he became a government major and learned how mainstream political elections, in the end, always default to the middle, his centrist tendency hardened into a life-long belief. His politics were consistent with his life view. He was not at all an idealist or an ideologue, any more than he could be called a fatalist or a moralist.

If Charles Lord gravitated toward anything, it was energy and enthusiasm. He was stylish and funny and shrewd, and he appreciated these qualities in others. And he liked to be in the center of things, so he tended toward offices – on the hill, in his fraternity, and as he grew older, in social and civic organizations. And the powerful impression he made upon others – his physicality, his affability, and his almost complete lack of any specific agenda, made him a very dangerous person.

His fraternity brothers saw great alignment with their particular point of view whenever they spoke with Charles. He liked them, and he reacted with genuine appreciation when they argued a particular issue. Charles would nod, and squinch up his big rugged face and utter a laugh that most resembled a polite sneeze. His brothers would smile when he laughed, "ehoo-ehoo," and then feel the warmth of his attention as he affectionately repeated the name of the person he was listening to. Invariably, Charles put an "ie" on a person's name; if the person's first name was not easily appended, he would use their surname.

It had not taken Charles long to find the political middle of Eta Chi. Once he arrived there, he never left it. When the Old Guard bemoaned the decline of Western Civilization so evident to them in the antics of the other houses on the hill (and certain sophomores in Eta Chi), Charles gave voice to their sentiments in terms that they found charming. But Charles was simply careful to restate for them what he was hearing, without endorsing any particular viewpoints. And when the sophomores rallied for abolition of the dress code, they could count on Charles to shake his head in vigorous commiseration with them. Carefully, he sought out different viewpoints across numerous constituencies, which permitted the more introverted or ambivalent brothers the sensation that they had been heard.

Even those seniors who were outspokenly members of the "Old Guard" found Charles a welcome addition to their fold. After all, he was pleasant and supportive of their positions. And so it was that Charles Lord was elected to be rush chairman before the brothers left the house in the spring of the preceding year. He had run against Tim Truesdale, a returning senior who, by tradition, should have been awarded the position.

Poor Tim Truesdale, of stiff and slightly awkward bearing, never had a chance against Charles. He expected to be awarded the position simply because he was a senior. But even the Old Guard who loved to visit Tim in his room and talk quietly as they listened to the Beach Boys, recognized that Mike was not a natural choice to lead the rush process. He was not a very convincing fellow. And besides, they told each other, Charles understood and appreciated the need to recruit a certain kind of boy to Eta Chi.

So Charles found himself in charge of rush as a junior. He came back to school holding the most important office in the house, but at the first chapter meeting of the fall, which was held the last week of September, he ran into a problem. It began innocuously, but quickly dissolved into the sort of political quagmire Charles feared the most.

The social director put up for a vote the decision on whether to have a rock and roll band instead of a jazz trio for the fall formal. There had appeared to be general consensus to liven up the affair going into the chapter meeting. But Tim Truesdale had decided to use this vote to presage the issue to be voted on subsequently – the relaxation of the dinner dress code.

So Tim stood up and declared that a move to a rock and roll band was the first step in the decline of the house into Delta Upsilon. He argued, stiffly and not very convincingly, that a jazz trio was representative of a classy, distinctive house, and that a rock and roll "formal" was an oxymoron. About a third of the brothers were unfamiliar with the word oxymoron, and thought he meant moronic. A number of these boys rose to respond to the charge that rock and roll was moronic. One boy even stood up and noted that the only rock and roll music that could be considered moronic was the Beach Boy songs in Brother Tim's room.

This rancor unsettled the seniors, who were unfamiliar with such a personalized attack during a chapter meeting. And so, for the sake of harmony in the house, they did not strongly back Tim's viewpoint, despite the fact that they would have preferred a jazz trio. So the boys voted by a two to one margin to have a rock band. In deference to Tim's position, it was agreed that this was experimental and would be revisited before subsequent events.

The next vote only exacerbated the split in the ranks. Without the Old Guard seniors from the year before, two juniors moved that the issue of the dress code be put up for a vote again despite the fact that the house had voted on the same issue at the preceding meeting. Initially, two seniors attempted through Robert's Rules of Order to table the matter as already voted on and resolved. But there was no legitimate basis for such a position in the by-laws of the house, and so the debate on the dress code resumed.

Charles had carefully considered the votes on the issue by counting the numbers of sophomores versus seniors, thinking that the juniors would vote two thirds in favor of relaxing the code. He had not anticipated that a number of sophomores would side with the Old Guard on this issue, which seemed relatively straightforward to him. But the debate was intense, and lasted for forty-five minutes. The entire senior class spoke ardently against any relaxation of the code, on the same theory of creeping DU-ism that had carried the day previously.

The New Guard couched their position in terms of individual responsibility. Why should the fraternity insist on coats and ties, as if the members of the house were unable to adhere to personal standards of dress appropriate for their fraternal responsibilities? One boy suggested that all the revised code would do is make coats and ties optional for their dinners, and that coats and ties would still be required for Wednesday date nights and social dinners on weekends.

But the New Guard had not counted on the fact that seven sophomores had found the dress code part of the allure of the house they had rushed, and were mindful of the seniors' cautionary tales. And so the second matter was defeated. Charles had spoken in favor of the measure, and felt completely naked when the Old Guard prevailed. He was desperate for political cover, and immediately proposed a third measure, which he guessed, without reflection, could return him to the center of the house.

Instead of the preceding relaxation of the dress code, Charles stood up and offered the following compromise: there would be a reduction of one night in the dress code requirements, which he suggested would be Thursdays. Coats and ties would continue Mondays through Wednesdays and on Saturdays as appropriate. No blue jeans or t-shirts would be permitted on Thursdays. And there would be no further votes on the dress code during the fall semester.

A palpable relief moved in a wave across the room. The New Guard saw this as a crack in the door. Old Guards saw this as a minor loss, with the protection of the balance of the dress code at least through the winter. Boys enthusiastically endorsed the "Lord proposal," as it was quickly dubbed, and there was a unanimous vote, save for poor Tim Truesdale who wore a pale cast on his face and stubbornly voted Nay in a loud voice. The boys laughed as his voice echoed in the room. And Charles had not only resumed the center, he had cemented his position as a leader in the house.

On the third Saturday of October, Charles sat in his room tapping his pencil on the yellow legal pad that was attached to his clipboard. Charles loved clipboards. They made him feel official and in charge - like a coach. He felt more organized when he held one in his hand. He kept four or five of them in his room. At this moment, he was noodling over the rush process, and developing his own power rush teams.

It would have surprised the boys how solitary Charles really was, and how much he kept his own counsel. He tended to make his own decisions, and then go off in search of the constituents he felt would most identify with elements of his plan. Most of the brothers, who, to be honest, did not think in terms of political agendas, believed that they were giving Charles the ideas for his platforms, rather than being led to Charles' agenda.

But Huff had emphasized to him that the decision on rush teams was the exclusive province of the rush chairman, so Charles spent consider-able time watching his brothers during the fall and forming conclusions about who would be the most convincing spokesmen for the house. The problem was that the more he thought about it, the more confused he be-came. As a sophomore, he had found the rush process a lark, and had run for the chairman's office instinctively. But now it dawned on him that the structure of rush and the selection of leaders during rush could have a pro-found influence on what the house ultimately was.

Some boys would have found this to be an exciting authority with which to influence what Eta Chi stood for. Charles found it intimidating and dangerous to his centrism. So he struggled on how to construct and empower the raft of strong personalities and viewpoints in the house, opt-ing finally to create a matrix with four points. People were either Old Guard or New Guard (a term he never shared with anyone), and they were either sharp or dull. His strategy was simple. He would divide the compo-sition evenly between Old and New Guard representatives, but skew the teams almost entirely toward the sharpies, as he began to think of them.

Charles relaxed as he drew this out on his clipboard. Finally he had a strategy that would work to his centrist tendency and appeal to the major-ity of the house. While there would be no vote on this, Charles always counted votes in his head. His count pleased him.

So, as he sat in his room designing his approach to formal rush, he felt confident and authoritative, in spite of his nagging concern over the potential impact of his decisions. After a while, Charles put down his clipboard, and lay back on his bed, with his hands behind his head. This evening he would be dancing with Holly Menard in the Great Hall, and with luck, they would end up in his room for the night. In fact, he was so sure of it, he thought he could smell her hair as he lay there.

Later that morning, Harold Wise walked from his room down the sophomore hallway in a great mood. He would pick up Martha Higgins at Kappa Gamma at about seven and they'd be dancing in the Great Hall long into the night. With any luck, he'd wake up with her the next morning. His roommate, Jim Steuben, had already agreed to sleep in one of the empty rooms.

The year had gotten off to a rollicking start, and Harold was effusive in his pursuit of sorority girls. He had promised his roommate at the beginning of the year to try to have a sorority girl for every date night, and suggested his roommate do the same. Jim told Harold he was oversexed, and Harold responded with a deep-throated chuckle, rubbing his right hand across his belly in a circular motion.

Harold and Jim had little in common, beyond the hotel school where they were enrolled, and a love for the dramatic. It had been Jim's suggestion that they take a double. He thought that rooming with Harold would be logical, since they were in the same school, and he liked how outgoing Harold was. Somewhere deep down inside he also thought it was safe, because he was not attracted to Harold.

Jim Steuben was tall with a slight build. He had a narrow, sharp chin and small, thin lips, and liked to drink martinis up. He could come across as haughty, a bit removed, but the brothers enjoyed his sharp, dry wit and clever way with words. He had rushed the house hard from the moment he saw it, and had really connected with the seniors and the juniors. He liked their style and felt at home in the dignified, conservative conversations that typified their exchanges.

When Bob Neff had made his Creeping DU-ism speech last year, Jim had stood and applauded, though he wished he had remained seated. He worried that by standing he was lining up with the older boys, and he was pragmatic enough to realize that the seniors were graduating. He would live with his classmates for the next three years. But he truly believed in the dress code, and he took Bob's challenge to maintain those traditional values as a personal responsibility. And he saw his responsibility as starting with his roommate.

Harold proved an easy convert. He matched Jim martini for martini as they reviewed the politics of the house over an occasional cigar. Harold's own conservatism and snap judgments found a welcome home in his roommate's far more strident ideology. But Harold had no particular interest in the symbolic traditions within the four walls of Eta Chi. He was not upset by what Jim saw as the declining civilization of the brotherhood, and, in fact, spurred on sophomores with a flair for the outlandish. But he agreed with his roommate on national politics (they both liked Nixon) and polity (each saw himself as chivalrous), and Jim mistook this as proof of Harold's traditionalism. But Harold, as he would tell anyone who asked, was only conservative from the waist up.

And he would have been shocked, and a bit frightened, if he had understood that his roommate, whom he called "Stoobie," was a little light in the loafers. But even Stoobie did not yet fully admit this to himself, and he managed to date girls throughout college, albeit conservative girls whom he could trust would not want to go further than decorum would allow.

On Harold's way down the stairs, he bumped into George, and gave him a hearty hello. It was only about the fifth or sixth time he had seen George the entire semester, although George technically lived three doors down the hall. Harold was glad to see him, and they stood on the stairs talking for a moment. George explained he was here for the weekend because Caitlin had gone home. Harold asked if he was bringing someone else to the formal, and George laughed. He hadn't even realized there was a formal that night, and didn't think it would be a good idea anyway.

Harold continued on his way to the kitchen to see Andy. The fraternity cook was all business when Harold spied him at the sink through the door. He was washing heads of lettuce and chuckling to Paul Harvey, who said "Good day" as Harold pushed through the door and greeted his friend.

Andy was tall, about six three, lean and sinewy. At fifty-eight, he had a sunny, calm disposition. Having shepherded the boys of Eta Chi for so many years, he was more of a father than an employee. Andy's wife worked at the Delta Epsilon Phi, and they lived about forty-five minutes out in the country where they had raised eleven children. All of their children had graduate degrees, except for the youngest, and he was on his way.

Whoowee! Andy yelled when Harold breezed in, what's my friend getting ready to do tonight? Harold laughed and asked Andy to take it easy, but Andy would have none of that. One morning about three weeks back Andy had entered through the back door to the kitchen and found Harold having sex with a girl on top of the box freezer. It was five thirty in the morning, and the girl had shrieked at the top of her lungs when she saw Andy in the doorway.

You going to have that same girl here tonight? He asked Harold mischievously. 'Cause I don't want to have to start knocking on the back door every time I want to come to work in this sin palace! The two laughed heartily. Harold rubbed his stomach while he told Andy that he was bringing a different girl tonight.

Andy hooted. My goodness, Harold, what about that last one? Andy remembered all of the boys who had grown up under his tutelage, and he had only known Harold a few months, but he already liked this boy a lot. It never would have occurred to him that catching Harold in the throes of passion on the box freezer made Harold nervous.

Harold was still cautious in the house. He knew that the house looked down upon inappropriate conduct. It was one thing for a girl to end up staying over on a Saturday night after a party. That was understandable, and a few seniors even had girlfriends stay the weekend if they were coming from a distance. But in general, girls who visited from other schools were expected to stay at a sorority with a friend or girlfriend of one of the other brothers. And if a girl spent the night at the house, she would certainly find a quiet exit in the morning, so as not to embarrass anyone.

Harold suspected that the brothers would not appreciate his sexual romp on the box freezer in the kitchen. That would surely be over the top, he guessed. So, for the next several weeks, he stayed particularly close to Andy, in hopes that Andy would keep his secret.

Out the kitchen window Harold saw his roommate lifting their tuxedos out of his car, and he went out to help him. Stoobie had agreed to pick them up, and he laughed when he saw the one that Harold had ordered – powder blue with a matching ruffled shirt. Stoobie's was traditional, of course: black with a conservative, white, flat-pleated shirt.

Interesting choice of a tuxedo, he began as Harold approached. I didn't realize you were performing in LasVegas this weekend.

Ooh, baby, baby, Harold hummed, smiling. Stoobie grinned and suggested that he would probably be able to sleep in his own room tonight once Martha saw that outfit. Harold scoffed good-naturedly. Wait until she sees my dance moves! he beamed.

Upstairs, Harold and Stoobie were walking their clothes back to their room, and Wally and Ronny ran out of a bedroom, laughing hysterically. From the bedroom, they heard an anguished voice scream, Is nothing sacred!?!

They must have farted on someone's pillow! Harold said to no one in particular. They run in, pull their pants down and fart on top of peoples' pillows. They probably did yours just before we came upstairs!

Stoobie shook his head in tiny, sharp motions. This was exactly the sort of thing he hated about the sophomores. In the room across from theirs, Wally Stimpson was sprawled across his bed, with his arms wrapped around his pillow. He was talking to his roommate, Nick, and another boy who sat on the floor with their legs stretched out. Their conversation ranged from the coming formal to Wally and Nick's most recent escapade as volunteer firemen. Nick, who volunteered for fire duty in high school, had persuaded Wally that joining the volunteer fire brigade was a great way to pick up girls. Wally had not needed much persuading.

Harold walked in and sat against the desk, taking in Wally with a quick glance. Wally greeted him loudly, and Harold nodded noncommittally. Wally aimed to please anyone he was near. Garrulous and funny, he wore a ready smile on his face and woke up every day wondering how to better ingratiate himself with his brothers. He volunteered for duties at the drop of a hat, was the first to join anyone who wanted to party, and craved the feeling of inclusion the fraternity gave him. None of his brothers could see how needy he was.

Harold listened as Nick and Wally recounted their last volunteer fire call. The smoke was billowing out of the front door, Wally said dramatically, when two men tumbled out through the door, coughing and shouting at each other. Then two girls came out, and you should have seen them!

They were prostitutes! Nick interjected.

Wally pretended to be one of the girls for the boys, complaining to a policeman that the two men were lunatics and that she needed protection. Ohhh, Aw-fisher, Wally mimicked, they are hawwwribble gentlemen!

The boys laughed, and asked for more details as Stoobie walked into the room. Nick described how he talked to one of the prostitutes, asking her how much she charged, and the room hooted in disbelief. Stoobie cleared his throat and said, Were you asking for yourself Nick, or did you plan on pimping the poor girl from your room?

The other boys willingly believed Nick's tale. Harold sensed that Nick was a pathological liar, and lost interest in the story as he looked around the room. The room smelled like Brandy, and the furniture was arranged to make room for the St. Bernard to sleep. Wally had leaped at the chance to be Brandy's caretaker over the summer, and when he came back in the fall, Brandy slept in his room with him.

At first, Nick had been irritated by having to step over Brandy's enormous bulk, especially when he jumped off of his bunk bed in the middle of the night. But Brandy was a lovable beast, and he quickly came around to thinking it was kind of cool. He even wished that Brandy would sometimes follow him up to campus, but the St. Bernard always seemed to go with Wally or one of the other brothers.

In 1964, a wealthy Cornellian had bequeathed millions to the school for the construction of the North Campus residential halls. The only condition required of the school was an unusual one. The benefactor loved dogs, and wanted the school to establish a campus-wide policy allowing dogs to run free anywhere. In classes, in the cafeterias, anywhere. The offer was too good to pass up. Except for the kitchen and food dispensing areas of cafeterias, dogs run free on the Cornell campus to this day.

In the mid-seventies, Brandy reigned supreme on campus. He was the largest, best-known dog and his handsome, squared head and gentle disposition made him a favorite with girls, except when he drooled. Unfortunately, Brandy drooled a lot, and his drool was often swinging from his massive jaw as he sauntered across the art or engineering quads. He accompanied Wally or one of the other brothers to classes and lunch and the libraries, and usually found a brother who was heading down the hill to walk him back to the house in the afternoon. In the house, he slept in the library under the piano until dinner time, and wandered upstairs after that.

As the boys sat around Wally and Nick's room, Brandy must have been downstairs. By now the room was quite crowded but the boys were barely moving as they talked. There was a feeling of slumber in the stale air that mingled with the pervasive dog smell that Harold couldn't get out of his nose. It made him want to scratch his arms and open the windows, so he left the room.

Up on Thurston Avenue, two Delta Gamma Nu girls and a Kappa were getting themselves ready for the formal, and although they knew each other, they were not aware that they were all going. Martha Higgins was shaving her legs in the shower and wondering why she had accepted Harold Wise's invitation. Actually she knew why, but still she wondered. She loved formal parties. It was a chance to dress up and unabashedly wear make up and dance with abandon. And she loved boys like Harold, whom she could count on to be pleasant and funny and full of testosterone. She would feel wanted and appreciated, and that was fun. So she put out of her mind that Harold had already dated two other girls in her sorority, one of whom had a crush on him. Besides, Martha said to herself, Diane isn't here this weekend, so she couldn't have gone anyway!

In the mirror in her room, she moved her hair around to see how she wanted to wear it this evening. She had "huge" jet-black hair, according to her roommate, whose thin, blond hair fell in wisps on either side of her narrow face. She tried her hair up, but it looked too wild, so she decided to brush it out in a classic, full look. Her lips were her favorite part of her face, and she pouted into the mirror to see how they looked. Then she smiled broadly and admired them open and closed. She could picture Harold's bright eyes when she flashed her biggest smile at him this evening.

Downstairs, Mitsy Smith was reading a book and occasionally looking out of her window at the fall day. She was looking forward to the formality of the evening with Jim Steuben, who reminded her of her father a little bit because he was such a gentleman. She knew that he would escort her carefully and not press himself on her and she loved that about him. So many boys at college were uncouth.

She had three outfits she thought of as formal, and she knew exactly which one she would wear – the navy blue round-necked one that went so nicely with the pearls her Mom had given her. She was slight, and careful in her bearing, and she always wanted to be thought of as elegant when she went to formals. She wiggled her toes and snuggled into her chair for one last bit of *The Brothers Karamazov*.

About a block down the street, Holly Menard was headed back to her sorority from the library where she had worked from eight this morning on her history paper. She knew that tomorrow would be a wash out, and had wanted to get it done if she could, but she had only written out about eight pages on the yellow pad that Charlie Lord had loaned her when she ran out of paper earlier in the week. She figured she had two pages to go.

Holly never gave a hoot about what she would wear – she'd find something in her closet. But she was thinking hard about what the evening would be like, and how much she liked Charlie. They were a great couple, and he made her laugh and feel special. He was…it wasn't that she didn't like the safety he offered. She did. But somewhere in the back of her head, Holly kept waiting for college to get kind of wild. Surely some darker character would enter her life! Then the old regret washed over her. She chided herself for being ungrateful. Charles is wild enough for me, she told herself as she walked. And he was exactly what she expected a boyfriend at college to be like. She exhaled heartily for emphasis. The air felt so good on her cheeks; she could feel them getting rosy as she walked.

⌒⌒

At Eta Chi, the boys on the social committee that weekend were setting up the bar in the Darling Room, helping Andy prep the dinner, vacuuming the downstairs and decorating the dining room with flowers. It was invariably boys in the hotel school who saw to the details, and made sure that each formal had a touch of class. They wanted every girl who walked through the door to feel that Eta Chi was a cut above the ordinary.

The boys upstairs eventually hit the showers and got dressed for the party. At six p.m., the first of the party-ers began to congregate around the bar set up in the Darling Room. Harold went with Stoobie to pick up their dates at Delta Gamma Nu. Charles Lord had told Holly that he would pick her up around six forty-five p.m., but in the meantime, he was wandering through the rooms, shaking hands with his brothers' dates, and surveying the preparations. He loved the beginnings of parties, before people relaxed and the night took on whatever shape it did.

Charles saw George Muirfield having a drink with Edward Stamer and a girl he didn't recognize, and waded into their space with a big shake of his head. George was a bit controversial because he was never around, and Charles wanted to probe this with him a bit. But Edward was speaking excitedly about his latest architecture assignment, and George's gaze was fixed on Edward's florid face. It would have been awkward to break in, and then Harold and Stoobie brought their dates through the front door, so Charles chose to intercept them instead.

He had seen Martha, Harold's date, before, but he did not remember her as being so…over the top. She stood five-feet five, but her hair made her seem much taller. She had a big, easy smile, and Charles noted her bright lipstick with a twinge of desire. She was someone to have some fun with! The girl with Stoobie was a different story. She walked through the front door with her right shoulder leading the rest of her lithe, compact frame. She wore a deep blue, satiny dress and a big string of pearls. She reminded Charles of his mother and he thought there must be something dull about her, but she shook his hand firmly when Stoobie introduced them.

Charles excused himself to go pick up Holly just as Maria Kitsoukjas walked through the door with Tim Truesdale. Tim proudly led Maria right to the bar and ordered them both Scotch and waters. Tim was certain that escorting last year's Darling not only gave him status, but satisfied an obligation to treat the fraternity Darlings with distinction. The brother behind the bar took tall glasses and filled them with ice, poured King Williams Scotch from a fifth into each glass, and topped the drinks with water from a stainless steel pitcher that was normally used for milk in the dining room.

Charles and Holly paraded through the front door, and Holly's face lit up when she saw Martha making Harold and another boy laugh deeply. Holly loved how gregarious and spunky Martha always was and this was the first time she had seen her at Eta Chi. The two girls exchanged spirited hellos and admired each other's outfits. Harold raised his eyebrows and nodded toward Charles smiling. Charles laughed – ehoo, ehoo.

In the great hall, the rock and roll band was setting up in the corner, and they took up more space than the jazz trio with all of their amplifiers and equipment. The fellow who appeared in charge looked like he had just gotten out of bed. Poor Tim Truesdale grimaced every time he looked over in their direction. The great hall was usually lighted by wall sconces on the two long walls and an enormous antlered chandelier suspended below the enormous rafters which gleamed with linseed oil that the brothers were sure to apply every fall. But tonight the chandelier was dark, and the wall sconces gave the room an intimate feel. Even without the main light, Charles still noted the glow of the wood ceiling.

The room had grown crowded. Most brothers had dates, and those that did not mingled freely with those that did. Every boy with a date wore a tuxedo, and only a couple of boys who were dateless had on a suit or jacket and tie instead. Charles watched Holly talk animatedly with boys and their dates. She was a beautiful girl, and people responded enthusiastically to the genuine interest she took in them. He was hoping that she would become the Darling next year, and thought that the boys would overwhelmingly endorse her.

The bar in the Darling room was noisy and busy when someone flicked the big chandeliers' lights on and off to signal that it was time for dinner. The boys gradually moved toward the dining room with their dates on their arms. In the library, a brother played a lively jazz number on the piano. Brandy stood next to the piano; his head was lowered, and just under the bottom edge of the piano about a foot away from the player. When the player reached the end of a stanza and lifted his fingers off of the keys for a moment, Brandy barked on cue. When he played softly,

Brandy let out a low pitched, prolonged howl. The girls who had not seen
Brandy perform before stopped and marveled over him.

In the dining room, candles were lit on each table, which were covered with white linens and decorated with golden and red leaves from the
yard. The leaves had been Stoobie's idea, and he pointed them out
proudly to Mitsy. Although the boys often sat with their closer friends,
there were no seating priorities or patterns in the house. Boys tended to sit
at different tables all the time, and formals were no exception.

Once the dining room filled, there was a moment of silence as the at-
tendees stood behind their chairs as the fraternity meal prayer was recited.
When the consul was absent, the pro consul, or vice president, said grace.
If both were unavailable, the rush chairman and the pledge captain, in that
order, led the prayer. Both the consul and pro consul were out of town this
weekend, so Charles said grace. He clinked his glass to begin, and then
intoned the words with a mock gravity –

> O Lord, bless this table
> As the guiding light of Eta Chi
> Reveals truth and honor
> In our lives together and
> Forevermore.
> Amen

The boys all said Amen, and held the chairs for their dates. Boys who
were by themselves waited until the girls at their table had been seated
before pulling out their own chairs. Beyond the windows that looked out
on all three sides, leaves fell from the trees in the cooling night air. The
pale yellow linoleum floor, scrubbed to spotlessness during initiation, was
heavily waxed before a formal like this. The floor squeaked beneath the
dress shoes of the boys.

Harold and Martha sat with Tim Truesdale and Maria Kitsoukjas,
Bob Woodbridge and his date, Lucy Fitzwaller, Wally and a girl Harold did not know, and Cullen Hastings, who was dateless. Lucy
Fitzwaller was tall, with shiny, almost polished skin and brown hair
that she dyed a slight red. Her prominent forehead was accentuated by
the way that she wore her hair swept up and off to the left. She always
wore it that way.

Lucy and Bob were both juniors, and though most of the house didn't
know it, they had started living together in College Town in the fall. Lucy
was as direct and forceful as Bob was mysterious. She loved her boyfriend, but she also loved to flirt. And boys were seldom prepared for how
aggressive she could be. On campus, Lucy wore low, rounded tops that
showed her ample bosom, and she loved to watch boys at the lunch table
stare at her when she reached over the table for something and gave them
an eyeful. She would do this with Bob nearby, and if it bothered him, he

never let anybody see it. But sometimes there was a steeliness in his smile that seemed forced.

Lucy completely ignored the other girls, and spoke to each of the boys with a disarming familiarity. Bob tried to engage Harold and Tim in a discussion about rush, but Harold found himself distracted by Lucy. She kept twirling the twizzle stick in her drink and looking suggestively at him. He made a comment to no one in particular about getting hot under the collar, and turned his attention to his date, who was growing irritated. Martha Higgins was not someone used to being ignored.

Across the room, Charles had made sure that he steered Holly toward the table where he saw George Muirfield talking quietly with another sophomore and a girl he didn't know. Charles was determined to get a feel for George, and he even suggested to Holly that she sit next to him, without explaining why. One of the reasons that they got along so well was that they could suggest things to each other without explanation, and work instinctively together.

Don't I have something of yours? she whispered to George, prodding him in his side good-naturedly, as she took the chair next to him. George just smiled and replied quietly, I am worried that my underwear will always come between us. He had not meant it to come off so suggestively, but Holly giggled, and said, There could be worse things! George heard what amounted to a giggle come from Charles as well.

Georgie, how are you? Charles asked. George was fine. He told Charles that he was looking forward to formal rush, and Charles immediately asked him how he thought rush was going.

No business tonight! Holly interrupted, and suggested the table play a drinking game she had learned at a party a couple of weeks ago. The game went like this: Each person told something that was either true or false about themselves. If at least half the table guessed wrong, everyone but the storyteller had to take a big chug of a drink. If the table guessed correctly, the storyteller had to finish the drink in front of him or her. But they were drinking wine, and the mood was not conducive to it, so the conversation moved quickly in another direction.

After dinner, the brothers sang the Darling Song as they stood behind their chairs in the dining room, and Charles publicly recognized Andy and the brothers who had served the dinner. Then the room moved through the library into the great room as the rock and roll band began to play. The music was loud, and at first discordant, but soon the lead guitar fell into a rhythm, and the rhythm developed a groove, and the room began to undulate to its call. The leader of the band, who still looked like he had just gotten out of bed, stepped up to the microphone to sing. His voice was growly, but insistent, and he somehow infused the words he sang with a layer of meaning that brought harmony to the ensemble.

There are moments in any community when stars align. It feels the same everywhere, in every culture and in every corner of the earth. People come together and share a special warmth and euphoric sense of connectedness. For whatever reason, the stars aligned in the Eta Chi house that night. It may have been the pulse of the music and frenetic phrasing by the singer, or the familiar walls and ambience of the great hall. It may have flown from the extraordinary sensuality one experiences from the clean fragrance of washed skin and perfumed lotion, combined with the silkiness of a cocktail dress or the starch of a tuxedo shirt. But it happened to the boys and girls laughing and dancing in the great hall that night. Sophomore or senior, New Guard or Old Guard, loyalist or sycophant, all felt a connection - the elixir of being - that captures the human bond.

The dance floor flexed and twirled and dreamed, and the music pushed and pulled. The singer let his voice reach for things he could not predict. The dancers danced with their partners, but with the entire room as well. There was a sway to the motion that complimented the musical pattern and made each individual feel connected to a bigger whole.

In the middle of the dance floor, in the middle of the evening, five couples danced relationally, like a star. To the north, Harold held Martha during a slow song, the two of them slightly damp with perspiration from the activity of the two previous songs. To Harold's left, Charles and Holly clung lightly to one another, with big smiles on their faces. Below them, but about three times as far away as the rest of the dancers, Maria spoke intently to George, their faces close and eyes magnetically energized.

To Harold's right, Stoobie and Mitsy danced with polish in traditional posture, his black tuxedo and her rich navy dress syncopated in late 1950s fashion. Just below them, Bob Woodbridge had Lucy Fitzwaller hung off of his neck, their torsos touching, but their heads turned out in different directions. Lucy had not taken her eyes off Harold since the slow song started, and now he was returning her frank stare with a mixture of defiance and fascination. Lucy kept imagining the inside of Harold's mind and ran her tongue around her lips to send him over the edge. She was determined to see him give in to her boldness from across the floor while he held Martha tightly in his grip.

Harold could not believe how Lucy stared at him, and feared that others could see her brazen longing. When Lucy licked her lips, it was all Harold could do to not lick his own in response, but he restrained himself. He saw clearly the measured interplay she was engaging him in, and instinctively became the hunted even though he was hunting Martha simultaneously. He also knew that there was a well-worn rule in the house that one brother did not pimp the girlfriend of another brother, and that Bob Woodbridge did not deserve this.

But Harold imagined his arms around Lucy as he held Martha, and could feel her hot breath on his neck. Then he imagined her in his arms, looking off at someone else, the same way she was with Bob, and a slight revulsion crossed his conscience. Why did Lucy do this when she was in Bob's arms? Harold wondered. In his arms, Martha moved slightly closer to him and smiled up at him, and he looked at her with a big grin. He was not being fair to her, and he refocused his attentions on Martha.

Martha had been thinking about Charles Lord. She had tried to picture herself dancing with him, and wondered how Holly was able to get comfortable with him being so much taller and bigger. She pictured her head against his chest while his big head moved easily above her, and liked the image. Charles was so easy to get along with, and so energetic, that Martha had trouble imagining what it must be like to kiss him. She wondered if Holly really loved him or not. They certainly were spending a lot of time together on campus. After awhile, Martha felt Harold's hand on her back and reacted with a smile and a snuggle. She still didn't really think of Harold as handsome, but he was so full of himself and so appreciative of her that she was drawn to him.

With each rotation in her dance with Charles, Holly watched Stoobie and Mitsy dance with a certain longing. They were so formal, so careful with each other, so sleek in the way that they moved with each other. Holly felt like a klutz. Charles could not have danced with her like that if he tried, and she wondered if it would make her feel different if he could. She and Charles sort of bounced around together, and it suited who they were perfectly. But it also made Holly wonder if there wasn't some ceremony lacking in their passion.

Charles was happily lost in the moment, holding onto Holly and scanning the room around him as they twirled. Holly smelled wonderful, the music was fun, and the champagne they had been drinking had gone a little to his head. All night he had been taking inventory of his brothers, confirming his thoughts from this morning about who should lead the house during rush as members of the power teams. He knew that picking the sophomores was toughest, and would be subject to the greatest scrutiny in the house, so he watched them with great curiosity. Stoobie was not a sharpie in his opinion. He liked Edward Stamer a lot. Edward had a natural presence and oomph to him.

Although he had not seriously considered George for rush – hell, he was barely a brother – Charles nonetheless could not help but be impressed by how easily George slid into conversations and lit up the faces of people around him. At dinner, he watched George effortlessly speak in formal reserve with Mitsy and Stoobie, sitting erect and fully at ease in his black, conservative tuxedo. If it were not for his long hair, he could have been F. Scott Fitzgerald. Then he would turn 180 degrees to flirt with Holly, and she would smile broadly at his boyish verve. Charles saw how Maria across the table kept wanting to engage George in conversation, and how smoothly George guided the conversation back toward Tim Truesdale. Poor Tim, Charles thought, even when he tries hard, he comes off dull. And now George and Maria were wrapped in each other's embrace on the dance floor. Hmmm.

Lucy reached her hands up to Bob Woodbridge's curly hair and pulled him close to kiss him on the lips. She had timed it perfectly to catch Harold's attention, but he did not look at her. Bob kissed her briefly, and pulled back. His eyes glistened and he observed his lover with detachment. It was what drove her crazy with desire, he knew, and it had the intended effect. Lucy wanted to feel desired, and when she felt Bob's reserve, she focused herself on him to pull him back into her web.

Bob had been wondering about character, and thinking about how two people as different as Stoobie and Harold could agree to be roommates. If they were opposites, it was not enough to simply conclude that opposites attract. There had to be some thread of connection between them, and Bob was thinking hard about what that might be when Lucy pushed her lips onto his. Lucy was a lot of work, but she was raw in her emotions, as ferocious as he was, and he loved her.

Mitsy was feeling the rush of her dancing with Stoobie, and the combination of animalistic gyrations from the fast songs and Stoobie's graceful control while they danced slowly made her cheeks blush. Stoobie was so distant and careful when he touched her that it excited her and made her want to suspend the moment. It was the moment between knowing and unknowing, between familiarity and intimacy, between wanting and commitment. She wished she could live in this moment until she found the boy she wanted to marry. It was so much more romantic than trying to fend off boors like Stoobie's roommate, Harold.

Stoobie was wondering why he didn't find himself more attracted to Mitsy Smith. She was elegant, attractive, and a wonderful companion. But he could not for the life of him get excited about *her*. He could get excited about the moment, about dancing with her, and going on dates with her, but not the girl herself. He hated that about himself. And his gloom went from bad to worse when he let his mind wander to his roommate's whisper at the bar when they were getting drinks during a break in the music. Harold had whispered excitedly to him that Wally and Nick were going to try to seduce one of the brother's mothers at parents' weekend next Saturday!

Whhhatt? Stoobie had replied, almost despairingly. Stoobie found himself increasingly at odds with the sophomores' plots and absurdities. Harold had already told him about having sex on the box freezer, swearing him to secrecy. That was wild enough, but how could boys want to seduce somebody's mother?

Whose mother? he asked Harold quietly.

Harold laughed so hard, the drink he was holding started spilling all over the carpet in the Darling Room. He had wanted to scandalize his roommate, but Stoobie had quickly moved from shock to details.

Well it sure as hell isn't going to be my mother! Harold replied, and they both laughed until they were red in the face. Oh my god, Harold went on, whose mother would you want to boink? Huh? Huh? He was egging his roommate over the top, and wouldn't stop. What about Mrs. Lord! She must be an Amazon! Stoobie started laughing so hard, he had to put the drinks in his hand on the bar counter.

Oh my god, Harold said again. Maybe we should all draw lots! What do you think? One poor sucker will have to sacrifice his mother for the good of the brotherhood!

As he danced with Mitsy, Stoobie looked around the room for Wally and Nick, but couldn't see them anywhere. He wished he could be as jocular as Harold, as able to let these things roll off of him, but he couldn't. He kept picturing Wally kissing one of the brother's mothers and it made him sick in his heart. He fully credited Wally with the capability to do something like that, and he felt miserable about it. It even occurred to him to tell some of the seniors, but what good would that do? What could anyone say?

After the band had played two slow songs, they ended the set with a loud and fast version of *Suite Judy Blue Eyes,* and the room immediately jumped into the fray. Charles started doing The Monkey with exaggerated gestures and everybody joined in. The dance didn't really work with the song, but nobody cared. People were hooting and raising their hands above their heads. By the time it came to a close, the entire room was out of breath.

⌘

The next morning Martha Higgins scooped herself out of Harold's car at nine thirty in front of Delta Gamma Nu. She was exhausted, but in a good way. They had stayed up most of the night, eventually going down to the diner on State Street at four in the morning for eggs and bacon. Then they fell asleep in each others' arms in Harold's room for a few hours. Martha had expected Harold to be flirtatious, even aggressive with her, and he was. But she had not been prepared for how tender he became when they moved from flirting to kissing. It was as if his body relaxed and the gentle side of him came out once his pursuit had born fruit. She began to understand why Diane had such a crush on him. Martha decided she would definitely see him again if she could. And when she got out of the car, she smiled and said, Call me sometime, to make sure he knew.

Holly Menard woke up in her own room at Kappa Sunday morning. By the end of the dance she was tired, and when Charles wanted to go upstairs and join a bunch of people doing whippets in Nick's room, she told him to go along without her. Charles cajoled her to accompany him, and even suggested that they just skip the whippets and unwind in his room, but she could tell he was still wound up. She caught a ride back up the hill from Stoobie and Mitsy, and promised her boyfriend she'd meet him for some fun tomorrow.

At brunch in the Eta Chi dining room, George Muirfield sat with Charles at a moment when the room was mostly empty, between the waves of brothers who came and went during the two hour meal. George had helped himself to scrambled eggs and four pieces of white toast that he covered with butter and jam as he sipped coffee. Charles was having Cheerios and some fruit while Andy made him a cheese omelet. It was a sunny day, and the sunlight poured in through the windows, making them squint their eyes a bit as they spoke.

George was telling Charles his impressions from last year's rush, and speaking rapturously about the experience. He looked intently at Charles as he spoke, and leaned in to describe the time that Charles had been in his room during formal rush. He was holding a piece of toast in the air as if he had forgotten it was there. Charles asked him why he had not been around the house at all, and George nodded his head vigorously as he re-discovered the piece of toast in his hand and wolfed it down.

I am not turning out to be a typical brother, am I? he asked Charles playfully, after he had swallowed his toast, and had begun to put jam on the next piece on his plate. Then he laughed a little, and cocked his head slightly at Charles and asked if Charles liked to get in line at toll booths, or take the far open lane instead.

Charles pushed his face forward slightly and studied George closely.

What does this house really stand for, Charlie? George asked the rush chairman next. Charles did not notice the irony with which George put an "ie" on his name. Then he went on before Charles would feel he had to say something.

I joined a house that struck me as unique, and vibrant, and even a little dangerous. Do you know what Bob Woodbridge said to me? He said the people in this house make the lights come up in the room a little when they walk into it. Hell, I don't think we can really say that's who we are if we are all a bunch of sheep who want to walk to class together every day.

George took a little bite of toast, sipped his coffee, and then continued on.

I am caught up in something that makes light bulbs go off in my head all week long. It's completely consuming, and I think it's a good enough reason to have limited time to spend at the house. I wouldn't be here much more even if I was sleeping here, Charles. So I think it's up to the house to decide what they want, not to me. But I will say this: I am fully prepared to give you my undivided attention during rush, and I think I can be effective in helping to get the right freshmen to see this house as the only logical choice on the hill.

As George finished his comments, he had used his hands expressively and his eyes had literally popped blue sparks at Charles. On the floor directly above them, a brother put Simon and Garfunkel on his record player, and the duo started singing in front of a gentle acoustic guitar.

Paul Simon was singing about sipping coffee and indifference, and Charles had no reservations left in his mind. George was a sharpie, and his passion was real. Charles said with some gusto, Georgie I want you to be a very visible part of formal rush! George stuck out his hand and the boys shook the fraternity handshake, and laughed together as they did it.

That afternoon, Charles sought out L.E.O. Pennington, and Bob Woodbridge and could not believe his good luck when he ran into Scottie in the library. He asked them which sophomores most impressed them, and guided the conversation toward George. He knew they sided with George, and he needed them to help him position George a little better in the house. The Old Guard was openly disdainful of George, and would not like the fact that Charles was going to put him on a power rush team. In their view, George had been a mistake to bid, and his absence from the house this fall proved them right.

In Tim Truesdale's room, when the Old Guard sat and complained to each other, they referred to George as "Moochfield" because, in their view, he was mooching off of the house with no intent of giving anything in return. Two or three of the boys, including, in particular, one junior named Bud Macher, called George "Moochfield" to his face. Hey Mooch-field, Bud would call to him, sarcastically, you got a call two days ago from somebody.

Bob and L.E.O. strongly supported Charles' viewpoint about George, and promised to help. Scottie smiled wanly, and said he would speak to George about showing up at the house a little more. He barely saw George, and found it humorous that anyone would think he would have luck influencing George. Hell, Scottie himself had not been to the house more than a dozen times this semester. And he didn't trust Charles Lord. But he felt he should try something since he was George's big brother.

CHAPTER EIGHT

Most organizations are a true reflection of their leader. In Eta Chi, the same could be said more easily about rush chairmen than the consul. There was a new consul and pro consul elected every semester, so their ability to make the house in their own image was quite limited. In fact those officers were often more a reflection of the house, than the other way around.

But rush was a process, and it was when the house really came together as a unit. And rush looked a lot like Charlie Lord. The freshmen who walked through the doors during the fall teas felt a loose, abundant energy in the rooms. It was serious, but not quite as serious as in the past, and there was an easy laughter that floated above the conversations. When Charles walked a freshman into the great hall and introduced him to one of the ready brothers, he chuckled (ehoo, ehoo) and left them with an off-handed, sometimes sarcastic wish for luck.

He kept his clipboard with him at all times, and made numerous notes to himself, both about the brothers and the freshmen. When he had a positive impression about a freshman, he tended to leave him with someone he favored. When he thought someone appeared dull, he guided them more toward someone in the Old Guard. For real losers, he immediately sought out Tim Truesdale.

He also relaxed the rules about the flow of people through the house. He wanted there to be a natural feel to the comings and goings, and instructed the brothers to trust their instincts about when to leave a room, and when to head back to the great hall. He also changed his mind more about who should do what based on what he saw happening. Harold, for example, was quite good at giving tours of the house – he was funny and loud and efficient, and so Charles picked him repeatedly to take strong candidates on tours.

He relied quite a bit on Buzz Delaney and Bob Woodbridge for their opinions about freshmen. Neither of these boys suffered fools easily. And the faith he placed in George Muirfield started to pay off quickly. George was quick-witted and sharp and challenging as he interviewed the boys who walked into the great hall, and he made them all feel as if they had stumbled onto the biggest secret at Cornell. He also gave Charles a pointed view about every boy he met, and their thoughts on people, while different, were not in opposition.

Charles was quite pleased with informal rush up through early December. The house had already racked up impressive numbers of freshmen visitors, and there were four boys whom Charles had already short-listed for bids. One of the boys, Patrick O'Hare, was not much to

Charles' liking, but he was Mike O'Hare's younger brother, and so he would be bid. Charles figured that the Old Guard would count him as one of their victories.

The second boy, Jimmy Dunbar, was zany, unpredictable, and funny. From Charles' simple perspective, Jimmy Dunbar would keep the place light and a little silly. The third boy, Joshua Finch, had a big pie-shaped face and a ready smile and a big head of curly hair. He was irreverent, but very bright and easy going.

The fourth boy was black. He would be the first black in the house since Charlie Vans had been bid three years ago, and Charles was determined to bid him on that basis alone. But as Wendell Denning quickly demonstrated as he moved through the gauntlet of personalities in the great hall, he was Eta Chi material anyway. He was already active on the hill, and he was quietly thought provoking in conversation. Charles knew he would be highly sought after by a number of houses.

And then a new boy walked into the last tea of informal rush, and the list grew almost instantly to five on Charles' short list. Danny Carvello was a transfer student. He had gone to a community college for two years and transferred in as a sophomore. He was scrawny, hyperactive and a genuine smart aleck. Although he didn't bother to tell anyone for quite awhile, he was also twenty-five years old. And he was ready to party.

Danny had gone off and joined the Air Force after high school, ending up as a computer programmer on flight simulation machines in Idaho. The Air Force made him grow up and see the world in all its comic and dysfunctional splendor. Bored out of his mind in Idaho, he played games on all the flight jocks who came through for training. He learned how to program the flight machines to include Pac Man on consoles in the simulators, and then warned the trainees about the dangers of sighting aliens while in the simulators. And because the pilots always wanted to meet local girls for entertainment while they were on the base, Danny became adept at rounding them up. He would sweet talk them, and cajole them, and make them laugh until they agreed to come for a party. He became invaluable.

In the meantime, he learned how to work the system. By the time he was discharged from the service, he had a jaded view on the morals of the world around him, and he was flabbergasted by the naiveté and short-sightedness of people. The world was waiting to be plucked, but he wanted to pluck it from on high, and he knew that meant college. He left the service, moved home, enrolled in the local community college and developed habits that would stay with him forever. His work came first, and he excelled academically. He was extremely efficient, working from four in the morning until eight. Then he would go to classes and chase girls in the afternoon. But he was always in bed by nine p.m.

For exercise, he followed what he had learned in the Air Force – he ran four days a week. Over time he ran longer and longer distances, until he could head out for an eighteen mile run when he was in the mood. It gave him time to scheme and laugh and vent and dream about what he wanted to do. After two years, he had a perfect 4.0, and applied to the engineering school at Cornell as a transfer student. He had taken electronics courses while in the Air Force, and he had a natural aptitude for it. Plus, computers seemed to be growing rapidly, and electrical engineering probably gave him lots of alternatives.

He had not known what to expect when he showed up at the Ivy League school, but he quickly concluded that the people were the same as they were everywhere else. Maybe a bit on the smarter side, but still caught up in their own underwear half the time. He started to have a ball.

When he walked up to the big hands and bobbing head of Charles Lord in early December, he had really just started exploring the idea of a fraternity. The first few months of school he had stuck to his routine. Up early, study early, go to class, play, go to bed early. Chasing coeds was so much fun and so easy, he couldn't believe it. After you have to work in the plains of Idaho to convince farm girls to jump in a hay truck for a ride to the air force base, flirting with smart girls who wanted to have sex seemed almost too easy.

But as Charles gripped his hand and welcomed him, Danny sensed intuitively an organized structure, and he moved immediately into military process mode. There was clearly a system operating here, and it had to be worked. He stood talking to Charles for a bit, whom he recognized instantly as an officer. He told him what a fine outfit Charles seemed to be running. Charles laughed, ehoo, ehoo, and liked Danny instantly. He asked Harold to give Danny a walk through the house, and Harold shook Danny's hand vigorously and nodded his head emphatically. On their way up the stairs, Harold chuckled and asked Danny what brought him to Eta Chi.

To be honest, Harold, Danny said, the fine reputation of the brothers here and an aching desire for sorority girls are my motivations.

Well, Harold replied, those are both admirable goals! He rubbed his belly and laughed heartily at Danny. Danny, who had no idea what Eta Chi's reputation was, thought he must have struck a chord, but was unsure how to read Harold's reaction. So he grinned and giggled.

Harold felt an instant distrust of Danny, but he didn't show it as he gave him a spirited tour and left him with Wally in the great hall. Harold didn't know what it was exactly, but it nagged him, and it would continue to for a long, long time. But Harold was relatively alone in his reservations about Danny, who worked the room efficiently and professionally, and left a considerable wake in the brotherhood that afternoon.

After all the freshmen had left the last Sunday tea of informal rush in December, Charles called the brothers together in the great hall for their final meeting before Christmas break. He stood at the enormous opening between the hall and the foyer while the brothers mulled about, laughing and talking animatedly about the afternoon. Charles put his fingers to his mouth and whistled them quiet, and the boys took their spots on the big gold rug beneath the antlered chandelier.

Charles was in a great mood. He had the brotherhood assembled before him, engaged in the life blood of their house. The afternoon had gone so well. He joked with them a bit, and they responded quickly to his humorous description of Mike O'Hare showing his own brother through the house. Mike smiled genuinely and yelled out that it was a hard sell to convince his brother that the brothers weren't retarded. Everyone laughed heartily. Then Charles put Patrick O'Hare up for a bid, but cautioned his brothers to consider Patrick on his merits. Do not, he cautioned, simply vote for Patrick because he is Mike's brother.

Mike nodded solemnly. He agreed that Patrick should be considered on his own merits. Tim Truesdale was the first to speak in Patrick's behalf, which made Charles have to control himself. Tim talked seriously about the conversations he had held with Patrick and what a fine person he was. When he finished, the room began to snap their fingers, but Charles held up his hand and recognized Bob Woodbridge. This, Charles thought, ought to be good. He knew Bob thought Patrick O'Hare was...sub par. Sub par was the expression Bob had used last night.

Bob stood erect in the front of the room and talked first about the collection of people he saw in front of him. He said that the bonds of brotherhood were not to be taken lightly, and that no one should assume that Patrick was right for the house or that Eta Chi was right for him, just because his brother was. He told the boys that he had looked at Patrick using the same high standards he applied to every boy who walked through the front door during rush. And then he said that Patrick O'Hare was an Eta Chi.

The room erupted in applause, and Mike blushed for his brother. He was so excited to hear the brotherhood speaking for his little brother that he could feel himself shaking slightly in the legs. Four more brothers stood up and spoke favorably about Patrick. Charles counted three out of the four as Old Guard, and was pleased with the count. He asked for a position, and one of the seniors said, Let's get him before another house does!

As the room began to click their fingers furiously, Charles said, All in favor? And the boys clapped loudly. No one opposed, and Eta Chi had its first pledge candidate. Charles followed Patrick with Wendell Denning, the black boy, and the room pulsed with energy over his candidacy. Three boys spoke about the importance of bidding Wendell early because there would be stiff competition for him on the hill. Buzz Delaney talked about the importance of thinking about Wendell without regard to the fact that he was black, and said he liked him as an Eta Chi, regardless of his race.

The group nodded seriously, and more boys stood and seconded Buzz' comments. More raised their hands, offering their support, but inquiring whether the vote was premature. Did they *really* know this boy? A vague, undefined uneasiness blanketed the room. L.E.O. Pennington got up and left the room.

George Muirfield raised his hand and spoke for the first time. He stood where he was and did not move a muscle as he spoke, until he slowly rotated his head to scan the faces of the boys in the room. He told the group that he thought it was impossible for them to not consider Wendell's race in his candidacy. He is black, and there are no blacks in this room, George went on.

We all know it, he said, and we should be proud of the fact that we want a black to join us. But his blackness should not be the reason we want him to become a brother. I think Wendell is an outstanding person who will add substance to our lives, and I strongly support his candidacy. And there is not a person in this room who doesn't also see Wendell as an asset to our reputation on the hill. So what are we waiting for?

The boys were silent for an instant, staring almost curiously at George. It was his first public comment during rush. Charles smirked at how perfectly George had cornered the room. If the Old Guard silently wanted to scuttle Wendell's candidacy (which he thought was a distinct possibility), they would now be in the uncomfortable position of appearing out of touch. The issue of race was a matter of serious debate and high sensitivity on the campus. Many blacks were choosing to live together in one dormitory devoted to African studies. Whites were unwelcome. There was a hostility and vehemence to the blacks' position that white students found oddly racist.

If the New Guard were unsure of Wendell as a person, Charles thought, they could not comment to that effect without appearing to be finding a false reason to keep him out of their house for discriminatory reasons. After the silence fell away, Charles put Wendell up for a bid, and the entire house raised their hands and cheered for their second pledge candidate. Charles nodded his big head, smiling, and told the room that they had bid two of the strongest freshmen on the hill, and the room cheered again.

***

What is real? And, more importantly, what is intended? L.E.O. Pennington picked his head up off his arm, where he had rested the side of his face while he tried to write in his journal, and sighed. He had walked upstairs to his room hoping that the momentary clarity of his thoughts would lead to a good journal entry. But then the clouds returned, and he slumped over his desk with his head as close to the page as his pen.

It had all started when he left the great hall in the middle of the rush meeting. He had kept his eyes lowered to avoid answering the looks of his brothers, who would wonder where he was going. As he moved he watched the tightly-woven, short pile of the great hall carpet turn into the pleasingly geometric simplicity of the foyer's tiles, and then into the warm hues of the lined hardwood on the library floor. He headed into the dining room, because something in him wanted to look out the windows at the woods below.

He was looking for a sign – something that might incline him to live. Certainly the foolish meeting he just left did nothing in this regard. Watching his brothers debate which freshmen should be anointed with the holy grail of an Eta Chi bid only exacerbated the ambivalence that wreaked havoc on his soul.

L.E.O. Pennington loved Eta Chi. It wasn't that. After a lonely so-journ through high school, the manic embrace of his fraternity satiated him to the brink of overload. It was his brothers' seemingly bottomless belief in their destiny that he could not swallow. In almost every word they uttered, he could hear their silly trust in their own importance. As if, he thought critically, the world was a collection of random moments through which they all marched in whimsical lock step. L.E.O. knew better.

These boys were not joined together out of their own prerogative any more than L.E.O. had chosen his own parents. There was a far greater gravitational pull at work here. It was obvious.

L.E.O. looked out of the dining room windows at the woods. The sunlight tried to reach down through the ancient trees to touch their roots, but the dense foliage defended the shadows well. This was not the first time his despair had consumed L.E.O. It had lurked within him before college in murky shades of gray. But recently it had taken on color and substance in his mind. He was tired of waiting for the future to reveal it-self. If the future was already foretold, what was there to debate? What meaning attached to the passion and determination of the boys around him, other than waste? Waste of self, of each other, of time?

The only real control he had over his life was its cessation. That was his dilemma. To live unfettered, he had to die in his own way. Didn't he? Of course, whenever he thought thus, he quickly worried that life was playing tricks on him. The gravitational pull wanted him to believe this, so he would succumb to its timetable. So, by choosing to die, and then forestalling this inevitability, he was defying fate. It was dizzying logic.

A blackbird moved between the trees, and he smiled. What if he were to bring himself to an end, here at the house? He pictured the looks on boys' faces, their shock and guilt. But that was not important. The only thing he would want is for his brothers to see the future more clearly. To recognize, as he did, the inevitability of life. He watched the tall oaks move imperceptibly in the glen. They were so tall that, even from their much lower place on the hill, they rose equal with the house. He squinted his eyes, and let the girths of all the trees blend together into a massive wall in his view.

How did trees manage so well? he wondered. They seemed to possess a regal disdain for the curse of time that life casts on everything else. L.E.O. pictured the trees absorbing the life force of birds, animals, insects, humans. Trees understood dying, somehow. In a way they died every fall, only to be born again the following spring. Perhaps that was a sign.

Maybe you had to die, like a tree, to get new life. Maybe life was really not about growing up, but growing outward, in circles, in a constant regeneration of self-determination that pushed inevitability further and further away. And maybe that is the source of all promise, destiny, youth...L.E.O. frowned slightly. There was something to all this, but he needed to write it out. So he walked through the kitchen and up the back stairs to his room, to write in his journal.

But the words weren't coming now. He pushed away from his desk, and looked around his room. He got up and dug around in his closet to pull out that painting he had found in the eaves. It had been sitting with a bunch of old boxes and discarded mattresses when he found it, and no one had wanted to hang it anywhere around the house. But there was something about it that made him want to keep it, so he shoved it in the closet.

The painting was a large, almost childlike simulacrum of a rush tea. At least that's what L.E.O. guessed. It was signed by Otto Kemper. '53. Otto had drawn the Eta Chi great hall from the perspective of the foyer. The picture was populated with boys in sport coats with the Eta Chi emblem on their breast pockets chatting with boys who looked full of awe and polish. L.E.O. appreciated the humor with which Otto had drawn the brothers, their open faces so replete with earnest self assurance and a sanctimonious wisdom.

In the center of the piece, a light emanated from an unknown higher source, and spread out in all directions, washing over all of the boys, suggesting a religious connotation. One brother stands in the far left of the image, his arm outstretched to the light as he speaks to three freshmen whose faces are shocked with revelation. Beneath the painting is the caption, "*Behold the true and guiding light of Eta Chi.*"

L.E.O. giggled as he examined the painting, and then propped it above his desk to look at it while he sat to write. When he had rushed the house, L.E.O. had been drawn to the boys, and to the feeling of the house. He understood that Otto was mocking the unquestioned fervor that so many boys embodied about Eta Chi. But it was also true that L.E.O. had found something here that resonated powerfully in him. And he struggled even now to understand what that something really was. There was a contradictory tension, a delicious and brightly illuminated but largely unspoken insistence that defined the core of this brotherhood.

As much as L.E.O. saw himself as waiting for the moment when his life's course would become obvious, as much as he understood that no person had the ability to really choose what he would do, or when he would do it, the dichotomy of Eta Chi nagged at him. His brothers hated boys whose vision of brotherhood was personal accommodation and subservience to its conventions. And yet Eta Chi had, by far, the strictest conventions of any house L.E.O. knew. It was, in L.E.O.'s view, as if the brotherhood wanted each brother to be a child at heart, and an adult in form.

That was it! L.E.O. picked up his pen and began to write in his journal. *I am surrounded by boys who taunt fate by acting like they have accepted their course, but who in their hearts refuse to succumb to the numbing fog of responsibility. That is the genuine source of mirth surrounding us all. We know that we are beacons of maturity to the people outside, as we collude with each sideways glance to subvert the yoke of adulthood by demanding that the brotherhood bow to the individual...*

L.E.O. sat back, and rubbed his temples. He knew this was only true in a theoretical sense, that if he tried to explain this to others, they would scoff at, or humor him. But it was absolutely clear to him. They were just like those trees - stopping their upward climb to grow in circles...What the hell was he talking about?

He looked up at Otto's painting, and wondered if the light of Eta Chi pulled them toward responsibility or irresponsibility. He understood the boys downstairs a little better now. They were playing along with the conventions of the house in order to be free. He wrote one last note to himself, to think about at some later point: *What is the real meaning of our conventions? Are we better off with them, or would fewer conventions spawn even greater freedom? And when I give up my childish things, will I give up that freedom? Will I even care, or remember? Does everyone grow up?*

⌒

Downstairs, the meeting had continued in L.E.O.'s absence, and the last boy Charles brought up for discussion was Danny Carvello. He did not expect to put Danny up for a vote, but he was curious to see what the brothers' reactions were, so he asked for comments, short of a vote.

A number of boys raised their hands. They spoke in glowing terms about their impressions of Danny. He was funny. He was shrewd. He was full of energy and enthusiasm. Charles was surprised at the number of boys who already had an impression of Danny, but then noted Mike O'Hare with his hand on his chin, wagging his head negatively. Charles asked him if he had a comment and he shook his head no, but then said he did, and walked to the front of the room.

Mike began walking up and down in front of his brothers, obviously agitated by the topic. Let me begin, he said, by telling all of you how proud I am of this house and of each of you. His thick, brown hair shook freely across his forehead. His face was as red as the sweater he wore.

I met this guy Danny, he went on. He was slick all right! But I couldn't get any feeling of real emotion out of him. It was like he was making fun of everyone as he spoke with us. And I don't know about the rest of you, I guess you didn't have the same reaction to him, and maybe I didn't see it, but I thought the guy was a jerk!

By now Mike paced impatiently, and he began to make a wider arc around the group, from the front of the house to the French doors that were closed to the patio in the back. He reached the doors and turned toward his brothers, and his face was bright red. His voice rose in a tremble. I don't want to begin to admit people to this house who won't be ...real! Who won't *love* this house! This is an important issue for me! *I love this house!* This house isn't something we turn over to some slick-talking guy who makes you laugh! I love this house! He yelled again, and with that he turned suddenly toward the French doors. With the heel of his right shoe, he began to kick furiously the wooden frame of the door nearest to him. Then Mike moved to the door to his right, and assaulted it with his left foot. All this time he kept screaming. I love this house! I love this house! *I love this house!*

As suddenly as he had begun, he stopped, turned and apologized for his behavior. He looked ashamed. The room stood very still, gaping in his direction. Charles had no idea what to do, so he laughed. Ehoo, ehoo. Mike moved away from the doors and reclaimed the space where he had been standing before he spoke. He thrust his hands in his pockets, and cast his eyes to the floor.

Harold Wise cleared his throat, and the room swung their faces in his direction. I think what Brother Mike was trying to say is that we don't know enough about this fella! Scattered laughter escaped around the room. Harold continued, I certainly don't. And I sure as hell don't want Mike to break the patio doors down! So let's vote to bring him back for formal rush! The room exhaled, and a few of the boys laughed nervously.

Charles scanned the room quickly to gauge the reactions of the brothers but he could not tell what most of them were thinking. They all looked embarrassed. He saw George Muirfield staring intently at Mike, his head leaning way out in front of the rest of him. George was so absorbed, he wouldn't have flinched if someone clapped their hands in front of his face. After a moment, Charles accepted Harold's point and called the meeting to a close. He reminded everyone that they were expected back for formal rush on the afternoon of January second.

George didn't move until he felt all of the boys around him getting up and walking out of the room. He could not believe how Mike had erupted in such raw emotion, and how the kicking of the door was somehow congruent with yelling that he loved the house. The day had been a blast but this was over the top. He had taken careful note of the looks on the faces of the boys who watched, and then observed how Mike somehow resumed his dignity and melted back into the room.

This was the third time in weeks that he had slept at the house after that weekend when Caitlin had gone home. He was beginning to establish a sense of the place, a comfort he had not really enjoyed before. As he went to retrieve the coat he had left in the library, Bud Macher walked along behind him and said, Hey! Moochfield! Awfully nice of you to show up for rush!

George winced inside himself, but kept walking steadily as if he heard nothing. Bud called him louder – Hey Moochfield! George kept walking. Mooch! George lowered his head as if he were deep in thought.

George! Bud finally yelled, exasperated. George turned attentively, and said, Hello Bud! How are you doing? Bud shook his head, and asked George if he had a hearing problem.

No, George replied with a concerned look on his face. Why do you ask?

I was calling you, Bud replied.

I'm sorry, Bud, what can I do for you? George spoke in a level voice.

Nothing, I guess, Bud answered, I was just saying I hadn't seen you around much.

George nodded. I know, he said. I haven't seen you either. We must have different schedules or something. With that he picked up his coat and left to walk back up to campus, to meet Caitlin at the library. He kept thinking about Mike O'Hare, and his mind returned to the formal a few weeks back.

The fall formal had never even occurred to George, so he was unsure what to do when he had met Harold Wise on the stairs that Saturday morning. The stairs were bordered on both sides by full walls, and there was little light. He had stood against one of the walls, catching up with Harold, who was as cheerful as always and hoping George might come to the formal that night. George liked Harold.

He had left Harold and gone to his room where he pulled out the tuxedo his father had given him to take back to school, and hung it on the bunk bed. George laid himself on the lower bunk and stared at the tuxedo's flat, black satiny finish. It was like his father was standing in the room with him, and he smiled at the thought. His roommate was up on campus playing tennis, and George enjoyed being alone in the room. He thought about how much he had wanted to join the fraternity, and how he had pictured himself in this tuxedo dancing at formals with Caitlin. Or maybe that Girl Outside The Library.

The first weekend back to college in the fall, the summer heat had not yet left upstate New York. Everyone was in shorts and tee shirts. George had sat for a moment on the stone bench outside Olin Library when he first saw the girl he now called the Girl Outside The Library. She had ridden up on a green, ten-speed bicycle and coasted to a stop, out of breath. She wore white khaki shorts and a blue, round necked top with a tiny little blue bow that dangled just off-center of the neckline. She wore anklet socks that barely poked above the white running shoes on her feet.

The first thing George actually noticed about the girl was her skin. A thin veil of perspiration made her tanned, healthy skin glossy in the sunlight. She rested her bike against the bench opposite his, and took a small backpack off of her shoulders and looked through it for something. Her back was to him, and George saw broad shoulders, a tiny waist, and a fanny shaped like a teardrop above muscular, shapely legs. When she turned around to sit down for a minute, George tried to look away but couldn't.

She looked at him briefly and smiled. Shoulder length blond hair framed a tanned, lively face. George was quite sure that he had never met anyone quite so…intimidating. It was not her body, which the girl somehow held shyly despite its stunning proportions. Nor her white, straight teeth or appealing nose. It was the blue intensity of her eyes, beneath strong, light brown eyebrows that sent him reeling. Her eyes were round, curious, and a shade of blue somewhere between sky blue popsicles and royal blue Dalton china.

As he lay in his bed looking at his father's tuxedo, George let the guilt of his recollections pass so he could imagine picking up the Girl Outside The Library for the formal tonight. She had paid him no more mind as they sat there on opposite benches in the summer sun. He did not speak to her, and if she knew he was ogling her she didn't let him know. After a bit she stood, and walked off across the Arts Quad pushing her bike along beside her. George had watched her fanny until he could no longer make her out.

What was it that made him think of her? He was happily united with Caitlin, almost inseparable, really. In fact, he had an almost desperate desire for Caitlin. He did not flirt or even think about other girls, but the Girl Outside The Library was seared into his most private moments. In September, George had arrived back at school from the summer on a mission. He had spent almost every day on the telephone with Caitlin over the summer. They had seen each other only three weekends, and the intervening days had stretched like taffy. The first night on campus, Caitlin had suggested that George sleep in her room, and he had never really left. They walked to campus in the mornings, met in the evenings at the library to study or after rehearsals, and walked back to her apartment together at the end of the day.

Caitlin's room had a single bed, and the two of them squeezed onto it, laughing and hugging. Caitlin wore a nightgown; George slept in his undershirt and pants. They rarely did more than kiss, and they spoke mostly of their work in the theater. Caitlin was determined to perform in musicals. George wanted nothing but serious, dramatic opportunities. And they were successful beyond their expectations.

At major play tryouts in September, George had been greeted warmly. On his way out the door afterwards, Steven Hurowitz, the short, wiry, black-haired professor, told him to be sure to check the callback board. Derek Steele had nodded to him, but was more noncommittal. At callbacks, in a second floor rehearsal room in Ridley Hall, Steve

Hurowitz asked George to read a black part. George picked up the script, read through the highlighted speech, and assumed a position in the middle of the room with his back turned to the other reader. The other reader was a six-foot-six graduate theater student who was black. He had a short, cropped afro, a pic in his back pocket, and one of the richest voices George had ever heard.

The scene was an argument between the two characters, and the part that Steve had given George to read was written in ghetto slang. The other reader began the scene, and George remained turned away from him the entire time that he pleaded with George not to do something stupid. George kept looking out the window at the early autumn night. The windows were open and the sweet, fresh air wafted into the room.

When it was time for George to speak, he whirled in place and pushed his face up into the black boy's. Luckily, the black boy lowered his head in response so that their faces were close. George put the script behind the taller boy's head and read over his big shoulder. He ranted at his reading partner, and began to embellish his accent as he went on. His speech was quite long, and out of the corner of his eye, he could see Steve Hurowitz transfixed and smiling.

George's reading partner began to fume in the long silence given him by the script, and moved his much larger body into the small space between them in a menacing way. George felt something in him giving way and opening up. He could feel the tension and awe in the others in the room who were waiting to read parts. He had already gone way over the top – usually callback readings were done without any theatrics, sitting on stools around the room, so that the director could hear the cadences of their speech and consider their basic physical attributes. George raised his voice as he started the final paragraph. His reading partner looked like he was about to slap him, and George read the final lines with vitriolic disdain –

Ain't no way any nigger like you is going to pull hisself up and walk the long white boy highway, so don' give me no bullshit. You nothing but a white-ass honkie lovin Unca Tom that wouldn't know ya daddy if you come home and found him in bed with yo' momma. GODDAM IT WILSON, you the sorriest excuse for a nigger I ever seen.

When George finished he stood staring into the glowering face of his reading partner, and the room did not move. No one breathed. The air came through the window, and George's partner finally began to smile, and George followed him. Then Steve erupted in laughter, and the room applauded. The two readers kept looking at each other, still in the moment, and George began to think the other boy was truly angry. So he turned, still in character, and whispered "I ever seen" as he looked out the windows. The other boy laughed and slapped him on the back. And George knew he had his first part in a graduate theater production.

He did not realize that he would be playing Mike Mafucci, an Italian gangster, in one of only three white parts in a black play called *No Place To Be Somebody*. For two days he actually wondered if he was going to be cast as a black man.

Caitlin tried out and received a significant part in the *Pirates of Penzance*, which thrilled her. She started taking private singing lessons, and her voice began to lift in the accomplished way that professionals fill a room. Together, they enrolled in a year-long course by a new theater professor entitled Progressive Experimental Theater, or PET. The teacher, a middle-aged thespian with a bitter edge to him, was trying to launch a new brand of theatrical expression that incorporated the precision and emotion of dance in performances with only single words uttered by the actors as they moved relationally across the stage.

In their first PET class, the instructor, Prescott Chilton Harris, had swept away the students' back-to-school enthusiasm with one withering gaze. He announced that his class would require professionalism and dedication, not college-aged whateverisms. The door would be locked at precisely one fifteen p.m. each day. Anyone late to class needn't knock, because they were deselected from the class and would receive an "incomplete." This would be true, he sniped, whether the tardiness was next week or the last day of the semester. There would be no class cuts permitted for any reason.

So don't come to me sniffling with illness, or apologizing for missing class because you just *had* to attend some funeral, because it does not matter, he told them. If you want to be actors, then behave like it and treat this class and your career, for the five percent of you who probably have one, like the most serious thing in the world. Now line up and let me look at you.

With that jaundiced start, Prescott Chilton Harris rocketed into their lives, demanding that they stand, move and feel with the same precision that modern dance artists point their toes. There was a binder with over one hundred pages of definitions and rules that the class was required to memorize and recite at a moment's notice during class. There was physical training that enabled the students to begin to move each part of their body as delicately and exactly as the professor demanded. And there was the professor himself, whose ego filled the room and invaded their skin with an awareness of their faults and miscues that astounded them. He knew before they faltered when and how they would, and glowered at whoever the offenders were at the exact moment it happened.

Caitlin loved the class and her life with George. She was recognized as a serious member of the theater community and she was in love with a boy who was willing to be as close to her as possible without immorality. Every day was a mixture of open theatrical expression and, paradoxically, a kind of domestic bliss. And she had persuaded Derek Steele to let her be his assistant while he directed *To Kill A Mockingbird*.

George chafed at Caitlin's assistant's role. But he was extremely careful to avoid discussing it with his girlfriend, because she immediately tied any suggestion of her romantic intention with Derek to George's relationship with Louise. And, God knew, George didn't need any more of that. He had spent the summer convincing Caitlin of his fidelity to her. By August, he believed it himself.

Rehearsals for *No Place To Be Somebody* were scheduled to move from the rehearsal rooms to the Straight theater the week following the weekend when Caitlin went home and George ended up at Eta Chi. On the Saturday afternoon before the formal George had found his way to L.E.O. Pennington's room. The boys sat listening to Ten Years After on L.E.O.'s KLH turntable, nodding in approval to *50,000 Miles Beneath My Brain.* George flipped through L.E.O.'s milk crates full of albums and talked about how excited he was to have a major part in a play. Around six p.m. L.E.O. put on a tuxedo and headed off to pick up a girl he liked from College Town, and George wandered back to his room. This would be a perfect time to go to the library and get in a five-hour catch up session, but the mood in the house made him feel he would be missing out if he left.

So he showered and pulled on his father's tuxedo, which fit him close enough. He brushed his hair across his forehead and around his ear and looked at himself in the mirror in the bathroom. Finally he wandered downstairs and immediately hooked up with Edward Stamer and his date in the Darling Room. He got himself a Vodka and Tonic from the boy behind the bar and chatted amiably with Edward as the room began to fill. From behind him, George felt a woman's hands cap his head and cover his eyes. The fingers felt cool on his face, and he smelled a kind of perfumed lotion. He twisted around slowly until Maria Kitsoujas' hands came off, and smiled genuinely when he saw her. Hello Mr. Actor, she said.

George told her how happy he was to see her again, and asked who she was with. She explained that she had seen Tim on campus and he had told her the Fall formal was this weekend. Since he did not have a date, she had offered to join him. George shook his head agreeably toward Tim, who stood near, with two drinks in his hand and a cool expression on his face. Maria asked if they could have a dance before the night was done, George said absolutely, and then Maria had taken Tim's hand and asked him to show her the decorations in the dining room.

Over dinner he ended up next to Holly Menard, and across from Maria and Jim Steuben and his date who had a name like Muffy or something. Maria spoke across the table to him once, but George could tell from the look on her date's face that he was not happy about it. Maria was so animated and comfortable, he would have liked to speak more with her, but he turned her questions back around to the senior with her.

George thought Tim Truesdale was a bit of a stiff, but he knew he didn't need any more animosity in the house than he already was feeling. So he was very solicitous even when Tim Truesdale didn't seem appreciative.

George got a kick out of Jim Steuben and whatever her name was. They looked like something out of the *Great Gatsby*, but they were personable and intelligent and enjoyable company during dinner. The girl was elegant, he thought. Steuben had an attitude, and George liked his convictions about things. Charles Lord had attempted to speak with him about rush, but Holly had put a stop to that right away. George thought Holly smelled like a spring night with whatever perfume she was wearing. He wondered if her hair just fell like that, or if she had to work hard at it to make it so rich and full.

After dinner George stood and sang the Darling song, looking at Maria as he sang the words he could remember, wishing that more of them would come back to him. Then he had wandered off and joined Wally and Nick at the bar who were in the middle of hatching their plot to conquer one of the boy's mothers the following weekend. They were drinking rum and cokes in short glasses and giggling as they looked around the room at the people dancing. At first George thought they were teasing him, but he began to see that they were high – their eyes were quite red – and seriously taunting each other about it.

If you guys are serious, you need a plan, George told them.

They looked blankly at him. There was the kind of pause that only happens with marijuana, and then they both broke up laughing again.

I mean it, George told them. Look around the room. Where do you think you will be able to do this? You'll have to get one upstairs alone to make it happen! George was having fun plotting the fantasy with them.

And you need to pick one whose husband drinks a lot so he won't notice that his wife is gone, he added.

George tried to picture the scene as he spoke and could not fathom seducing a woman his mother's age. He was sure that kind of thing happened, and he absolutely wanted to be there to see this, but only out of a disgusting prurience. After a while more boys joined those getting drinks for their dates and the word of their silly plot began to spread. George promised to be there to monitor their success and they renewed their talk as he walked off.

He had seen Maria making a face at him over Tim Truesdale's shoulder on the dance floor and he decided to cut in for his dance with her. Tim seemed fine when George tapped his shoulder and said, Take care of our darling! brightly as he left the floor. The song was fast, and Maria moved her shoulders and swayed her hips, smiling at George as he started to dance. She leaned close to him so he could hear her and said, I'm not his date, you know!

George laughed and nodded in understanding. He leaned forward and yelled into her ear, Thank God for that! and they smiled at each other.

George began to let his body move to the music, making angular, dramatic motions with his arms, and sweeping arcs with his feet. Maria laughed and copied him. It was more like modern dance than normal dancing and it looked cool to her. When a slow song started Maria wrapped her arms around George's neck and looked into his eyes as they moved slowly in a circle. They were talking softly, and when George asked her what she planned to do with her life, she talked about wanting to be a psychologist. George listened intently.

George knew there not a shred of romance developing between them, just a kind of pleasant attraction and shared zeal about the lives they were leading at school. He told her about being in a play with all black actors, and their mouths were so close they would have kissed if their attraction had been different. But Maria was so comfortable in his arms that when the song ended they stood there swaying slightly, talking intensely with each other, their eyes and faces close.

How did you end up here? she asked him as they stepped away from each other. He looked at her carefully for a moment until she motioned around her, indicating she was speaking about Eta Chi.

This house suits me perfectly, Maria, he said. I was drawn here by its character and formality. It's very much like the way I grew up. It's the way I dreamed college would be when I was in high school. The better question to ask is: how did this house end up with me!

Maria shook her head lightly, and said Hmmm. She reached to him and kissed him on the cheek and said, I am glad this house found you, George. There's something to this house I only vaguely understand, but I see it in your eyes. It makes me warm.

George stared intently at Maria Kitsoujas, hoping she would say more, but she left him to go to the ladies' room. At the end of the evening, George bid Maria goodbye as she and Tim Truesdale walked out the door. He was pleasantly inebriated, and in the middle of a lively conversation with Cullen Hastings about architecture. Maria was a hip person, he noted. Tim walked like a moron.

The next day, after brunch, George headed to campus and went to the room in the library where he and Caitlin usually studied. The sun was out, but it was the cooling, golden light of autumn that magnifies the colors in the trees and makes the world stand out in bas relief. George relished the day. He did not miss Caitlin at all. And that made him think.

He was more than a little surprised to find himself sitting in the library on the last Sunday in October, not missing his girlfriend. They were almost desperately close, and would spend at least some portion of every evening in the library off in a corner wrapped in each other's embrace. George had never really become comfortable with their public displays of affection, but Caitlin's intensity at those moments made him forget himself. She was so insistently affectionate with him, that her reserve when they were in private confused him. He knew somehow that it was the thrill of being daring in front of others that made Caitlin so profuse in her romantic demonstrations. And he liked the fact that she was aroused this way, but why did her ardor not carry into their moments alone?

He watched people passing his table in the library, noting their body types and the way they slouched or tip-toed or swayed through the room. He could feel the book in his hands, but it seemed to be very detached from him, as if he would be unable to even make out the print on the page, were he to glance down. He saw a shadowy image of himself in the glass between his room and the main corridor beyond, but he could not distinguish his features or the frame of his body. It was a sensation he did not want to end, and he sat still for several minutes.

Eventually he resumed studying, and he worked well until it was time to walk back to the fraternity. The air was unseasonably warm as he walked through the arts quad, across the suspension bridge, and down Thurston Avenue. The sky was light, and it was easy to see where he was going, even where there were no streetlights. Caitlin was not coming back until the morning, so he would not see her until PET class. When he arrived back at the house, the Sophomore Hallway was buzzing with rumors about how Wally and Nick were planning their deflowering of one of the mothers.

Steve Stilton told Wally to stay away from his mother and Wally asked Steve what she looked like. At one point, the boys started hearing that Edward Stamer was going to compete with them to see who could do it first, but Edward hotly denied that he had meant it. George got right into it, telling his roommate, Jason, he guessed Fritz's mother might be attractive. Jason started choking, and went down the hall to tell others that George had a crush on Mrs. Hublein. Down the hall, George heard Fritz yelling, No Way!!

Parents weekend at Eta Chi came and went. George actually showed up to see if Wally and Nick would really try something. And while the two boys swaggered into the dining room as if they were sizing up all of the mothers who were there, they ended up sitting with Steve Stilton's parents. Mrs. Stilton was wearing a tan cocktail dress that matched the color of her hair. George leaned over to Harold and asked him what he thought, and Harold groaned at the thought of it. Nice rack though! he said under his breath. The two boys eyed Wally over Mrs. Stilton's shoulder and winked toward him, nodding. But Wally had actually taken a liking to Steve's mother and even told her how much he missed his own mother.

Mrs. Stilton leaned in, touched Wally on his arm and told him his mother must be so proud of him. Wally smiled and said, You think so? He put his hand on top of hers and winked at Steve. All around the room the brothers watched carefully. That was as close as he got.

A number of boys had stared incredulously at George when he showed up for the dinner party, because his hair was cut short, in a round pattern, and was jet black.

What the hell happened to you? Cullen Hastings had asked.

George explained he was playing an Italian mobster in a play, and had to look the part. Actually he had been surprised when Stephen Hurowitz had sent him to the wardrobe room on the first night of rehearsals in the Straight Theater. No one had forewarned him that they were going to cut his hair and dye it black. He just was told to ask for Rose, and when he got to the room, Rose squealed and pushed George into a chair and told him to close his eyes.

When George protested, she pushed gently on his chest, with her face up close to his and whispered, Director's orders! Rose had huge, round brown eyes, accentuated with striking black mascara, and the largest chest he had ever seen. She was one of the stagecraft people who wanted to work backstage in the theater, and George liked her. So he trusted her instruction, closed his eyes and sat still while she cut huge chunks off his hair and snipped what was left into a round bowl cut. Then she led him to a sink to wash in the dye.

Wait a minute, George said, is this dye permanent?

Of course not, silly, Rose said as she winked to someone else. It may not even last through the play!

CHAPTER NINE

When Stephen Hurowitz had cast George as Mike Mafucci, it was not because he had done a good job as a black man, though he had, in fact, blown away the room with his impersonation. It was the tension he felt between George and Duncan, the tall black actor who would have the lead in the play. He needed George to get under Duncan's skin, and he had pushed him so hard in the tryout, Stephen knew it would work well on stage. But he worried about making George seem Italian, so he had given George a book, *How To Be Italian*. He insisted that George use his hands all the time when he spoke. George was very coachable and developed a wonderfully sardonic tone with his accent.

As the play approached, Stephen began to talk to the cast about what it would be like to do a show *for* blacks. Other than Duncan and one other black boy in the theater department, all of the other black actors had been collected through advertising in the Cornell Daily Sun, and by Stephen going to the all-black dorm and posting a want ad. He told them that he was advertising the play in the regional newspapers with an explanation that it was a black play with black actors, to encourage a black audience.

Now, I don't know what kind of turnout we can expect, but I will tell you this. Black audiences are far more vocal than a white audience. The cast looked at him quietly. You know how white people sit in their seats and try not to sneeze? They all laughed.

Well, black audiences like to react to what they are watching. They speak to characters on the stage in the middle of scenes. They cheer when Duncan does something heroic. They boo when the bad Mike Mafucci comes on stage to collect money from the bartender. They like to be part of the show they are watching.

One of the boys had been looking at George and asked him in a loud voice what he was confused about.

What do we do when they talk to us, do we talk back? George inquired. The cast laughed.

No, no, no, Stephen Hurowitz replied. Stay on script, but enjoy the visceral, joyful interactions. Play to the audience a little!

The cast looked around at each other, smiling. They had all grown close during the rehearsing, and were looking forward to opening night in two weeks. At the final dress rehearsal, Rose told George she needed to do his makeup and when he went upstairs, she patted him into her chair. He told her he could do his own base but she said she had to do his hair first, and he looked at her funny. She picked up a curling iron, and ordered him to sit still, while she went to work.

The first time she released the steam from the iron to make curls in his hair, George yelped loudly.

What the hell are you doing to me? That burned my scalp. The girls in the room all giggled.

Don't be a cry-baby you big tough gangster you! Rose scoffed. She took another tuft of hair and twirled the iron around to make another row. She whispered in his ear, I'll try not to burn you, but that happens when you curl short hair sometimes.

I feel like I'm in a dentist chair, George mumbled morosely, but he promised himself he wouldn't give in to the pain. When Rose was done, she took a mirror and held it up for him to see, and he smiled broadly. You're a masochist, Rose, but a good one. He looked so different, he couldn't believe it.

George was using all of the acting training he had received so far to create the character of Mike Mafucci. Before the dress rehearsal, he showed up at the stage three hours early. He had to find a way to sneak into the theater, because it only opened two hours before rehearsals or shows. There were safety lights illuminating the stage and the orchestra, but the theater was mostly shadows. George walked to the exact middle of the stage and sat cross-legged looking out at the empty seats, imagining them full.

Then he breathed rhythmically and meditated for a while, before he stood, stretched, and slowly worked his body into the neutral position. He was becoming good at finding neutral, and could tell when he was there by how relaxed his body grew.

Without moving, he went down a mental checklist of his character's body. It was much stronger and muscular than his own, and older, and tired. From the orchestra, it looked like a puppet was slumped in the center of the shadowy stage.

Finally he let his center spin and swirl deep in his middle, and begin to send instructions to the rest of his body. He always tried to work through his center, as he had been taught, and would slowly sense his arms and legs and torso taking on the feelings that Mike Mafucci felt everyday.

By the time he was finished, he was standing slightly off center, his hip thrust out wider than his ever was. His head was back and angled slightly upwards, as if the center of his neck was on the back of his shoulders. He began to feel disgust as he looked around the stage at the set, which was a run-down bar in Harlem. He hated when the boss sent him down to this scumbag's place, and wished he could be somewhere else.

He cleared his throat the way Mike always cleared his throat, and delivered his most important lines to an imaginary character across from him. The words themselves seemed to sneer.

George knew that the trick was to get into character and stay there, even during makeup and when the doors opened and the audience began to shuffle in. But he couldn't do it fully when he went to makeup and Rose curled his hair. He managed to keep his body in character, but spoke like George when he was with her.

On opening night, a Thursday, there weren't many black people in the audience, and no one booed George, which disappointed him. He would have used that to fuel his dislike for the main character. But the next night about half the audience was black, and George could feel the difference from backstage. He did not come onstage early in the play, so he watched the actors work though their lines and saw the audience laughing and occasionally uttering " All right!" or "Awww."

Then he strode through the stage door into the barroom and called out his first line, "Hey Johnnycakes, how's business?"

George could not help but hear someone in the audience say "Uh-oh" in a loud voice followed by a laugh from some other part of the theater. But he was deep into his character, and so intent on pissing Johnny off that the rest of the noise from the audience went unheard. From his place in the audience, Stephen Hurowitz smiled widely. Mike Mafucci looked and sounded like an Italian thug, and the boy playing Johnny was genuinely rankled by the sight of him.

Mike Mafucci was not a big role. He came on stage a total of twenty-one minutes out of one hundred and twenty-five. But George treated it like a lead role, and relished every moment. He was playing a character in front of four hundred people who were paying five dollars to see him be an Italian gangster. He was in heaven.

When the local paper reviewed the show, there was a fleeting reference to a gangster and George was ecstatic. The reviewer didn't think much of the play or the production, but that was totally irrelevant.

The Saturday of the sixth, penultimate show, George went in the morning to tryouts for one act plays directed by graduate students. Caitlin wanted to be in a one act, experimental opera, and was assured of the role she wanted before tryouts. George went and read as if he were reading for the first time. Inside his head, he was trying to force himself to be humble, though he knew that he would get a part. After the tryouts, two of the directors approached him together and asked if they could speak with him. They told him they both had parts for him, and had decided to let him pick the one he wanted.

There is little elixir stronger than the feeling of being desired by many, and George's humility drained away instantly. He nodded his head, and suggested that he spend a little time with each of them so he could understand the roles and the plays. The graduate students flinched slightly.

Let's just resolve it now one of them said. My role is an army captain during a war scene, and his role is a young virgin who's being pursued by a homosexual. Which of those two appeals to you? The graduate student speaking thought the choice was obvious.

George looked at him silently a moment, and said, I'll take his then.

The other director, James Shelton, hooted and told George rehearsals started Monday. George nodded, and looked at the first director, who was fuming. He said, I did a play like that two years ago. This will broaden me more. The student shrugged and walked off. George regretted his decision a little, but figured it really did make sense to try something new.

The last performance of *No Place To Be Somebody* went well, and George expected the cast to have a wrap party afterwards. But the blacks in the play seemed uninterested, and Stephen Hurowitz simply thanked everyone for their fine work. George wondered if this was how professional theater worked, and was a little unsettled. He walked to College Town to Caitlin's apartment and found her studying. Her roommate was not home, and they made tea in the kitchen and talked quietly about the last show. He suggested that they go out for a drink, but she told him she wanted to climb into bed and hug him ferociously until they fell asleep, and that is what they did.

At the first rehearsal for the one act play the following Monday, James Shelton explained that the cast would be going through a series of exercises for the first week, and not working from the script. He choreographed improvisational routines with the seven people who were acting in the play. His goal was to develop subtext between the players at the subconscious level, which would end up extending to the players once they began working from the script.

George thought the work was fun, but strange. On the third day, the director asked George and the boy who would eventually be playing the homosexual to stay and told the rest of the cast they could leave early. They were in rehearsal room one, near the department administrators and deans' offices. It was warm in the room, and daylight was fading outside the windows.

James Shelton handed George a little rubber ball that fit in the palm of his hand, and told him he had to keep it in his hand. He then turned to the other boy, and told him that his job was to get the ball out of George's hand.

That's it? they both asked.

That's it. George, your objective is to not let that ball out of your hand, no matter what.

The two boys looked at each other and grinned. The graduate student went and hoisted himself up on the window sill and watched without saying another word.

George moved away from the other boy, walking aimlessly around the room, waving the ball in a taunting manner when he was a good distance from the other boy. The other boy was a bit shorter than George, and not as strong. For a while George simply held the ball in his fist with his arm straight up, so that the other boy couldn't reach it. At first the other boy just tried to swat at it and stayed away from actually putting his hands on George.

Jesus, try harder, will you, George muttered. We'll be here all night at this rate.

The director shushed George and said, No talking.

The boy began to press more insistently for the ball, at first pulling on George's arms, then wrapping his arms around George to try to stop George from moving around the room. George resisted him easily, and grew almost bored as they continued the silly improvisation.

After almost an hour, the boy was no closer to wresting the ball from George's hand, which by now was a little sweaty. The day was gone, and the only light that filtered in through the windows came from the distant streetlights on the avenue behind the building. Finally George let the boy push him to the rubber mat, though he knew that he could have resisted him still. Maybe this would make it easier for the boy to get the stupid ball and end the exercise.

The boy straddled George, and actually gripped George's hand for a moment, but George kept writhing beneath him and the boy had to let go of George's hand to steady himself. The boy cursed under his breath.

George extended his hand with the ball clenched in his fist and stared at the other boy. The boy gripped his hand and tried to pry his fingers apart, and George stayed still on the floor with his eyes closed, concentrating on his center. He was willing his fingers to stay wrapped around the ball, and the boy, whom George realized was really quite weak, started to pant as he tried to get his prize.

It was now a quarter to six and they had been at it for close to two hours, when the director said Out!

The boys stopped and sat on the floor looking toward him. They had almost forgotten he was still there. The director looked pleased. George felt the whole thing had been slimy and too long. The other boy looked sheepish, and tired.

Okay, what have each of you learned? the director asked, staring out into the middle of the room.

The two boys were silent. Then the other boy, whose name was Lincoln, said he felt unhappy, and that it was much harder to get George to give him the ball than he had expected. He was rubbing his leg where George had pushed hard against him while they were on the floor.

George?

You know, I wanted to give him the stupid ball after a while, just to get it over with, but I found strength through my center to stay true to the rules.

Good! exclaimed the director, leaping up and beginning to pack up his things. For each of you, I want you to remember this when we start reading next week. The ball is your virginity George. And Lincoln, you really want that ball.

The two boys looked at each other, and smiled.

Fat chance, George said evenly as he looked at Lincoln.

Yeah, baby! Lincoln said, and they laughed together.

When they began reading, the director had tried to design similar types of improvisational exercises for the other characters. George doubted that it had been worth a week of rehearsal, when he could have been building his character's body and voice, but he appreciated the effort the director had put into developing the play in an innovative way.

The play was a comedy by Terrence McNally set in New Jersey, and George played a hapless young man who couldn't see what was happening around him. George loved how clueless his character was, and imbued him with a superficial irritation at not being able to understand the meaning of things. He was a virgin who was afraid of having sex with the kittenish girl who wanted him and didn't even know that Lincoln's character was pursuing him sexually. He worked hard on his character, and concentrated on getting into character and staying in it before, during and even after the rehearsals.

The rehearsal schedule was tight – a matter of weeks – and so the actors worked long into the night in the little black box performance room in the basement of the theater building. The director was painstaking in blocking out the play. He insisted that the actors move to precise positions in the performance area. As the performances loomed, George came down with a fever and a slight cold. His head was a little foggy, but he met all of his deadlines for lines, blocking and character development.

One act plays ran three nights, and on the first night George was exhausted. Final examinations were beginning, the rehearsals had been long and he was behind in his studies. The stage area was indicated only by the walls and a dirty white painted line on the floor, about three feet from the first row of chairs in the tiny square room.

George began the play on stage, shaving his face in an imaginary mirror which was located stage left in the audience. Once the audience was seated, George walked out casually from the side door, almost as if he were attending the play, then stopped, swiveled and put his hands up to his face, one hand pulling at the skin, the other holding the imaginary razor, and froze. He was in his underwear.

He was required to stand totally still until the audience grew quiet looking at him as the lights came down to signal the start to the play. There were only four stage lights on the whole stage, and three were dark while the fourth shone directly on George's face.

He loved this part of the play, because the director had instructed him to begin only when he felt both he and the audience were ready. So he stood there at least a minute, until he heard a slight cough from someone in the audience and then began to shave and launched into his lines. He always waited for a sound from the audience in the quiet, because he knew that the audience would be thinking about that sound, that cough, and would focus immediately on him once they were focused anyway.

He was only in the first and the last part of the play. The entire middle section involved the other characters, as Lincoln tormented everyone in his path. But in the first scene it was only George and the girl playing the ingénue, who knocked at the door to George's little apartment looking for someone else. When George let her in the apartment, she looked around and was getting a kick out of George in his underwear, before she realized she was in the wrong place. Within minutes, George was lying on the stage floor, having feinted from distress, and the girl had removed her shirt and was leaning over him in her bra, with her breasts close to his face when he awoke.

She wanted action. George's character wanted escape. The audience was laughing hard. A knock on the door broke the scene, and George hurried into his imaginary bedroom, behind the one tall black partition at the back of the performance area, where the other actors waited to go on. They entered the apartment around the other side of the partition as George left the audience's view, and the play began in earnest.

George had almost twenty-five minutes to stand by himself behind the partition before he returned to the stage. With his fever, even standing was exhausting. To rest, he decided to put himself into neutral, and within minutes his body was naturally positioned on itself in a puppet's slump. It felt so peaceful and his forehead felt so warm that the next thing he knew, George was asleep standing in neutral backstage during the performance. He did not wake up until one of the actors left the stage and woke him with a whisper. There were thirty seconds before George's cue to return to the stage, and it took George half that time to clear his brain and realize where he was.

But he knew his lines perfectly, and when he breezed onto the stage as his character, he hit the lines perfectly, and even felt a little rested. The end of the play was one laugh after another, as Lincoln's character pursued George's and the girl chased both of them, and George tried to get all of these people to leave his apartment. McNally's sarcastic and slightly perverse view of society hit the mood of the audience just right, and the show was well received.

The last night of performance, the director had made a blocking change before the show. In the final scene, he wanted George to move three spaces upstage, rather than downstage when he was talking to Lincoln. George was not feeling any better, and absorbed the direction slowly, but understood before he went off to prepare. Unfortunately, during the play George had already ingrained his blocking into his head, and moved instinctively downstage toward the audience, as he had the previous two nights. He didn't even realize that he had forgotten the instruction until the cast party after the show when the director curled his lip and snarled at him about it.

The director's ire snapped George out of character, much to the delight of the cast, who tired at George's insistence that he remain in character after the show. But in truth, George did not consciously try to stay in character when the show was over. It just took him some time to stop thinking and feeling like the character, and he didn't rush the release.

At the end of the evening, he was walking across campus with Arthur Conde, who had played one of the other characters in the play, and asked him if he knew why the director had gotten so mad.

I mean, for chissake, Arthur, we did the show that way the first two nights and it went fine. What on earth was so important about that blocking change on the last night?

Arthur laughed with high pitched glee.

You're an idiot George. You know why.

George looked at Arthur earnestly. I do? he asked.

Oh my god, you don't! Arthur replied and chortled again. Actually if you really don't know, I am not sure you're ready to handle it, he concluded.

What? George asked, now intent on his companion.

I suppose you don't know that our esteemed director is in love with Lincoln?

George's mouth gaped. You mean in love, in love?

Arthur cackled again. Jesus, you are a rube. Yes, I mean as in emotionally and, he paused for emphasis, *homosexually* in love!

No, I did not realize that. George replied. He was stunned. The director had played his sidekick in *No Place to Be Somebody*, and they had spent a lot of time backstage together, but George had no inkling he was homosexual.

So what had that got to do with the blocking change? George finally asked, recovering himself.

He was jealous! Arthur explained. George was lost again.

Okay, you know how you always got that big laugh when you went downstage in that scene? He thought you were getting the laugh that his lover should have been getting, so he wanted to reverse the blocking so that Lincoln would be downstage and be able to play to the audience better. But you forgot, and you got the big laugh again. It made him furious, because he thought you knew why he was trying to do it, and purposely ignored his direction. Arthur paused, and looked up at the sky. Now that's hilarious, he said, and waved George off as he headed toward west campus. George trudged toward Caitlin's apartment.

When he saw his girlfriend, he asked her if she knew that the director and Lincoln were lovers. Nooo! Caitlin squealed. But I'm not surprised. Why? As George told her the story, he became incensed that the director had been preoccupied with getting his lover laughs instead of focusing on the dramatic delivery of the play.

Oh, for heaven's sake, Honey, you're not on Broadway! Caitlin said gently as she rubbed his arm. Besides, you make a beautiful virgin. George smiled weakly, and let the issue pass.

In January, George left his parents the morning after New Year's Day, and drove up the Massachusetts Turnpike toward New York State. Snow was trying to fall, and he occasionally turned the wipers on to clean the windshield, but it mostly flurried until he got off the throughway and began driving old Route 20 across the state. George loved the drive, which made a straight line parallel to the highly traveled throughway, but rose over and through the hills and valleys of New York.

Route 20 was an old, four-lane road that connected villages and hamlets. Between the towns, the roads were almost always empty and George drove fast. Though the towns were empty whenever he passed through them, he tried to slow down close to the speed limit when he reached them, guessing that a local policeman might be waiting on the edge of town.

He blasted music through the stereo he had installed himself in the new car – a customization mostly unheard of in the early seventies. He slipped another cassette into the stereo and Bonnie Raitt's slide guitar began its snake-like howl. She was singing *That Song About The Midway* and George tried to join in but could not hold the notes. He did not know how to sing. The Camaro was light in the rear and he could feel the back end swaying a bit as he drove through the slush forming from the wet snowfall on the concrete.

One of the main reasons he drove Route 20 instead of the throughway was to stay awake. The throughway was straight, flat and sleep-inducing, and Route 20 provided him with variety and curiosity about the people who lived in and in between these little towns. He could not imagine for the life of him, what possessed these people to choose to live in the absolute middle of nowhere.

He smiled at the thought, and felt his center spinning in the absolute middle of his personal universe. He could see its brass glow and finely hammered shape deep within the middle of his core. He popped open the glove box and removed the package of Energets he had bought for the ride. Energets were coffee flavored caffeine candies that he loved to suck on instead of stopping for coffee and wasting time. Sometimes he went through so many of them he got a stomach ache and started to shake, but by then he was usually just about to Ithaca.

He arrived at Eta Chi at one in the afternoon, and pulled his car up close to a bank of snow that ringed the semi-circular driveway. Boys were pulling in and unloading clothes and Christmas presents, and yelling happily to each other as new boys arrived. George carried some things up to his room, which was cold because the heat had just been pushed back up a few minutes ago, and had not yet warmed the house. Frost lined the window that looked northwest into trees and toward the lakes. George pulled out a sweater and left to find others to have fun with before the meeting at five p.m.

Charles Lord called the boys to order at about ten past five in the evening. Outside the darkness was lessened by the white flurries of snow that fell silently, piling up on the cars and driveway. A fire roared in the great room, and the boys sat toward the fire, for warmth. Charles reviewed the coming days, explained responsibilities during the teas and room visits. He announced that he had just posted the room teams in the upstairs hallway. He cautioned the boys to remember to check the board each day, since he would be making changes each day as necessary.

The boys raced upstairs to see which teams they were on and joked about which teams would be the most successful. Harold was on L.E.O. Pennington's team. Edward Stamer was with Bob Woodbridge. Stoobie was grouped with Tim Truesdale and Tim's roommate. George was on Charles Lord's team with Buzz Delaney and Scottie. None of the sophomores were sure which of the teams were considered the power ones, beyond Charles'. The seniors raised their eyebrows at the team Charles had selected for himself, but said nothing.

The skies had cleared for the first tea the next morning, but it was blustery and cold, and the freshmen wore parkas when they came. Some threw their coats into a pile on the floor of the great hall, others just kept them under their arms as they toured the house and chatted up the brothers. Charles watched on, clipboard in hand, and sent seniors to rescue sophomores stuck in a corner with a talkative candidate. The day was going extremely well, though he wondered if the same numbers of freshmen were coming through the house as in past years. He wished he had kept the counter with him that Huff had presented him last spring.

That night, the brothers gathered after room visits and reported that they had received great feedback on the house from the freshmen in their dorm rooms. Phi Delta and Chi Psi were identified as the key competitors for the boys they considered the best candidates for Eta Chi. Bob Woodbridge stood up and reminded everyone of the rule against speaking negatively about other houses. The seniors were a little taken aback at the relative informality of the meeting. Charles seemed content to let a number of boys lead different portions of the meeting, which was peculiar.

Afterwards, Charles called Bob, L.E.O. and Buzz to his room and they reviewed the strength of the power teams. They decided to move people around, based on each other's descriptions of how the boys had interrelated. They decided that Harold and George should be on the same team together, because they complimented each other in extremely different ways. Charles decided to put two seniors on his team for the second night (to appease the Old Guard, though the other boys didn't quite understand his motive). So Bob Woodbridge volunteered to take Harold and George, and then they struggled over who would be a logical anchor to those three, finally settling on one of the quieter seniors, a boy named Rich Bennet.

Bob recommended that Edward Stamer, who had really impressed him tonight, go with L.E.O. L.E.O. agreed that Edward made a lot of sense.

The next morning Charles directed George to stay in the great hall, instead of moving about the house. He had noticed how George shined when he greeted freshmen there, and picked up the tempo in the room with his clear, firm voice and ready laugh. His enthusiasm was contagious for his brothers and for the freshmen.

George also put the freshmen on the spot almost immediately upon greeting them, and his aggressiveness set a tone that Charles liked. Boys who chafed at his challenging questions got an immediate sense of competition and passion which helped to sort out those who Charles would consider too dull to bid. As the morning wore on, he watched Harold and George developing an interplay with each other as they passed freshmen off to each other. Edward Stamer began to copy George's approach in the great hall after he saw him in action, and Charles told the two of them at the end of the tea that they would be the anchors for the room for the balance of rush. Both boys beamed broadly and high-fived each other.

That night Bob Woodbridge's team was awarded two bids to deliver. One to Danny Carvello and one to a pleasant, brown-eyed engineering student and 150s football player named Joey Padillo. On the way to West Campus, Bob's team discussed their approach. George thought they should improvise and Bob and Harold chuckled. Rich said he wanted to talk about what the house was looking for in pledges, and Bob gave them each a topic to cover. Rich would speak about friendship, Bob about achievement, Harold about character and George could improvise about individuality.

When they reached Danny's room, he greeted them warmly, with an almost silly grin on his face, and a mock seriousness of purpose. In fact, he was quite impressed with the boys who were in his room tonight. They were smart, cagey and passionate. When Bob extended him the bid, Danny stood up and wiped his forehead with exaggerated zeal and shook everyone's hands. He was smiling widely, and spoke quickly about how happy he was. George stood back until he had finished with each of the other boys, and gripped Danny's hand hard. Danny nodded sagely into George's serious gaze.

Then George said, Whatever. Danny giggled slightly, and the two boys shared something between them without speaking another word.

What was that last thing about, George? Bob asked out in the hallway.

You mean, Whatever?

Yeah.

He's playing us Bob, and I wanted him to understand we knew that, and we're cool with it.

Bob shook his head, thinking about it. What's the chance we'll lose him? He finally asked.

None, George replied, smiling. He's ours. We just have to find out how.

The two boys caught up with Harold and Rich as they were beginning with Joey Padillo, and they went back into their game plan. Danny Carvello had made it clear that he and Joey were looking at the same houses, and wanted to get bids together. But Joey was not half as coy as Danny. He said he was thrilled to be bid, and would most likely accept. He didn't say yes, though, and this troubled Bob.

⁂

Each year in rush the newest brothers accelerate through a learning curve on how to speak about a pledge, and how to question each other's judgment on a candidate. By the middle of formal rush they are outspoken about whom they like, and why, and the debates in the bidding meetings grow intense. It was no different in the winter of 1975, when the sophomore class developed its rush persona. But 1975 was distinctive in that, for the first time, the sophomores tended to ignore the viewpoints of the seniors. Charles Lord's relaxed, centrist style tended to favor those boys who were passionate and outspoken, with little regard to their experience level.

Larry Dobrinski is perhaps the best example of this shift in the house. He was raised three times for a bid, with the seniors speaking ardently in his behalf, and the sophomores, in increasingly strident tones, rejecting the profile offered in support of his candidacy. While in the past, the sophomore class would have yielded to the collective wisdom of boys who had gone through this three times, this sophomore group did not back down easily. They would raise enough concerns about a candidate like Larry to insist that he be brought back for further evaluation.

Larry was a jovial show-off. The seniors loved the way he played show tunes on the piano and led them in singing the old standards. Harold, Edward and Cullen Hastings thought he was an egotistical jerk. They repeatedly told the story about how Larry sang and played the piano in the student union as if he was the next Frank Sinatra.

In the end, Charles had maneuvered Larry into the big victory for the Old Guard by imposing on Bob and Buzz to speak favorably about him. He figured Larry was better than someone else the Old Guard might get focused on, and packaged the vote on Larry with boys whom he knew the Old Guard were cold about, but whom he liked.

Charles actually worked the sophomores like a constituency, and swapped Dobrinski for three boys he knew they liked. He made sure that they understood that their three picks were vehemently opposed by the seniors, although this was not really the case. So on the third and final discussion about Larry, which followed the bidding of the first of the three candidates the sophomores liked, the sophomores spoke in opposition, but only in a mild way, and swung their votes for him after the seniors had extolled his virtues. The next two candidates were voted in, though one was voted Bring Back and voted in at the next meeting.

At the end of formal rush, Eta Chi had bid twenty-seven boys, and twenty-five had accepted. One decided not to bid any fraternity, and the other decided to make no decision until he could spend more time at the house. This last boy would end up joining Eta Chi three weeks into the spring semester, only to quit the house the week before initiation. Charles was pleased with the pledge class, whom he thought were sharp, and quite a lot of fun. The sophomores knew nothing different from what formal rush had been for them as pledges, and thought the process had gone according to tradition.

But the seniors noted amongst themselves that the house was different, and that the process of rush had been more fractional and less unifying. It was difficult to put a finger on, but the old sense of values and measured resolve to seek the best and the brightest was, in some vague way, more artificial. There was an edginess to the incoming pledge class, but as the boys sat in Tim Truesdale's room and reviewed the pledges, each of the boys seemed qualified and of high caliber.

We've been hoodwinked, intoned one senior as they sat together in Tim's room. But for the life of me, I don't see how.

The other boys looked at the speaker with reserve. Then Tim Truesdale himself spoke up, and all the boys turned to listen to him.

It will be fine, Tim assured his audience. It's a fine pledge class, and we're just seeing the ghost of Christmas Future. We can't be old scrooges!

None of the boys had a clue what he meant, but Tim often struggled to express himself, so they let it ride.

CHAPTER TEN

On the Friday of the first week of classes in January 1975, George and Caitlin walked briskly in the wintry, wet slush along the arts quad to tryouts for the spring plays. They had left the warm, well-lit rooms of Uris Library, and laughed as they hurried across the Quad in the stark whitewash of bleak daylight that filtered through the low cloud cover above them. Caitlin never seemed to notice the cold, but George felt himself shiver slightly beneath his blue parka with the fringed hood draped down his back.

Inside Goldwyn Smith Hall, they stomped their feet to knock some of the slush from their feet, and took each other's hand as they walked down to the basement and along the dim hallway to the amphitheater. By now, they should have been content to compete for key parts in the best productions, but actors are a notoriously insecure bunch. Each of them privately fretted about not being called back.

Still, George marveled at how differently he approached tryouts now. The goal was to get up, read and get out, and not linger to watch the competition. As they entered the chamber, Caitlin moved away from him and ran up to Derek. She kissed the professor on the cheek as she pulled her hair to one side. George moved toward the stage to get in line to read, ending up beside James Shelton, his jealous director. James said nothing, and nodded curtly to George. George greeted him softly using James' character's name from *No Place* . Neither boy referred to their one act play. George thought about the improvisational exercise James had put him through with the rubber ball, and wondered if the two boys had been lovers when Lincoln tried to take George's virginity symbol from him. The image of it made him queasy.

He went on stage after about eight others and read the script standing very still. He projected his voice as Stephen Hurowitz had taught him, with deep breath from his stomach, so that the words were crystal clear in the back of the chamber, and rang with authority. The last line he whispered, so harshly, so fiercely, that the entire room went still for a moment –

> *I will not suffer such indignities, betrayed at your feet and prostate before you, only to justify and give legitimacy to your pity.*

George did not know where the reading selection came from, and had read it in an almost improvisational way, but as he walked off stage and down the shiny wooden steps to the orchestra, he glanced quickly to note the reactions of the professors. Each of them was jotting notes to themselves, which meant interest, and he grinned to Caitlin who still stood next to Derek, smiling.

George circumnavigated the seated students to reach his girlfriend, and tugged her arm from behind. She turned to him, her face flushed and eyes wide, and whispered, Derek is going to direct *A Streetcar Named Desire*! And he wants you to read for the part of Stanley Kolowski's friend! They hugged each other excitedly. That was a part that would ordinarily go to one of the graduate students. Caitlin raised her eyebrows and told her boyfriend she really wanted to be in *Streetcar*. Her eyes poked toward him, the whites of her eyes accented by the deeply freckled skin of her temples. Her freshness, from the clean smell of her skin to her childlike exuberance, never failed to draw him in.

George smiled and told her to go get up on the stage and become Stella. They hugged again, and she moved toward the stage. He watched her walk fluidly up the steps when her turn came, and saw the boys in the audience watching her intently. She stood languidly in the center of the stage and read the female script in a lyrical, demure voice that made her seem like a little girl.

Not a bad trick for a voluptuous, five-foot-eight woman, George told her as the door swung shut behind them and they headed across the quad again in the cold air.

Was I positing? Caitlin asked, gazing up at the neutral sky.

George understood her question, which was a technical one. She wanted to know whether she had posited enough before the audience to be considered performing, in the vernacular of Prescott Chilton Harris. They had both grown fond of the technical jargon required in their PET class.

You're in, sweetheart, George replied firmly. She loved it when he called her that and she looped her arm through his and gripped his hand in the pocket of his parka.

At callbacks, George was on two lists, and Caitlin was on *Streetcar's*, so they were both thrilled. In addition to *Streetcar*, George was on the list for *The Miser*, by Moliere, which was being directed by the Dean of the Theater department, whom George always referred to as Abe Lincoln.

Callbacks were at the same time, so George divided his time between the two rooms. *The Miser* was in the same room he had auditioned for *No Place*, and *Streetcar* was down the hall. The mood in the two rooms could not have been more different. In *The Miser*, Abe Lincoln sat in the middle of the first row of chairs facing a small space for the auditioners to stand. The Dean was tall and gangly and formal, and he spoke precisely in a clipped, careful tone of voice. He gave his callbacks specific instructions, telling them about the characters they were about to read, and sat very still as they read.

In the *Streetcar* audition room, Derek Steele roamed around the perimeter of the empty room like an impatient animal. Auditioners sat on the floor against walls, or in front of others against the walls, while readers tried to get through a paragraph of script before Derek would interrupt them and tell them to sit down or swap characters in the scene, or stop fidgeting, FOR GOD'S SAKE!

The clique of established actors relished his antics, but the newcomers felt disoriented. George loved the feeling in the room, and was about to read a part, when one of the graduate students came in and handed Derek a note.

George, you're needed in the other audition, Derek said wearily. George handed his script to the person next to him, and ran down the hall to the other room. This was something new!

The Dean nodded at George as he entered, raised his finger to indicate a brief wait, and returned to watching two people read in the front of the room. When they finished, the Hastings thanked them and told them that was all, and then asked George and Duncan to read two parts for him. George joined Duncan in the front of the room, and when George looked back at the people sitting in wait to read, he felt a tension stretching like a veil across them. Then he realized it was not tension, but boredom. The people trying out for the play were actually *bored*. He couldn't wait until he finished, so he could scoot back to *Streetcar*.

He read plainly, sitting down, while Duncan chose to pace around him. The language of the play was stilted, and formal, like the Dean. George hoped he wouldn't do well. After he finished, the Dean sat looking at the two of them for a moment and then excused them. Duncan stayed in the room, and George returned to the palpable energy of the room down the hall.

Derek was standing still, nodding, as Alex read the part of Stanley and Caitlin read Blanche Dubois. When Caitlin finished the part – " I, I, I took the blows to my face and body!" – with histrionic exasperation, the room clapped at her mocking tone and Derek yelled Out!

Derek looked at his notes and then told others to read, so George slumped down against a free wall to watch. He held his thumb up to Caitlin across the room and she glowed in return. They both knew that the two leads would go to graduate students, but they could dream.

The auditions were almost over before Derek asked George to read Stanley, and George frowned. He had hoped to read the part he was really competing for, and the girl reading Blanche with him was not very interesting. He began to wonder whether Derek could be enough of a maverick to give Stanley and Blanche to him and Caitlin. He began to read with more gusto, but the woman with him was unresponsive and he felt unsupported. Derek looked on impassively, and then yelled Out! and called it a night.

The next two days George and Caitlin took turns checking the callback board to see if the parts had been posted. It was the time Caitlin called actors' purgatory, the suspension between heaven and hell, when the actors didn't know if they would be admitted to heaven, or cast into the milky subspace of waiting for the one-act tryouts. On the morning of the third day, Caitlin walked impatiently into Derek's office and asked when the parts would be announced.

Derek leaned back in his chair, his hands behind his curly hair, and grinned under the bushy red contours of his moustache. Anxious, are we? He asked.

Come on Derek, I want to know. What could the problem possibly be? Caitlin had her hands on her hips, and her pressed, straight blue jeans made her look about seven-feet tall.

You know, Caitlin, you are one long drink of water, Derek offered musingly.

Caitlin let her long hair fall a little forward. She felt her face flushing slightly, although she wasn't really sure what Derek had meant. Then she flipped her hair back slightly and asked her professor what that meant.

It means, he said, sitting up slightly and putting his face closer to hers, that you are more stunning than you are innocent. He leaned back again and looked at his student impassively. He wondered whether he was right about this. Caitlin came across as a sophisticated babe, but there was something naïve about her, something innocent he could not define. He knew that she and George lived together, and George was clearly no innocent. But still, there was something.

Caitlin tried to harrumph, but it came out sounding more like a purr, and Derek mistook her response. It is in such ways that reputations are created out of absurd innuendo, but Derek wasn't one to care about reputations anyway, so Caitlin's, or at least the one he formed of her in his office that day, would remain an isolated illusion in his mind.

So, Caitlin said, pressing an imaginary wrinkle out of her jeans, am I in your play or not?

Derek laughed. You know the rules kid, he replied, until the list goes up, there is no advance info. But I will tell you that I have put you in for a part in *Streetcar*, and there is no conflict about that in the department.

Caitlin looked at Derek with genuine curiosity. What did he mean about conflict? What happened within the department that would have anything to do with casting decisions?

Derek sat quietly for a moment, and then decided to explain the process to the young girl whom he liked having as his assistant and more than once had imagined as his lover.

The Dean and I are debating over some casting decisions, he told her. But the Dean is the Dean, and I am only a maverick untenured professor. So he is being kind to me and pretending to consider my thoughts on the matter before pulling rank.

Caitlin's mind was working furiously to remember who had been called back for both productions....beside George. This couldn't be all about George could it, she fretted to her herself. She felt tinges of jealousy and anger and resentment, and Derek watched those emotions roll across her face with compassion and understanding. He knew what it felt like to compete, be really good, and still feel like the second banana.

The theater was a luminous beast. It consumed actors like air so that the privileged few who popped out at you could dazzle and sear themselves into your subconscious. He also genuinely liked Caitlin, and thought she had a chance to make it. He knew she had the determination, and she was good looking enough, and those two are often enough, especially when the person has brains. Caitlin appeared to have plenty of those.

George. Caitlin said matter-of-factly.

George. Derek replied, carefully. He would be a very good spoil to the person I have cast as Stanley.

Do you think he is really good?

Derek studied Caitlin's face for a moment, and then told her the truth. He's a rookie, Caitlin. He sucks up everything at a hundred miles an hour, but I don't know if he will have staying power. But for the moment, yeah, I think he's good, and he makes people on stage around him better, because he demands that they act with him.

Caitlin nodded. Part of her was envious, and part of her delirious. She loved George, after all, and she loved being Derek's confidant almost as much.

You are my hero, Derek, Caitlin said quickly. The words had come flying out of her, and she wasn't really sure she had actually said them, but as she looked intently toward him Derek closed his eyes. He inhaled her words and paused before he opened his eyes and smiled slightly at her. Get out of here, he said. And she did.

The next day George and Caitlin walked together to the callback board at lunchtime and saw the department secretary posting the castings for the spring plays. They looked at each other expectantly, waited for the secretary to finish and walk away with a smile, and approached the typed lists. Caitlin had not said a word to George about her conversation with Derek. She was beside herself as a result.

Caitlin was cast as the Kowalski's' neighbor in *Streetcar*. George was Cleante in *The Miser*.

George groaned. I can't believe I got Abe Lincoln and not Derek, he said. And you've got Derek and *Streetcar*!

Shut up honey, Caitlin whispered sternly. You have a lead, and I have another small part. You should be jumping around with joy. She looked at her boyfriend fondly. And now I can tell you what Derek told me. She told George about how the Dean and Derek had actually *fought* over him. George said that made him feel worse, because now he knew that Derek had actually wanted him for the part. Caitlin tisked loudly. Pride goeth before a fall, you know. At that instant, the Dean passed them in the hallway.

Hello George! The Dean said jovially. I am excited to begin work with you on Moliere's funniest satire!

George pulled himself up, smiled broadly and replied, Thank you Dean! I can't wait to get started! He wished he could remember the Dean's name.

The Dean looked carefully at George and nodded stiffly. He seemed to think before every sentence. This will be a good experience for you, he said directly, but in a friendly way. You will have an opportunity to get a period piece under your belt, and expand your horizons.

George was watching the Dean's goatee jab up and down as he spoke, and then focused on the man's red-rimmed eyes fluttering above the coarse, gray skin of his cheeks. But when he looked up into the Dean's eyes, there was a softness and depth there as well.

When do rehearsals begin? George asked.

Not for a few weeks, the academic answered cheerily. He waved and walked off down the hallway.

Some teeth, George whispered to Caitlin. The Dean's teeth were long and discolored, probably from cigarettes and coffee and disregard. They giggled, and Caitlin elbowed her boyfriend in the chest. Come on Cleante, she said, I want to go sip tea in the Green Dragon. So George followed his girlfriend out the door and they headed to the right where the architecture building stood tall on the edge of the arts quad.

Rehearsals for *Streetcar* began immediately, and Caitlin was consumed by the play and Derek. George focused on their PET class and the rest of his classes, and began to spend some of his free time at Eta Chi. As Caitlin rushed off to do something before going to the Straight Theater for rehearsals, George would walk to the house from the library in the cold, late afternoon, after darkness had replaced the sullen overcast sky.

For some reason he had always loved to walk alone at dusk, when the daylight was fading, but not quite extinguished. There was a sense of coming warmth and food, and a secret, solitary solace brought on by the edge of day that could be savored before reentering the pleasant din of family or friends. As he walked slowly past the sorority houses and faculty homes, he imagined the people inside.

Sometimes there were lights on inside, and he would imagine the people moving about the kitchen preparing supper. When the houses along Fall Creek Avenue and the little side streets that led to Thurston Avenue were dark, he pictured girls or old ladies sitting still at the edge of a window in a darkened room, watching him slide by the universe of their moment. He would imagine himself in their place, and then do something silly, like dance a jig, to make them laugh in spite of themselves.

At the house, he would always shudder after getting inside, to rid himself of the wet chill, and take a moment to acclimate to the sounds and movements of the house. He liked it best when there was no one in the great hall, but the bustle of activity in the dining room assured him that dinner would be lively. Then he would shoot upstairs and change into a coat and tie, usually his tan corduroy jacket and a plain blue knit tie that could blend with whatever shirt he happened to be wearing. In the winter he wore wide wale corduroy trousers, and his hiking boots which were supposed to be waterproof. He expected waterproof things to be warm, but these boots always made his toes cold.

Then he would bound down the stairs and enter the library where boys would be gathering before dinner. After he had been cast in *The Miser*, he had decided to grow a beard, and by February, he had an uneven mess of facial hair with significant splotches of skin that had not filled in yet. He was also letting his hair grow, and the back of his hair now fell well over the back collar of his shirt. He still kept his hair off his face by sweeping it up and around his right ear.

George was surprised by how many pledges from rush attended dinners during the week, and he made an effort to get to know them. He thoroughly enjoyed the dinners, which smelled so good in the kitchen and were served home-style by brothers who then sat and ate with everyone. All brothers rotated serving duties, and George found he even liked to do that. The banter around the tables was often clever, and always respectful. George always felt the room grow warm during dinner, from the hot food and the large number of boys in attendance.

After dinner, George would sit upstairs for a minute with whichever boys were around, and then pull on his parka and head back up the hill to Uris Library. Often, George accompanied pledges who had no reason to stick around after dinner, and on the darkened sidewalks the boys would laugh and ask each other questions, or tell jokes and tall tales.

As they walked, George would secretly mimic the boys he walked with, matching their gait, and the way that they swung their arms or shoulders, or turned their heads to speak. He reveled in practicing the expressions on their faces, and the way that their bodies moved when they laughed. It was for him a kind of respect for who they were, and an exploration of different styles and characteristics that he could associate with their personalities. He figured he would one day use some portion of a smile or look of surprise, or distinctive walk to build a character in a play. And he also, unwittingly, began to develop a sincere appreciation for a number of boys whom he might otherwise have paid little attention to.

He was careful never to overplay his subjects, although he began to incorporate slight attributes of boys even as he sat with them at dinner. And this caused him to be struck by how little the people around him actually observed about others. He could mirror a boy's style directly across the table from him, and not a single boy at the table would even cock an eyebrow or notice the redundant dynamic of the conversation. But he was careful even then not to overplay the moment, for he did not wish to seem cruel or odd.

And so January turned into February and then to March before *Miser* rehearsals began in earnest. Caitlin was deeply into her character, a southern wisp of a thing, at once tantalized and demoralized by the gritty world of New Orleans as depicted in the famous play. She snuggled with George at night in a comfortable, tired way, and in the morning they would walk up through the stone arch to the campus from her apartment in College Town, traipsing through the drifts of snow, hand in hand. Caitlin wore the same dark red elf's cap all that winter, and George would stare at the little yarn ball at its tip whenever she walked ahead in the narrow, shoveled path on the sidewalk.

On the first day of *Miser* rehearsals, the Dean looked at George and asked if he understood that he would need to shave his beard for the performance. George nodded quietly, and then the Dean asked George to go and stand next to Duncan who played the Miser, and was the father to George's character. It was George's first experience with a director who began to block the play from the very first day, and the rigor of it depressed him. He thought it would take all of the spontaneity out of the performance if they were expected to stand just so through two months of rehearsals. But the Dean quickly demonstrated that he would move the actors quite a bit as he thought about the play and watched them grow into their parts. In many ways, the dynamics of the scenes were explored more fully with this approach, and George began to appreciate the dedication and the thoughtfulness with which the Dean was actually *directing* the play.

Cleante was a young, vain fop of a son to the Miser, who saw only avarice and duplicity in everyone around him. George and Duncan began to warm to the roles, and the clever, if somewhat contrived, humor of the piece. Duncan developed a crotchetiness, and a stoop and George built Cleante into a clueless and whimsical boy who rushed onstage barely knowing which room he was entering. Then his father would reduce Cleante to a desperate schemer, too immature to actually convert any of his schemes to reality.

In early April, the Dean displayed the costume designs to them, which were drawn in minute period detail by the stagecraft class. The Miser was drawn with a cane, and in old rags of clothing. Cleante wore a stylish wig, and a bright blue trimmed waistcoat, pantaloon britches and a ruffled shirt. Duncan and George giggled as they stood looking at the drawings and the girls measured their bodies for the costumes. I am going to get through my entire graduate program wearing rags, Duncan said solemnly.

The following weekend *Streetcar* opened, and George walked Caitlin to the performance about two hours before curtain, and sneaked into the theater and took a seat in the middle of the orchestra, in the third row. He could hear slight, muffled sounds offstage as the crew and actors prepared for the play, but the theater was silent, and the huge, ornately adorned walls and rows of hundreds of chairs gave George a powerful sensation.

He did not understand why, but sitting in the center of this enormous, lonely, empty structure seemed to amplify the prickly sensations on the skin of his arms, and sharpen his sense of self.

When the doors opened, the ushers looked curiously at George, but said nothing to him, and he settled into his seat to anticipate the show. Caitlin had talked constantly about it, but George did not have a good sense of what he was about to see. Caitlin talked more about Derek's intensity and emotional edge than the production of the play, and George knew that the actors would be stretched to their limits by Derek's visceral exhortations. He fully expected Derek to do to *Streetcar* what he had done to *Oedipus*. He saw the stagehand move to the curtain rope and focused to be sure he caught every nuance from the opening moment.

The curtain opened and the audience saw a sparse, depressing set that looked like it belonged in a black box production rather than on a real stage. This made total sense to George, and he breathed in every tiny detail with excitement. Then the play began and the actors labored through their lines, standing apart on the stage as if they were in silos and could not even see each other. The feeling Derek had imagined and Caitlin had seen − of lonely people caught in prisons with invisible walls, of squalor suspended in the middle of middle class opulence, of rage − never really moved between the actors and evaporated before it left the stage. What the audience was left with was a disturbing and tiring disjointedness, and élan.

George knew instantly the disappointment of the play, felt both the effort and the daring and the total lack of community between the players and the viewers, but nonetheless tried hard to salvage the good in the production. Caitlin in particular was luminous, almost haunting. But her part was not big enough to carry the play and Stanley and Blanche (who in reality disliked each other offstage) spoke past each other into the dusty gloom of the stage set.

George still found much to admire in the play, and he talked to Derek afterwards about the positive subtleties stitched into the fabric of the show, but they both knew it was not what it could have been. After the first night, before the reviews came out, Derek took the cast out for pizza and George told Caitlin what a strong performance she had turned in. But there was little real buzz in the group as they sat at Johnny's and chewed their dinner.

Caitlin managed to spark everyone's spirits with a mock rendition of Blanche's maudlin speech to Stanley at the end of the play, and Derek was as bellicose as ever, but the mood was cautious. George held Caitlin's hand tightly on their walk back to her apartment, and there was a warmth to the air that foretold the coming spring that helped distract them from the play.

George went to the next two performances, and supported his girlfriend fiercely as she fought through the poor reviews in the Daily Sun and local press. He was excited that she had received such strong mention in the reviews, and reminded her that they were learning the craft, not depending on it for their livelihood. Caitlin found her boyfriend's attitude disloyal, somehow, and irritating. She wished he would stop talking so much about it, and told him so. He would smile in response, and nod, and wait a moment, and then dance a jig, and then resume what he was saying. That made her madder, but happier at the same time, and this went on until the play was done. He stopped speaking about it the day after it was over and that made her mad too, though she never told him that.

The *Miser* was now in full swing, and George was as busy as Caitlin had been with *Streetcar*. On the Wednesday following the last *Streetcar* performance, George walked down to Eta Chi for dinner before he went to the Straight Theater for rehearsal. He should have met Caitlin for dinner at the Straight, but didn't. He had developed a fondness for his routine and while Caitlin's new-found availability was pulling him strongly back in, something more subconscious than apparent carried him back down the hill for supper. When he told Caitlin what he was doing, she smiled and did not seem to pay much attention to it.

He took his solitary walk to the house in the cool, but warming spring air, crossing the suspension bridge slowly, and listening to the water rush by far below him. There is never enough smell to lakes and rivers, he thought, pausing to look over the little metal prongs that were intended to keep the curious careful. But the speed of the moving water did kick up a spray that put moisture in the air, which gave off a clean smell. The bridge flexed slightly, and George looked back to see others beginning to cross the bridge, making it move. As strong as the bridge was, with thick, steel suspension cables, concrete footways and steel under-supports, it still swayed under the force of people stepping across it.

George moved off on his way, his solitude momentarily intruded upon by the on-comers, and began to think about what might be for dinner. He hoped it would be Andy's meatloaf, which was always spiced nicely, or the flank steaks he sometimes cooked up with peppers and onions. He turned onto Cayuga Heights Road and crossed over to the far sidewalk, picking up his pace as the night darkened around him. He saw a boy ahead of him turning into the Eta Chi driveway, and wondered who it might be, but he did not try to catch up to him.

When he entered the foyer, a boy was getting ready to bound up the stairs, but stopped when he saw George walk in, and said, Hey, somebody was just looking for you George. Something about an important call from home.

George thanked him and followed him up the stairs to change his clothes, but Mike O'Hare stopped him at the bulletin board, and said, George, you need to call home. I know, George said, somebody just told me. George looked at Mike, who was looking carefully at him, so George shrugged and returned downstairs to the mailroom where the main house phone hung on a wall, and dialed his parents' number collect.

A collect call from your son, will you accept the charges? asked the operator of his sister who answered the phone.

Yes, we will operator, his sister replied. She paused. George?

Yup, what's up? George said jauntily. He was still thinking about dinner, and looking at his watch to see how much time he had.

Hold on, sweetie, Mom wants to talk to you.

George's mother came on, and heard his voice. He was asking his sister what all the hubbub was about.

Honey, his mother said, I don't know how to tell you this, but he's gone. Daddy's dead, honey.

George told his mother he was sorry, but he really didn't understand. His mother was weeping softly, and trying to tell her child what had happened, but George was thinking about dinner, and rehearsal, and was having trouble hearing, or at least connecting his words with the sounds coming through the black plastic phone with the thick silver coil that connected it to the black and chrome payphone that said, "New York Telephone Co."

You have to come home honey, but I don't want you to drive so we need to get you an airplane ticket. I'm sorry I can't be there with you, I know this is a shock. I'm still expecting your father to show up. Are you there, honey?

George was thinking furiously about the Miser, and the fact that the play was opening in a few weeks. He could not yet make sense of what his mother was saying, and he felt terrible, but he had obligations to the Dean and the cast.

Mom, I really can't come home right now, I have rehearsals all this week and next, and I can't miss them. This sounded totally logical to George. In fact he felt proud of himself for being strong and focused on his commitments.

His mother broke down and George heard the phone changing hands and a number of people talking in the background. Then his other sister came on the line, and said, George, you need to come home. Daddy's dead, and we need you. You are in shock, George, this is terrible. His sister began to tear up and George heard her voice weaken. George, we will call and buy you a ticket to fly home tomorrow morning. We will call you back later, okay?

George said okay, and replaced the handset on the chrome stirrup of the pay phone. He was alone in the mailroom, so he looked to see if he had any mail. Then he walked slowly back up to his room, and sat on his roommate's bed. Mike O'Hare had been sitting outside the mailroom, and when George walked past him, he rose silently and followed George to his room. The window was dirty, and the bedclothes were a mess on the beds, but the room was otherwise orderly.

Mike O'Hare's face was beet-red, and he desperately wanted to say something, but instead he kind of leaned against the window sill and looked down at the floor. He had answered the house phone when George's sister had called, urgently looking for his fraternity brother, and in the course of the conversation, George's sister had explained the reason for her call. He promised her that the fraternity would find George quickly, although he had no idea how they might do that.

Then George had walked in and Mike resisted the urge to grab him and hug him hard, and instead just made sure that George went right to the phone. And then he had waited. Now the boys were down at dinner, and he was in George's room, looking at a boy he did not know well, and he wanted to cry more badly than George, but George was solemnly silent, and almost surreally calm, and Mike did not know what that meant. And then George covered his face with his hands, and began to cry hard.

It was not until George was sitting in the little den off his mother's kitchen three days later that he began to puzzle in silence over the fact that his center – the spinning, golden orb that descended to a point deep within him - had stopped spinning. He was sitting with his sisters, his mother and his grandmother, and there was that fragile air between them that seems to envelop mourners. Sometimes someone would say something, and sometimes there would be a distracted silence that betrayed the exhaustion and rawness of grief.

George had been looking at his left hand which lay on the arm of the couch. He was thinking about how he had never before even thought about, let alone felt, the inside of his skin. But there was his hand and in his mind's eye he was inside that hand, looking at the sinuous backside of his epidermis, next to where the bones and veins and tendons lay waiting for his brain to give an instruction. Then he suddenly noted the stillness within him. His center was suspended, and rock-still, and he had never felt it stop. Had it stopped suddenly? He knew it hadn't – he surely would have recognized something like that. It must have spun slower and slower until it gradually came to rest in its place.

He took inventory of the last three days, to pinpoint when the spinning must have started its deceleration. The night he had called home and then sat in his room with Mike O'Hare (something inside him wanted to think about Mike O'Hare, but he filed that away for some later reflection), he had vacillated between sitting silently and crying, and listening to Mike try so earnestly to simply be there and share some of George's pain. Then he had climbed up into bed and slept.

The next morning he rose and walked into a small bathroom that was different from the one he normally used. He wanted to avoid the boys he would normally see, and he wanted to shave off his beard. He had never tried to shave a beard off before, and by April the growth on his face had filled in and thickened. It took him three lathers to get it all. He kept looking at himself in the mirror, and took numerous opportunities to lean close to inspect his cheek or his chin, but in reality he wanted to look hard into his own eyes. He saw nothing of note – no sadness, no fear, no change. Perhaps this was when the spinning began to slow, he thought.

Sitting in the den, he could not recall quickly how he had learned about the flight he would take to get home. Someone must have told him. Mike O'Hare drove him to the little regional airport, and told him to call when he was coming back. George thanked him, headed for the counter, turned back and thanked Mike a second time before he drove off, and then flew home. His mother nearly collapsed against him when he arrived at the house. She looked like all the air had gone out of her, and George hugged her for some time, before he suggested she sit down.

She seemed suddenly irritated with him, and he frowned. He could not have known that looking at George's resemblance to his father, hearing him suggest she sit down just the way her husband might have - made his mother resent him and smolder inside. Or that this wave of resentment made her feel guilty and confused. After a moment, George said he was going upstairs to put his things down, and that seemed to help.

He sat on one of the twin beds in his room and looked around at the walls, and wondered when his father would come home and make all this right, and for the first time since the day before George realized that his father would not be coming home. He grinned at his own stupidity, and walked back downstairs and into the arms of his sisters and grandmother and uncles and aunts and others who were stopping in through the afternoon.

CHAPTER ELEVEN

Henry Muirfield had been a driven man when he dropped dead of a heart attack. He was loved by his friends, and being both ambitious and charming, he had made scores of friends. He was both generous and orderly by nature, often making lists of the things he wanted to do for others, and this purposeful kindness made him an icon where he worked. It was no surprise that legions of people – coworkers, neighbors, politicians – turned out to wake and bury him.

For two long days, George stood alongside his sisters, his mother, his uncle and others, greeting an endless stream of people who came to pay their respects. In the morning he got up and showered and dressed, and tried to look nonchalant until it was finally time to drive with his family to the funeral home across the street from their church. The afternoon wake was quite business-like, but at night the people tended to stay and the room grew loud and comfortable with conversation.

George watched the people standing and chatting amiably with each other in the primly decorated rooms of the funeral home, and then turned to see his father lying in the open, brushed-metal casket, and then returned to greeting someone else in the line. He did not know many of the people, but they seemed to know him, and many told him they understood how hard this was for him.

George smiled and shook their hands with vigor. Inside he seethed. It was not merely presumptuous of them to say they understood how he felt. It was appallingly naïve and dim-witted. He had no idea how others felt at such moments, but he was glaringly sure that no one had even a remote sensation of the blinding dissonance reverberating through him. They couldn't pretend to see the deep waters of his soul darken and then freeze, only to crack, and then boil. And still, there was an inside-out quality to all of this that he could not reconcile. He would think of his father and feel remorse, and longing, and at the same time struggle to push away the sarcasm and humor with which he secretly watched others express their grief.

There were dozens of times in those two days when George giggled with one sister or another, laughing at the folly of past family outings, or the funny way that someone's hair stuck off the side of their face. The thought of laughing made his brain feel hot. And then he would crumble inside, and waver slightly on his feet, and his amusement would dissolve into a maudlin despair.

After the first night of wakes he sat with his family in the den and let the exhaustion creep across his insides and replace the thick numbness that had taken hold of him. He looked at his sisters more than his mother, who teetered on the edge of her own private debilitation, and whose face was too painful to explore. Penelope, the oldest sister, was making her way carefully through her emotions, and insisting of herself that she be strong and cogent for now. Marge was intent on finding something funny to laugh about at least once an hour, and stroking her mother's arm whenever she was near.

The uncles and aunts and family friends that moved slowly through the house, lifting dishes off the table and making drinks for people, floated by, murmuring to each other. George was almost comfortable in the rhythm of it all when Penelope began to speak about what she wanted to say to Daddy.

George and Marge looked up from their laps and cocked their heads while Penelope announced that she intended to write something to their father and put it in his casket so it would always be with him. Marge thought it funny, and began to joke about the things they could finally say to him that they wouldn't have dared say before. But Penelope said she was serious, and George was already in some other place wondering what he might say to his father. What do you say to anyone that is good enough to hold up for eternity? he wondered.

After a minute, he said he was going to bed, and stood up. He raised his eyebrows at his sisters and shuffled off to his bedroom, listening to his sisters' banter about the idea fade in his wake. He felt his leg muscles lag as he climbed the stairs, and knew he would sleep soundly if he could make it the next fifteen feet to his room. When he reached his bed, he pulled off his shoes, undid the striped tie around his neck, and stretched out on his bed. The morning light filtering through the pale yellow window shades was the next thing he saw.

Death, as we all know, is a curious thing. It extinguishes so much in its aftermath, depleting the will and vibrancy and expectations if its constituents, that its creative force can be overlooked. It creates negative life energy in the shape of anger (or fear), and resentment, and greed. But it also innovates perspective, and the freedom to explore whatever lies unknown.

When George woke on the morning of the second day of wakes, he sat at the small maple child's desk in his bedroom where he had always done his homework, and looked out the window into his backyard. The grass was dark green, and dormant, and the tepid April sun made the yard look tired. By June, the grass would be thick and lush, but now its bare spots rutted the hardened dirt. He was still in his clothes from yesterday, but he felt refreshed, and optimistic. And he kept thinking about what to say to his father.

Secretly, he had been speaking with his father in his mind, but the idea of saying one thing to him in writing was different. It was irrevocable once that casket was closed.

What was more, he did not understand how he was supposed to get the message into the casket, or where he might hide it so that the undertakers would not find it (did they look for such things, he wondered?). The only way that he could think of was to go to the kneeler in front of the casket, and try to shove it quickly somewhere when he thought people were not looking. But the wake was so full of people, wouldn't they see him? Maybe it would look like he was taking something!

He had no idea what he would want to say, but it troubled George that if he did not do it, he would have missed a once in a lifetime opportunity. So he decided to work on how to get the message into the casket at the next wake. Once he was sure that it was even possible, he would begin to work on what to say.

The afternoon waking hours were two to four, and the first people walked through the door at two p.m. on the dot, so George walked quickly over to the casket and knelt in front of it. He looked at the plastic, slightly-gray caste to his father's face with the lips drawn so strangely tight, and then to the hands in which rosary beads were strung to look as if he was holding them. George smiled to his father in the casket, and reached over to lay his hand on Henry Muirfield's arm.

He had hoped it would look like he was in contemplation, but in truth he was testing his reach to see if he could unobtrusively slip something like a piece of paper into his father's suit coat pocket. It was farther than he expected, and he had to lean his body far across the space before he could touch his target. Right then George felt a hand on his shoulder and jolted backwards in fright. His mother stood behind him, telling him it was all right. She must have understood what he was doing! He felt compelled to speak.

I didn't mean any harm, Mom. It was just a test.

His mother looked sadly at him, nodding. Then a puzzled look came over her face, but Penelope called her to come over to see someone in the receiving line, so she wandered off without another word.

George walked quickly over to join them, and for the next hour he greeted people, and slowly relaxed after realizing his mother had simply been consoling him. When he got the chance, he broke away from the line and walked aimlessly through the rooms of the funeral home that were not filled with people. The Muirfield wake was the only one scheduled for the day, so the suite of rooms on the opposite wing of the building was empty.

George spied some paper sitting on a table in one of these rooms, and he walked over to examine it. They were blank sheets from a guest register, which he replaced on the table after examining them, and one of the directors of the home saw him and approached him from the main middle corridor. As he approached he nodded his head, as if he understood what George must be thinking.

Is there anything I can help you with, young man?

George didn't know what to say for a moment, and stood there eyeing the man in the somber black suit with his hair slicked straight back off his forehead.

No, thank you, he finally said. The older man nodded graciously. George thought nodding must be an important part of this man's repertoire. George pulled his mouth up in a straight line, and nodded slightly in return.

As the man turned away to leave George in his solitude, George suddenly had an idea.

Actually, there is something you might help me with, he said softly.

The funeral director turned and smiled wanly.

Do you have an envelope with the name of the Funeral home on it, that I might have? George asked.

The older man studied George for a brief moment, nodding as he blinked rapidly in thought.

In the background, from the other side of the home, George could hear his uncle telling someone the story of the time his father had taken the family on a fishing trip in a rented dinghy. Henry Muirfield had driven the little boat up onto a sand bar, and asked Penelope to get out and shove them off. When she did this, the boat began to drift away, and Henry had yelled to Penelope to jump back on board. Penelope tried but missed, and was clinging to the side of the boat with her entire body in the water. So Henry tried to pull his daughter back into the boat with one hand, while he held the engine tiller with his other hand. Unfortunately, the more he tried to pull Penelope into the boat, the more she resisted because her face was heading into the bucket of squid bait sitting below the gunwale.

Pull! Henry was yelling at his daughter.

No! Penelope was screaming.

Henry! Mrs. Muirfield complained, just before the boat tipped just far enough to send Henry rolling over its side.

There was a pleasant, diversionary laughter from the other room, and George smiled at the funeral director.

Is it important that the envelope have our name on it? the funeral man asked carefully.

George tensed a little, and then sputtered, No, of course not, I just... you know, I thought if you had an envelope lying around, it would probably have your name on it, and I wanted you to understand that would be okay. I just want an envelope to put something in.

In truth, George had thought that the funeral home envelope might avoid suspicion. The funeral man nodded quickly. Of course, just a moment, he said and walked smoothly off to the stairs where George knew the office was. He returned with two envelopes, one with the name of the funeral home on it, and the other blank.

I brought you both just in case, he told the young boy with the anxious frown on his face. George relaxed and thanked the man, pocketed the envelopes and rejoined his family in the other wing. He was very pleased with himself, because the funeral director had innocently given him both a test envelope *and* one with the funeral home's name on it that he could use later for the real thing. Before he knew it, it was time to go home.

In the evening, George began to scope out his father's casket again, thinking that perhaps there was a place in the lining or under the pillow that he might be able to conceal his missive, but his sisters asked him to stay with them in the line. So he could only look across the endless starched arrangements of flowers at the casket as he greeted more people he did not know. He was too far away to see what he wanted to.

It was in the last thirty minutes that George found the break he had been hoping for. His father's sister, an aunt he had always loved, and who tended to the dramatic, had been speaking breathily with his mother and sisters near the casket when her emotions overcame her. Her voice elevated somewhat, she told the assemblage that she simply refused to believe that her brother was dead.

George moved closer to be near them, and ended up next to his aunt, who leaned on him in her grief. She was a solid, substantial woman, and George rocked back a bit under the unexpected weight of her body.

He reached into his pocket for a handkerchief to offer her, but instead his hand found one of the two envelopes the funeral man had given his that afternoon. Just then his aunt convulsed and then threw herself over the gilded, metal edge of the casket and onto her brother's body, weeping profusely.

No one moved. Someone gasped. George's sister, Marge, giggled. George's aunt gripped her dead brother's body and continued to wail.

By now, George had withdrawn the envelope from his pocket, and impulsively moved to the casket's side to help pull his aunt away. As he rested his right hand on his aunt's back, he moved his left hand into the casket near his father's head, and suddenly realized that this gave him the chance he had been waiting for!

As others rushed to help him with his aunt, he methodically moved the envelope – first along the lining on the side, but there was nowhere there to deposit it – and then under the pillow where his father's head was being jostled by the movements of his aunt and the people trying to help.

The satin pillow was stitched into the lining! There was no room for anything to be hidden under its tiny tuft. His aunt was now being led to a seat, so he took the last moment of opportunity and slid the empty envelope under his father's shoulder. If you stood directly overhead, it was clearly visible, but from most angles it could not be noticed. This, George said to himself as he turned to join the stunned audience of this melodrama, was not going to be easy.

Marge was looking curiously in his direction when he turned.

What are you doing? she mouthed to him across the small space between them. George smiled, and nodded toward their aunt compassionately, as if to suggest that he was concerned for her. Marge frowned, and moved around the room to stand next to him.

What the hell were you doing in the casket, George?

I'll tell you later, he whispered, and then walked outside to get some air.

Outside George looked up at the late afternoon sky and breathed deeply to calm himself. The air was cool, and damp with the soft moisture of a tardy spring. He knew he would have to confide in Marge, but that seemed okay. She would find it humorous.

After the wake, the family made the trek back to the house, and Marge pulled George into the living room as soon as she could.

So tell me. She looked at her little brother sternly.

George explained what he had been doing, and he had been right. The two of them laughed about it, and then almost became hysterical reliving their aunt's dive into their father's casket. You know sweetie, I think you will have a chance to put something in the casket. I don't think you need to be shoving it in there like a secret agent! This made the two of them snicker again.

Penelope found them and wanted to know what they were laughing about. So George explained it to her, and she was laughing too.

Did you realize that the pillow is actually stitched into the lining? George asked his sisters. This made them all choke with laughter. When they calmed down, Penelope explained that they would each have a time alone with the casket in the morning before it was closed, and this was the time she was planning to leave her letter with Dad.

I always knew I was a moron, George said. And I may still try to sneak mine in there, he added. The three of them smiled and cleared their throats. The moment of levity was gone, and the residue of reality left each of them a little uncomfortable.

George went to his bedroom and sat back down at his children's desk, looked out at the darkened night, and reached into his backpack for some paper. He sat still, listening acutely to the hum of voices and activity downstairs, and then drowned out that noise with the ringing comfort of the still air in his room. Finally he scooped a pen out of the center drawer, and began to write –

Dear Dad,

I don't know what to say to you yet, but I guess time is

George crumpled up this sheet and tossed it into the empty wastebasket nearby. Then he picked up his pen and started again –

Dad,

I don't know why this happened. I don't know what this means. I wish I could think straight, and I know that you would want me to be strong and deliberate. I try to picture you here, and what you would do to help people.

George sat back and looked at his words and frowned. He wanted to tell his father how much he missed him, how hollow and furious and lost he felt, and how deeply he loved him, but none of these words would come from his hand. He wanted to be jocular, and make his father laugh, or find some secret code or message that he would feel they could share in perpetuity. Then he wrote –

Do you remember when I was a little kid, and we would go swimming in the ocean at the Cape? You would pick me up, and twirl me around, and then throw me off into a wave while we both roared laughing. And then once when you had me up in the air, you stopped because of the look on my face, and asked me what was wrong. And I told you that when I looked at your face, I could see myself?

George stopped breathing normally, and put the pen in his mouth to make himself relax. Then he said," God" out loud, and stuck the pad of paper in the desk drawer, and moved to his bed to lie down. The posters he had put on his walls as a young teenager still were scotch-taped above the beds. Over his head, W.C. Fields looked out from under a fedora holding a poker hand of playing cards. George tried to close his eyes, but he couldn't lie still so he leaped up and moved downstairs.

It was late, but in the dining room there were pies left out. Some were store-bought, but there was a mince meat pie that someone had baked, and George took a slice. His grandmother passed through the room.

Can't compare to mine, can it? she asked her grandson.

Nope, George answered, and the two of them paused to nod at each other and smile. His grandmother rested her hand on George's arm. Her fingers were bony and gnarled from old age and arthritis. She patted his arm, and George put his hand on hers and muttered, Unbelievable, isn't it? His grandmother shook her head, but otherwise kept her own counsel.

George returned to his bedroom and sat again at the desk. He pulled out the pad of paper and read what he had written earlier. It was okay he thought to himself, but why did he want to say this? He thought for a moment and was tempted to write on the next line –

I'm still that little kid...

But that seemed too hokey, too cute.

He would have torn the sheet out and started over, but his mind was like a padded cell. Whatever outpouring he might have wished would come, he could tell would not. So why frustrate himself with a blank sheet of paper? He sat for a very long time looking out his window, even though he couldn't see anything because of the illuminated reading light on his desk. He was wondering what he really wanted to say to his father. He began to doubt if he should put anything in the casket. Better safe than sorry, he thought for a moment.

George sighed, and reached for his backpack. He had stuffed text-books and the PET manual in the main pocket, and he took them out and threw them on the floor. In the side pocket he found the script for The *Miser*, and considered putting that in the casket. The thought of it made him giggle. It would be a symbol. But a symbol of what? Of his acting? Of himself? Perhaps he was thinking wrongly about this idea. Maybe he should put something in the casket that he valued – something he would give to his father as a keepsake, or expression of his love. No, not his love. His honor.

George shrugged, and continued to shuffle about in his backpack aimlessly. There was nothing in it that could give him inspiration. It was just enabling him to take a break from the issue. Then his fingers found a tiny plastic box deep in a side pocket, and when he withdrew it the white light of Eta Chi glinted beneath the cheap, clear plastic cover. It was his fraternity pin.

When a boy pledged Eta Chi he received a pledge pin, and when he was initiated into the fraternity, he received his fraternity pin. George could not remember what use the pledge pin was supposed to serve, but the fraternity pin, which was larger and more ornate, was intended to be given to a girl the fraternity brother was serious about. In the fifties, boys pinned girls they intended to marry.

It crossed George's mind to put his fraternity pin in the casket, but he quickly dismissed the idea. The image of pinning his father was disgusting! And besides, he wanted the romantic experience of giving this pin to someone he cared about during college. He mused for a moment over the fact that he had never once thought of pinning Caitlin, though to be fair, he had not remembered where the pin was until he found it a moment ago.

Still, the thought of the pin helped him to think more about leaving a symbol of something with his father, rather than a written message. Something that might carry, rather than delineate, a lasting meaning between them. He turned some expressions over in his mind – well known sayings in Latin (*Illegimati Non Carborundum*, for example, or *Spes Sibi Quisque*). But this struck George as too forced, too impersonal.

The Eta Chi pin began to gain favor in George's mind. It was something he did not want to give up, so placing it in the casket would have a meaning. As he thought about it, the pin stood for a collective value of some kind. And while he did not necessarily get exactly what kind, or even whether he was committed in any serious way to it, it didn't matter. His father had stood for something, he wanted to stand for something, and the pin stood for something. It was an undefined symbol of meaningfulness. And when it occurred to George that he would still have the pledge pin to give to a girl, and thus he would definitely *not* be pinning his father, his decision was made. It just took him until the morning to realize it.

In the morning, George awoke and immediately grimaced at his thinking of the night before. How stupid he had been to think of putting his Eta Chi pin in his father's casket. But when he sat down at the little desk and rolled the pin about in his hand, he realized that he was going to do it, and that the oddity of it suited him somehow. Whatever his relationship with his father had been (and he would spend some time over the next few years awakening to what it had been), it was unfinished. At its most elemental, the fraternity pin stood for a bond between men, and the bond between George and his father was important to memorialize.

George took the pin and found the envelope with the funeral home's name on it and placed it inside, but did not seal it. He wasn't sure yet if there wasn't something he should write in addition, so he placed it carefully in his suit coat pocket, and went downstairs to eat breakfast. Penelope sat with her chin on her hand at the breakfast table, dipping a tea bag into hot water in a small teacup. She looked distractedly at George as he fumbled around in the cabinet for some cereal, and said Hi in a soft voice.

Now it begins, she said next, looking at her tea. George placed a bowl with Cheerios and milk on the table, pulled out the chair and sat down, before he replied.

Yup, I guess it does. He did not have a feel for what might be beginning, but he was pretty sure he didn't really want to know either.

At the funeral home, the Muirfield children each took their moment with the casket alone, Penelope first, Marge second, and George third. George tried to gauge the time so that he did not take any more time than his sisters, and he knew that his mother needed to be last, and longest. When it was his turn, he stood quietly next to the shiny amber metallic box and looked at his father's face. He smiled, pretended his father's face smiled back, and then withdrew the envelope from his pocket. He reached over, and carefully inserted the envelope in the inner right breast pocket of his father's suit coat. It slid in easily. He barely had to lift the perfectly pressed wool of the suit.

He felt no tears welling up in him, no loss of control. He knew he had chosen the right thing to do, could feel his father's approval, somehow, and his understanding. For years, George would have two kinds of communications with his father in his mind. Some would be dialogues, but some would be like this – wordless, knowing, smiling, peaceful. He was pleased they could conclude this way.

The funeral mass and the burial went at their own pace, in their own way, with people in tears, and emotions splayed unevenly and collectively. George could not hold back his tears at the mass, but found himself more irritated than sorrowful at the burial. There were so many people at the cemetery that dignity seemed displaced by ceremony. Then it was over, and they were home with nothing left to look forward to.

Friends came by later in the week and over the weekend as relatives departed. Food continued to arrive from neighbors and friends, but in diminishing turns. George sat with his mother and spoke in generalities about the future. He guessed that they would be all right financially, and she agreed. She thought they would do fine. He told her he needed to go back to school. She told him that of course he did. We will talk a lot on the phone she told her son. And when you come home for the summer, we'll spend time together.

On Sunday afternoon, a friend from high school drove George to Logan Airport and he boarded the little Allegheny Airlines plane that would take him to Ithaca. There were only a handful of people on the plane, including one girl whom George recognized from a government studies class. His seat assignment was in the row immediately in front of her, in the window seat. He had always found her sexy from a distance, and up close she did not disappoint him. She was petit, and intense, with a sly smile. He smiled briefly toward her, and took his seat to watch the plane take off.

After take off, the girl leaned forward so she could see his face between the inner wall of the plane and his seat back, and asked him what had brought him to Boston.

The question surprised George, and he had to think how to answer her. He did not want to appear maudlin or needy, or to make her feel bad about his predicament, so the first thing he did was smile broadly toward the part of her face he could see peeking through the little space. Then, in an offhanded voice, he informed her his father had died, and he had been home to attend the funeral.

The girl laughed.

George felt his face flush. She had thought he was being sarcastic, or silly. For a second he felt her flirting with him, but he knew he was trapped by the reality of the moment. He smiled again, so as not to embarrass her, and said, No, I'm serious. My dad did die. And with that, he turned his face to look out the window where she could see his profile, and absorb the truth of his statement.

For a long moment the girl said nothing. A look of disbelief crossed her face, followed by blinking, uncertain eyes. I'm really sorry, she said finally. George thanked her, and told her it was okay. The rest of the flight he spent looking out the window, wondering why he would say it was okay, when it wasn't. And he puzzled over the right way to tell people. The girl and he exchanged no further words, but he noticed that she studiously avoided his looks in classes for the rest of the term. It wasn't my fault my father died, he would say to himself as he looked at her across the big lecture hall. What the hell is her problem?

Once in Ithaca, he took a cab back to the fraternity, and was pleased to see some of his brothers. He noticed that some of them felt uncomfortable with him too, though they were kind and put hands on his shoulders as he passed them in the hall. He unpacked, and went downstairs to the mailroom to call Caitlin. He felt bad that he had spoken so little to her, but there had been no time and they had agreed just to wait until he returned. There was no answer in her apartment, and he guessed she was in the library. He hung the handset in its chrome stirrup, and walked back upstairs. He had no library in him that night. He told his roommate about the funeral, and a few of the boys came in to listen. One of the boys said his grandmother had died, and described what that had been like. Another looked solemnly at George and told him he could not be him – so calm, so rational. George said, you'd be surprised, and then suggested they catch him up on what had happened in his absence. The boys heartily took his lead.

On the way to campus in the morning, George remembered what Prescott Chilton Harris had said on the first day of PET class – that class cuts for any reason, even a funeral, were inexcusable, and would result in dismissal from the course. He wondered if that could be true, and thought he should check with the administrators before the class started. He had spoken with Caitlin before breakfast, and they had agreed to meet at the Green Dragon for a bagel at nine. Caitlin had told him to forget about morning classes, and he had agreed.

Caitlin met him outside the short set of steps down into the basement coffee house, and hugged her boyfriend ferociously. She roped her arm around him, and guided him inside. She walked him to a table, and they sat down. They talked for two hours, with Caitlin asking dozens of questions and George telling her the funny moments and the strange ones. Their eyes barely left each other's, and by noontime, George felt some semblance of spirit within. His center remained still, and seemingly immovable, and he told his girlfriend that too. Caitlin nodded emphatically, and squeezed his hand.

They walked together to PET class, and George said he would join her in a minute in the classroom. After she was out of earshot, he approached the two departmental secretaries and began to explain about his father. The two ladies said they knew, they were so sorry. What did he need?

He explained about Prescott Chilton Harris, and the two of them looked doubtfully at each other, and told George to stand right there until he arrived. The teacher walked straight up to the counter to ask for his mail, and the secretary to George's right stood and told him in a soft voice about George. When she told him that George's father had passed away, and that was why he had missed class the preceding week, Harris absorbed the information without comment or reaction.

The teacher turned slowly toward George, and let his eyes fall into George's gaze and stay there a moment. Prescott Chilton Harris's eyes were not what George had expected. He looked beaten, and misanthropic. Then the teacher placed him arm around George's shoulder, and silently moved with him into the classroom, whispering that he was so sorry, and then resumed his normal imperiousness in the center of the room. George found it impossible to concentrate for the entire class, but the teacher never noticed him.

At the Green Dragon, Caitlin had told George how she had attended *Miser* rehearsals twice while he had been gone, and that the Dean had assumed the role of Cleante so that rehearsals could continue. She told him how interesting it had been to see how he played the character, which was different from George's portrayal. As the afternoon wore on, George tried not to think about the play rehearsal that evening, but went to the Straight Theater early, and sat in the middle of the stage by himself before anyone else arrived.

He had not looked at the script since he had left, but he was certain he would pick the scenes back up where he had left them, and spent his time just looking at the empty seats of the orchestra. Caitlin had said that the Hastings had been much sillier, and more over-the top, so George thought about how he might adjust his character that way. The thought of it made him tired. The cast showed up together, and they all hugged George and stroked his arm. The Dean was solicitous and warm in his funny, formal way. Then he asked George whether he was up to rehearsing, and George said he didn't see much choice. So the Dean said, Fine, well, we are supposed to begin this evening with Act Two, Scene Three.

George went off stage and prepared to enter the Miser's living Room in the middle of a heated discussion between the Miser and the maid. Although he normally rushed in in a huff, George thought it would be all right if he took it easy at first, and simply walked on stage. The other actors turned and waited expectantly for George to speak.

Nothing came.

George looked hard at Alex and said nothing. His first line began with "Father!" and the word would not come out of his mouth.

The actors and the Dean stood totally still. A silence enlarged as breathing dwindled. The pain in the room was palpable. Finally George said, Well, I guess I wasn't quite ready. He was amazed at how uncharacteristically he was behaving, but he did not care.

All right, the Dean said from the orchestra. What would you like to do? His voice was raw with compassion.

I want to start again, please. George said to him. Can we begin the scene again?

Of course, the Dean replied.

George took himself backstage, and cursed under his breath. He tried to put himself in some semblance of character. When his entrance came, he bolted onto the stage, pretending to hold the handkerchief to his nose as the Dean had instructed him, and said "Father" with a dramatic flourish.

Alex peered at him with a sneer.

What does my spendthrift son want now? He complained. And Cleante half-heartedly emerged from George's subconscious to finish their repartee.

❦

The Girl Outside The Library bicycled back into George's view later that week, as he walked across the arts quad on his way to English class in Goldwyn Smith Hall. She was riding her bike slowly along the paved walkway that led from Goldwyn Smith to Uris Library, smiling and laughing with a second girl who rode a bicycle next to her. As she approached George he felt his pulse quicken. If she would only smile toward me, he thought, my day will be made.

The Girl Outside The Library was wearing blue jeans and a cabled, bright blue crew-neck sweater. Her hair was parted to one side, and pulled back behind both ears, which were slightly red from the air. Even in April, George thought she looked tan, or maybe she was just rosy. She was still stunning, and the way she smiled and laughed so freely with her friend had George convinced that she was as wonderful inside as she was out.

Unfortunately, The Girl Outside The Library either did not look at George or simply did not recognize him. He wasn't sure which, since she only seemed to look his way quickly as she needed to pass by him on the walkway. He gave her a big smile, but felt a bit foolish when she did not reciprocate. And then she was gone. He watched her rolling away. He guessed that if he did not get a chance to see her soon, any hope he might have of her recognizing him from before would be lost. Nevertheless, the incident perked him up.

As he turned to go to class, George met Holly Menard and a girl he did not know. Holly called out his name with pleasure and hugged him hard. She introduced George to her friend, Althea Redmonton, explaining to her friend how George had just lost his father. George grimaced inside himself. He hated being introduced as the guy with the newly-dead father. But Althea Redmonton did not make too much of it. In fact she tossed her head slightly, said I'm sorry, and smiled at George in a casual way. When George looked into this girl's eyes for a moment, to capture the meaning of her reply, he had the sensation of going down the rabbit hole.

Althea Redmonton's eyes were hazel colored, except for a tiny streak of brown that left the center of her right eye and lateralled right to the bright whites of her retinas. It was a little streak that one did not notice on first glance. Instead, there was something arresting about her look that made one want to keep looking, to detect the source of the curiosity. And the streak, which was naturally accentuated by the soft, slow manner in which Althea Redmonton blinked, was both alluring and symbolic. For Althea Redmonton had a little streak running all the way through her.

She was a substantial, shapely woman, with the kind of naturally blond hair that you only see in advertisements. Her face was strong, and clean, and graceful, and she had a ready smile that showed her straight, but not perfect, white teeth. When she smiled, she tended to move her arms in a circle, or fold them behind her back. When she rotated her arms like a little locomotive, the impression was that she was on the go. If she folded her arms behind her, she leaned slightly back, and subtly welcomed you into her own private, invisible bubble of space. You didn't so much meet Althea Redmonton as experience her. By the time George pulled himself back from the rabbit hole – an event that took only a moment, but felt like several minutes - he thought he may have felt his center move. What a day he was having.

The two girls moved off on their way across the quad, and George resumed his trek to English class. He felt guilty, giddy, and confused. He also felt relief. Whatever mourning was supposed to bring, he doubted it included the sensations he had just had. How could he be flirting when there was a crater in place of his emotional reservoir? Wasn't he defrauding his own sorrow? Was he so heartless, so callous, that he could forget his despair with one look from a girl? He answered himself with a loud NOPE! As he pulled open the door to Goldwynn Smith Hall.

He bounced up the stairs with a new revelation. His pain was real, and deep, and distortional. He knew that. But the imprint of his soul could still be tickled by the sweet, secret rush of intrigue. And that was okay. Somehow, a little color crept back into the edges of his view – a sepia tinge that warmed the muted, dusty hallway on the second floor. He had not realized how gray and colorless the world had become.

George focused hard during class on his center, urging it mentally to break loose and spin. But he could do nothing to influence its weighty stillness. That would have to wait. After class he headed down the hill to Eta Chi for a chance to study before dinner. Since he had returned from home, he had tried to catch up on his studies by going to his room and lying on his bed with the door closed.

Dress rehearsals came the following week, and George laughed in good natured fashion as the costumiers fitted him with the frilly, large ruffles and bows that Cleante mistook for fashion. Privately, he found it hard to generate excitement about the show, but the cast had grown to love the old play, and the Dean's profuse elaboration on the ironies and subtexts in which Moliere cavorted. The Dean not only brought the period alive, but inserted the minute details of French theater from the era the play was written. The one detail he could not decide upon, to everyone's amusement, involved the tradition of opening the play by the clanging of a pipe offstage to gather the audience's attention.

The pipe was supposed to be struck twelve times in slow, purposeful fashion, during which time the unruly audience would quiet down to watch the play. So the Dean told the cast he was considering banging the pipe only eleven times, to signal that the production would indeed be *miserly*, even with its sounds. George could not fathom who else in the audience besides the erudite Dean would even know of the tradition, let alone count the sounds. Perhaps the other theater professors? But the Dean fretted that it might be misunderstood as a gaff – an erroneous replication, rather than a humorous one.

George's wig smelled of powder and scratched his ears, but it also helped him into character, and to be more foppish than he felt. In the actual performances, Alex did a wonderful, if somewhat overly-dramatic turn as the miser, and the audience laughed well, but not energetically. The production received good, but tame reviews in the local press. George was just glad to see it end. He appreciated it more than he realized when the Dean stood with his arm around him on the last night. It was a fatherly thing to do, and George's body slumped imperceptibly in response.

CHAPTER TWELVE

It was May, and the warmth of spring arrived to fill the evening air with moisture and promise. Nature's delicate perfumes – hyacinth and honeysuckle - and the strong, musky odor of new growth tantalized George as he walked down the hill to the house in the early evenings for dinner. Occasionally he heard crickets chirp. He certainly did not recognize it, but the weeks had turned to months and his trips across the suspension bridge and down through the neighborhoods for dinner at Eta Chi had turned from novel to comfortable.

He anticipated the darkened houses, and smiled when they were lit up. He foresaw the cracks in the sidewalk where the stone was made uneven from frost heaves, and walked the same, certain way over them each time. He girded himself against the tingle of fear that went through him every time he passed the deep glen that fell to his left as he neared the house. It was overgrown with trees and brush that seemed so mysterious and gloomy even in daylight. And he touched the thick granite slab atop the stone wall at the edge of the property in the same place every day.

After dinner he would return to campus and the well lit quiet of the ornate Andrew Dixon White library within the Uris Library. There he would sit below the wrought iron balconies across from Caitlin, their legs folded in with each other's. When the library closed they would walk back to College Town to her apartment, speaking softly in the darkness.

George knew there was something ajar inside him. He could tell it every time they spoke about their majors. It was the end of sophomore year and time to declare majors. Caitlin was majoring in theater arts, of course, but George was perplexed. He could picture himself a theater arts major, and certainly received encouragement from the Dean and other professors, but committing to the theater as a life pursuit rang hollow. He did not believe he was good looking enough that breaks might come his way, and he knew competition was fierce in the theater for paying roles. In his confusion, he kept reciting to himself a line from *The Miser*. Throughout the play, whenever his character had a ridiculous, vain idea, his father, the miser, would scold Cleante, saying: Man does not live by bread alone!

There was also the nagging matter of fragility, which he now fully embraced and used to his advantage as an actor. He was taking on that rubbery persona all the good actors had – a changeable, adaptive emotional state that enabled them to move quickly and believably into different characters. But this emotional, chameleon-like ambivalence troubled him too. It seemed weak, non-heroic, unprincipled. When he tried to explain himself to Caitlin, she bristled.

We are always surrounded by people that break apart and remake their emotions the way construction workers make buildings, he would say.

So isn't that what is so incredibly exhilarating about it? she would reply.

Yes, I guess, but over time doesn't this make all of us sort of false? You can't tell me that you trust when Alex or Maxwell look at you and share some emotion with you. They might be in character, or trying out some nuance, or maybe not even sure what they feel, because feeling itself has become so...fungible.

I trust you. What's so difficult about that?

George would look at Caitlin and wonder. What was so difficult about that?

By the time George informed Caitlin that he had decided against being a theater arts major, she had known for some time that he was heading there. There was too much doubt in his voice. She wondered if his father dying had anything to do with it, but never raised the question. He had been positively prickly about that topic since he had come back to school.

Caitlin wasn't even sure whether she wanted George to be in the theater arts department with her. Part of her liked the idea that she would be the one truly dedicated to the theater. She loved him, she knew that uncontrovertibly. But they seemed fully able to coexist on the different plane they had found together, regardless of whether they shared classes or productions together, or only saw each other in the library. They both knew that George, or anyone, could act in the productions without majoring in it. So it did not occur to her until long afterwards that George was making choices about whom he would be. She missed the notion that the single-mindedness George had demonstrated in acting might be redirected to something else entirely.

When George had arrived on campus as a freshman, he had been assigned an English professor as an advisor. So he scheduled an appointment to see him, and sought his advice about what to do. The advisor was a tired, quiet academic but one of the few faculty that genuinely liked to advise students. So he listened carefully to George's story.

The man and the boy sat across from each other in the professor's office in Goldwyn Smith Hall in the late afternoon with the windows open. The linoleum floor was dirty, and George was leaning forward in an old oak chair that creaked as it moved.

Are you sure that the theater doesn't call you? the advisor asked. It sounds as if you have put great energy into it and have been received well.

George found it irritating that he would probe this again, but he answered the man. He told him that he did not want to limit himself to the theater, and didn't the advisor think that it would limit him?

The advisor thought it could.

You seem to know what you want. The advisor said next.

George nodded slowly and looked out the window. They had discussed all the possible options. History. Government. English. Comparative Literature. George didn't understand what English was, if it wasn't comparing literature.

The advisor grinned.

He hated math, didn't take too well to the sciences, and saw no purpose in foreign languages.

They settled on English.

George never told the man the significance his family had always placed on writing. He failed to mention that his father and Penelope and Marge had all majored in journalism. Or that his mentor in high school, a teacher who had taken George under his wing, was in charge of the English department. Or that reading fiction was close to an erotic experience for him.

It was the way that a fresh, untouched hardcover book of fiction smelled when George first opened its pages. He would lovingly smooth out the pages in small sections to break in the binding, enthralled by the idea that the story would be different than it appeared. The books with beautiful covers could be boring or dense once devoured, while the slim, nondescript volumes could turn out to be thrilling rites of passage. Almost every novel spoke to him in an enticing voice that solicited him to explore new truths. With the good authors, the voice would begin to modulate and become familiar, trusted. Fiction was the great art of telling the truth in an intimate setting. With focus, great books touched all the senses.

But George and the advisor settled on English because it was the most logical major for him, given their analysis of his interests. Majoring in English would allow him to study a number of other liberal arts, and continue in the theater if he chose. It kept the most options open for him. George left the advisor's office satisfied that they had appropriately vetted his choices and logically chosen a good path for his undergraduate degree.

At Eta Chi, the warm weather brought the boys outdoors, to sit by the pool or in the semi-circular lawn in the front of the house, and read for their final examinations. Eta Chi was one of two fraternities that had a swimming pool, which went largely unused in Ithaca's long winters. But for the last few weeks of classes, the boys filled the pool and invited sorority girls to come over and study by the pool in their bathing suits.

The water never really warmed until the middle of June, so people had to be pushed into the pool in May, and the tranquility of the afternoons would be split by the piercing screams of a brother or a visitor who was sent unexpectedly into the cold water. Sometimes a brother would set up his stereo on the slate veranda overlooking the pool, and if you closed your eyes to listen, you could hear the hiss and crackle of the needle on the record, before the Rolling Stones, or the Doobie Brothers, or Led Zeppelin echoed across the property.

The final chapter meeting of the year was scheduled for Sunday evening of the last week of classes, and George decided to go. He had missed every chapter meeting this year, which made him uncomfortable, but he had been spending enough time at the house to be more accepted by the boys. And the jokes he overheard about antics at the meetings made him curious.

When the time for the meeting neared, there was a great rush of activity as boys on all three floors began to run down the hallways and the stairwells toward the Chapter Room. George followed his roommate down to the foyer and then to the basement. There were boys behind him, and one of them was hooting for no particular reason. When they reached the door to the chapter room, the guardian of the door intoned deeply a phrase George had not heard since initiation. It was at that moment that George realized that he had missed initiation this year, when he had been home for the funeral. Inside the chapter room, Danny Carvello kept walking back and forth, suggesting that there very well might be Phi Delt imposters in the room, which might require strip searches. Everyone was laughing.

The consul called the meeting to order and the door was shut and the boys quieted down. After some procedural matters were covered, the social chairman stood up to propose that the fraternity have a final party next Friday with Kappa Psi – a chugging contest to be held in the late afternoon. The boys enthusiastically endorsed this proposal, and then elections for next year's officers took place. Any boy running for office was required to step out while people commented on his candidacy. When all comments were exhausted, each brother placed his written ballot in a large wooden box directly in front of the consul's podium.

Charles Lord was elected consul for the fall term and the room hooted in approval. Charles beamed from his chair, and a boy who had become a sidekick of Charles was named pro consul.

Edward Stamer had put his name in for rush chairman, and he was running against Mike O'Hare, who would be a senior. George found the decision difficult, but in the end he voted for Mike. He hoped that Edward would win, because he thought Mike was too intense and emotional to run the rush process. He might start kicking the doors in the great hall, or something. Still, George felt he owed him his allegiance. Fortunately, the rest of the brotherhood had the same reservations about Mike, so for the second straight year, a junior was tapped to run rush.

Just as the remaining posts were about to be voted on, there was a knock at the door. The guardian of the door, a senior who was Tim Truesdale's roommate, stood and formally approached the door with a serious look on his face. He rapped his knuckles on the inside of the door seven times, and waited to hear the reply. If the boy seeking admission to the meeting was truly an Eta Chi, he would know that he was supposed to then knock on the door the number of knocks that the guardian of the door had rapped, minus four. The boys inside heard three knocks in reply, and the guardian of the door unlocked the door to admit a junior who nodded curtly and took the nearest chair.

George leaned to Cullen Hastings who was sitting next to him, and inquired softly why anyone other than an Eta Chi would want to gain admittance to a chapter meeting in their basement. Cullen smiled, but did not respond.

Immediately after the meeting, Edward Stamer approached George, and George congratulated him on his new post.

Thank you George! I hope you and I can work closely together! You and I seem to see eye to eye on people. Edward said. George nodded. He was surprised that Edward had any inkling about how George saw people, but he told Edward he was flattered and looked forward to the opportunity.

❦

Althea Redmonton was a Kappa, but a renegade one. She had rushed the sorority on a lark, never intending to live in the house. In truth, Althea Redmonton didn't like hanging out with girls. I don't know why, she would tell boys she knew, but I just don't have as many girl-friends as I do guy-friends. She always said "guy," and not "boy," so they would not be confused into thinking that they might be her boyfriend.

Boys liked Althea. She was approachable, compassionate, and exciting to look at. She had a full figure, and knew what clothes to wear to accent her curves. She was also a bit zany, and boys liked that about her too. She was not, however, that easy to get to know. She tended to be reserved in social settings, hiding and watching behind her nice smile and hazel eyes. This led lots of boys to ask her out on dates (she did not seem the type to just walk up to and start a conversation with), but she hardly ever went. She would not tell them no flat out, but suggest that she wasn't sure, and then wander off to find someone she knew.

In truth, Althea Redmonton was attracted to the types of boys who wouldn't ask her out so nicely. My god, her friend Holly would say to her, every boy you like is a scoundrel! And they would snicker, and Althea would puff on her cigarette, blow smoke from her mouth, and say, Sweetie, I like them bad to the bone. Then the two girls would guffaw, and Althea would elaborate.

Holly, I think Charlie's a nice enough guy, but that's his problem. He's always going to treat you so nicely that you won't see the train coming. And you won't get that… thrill.

That thrill?

You know, the thrill of the chase, the uncertainty of their loyalty. Even the sting of their cruelty.

Holly shook her head to reject the idea. There is no thrill to cruelty, Althea. Someday you'll want that boy to be good for you, and you'll be with the wrong type.

The exciting type, Althea replied, blinking slowly as she smiled.

They were sitting in the Straight cafeteria watching boys go by. Tomorrow was the last day of classes for the spring term.

We're going to Eta Chi tomorrow for a chugging contest, Holly said after a minute. Do want to come and find a bad boy there? Holly was always trying to get Althea to come with her to Eta Chi. Secretly, she wished Althea might find someone she liked there. Aside from her weird taste in boys, Althea was a decent companion, and Holly had been named Darling for the following year.

Althea shrugged. I dunno. Maybe I'll catch up with you.

Holly smiled. She knew Althea didn't want to have to go to Kappa first.

I'll pick you up at your apartment at three.

Althea reached to her little purse for another cigarette, and nodded her acceptance with another shrug.

The next day, Holly arrived at Althea's apartment at three ten and Althea was in her underwear.

What do you wear to a chugging contest? she asked Holly. Holly looked at Althea's curvaceous body with a raised eyebrow. She could wear a paper bag and look great. Holly was wearing a denim skirt and a pale yellow top.

Jeans. She finally said. Something you can throw up on. They both giggled.

At Eta Chi, the boys arrived back from campus at various times, and pitched in to help arrange the tables in the dining room in two long rows. Two of the boys rolled a beer keg out from the kitchen, and began the arduous process of installing the tap. No one ever seemed competent at doing that. Others threw plastic table cloths over the long line of tables, and pushed the chairs back to give everyone plenty of room.

Around four p.m., girls from Kappa started to arrive, and as they walked into the dining room, they would roll their eyes and groan as if they were dreading the drunkenness they had come to enjoy. Some of the boys were sipping beers and offered some to the girls but most said they'd wait a bit. By four fifteen, the room was buzzing with laughter and the anticipation of the beer fest to come. The social director pulled a bright orange baseball cap from his back pocket, put it on his head, and put a coach's whistle to his mouth and blew the room silent.

Let the games begin, he yelled, and everyone clapped and headed for the tables. The majority of the boys and girls had been through this routine before, and were explaining to first-timers the rules of the game.

Harold Wise and Jim Steuben were anchoring one end of the boys' table. Beside them was Danny Carvello, who had a huge smile on his face and was calling out questions to the girls behind the other table.

Can one of you please teach me how to play this game? Is this like strip poker?

The girls laughed, and scolded him.

Edward Stamer was in the middle of the table, asking technical questions of the social director. Do you really have to finish the whole glass? Who makes decisions about whether a team has really won? (In truth he was doing this for the benefit of the third girl from the right, who was a first timer, and a little intimidated. He never took his eyes off her while he raised the questions.)

Beyond Edward a number of boys stood along their table – Mike O'Hare and his little brother Patrick, Fritz Hublein, Wally Stimpson, and two new brothers, Joshua Finch, and Bill Wygott. The two Canadian hockey players, Jim Dart and Brian Woodson, anchored the far end.

There were many variations to the chugging contest, but the simplest version involved the first three people at the same end of each table chugging the beer placed in front of them, racing the three people opposite them. When you finished your chug, it was customary to slam the little seven ounce plastic cup down on the table in front of you, upside down as proof that you had finished your beer. Whichever side was slower lost, and that side had to drink the beer in front of them (except for the three who had just competed).

It was not always boys against the girls. Sometimes the participants would agree to "mixed doubles" (usually when the girls complained that the boys had an unfair advantage). Sometimes there were face-offs involving only one person on each side. As people joined or left to use the bathroom, or sit down for a minute, others would take their place at the table. It was only with these relaxed guidelines that the party could last any length of time before the entire room was too drunk to continue.

After the boys won the first chug, there was a great hooting and complaining throughout the room. The girls grimaced and grinned to one another as they sipped the beer in front of them. The boys hollered at them to drink up and not take all day. The chugging contest had begun.

Holly and Althea arrived at the house just as the girls were drinking their first beer of the day to the hooting insistence of the boys opposite them. Holly led the way, her eyes lit up with anticipation. This was only the second time she had been to the house after being named Darling, and she knew she would receive a warm reception.

As they passed through the foyer, George bounced down the stairs from the second floor with his backpack slung over his right shoulder.

George! Holly yelled. Where are you going? Aren't you coming to the chugging party?

George had not even thought about the party. He was headed up the hill to the library to study. Finals were only days away.

Oh my god, Althea said in a dry voice, I think he's going to study!

George looked at Althea and smiled brightly. Actually, he replied, that was exactly where I was headed. Althea had on tight fitting jeans and a tan blouse that made her blond, bobbed hair look even shinier than George remembered.

I'm not sure I'm the chugging type, he offered. Holly roped her arm through his and pulled him with her as she and Althea headed for the dining room.

Well, let's just find that out, she said. Darling's orders! She smiled excitedly toward him. Then they were in the dining room, and the boys all clapped at the sight of Holly. She bowed, and rushed to join the other table. Althea smiled distantly and walked to a chair behind Holly to watch.

George just stood there at the entrance to the dining room and watched the second round of chugging. The room was hot with people and beer, and he wanted to stay and have fun, but knew he should go. Before long, he had set his backpack in the corner of the room and was cheering on the boys as they drank their third and fourth rounds. The boys won the first two rounds, but the girls came back and beat the other end of the table in rounds three and four.

When Mike O'Hare took a break, he told George to get in there and fight for the cause, and George stepped to the table to chug. He was opposite three girls he did not know, but all of whom were kind of attractive. He had no idea that certain sororities were considered to have better looking girls, and that Kappa had the "blond, blue-eyed babe" reputation on campus. On his right Patrick O'Hare was getting ready, and telling George to be quick about it. To his left, Edward Stamer has stepped in for the round.

I've got the one on the left, George. Edward whispered under his breath.

George looked at him and nodded. You can have all three of them, he replied. Out of the corner of his eye, he saw Althea Redmonton watching him as he bantered with Edward. All but that one, he said to himself.

George was a fresh contestant, and easily out-chugged Edward and Tommy. But he was second to put his glass down. The girl to the left that Edward favored was first overall, and she smiled knowingly to George.

The chugging continued twice more, and the boys lost both times, so George now had three cups in him in ten minutes. He looked at the cup and figured that he had really only consumed about one full beer, which wasn't so bad. Then the social director who was still blowing his whistle for effect yelled Face-Off! And people on either side of the table started yelling names of who they would be willing to face-off.

I'll take Susie! A boy yelled. Susie waved her hand to say no thanks.

Edward yelled over to the girl he liked. Come on Betsy – our turn! Betsy told him he was too slow, and Edward laughed.

Darling! Darling! some of the boys started to chant. But Holly wagged her head in exaggerated fashion, yelling out that it was unlady-like. Everybody laughed.

Then Betsy called to Edward and asked him the name of the boy next to him.

George! Edward yelled with gusto. Other boys yelled his name too.

Think you can handle me George? Betsy teased. People whistled and hooted.

George smiled and shrugged. Then the social director yelled Double Face-Off! And everyone roared their approval. This meant that George and Betsy would compete with two glasses, instead of one.

George moved to the center, opposite Betsy, and took the beers in his hands. She must do this for a living, he thought to himself. The whistle blew and he drank the first beer, slammed it down and lifted the second cup to his mouth. Betsy was already drinking her second cup. The girls were cheering. George chugged the second beer faster, and their cups hit the tables within an instant of each other.

Kappa wins! Yelled the social director. George protested, and yelled Face- Face-Off!

Betsy yelled, you're on! There was confusion for an instant. George had made it up, but the boy pouring the beers from the pitcher got his point, and refilled the glasses in front of George and Betsy.

Come on Georgie! Yelled Charles Lord, who had just walked in. He walked over and hugged Holly and said hello to Althea, as George and Betsy smiled at one another. Then the social director blew the whistle, and George was chugging again. He realized that the first beer was the more important one, and he opened his gullet and poured it straight down as people cheered. He was ahead after the first glass, but had to gulp the second glass. He could feel the beer filling his stomach, but could see Betsy struggling herself, and he finished ahead of her. The boys cheered. George took a big breath, and smelled the stale beer in his nostrils. Then he slapped Edward's raised hand, and took a break while the girls' table drank their penalty cups. Across the room from him, George could feel Betsy looking his way. She was pretty. And she obviously wasn't thrilled over Edward. Hmm.

For awhile, George just sat and watched as others competed. He could feel the swell in his head, and noticed he was smiling without meaning to. He watched Althea stand at the girls' table and chug her first beer. She drank it smoothly, and wiped her lips with her sleeve afterwards. He kept looking at her lips as she spoke with people next to her and waited for the next contest. It wasn't that her lips were distinctively full or shapely. He wouldn't say they were pouty. But they were so soft and creamy. He bet they tasted sweet. He tried to feel guilty about Caitlin. But Caitlin could not come into much focus in his head.

It was about six thirty now. The party was still in full swing, and Althea stood in at her table for several more beers. After a while, the social director called for mixed doubles, and boys and girls crisscrossed to each other tables until there was about equal representation. Althea stayed where she was and a boy moved in next to her. It was a freshman George did not know well, and he felt an immediate pang of jealousy. But he smiled as Althea quickly put him in his place and began to scan the room to avoid him.

Across from George, Danny Carvello had positioned himself next to a dark-haired girl with a slender build and a huge, white smile. Danny was leaning his head in close to the girl and acting with mock surprise over what she was saying. George wondered what color Althea's teeth were. Then the chugging started up again and George watched Danny in the competition. Danny held the cup to his mouth, and jerked his head backward as he drank. He arched his eyebrows repeatedly to emphasize his effort, but was the last one to put his glass down. As he set it down, George realized it was still full.

No one was paying attention, and Danny was simply faking it. George wondered how long he had been doing it. Then Althea yelled Face-Off and Holly joined her in the yell. People started yelling names again, but Althea was pointing directly to George, and the table nearest him hooted and dragged him up to the table.

Althea was smiling at him. George was looking at her lips. Someone handed him a beer, and the room started clapping. People chanted, Face-Off, Face-Off, Face-Off!

George and Althea chugged their beers. The social director declared a tie, and directed a re-chug. Conspiracy!, George protested. Althea wiped her lips and said, Oooh, poor little boy. George smiled, and took the next cup of beer. This time he lost, but as he did, he put the cup upside down on his head, and everybody laughed. He thought he noticed Althea sway. By this time, he had no idea whether he was swaying, but he hoped he wasn't.

George stepped away from the table after that and took another beer off the end table and walked out to the foyer and outside into the night. He needed to clear his head. After a minute, he walked back inside and on an impulse walked into the mailroom to see if he had any mail. No mail. He began to scan the other cubby holes to see how many boys did have mail, when Althea walked out of the bathroom behind him. There was a small bathroom reserved for girls in the back of the mailroom.

What are you doing? Althea said in a loud voice. She was moving her arms in a little circle and smiling as she said this.

George told her he was looking at empty mail boxes. As he did this, he copied her rotating arm movements. They both laughed hard. George looked at her lips again. Althea thought through her alcoholic haze that George was making fun of her.

Don't make fun of me. She said. She pulled her cigarettes out of the pocket of her jeans and reached back in for matches.

Smoke? Althea asked him. Her eyelids batted slowly over her eyes, and George zoomed in for an instant. The rabbit hole sucked him in.

George didn't smoke, but he had tried smoking enough in high school to go along with her. He slowly took the pack of cigarettes from her hand and said, Actually, no. Then he shook two of them loose, put them both in his mouth. Althea was trying to strike a match, but the match she first removed had its cover smudged off.

George interrupted her, and took the matchbook from her. He pulled off a match and struck it once. She was looking unsteadily toward him, smiling.

It's a good thing we're drunk. He said softly. I think I look ridiculous. As he said this he pulled the cigarettes from his mouth and shook the match out.

Althea told him she didn't think so at all. She told him she thought he looked like a cowboy. George laughed. No one would ever mistake him for a cowboy.

He put the cigarettes back in his mouth, lit a second match and held it to both of them and puffed until they glowed. Then he withdrew one and handed it to her and she took it between her two fingers and held it to her mouth. George watched the cigarette go between her lips, watched her cheeks flex slightly, saw the glow of the cigarette brighten and then fade. Then Althea blew the smoke slowly off to the side.

The mailroom was small enough to create a sensation of intimacy.

Wait here for a second, George told her. He walked out to the dining room and grabbed two fresh cups of beer off the end table, and returned to the mailroom.

Althea was leaning against the mailboxes, smoking. George handed her a beer, and she took it carefully from him. She was not looking at the beer. She was staring at George as if for the first time.

Shouldn't we be leaving the powder room? Althea asked. George told her it was the mailroom. A minute later, he said, I want to ask you a question.

Oh god, Althea thought. She did not want this guy to ask her out on a date. She was just beginning to like him.

George smiled and asked Althea what her favorite feature was.

What do you mean? Althea asked.

I mean, what feature of your physical appearance do you like the most?

Althea considered the question a moment. She decided to go along. Actually, she said, my favorite feature is my skin. Actually, my face and my skin. She could not believe she was saying what she was saying. This was weird conversation.

You have a strong face. George agreed. Althea smiled.

I would have said your lips. George said next.

A strong urge passed through Althea's head. No one had ever said anything to her about her lips. It was always her eyes, or her figure. She watched George take a sip of his beer. She wanted to flirt with him, but felt unsteady. Too much beer.

She reached for the cigarettes that George had placed in one of the mail cubicles, and took one out. George reached for the matches, lit one and held his hand up to light the cigarette in her mouth. Althea put her hand on his hand holding the match. Then she pulled the cigarette out of her mouth, brought her hand up to George's face, and pressed her soft lips against his.

Althea Redmonton's kiss developed and built on itself. It was to etch and leave a permanent streak across the lines of memory in George's mind. For a long while, their lips pressed together so lightly that George could feel the most minute edges and contours of her lips almost pulling away from him.

Other than her hand on his face, their bodies were not touching until George lightly put his right hand against her hip. He felt her hip move slightly in response. Then Althea's lips began to press his own more firmly. Every nuanced pull and push of her mouth against his sent sensations across his body. He could smell the cigarette still burning in her other hand, taste the smoke as their mouths opened and closed. The way that Althea delicately pulled herself back, as if their kiss might break off any instant, only to return with more insistence, made him ravenous.

Althea's mind had started in a different place. She kissed George on an impulse because he had made her feel sexy. She had expected only to kiss him lightly before suggesting they move back into the main part of the house. But George was tender, tentative, and his lips tasted rich on her mouth. So she began to kiss him more genuinely, and felt herself becoming aroused. He seemed in such control, and detached from her that she wanted to make him lose control.

They kissed for several minutes before Althea let the tip of her tongue enter his mouth. His response emboldened her. George pulled her tongue into his mouth and moved his hand from her hip to the small of her back, but held his own tongue back for a moment. Then his tongue was in her mouth and the tempo of their kiss intensified. Althea could smell his skin and had moved her hand from his face to the back of his head, where she began to clutch his hair.

George wanted to explore her body with his hands, but resisted. His instinct warned him not to push too much, too soon. He had no idea that crossing Althea's mind was the thought that, if she was ever going to have sex in a mailroom, this was the time. Then the mailroom door bumped open, and they pulled apart.

George and Althea stood close to one another, and Althea said hello to the Kappa who walked in to use the little bathroom. The sorority sister smiled at them as she closed the bathroom door. George looked nonchalantly at Althea. His mind was on fire, and he really wasn't sure what to do.

George Muirfield, he finally said, extending his hand to shake hers. Althea took his hand, held it close to her body, and smiled. George could still taste her lips, and was drinking her in with his eyes.

Althea searched his eyes, saw the clear intensity behind an exquisitely complex bundle of connections racing back and forth between them, and whispered her name in reply. His gaze seemed to anticipate and challenge her own. It was like his eyes were asking her to be naked for him, but promising never to tell or demand it of her. It was almost as good as their kiss had been.

Have you two met? The Kappa teased them as she emerged from the bathroom and saw the two of them so intense. The three of them laughed.

I think we just did, George replied, and broke his look with Althea to see and smile at the other girl. I'm George, he said to her, and extended his hand to her. He didn't know what else to do as the three of them just stood there.

I know, she answered. George cocked his head inquisitively. I'm Suzie, she said pleasantly. Well, I am going to leave the two of you alone now. She left the room.

When George resumed his look at Althea, her eyes had never left him, and the raw nakedness of her gaze overpowered him. She would tell him much later that she could not account for why this happened. She could feel herself removing all of the pretense and safety nets we normally layer over ourselves, all the cynicism and aggression that clouds our eyes to shield us from others. It was as if she were somehow unveiling herself to him. It was how he had turned and spoken to her sorority sister, something in the way in his conduct that had taken her back into some childhood memory, after such an intimate moment between them.

It was as simple and as complicated as any deep connection between two people. But what would astound them both was the risk she took with him at that moment. They barely knew each other, and their two encounters had been as fragmentary as they were intense. But when George returned to looking at Althea, and received her gaze, his own eyes refocused in curious disbelief, and then slowly, awkwardly, opened to hers. There was a powerful, almost physical conduit between them. No corners of their souls remained unclaimed. And for the rest of their time, they would share ownership in each other's deepest sensibilities, instincts, and fears. It would be both a blessing and a curse.

On Saturday morning, George awoke in his room at Eta Chi and literally leaped out of bed. He was only slightly hung over, and wound as tight as a coil spring. He dressed, walked out to his car, drove downtown into Ithaca, and stopped at the first place that looked like it sold cigarettes. He walked in, bought a pack of Camel Lights, picked up two books of matches from the flimsy cardboard case on the counter and walked outside and down the sidewalk. When he came to a bench that looked out over a little park, he sat down, opened the cigarette pack, and pulled a fresh cigarette out. He brought it to his nose to sniff its full length, then placed it on his lips and lit it. Only then did he allow himself to begin to think.

Althea Redmonton raged in his mind, and the cigarette he smoked gave him a visceral sensation of her presence. It also made him dizzy, so he let it burn down in his hand while he thought. He closed his eyes, leaned back and reenacted their kiss in the mailroom in his mind. But it was what happened after they kissed that swelled in his brain and made him shiver. There was more between them at this moment than… he began to think about Caitlin. Was that possibly true? He didn't even know Althea, and Caitlin and he had been soul mates for close to two years. Hadn't they?

He forced himself to think about Caitlin, about the way they looked at each other, and touched each other. Caitlin Fossburgher was beautiful, and smart, and loving. She was a lot of fun to be with and they loved so many of the same things. She was so giving to him in their relationship, and he learned from her how to be giving in return. But what did she give? George shook his head as if to clear it.

It was no use. As he walked himself through his relationship with Caitlin, Althea Redmonton was looming as large as a right whale in his head. For a moment he actually wondered whether he was being disloyal to Althea by thinking about Caitlin! Then he remembered the time that he had pulled his groin muscle during *Oedipus*, the same way that he used to when he played hockey in high school. It had been a bad pull, and he had fretted to Caitlin about how long it usually took to heal. He had to be up on the stage piping the next several days, and was afraid he wouldn't be able to do it with such a bad muscle strain.

The following morning, his groin muscle was perfect. No tenderness, no residual limitation in flexibility. It was a miracle. Then Caitlin had shyly asked him how his muscle was and when he explained how it had literally disappeared overnight, she beamed at him.

What? he asked.

I prayed for you. Caitlin replied softly. She had been teaching George all about the tenets of Christian Science, and how prayer could be powerful enough to not only heal oneself, but others. George had scoffed at the notion, but from that moment on, he believed her unquestioningly. And he had found her care for him extraordinary.

Althea Redmonton's religion was an unknown, of course, as was just about every other detail about her life. Except for her soul, which George felt connected to right at that moment. He could almost speak to her as he sat there. It was incredible.

CHAPTER THIRTEEN

U p in College Town, Althea Redmonton was waking up in her bed with a dreamy smile. She was having that same dream again, the one where she was in a cave, next to other caves where her mother, father and brother were. It was always the same. She would wake up in her cave, and feel frightened, alone. She knew her parents and brother were nearby, but she couldn't speak with them. It was frustrating, as if she were tied up, even though she was free to roam around her cave.

Then the large man came into the cave. He was huge, and muscular, and dressed in rags. He didn't look directly at her, but he was there for her. She would tell him that this was her cave, but he would act like he couldn't hear her. Then he would pick her up. She was nearly weightless in his massive arms. It made her feel both helpless and safe. But there was something she didn't understand, because he would then slap her face. Not hard, but brusquely. He was not trying to hurt her. Was she falling unconscious? She never understood. Then he would carry her out of the cave and lay her in the tall grass behind the beach. She would think she was sitting up, watching him kneel in front of the water and drink with his hand. Watching him aroused her. Then her family would be standing over her in the tall grass, calling her name, and she would wake without moving. Her arousal would continue without them knowing, making her feel ashamed. And elated.

Althea rolled over in her bed, and sighed contentedly as she wrapped her arms around her pillow. This time, before he slapped her, the huge man had kissed her, so gently, that she had been like soup in his arms. Althea's head began to clear, and she rolled off her bed and walked naked to the refrigerator for cold water. She loved to sleep naked, although she did it rarely.

She poured herself a tall glass of water from the gallon milk container that she refilled with water from the tap, and drank it standing at the refrigerator with the door open. Then she walked to her closet and took her old cotton bathrobe from the hook on the door, wrapped it around herself with the thick, soft sash, and sat at her kitchen table.

The matchbook George Muirfield had folded backwards like a tent sat on the table, next to her cigarette pack which was crumpled, and almost empty. Althea pulled her knees up close to her chest and looked at her toes. Maybe she should paint her toenails, she thought. She walked across her little studio that was shaped like an L, to her dresser around the corner, and picked out a pink polish. She moved back to the kitchen table, resumed the same position, and twisted open the polish with effort.

Althea did not use nail polish much, and usually put clear polish on, but today was definitely a day for color. She leaned around her knees, resting the side of her face on the soft nap of her bathrobe, and lightly applied the polish to each toe, starting with her pinkie. She was thinking hard about what had happened between her and George Muirfield. She kept wondering if all the beer had made it seem different than it really was. She knew that she had gotten drunk, but what had happened stood out in her mind with sober clarity.

George Muirfield frightened her. He was so solid and unequivocal when he looked at her that she lost the control she kept over most boys she knew. She thought about her on again – off again relationship with Matthew Stollings. Matthew was hard with her, and could be irritatingly self-centered, but she still managed the tempo between them. It was as if Matthew only needed to *think* he was dominant. So long as she let him see their relationship that way, she got him to do pretty much what she wanted.

She guessed George Muirfield was very different. He was awfully serious, which she didn't think she liked. Serious boys could be so ponderous, and exacting, that nothing spontaneous ever happened. Holly had said something about him being in theater. That might be cool. She didn't have any interest in theater, but it was likely that people into theater had a wild side to them. She thought about the two of them standing so close together in the mailroom, touching without touching, and could easily imagine a wild streak in him. That's what he would be – her wild boy. This made her smile.

She finished polishing her toenails and took one of her last two cigarettes out and lit it. The smoke tasted strong and full in her mouth, and she exhaled through her nostrils. She had a sudden sensation of being with George, of watching him put a cigarette to his lips and inhale. She shuddered for a moment. He definitely scared her, and she had no clear idea why. She hoped he wouldn't be presumptuous with her, because of the bizarre way they had looked into each other. She didn't like being so exposed with someone she didn't even know if she liked. That was wrong. She knew she liked him. She just didn't know what to do with him.

She put her cigarette out in the little dish she had made into an ashtray, and looked around her apartment. The old refrigerator with the big thick white door that reminded her of ice cream trucks when she was a little girl hummed loudly. There was an electric stove next to it, with its oven that sometimes didn't work right. The sink was old and tired, and she wasn't very good about keeping it clean, so it looked pretty sad. Across from the kitchen area, she had a couch and a chair that came with the place and the table she had brought from home. Her bed was around the corner with her dresser. Maybe this is my cave, she thought, thinking back to her dream.

Later she would think hard about whether this was the moment when George had sneaked up to her door and placed a rose on the doormat. She didn't find it for a couple of hours, after she had showered and dressed and begun to leave for campus. Seeing it in its green wrapping made her freeze and look up and down the street. It had to have been George. If Matthew had brought her a flower, he would have pushed it on her as some way of wanting something. Matthew was a piece of work, but she liked how pushy he could be. He knew what he wanted and made no bones about it. And he had never given her a flower, although once he had bought her a silver bracelet.

Althea took the pink flower inside and unwrapped it. She held it in her hand as she rummaged in the cabinets for something to put it in. She had nothing tall enough to make it stand, so she found her scissors, cut the rose in half, and stuck it in her tall water glass. She held it under the faucet and watched the water fill to the top, poured a little back out, and set the glass on her kitchen table. Then she sat back down, and smoked her last cigarette.

Why hadn't he knocked on the door? She imagined herself answering the door in her bathrobe, seeing him standing there holding the flower, and saw why he had chosen to leave it. She looked at the rose, leaned into it with her nose, and sat back.

What did this mean? It made her feel good, and made her want to see him. But she had no idea where this was really headed, and wondered what conclusions he had reached to drop the flower off at her apartment. Impulsively, she reached for the campus telephone book and looked up Eta Chi. She dialed the number, pictured the mailroom where the pay phone was, and asked for George Muirfield when a boy answered the phone.

Just a minute, he said. Althea could hear him leave the mailroom and yell out whether anyone knew where Muirfield was. Then there was silence for a couple of minutes, and she wondered if the boy who answered the phone would ever return. Then he came back on the line.

Sorry, he's not around. Want to leave a message?

Yes, she answered. Then she balked.

Hello? the boy asked impatiently.

Just tell him Althea called.

Spell that?

AL – TH – EA.

Got it. Does he have your number?

No. Althea gave the boy her telephone number. Then she hung up and went to her closet and looked at her tops again. Maybe she should put on a different one. She was supposed to study with Matthew tonight, but she was thinking about George. She walked to her mirror and stood close to it so she could look into her own eyes. Then she smiled at herself, and headed up to campus.

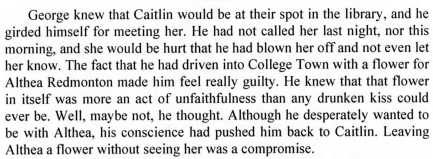

George knew that Caitlin would be at their spot in the library, and he girded himself for meeting her. He had not called her last night, nor this morning, and she would be hurt that he had blown her off and not even let her know. The fact that he had driven into College Town with a flower for Althea Redmonton made him feel really guilty. He knew that that flower in itself was more an act of unfaithfulness than any drunken kiss could ever be. Well, maybe not, he thought. Although he desperately wanted to be with Althea, his conscience had pushed him back to Caitlin. Leaving Althea a flower without seeing her was a compromise.

George walked into Uris Library at a quarter to one in the afternoon, and went straight to the Andrew Dixon White Library. Caitlin's books were there, but she was not in the room. George sat down opposite her things, and took out his books. He looked around the room at the other people studying. There were girls and boys at the little desks up in the balconies, and there were three girls at the other large table. Between the three girls there was a package of red Twizzlers, and George could smell the sweet licorice candy one of the girls was slowly chewing as she read.

George had just begun to try to read through the underlines and notes in his economics 102 textbook when Caitlin shuffled into her chair. He looked up apprehensively and she looked coldly into his eyes.

Did you have fun last night? she asked.

George felt the hairs on the back of his neck. Actually, I did. He replied.

Do you have any idea how cruel that is? I had no idea where you were. *Where* were you?

At the house. I ended up in a chugging party, and things got out of hand. (She had no idea how out of hand, George thought guiltily.)

What the hell is a chugging party?

It involves a lot of beer, and competing with teams to see who can drink the fastest.

So how drunk did you get? (George thought that was an interesting question.)

Drunk enough to not call you, he said in a regretful tone. He did feel regret – he should have called her.

I'm really angry, George. George could tell that this was the end of the conversation as far as she was concerned. She started looking at the book in front of her. He didn't know what to say. If nothing had happened – if Althea had not happened – he would have worked harder to find a way to apologize. But he was confused about what he wanted, and did not want to lie. He knew that Caitlin would just put her mind to her work. She was incredibly disciplined in that way. He was not going to be able to study. For a long time he sat looking out the window, down toward Cayuga Lake.

Eventually he picked up his textbook and moved through it, but none of it was sinking in. Around three p.m. Caitlin looked up, stretched, and asked her boyfriend if he wanted to go back to the apartment and study there. George said okay, and they packed up their books and walked together out of the library. Caitlin had been fretting about their conversation, and wanted to break the silence between them. If George wanted to get drunk with his fraternity brothers, what did she really care?

They walked past the Straight toward College Town, and Caitlin took her boyfriend's hand in hers as she scolded him again.

I ought to kill you, you know.

Yep.

They walked in silence for a minute. George asked her if she had been able to study the last few hours. Caitlin told him not very well. George told her that was better than he had been able to do, and Caitlin squeezed his hand tightly.

That was the moment that Althea Redmonton saw George, coming the other way. He was walking with a tall girl who moved like a swan, and held George's hand in hers. George and the girl turned to their right as they passed over the bridge that brooked the little gorge on the south side of campus, and George looked toward Althea just as they were turning. It was a momentary view since George and Caitlin's path then went behind a building. George's heart leaped into his chest, and panic gripped him.

Althea's face had been noncommittal, but George knew what she was thinking. He was thinking it himself. Caitlin had been speaking about something, and he made a sound to indicate he was listening, but the image of Althea walking onto campus was making him sick to his stomach.

They walked underneath the stone arch and down Eddy Street to Caitlin's apartment. Caitlin was feeling better, and was talking about what she could make them for dinner, if George wanted to just hang out for the rest of the day. Caitlin asked him what he was hungry for. George told her he didn't know. I'm hungry for Althea Redmonton, he thought to himself miserably. It made him feel lousy to think that. Caitlin deserved better.

He walked up the steps to her place behind her, watching Caitlin's graceful frame flow up the stairs. She barely moved her hips laterally when she walked. Then they were inside and on the couch, pulling out their books. Caitlin snuggled up against him and began to focus on her work. George took out a history book to try a different subject. He found it harder to concentrate when he was sitting so comfortably against his girlfriend, but he was not about to move. Then Caitlin leaned her face into his shoulder and smelled his shirt.

Is that cigarette smoke? Did you smoke cigarettes? Her voice was incredulous.

Yeah, I did. George replied. Gives you some sense of how drunk I was.

Caitlin pulled away a little but left her stockinged feet touching his.

Good Lord. She said disapprovingly.

George didn't share Caitlin's reaction. He was thinking how good a cigarette would be. Then he pictured Althea at the library, fuming about the mess he had just made. At least he hoped she was fuming. If she wasn't, then what was she doing? He imagined her hand on her hip, and the way she had swayed at the chugging table. Then he looked at Caitlin.

His girlfriend looked serene as she studied. She had already gotten over the cigarette smoke and was reading *Technical Stage Production, 2d ed.* He marveled at her, and tried hard to think about what he wanted. He loved Caitlin. He had a deep respect for the principled, passionate way that she approached her life. They were simpatico in so many ways. But she did not make his blood boil. There was a measure and a cadence to their relationship. It was like a governor on a go-cart. It was just too safe.

George did not consciously say to himself that he was going to leave Caitlin. But at that moment he knew it, the way that you know something in your heart but have not had the gumption to articulate to yourself. He felt relief.

Althea Redmonton just kept walking to campus after she saw George. She had seen the look in his eye, however brief. That startled, caught-in-the-act look that boys always had. The first thing she felt was anger. She didn't care that George was with some other Swan-girl. She could hardly expect him to be hers. And she was going to be with Matthew Stollings tonight herself.

She told herself she didn't even care that George had been holding the Swan-girl's hand about two hours after he had been sneaking a pink rose onto her doorstep. That just proved he was an egotistical bastard. What made her angry was the fact that she had called him at Eta Chi and left a message. And now she couldn't get it back. The son of a bitch, she said under her breath.

While Althea Redmonton was not prone to be introspective, her brow was furled a bit as she entered Uris Library. In some corner of her mind, a doubt nagged at her about why a boy like George Muirfield would behave as he had. What was it about her that would let him do this to her? People always told her how attractive she was. She knew her looks pretty well, and was sure of her appeal. Was it something inside her? She began to think about Matthew's nonchalance around her. She knew Matthew saw other girls on occasion, and she sometimes went out with others. It was an understood arrangement between them. Althea thought of Matthew holding hands with some girl. She pictured him kissing her. It wasn't comfortable, but it didn't make her furious.

It was just that stupid moment in the mailroom that irked her. She had opened herself to George Muirfield. The fucking bastard knew it, and there he was walking into College Town with a big red swan. So why hadn't their moment together been as special for him? Althea began to doubt her self. She turned around, left the library and walked to the Straight to buy cigarettes. She bought two packs, and took one matchbook off the counter. The son of a bitch.

Althea walked outside, sat on a bench and smoked a cigarette. Students were walking around, and two girls were standing in front of the Stump, talking dramatically with each other. The Stump was a Cornell institution. When Dutch Elm disease had ravaged every tree on the Arts Quad, and claimed the beautiful elm in front of the Straight, the university had removed all of the trees, but the workers had left the Stump in front of the Straight. It was about five feet tall, and three feet in diameter. The Stump had quickly become a medium for student expression. In the middle of the night, students would paint the stump in psychedelic colors or paint messages on it. Sometimes they stapled posters all over it, announcing some event. The Stump grew into a shrine, a symbol of Cornell.

Althea walked back up to the library, and looked for an empty desk in the main room where the reference desk was located. It was crowded with students prepping for final examinations. The room was quieter than usual. She saw Holly Menard sitting with Charles Lord, and walked over to say hi. Charles smiled, and returned to his book. Holly got up and dragged her friend out to the corridor where they could speak.

So? Holly looked expectantly at Althea.

What? Althea said, though it could only be one thing.

Suzie told me you and George were pretty intense outside the bathroom last night.

Althea rolled her eyes.

I was drunk. It was a mistake. He's a creep. As Althea said the words, she didn't trust herself. The picture of George in her head was the opposite of a creep. It made her pulse quicken.

Holly wanted to know details, and Althea demurred. It wasn't anything worth telling, she lied to her friend. Then she asked Holly what she knew about the Swan.

What swan? Holly asked, pulling her head back and squinting.

The tall, red-haired one he's obviously with, Althea replied.

Holly smiled knowingly. Ohh, what's her name...Caitlin, I think. So nothing happened? And you want to know about his girlfriend? Want me to ask Charles?

No! Althea whispered. It doesn't matter. He's not my type anyway. Not dangerous enough for yours truly.

Holly looked at her friend carefully and told her she liked George. Althea smirked and told her about the rose. Then she told her about seeing George and Swanny on their way to College Town. Holly was appalled. Their conversation ended when Matthew Stollings interrupted them. He leaned into Althea and kissed her cheek, and said hi to Holly.

Holly couldn't stand Matthew Stollings. He was arrogant and mean, and she didn't even think he was good looking. But she knew Althea liked him. She looked at his high forehead and blond, tight curls of hair and told Althea she would catch her later. Althea murmured a goodbye, and walked off in the other direction with Matthew.

Caitlin sent George up to the corner to pick up some peppers at the little convenience store in College Town. It was seven p.m. and she had taken some frozen chicken out of the freezer to make a chicken stir fry. The chicken was caked with frost. George walked up to the corner of Eddy Street and College Ave., and looked up the hill in the direction of Althea's apartment. It would only take him five minutes.

Althea's apartment was empty and dark when George got to it, but he went up and cupped his eyes on the window next to the door and peered inside anyway. Daylight was fading, but he thought he made out the rose standing on the kitchen table. He stood with his back to the door, looking down the steps and along the little driveway next to the house that led to the street. What if she came up here right now, he wondered? He didn't know what he was doing here, and would have felt ridiculous if she found him at her back door, so he started to leave.

As he moved down the stairs, he felt around in his pocket for the cigarette and the matchbook he had slipped out of his backpack as he left Caitlin's house. He stopped on the stairs, put the cigarette between his lips, and lit it. He inhaled and stood still as the smoke entered and left his mouth. It tasted sweet, and familiar. George started to slide the matchbook back into the thin pocket of his corduroys, and drew it right back out. Turning, he folded the matchbook cover like a tent, so the matches stuck out on one side, and placed it on the railing at the top of the steps. He looked at the matchbook and doubted it was a smart thing to do. What the hell would it mean?

So he picked it up again, fished in his pocket for a pen, and stood with the cigarette dangling from his lips, trying to think about what to write. The smoke kept curling up near his face, which made him keep shifting around as he bent over the little matchbook. He giggled, wrote the message on the inside of the cover, bent the cover back to its original side, and then left it opened like a tent on the railing, near the corner. That way the matches would be protected, but it would still stick out a little bit when she walked past. Then he went to the little store, bought a green pepper and a red one, an onion, a pint of chocolate ice cream, and a pack of peppermint gum for his breath. He chewed two sticks at once on his way back to the apartment.

Caitlin was reading and asked George to cut up the peppers. He told her he had bought an onion, too. Caitlin said Yum and went back to her book. George took a plate down from the cabinet, and sliced the peppers and the onion while olive oil was heating in the gritty old pan that had come with the apartment. It was caste iron, and heavy. He placed the vegetables in the oil and watched them sizzle.

The small, circular fluorescent light above the sink spread a harsh light across the kitchen, but the onion smelled good as it browned. He sprinkled salt and pepper over the mixture, told Caitlin he was adding the chicken, and heard her close her book and get up. She looked approvingly over his shoulder, and started to hunt around in the little refrigerator until she pulled out some left over broccoli. She opened the baggie and shook the broccoli on top of the chicken and vegetables, and stirred it around with a wooden spoon.

George was watching her, and thinking about the matchbook. He regretted leaving it on Althea's porch, and wondered if he should go retrieve it. The message he had written, while he still thought it clever, was too much. It wouldn't entertain Althea, it would come across as…weird. He didn't think he needed that on top of everything else. Then dinner was ready, and Caitlin spooned a big pile of the stir-fry onto two plates, and George got them both a tall glass of milk. The quiet around them was broken by the occasional scuffle of someone walking down the street, or the yipping bark of the neighbor's Scottie.

What are you looking at? Caitlin asked George, after he had helped them both to a coffee cup filled with chocolate ice cream, and sat back down. He was watching her scoop her ice cream with a little spoon, and place it delicately in her mouth. She loved ice cream and her shoulders lifted up and scrunched forward as she ate.

I like watching you eat ice cream, he answered her. It made him feel guilty when he said it. Not because it wasn't true, but because it implied other things. Caitlin beamed at him. He smiled back. Everything was making him feel guilty. He worried that he was disappointing Caitlin when he smoked the cigarette. He felt like he was cheating when he bought the gum. Even buying the ice cream made him remorseful. It was obviously a peace offering of sorts, when he wasn't really making peace.

After they finished cleaning up and George had dried the caste iron skillet with a paper towel, he informed Caitlin that he was going to go to the house. He couldn't concentrate on his work as he sat with her, needed to be alone to study, was worried about his finals. He looked at her for her approval, and Caitlin nodded her head understandingly as she stared at him.

They had been doing this lately, since he had returned from his father's funeral. He still stayed with her, but some nights he would decide to go to the fraternity. He always had a reasonable excuse, but Caitlin knew that they were excuses nonetheless. She believed George's point about being able to study. She knew what distracted him, and that he needed more solitude to work than she did. She liked to study with music playing. He needed silence. And she recognized that he had not had his head in his studies since he had returned, so he really did need to concentrate. But there was something else underneath it all, something she had concluded was related to his father.

George had been curiously, and stubbornly unemotional about it. It wasn't that he refused to face it. He spoke to her about how he felt, shared how scary and confused it made him to think about his father. But there was something clinical and reserved about his assessments, and he kept telling her that he resented the fact that it labeled him. That was the word he kept using – labeled.

Caitlin had little idea what he meant when he talked about being labeled. She could only guess what it must feel like to not have her father. It was close to unimaginable for her. Her dad was so strong, so complete an individual that she could only picture herself sobbing, and letting her emotions tumble if he were ever to die. If there were any tumbling going on inside of George, it was not obvious. Except for the fact that he occasional wished that his center would resume its spinning. The center she had found within herself did not spin or move at all. Hers was like a tall steeple out in the middle of a large expanse of space. But she could grasp what he was saying.

She watched him pack his backpack, hugged him, and asked him if he wanted to do something tomorrow. He nodded, and said he would call her in the morning. Then he thanked her and left. What he thanked her for was a puzzle, but Caitlin forced herself to stop analyzing her boyfriend, and went to take a shower so she could go to bed with her hair wet. She loved to do that.

George walked up Eddy Street, knowing that he was going to turn and head up to Althea's apartment, but pretending he wasn't. Then he turned and walked slowly up across College Avenue, past the Palms where he had drunk tequila with Louise so long ago, to the house where Althea's apartment was out back. This time her lights were on, and he stopped uncertainly. He wondered if she had noticed the matchbook, and debated whether he could get close enough to see if the matchbook was still there. He sidled along the edge of the house until the light from her apartment spilled down close to his feet. The main house was dark, which he hoped meant that no one was home. It was exciting to be so close to her, and anonymous. It was as if he was in a movie.

Then he peered around the edge and looked up to try to see the matchbook. What he saw was Matthew Stollings' head through the kitchen window. He ducked back out of view, breathing harder. He nodded to himself. There was symmetry to her being with someone; but he still felt sick to his stomach. He thought to walk away, but really wanted to retrieve that matchbook now, if it was still on the ledge. What a fool he had been to leave it there. He tried to picture the steps, and wondered if he could climb the side of the stairs just high enough to reach his hand up to where he had placed the matchbook.

He had to try. He placed his backpack silently on the little driveway, and walked quickly around the edge of the front house toward the side of the steps, as if he lived there and always did that. The only way that they would have noticed him is if they were looking straight out the window, and if they were looking out the window, he certainly did not want them to see him creeping around.

The steps were not that high. He could reach the top landing with his hand as he stood next to it, covered in the shadow of darkness created by the little outside light on the wall next to the door. He could hear them talking inside, but could not understand their words. He heard Althea laugh lightly, followed by his deeper voice. The side of the little porch was covered with flimsy lattice work, and with one feel of his hand, he rejected the idea of attempting to climb it. From the angle he was at, he could not see whether the matchbook was still there.

Suddenly the door above him opened, and Matthew Stollings was outside, bouncing down the steps and heading out the driveway to the street. George froze in fright. He tried to picture his backpack where he had left it, and hoped that this boy would not notice it against the little side wall of the main house. It was in the dark, so there was a fighting chance. He listened with adrenaline intensity, and heard the boy walk out to the street. Then he lost his trail. He began to relax. Once he collected himself, and was sure that he was alone, he would be able to get out unnoticed.

Then Matthew Stollings walked back into the driveway, and George stood motionless as he heard someone approach. What the hell had he thought he was doing, he wondered. This was embarrassing. Matthew Stollings whistled as he roped up the little steps, feet from the top of George's head. He noticed the matchbook George had left on the railing, grabbed it, and stuck it in his pocket as he went inside. George heard the door close, and Matthew ask where the wine cork was. George moved immediately up on the second step, made his eyes adjust to the light and looked for the matchbook. It was gone. He walked rapidly around the corner of the main house, scooped up his backpack, and ran out onto the sidewalk and down about three houses. Then he slowed to a walk, breathing heavily, and turned right onto College Avenue to head across campus.

He was perspiring, and his stomach was whirling with adrenaline. It was too late now. Whatever would happen would happen. He wondered what had happened to the pink rose, and he smiled with the hope that it was sitting there in front of the boy with the wine. Maybe it would be a secret reminder to Althea.

When Matthew Stollings walked into the house, he called out to her for the corkscrew. Althea was in a great mood tonight, and had suggested they blow off the library and have some fun. He never knew with her, but when she was frisky like this, that usually meant she was horny. So far so good, he thought as he poured the sweet Riesling into two different wine glasses.

Matthew had a thin face with smooth skin, and long, white hands that always made Althea think of the white alabaster statues in the Temple of Zeus. He even had a habit of looking down and away from himself, like those statues. Sometimes his thin lips would curl to a sneer before he made dismissive comments about something or someone. Usually what he had to say was quite funny, taken the right way, and Althea interpreted his pursuit of her as a high compliment, given his disdain for so much.

He was tall, and lean, and wore expensive clothes. Clothes looked good on him. When Althea left the bathroom, where she had placed the rose when she got home, she giggled as she entered the kitchen and saw Matthew holding the bottle between the legs of his khaki trousers and fighting with the cork. She sat at the table, lit a cigarette, and exhaled slowly while he filled the glasses. What she had really wanted to do was go dancing somewhere, but neither of them could think of where. After their second glass of wine, Althea stood up, turned on her clock radio and instructed Matthew to get up and dance with her. She pulled him to her, and they moved slowly around as the radio played *Dust In The Wind*. She didn't have to wait long for Matthew to make the next move.

It was Sunday afternoon before George looked in his mail cubby and saw a little slip of paper. He pulled it out and looked at it –

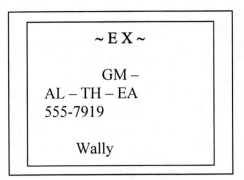

~ E X ~

GM –
AL – TH – EA
555-7919

Wally

George stared at the message for a minute. Althea Redmonton had called. Had she read the message on the matchbook? She must have. There could be no other explanation. Why else would she call? George grinned at the image of himself crawling up her steps to get it back. He fished for a dime in his pocket and inserted it into the pay phone and dialed her number. He could see her picking up her telephone in his mind's eye.

Hello?

Althea, it's George Muirfield. Silence. I'm really glad you called.

Althea was sitting at her kitchen table and reached for her cigarettes.

I wanted to let you know I don't see boys who are involved with other girls, she finally said into the phone. Her heart had started to race, and she told George she needed to put the phone down for a sec. She walked away from the phone, lit her cigarette, blew smoke at the ceiling, and came back.

George was imagining her, seeing her eyes, her face. He pictured her body curled in a big, round chair.

You wouldn't have called if you didn't get a hoot out of my message, George told her when she announced she was back. I meant it and I can explain. He listened to her inhale, and saw her smoking. He felt in his pocket for cigarettes, but they were in his backpack.

You explained plenty, pal. Althea liked the way she said "pal." I don't want to sit and listen to your Poor Me routine.

George stared at the mailboxes. He didn't really know what to say. This was complicated.

What happened between us was real. I know it. You know it. I know how you must have felt because I felt the same way last night when I saw you with someone.

Althea sat up alert. Where had this guy been where he could have seen her?

You saw me with someone?

George's stomach began to churn. How could he explain how he had seen them at her apartment without looking like a loser? But he decided to go with the truth, sort of.

I actually went to your apartment last night because I had decided I thought the message may be too much, and wanted to get the message back before you got it. But I didn't because you were there with someone. So I left.

Althea looked alarmed. She had no idea what he was talking about. He wanted to come and take his flower back before she got his message? This guy was weird. It was time to cut this off and move on.

George, you and I had some weird connection the other night. It was nice. But I am not in a position to…look, just let it go. Concentrate on the Swan. And don't call me any more.

Click.

George stared at the receiver, with his head cocked. His first re-action was to feel sorry for himself for telling her too much. Sometimes the truth got you in trouble. Then he pondered what she had said about a swan. That was pretty strange. Maybe this was for the best. He shuddered to think how obsessed he had been the past two days. But he knew he wasn't going to be able to shake her out of his mind just like that.

Althea sat and stared out the window. The house next door looked big, and solid, and bright white in the sunlight. She had done the right thing. For all she knew, George Muirfield could turn into a stalker. She looked at the clock, and realized that it was Sunday. She had gotten almost nothing accomplished since she had been in that mailroom with him on Friday night. She wanted to go to the library, but worried she would end up seeing Holly, or Matthew, or even George.

So Althea chose to stay home, and she spread her books out on the kitchen table, and after a few fits and starts, her head was back in gear. It was warm, and she had the back door open to let what little breeze there was filter through the half-screen door. She wore athletic shorts and a Cornell tee shirt.

She paced herself through the afternoon with her cigarettes. She didn't usually smoke so much, and also wanted to make her cigarettes last, so she smoked no more than one cigarette an hour. If she didn't notice, she would sometimes go an hour and a half between smokes. She was getting a lot done; reading through her economics notes, reviewing the history prelim and preparation guide the history professor had handed out, and reviewing the French quizzes for the semester.

When she stopped to light her cigarette, she would look out the window, or at her refrigerator with the noisy hum, and blow the slightly blue smoke in a steady stream out from her lips or nostrils. And every time she smoked, Althea pictured George with two cigarettes in his mouth lighting the match. God, he had been cute. She stood up, went into the bathroom, and picked up the rose as she checked herself out in the mirror. Then she brought the rose back and put it on the table as she studied. No reason to let it go to waste in there.

She studied straight up to eight p.m. when she got hungry. She had no food, and didn't want to go onto campus for cafeteria food, so she walked down the block to the University Deli. Inside there was a line of six people waiting for sandwiches and submarines to be made by the two girls wearing hairnets who stood behind the counter. Althea read the list of offerings on the board high up on the wall. She never liked the way the Uni Deli smelled. She thought it smelled like old lettuce. But their food was actually okay.

Althea ordered a Greek salad with extra garlic bread, and paid the boy at the register. Then she moved off to the side to let the person who had been standing in line behind her reach the counter while she waited to get her dinner.

When she saw it was Caitlin Fossburgher, she literally flinched. Caitlin was five inches taller than Althea, and her long, deep-red hair flowing behind her made her seem even bigger. Caitlin was smiling at the boy at the register, and ordering a turkey submarine with oil and vinegar and all the toppings. Althea was staring. She had probably seen this girl before and never really taken notice, but now she was here, soaking in her freckled skin, and pretty face. She really did flow like a swan, Althea thought as Caitlin moved away from the counter.

For some reason she wanted to make eye contact with her, but Caitlin was looking at a notice posted on a bulletin board. Caitlin looked like a bit of a granola head, but so what? Then the thought crossed her mind to tell her about George. If she were Caitlin, would she want to know? Of course, she actually didn't know much about their relationship. Her salad was put up on the counter for her to claim. Caitlin looked up and then resumed reading the items on the bulletin board. Althea picked up her salad, and headed out the door. It was too much. She had to go back and study.

The next day and the next day happened. Althea took one examination on Monday afternoon, and two on Tuesday. She had one scheduled on Wednesday, and her last final on Thursday. But that one would be easy. She felt lucky. There were some people who actually had finals on Friday and Monday after that.

On Wednesday she took her history final in the morning, and headed back to her apartment to study for the afternoon. Matthew had called to say he wanted to bring pizza over for a quick dinner so he could say goodbye before they left for the summer. It was hot out, and there was little cover between campus and her street, so Althea was moist with sweat by the time she arrived home. She stripped off her clothes, and took a quick, cool shower, before she changed into something fresh to study in. Even with the heat, she was comfortable in her halter top and white short-shorts. That ought to turn Matthew on a bit, she thought.

As she worked through the afternoon, she smoked through her second pack of cigarettes. She had used up her matches, and every hour or so, she'd turn the stove on, wait for it to turn red, and then hold her head down with the cigarette between her lips to light it. Smoking was actually pleasant in the heat.

Matthew arrived at six fifteen, with a large pizza from Johnny's Big Red Restaurant. Johnny's had a hot truck on campus and also had a pizza place a stone's throw from Althea's apartment. Matthew was in a snit. He had taken two finals today, and had to take two more Thursday. Althea commiserated with him.

Into your preppy look? she asked, teasingly. He was wearing Nantucket red shorts and a white polo shirt. Matthew smiled and looked down and off to one side.

Althea stood up, and put a cigarette in her mouth as she walked to the stove and turned it on. Matthew asked her what she was doing.

I'm out of matches, Althea said matter-of-factly. She disliked the way he was always commenting on her smoking.

Matthew grimaced slightly. He didn't mind her smoking, but he only smoked on rare occasions. He would have preferred she smoke less.

Well, I shouldn't be encouraging you, but here. I've been carrying these around for you since Saturday anyway. He pushed his hand into his shorts and pulled out the pack of matches he had scooped up from her railing. As he handed them to her, he asked if he could use the bathroom, and Althea said of course. She turned off the stove, and returned to her studying spot at the kitchen table.

Althea opened the matchbook, pulled off a match, and struck it on the grit. It didn't light the first time, so she threw it in the trash, opened the book again and started with a fresh one. This time her eye caught something on the inside of the cover, so after she had lit her cigarette, she inhaled, put her foot up on the other chair and took the matchbook into her hand. She could hear Matthew's tinkle splashing in the toilet.

She held the matchbook up with one hand, and opened it fully. This is what she saw:

A –
I'm
Smoking
For
You.
  G.

Althea exhaled the smoke from her mouth in a rush. She blinked her eyes, read it again, and then burst into laughter. She couldn't stop staring at it. That bastard! But then the thought of it began to make her giggle. Actually, she loved it. This was just too much. Somehow, her elegant boyfriend with the nice clothes had been carrying George Muirfield's hot innuendo around in his pants for days. And he had handed it to her just as he had been chiding her about her smoking. The smile on her face was enormous when Matthew came out of the bathroom.

What? he asked curiously.

Althea tucked the matchbook into a nearby textbook, and didn't miss a beat.

I was just thinking about how sweet it was of you to have matches for me.

Matthew smiled. Sometimes he thought Althea was a little dense. But she had one hell of a body.

CHAPTER FOURTEEN

I n the fall of 1975, music invaded the soul of Eta Chi. And it started, presciently, at the moment the boys returned from summer break, driving and flying from all points on the compass to Ithaca, New York. It started with one boy, a sophomore from New York City, who had spent the summer staring out at an empty sky from his uncle's barn in rural Ohio. As the clouds scrolled past, he smelled the hay and dreamed of many things as he listened over and over to The Jimi Hendrix Experience.

So the boy made a tape of *Are You Experienced?* that played the title song sixteen times. If he had known how to tape the song once and then fix the tape so it repeated, he would have. But he didn't know how to do that. So he just taped the song sixteen times. Eight per side. Then he drove from Ohio to Eta Chi in time to be sure he would arrive before anyone else. He left at ten p.m. and got to the house at eight in the morning. On the way, he didn't listen to the tape. He played the Rolling Stones singing, *You can't always get what you want.*

When he arrived at the house, he carried his stereo upstairs, but instead of going to his new room, he bumped the door open to Harold Wise's room on the third floor. Harold and Fritz were going to be roommates in a double that looked out over the front yard. He set up his stereo so that the speakers were wedged in the window, facing the yard. And then he waited until he saw the first car pull into the driveway. He was lucky he left early, because Charles Lord felt it his obligation as consul to be at the house when everyone arrived, so he arrived at nine fifteen. Charles was just getting his large-framed body shaken loose from his drive when the song started to bleat from the third floor. Charles looked up at the speakers sticking out from the window and chuckled. Ehoo, ehoo. The static-y, hypnotic shuffle beat of sound that opens the song gave way to Hendrix, and the year began. The song kept playing.

Danny Carvello had tapped his left foot and bopped to the music on his radio from Massachusetts to Ithaca, and jumped out of his little, blue Volkswagen beetle a bundle of nerves. He had spent an impatient summer doing engineering clerical work at General Electric, thinking about the coming fall. He walked up to Charles Lord and saluted, then giggled, and exchanged the secret handshake with exaggerated flair.

What the hell is that? He asked the consul. They both looked up at the third floor. Danny dipped his eyebrows toward the center of his face in a mock scowl, and shrugged. Then he began to walk back to his car, dipping his right shoulder to the music.

George Muirfield's maroon Camaro squealed into the parking lot, and swung itself next to Danny's beetle. George looked out his window as Danny approached.

The two boys greeted each other excitedly, and began to lug their belongings into the house. Soon many cars slowed as they approached the semi-circular driveway, and began to crowd the parking lot. Jim Steuben was let out by a taxi. Fritz Hublein carpooled with two sophomores from upstate New York. Wally met Cullen Hastings at the airport and they met a sophomore from Hawaii, and the three of them commandeered a taxi van to transport all their luggage together. Two cars from New Jersey arrived convoy-style, and four boys piled out. One of the cars was driven by a boy's mother, who looked uncertainly at the speakers blaring "that psychedelic music."

Around two p.m., which was the scheduled time that all brothers had been asked by the social chairmen to arrive, Harold Wise was driven into the parking lot by his sister who was dropping him off. The parking lot was totally jammed with cars, and boys were walking all over the property. Two brothers leaned out windows, watching the others. Harold pulled himself out of the car, and looked up at his room.

What the hell!! Harold yelled. Forgetting his sister and the car, he marched right to the front of the house. His new roommate was standing at the door, and Harold asked him what the hell was going on.

Fritz told him that someone had set up a stereo in their room and that the same song had been playing for hours.

Whaaaaat? Harold said. Then he started up the stairs, muttering Uh-oh, Uh-oh. Ohhh-no. A moment later the boys at the door heard the music go silent, and saw the cassette tape coming flying out into the yard.

Heyyy! Jimmy Dunbar yelled. That's my tape! And then the stereo was blasting again. Only this time, Earth Wind & Fire were singing –

Hearts of Fire, create love desire,
Take you high and higher to the world you belong

Hearts of Fire, create love desire, high and higher
To your place on the throne
We come together on this special day
To sing our message loud and clear (Mmmmn)
Looking back we've touched on sorrowful days
(Wooowww)
With future pass they disappear...

Woman don't you hear me now, don't you hear me now
Woman don't you hear me now, woman won't you hear me now

Harold was leaning out the window above the speaker. Boys were standing in the circular grass cheering. And then everyone started to dance. Charles Lord was doing the Monkey again, and even Jimmy Dunbar started shaking his shoulders to the beat. There were at least fifteen boys at cars, or standing in the grass, waving their arms and stepping to the beat. Then Danny Carvello stepped up on the bumper of someone's car and shouted, HAVE MERCY, LISTEN TO ME, YEOW!! That's how it began.

Holly Menard couldn't get the katydids out of her head as she sat in the backseat of her parents' Ford Country Squire. For some reason, both her parents had decided to make the drive to Ithaca from Dover, Massachusetts, where the katydids hid in the tall grass outside Holly's window. Usually her mother drove her up to school, and helped her carry her things into Kappa Psi. They drove without the radio on so they could talk. Holly's father, a high school chemistry teacher, was trying to talk to Holly about premarital sex. Her mother looked out the window, smiling. She knew it was a little late for her husband to be having this discussion, but it didn't hurt anything. She had made sure her daughter was on the pill.

Holly listened to her father stumble through the biology of reproduction, the need to be careful about diseases and the natural desires of boys. It was as if he was instructing a class. She pictured Charles sitting in the backseat with her, with his hand over his mouth trying not to laugh. But she didn't mind. She loved her dad, and liked the fact that he was trying. Outside, the New York countryside flattened out and rolled slowly toward Syracuse. By the time they were past Schenectady, the katydids had been replaced by the hum of the tires on the throughway's macadam, which was louder and scratchier sounding than the smooth pavement of the Massachusetts Turnpike.

Holly was looking forward to seeing her sorority sisters and the boys at Eta Chi. She had that same churning in her stomach that had preceded every first day at school since kindergarten. Cornell was such a beautiful place to go to school, and it was so familiar to her, now that she was a junior. When they turned south on Route 81, she could barely wait. She was so excited it was hard to concentrate.

Lucy Fitzwaller pulled into College Town in her Ford Pinto, going too fast. She loved to drive on the old back roads into Ithaca, and was listening to the college radio station. Her thick hair, now dyed blond, was flying around from the rush of warm air coming through the open windows. She wanted to reach the apartment before Bob, so she could walk into the place and make it hers. She loved living with him, but somehow wanted to feel ownership of the place, even though they shared it fifty-fifty. Her parents knew that she was living with Bob, and didn't love the idea, but she had been independent and strong willed her whole life, so they knew better than to argue. Besides, she was twenty-one, and would be on her own at the end of the year anyway.

Bob Woodbridge knew about his girlfriend's idiosyncrasy, and made sure that he did not arrive at the apartment until five in the afternoon. He had gotten to Ithaca around one p.m. and spent the time at the house, reconnecting with the brotherhood. He loved Eta Chi, even though he spent less and less time there. In a competition, his girlfriend won ninety percent of the time, and she only liked to go to the house when there was a big social function where she could dance and flirt with the cute brothers. When she wanted to egg Bob on, she would talk seductively about coming on to one of the innocent little sophomores. That always got him going.

When he got to their place at five, Lucy had already unpacked her things, and popped the cork on a champagne bottle as he walked in the door. She was wearing a loose fitting silky shirt, and had her hair pulled back and around over one shoulder. Her skin glistened from the moisturizer she had applied. Hubba, hubba, Bob said when he looked at her. Damn Lucy, you are one sight for sore eyes. She handed him the wine glass filled with champagne, and said, welcome back big boy in the best Mae West she could muster. But they had been away from each other too long, and the whole exchange felt sort of forced.

Althea Redmonton's younger brother was accompanying her on the trip back to college from their home in Vermont. He was seventeen, and wanted to go with her, and then drive the car back by himself, and their parents had said okay. Her brother was going to be a handsome kid, but he was still kind of awkward, as if he had not grown into his own body yet. He lived a separate life from his sister. Even though their rooms were back to back, they really didn't see that much of each other in the summers when she was home. He had an odd collection of friends, and she teased him about how weird they seemed. One of his friends wore a Mohawk in honor of his football team, even though he wasn't on the squad. Another always shook his body as if he was trying to shake off the demon, which he did to make the others laugh. Althea burst into laughter when her brother told her that they fantasized about her all the time.

When they reached Ithaca, Althea took the long route that let her drive past Eta Chi. She had been thinking hard about George Muirfield, whom she had not seen since that one night at his fraternity. She pointed out the house to her brother, and the thought of being back at school when she could find a way to bump into her Wild Boy was making her nervous and energetic. She had gone over to Eta Chi to see him before she left school for the summer, but in the words of the boy at the front door to the fraternity, George had already swooshed out of here two hours before. Something about needing to get home, the boy added over his shoulder as he walked back into the dining room where he was studying. He left her standing in the foyer, near the mailroom.

Eta Chi was quiet when she drove past, and she and her brother continued on to her apartment, which she had not even bothered to sublet during the summer. She liked it just the way it was, and it brought a smile to her face when they pulled the car into the little driveway. When her brother helped carry her bags in through the kitchen, he said, "Cool."

Martha Higgins shoved her suitcase into her closet at Delta Gamma Nu in a snit. She had been a wreck for the last two weeks, and the fray on her nerves had been exacerbated by having to get back to school. It wasn't that she was unhappy to be back. It was actually a relief, because the summer had been so hard. She had gotten a room in New York City through a friend, in a nice apartment on the upper west side. It hadn't been too expensive, and the summer had started out so promising. She was interning at Bloomies. Or at least that's what they called it. She wasn't much more than a glorified sales clerk, but she had been told that this was a great way to get her foot in the door as a junior buyer when she was ready to graduate, and retail seemed like so much fun to her.

Then she had met people easily, and the summer was working out perfectly, before she missed her period, and knew something was wrong. She felt different, somehow, and wondered if she could possibly be pregnant. How could that happen to her? She had been having sex, of course. It was theoretically possible, but she thought it was highly unlikely. If she was pregnant, it must have happened before she left school. As she went back over her last weeks as a sophomore, she knew it was a real possibility. Still, it was so unlikely.

Then she had realized she better find out, so she went to a clinic where they drew her blood, and called her three days later with the news.

I have great news! The woman on the telephone had said. You're pregnant!

Thank you, she had replied, and hung up the phone. Then she looked for the telephone book, and flipped to the yellow pages, and looked under "abortions." There wasn't anything listed. Then she looked under fertility clinic. She found eleven listings, called the first one, and asked if they did abortions. No, they didn't, but they gave her the name and number of a clinic that did. She called that number, made an appointment, and hung up the phone. There was no question that she had to have an abortion, and have one fast.

Three days later, she left the clinic in tears. She had tried not to think about what an abortion did, or how it might feel. The waiting room had been filled with girls of all ages, including one woman in her late thirties who was telling the teenager next to her that it was absolutely the right choice for her, and that she couldn't let the boys in her life control her. Then it was Martha's name that was called, and she had gone to a little room where a nurse explained what would happen, and asked her to change into a hospital gown. The bed that she sat on as she talked to the nurse and swung her legs was stiff, and covered with a flimsy white rolled paper.

A different nurse asked her to follow her, and Martha stood up, clutching the back of the open johnnie so people could not see her fanny. Her fanny was simply too large for people to see. But there was nobody behind her to look. She followed the woman, who was older, and acted tired, into a room where she was asked to lay down and put her feet up in the chrome stirrups. She did, and then she waited for hours. It was actually minutes, but that's how it felt. Then the doctor came in. He was young, efficient, impersonal. Martha thought he would be handsome if he only loosened up a bit. Then he told her what she could expect. She had had images of scraping and scalpels, but he told her that he was going to suction the fetus out of her. It was like a large, industrial vacuum.

Afterwards, she thought about the pain, and how much it had hurt. She was so relieved it was over, she wanted to party, but her body told her to go home and rest. She ended up in bed for two days. When she got back to Bloomies her supervisor for the summer tisked, and suggested that Bloomies interns had to work through little colds. She replied that her uncle had died, and she had gone home for the funeral. Then she had looked levelly at the supervisor, and asked her if her uncle was still alive. The supervisor walked off with a shrug.

So here she was, only four weeks later, back in her sorority room, waiting for her new roommate to bop in all cheerful and excited about the year, and she felt like screaming out the window. She was pale, had not been able to get any sun the last few weekends, and she was miserable. No one had forewarned her about her emotions. No one had told her about the remorse and sinfulness that pervaded her thoughts. No one had told her that her body had to physically and physiologically unravel the complex hormonal transitions that her body had begun when the sperm met the zygote. And she couldn't for the life of her get her goddamn stupid suitcase into the fucking closet.

Caitlin Fossburgher was sitting in the passenger's seat of her father's Buick, quietly panicking about her return to school. Her parents had given her a car over the summer, but something happened to the engine, and it had to be repaired, so her father was driving her up to school and coming back for her in two weeks so she could get her car. He was a little grumpy because he had bought her the car to avoid having to drive her back and forth to school. But he loved his daughter unconditionally. He would drive her to Alaska if she asked him to. But Caitlin had been so hostile the last several days that he realized she must be nervous about returning to school. He hadn't a clue why.

Caitlin was waiting in her mind to see George. She had to see him and understand what he was doing. She knew already that he had moved on, but it was important for her to understand why. They had left for the summer without real plans about how to communicate and see each other. Caitlin realized over time that this had been intentional on George's part, or at least in his subconscious. She spoke to him three times the whole summer. Twice she called him. Once he called her. Getting together was clearly not in the picture. It had been four weeks since they had spoken. The pit in her stomach was huge. She was convinced that the reason had to be some other girl. And she knew instinctively that George had slept with her. That had to be it.

She had to get rid of her father and get on with it. It was going to be awkward, but she still loved the dumbbell and needed to know. She saw that he had obviously chosen to take the easy route. In a way, this helped her resolve to remain celibate until her marriage. There was a beauty to celibacy, a spiritual independence and honesty that the people around her could not reach. George had turned out to be just like the rest of them, apparently. She had had high hopes for him, but so be it.

⌒⌒

At Eta Chi, the brothers met at four thirty on the first day to receive the duty rosters that had been prepared by the house managers. There were eight teams with team captains assigned to dust, wash and vacuum the downstairs, rake the yard and sweep the driveway. The kitchen had to be scoured after a summer of misuse by the few boys that had stayed on. The entire wooden ceiling of the great hall and all of the downstairs woodwork needed to be cleaned and rubbed with linseed oil. The dining room needed to be emptied, the floor waxed, and every window washed inside and out. Fall clean up took the brotherhood four full days.

The mood throughout the house was jovial and energetic as the boys rekindled friendships and laughed about their summers. The newer brothers had to be shown the ropes, and were generally amazed at the industry and care the seniors and juniors took to make the house immaculate. And through it all, Jimmy Dunbar's stereo, which he had moved from Harold's room to the great hall, blasted out music – Earth Wind & Fire, Barry White, Aretha Franklin, The Supremes. Danny Carvello snapped his fingers and hummed as he walked through the house. Harold Wise tried to match Barry White's deep, resonant voice. And four sophomores – Joey Padillo, Rick Frye, Hank Broussard and Dexter Billings – lined up in the Great Hall just like Diana Ross and the Supremes and delivered a spirited interpretation of *Stop In The Name of Love*.

Three of the boys stood in a line behind the fourth boy who took the Diana Ross role, and ran through the whole finger pointing, arm-rolling act as the song blared out from Jimmy's speakers. The boy pretending to be Diana Ross swooned around in front of them, mouthing the words dramatically. The rest of the room stood still for a moment as the performance unfolded, and then erupted in applause and laughter. Quintin Wells, a senior, and a self-proclaimed surviving member of the Old Guard, watched from the second step where he had been heading up to the second floor with cleaning materials. This was unusual, he thought. He wasn't accustomed to boys singing like girls. It made him a little fidgety.

By Saturday afternoon, the house shined, and the boys were ready for the last weekend before schoolwork loomed over their heads. Joshua Finch answered the payphone in the mailroom, and went to find George Muirfield. George and his roommate had taken a tiny suite of two rooms on the third floor, and it took Joshua a minute to remember which room was theirs, and climb the two sets of stairs to get there. George asked who it was. Joshua said he didn't know. George ran down the stairs to the phone and said hello.

Hi George, it's Caitlin. George couldn't tell, but Caitlin was fidgeting furiously with a button on her blouse. George said hi softly.

I need to see you, she told George firmly. George agreed. He suggested they meet at the Straight, and Caitlin's jaw dropped. She couldn't believe how impersonal and cold a choice that was. Why couldn't he just come over to the apartment? Fine, she said. What time George? The anger in her voice was spilling through the phone line. George breathed in and out, and said, Four? They agreed on three.

At three p.m. George walked into the Straight and headed for the huge sitting room behind the main entranceway where they had agreed to meet. The ceilings were forty-feet high, and tall windows lined the top ten feet of wall on all sides. Below the windows, ornate wooden paneling gave the room a clubby feel. Oversized, comfortable chairs and couches were discreetly positioned throughout the enormous room to create a sense of privacy.

George saw that Caitlin was not there yet. He was pleased he had made himself be on time. He sat down in one of three large leather chairs, and waited. Across the room he watched a boy sitting by himself in a chair, silently mouthing words and ticking his head convulsively. The boy had long, stringy hair and a beard. The entire time George was in the room, the boy did not stop his imaginary dialogue with the spirits that apparently surrounded him.

Hi George. Caitlin stood over him. She was wearing shorts, and a sleeveless, ribbed top. George could see the graceful lines of her figure, and the smooth skin of her legs at eye level to his face. He looked up. Hey.

Caitlin took the chair next to him, and leaned over across its arm to be able to speak softly. George thought she looked beautiful. Her hair was pulled back in a loose braid, and her eyes were bright.

So, how was your summer? She started off. This was going to be harder than she thought.

George exhaled. It was long and quiet, and nice, he replied. Yours?

I want to know what happened, George. I think we have been together long enough to merit a discussion before we just walk away from each other. Caitlin had chosen her words carefully. She felt like she was about to vomit, but she had to make this a mutual act.

George looked almost longingly at the girl whom he knew better and liked more than anyone else. He was not going to be able to explain himself to her. He couldn't tell her that it was him he didn't trust. That he could easily end up in a ferocious hug with her right now, and spend the next two years arm in arm with her. That he was so comfortable with her that this was as painful for him as it was for her. That if he had gone to see her in the apartment, he knew he would have ended up with her on their bed, whispering to each other, and feeling a temporary remorse for his summer behavior.

What he could not explain, because it was buried too deeply in his subconscious, was how different everything now seemed. How the theater was now frivolous and childlike, how Caitlin struck him as unrealistic and idealistic in a world where neither of those traits were valuable. How life now seemed starker and more serious. How his eyes now saw purpose instead of a rainbow. He cleared his throat.

This would be so easy, Caitlin, but it wouldn't be right. As weird as it sounds, I have way too much feeling for you to be dishonest, and that's what I'd be doing.

You're already with someone aren't you? Just tell me. Have you met someone else?

George thought about Althea Redmonton. That was someone he had "been with" in ways he had never been with Caitlin.

Yes. He felt like he was lying, and this made him look guiltily to Caitlin.

And you've slept with her, haven't you?

What???

George, you have. I can see it in your face. And that's okay. I just needed to know.

George felt like laughing at his own predicament. Of course he had slept with Louise, over a year ago. And he had certainly wanted to sleep with Althea, for one, more recently. But he felt violated by the way that Caitlin was accusing him.

Caitlin, that's none of your business. I can tell you with total honesty that that has nothing to do with this. He put conviction in his voice.

I knew it, Caitlin said, nodding to herself. So. This is it. I am okay with this George. I can see that we are not on the same plane anymore. Actually, I think you're right. I'm glad we didn't prolong this.

Caitlin reached over and kissed George on his cheek. He could smell her skin, and her warmth. I did love you George. Take care of yourself.

George watched Caitlin walk away. She wasn't wasting any time. George felt the hole in his stomach turn, and worried that he had done the wrong thing. Then he shook his head, looked across at the boy who was furiously debating something in silence with the imaginary people around him, and stood up to head back to the house.

In the seventies, the legal drinking age in New York was eighteen. If boys were old enough to be sent over to fight for their country in Vietnam and come home in body bags, then they were certainly old enough to drink beer in a tavern. States all over America lowered the legal age. So the bars in Ithaca were plentiful, and packed. The university even provided bars in the residential campus student unions that were open seven days a week from four in the afternoon until midnight.

In College Town, bars lined the main street and the byways. There was the Number 9, a bar modeled after Fire Engine No. 9, which everybody called the Nines. Bartenders stood behind the shell of an old fire engine which took up the entire middle of the bar, and served kids four deep at the bar. And there was a new bar called The French Connection, just two doors down that offered a more upscale feel, but which also smelled overwhelmingly of popcorn. The popcorn was free, and constantly popping.

On the road that bordered West Campus, The Chapter House stood on a corner about four blocks beyond campus. It was an older bar originally themed to address the popularity of fraternities and sororities. But the décor had not changed since the fifties, and the inside was a wide open wooden floor where people stood and drank in front of pictures from the forties. A small eating area with a limited menu was off to one side, but food was not served on weekend nights when the overflow of people just wanting to drink and flirt with each other took the entire space.

Downtown, there were any number of bars, but the most popular was The Haunt, a place with both free popcorn and a roaring gas fire in a round open hearth where you could put your feet up on cold winter nights. That was a favorite Friday happy hour spot, with ten-cent beers and lots of people looking to jump start the weekend. Every weekend looked best on Friday afternoons at happy hour.

There was also the Fall Creek House, known affectionately in Eta Chi as "The Creeker." The Creeker was off the beaten path, below Eta Chi in a residential neighborhood. When the boys from Eta Chi (or one or two other houses) weren't there, it was more of a local pub than a college bar. So on the first Saturday before classes, The Creeker was the last place the Eta Chis were going to head. After all, the only girls who went to the Creeker went with them.

Danny Carvello had gone to Charles Lord Saturday morning and asked how he might help lead the social efforts of the fraternity. He knew that the social chairmen were elected posts, and he wasn't trying to interfere, but he wanted to be a part of it all. Charles enthusiastically agreed, and called Harold Wise and Stoobie over from their work detail to see what they thought. Harold and Stoobie were the social chairs for the fall semester.

It was agreed that Danny would be great at organizing the Eta Chi freshman tea. In the middle of October, Eta Chi held a tea for freshmen girls that were known on campus as a special and highly selective formal affair. Invited freshman girls had two Eta Chis dressed in suits and ties knock on their dorm room door and present them with an engraved invitation on heavy stock stationery. The envelope was addressed with each girl's name in calligraphy. When the girl thanked them and afterwards began to inquire about it, she would hear that it was an honor and that she had to go. Many girls went out to buy dresses and have their hair done, once it was described to them.

What Danny was asked to do was organize the selection of the girls for the tea. Charles and Harold and Stoobie explained to him that only the best looking girls in the entire freshman class could receive invitations. They suggested he start with the freshman picture book, but it was important that all girls proposed for invitation be examined personally before their names were added to the list. When Danny asked whether it was indeed a tea, the boys giggled and explained that yes, it was held in the afternoon, and tea and finger sandwiches were served. But there was also a punch that was always heavily spiked. Danny needed no more prompting. He was a man on a mission.

By Saturday evening, Danny had sought out dozens of brothers and given them strict instructions to be on the prowl for terrific looking freshmen. Don't waste your time with the sophomores and juniors, he warned. Zero in on the girls who look like they don't know where they're going. And get names!

The boys enthusiastically responded to Danny's exhortations. When George walked back in the door from meeting Caitlin, Danny reminded him of his important obligations regarding the freshman tea. George looked at him bewildered. He told Danny he was unaware of this. Danny looked strangely at the junior.

I thought this was a big deal. You're a junior and don't know anything about it?

George told him he had been off on other adventures last year. Danny nodded. Well, you're now commandeered onto my committee. Want to come with me tonight? We have to start our advance scouting immediately! Danny's enthusiasm was a welcome tonic to George's confused state of mind. And it sounded like a lot of fun.

Althea Redmonton telephoned Holly Menard Saturday afternoon to ask where she would be going tonight. She wanted to go out, and she didn't want to go alone or with Matthew. She had told Matthew she'd find him at the Nines. She wanted to go with Holly so that she'd be able to bump into George Muirfield, or at least get some fresh information about him. She looked at the matchbook with his message written on it. It was open and held by a stick pin on her little bulletin board. She had kept it in her room all summer, and had stuck it in her pocket when she headed back to school with her little brother.

Holly was so up that Althea could hear the rush in her voice. Everybody was going to start out at the Nines, and see what led from there, she told her friend. They agreed to meet at seven thirty at the bar. Althea got off the phone and poked through her closet, trying to decide what to wear. She had several new outfits she had bought with her mother in August. She picked out navy blue culottes with a simple white jersey that she would tuck in. It was a little too preppy for her, but it would show off her tan and was only good until about mid-September when the summer warmth unraveled. She had a sudden urge for a cigarette, and sighed. It had only been four weeks since she had quit.

It was eight in the evening before the first Eta Chis crammed into a car and headed for College Town. The bars would serve until one and be open until one thirty. There was plenty of time. Some of the boys started at the Nines, and some at the Chapter House. Danny, George, Charles and Buzz Delaney decided to start at the Chapter House. They parked as close as they could, and agreed that the rest of the night would be walking. If they got separated, it was only a twenty-five minute walk back to the house anyway.

Danny moved quickly through the crowded bar, surveying the scene. Within minutes, he was talking to a tanned blond girl about five-feet ten, who wore a Lily Pulitzer dress. He guessed that the dress was a dead give-away that she was a freshman, but it turned out she was a sophomore. She also wanted nothing to do with him. She was waiting for someone, she told him politely. Absolutely, he replied. I was looking for a freshman anyway, he said. He spread his hands and pushed them out from the sides of his face as if to say Oops! before he walked off.

George asked him how he was doing. He told George he had met one sophomore dyke, and they both laughed. Then two girls walked in the front door and asked them if this was the Chapter House.

Bingo, Danny said. George smiled and said Yes it is!

They were about the same height, and smiling broadly. Danny asked them if they were graduate students and they giggled and said they were freshmen from New Jersey.

You must be the only two! There's a quota on female freshmen from New Jersey this year. Danny was nodding and smiling at the two girls. The girls glanced at each other questioningly, before the girl on the right laughed hard.

My god, she said, I am going to have fun at college!

George was looking at each of the girls, trying to decide whether they were pretty enough for the freshman tea. They were cute. Danny sug-

gested that the girls circulate through the bar and get to meet everybody.
The girls giggled and walked deeper into the bar, and Danny turned to
George. If you have to ask yourself, then they don't make the cut, he said
simply. Then he was gone.

George went up to the bar and waited until the bartender got to him.
He asked for a boilermaker, and the bartender nodded. He placed a beer
glass under the tap that said "Genesee Pale Ale," and while it was filling,
he poured a shot of whiskey and put it up on the bar. George drank the
shot, and took the beer while he handed the bartender money. The bartender grabbed the shot glass off the counter, rinsed it, and moved on to
the next customer. George had always listened to his grandfather talk
about boilermakers, and had always wanted to try one. The whiskey was
rough, but the beer chaser tasted great.

He was about two thirds done with his beer, and had started talking to
a brown haired girl next to him when he saw Holly Menard and Althea
Redmonton walk in. His pulse quickened. Then he saw the blond haired
boy from Althea's apartment walk in behind her. He returned to talking
with the girl next to him. Inside him a jumble of flashes were going off.
The girl next to him was actually quite good looking. She had shoulder
length shiny hair and high cheek bones. George asked her if she was a
freshman, and the girl groaned and asked if it was that obvious.

George smiled and said no, he had no idea. He felt something inside
himself, and stopped moving for an instant. And then he smiled brightly
to the girl whose name he did not know yet.

What did you just say? he asked her. It got too loud for a second. The
girl leaned up to his ear and asked him if he could tell her what other bars
were popular around here. He nodded, excitedly. Deep in the middle of
his insides, his center was slowly spinning, and gaining momentum. He
was back. It was like an adrenaline rush.

He suggested that he could walk her up to College Town since he was
headed there anyway. She looked dubious. It's all right, he told her, I'm
not asking you on a date, you can even walk behind me if you want! The
girl looked strangely at him, and said she might. George told her to take
care, and walked out of the bar. He could have cared less about the girl.
And besides, he had had to ask himself, so she didn't make the cut.

Althea Redmonton watched George through the little window in the
front of the bar. She slipped her finger along the front waist band of her
culottes. She had seen him talking to a girl at the bar who was clearly not
the swan, and then he had walked out alone. Had he seen her? Of course,
if he did, he undoubtedly also saw Matthew who had latched onto them.
Until she saw George, she had been having a nice time listening to Matthew's churlish account of his summer in the Hamptons.

Althea was standing next to Holly, who was looking up at Charles
with a big smile on her face. Althea thought Holly was one of the most
perfect looking girls she had ever met. She had a fresh, classic look. But

the steadiness of her temperament made her come across a bit frosty until she really liked you. Althea looked at Matthew standing across from her, trying to talk to Charles over the din. He was almost as tall as Charles and he was leaning close to him, grinning about something.

George walked quickly up toward College Town. He looked back once to see if the freshman was following him, but was not surprised to see she had not. His center was twirling, and his energy level was higher than it had been in months. He smiled happily as he walked. He thought about Althea Redmonton wistfully, but was in no mood to get himself wrapped up in someone who was involved with someone else. He knew what that was like. Still, when he walked past the little market in College Town, he abruptly turned and pushed the wooden screen door open to see if they sold cigarettes. He had not smoked since the end of school, but he wanted to all of a sudden. And the freedom he felt to do it if he wanted, without disappointing Caitlin (or his father, he thought briefly), was delicious.

He said hello to the boy behind the counter, who said nothing in return. George asked him for Camel Lights, and the boy searched in the rows of cigarettes for the brand. He asked George whether he wanted hard pack or soft pack, and George said soft. Althea's pack had been soft, and it felt better in your pocket than the hard pack did. The boy put the cigarettes on the counter and placed a matchbook on top. The matchbook cover said "Lucky Strike."

George left the market and walked up to the Nines. He knew he'd find a bunch of his brothers there, and decided he would find at least one freshman worthy of the freshman tea. The Nines was even louder than the Chapter House, and George pushed his way through people holding long necked bottles of Budweiser and Miller and green, fat Heineken bottles, until he found someone he knew. Cullen Hastings was talking animatedly with Jimmy Dunbar, and they slapped George on his back heartily. What are you guys doing? George asked.

We're in search of the bionic fuck, Jimmy yelled over the noise.

George nodded seriously. I'm afraid to ask, he yelled back. Besides listening to the Jimi Hendrix Experience all summer, Jimmy had watched reruns of the *Six Million Dollar Man* on television. Lee Majors had six million dollars of bionic enhancements, giving him superhuman abilities. George had not really considered *that* kind of bionic enhancement before.

Just picture the Bionic Man with Wonder Woman, Jimmy yelled. Think about the possibilities! That's my goal this year!

Cullen Hastings was laughing and wagging his head at George. George asked them if they had found any freshmen women yet, and they nodded negatively.

George felt himself bump into someone and turned to apologize. One look, and he prayed the girl behind him was a freshman. He told her he was sorry.

What for? She yelled, smiling. George explained that he thought he had bumped her, and the girl giggled. I've been bumped all night, she answered. George saw that her beer was about empty, and asked if he could get her a beer. She nodded her head vigorously. She had a boy's haircut, short and parted. George could smell her perfume. It was clean smelling. He told her he'd be back, and started to make his way to the bar. By the time he got back, he wondered if she'd still be there, but she was. She was a freshman.

They had been talking and laughing for awhile when George spied Danny Carvello, who raised his eyebrows and nodded his appreciation from across the room. The girl with George was stunning. High cheekbones, a fine, straight, model's nose, and a genuine, toothy smile. Danny made it over eventually, and George introduced them. Before long, Danny had the girl in stitches, and George winked to his brother and headed off. George had had enough of her already. They had talked past each other, amiably, for long enough and needed an excuse to part.

It was eleven thirty before George saw Althea again. He was at the bar, which had thinned out enough for him to be standing at it with three of his brothers. She walked in with the curly-haired guy and Charles and Holly. The four of them walked up to the four boys at the bar, and everyone was greeting each other. George looked at Althea, looked away, and then looked back. She was standing next to Holly and smiling at something Charles had said. Finally she looked at George and tipped her head slightly and said, Hi George. George stuck out his hand, and told her he was glad to see her again as they shook hands. Her hand was warm, and she gripped his hand firmly, and for a long time.

Matthew Stollings saw some of his fraternity brothers and wandered over to them for awhile. Holly was watching her friend and George musingly. The energy between them that each of them was trying to ignore was obvious. Holly asked George how his summer had been. He looked at Holly as he answered, felt Althea looking at him, listening. His neck was hot. He asked them if they had ever had a boilermaker. They hadn't, and wanted to know what it was. When he described it, Holly wrinkled her nose in distaste, and said, Not for me! Charles was handing her a gin and tonic.

George looked at Althea and asked her if she was game. Althea smiled so brightly at George he wondered if she was one of those girls that make fun of everyone behind their backs. Then she told him she was ready to try anything, and he sidled up next to her as they asked the bartender for two boilermakers. This bartender filled the two glasses of beer first and set them on the counter in front of the two. Then he poured two shots of whiskey, and ceremoniously held them above the beers, before he dropped them into the beer. Shot glass and all. The shot glass was sitting at the bottom of each of their glasses and the whiskey was swirling up through the amber ale.

George looked uncertainly at the bartender. Was this a joke? The bartender acted normal. So George picked up his glass, clinked it against Althea's and said, You learn something new every day, before he took a long pull on the drink. The whiskey in the beer was strange, but not as disgusting as it looked. Althea took a sip, and George said that these were obviously not meant to be sipped. They both laughed. As Althea took a much larger gulp of her beer, George fished the cigarettes out of his pocket and held them up for Althea to see, smiling.

That was the first time their eyes had really met, and they looked at each other carefully for a minute. Althea put her hand on George's arm, and leaned her face close to his, so she could say something softly into his ear. He could feel her close to him, and smell her skin. Her whisper was slightly hoarse –

I haven't smoked in a month because of you.

It wasn't true of course, but Althea had been thinking furiously about how to bridge the moment she opened his matchbook last spring to now. It was the best line she could think of. And it sounded cool.

George was looking at Holly who was watching them, and at Matthew whom he could see across the bar behind Holly. Althea pulled herself back, and looked evenly into George's eyes. She slipped her finger along her waistband again, unconsciously. She knew that she had lost ten pounds over the summer, and looked good. George stared at Althea. He could sense no one else around him. But he grasped that what she was saying was somehow true.

Neither have I, he finally said. Althea tucked her chin in and wiggled her head slightly as she continued to look at him, and he laughed loudly. Charles and Holly looked over for a moment, but then resumed talking with Cullen Hastings. George asked if she thought it was a good idea for them to start up again. Smoking, he added for clarification. Althea wanted a cigarette so badly, she could taste the tobacco in her mouth and nostrils. George saw her nostrils flare.

He withdrew two cigarettes from the pack and handed her one. Then he pulled out the Lucky Strike matches, smiled as he pointed out the cover to her, which made her beam, and lit her cigarette first. When she put her hand on his as he did, George thought he was going to explode. His center was spinning like a top, and glistening. He realized that she must have gotten his message on the matchbook from last semester. Everything seemed possible.

They smoked the cigarettes together, inhaling as they looked at each other, and then looking away to blow the smoke up at the ceiling or toward their feet. George felt the same rush and dizziness as last time. Althea said she felt dizzy, it had been so long. I know, George replied.

Matthew Stollings wandered back over and stood next to Althea. He was about four inches taller than George, slighter, and tauter somehow. Matthew stuck out his hand to George and introduced himself. George did not look at Althea again that night. He was polite, even boisterous with Matthew, and they stood there for at least twenty minutes. He did not once return Althea's glances. Inside he was roiling, like a little dinghy in six-foot swells, but no one would have known it. Except Althea, who had the exact same sensation, and felt the same seasickness. Then George said goodbye, told Matthew it was nice to meet him, and walked off briskly to catch up with Cullen Hastings who was headed out the door.

By the time George woke up and found his way to the bathroom Sunday morning there were two boys standing in front of the bulletin board at the top of the stairs, looking at photographs of freshmen girls, which had been cut out of the Pig Book. The Pig Book was the register of photographs of all new students. Danny had cut out about twenty-five of the best photographs of girls and scotch-taped them to a poster board. He had hung the poster board next to the bulletin board, and placed a long sheet on the bulletin board itself, entitled, "Freshmen Tea Nomination List."

The boys were arguing about one of the girl's photographs. The boy on the left swore that he had met her the night before and there was no way she was that good looking. The other boy was challenging him based on the photograph, and suggesting that either he had not seen her, or that he had no taste, he wasn't sure which. Then the first boy asked if the other had a pen, and when the other boy handed one to him, he wrote on the poster board next to the girl's photo, No Way!

George looked at the girl's picture. The photograph was obviously professionally done, and he recognized the care that had gone into making it. It was like a photograph from his stage productions. He opined that she may not look quite as good as the picture. The boy who had seen her, said, SEE? The other boy just shook his head. George looked over all of the pictures that Danny had cut out. Girls' faces looked out from the photos, trying so hard to be...beautiful. George wondered aloud whether effort affected beauty.

Then he left the boys as they scanned the rest of the pictures, and walked downstairs for brunch. He saw Jimmy Dunbar coming in the opposite direction and said good morning to him. "Beep," Jimmy responded to George. George pulled his head up and gazed at the boy who was walking so close to the wall his hand was brushing it. Jimmy's head was slightly lowered, and off to one side.

Beep? George asked.

Jimmy picked up his face a bit, and his long, straight hair drifted to the left so he could look George in the eye. Jimmy's blond hair hung the full length of his face on both sides. He had a lean, nondescript body. George could see only one of Jimmy's eyes.

Beep, Jimmy said again, looking away.

George raised one eyebrow and shrugged. Okay, he answered.

Jimmy Dunbar was a physics major. He would tell people that you had to be a little strange to be a physics major. No one was ever sure whether he acted strangely because he felt he needed to be in order to be a physics major, or whether he really was odd. But in any event, Jimmy was a character, as George discovered on his way into brunch.

At brunch, George ate an enormous plate of scrambled eggs and sausages. He was ravenously hungry. There was a coffee urn on a table near the door to the kitchen, and George refilled his cup four times, as he sat and watched people come and go to brunch. The coffee was hot, and bitter. The room was warm and the air floating through the window was humid.

Danny walked in and sat next to George. He congratulated him on scoring. George smiled. You think so, he asked?

Danny nodded his head slowly. She's confirmed, Danny told him. George was thinking about Althea, but he knew Danny was speaking about the short-haired one in the bar. George thought Althea Redmonton made all of the women around her look like margarine. But he understood that for the purpose of the freshman tea, he was going to have to come around.

In the first week of classes, George had to face what he had been avoiding since last spring. He knew already that he was not going to try out for the fall plays. But he had not actually concluded it with finality. He did not know what he had already planned in his head. But breaking up with Caitlin somehow went hand in hand with breaking up with the theater. It was not until Friday, when he knew tryouts were to take place, that he stood in the Straight, staring at the bulletin board at the notice of tryouts in Goldwyn Smith Hall. A girl came up behind him and tapped him on the shoulder. It was a girl from his freshman biology class named Carol. They each said Hi! excitedly, and George asked her if she wanted to go downstairs for something to eat.

Carol said she'd love to, and George looked one more time at the notice, and then turned his back on the both the theater and the bulletin board. Carol had the shiniest deep blond hair he had ever seen, and it still glimmered the way he remembered from biology. They had flirted a little freshman year when George was just becoming serious with Caitlin. Then the prelim results had come back, and Carol had rushed into George's arms in the Straight and started bawling. George had held her tightly, then asked her what the trouble was, and she told him that she had scored a 31 on the prelim. George nodded and giggled. She stopped sobbing for a moment and looked at him.

What's so funny?

I got a 27! You did well!

George had meant for it to be funny. But Carol backed away from George horrified. You got a 27 and you think it's funny?! Carol was from West Virginia, and her accent made her indignation sort of sexy.

George shrugged and grinned and started to explain, but Carol told him she didn't need to associate with boys who flunked out. That was the last time George had talked to her. Now he was walking behind her down the wide steps to the cafeteria, and admiring her hair and wondering what this might bring. Carol was lithe, almost flat from head to toe, and her chin came to a pretty point. She was tinier than George remembered.

They ate lunch and talked for almost two hours. George was happy to sit with her, and he entertained her with stories from freshman year, but puzzled over the entire incident. She didn't seem to be flirting with him, and yet she wanted to keep talking with him. The Straight cafeteria emptied out. It was Friday and most people were headed for happy hour somewhere. George finally asked her if she wanted to go for a beer, but Carol shook her head no.

George, you are a good person. George nodded, noncommittally.

When I saw you at the bulletin board, I just came up to you...because I...

George raised his eyebrows and cocked his head ever so slightly. Go on, he said.

I just needed someone to talk to.

That's okay with me. It's been nice. I only asked you if you wanted to go to a bar for fun, he assured her.

No, no, that was fine. Can I just tell you something? George told her that she could absolutely tell him something.

Over the summer I met this guy. George's antenna went up.

Anyway, I got pregnant. George nodded. She didn't look pregnant.

So I couldn't have a baby, and I...took care of it. George took this in, smiled and said he understood, and how could he help?

Carol looked at George carefully.

You just did, I guess. I just needed to tell someone. I couldn't tell him. I sure as heck couldn't tell my mom. When I got back to school, I just kept thinking about it. It eats away at me, like you wouldn't believe. This afternoon I have been walking around telling myself I have to stop thinking about it. Then I saw you upstairs. You swear you will never tell a soul, right?

Suddenly the fact that she didn't know this boy made Carol skittish. She felt so stupid to have told him. What might he do?

George told Carol that he knew no one to tell, and he wouldn't tell anyone. He told her she had done the right thing, and that she shouldn't feel bad about it. Jesus, he said, why worry so much? Her reaction told him that hadn't been the right thing to say, but he had meant it. He asked her what religion she was. She was a Methodist. Well, he said, I don't know about Methodists, but I am a Catholic, and I still believe you did the right thing. It's what I would have done. He shook his head firmly once for emphasis. He had not known until then that was what he believed. But he was adamant.

They spoke for another twenty minutes or so. Carol thanked him for listening. They picked up the trays they had used and brought them to the gray conveyor belt that carried the trays behind a wall. George walked the girl upstairs and outside into the hot afternoon air, and patted her on the shoulder. Then he headed up onto the Arts Quad, to walk to Eta Chi. Carol watched him until he disappeared, and then turned in the other direction to go see a friend of hers in College Town.

On his walk down to the suspension bridge, and across it, George saw Matthew Stollings lying on the grass not far from the suspension bridge. He was lying next to a girl with their heads close, and George strained his eyes to see if it was Althea. It clearly wasn't. Then the girl raised herself up on her elbow and leaned over to kiss Matthew. Matthew put him arm around the girl. George smirked to himself, and moved along out of view. He had sworn to himself that he was not going to call Althea. He had even begun to stop thinking about her. And now this.

Of course Matthew Stollings had just done nothing more than what George had done with Althea last semester. It meant nothing. Or maybe nothing. It could mean everything. Even if it meant nothing to Althea, or to Althea's relationship with this guy, it meant something to George. Matthew Stollings was putting Althea in play by kissing this other girl. George smirked again. I hope she's worth it, he said in his mind to Matthew Stollings, because I just caught a break. He pumped his fist excitedly. And when he reached Eta Chi, he walked to the pay phone, inserted a dime and dialed her number from memory.

There was no answer. George was undaunted. He headed up to his room on the third floor. As he rounded the newel post on the second floor he heard singing in the far room opposite the staircase and twirled around to see what was happening. It was Rick Frye's room. Rick was George's little brother in the fraternity. In the middle of the room, four sophomores were standing in formation, singing the words as Diana Ross sang *Ain't No Mountain High Enough* on the record player. Half a dozen boys lay on the bed and floor around them, calling out instructions.

No, no! You've got to twirl your arms the opposite way!

Come on, belt it out! I can't even hear you over the record player!

A couple of the boys acknowledged George, but then returned to their instructions. One of the boys in the Supremes fell out of line, saying he'd had enough, and another boy on the floor leaped up and took his place. The music was pulsating through the room. It was four p.m. and a number of the boys were drinking scotch on the rocks from Rick Frye's Dewar's bottle on the bureau. Rick insisted on making George a drink, so George slumped down against a wall, and began sipping scotch. It had the smooth burn that no other whiskey can match, but it still burned.

He was watching the boys try to imitate the Supremes, and thinking about Althea Redmonton. They switched the record back to *Stop In The Name Of Love*, and two boys picked themselves off the bed and insisted they get a turn. They had obviously been at it previously, because they worked right into the rhythm of the song and embellished their movements in unison. The boys around them hooted. Rick insisted his big brother have one more scotch. Come on, big bro, he said smiling. Bottoms up.

Rick Frye was 158 pounds of skin and bones, and about a million freckles. He had sandy, short hair, and a nasally way of speaking. His upper lip tended to curl slightly when he talked. He was an engineer, and a party person. He was also a staunch Republican, and often started heated debates about politics. He loved Richard Nixon. Richard Nixon should still be president. That was for sure.

That night George drove himself to the bars. First he drove past Althea's house, and prepared himself to stop in if she were home. There were no lights on, so he drove past, turned around in a driveway farther up along the road, drove back past slowly to be sure, and then headed for the Nines. It was the obvious place to start looking. Unfortunately, he didn't need to look far. Althea was sitting in one of the few booths with Matthew, and another couple he didn't recognize. He wondered for a moment if the other girl might be the one from this afternoon, but shook his head to tell himself not to be stupid.

He had not been prepared for this of course. So he walked up to the bar and ordered a Dewar's on the rocks, and then turned around to get his bearings. There were no Eta Chis in sight, which made him nervous. He couldn't just stand there by himself. He didn't realize that Althea had seen him at the bar and was studiously avoiding looking his way in hopes he would not see her. She had waited all week for his call. And now this.

George drank his scotch in one long gulp, and motioned to the bartender for another. The bartender looked at him for a moment, refilled the glass, and then told George to take it easy. George nodded sheepishly, and smiled. He turned back around again, and saw Matthew get up and head for the bathroom. In retrospect, he would always be proud of this moment, though he would claim the Dewar's helped.

He walked straight to the table after Matthew strolled away, and stuck his hand out to the boy who was sitting opposite Althea. George Muirfield, he said pleasantly. The boy said his name but George didn't listen. The unfamiliar girl smiled up at him. George turned to Althea and said, Althea I'm sorry to interrupt, but would it be okay if I spoke to you about something for a minute?

He turned to the other boy and girl, and told them it would just be a moment. He was sorry. He needed to ask Althea something personal.

He looked back at Althea who was staring at him with her eyes wide.

It's not anything bad, he went on, just come outside for a sec so I can find out something about someone you and I both know. Althea looked at the other couple and told them she'd be right back, with a shrug of her shoulders.

Outside the night air was still warm, but beginning to cool. You could smell fall coming. George took Althea's hand, and walked around the corner of the bar. Althea asked what he was doing, and he just pulled her gently along into the cover of the building's shadow in the gathering night.

Come here, he said, and pulled her close to him. This is important. He could feel her hands, which were damp, and see apprehension in her face.

Is this all right? he asked after a moment. He was still holding her hands, and felt his chest move from his breathing.

Yes.

George released her hands, put his hands around her head, and pulled her face up to his. He could almost sense her tense up, so he stopped moving, and simply gazed at her. Their eyes met and caressed each other. Then he kissed her. Althea felt his lips, tasted the scotch from his mouth, and wrapped her arms around his shoulders. She was shuddering. He had one arm around her head and the other around her waist, and was pulling her to him. She felt their noses touch and his hand on her back. Their legs pressed firmly together. George finally pulled himself away slowly, but kept their waists tight together with his hand on the small of her back.

Althea was looking at him and smiling uncontrollably. She didn't think she had ever been in love before, and wondered if this was how it started.

I want you, George whispered simply. The words were flat, declarative. His eyes were almost defiant. Althea didn't breathe. Me too, she finally said.

George let his hands drop and backed away slightly. He gazed up at the side of the building beside them, and then returned to looking at her. Her eyes looked almost totally green in the faded light.

Aren't you needed back inside? he asked her carefully. Part of him wanted to yank her down the street. Althea put her hands to her temples. She thought for a minute.

Meet me somewhere in one hour, she said firmly. I can't just walk out and never come back.

George squinted his eyes for a moment, and tried to picture himself with Caitlin. He hated it, but he thought he would want time too.

One hour? he asked. Althea reached up and kissed him hard. It started to last too long.

So she pulled away and told him one hour. He told her he'd be at the Chapter House, and walked away without another hesitation. Then he stopped and watched her as she reentered the bar, pulling her skirt down as she walked through the open door. He pumped his fist again as he headed down the hill to the other bar.

Matthew Stollings may have appeared nonchalant but he was shrewdly observant. He paid attention to the way that people held themselves and the way they posed. Had he watched Althea enter the bar, he would have immediately noticed something in her haste, or preoccupation, and stewed over it. But he was listening to his roommate's story about being a pizza delivery boy all summer when Althea came up to the table and said she had to go to the ladies' room. He looked at her and smiled and told her he'd ordered her another drink while she was gone.

Althea went to the bathroom, and put both hands against the wall when she got inside. She was going to have to regain her composure, but it wasn't coming easily. She kept reliving how George had dragged her into the shadows and kissed her. It made her feel like she was blushing. But when she looked in the mirror, she didn't look flushed. She looked radiant, and this brought an enormous smile to her face. Goddamn, she said to the mirror. She went to the bathroom, reapplied her lipstick and took a deep breath as she headed back out. She didn't have a clue what she was going to do.

Are you okay? the other girl asked her when she sat back in their booth. She told the girl she was okay. She mouthed the word "cramps." The other girl nodded in appreciation. Matthew wanted to know what what's his name wanted. All three people stopped to hear.

He likes one of the Kappas, and he thought I could tell him whether she was available, and where he could find her tonight, Althea said in a rush.

Matthew put his arm on the back of the bench behind her shoulders. Which one, he asked curiously. Althea said Suzie, without thinking. It was the first name that popped into her head. She wished she hadn't said it, since Suzie had been the one in the mailroom with them last spring, but it was too late.

Matthew offered that he didn't think Suzie was very attractive, and both girls immediately protested. The girl sitting opposite Althea sort of looked like Suzie, but she wouldn't think that, Althea guessed. She had just complained on principle. Matthew and his roommate began to talk again about the summer, and Althea made small talk with the girl. It was easy to smile and nod, and the other girl thought Althea was enjoying the conversation. Althea felt Matthew's roommate looking at her. He was always doing that. Althea thought his leering a bit creepy, but he never hit on her. Then he asked her if she was okay.

Althea looked at him, questioningly.

You look sort of pale, he explained.

Matthew turned and examined his girlfriend, and asked her if she was okay. She told them she was fine, just a little out of sorts. Girl stuff. The boys chuckled. Then Matthew's roommate suggested they try out the Chapter House next, and Althea felt her heart drop. She looked at her watch. She guessed about half an hour had passed since she came back inside. And now the four of them were headed to him.

She could have told Matthew she wasn't feeling well. He would have believed her – it wasn't the first time her menstrual cycle had kept her home. She could have taken Matthew aside and just said to him that she was breaking up with him. Or that she needed to do something else tonight. But she didn't. She wouldn't say it to herself, but she wanted to keep Matthew somewhere in her life until she understood what this incredible thing with George Muirfield was all about. It wasn't that she didn't trust her instincts about George. He was all she could think about, and she even believed she could feel him when they were apart. But there was still something, an unknown quality to their connection, that led her to want to hedge her bets.

So she went along with the group's idea to go to the Chapter House. She spied George the instant they walked in. The pub was packed with people, but she looked directly to him and widened her eyes to signal a problem. He was standing with three boys she recognized as Eta Chis, and they were talking loudly to each other. George had no visible reaction to seeing her with Matthew and the other two. But she felt the twinge of his seething in her stomach. There were dozens of people between them, and George turned his back to talk to his fraternity brothers. Althea felt like she was breathing in unison with him, and he turned curiously to look at her when she exhaled with her lips pursed.

Matthew left the others to go to the bathroom, which was past the spot where George was standing. He pushed his way between people standing in every possible direction, and his path brought him right next to George.

Hey! Matthew said, in a friendly way. Still haven't found Suzie?

George laughed noncommittally and nodded his head. He didn't have a clue what Matthew was talking about, and didn't want to. Matthew tossed his head good-naturedly, and kept snaking his way to the bathroom. George looked quickly over to Althea who turned and walked straight out the door to the outside. George handed his beer to his fraternity brother and told him to finish it if he wasn't back in five minutes. His fraternity brother nodded, and took the beer in his left hand as he drank from the beer in his right.

George shuffled through the crowd to the door, looked back around toward the bathroom, and walked outside. It took a moment for his eyes to adjust to the darkness, and then he saw Althea facing the other direction about twenty yards away. The streetlight illuminated the swell of her hips from behind. He approached her and she waited until she could feel him directly behind her and then she turned and pulled him into her arms. Her mouth was on his, and he managed to pull her with him onto his lap as he sat himself on a stone wall to her left. She was heavier at first than he expected, but her soft, round frame cradled gently into his arms and legs.

Their kissing was a mixture of insistence and languor. When George opened his eyes, so did Althea, and they pulled their lips apart by an inch. George asked her what they should do. They could feel each other's breath. Althea moved slightly and felt his erection against her khaki skirt. George's right hand slid up and down the soft material of her blouse, along her backbone. Whatever reluctance about Matthew had been in Althea's head melted away. She looked at George levelly, and as George began to feel himself pulled down the rabbit hole, Althea told him to take her home.

And that was that. George lifted her in his arms as he stood up, let her gently down, and the two of them walked arm in arm to Althea's apartment in the back of the big white house with the little driveway on the side. They barely spoke, and their minds were racing. When they reached the door, and entered the kitchen area, neither of them knew exactly what to do next. They stood looking at each other and smiling. I think I hear my heartbeat, George finally said.

Making love with George that first night was a different experience for Althea. She had slept with two other boys, Matthew and that silly kid from high school, and both of them had been pretty straightforward about it all. But making love to George was like a swirl of increasing passion that took forever to get started. They had lain on her bed, first in their clothes and then slowly in fewer clothes until they were naked. They had left a little light on in the kitchen, and Althea watched George take in her breasts and stomach and legs and arms as he lay there next to her. They were facing each other with their heads propped up on four pillows, gazing at each other with building anticipation. The air that came in through the window at the head of the bed felt cool, and gave them both goose bumps. Their breathing seemed to syncopate, and then increase, and then finally he was on top of her and inside her and their bodies rocked together for a long, long time.

For George, the wait for Althea – the portend of her body and soul joining his in what he envisioned to be an ultimate possession – was so consuming that when he actually touched her, felt her breasts and her hips and the crook of her elbow in his hands and mouth, it was almost too much for him to bear. The roundness of her body and the soft warmth of her skin became symbols in his mind for what passed between their eyes and mouths. He was in a dream state.

And when, the next afternoon, they were making love for the third or fourth time, having barely been apart from each other's touch in fourteen hours (the exception being when each used her little bathroom), the world was defined by their nakedness inside the walls and the windows of Althea's tiny place. George was sitting up with his legs apart in the middle of her bed, as Althea straddled him with her legs behind his back. Her arms were draped loosely around his neck and they were gazing at each other with locked intensity. They had been in this position for some time, and barely moving when Althea felt herself giving way and unraveling. She began to move more, her breathing turned ragged, and she experienced her first orgasm with a boy.

Afterwards, she pressed her face against his shoulder and began to cry softly. George held her tightly, knowing intuitively that her weeping was a natural, and not distressful act. The word love formed in Althea's mind, and George immediately stroked her arm and told her he knew. Althea looked at him, half in fear and half in awe. They were both exhausted, and sore. Like it or not, it was time for them to rest.

George suggested they eat and drink, and peeled himself away from her to walk naked into the kitchen to see what Althea might have in her cabinets. There was basically nothing. He fished the cigarettes out of the pocket of his pants that lay on the floor and lit one in his mouth and blew the smoke up at the ceiling. Althea approached him, put her hand on his shoulder, pressed her breasts against his back and took the cigarette from his hand. She inhaled deeply, exhaled and said she was going to get in the shower. George took the cigarette back and told her he wasn't sure he could bear being away from her that long. Try, she said, and went to her bathroom. George watched the bathroom door close behind the bare curvature of her back. He pulled on his pants, picked up his shirt and shoes, and left a note on the table. "Back in a sec."

Walking to his car made him realize how sore he actually was, and this made him giggle uncontrollably. He drove to a little strip of stores downtown where he knew there was a liquor store, but thought he also remembered a little grocery. He bought a six pack of Narragansett beer, a fifth of Popov vodka, and a bottle of Greystone champagne. In the grocery, he had hoped to find something for dinner, but there was nothing that made sense, so he purchased orange juice, cranberry juice, a loaf of French bread, two cans of Geisha white albacore tuna, Hellmann's mayonnaise, Wise potato chips and a head of lettuce. There was no iceberg, so he took romaine. It had been close, but he still had enough money left for another pack of cigarettes, which he guessed might come in handy.

Althea was sitting at the kitchen table when he returned. She rose quickly, and gave him a long kiss as he stood at the door with the bags in his hands. Then she pulled away and told him not to do that to her again. He said okay and handed her one of the bags. You told me to try, he said sweetly. She asked him if he was sore. He assured her he was.

Too sore?

After they were finished, George sighed and said that maybe he really was too sore now. Althea cupped herself in his arm as they lay on her bed. She asked him how long soreness was supposed to last. He replied that it was his understanding that soreness usually lasted about half an hour, and they both laughed as if they had been hilariously funny. George got up, opened two beers and brought one to Althea, still lying on the bed. The sheets were strewn all over the floor, but she had pulled her bathrobe over the middle of her body and watched him as he moved through her apartment. She rose and took two pillows and walked to her couch and curled herself up against them to sip her beer. George found a can opener and mixed the tuna salad, cut the French bread length-wise, fiddled with the stove until he got the broiler to work, and laid the bread on the oven grate. He looked in the cabinet for spices. He found black pepper and cayenne pepper, and dosed the tuna salad heavily with the black and lightly with cayenne, and then remixed it.

He washed the lettuce under the stream of water in Althea's tired looking sink, shook it hard, and then pressed more water out of it and laid it on the counter. He found two plates, removed the bread from the oven as it started to crisp, smoothed the tuna mixture down one entire length, covered it with the romaine and placed the other length of bread on top. Then he cut it in quarters and divided the sandwich onto each plate. He opened the chips, spilling some on the plates, and brought them to where Althea was sitting.

The entire time Althea had been watching him, and occasionally saying something, she marveled at his naked frame. He was completely uninhibited as he moved around in her little kitchen. He acted as if no one was there to see his rear end, or his sex. He put the plates down, and walked over to the bed and pulled his boxers on. Then he mixed two strong drinks with the vodka and the cranberry and orange juice, and sat down opposite Althea in her chair as he handed her one. This is good for soreness, he told her. He took a large gulp of his drink.

Then a look of concern came over his face, and he paused. I hope you like tuna fish, he said. It was all I could find. Althea took a large sip of her drink and nodded. I do, she said. The naturalness of their exchange frightened her. So much had happened in the last twenty-four hours that this seemed surreal. And the thought of leaving Matthew in the bar last night returned to a corner of her mind.

CHAPTER FIFTEEN

On Sunday evening, Eta Chi held its first Chapter meeting of the year. Charles Lord rapped a gavel to bring the meeting to order, and suggested that they review Robert's Rules of Order to ensure that the meeting was conducted fairly. He asked the pro consul to begin, and the boys listened carefully to his recitation of the key elements of the structured meeting format. Charles was not predicting any disputes, but L.E.O. Pennington had complained to him that certain measures put up for vote tended to be ram-rodded through without regard to proper voting, and could thus be deemed invalid. So Charles had gone to the library and taken out the little abridged version of Robert's Rules.

He followed the format in the book and asked for procedural issues (there were none), old business (it being the first meeting of the year, there wasn't any old business either) and then came to new business. Joshua Finch raised his hand and said he wanted to make a proposal. Charles asked him to describe his proposal, and Joshua explained that the proposal was to eliminate the dress code at dinners, except for formals. Someone along the back wall seconded the proposal.

We have a second, Charles intoned officially. Is there any debate or commentary?

A number of hands were raised. Charles was watching the faces of the brothers carefully. This topic was always a lightening rod, and he never knew which way to lean. He personally thought the dress code was stupid, but he didn't exactly object to the dress code, either. The will of the majority should prevail on the topic. The vehemence with which so many of the boys in the Old Guard decried the loss of propriety and honor when this topic was raised was simply lost on Charles.

As the debate unfolded, Charles watched the veins of conservatism surface in a different collection of people than he might have guessed. Danny Carvello and Frank Deming, whom he would have thought would ardently support abolition of the dress code, sided with Stoobie on the importance of maintaining their image. Harold Wise, and Rick Frye who sounded like they were politically to the right of the John Birch Society, wanted to see the dress code eliminated. There were people in the middle like Cullen Hastings and George Muirfield who thought that there needed to be some philosophy about the dress code, rather than continual votes about it. Whatever that meant.

In the end, the vote to abolish the dress code was struck down, but then another boy proposed that the dress code be reduced to Mondays and

Wednesdays. This brought fresh debate, but finally passed by a slim margin. Joshua Finch had a wide smile and a vacant look in his eyes for the
rest of the meeting.

Date Nights began the following Wednesday, and an unusually large
number of brothers brought dates. Harold brought Martha Higgins. Stoobie escorted Mitsy Smith, who wore a pair of white slacks and a black
top. Holly was there, of course, with Charles. George showed up with
Althea Redmonton in a simple tan dress that accented her tan and outlined
her figure. Jimmy Dunbar arrived with a girl no one had seen before. She
looked sort of macho, with short hair and a strong chin. Seeing her caused
Harold Wise to lean over to Cullen Hastings and suggest, That one would
tear you apart! Bob Woodbridge came in just as dinner was about to begin, squiring Lucy Fitzwaller on his arm. Lucy waved to boys she knew
and the simple bangles on her arm clinked as she did.

After dinner the boys rose and stood behind their chairs and sang the
Darling song to Holly. Althea had sat next to Holly and she looked openly
at George as he sang the song looking directly back at her. If you had
asked George where Holly was in the room, he wouldn't have been able
to tell you. But Holly was looking at George and Althea with a maternal-
istic grin. She was so excited that they were together, and that it looked as
if Althea would be with her a lot at Eta Chi. Althea seemed so peaceful
for a change.

Some of the sophomores who didn't have dates and had sat together
at a far table, put their arms around each other as they sang. They looked
at each other occasionally and smirked as they sang. One of the boys,
Jack Ellis, could not hold a tune, and raised his voice mockingly to make
it look like he was singing off key on purpose.

After dinner, Harold told Martha that she had to come upstairs and
see what he and Fritz had done to their room. Martha was glad to be out
and social again. Life was returning to its normal form. She followed her
date and Fritz up the stairs to the third floor. They turned right and walked
down a dark corridor to their room on the left at the end of the hallway.
As she entered their room, she stopped and gawked. The entrance was all
black – the walls *and* the ceiling. Their room was U-shaped, and the entrance was like a narrow hallway of its own, until you walked to the
bottom of the U and turned into the room. From the doorway, your eyes
went down the little corridor to the far wall with the window that looked
out onto the front yard. The floor was bright red. Martha thought it resembled a haunted house at an amusement park.

When she followed Harold into the interior of the room, Harold
turned to see her expression as he rubbed his stomach and laughed heartily. The entire room – every square inch – was painted red and black.
There was not any uniformity or pattern to the colors. A six by six wood
beam that protruded about ten inches into the room from one wall was

painted black on all four sides, and red on its face. The ceiling in the interior was red, and the floor was black, with a tan throw rug covering about a third of the wood flooring.

Harold put on a Barry White record, as Fritz described how they had worked all weekend painting the room. The colors had been Harold's idea. Harold asked his date what she thought. Is this a room to die for, or what, he asked her, beaming. Martha broke up laughing. It's a bordello! she cackled. The boys nodded. Precisely, they thought, winking at each other. Barry White's baritone was growling around them.

George and Althea had wandered upstairs after dinner so Althea could see where her new flame slept, and George dragged her down the hall when the music started playing. When they turned the corner into the bordello room, George yelled, Oh my god! Althea just stood wide-eyed. Barry White said, *You're my everything.* Althea had her hand stuck in the small of George's back, over the edge of his corduroys. She tugged on him to suggest that they move along.

Downstairs on the second floor, in the sophomore corridor, one poor brother started playing a John Denver record. As soon as *Country Roads* began, the boys up and down the corridor booed and hissed. David Dalrumple, a sophomore with large, pale eyes, yelled out that he thought John Denver was a homo. Everybody laughed. Then a few of the boys who had hooted the loudest at David's remark began to make up their own version of John Denver's song.

It took them some time and some disagreement, but by the time boys were heading up the hill to go the library, they were singing it at the top of their lungs.

Muddy Roads, take me home
To the place I belong
Up the Poop-chute
Hershey Highway
Muddy Roads, Take me home

Perhaps it was gallows humor, Quintin Wells thought as he passed by the corridor and heard the refrain, but it's all in good fun. Stoobie smirked and shook his head in mock despair as he walked by. He hoped Mitsy, whom he had left downstairs for a minute while he collected his books, couldn't hear them. Before it wound down of its own accord, most of the boys still in their rooms were singing along with gusto.

Stoobie and Harold had laid out the fall social calendar at the chapter meeting, to much applause. There would be a great variety of events, from formals with great bands, to keg parties and special Wells College nights. Wells College was a small all-girls college about fifty minutes from Ithaca. According to legend, Wells girls were easy and really wanted to marry a Cornell boy. So Harold proposed hiring a bus to transport the

Wells girls to Eta Chi. They could post notices of the party on the Wells College bulletin boards. And, Harold noted to much laughter, the posting would indicate that bus transportation would be provided to Eta Chi. It would not highlight the fact that return transportation would not be offered. Stoobie had shaken his head dramatically as if he couldn't control Harold, and the entire chapter meeting had hooted and clapped.

As Stoobie walked Mitsy back up the road to Delta Gamma Nu so she could change clothes and get her books, he invited her to the first formal, even though it was nine weeks away. Mitsy pushed her arm through his, and gripped him tight. She told him she'd love to go. She was thrilled that they were continuing to see each other, even though she wondered occasionally why he never tried to kiss her. When he said good night, he always kissed her formally on the cheek, and told her how lovely she was. The truth was Mitsy had grown attached to Stoobie. The strength of his character lent him a maturity and humility that she found charming. Perhaps soon she would kiss him differently.

The Eta Chis continued their hunt for the best looking freshmen girls over the next several weeks. The Pig Book was gone through dozens of times in rooms all over the house. Boys would come back to the bulletin board and put the name of a girl they had met at lunch, or with a friend, on the bulletin board. Their picture would be cut from the Pig Book and posted on the board next to the nomination sheet so other boys could comment. The list grew from the original twenty-five that Danny had posted to sixty or seventy by October First.

In the bordello room, Harold sat with Fritz and Ronny on Friday afternoon before they were to head out for Happy Hour. Ronny was leafing through the Pig Book, commenting on the pictures. My god, he would say, look at how ugly this one is. Why would someone like that send her picture to the school? Harold was nodding his head, but not listening carefully. He was thinking about Date Nights, and how to add some pizzazz to them. He had brought a girl every week to Date Night. He was the only one other than Muirfield and Carvello who managed to do it. Muirfield kept bringing the hot chick with the voluptuous body. Carvello brought a different girl every week, but they were always the same – thin girls with big, bright smiles that had that fresh-faced, dewy look.

As social chair, he thought it was his responsibility to do this if only to encourage others. This past week, he had invited a girl in his accounting class who was not very attractive, but whom he found sexy in a weird way. She was a thick girl. She had thick legs, a thick waist and eyes that didn't exactly look straight. But she had this wicked smile that made him fantasize about her during class, and he figured Date Night would be an easy way to explore things with her. It had turned out unbelievably. Boys gave him sideways glances when he escorted her into the dining room, but afterwards, when he showed her his room, she had pushed him on the bed and given him an incredible blow job. The whole time she did, she looked at him with her slightly crossed eyes. It was the most erotic thing that he could remember.

He pulled himself back into the conversation, and had a sudden inspiration. He heard Ronny say, No wonder they call this the Pig Book.

He said, THAT'S IT!!! Ronny and Fritz jolted at his yell, and looked at him curiously. Harold said, Boys, We're going to have a Pig Night!

He hurried on to explain. On one of the upcoming Date Nights, we'll tell everybody to bring the ugliest girl they can find to dinner. The more outrageous the better. That will get everybody revved up about Date Night. Ronny and Fritz told Harold he had lost his mind. Then he told them what had happened to him two nights back, and they told him he was positively disgusting.

On the next Sunday, before the freshman tea, the brotherhood of Eta Chi turned out in force to deliver the invitations. Earth Wind & Fire was playing loudly somewhere in the house as boys got suits out of their closets. Some boys ironed their shirts. All of them went to the bathrooms and carefully combed their hair. Charles Lord and Danny Carvello had stressed at the chapter meeting how important it was for all of the boys to be well groomed. First impressions, even at the door to a dorm room, were everything.

Harold Wise and Edward Stamer teamed up to deliver invitations. There were twenty teams of two boys, and each team had either three or four invitations to deliver. It was agreed that the best chance of delivering the invitation to the girls in person was Sunday evenings. Harold and Edward drove in Edward's green TRW to West Campus, and parked in the south parking lot.

Reminds you of rush, doesn't it? Edward asked his companion. Harold was humming That's the way of the world, and fixing his tie.

This is going to be awesome, he answered.

The first girl on their list lived on the third floor of West Campus No. 3. They walked in through the open door, past freshmen boys lounging on couches in the common rooms, and hopped up the steps to the third floor. One girl walking down the stairs said Wow! as they passed. They smiled brightly at her. Dorothy Versailles opened her door in her bathrobe. She thought it must be her friend from next door.

Dorothy Versailles? Edward asked. Dorothy nodded quickly. She looked at these two boys in suits and ties, cluelessly. Her blond, rumpled hair was still wet from her shower.

We're from Eta Chi fraternity, Harold said. And we would like to invite you to our freshman tea next Sunday. Harold smiled and nodded as he took in her face, and imagined the body hidden behind her thick, cream-colored robe. What a looker, he thought to himself.

Are you sure you're looking for me? Dorothy asked. I don't know anything about this.

Harold handed her the invitation with her name on the envelope in calligraphy. We're sure, he answered. He liked the kind of wild look in her eye. She was a tiger. Dorothy thanked them, and was looking at the invitation as she closed her door. She picked up the phone in her room and called her sister who had graduated from Cornell four years before.

Oh my god, you got invited to the Eta Chi freshman tea? Jesus, Dorothy, that's wild. It's like...god, I don't know. I am so jealous. I knew these three girls who went. They talked about it the entire four years I was there. You have got to go. And buy a dress!

Harold and Edward went to the next room on their list. It was locked so they asked the girl in the next room if the girl they were looking for was around. She told them that the girl was at the library. They thanked her, and slipped the invitation under her door. The last girl on their list was on North Campus, and they drove up there laughing about the coming party.

Edward told Harold he thought he had met the next girl, and wanted to do the talking. When they got to her door, there was loud Bee Gees music coming from inside. Edward knocked on the door, and knocked again after there was no answer. The music was turned down, and a girl peeked around the door cautiously. Can I help you? she asked. She looked behind her and giggled to someone in her room. Edward asked if she was Hope Woodbury, and explained why they were there.

You're kidding, right? the girl said. A boy's voice murmured from behind the door. Harold told the girl that they understood she was preoccupied at the moment, but that the brotherhood hoped that she would be able to make it next Sunday. The girl had gorgeous, chestnut brown hair that cushioned the sides of her face, and full, sexy lips. Edward was tongue-tied. She flashed her eyes at Harold and then at Edward, and pushed her face out into the hallway where they stood. Edward was holding the invitation in his hand, and she looked at it curiously.

Will it be fun? she asked softly. They assured her it would. She stuck her bare arm out and plucked the stiff envelope out of Edward's hand. Thanks!! She whispered, gleefully.

Looking forward to it, Harold told her. As they walked away, Harold turned to Edward, and put his hand on Edward's shoulder. Nice work Romeo, he said. Then he guffawed, and said, Did you see those knockers!! Harold himself had not been able to see anything, but his imagination had taken him places his eyes couldn't go. When they got back to the house, they told everyone about the girl they'd caught having sex, but who still agreed to come. That, gentlemen, Harold intoned, is the power of Eta Chi!

The boys worked hard to decorate the house for the tea. They rented nice linens for the tables, and placed fresh flowers in small glasses on all the tables. When Cullen Hastings asked where the flowers had come from, two of the boys working with him told him not to ask. Then one of the boys said that there were lots of flowers growing all around them, and the two boys chuckled.

Danny walked through the house surveying the progress, and was pleased. There were rented champagne flutes in rows on the table next to the punch bowl. Two boys were standing over a recipe and adding ingredients carefully. It was important that the punch be spiked, but delicately. He had Edward put his TRW near the front door, in front of another brother's 914 mid-engine Porsche. The Porsche didn't run, but it looked sleek.

The first three girls arrived at two, walking side by side in the pleasant autumn sun. It was warm enough that they didn't need coats, although one girl had a sweater thrown over her shoulders for the walk home. They had been at Cornell seven weeks, and were beginning to get their bearings. They didn't realize just how long a walk from campus it was, and were beginning to complain by the time they arrived. They were wearing short sleeve, plain cocktail dresses and medium heels. Then the house loomed before them, and they could hear chamber music floating out the windows.

One of the girls said Wow! The girl next to her said, Well all right! They had not really known what to look forward to, as this was their first visit to a fraternity. The majestic sweep of the house and circular drive, and the rock wall lining the property were more than they expected.

Two boys in suits were standing at the large oak front door with big smiles on their faces. One, a sophomore, turned to the other, and mentioned that now he understood why he could never find good looking girls when he was a freshman – they were all taken up by the frats! The other boy reminded him that "frat" was not an accepted word, and then the three girls were upon them. The older boy stuck out his hand, and said that it was his lucky day when the first three freshmen to arrive were also the prettiest.

The girls groaned, but smiled brightly. The boys showed them inside, and asked if they could get them something to drink, or would they prefer a tour of the house, since they were first to arrive? The girls looked at each other uncertainly, and said they thought they could just wait here in the main room for others to arrive.

Absolutely! The older boy concurred, and immediately introduced them to four brothers who were standing near the punch bowl.

Hope Woodbury, along with seven other girls, had called and asked for a ride to the tea. So boys were dispatched at exactly two p.m. to escort them. Fritz and Ronny had insisted that they pick up Hope Woodbury, the girl they had heard was having sex when Harold and Edward had delivered the invitations. When they got to her door, she popped out with a huge grin on her face. She was wearing a yellow and pink Lily Pulitzer print dress and low heels, and acted like she couldn't believe her own luck. Her brown shoulder length hair was combed out straight, and fell on either side of her face. She swayed as she talked excitedly to them, as the three walked down her hallway.

So this is really legit? she asked them coyly. Fritz assured her that it was indeed legit, and they were pleased to escort her to the tea. Ronny was looking at the girl's figure appreciatively, and thinking how much he liked her giggle. It was knowing and naughty. He leaned out to look toward her and asked if she would mind if they picked up one other freshman. Hope thought that would be fun. Fritz and Ronny looked at each other, and thought the same thing – this girl was wild.

They stopped at Donnelly Hall, an all-women's' dorm, and Ronny waited in the car with Hope Woodbury. Ronny was a realist. He knew that not every girl was going to be receptive to his advances. He was short, and had small dark eyes and a receding hairline. But he also knew that you never knew which girls would be receptive, so it was best to try every one. And he had an enormously appealing sense of humor, and could tease a laugh out of just about anyone. So he went to work slowly on Hope, asking her where she grew up, whether she had gotten tired of college yet, and what her favorite shampoo was. By the time Fritz returned with the second girl, Hope was laughing so hard at Ronny's stories about the kinds of shampoos he came across at the fraternity that she was holding her hand over her mouth. You never know, Ronny thought to himself.

The tea was in full swing by two twenty, and Danny Carvello was in his element. The girls in his line of sight were spectacularly dressed, well groomed, and distinctly good looking. The boys circulated among them in their suits, and a three man band played the flute, bass fiddle and piano in the library. The flautist was a woman in her forties in an aquamarine cocktail dress. She closed her eyes and concentrated when she played. When she opened her eyes, she watched the people dispassionately.

Danny was convinced he would find a girlfriend for himself in this convergence of beauty. And he loved the formality of these types of things. The girls were so clean and fresh and bright-eyed. It was that unspoken balance between proper decorum and delirious abandon that made the exchanges between boys and girls so exquisite. If he could just find a beautiful girl who was raised with real values, but who wanted to be both proper and crazy, his life would be complete. And where better to begin the search in his junior year at Cornell, than at the Freshmen Tea?

Harold, Fritz and Ronny had more immediate intentions, as they were hoping to score with someone. As Harold put it, it really didn't matter which one you ended up with when you stacked the deck this way. George, Cullen Hastings and Stoobie were more innocent about the whole event, and were just looking forward to being around beautiful women in cocktail dresses. It is fair to say that none of the boys were thinking about the ripple effect of the freshmen tea – that the eighty or so best looking women in the freshmen class would have a special place in their heart for Eta Chi. It was usually the first fraternity they were exposed to, and it was a class act. And that's what they would tell everyone who wanted to know for the next several years. Including their younger sisters.

By three thirty, the party had moved beyond awkward introductions and feigned exclamations to genuine socializing. The girls did not know each other and knew few, if any, brothers. But everyone was dressed in suits and cocktail dresses for the first time since arriving on campus, and the punch was starting to take effect. Certainly all the girls in the room were attractive (which, of course, led some girls to compete for attention). And the boys, although they spanned the spectrum when it came to looks, were smart, and funny, and exceedingly thoughtful.

Hope Woodbury had zeroed in on Harold Wise as soon as she saw him. She was a party girl, and while she had gotten a huge kick out of making those silly boys in their suits think her brother (who was in her room when they came calling) was an impatient lover, she was clearly on the prowl. Fraternities were supposed to be wild, and while she had guessed correctly about what to wear, she was a little disappointed that the party was so...boring. These guys were clearly not about to swing from chandeliers any time soon. Then she spied Harold, and saw an adventure waiting to happen.

Harold was engaged in conversation with Dorothy Versailles when Hope walked up and said, Hey there stranger! Harold smiled, and introduced Hope to, umm, Dorothy. Dorothy was tall and statuesque. She had an impressive head of long, blond curls, and a vacant look in her eyes. Harold had already concluded that nobody was home, so he concentrated immediately on Hope. Dorothy quickly moved off to the punch table.

So what happened to the wild fraternity parties I always heard about? Holly asked with a mischievous grin. She was looking at Harold's tie, which was black with white polka dots.

It's right here waiting for you, baby! Harold said pleasantly. Then Hope looked up in his eyes and Harold resisted an impulse to start rubbing his belly. He asked her if she would like to see the rest of the house, and extended his arm for hers. Hope pushed her arm through his, and the two walked toward the staircase.

Danny saw Janette Emilio across the great hall and stopped moving for a second. Who was that? He recollected the photographs from the Pig Book that they had taped to the wall upstairs. She was definitely different in person. Janette was quite slender, with shoulder-length black hair and creamy skin, and an enormously wide smile. She was wearing a medium blue cocktail dress and red open-toed shoes. She was the first girl that Danny had seen since he arrived this semester whom he actually wanted to know.

An hour later, the musical trio had stopped playing and was putting their instruments away. The sky outside was edged with blue wisps, and felt cold enough for a sweater. The wall sconces in the great hall cast an amber light against the walls and up into the rafters that glistened with linseed oil. Somewhere upstairs, music was beginning to flow faintly out the windows from record players. Some girls had left together to walk back to campus, but most of the girls accepted rides from the brothers they had met.

Fritz, Ronny and Wally were standing in the foyer, laughing with four girls who were thanking them for a nice afternoon, and talking about going out for pizza. Cullen Hastings and Stoobie were escorting two girls who looked tired and a little tipsy toward the front door. George was speaking seriously with a petite girl in the library where the musical trio had been. Harold Wise and Hope Woodbury moved down the steps from the second floor. Harold was adjusting his tie, and looking flush. Hope looked nonchalant.

Danny Carvello and Janette Emilio were sitting on a couch speaking softly to each other. Danny was on the edge of the couch with his hand on his chin. Janette was leaning back and looking at him. Danny turned to look at the scene and smiled. The freshman tea had been a hit. And he had met someone.

❦

Matthew Stollings was sitting in Olin Library. Olin was the graduate library, directly across from Uris. It was Sunday, and he was engrossed in his history paper which was due in a week. He loved to research but found the writing difficult, and he had to force himself to focus. He was at one of the large tables on the first floor, behind the row of desks that lined the wall of windows facing the Arts Quad. People he didn't know sometimes took other parts of the large tables where he sat, and he liked that. He enjoyed watching people put their things around on the table to create their own little space.

He looked up after a while and saw Holly Menard and Althea Redmonton push their way through the wide, flat metal arm that served as a barrier to the exit, and come into the room. He waved to them and they waved back in a distant, oh-no sort of way. He smirked at their reaction. Did they actually think he was going to engage either one of them?

He had been taken aback weeks ago, when his roommate told him that Althea had just walked out of the Chapter House. Eventually it became obvious that the Eta Chi – what was his name? – who had come up to the table in the Nines had whisked her away. He couldn't stand Eta Chis. They were so taken with themselves and their house. Matthew had rushed there briefly, but found Phi Gamma much more to his liking. Phi Gamms saw the world for what it was.

That night had actually turned out fine. Matthew ended up running into the girl he had been messing around with near the suspension bridge, and she was drunk. They had a great time, and he was still seeing her occasionally. He liked to see more than one girl if he could. If you focused on one, she always had too many expectations. It wasn't as casual and free as it was when you both understood that you weren't committed to each other. Matthew had enjoyed Althea, but he wouldn't have stopped seeing other people for her. He had to admit, though, she looked fantastic across the library from him.

After that night he had not seen Althea for a week or two. There was no way that he was going to call her, and he was getting preoccupied with the other girl anyway. But when he did run into her on campus, they had stopped and talked awkwardly for a minute. She had told him she was sorry about how she ditched him. He told her it was probably just as well, anyway. She cocked her head and squinted at him as if she was trying to read his mind, but he did not let her in. In his thoughts he was slapping her across the face, and then leaving her on the ground without another word. She had never seemed very bright to him.

Holly and Althea decided to go downstairs to avoid Matthew who waved to them from across the large main room in Olin. They both needed to study, and had opted to try Olin, to avoid getting into conversations with all the people they normally ran into at Uris. Holly pointed out that Charles and George were at the freshman tea today, so they wouldn't be around. Althea asked Holly what the freshman tea was, and Holly described how the brothers had a formal tea for freshmen women. Althea grunted and asked how the girls got picked to go. Holly said she wasn't sure, but she had gone her freshman year and had fun. They get all dressed up like it's a formal, and have finger sandwiches and punch, she told her friend. Althea pictured George in a suit flirting with some little freshman, and smiled.

She closed her eyes and tried to speak to him mentally. You can look but don't touch, she willed him to think. Holly asked her what she was doing. Althea opened her eyes and said she was telepathically telling George to keep his hands to himself. They both chortled softly. Their lovemaking over the past several weeks had been so intense that Althea doubted George could actually do something with someone else. Then two boys who had been looking at them walked up. The boy nearest Althea asked if they wanted to get coffee at the Straight. Althea smiled pleasantly. He was quite tall and good looking. She liked how his prominent teeth gave his smile an earnest quality. She thanked him but said she had to study, and opened her books as he walked away.

The one on your side was kind of nice looking, Holly whispered. Althea nodded, and wondered again about George at the tea.

I don't suppose there were many ugly ones at this tea when you went? she asked Holly. Holly had pulled out a clipboard with "Charles Lord" written on it in permanent ink. Nope. Not a one, she replied. Then she added, Good lord, Althea, George only has eyes for you. Believe me.

Althea wondered why George had not told her about this tea ahead of time. He had just said he had something going on at the house. But he had also said he would meet her tonight at the library. It crossed her mind to go talk to Matthew Stollings, as a sort of payback. Then she shook her mind clear and started to study.

In the days after the freshman tea, Harold Wise continued to muse over the idea of a Pig Night. When he explained it to his social co-chair, Stoobie gasped and told him he was completely disgusting. Think about the feelings of the girls who would be invited, he said in an exasperated tone. It would humiliate them!

But Harold replied that the girls would love the chance to come to something at Eta Chi. He chuckled. We'd be doing them a service! he exclaimed. He began to talk up the idea around the house, and found receptivity along the sophomore corridor. They began to come back to the house with girls' names they were thinking of as dates, and point them out on campus. It became a small competition to see who could identify the ugliest girl in sight.

When the boys asked Harold what they would do with all of these ugly girls, he told them he had a plan. A perfect plan! They would ask the girls to wait in the library while the boys all went into the dining room behind the closed doors. Then, before the doors opened for dinner, the boys could all drop their pants as a fitting welcome to Eta Chi!

Harold spread word that the second Wednesday in November would be Pig Night. He knew that the event was for real when a sophomore came to tell him he was having trouble getting any ugly girls to accept his invitation. Harold told him to redouble his efforts and treat them just as he would treat a pretty girl. Then he raised his voice. Just because they're ugly doesn't mean they're stupid, you chucklehead!

Of course not every brother was amenable to Pig Night. There were boys, like Stoobie, who took a principled position that this sort of thing was bad for the house. Others wanted to take their regular dates to date night, including George Muirfield and Charles Lord. Danny Carvello was against it for two reasons. First, he really didn't want to take any ugly girls out, and second, he was working hard on Janette Emilio.

On the second Wednesday of November, Jane Quissling was sitting in labor relations history class in the ILR school. Jane Quissling thought she had the highest IQ in her class. She didn't. But she had always pretty much been the smartest when she was younger and old habits die hard. In Jane's case, though, this was also a defense mechanism. On her left temple, Jane had a prominent growth. As a child, her mother had always referred to it as her hot button, or the extra space her head needed for her substantial brain. It was easier for her to go through life knowing she was smarter than everybody in the room, since she had the burden of this disfiguring lump on her forehead. It was an enormous lump, which tended to distract people from taking in the rest of her face, which was plain, but by no means unattractive.

Since the class had started, Jane had sat next to Fritz Hublein. He had been affable from the start, and she looked forward to sitting with him in class. He had curly brown hair, glassy brown eyes, and a carefully groomed moustache. She liked the way that he was always raising his eyebrows. When the professor said something controversial or funny, Fritz would look at her, pull his mouth up tight and raise his eyebrows. Then he would smile and his eyebrows would move up and down. She found his amusement pleasant, and she would smile back at him. Plus, she never saw him looking at her hot button, like so many people did.

So when Fritz invited her out of the blue to come to his fraternity for dinner this evening, she was pleasantly surprised, and said sure. He told her what to wear, and they agreed on a time when they could meet on the Arts Quad so they could walk down to his house together. She was a sophomore, but had not been to a fraternity before. She wasn't the type to go alone to the big open mixers she heard about, and the friends she had made found the whole Greek thing kind of gauche.

After classes, Jane walked to her dorm room in Mary Donnelly and sorted through her closet to get ready to meet Fritz. She began to wonder whether she had misjudged his interest in her. She had assumed that he was in the friendly-but-not-interested category, but now his invitation made her reconsider. She tried pictured herself kissing him. It might work.

At five p.m. she left her dorm to head back to the Arts Quad. She had brushed her brown hair out and pulled it back with a clip, and had put on a very subtle lipstick. She didn't usually wear makeup. With her hot button, it seemed kind of silly to. She had picked out a plaid skirt and a crème colored blouse and low heeled pumps. It had been a cool day, so she wrapped her favorite cardigan over her shoulders, and raised her eyebrows at herself in the mirror before she left.

When she got to the Arts Quad, she did not see Fritz yet, so she stood near the entrance to the mathematics building, where they had agreed to meet. It was getting colder, and as dusk approached, the little sunlight that had been trying to find its way through the dreary, overcast sky started to concede the day. Jane saw two boys and a girl coming from the direction of the libraries. There was an enormous Saint Bernard walking with them, and she thought she made out Fritz on the left.

Soon the Saint Bernard shuffled up to her, panting heavily. Fritz waved to her as the three people approached. Jane Quissling loved dogs, and she rubbed the dog's head as Fritz introduced her to Ronny and Angela. She had seen Ronny before in the ILR school. He was small and wiry and hard to get a sense of. The girl with him was wearing a beautiful dark red dress and a small white sweater. Her face was covered with acne, but she had the glossiest light brown hair Jane had ever seen.

Fritz introduced her to Brandy, whose head she was rubbing, and the four of them headed over to the concrete steps that led down to the suspension bridge and over the rushing gorge. Fritz and Ronny started explaining where their fraternity house was, and Jane asked Angela if this was her first time there as well. Angela wagged her head up and down in abrupt little motions. She had a high pitched voice, and said it was *absolutely* her first time too. Fritz looked at Jane and raised his eyebrows repeatedly. Jane smiled and shook her head as if she understood.

Eta Chi looked like a forlorn castle in the early evening mist as they arrived. The outside yellow lantern light was glowing and there was a fair amount of activity as people drove into the driveway, and walked along the sidewalks toward the house. Jane knew she was going to have a good time.

Inside, Fritz and Ronny escorted their dates to the library, and excused themselves to go upstairs and change into their coats and ties. There were only a few people in the library so far, and everyone introduced themselves next to the grand piano. Angela sat at the piano and tested it to see if it was in tune. Then she played one of the college drinking songs, and Brandy, who had walked in and stuck his head under the piano, began to howl. Everyone laughed, and when she was done, people clapped their hands.

People continued to gather in the library. Harold walked in with the girl with the slightly crossed eyes. He felt sort of funny about inviting her, but they had been flirting in classes since their last date night, and Harold figured what the hell. She was ugly and sexy! She grinned wickedly at him when he invited her. Oh boy, Harold thought.

Then David Dalrumple walked in with his date. David was not what you would call handsome himself. His eyes seemed to bulge out from his face, and he had wispy hair that you could just tell would be stretched over a mostly bald scalp in a few years. The girl with him was so plain looking that there was not a single feature on her face you could remember if you tried. She didn't have much of a figure, and she wore a brown and white plaid dress, which made her body look bumpy. The truth was that David was secretly enamored of her. He had used Pig Night as an excuse to have her come to his fraternity without getting razzed by anyone.

A number of boys showed up soon after, and, more than anything, the collection of girls they escorted looked simply unorthodox together. There were girls with nice figures and distressful faces, and others with uneventful faces and awkward frames. There was only one immense girl, who came into the room with Jack Ellis. Her head was lowered as if she was afraid that someone might tell her this wasn't real. Jack looked for Harold to give his stamp of approval. But Harold was in conversation with his date and George Muirfield.

George had tried to avoid this date night for days. He certainly was not going to invite some ugly girl to dinner, even if that was the game, and he had Althea to think about. Althea had come to every date night since the first night he asked her. So he puzzled over whether to simply suggest to Althea that they do something instead of date night, or just miss it somehow. But part of him, guiltily, was curious about just what would happen tonight.

In the end, Althea made the decision for him. Holly had asked if she was coming, and Althea had said yes, even though they hadn't specifically talked about it. Was that okay?

Yes. George replied. Of course it's okay! So they agreed that Althea would just walk down the hill and meet him at Eta Chi, but she hadn't arrived yet when he was speaking with Harold and his date. George looked at the girl with Harold and thought she was on the unattractive side, but she certainly wasn't outlandishly ugly.

Then Joshua Finch walked in pushing a girl in a wheelchair. He had an enormous, sunny smile on his face, and was squinting his eyes. He was followed by Cullen Hastings who came into the room with Althea Redmonton on his arm. George beamed at her. Her cheeks were rosy from the walk, and he felt the warmth in her smile as their eyes met. Cullen walked her up to George. Althea removed her arm from Cullen's, and put her hand on George's face, to let him feel the cold. Cullen scolded George for letting Althea walk alone to the house. George knew that Cullen had a huge crush on Althea, who was always playful with him. Cullen had also assured George that he would never pimp on a brother, and George trusted him.

Charles Lord and Holly Menard entered the room. Holly did not have that same halo of cold fresh air that had encircled Althea and others who walked into the room straight from the outside. The chill from outside had already been rubbed out of her arms. Holly scanned the room, and saw almost no girls she recognized. Then she saw the heavy girl with Jack Ellis and walked immediately up to her, extending her hand in greeting. She recognized her from one of her classes. Then she said hi to Jack, who looked funny to her.

Are you okay? she asked him. Sometimes she felt like such a mother to these boys!

Jack assured her he was fine.

Not long after, Danny Carvello appeared at the doorway with Janette Emilio, followed by Nick Cohen with a girl clinging carefully to his arm. The girl had a walking cane in her free hand. It took a moment for the boys in the room to realize that Nick Cohen had not only brought an ugly girl to dinner, but a blind, ugly girl. Joshua Finch wheeled his date over to Nick and the blind girl to say hello. Althea Redmonton, who had sat down on one of the couches while George went off for a minute, observed the room with curiosity.

The girls at dinner looked out of place to her, and there was something in the boys' antics that made her suspicious. And God, what was happening to the tastes of these boys?

Harold raised his voice in a mischievous way, and asked if his brothers could join him in the dining room for a moment before dinner began. He opened one of the doors that shut off the library from the dining room while the tables were being set, and motioned for the boys near him to get moving. He apologized to the room of girls, said that there was a fraternity matter that had to be taken care of. They would be right back. The girls started talking to each other. Nick Cohen left his blind date with her hand against a window sill, and told her he'd be right back. The girl in the wheel chair had started talking to someone seated on a couch, so Althea walked up to say hello to the poor girl with the walking stick. This was turning into such a bizarre night.

After the doors were shut, the boys gathered around Harold who was shushing them to be quiet. Nick Cohen said he'd never had a blind date before, and the room erupted in laughter. One of the sophomores accused Harold of cheating. He brought a girl he had already taken to a regular date night! Harold told him to mind his own business. One of the quiet juniors, a tall, taciturn boy, opined that this was cruel. David Dalrumple objected. He told the junior he had brought a girl he sort of liked. He felt his neck get hot as he said it.

Gentlemen, Harold intoned, the honor of Eta Chi is at stake. Are or are we not going to show these women our manhood? Some of the boys had not heard of Harold's plot, and asked what he was talking about. Then there was another gaggle of voices as boys tried to explain to the others asking the questions what the plan was. Harold undid his trousers and paraded around the room with them around his knees, laughing. He had pink boxer shorts on underneath, and the room cracked up.

Cullen Hastings said he did not think this was a good idea, since some of the boys had real dates with them. He was thinking mostly about Althea, and a little about Holly. A boy behind Harold said it would be no harm – it was all in fun. Someone suggested that they could all sing a refrain of Muddy Roads instead of the Darling Song, and a couple of the sophomores started singing it softly. Stoobie told them to stop that. He had been standing quietly and watching the crowd, but he couldn't take much more of this. He sniffed, and said that the tradition of singing the Darling Song was not going to be thrown out by a bunch of idiots standing with their pants at their ankles.

Even Harold agreed that was too much, and the two sophomores who had been leading the insurgence – Jack Ellis, Joshua Finch – backed down. Danny Carvello entered the dining room with George Muirfield at that point. They had been upstairs and missed the gathering. Danny shook his head very seriously as they approached the huddle of boys, and said he was concerned. He believed he had sighted a beached whale in the library.

The room broke into hysterics again. George looked at Cullen Hastings and asked what they were doing. Cullen told him that Harold was trying to get everybody to drop their trousers. George said he would get totally naked, but he would not go halfway. When some of the boys tried to dismiss such a ridiculous notion, he told them he was serious. There was a moment of awkward silence. One of the boys who had set the table came out from the kitchen and announced that dinner was getting cold.

Harold took charge and instructed the boys to sit down. When the girls come through the doors, he said, everyone should stand up and drop their drawers. A number of the boys thought that sounded like an acceptable compromise, and began to move around to chairs and sit down. Harold joined them, and urged them to unbuckle their pants now. But a number of the boys were starting to protest as they moved about, and George was yelling it should be all or nothing.

Open the doors!! Harold yelled.

The boy who had been impatiently waiting to serve dinner moved to the doors to open them. As the doors opened, Harold and about six or seven other boys who had readied themselves, leaped up and let their pants fell to their knees. As the first girls started to filter into the dining room, someone yelled, Welcome to Eta Chi!!

Harold, who was clutching his pants with his hands, laughed hysterically as he looked down and re-buckled his pants. The girls couldn't see much of anything, because a number of boys were still milling about in a state of generalized confusion. All around the dining room, boys were messing with their belt buckles or moving to meet their dates. Most of the girls looked bewildered.

Holly Menard marched up to Charles Lord and asked him what in god's name was going on. But Charles had actually missed everything himself, and had arrived through the kitchen just as the doors were opening. When she spied one of the sophomores zipping his fly, she flinched and looked sternly back up at Charles. Charles was scanning the room, chuckling. Ehoo, ehoo.

Danny Carvello found Janette and took her arm as he guided her to one of the tables, and Althea strolled in with the blind girl, until Nick Cohen approached them and took her arm. The girl in the wheelchair wheeled herself in.

Dinner was marinated flank steak, mashed potatoes and green beans. They had ice cream with chocolate sauce for dessert. The conversation over dinner was lively. Perhaps because the boys were on edge, or perhaps because some of them felt bad, a number of spirited exchanges had different tables laughing hard and sounding more boisterous than usual. George and Althea sat with Nick Cohen and his blind date, Fritz and Jane, and Ronny and the acne-faced girl in the pretty red dress.

For some reason, George kept thinking about the fact that the blind girl, who had a chubby, round face and a great sense of humor, couldn't see the protrusion on Jane Quissling's forehead. Fritz seemed to be enjoying Jane's company, and even casually rested his hand along the back of her chair near the end of dinner. Ronny acted sullen, and his date didn't say much, other than to exchange some recollections of Vermont with Althea, when she learned Althea grew up there.

Across the room, the girl in the wheelchair was making the over-weight girl and Nick Cohen laugh loudly with her imitation of an orangutan she had seen at a zoo. The overweight girl, whose body rose and fell as she chuckled at the story, no longer felt uncomfortable. Quintin Wells and Joey Padillo, neither of whom had brought dates, were sitting across from them with looks of disbelief on their faces. Quintin looked to the table next to him, where he thought the girl with the crossed eyes was leering at him. Next to her, Harold Wise was chuckling with Charles Lord and Holly Menard. Quintin thought the color of Harold's face matched the outlandish pink of his boxers.

David Dalrumple and his date were sitting quietly at the table oppo-site Harold and his date. Harold winked at him, made his lips form into a kiss, and shook his head in the direction of David's date. David had no idea whether Harold was encouraging him or making fun of him, but he put his arm along the back of his date's chair to send Harold a message. His date smiled at David, and leaned a little closer to him.

Before dessert, the boys rose and sang the Darling Song standing be-hind their chairs. Jack Ellis tried to move next to Joshua Finch and put his arm around his shoulder and rock back and forth as they sang, but Joshua's date's wheelchair was in the way. He moved back to his chair and sang softly. Across the room, George was standing formally behind Althea's chair. Before the singing began, he had put his hands on her shoulders and leaned down to her ear to whisper something. Althea craned her head around and up to see his eyes and whispered something in return.

Althea felt hot. She was blinking her eyes and looking at the spoon that was to be used for the ice cream about to be served.

George had whispered, I love you.

He had not intended to say that. He had been thinking about how much he wished he could hold a tune, and what a beautiful voice Althea had. She was terribly shy about it, but sometimes when they were com-fortable in her apartment and Bonnie Raitt came on the radio, Althea would sing along with her. George thought her voice was smoky and me-lodious and plaintive. And when he encouraged her, she sang with a little more gusto. He loved to hear her. But that's not what had come out of his mouth.

They had beaten around the issue for weeks and weeks. The depth of their ardor was not something they avoided talking about. But they had scrupulously avoided the L word. George thought they had used just about every other word in the English language to describe their passion. So he was glad to finally say it. But now he was fretting over her reply.

She whispered, What did you say?

As George sang along, he was furiously trying to decide whether she had not heard him, or was taken aback by his declaration. Actually, Althea had not expected, and at first, not heard what George said. So she had asked him what he said, and turned back around as the singing began. Then his words came alive in her mind, and made her queasy.

Althea had been in love with George, probably since they first kissed in the mailroom, if that was possible. But she did not trust herself, and could not believe how love felt. It was heady, and consuming, and weakening somehow. She wanted to be near him, could feel him with her eyes closed as they sat next to each other, and sometimes felt her thirst for him in her throat. But what was that? That could be a lot of different things besides love. She knew they were working their way around it, trusting each other with each other, in a way that was extraordinarily different from anything she had ever experienced with Matthew or other boys. It was frightening to her.

And now this.

The Eta Chis finished their song, and sat back down for dessert. Jane Quissling said that was one of the most beautiful things she had ever experienced. Althea looked at her, and for the first time of the evening didn't see the enormous growth on her head. She just saw Jane Quissling. Fritz smiled at Jane and raised his eyebrows. The blind girl sighed and thanked the boys at the table. Althea glanced at George, who was looking across from him as if he was trying not to look at her. She felt the tension in his face. But she wasn't ready to say anything to him.

The dinner ended and everyone stood and began to find their way out through the library. Althea took George's hand as they walked. He was laughing with Ronny about something, but he gripped her hand firmly and squeezed it. As they moved along he leaned close to her and said it was a good thing she hadn't heard what he had to say before the Darling Song. Althea just looked at him, cautiously. George smiled and said, Never mind, I'll tell you someday. She smiled sweetly at him. God, he looked adorable when he was afraid.

Holly asked Althea and George if they wanted a lift up to the library in Charles' car. Althea and George looked at each other, understood what the other was thinking, and turned and said sure. They piled into Charles' tiny car, and laughed at how cramped they were during the quick ride up to campus. Charles parked as near to the library as he could find a space, and George and Althea were all arms and legs as they tried to extract themselves from the back seat with their books. As the four of them walked to Uris, Holly spoke up in stern voice. All right boys, what the *hell* was that all about tonight!

Charles chuckled and George said, What do you mean?

Holly told them not to give her that. Then she pushed her arm through Charles', and said she was going to get it out of him one way or another.

Once in the library, the two couples separated. George and Althea headed up to the stacks where George needed to search for some critical research. Charles and Holly went to the main reading room.

George and Althea piled their books on two adjoining library desks in the upstairs stacks. There was no one anywhere near them, or even on the floor from what they could tell.

Tell me, George.

What?

Tell me what the hell was going on tonight. Why were all those girls at date night? I don't care, and I liked the ones I met. But all of you were looking too...naughty. Althea looked at him hard.

George stalled for minutes, suggesting that he didn't know what she was talking about. But he knew he was going to end up telling her. Jane Quissling's hot button kept passing through his mind.

All right. You absolutely have to promise.

I promise, I promise. So?

George thought for a moment about how to explain it. You know how everybody calls the Pig Book the Pig Book? Althea said she did.

Well somehow the idea came up that we could...have a Pig Night. He started giggling in spite of himself.

Althea looked saddened. You mean that those girls were asked to come to dinner to humiliate them? An awkward moment passed between them. And you think it's funny?

George tried to explain.

Look, you saw what happened. It started out as a wild idea, and maybe it was in poor taste...but it didn't turn out to be a humiliation. Hell, I think Fritz wants to date Jane! And plus, you have to admit – it was comical! George grinned at his girlfriend, hopefully. He desperately wanted her to see the humor in it.

Althea wondered if she knew the boy in front of her. She thought it was the cruelest thing she had ever heard. Then it dawned on her.

You invited me to Pig Night? Her hushed voice hung in the air of the stacks like dust particles.

George looked at her in earnest shock. No! he exclaimed. *You are the Anti-Pig!*

The two of them glared at each other and then suddenly began to laugh. They laughed until they were both holding their sides and their eyes were wet. Each time they tried to stop, one or the other would restart until all was rung out of them. George was still concerned. He moved close to her, and put his arms around her waist.

Listen. I am glad you came tonight. For reasons maybe I'll explain to you someday. But I wasn't about to ask some other girl, let alone an ugly girl. I didn't know what to do. Then you told me you were coming, and I just went with it.

George went on to tell her how hilarious it had been when the boys went into the dining room. They were trying to get up the courage to drop their pants as a prank, he told her laughing. Althea's eyes got bigger and she asked George if he would have dropped his pants. Her hands rested on his arms. They sensed each other, like you feel a tingle rush across your skin.

No, he told her. I said we had to get totally naked or do nothing at all. He had expected a laugh, but her eyes looked deeply into his as he said this, and she said nothing. She kept peering into his eyes, searching. Something unknown dislodged inside her head. They breathed quietly for a moment.

I heard you, Althea told him.

George said nothing. She thought she could sense his insides coil, but it was his center, spinning wildly.

I love you too.

CHAPTER SIXTEEN

Jane Quissling didn't kiss Fritz Hublein goodnight when he drove her back to Mary Donnelly after date night at Eta Chi. He kissed her. And that was remarkable, because Jane always had to be the first one to kiss the boy. Once boys kissed her, they found her to be a terrific kisser. But the few awkward boys in high school who had seemed interested in her wouldn't take that first step – she assumed because of her hot button – so she became adept at finding an impromptu moment to catch their lips with hers. Then she would lock onto their mouths and nuzzle them, and they wouldn't want to stop. She had lots of fantasies about her ability to control boys once she had them on her lips.

But Fritz actually leaned into her of his own initiative and kissed her. They were in front of her door at Mary Donnelly and after a moment of surprise, Jane locked her lips passionately on Fritz Hublein's and nuzzled him. His lips were thin, and his moustache soft, and she felt his body grow excited quickly. She didn't know how far she might be willing to go with Fritz. Part of her wanted to continue the moment and pull Fritz into her room. But the other side of her was leery of him still. This was all too soon, too different to believe yet. So she kept her passions in check, and although by now they were wrapped pretty tightly around each other as she continued her assault on his lips, she broke it off and smiled genuinely at him.

I had a lovely time tonight Fritz. Maybe we can do something else sometime.

Fritz looked at Jane, and her hot button no longer seemed to exist on her face. He said he'd like that in a husky voice. Then he raised his eyebrows a couple of times. Jane squeezed his hand and then slipped behind her door. As it turned out, this was the best thing Jane could have done. Fritz walked away from her door in a state about her, and headed back to the house to talk with his roommate.

ROOM!! Harold boomed out. They had started calling each other "Roomie" but it had shortened almost immediately to "Room." When Fritz said "Room" he did it in a low, fast, clipped voice. Almost like a cough. But when Harold said it, he bellowed the word. It had become a term of affection between them. Harold looked accusingly at his roommate.

So?

Fritz looked at Harold dispassionately and asked him, What?

How did it go with the Unicorn? Harold burst into laughter. Fritz grimaced.

Ohhhh, ho-ho-ho!! Harold said in astonishment, you like her! Fritz told Harold he thought he might. He said she was an unbelievable kisser. Harold nodded and said, Okay. He had to backtrack fast. He had been referring to Fritz's date as the unicorn since dinner had ended. He didn't want Fritz to be angry with him.

Fritz inquired about the girl with the crossed eyes. Had Harold had another erotic adventure? Harold said he had not been as lucky this time. And she's not as good a kisser as...what's her name anyway? Fritz said Jane's name. The two boys looked at each other. Whatever boundaries form between roommates began to form between them.

When Fritz walked into his next labor relations history class, he didn't see Jane Quissling. He had been fantasizing about her, and hoped she would arrive in time for them to talk before class began. Jane walked in and smiled at him, and he raised his eyebrows and returned her smile. Her hot button wasn't invisible to him now – it was larger than he had made it in his memory, and the desire he had carried for her since Wednesday dipped. Then he recalled her kiss, and felt her sitting down beside him. He looked at her silky, bluish-gray skirt and pale blouse. Jane Quissling had a nice figure, and she looked good. Then she leaned closer to him and whispered Hey! He felt his ardor returning. So he asked her if she wanted to go out for beers tonight before he lost his nerve. Jane beamed. Maybe this wasn't a fluke, she thought.

Fritz picked Jane up at her dorm room. It was quiet in the hallway, and Jane had changed to blue jeans and a red, thick turtleneck sweater. She wore red lipstick. Fritz couldn't stop looking at her lips as he walked her down the hall. Jane was trying to be coy, but she had loved going to Fritz's fraternity, and felt him looking at her out of the corner of her eye. She told him to stop for a moment, and close his eyes. At first he asked why, but she insisted, and then reached up and kissed him. It was one of the ways she had used in high school, and she wanted to feel the dominance again, even though she had planned to wait him out.

She kept her eyes open, guessing that Fritz would keep his eyes closed. She was right, and she felt his arms wrap around her as she nuzzled his lips again. Fritz would have stood there all night. But Jane pulled herself away after a bit, brushed his lips with her thumb to wipe away her lipstick, and told Fritz she thought he was supposed to be taking her out. Fritz was clearly aroused, but he said, Right, let's go! As they walked to his car, Fritz took Jane's hand. It seemed to him as if she curled up next to him as they walked. It felt great.

They went to the Nines, where the crowd was loud and packed, and pushed their way through until they found some open space. Fritz asked her if she wanted a drink or a beer, and she said she'd have what he was having. He came back after a long absence with two Rolling Rocks. As she took the bottle from his hand, she leaned up close to his face, purposely putting her mouth near to his, but talking as if she was just trying to be heard.

I'm really happy you asked me out, Fritz, she yelled. Fritz smiled at her in the din. I didn't think you would after all the time we spent sitting next to each other, she added.

Fritz nodded his head. He wondered about his motives in asking her to Pig Night. He really didn't think this would have happened, but here he was. Jane leaned in to him again.

When are we going to talk about it?

Fritz tensed. He widened his eyes to see what she was talking about.

This! Jane shouted. She pointed her green beer bottle subtly toward her forehead. She had been through this before. She knew it was better to get it over with now, even if it felt uncomfortable.

What about it? Fritz asked. Jane grimaced good-naturedly. You mean you've never noticed it before? The two of them laughed. Fritz looked at her hot button for a moment after they stopped laughing. It was like a miniature mountain on the plain of her forehead. He leaned in close to her. Sometimes I see it and sometimes I don't, he yelled softly.

Jane's pleasure was apparent on her face. That was the best answer she would ever hope for from anybody. The fact that he had looked at her just once and not seen it made her skin tingle. Unless he was lying. She had never really trusted what boys said to her, and was always looking for hidden meanings. She told him not to lie to her, ever. It came out of her mouth a little with force, and Fritz recoiled a little.

Okay, he replied. For a minute Jane started to panic, but they kept drinking their beer, and Fritz seemed fine after a bit.

Jane felt she had better do something to recover, and she did what her mother had always told her to do. She told the truth. She told Fritz she was sorry, that she hadn't meant it the way it sounded, and that it was the nicest compliment she had received in a while. Then she told him she hoped she hadn't scared him away.

Fritz listened to Jane curiously. She was clearly a little intense for him, and he wasn't sure what she was so fired up about. But he had obviously said the right thing to her and wanted to put it behind them. Then he saw three Eta Chis waving to him from across the room and waved back. He asked Jane if she wanted to join them, and she said sure, even though she didn't. She had lost her control.

Fritz introduced Jane to his brothers, and she could feel them glancing at her hot spot. She didn't mind that – people did it all day long – but she was worried that Fritz might still get cold feet with her if he felt her forehead was too much of an issue in the world around them. But he continued to act fine, and he slipped her hand into his as they all talked. It made her feel proud, and secure about him. It was like he was signaling to his brothers that she was not to be made fun of. And, in fact, that was exactly what Fritz was doing, although it was his subconscious at work. His conscious mind was just thinking how much he liked holding her hand.

At the end of the night, the cold November air jolted them out of their tipsiness, and they drove back to Jane's dorm making casual conversation about the people they had met. The car had barely heated up by the time Fritz got out and walked around to help Jane out of the car. They walked arm in arm into her dorm, and up the two flights of stairs to her floor. Jane's room was at the end of the hallway, and it was just as quiet as when they had left. Fritz asked her if it was always this quiet, and Jane told him it was pretty boring. Most of the girls kept to themselves.

Fritz stammered a little, and then told her that it was a little early for him to be doing this, but he wondered if Jane would like to come to the Eta Chi Christmas formal the first Saturday in December. He was looking at her lips as he said it, but then looked up into her large brown eyes. He couldn't believe that he was asking her. Part of him regretted it as quickly as the words spilled out of his mouth. Could he really walk in the front door of Eta Chi for the Christmas formal with…the Unicorn?

Jane felt back in control. She knew deep inside her that too much was going right too quickly with Fritz Hublein. But she also knew that she was never going to get anywhere unless she trusted some things to fate. She took Fritz's hand, asked him if he was sure. He wasn't, but he was not about to say that. She told him she would love to be his date for the formal. She started kissing him hard, and turned the door handle to her room so they could move inside as they kissed.

❧

The second informal rush afternoon tea was scheduled for the Sunday following Pig Night, and Eta Chi was in form. Edward Stamer had assumed the mantle of rush Chair easily, and orchestrated informal rush as he had seen his predecessors do it. As a person, Edward was tall, and distinctive in his looks. But his style and his image were not a match for the debonair effusiveness of Will Houghton or the carefree ebullience of Charles Lord. Edward was a bit more introverted, and less loquacious than either of them. But he was organized and motivated to succeed, and the brotherhood fell in line behind him.

There was a new jauntiness to the teas. Some of the cavalier attitude of the Charles Lord rush spilled over into Edward's year, and the sophomore class that Charles Lord's rush had yielded was more prone to excess. Plus, the senior class from the prior year, with its contingent of the Old Guard, was gone. Quintin Wells would complain to Edward that it was haughtiness, and damaging to the house. Edward didn't disagree. He had liked the formality of the house when he joined, but he did not see a way to steer the ship any better than he was doing.

Andy had prepared peach cobbler for the tea, and the boys had cut the cobbler into pieces that were a little too large. Plus, the cobbler was slightly runny, and goopy, which led the freshmen to have to be careful as they ate it on plates. Most of the Eta Chis were too busy rushing the freshmen to eat the cobbler themselves, and so the picture Edward watched unfold at the second Sunday tea was of freshmen struggling to eat the runny cobbler while his brothers swirled in and around them, urging them to enjoy themselves, as they sized the freshmen up.

David Dalrumple stood in the great hall with one boy who had taken a large slice of the peach cobbler onto his little plate, but had neglected to take a fork with him as he moved away from the table. He was nodding in response to David's exhortations about Eta Chi and trying to pick the cobbler up in his free hand. As the boy moved the cobbler toward his mouth, it began to slide out of his hand toward his shirt. The boy tried, unsuccessfully, to angle the plate in such a way as to catch the falling confection. David stared at the light brown crust of the cobbler as it slid onto the front of the boy's shirt.

Can I get you a napkin? David asked him carefully. He didn't want to embarrass him. Then the boy tried to rescue the cobbler off his shirt and get it into his mouth. But the sweet dessert by then was not holding together, and it fell utterly apart, and all down the boy's shirt and pants.

Or perhaps a tablecloth, David suggested?

Across the room, Harold Wise was entertaining an engineering student with a chunky build. He asked Harold a number of questions in quick succession, as if he had them memorized. How many pledges do you bid? Why would I want to join this house? What is the social calendar of the house like? Do the frat brothers study together? What percentage of the guys are in the engineering school?

Harold did his best to answer the boy's questions. The boy annoyed him, but Harold appreciated the fact that he was trying to understand the whole thing. It was early in the process, and lots of freshmen asked these questions. Then the freshman pulled himself up stiffly, and tried to look deeply into Harold's eyes. He said, Show me the guts of this house! When he said "guts," he emphasized the word by slowing his speech down and squinting his eyes.

Harold said, Oh, you want to see *the guts* of the house? The boy nodded seriously. Harold told him to follow him, and walked the boy down to the basement, past the chapter room. The freshman asked him what that room was. Harold said, That is the chapter room, but don't be misled. That is not the guts of the house. If you really want to see the guts of the house, follow me! The boy followed Harold as he squeezed along behind the old washer and dryer. He was excited by the intrigue.

Then Harold pushed open the heavy door to the boiler room, where the heating plant to the house hissed and crackled. It was dark, except for the glow from the boiler itself, and extraordinarily filthy. The black soot was caked onto the walls.

You wanted to see the guts of the house, Harold said in the dim light. *This* is the guts of the house! He nodded seriously at the freshman, and didn't say another word.

The freshman stared at the boiler. The boiler burped. The freshman peered in the darkness at Harold.

I understand, he said solemnly. After a moment, Harold suggested that he needed to return the boy upstairs. Boy oh boy, he said, my brothers would be really upset if they knew that I was showing you this on your very first visit! The boy thanked him for his trust, and followed Harold back past the washer and dryer and up the stairs. Harold guided the boy to the door, making note of his name on his name tag.

Listen, he told the boy, you need to see the difference between our house and the other houses, and the only way for you to do that is to get around during these teas. So get going and examine the other houses as closely as you have looked at us! And listen, be sure to insist that you see the guts of all the houses. The boy thanked him and headed off to Phi Delta, where Harold told him the guts were particularly impressive.

In the rush meeting that followed the end of the Sunday tea, Edward led the brothers in a freewheeling review of the freshmen who had passed through their doors that day. Edward was keeping the traditional information about their progress – numbers of visitors, numbers of repeat visitors, and so on. He shared this information with the assembled boys, who clapped and snapped their fingers in appreciation. They were thirty-two repeat visitors ahead of last year at this time. But Edward cautioned the group that this did not mean that it was the right thirty-two.

Then he called out the names from the guest register of every freshman who had signed in. He put check marks next to names of boys people liked, or x's next to others to indicate no interest. When someone had made a distinct impression, Edward wrote a note to that effect. When he yelled out the name of the boy Harold had shown the guts of the house to, Harold raised his hand and asked to be heard. Edward asked the group to quiet down, since a number of low voices were comparing notes about boys they had met. Harold cleared his throat, and moved next to Edward.

I have a proposal, he said in a big voice. I know traditionally that we put freshmen into two categories. We either vote to bring them back or that we have no interest in having them come back. But this young man I met today belongs in a different grouping. I propose we create a new category called "Bring Back and Abuse"!

There was a moment of silence followed by bursts of laughter around the room. Edward didn't appreciate this but Harold had the floor. He told the boys the story of taking the freshman down to the boiler room, and the room laughed and applauded.

For these kinds of freshmen, I say we should invite them back and have some fun with them! Harold concluded. Do I hear a second?

A number of voices chorused a second. But Edward stepped forward and told the group to wait. He found the story as funny as everyone else, but this was serious business, and as rush chairman, he was going to bring this to an end right now. There were one or two cat calls, but Harold raised his hand, and announced that Edward was rush chairman, and that the room shouldn't take everything he said so literally. Nonetheless, Bring Back & Abuse became an informal category that day.

Even as Edward went through the remaining list of names, some boys would call out Bring Back and Abuse!! On at least two occasions, Edward placed a check mark next to a name because he only heard the words, "Bring Back."

At the end of the meeting, Edward announced something new for this rush season. He had read the IFC rules carefully and concluded that there was a minor, incidental contact exclusion that would cover a brief hello on the phone. So he assigned brothers to call freshmen everyone liked, to invite them back. Most boys simply made a quick call, but a few took the opportunity to spend a minute on the phone to chat up the house. And for reasons unknown to the brothers, Harold referred to himself as Harry when he made his calls. Nobody would have called Harold "Harry." It just didn't fit. But when Harold telephoned the freshman, he boomed his name into the mouthpiece, like this: Jim? Harry! Harry Wise at Eta Chi!

Harold would move quickly though the conversation, and insist that they call him back at a later time with any questions they had. Harold's high-octane approach proved quite effective. Freshmen found Harold fun and supportive. So from these series of calls, a number of boys took him up on his suggestion and called him back as rush progressed.

One freshman, a boy named Frank Shanahan, called for him and asked David Dalrumple, who answered the telephone, if he could speak to Harry-Harry Wise. David confirmed into mouthpiece that the boy wanted to speak to Harry-Harry. Then he went running through the house yelling Harry-Harry! Harry-Harry!

He found Harold in the kitchen talking with Andy and told him a freshman named Frank was on the phone. Harold went to the phone, picked up the handset dangling on the silver coil, and said it again. Frank? Harry! Harry Wise! And for the rest of his college days, Harold was known informally around the house (but rarely to his face) as Harry-Harry Wise.

As Harold chuckled into the phone, Jimmy Dunbar entered the mail-room, looked at Harold as he checked for his mail, and said, Beep. Harold ignored him as he chatted amiably with the freshman. He thought Jimmy Dunbar was a weirdo. But Jimmy listened carefully to Harold as he talked, and when Harold hung up, Jimmy asked if he believed what he had just said.

Harold eyed Jimmy suspiciously, and said, What?

What you said to the kid on the phone. Do you believe it or were you just spinning fairy dust? Jimmy looked intently at Harold, and it made him want to leave. But he told Jimmy that he did, indeed, believe what he had said. As the two boys wandered out of the mailroom, Jimmy said he wouldn't have guessed that.

Harold studied Jimmy carefully. What Harold had told the freshman on the phone that Eta Chi stood for honor, and for achievement, and for integrity.

That's what this place is all about Jimmy. Harold finally said. Jimmy was unfazed.

I believe in having an outrageous time as much as we can, Harold went on. That's what college is all about. But it wouldn't be worth living here or making this place our home, if we also didn't recognize each other…you know what I mean? What I feel in here (he pointed to his heart with his thumb) about the friendships that make us brothers has nothing to do with being wild. It has to do with believing in each other, and being there for each other. Harold started to laugh a little. I don't know what the hell I am saying but I know what I mean. Jimmy nodded.

I like this house because it makes me not feel lonely, Jimmy said after a minute. Harold felt like rolling his eyes, but resisted. Thanks for telling me how you think about it, Jimmy added simply, and then retreated inside his own mask.

Harold missed his retreat. He told Jimmy that he hoped that the social events helped too. Jimmy smiled and said Beep! Harold looked at Jimmy, and wondered if the boy in front of him was AC-DC. He sometimes worried that those types might like fraternities.

Bob Woodbridge walked through the library to the foyer and up to Harold and Jimmy. In his deep voice he asked if they were contemplating the meaning of the guiding light, and Jimmy offered that Bob had surmised the truth. Bob arched his brows in a pause and then shook both their hands, telling them to have a great Thanksgiving. It was only days away, and he knew he wouldn't be back at the house for a few weeks. And that broke the séance up.

Dottie Redmonton loved washing her hands in really hot water in her kitchen sink. That's what she was doing as she looked out the window to see Althea in the passenger's seat of her husband's car crunching up the stone rock drive that led up from the road in Whittlesboro, Vermont, where they lived. Alexander Redmonton had offered to drive up to Ithaca on his way out of Manhattan on the Tuesday before Thanksgiving, so that Dottie or their son didn't have to make the trip. It was an unusual offer, and Dottie thanked her husband for the help.

Dottie was a stern, no-nonsense woman with striking cheekbones and a full, muscular figure. She played golf and tennis, and worked hard in her garden. She had met her husband at Cornell, when he was an economics major on his way to business school. She had grown up in Connecticut, but Alexander's family was deeply rooted in Vermont. There had been little question as to where they were going to live, even though he worked in Manhattan three to four days a week.

But Dottie had come to love Vermont. It was private, and pristinely beautiful. They purchased an enormous, old house on a farm that Alexander let out to others to work, and it suited her. It had been a little isolated for the kids, but they had taken pains to spend holidays in New York, and to travel to Europe twice so that the kids had some worldliness in their character. She thought Althea had turned out well, and Ethan was coming along.

Dottie smiled at her children's' names as Althea huffed through the kitchen door with her big suitcase. Dottie had never liked her own name because of how hard it sounded. It started with a hard consonant, and was punctuated with a hard T sound. She would have preferred the softness of her given name, but no one ever called her Dorothy. "Dorothy" had softer sounding vowels, as well as "TH" instead of "T." But she was always Dottie. So she picked names for her children that both started and ended softly.

Althea would have been surprised to learn this about her mother. Her mother always seemed so strong and full of purpose, that the sharp sound of her name fitted her perfectly. Her preference for soft-sounding names was incongruent. Althea dropped her suitcase on the kitchen floor, and gave her mother a big hug. Alexander strode along behind his daughter, and gave his wife a reserved peck on the cheek as she welcomed her daughter. He always kissed her cheek when he arrived home, and though it was a small and distant gesture, they had always greeted each other this way. Even when they were in college and Dottie would return to Wells College after a wonderful college weekend in Ithaca, that was how they had said goodbye to each other.

Alexander was tall, and thin, and handsome in an angular way. He had a square chin, and a long face, and slightly hazel eyes that were hard to read. On weekends he wore LL Bean chinos and corduroys. In Manhattan, where he was an investment banker on the sell side in a small firm off Wall Street, he wore plain gray Brooks Brother's suits. Dottie often kidded him about his uniforms, but he was neat, and pleasant in his appearance, and she really couldn't complain. You would not have guessed it from looking at them, but Alexander and Dottie enjoyed a robust, if conventional, sex life. She was probably slightly more sexual than he, but they accommodated each other nicely.

Alexander headed off to their bedroom to change clothes and called back over his shoulder to Dottie to ask her daughter about her new beau. Dottie smiled and Althea told her that Dad was exaggerating, but it was true she was seeing someone new. Ethan walked in and greeted his sister with a pretend punch to her arm. Behind him his two pals shuffled in, and

Althea gave them both a big smile and asked how they were doing. The room was warm and smelled of fruit pies. Althea wished George was there with her.

Thanksgiving morning was a blur of people in the kitchen, cutting up fruit and cooking vegetables and three different sorts of stuffing for the turkey. The frost did not leave the morning lawn until close to eleven, and the wind made Althea's face flush every time she walked outside to put something on the porch because the fridge was too full. Alexander's parents and his brother's family were coming at noon, and Dottie marshaled every detail of the preparations. Dottie asked Althea to set the table when she was done with the green beans, and Althea smiled cheerfully. She loved the smells of the kitchen and all the activity allowed her to decompress without having to talk to anyone.

Althea heard her grandparents arrive as she set the table in the far dining room. The far dining room was centered by an enormous, oak harvest table surrounded by beautifully carved chairs with red cushions. The room was windowed on three sides, jutting out of the rear of the house toward the fields and away from the road. She listened to her grandmother's shrill voice asking where Althea was, and then heard her approach the dining room calling out her name. She loved her grandmother. They hugged, and Althea stayed in her arms for a minute while they laughed and exchanged hellos.

When dinner was finally ready, daylight had already faded. It was four p.m., and the parents and grandparents toasted the holiday with a manhattan (Dottie and Alexander always had one cocktail before dinner, usually a manhattan). Alexander's brother had brought champagne, which Althea and Ethan shared with their cousins. Althea stepped outside with her champagne flute to smoke a cigarette by herself. Her parents did not object to her smoking, but she was not allowed to do it in the house. She inhaled and then exhaled up into the cold Vermont sky and hoped George was matching her at his home. She wondered where he was right then.

Althea, telephone! Her brother yelled across the interior of the house. Althea took one last pull on her cigarette, exhaled quickly, put it out under her shoe, and walked inside. It was freezing cold anyway. She went to the phone in the study and picked up the white princess handset and said hello. It was George, and she immediately asked him if he had just had a cigarette. He laughed and said, yeah, about fifteen minutes ago.

They both thought it was really cool that they had shared a moment together, so far apart. George had already finished dinner, and was helping with the dishes, but he wanted Althea to know that he was thinking incessantly about her. Althea told him she would love to have him with her when she went into dinner in a minute. He asked her what she was doing the rest of the weekend, and she told him she'd just catch up on her sleep and hang out with her family. He told he was probably seeing some high school friends Saturday, but that was all. Althea was called to dinner, and she told George she loved him, and to call her tomorrow. Love you too, he replied, in a quiet voice as he hung up.

Althea sat in the middle of the harvest table at dinner. Alexander and Dottie were at the ends, and her uncle and aunt sat across from each other, on either side of Alexander. Her grandmother was opposite Althea, and she gazed at Althea intently as dinner progressed. She was a compact, wiry woman with bright eyes and a quick tongue. Men loved her because she was challenging and saucy with them, and had strong opinions. She thought Althea looked beautiful. Although her cheekbones were nowhere near as pronounced as her mother's, Althea had a healthy, full face, and a knowing look that her grandmother thought she got from her. She liked the way that Althea carried herself – she had gumption, and held herself with poise.

The conversations passing over the table were as numerous as the platters circulating around the table. Victor, her uncle, defended the nation's choice of Jimmy Carter for President as Alexander scolded him and handed him yams. Dottie asked her nieces and nephews about the fall sports season while their mother scooped squash onto her plate and told Althea's grandfather she was done with television. Althea's grandmother's eyes were dancing with mirth as she asked her granddaughter if she had a sweetheart. Althea stuck her fork into a piece of turkey and swished it around in gravy as she nodded her head and smiled with her eyes lowered. Ethan handed Althea a bowl of stuffing and she passed it along without sampling it.

So? Tell me about him. What does he look like? Althea started to answer and the conversations on her mother's end of the table ebbed as she spoke.

He's nice looking – you know, kind of a strong face with these intense blues eyes. Her father and her uncle and grandfather were laughing about a story Alexander was telling, but her mother was obviously listening to her daughter carefully.

Her grandmother asked her if it was getting serious, and Althea blushed slightly and said no. Then she said that was enough focus on her dating habits, and put a big forkful of mashed potatoes in her mouth.

I dated a boy in college once with these unbelievable eyes, Althea's aunt offered. I always wondered what had happened to him! Althea grinned at her and said Aunt Elaine! Victor's ears perked up and said that he was getting jealous, and everybody laughed.

Victor looked down the table and said that he had fallen for Elaine the moment he saw her, but that it took her much longer to come around. Dottie said that was sentimental rubbish. Love at first sight was nothing but trouble for girls.

Althea's grandfather protested, and asked why it was more trouble for girls than boys. Her grandmother winked at Althea. Then she asked Alexander how long it had taken for him to fall for Dottie. But before Alexander could answer, Dottie replied that both she and Alexander had seen numerous people while they were dating at college. It was normal for boys and girls to play the field while they could. As Dottie spoke, she brought her hands together over her plate with her elbows resting on either side. Her hands had the red, scrubbed look of just being washed.

Why! Elaine protested. There's plenty of room in the world for all different kinds of romances. I knew a couple who dated all the way through college, and are still happily married.

Dottie smiled pleasantly, and suggested that being "in love" before you really knew the person only clouded your judgment. True compatibility for marriage was something that two people needed to address *dis*passionately! Althea looked at her father, but his eyes were impassive. In the car he had told Althea he thought it was nice she had found someone she liked so much. But he was always pleasantly noncommittal with her.

The conversation turned away to other things, and the dinner turned into desserts – apple, blueberry, and pecan pies and vanilla ice cream. The smell of freshly brewing coffee filled the air. As Althea cleared plates, her grandmother casually followed her, and when they were alone in the kitchen she asked Althea if she was in love.

What? Althea asked. She felt uncomfortable. It's in your eyes, sweetie, her grandmother whispered. Don't listen to your mother. Trust your instincts. Althea told her grandmother she didn't know what she was, but it was possible. And that was the truth. It was one thing to say it to George, and another thing to say it to her grandmother. That was so weird!

Althea hugged her parents hard when she left to go back to school on Sunday. The weekend had slid by, and when she woke up on Sunday, she had lain in her bed under the big comforter and drawn lines in the frost on the window pane next to her with her fingernail. First she drew a heart, and then a box, and a bunch of squiggly lines. When she stood up, the wooden floor was cold to her feet, and she hurried to the bathroom that had a rug.

Then she packed her suitcase with the clean clothes her mother had put out for her, and went downstairs to the kitchen where Ethan was sipping on some hot chocolate. He was driving her back to school, and they had to leave early so that he could get back before it got too late. She ate the last piece of apple pie from the fridge, and then her parents came in from the den to say goodbye. Alexander gave his daughter a hug and a kiss on her cheek, and her mother pulled her to her and hugged her gently, and wished her luck on her exams. Somewhere in her abdomen, Althea felt the slightest curl of insecurity, but it lasted only until she got outside in the fresh, Vermont air.

By the first weekend in December, snow covered the ground in Ithaca and stuck. There wasn't much, only an inch or two, but winter had come along and brushed the last of the leaves out of the trees. Eta Chi looked like a grand old lady in the wintry dusk.

Jim Steuben had asked Mitsy Smith to help him decorate the house for the Christmas formal, and the two of them were putting pine cones and glitter on the huge Christmas tree that some of the brothers had cut down at the local tree farm. They didn't have many strings of lights, so Stoobie and Mitsy carefully strung them in even intervals around the tree. Mitsy took every opportunity to lean against her boyfriend, or touch him as they decorated. It was such a family type of moment, it made her warm and flirtatious.

Stoobie was determined to restore some of the elegance to his fraternity's formals, and he had told the brothers at the last chapter meeting that tuxedos would be required. Some of the boys protested, but Stoobie had pointed out that second hand tuxes were available in the mission downtown for a few dollars. He had found a beautiful one there for seven dollars. So those who did not want to rent them for twenty-two bucks had alternatives. He pointed out that the girls would be in gowns, and it was only proper for the boys to dress up too. Then Harold had stood and announced that the band was going to be the Buck Trellins Jazz Band, and the brothers clicked their fingers. We're going to have some hot jazz! he told them.

There would be a flower for each date on the dining room tables, which they could pin to their gowns, or carry in their hands, Stoobie went on. The band was going to play some Christmas carols before dinner, and then dance music after dinner. Harold then announced that the Wells College Extravaganza had been postponed until January. It would be a good way to give the new pledges a night to remember, in addition to the annual songfest at the Stables. He hoped that there would be at least two Wells girls for each brother and pledge. The room hooted. Even Stoobie grinned.

Snow fell on Saturday morning, and gave the lawn and roof to the fraternity house a bright, clean Christmas look. About four in the afternoon, the jazz band began to arrive, and Stoobie showed them where they should set up. The first five men that Stoobie met just laughed when he showed them the corner of the room he suggested.

Man, there ain't no way we gonna fit in that corner! said the tallest of the bunch. He was about five inches taller than Stoobie, and had the smallest waist Stoobie could recall ever seeing. Stoobie told them to do their best. Then he asked why they thought they needed more room. Another of the men looked at Stoobie and said, Where's Harold?

Stoobie said he didn't know where Harold was. Why?

'Cuz he the one that saw us playing. He'll understand.

Stoobie looked at the men and sniffed. He told them to go ahead and set up, and walked off. The rest of the sixteen man band arrived and carted in their instruments, and a large blue bandstand that said " The Buck Trellins Jazz Standard" in sparkly red letters. Stoobie had gone up to put on his tuxedo, and by the time he returned downstairs, the band had spread out across one entire wall of the great hall. The Christmas tree was now squashed in behind the saxophonists. Stoobie stared at the room, turned toward the dining room and muttered Oh my god three times. There was nothing he could do about that, so he wandered in to see that the dining preparations were ready.

Mitsy Smith went out that morning and bought a bright red cocktail dress and patent leather high heels. When Stoobie picked her up, he thought she looked stunning and told her so. He was in an old fashioned tuxedo and his hair was immaculately parted and combed across his head. A number of Delta Gamma Nu's were going to the formal, but Stoobie was the first to arrive for his date. Mitsy had asked him to come early so she could be there with him from the beginning.

Stoobie took Mitsy's arm and guided her across the slick walkway to his car. She pressed tightly against him, and said she wanted to have a really special time with him tonight. Stoobie gave her a big smile, and agreed that it would be a wonderful evening. They drove back to Eat Chi holding hands in the car.

Danny Carvello picked up Janette Emilio not long after. Janette Emilio was giving Danny Carvello fits. She was as aloof as he was pushy, and while it was clear to Danny that she liked him, she deftly avoided his attempts to become romantic. He made her giggle, and she would be warm and touchy with him, but if he suggested that they sneak off somewhere privately, she stroked his curly hair, told him he was adorable, and kept talking to him as if he had never said anything. Danny found himself in uncharted territory. If any other girl had pushed back so much, he would have dropped her instantly, but something about the way Janette did it made him desire her more.

Danny had had such an easy time with girls at college. It seemed like all he had to do was spend one night with a girl, and she was a willing partner. He always had fun, but the conquest was sweeter than the aftermath, and he rotated through girls every week. Sometimes he slept with them, and sometimes not, but he restlessly moved on. He wasn't really sure what he was looking for. And with respect to relationships, he did not have much to go on for role models.

He loved his parents, but their relationship had been strained for as long as he could recall. When he was little, he thought his father was uncompromisingly critical of him, and his mother sweetly loving. But as he grew up, his parents slowly replaced each other in his childhood universe. His mother, a sullen, quiet woman who did not believe she had gotten a fair shake out of life, increasingly ignored him. She would look impassively at him when he asked her permission to do something, as if she didn't care whether he ever got an answer. Soon he stopped asking her and did whatever he wanted. It took him a long time to see that this was the identical way that she dealt with his father.

Mr. Carvello eventually transformed into Danny's mentor, in an unusual way. He often sat by himself in quiet contemplation, angry at his wife, and unwilling to do anything about it. He was taciturn by nature, and his marriage exacerbated his natural inclination. But as his son grew older, he would put his hand on Danny's shoulder and try to give him advice in the way that his own grandfather had done to him. Danny struggled to see the value of his father's adages (Danny's favorite being, " Life has as many bends as your intestines"), but he felt the love in his father's touch. He knew that he could always return home to his father for that touch and advice, which is often all that a son needs. Regarding relationships, though, his parents offered no model either in words or behaviors, and he felt very much alone.

He knew the type of look that attracted him. He loved thin women, with lots of energy and sparkly eyes. And while he dated lots of different looking girls, invariably he came around to dark haired girls. It was their motivations that he was clueless about. He was quick to surmise what made girls tick – they were open about themselves, and inevitably disappointed him. He could not see that what he was searching for was someone in his own image. Someone as independent and discriminating and intense as himself. He also wanted to find a woman he could have a relationship with that was the exact opposite of his parents'. And it was precisely because he intuitively saw himself in Janette Emilio, but could not perceive it consciously, that he kept coming back around to her.

When he brushed through the doorway in Delta Gamma Nu, Danny saw a couple of girls he knew and greeted them with a big grin and asked them if they were ready. They laughed, and said they weren't his date. You never know! he exclaimed, giggling. When Danny giggled, he kept his chin down and the sound stayed inside his mouth. He peered at them knowingly and asked if he should wander upstairs to see if Janette was ready.

One of the girls groaned and said, Down, boy, I'll go tell her you're here. She didn't bother to add that boys were not allowed on the second floor. All the Eta Chis knew the rules. Danny walked in the living room and looked around restlessly.

Janette entered the living room a few minutes later, and Danny said Wow! She asked him if he was ready, and he nodded his head. Janette had on a silver sequined dress, and her shiny, black hair was combed in a perfect arc around her face. She flashed her long, bright teeth at Danny, and asked him if he liked her dress. Danny put his hand up to his heart and pretended he was having a stroke. Then he giggled and said, What dress? as he extended his arm to her. Her thin arm and long fingers seemed to fit perfectly on his arm.

At Eta Chi, Fritz Hublein sat on the bed in the bordello room in his pants and an undershirt. The noise from two floors below was already audible, and Fritz watched Harold splash after shave on his face just before he headed out to pick up his date. Harold had his trademark powder blue tuxedo on, and was in a great mood, but he couldn't believe his roommate.

You can't just sit there all night and blow her off, Fritz!

Fritz had cold feet about taking Jane Quissling to the formal, and had told Harold moments before that he was just not going to attend. It had been growing in his mind for days, and the protrusion on Jane's forehead had grown bigger in his imagination in lock step.

I'm not going. He said simply. You've seen her – she's a unicorn. There's no reason I should be taking her anywhere when there are lots of pretty girls with regular foreheads I could be taking.

Harold grimaced. Sometimes he opened his big mouth too much. He told Fritz it was not the gentlemanly thing to do. Listen Roomie, you invited her and the poor girl is waiting to be picked up. It was too late for you to back out! Besides, think about what she did to you in her room!

Fritz thought about it. He had not really told Harold anything, except that she had pulled him into her room. And she had been incredible, sitting on his lap in her desk chair and kissing him all over his face. It had been the most erotic kissing he had ever had. But they did little more than sit there and grope each other, and kiss, until he left. And the mountain on her head stayed in the front of his brain.

A sophomore knocked on the door and called out for Fritz, telling him a girl named Jane was on the telephone. He yelled back to tell the sophomore to say he wasn't here. But Harold scolded him and ordered his roommate to go downstairs and tell the girl to her face. That was the absolute least thing he could do. So Fritz pulled himself up, and put his shirt on as he traipsed down the stairs. Harold was right. He couldn't be a total schmuck.

Hello?

Hey Fritz, it's Jane! Her voice was so excited that he felt guilt overriding his stubbornness. What was he doing? She was so upbeat!

I'm glad you're late! She told him.

What?

Well, I'm late too, and I wanted to make sure that you parked on the other side of the dorm and came the short way. I'm wearing very sexy, but very impractical high heels. Jane couldn't believe she had just said that, but she was going for broke tonight. She looked at herself in the mirror, admiring the cobalt blue dress she wore. Her mother had sent her back to school with it after Thanksgiving. It looked fabulous.

Fritz coughed. He told her he'd be there in ten minutes, and apologized for making her wait. He hung up the phone, and couldn't believe he had almost thrown this away. She was going to be a blast tonight!

George Muirfield put the little jewelry box in the glove box, and headed over to College Town to pick up Althea Redmonton. He was wearing his father's old tuxedo, and feeling great. Since September, George had received a monthly check for forty-five dollars from the government. It was a death survivor benefit from Social Security that he would get until he turned twenty-one. He had tried unsuccessfully to save it all for something, but by December he had still managed to hold on to ninety-one dollars which he had taken downtown this morning to buy Althea something.

It had taken him about ninety-one minutes in the jewelry store to pick out what he could afford. It was an amethyst ring with tiny little diamond pieces in a star around the stone. He had gone through bracelets and necklaces, which he thought would be more practical, but he kept returning to the ring, and the girl behind the counter assured him that she would *love* it if her boyfriend gave her that.

He ran up the steps to her apartment in the frisky air and knocked lightly on the door. He could see her walking around inside, and she waved him in, so he entered the warmly lit room. Waiting for an invitation out there? Althea teased him. She thought it was so funny how he still knocked when he came over. She wore a navy blue dress and pearls, and stuck pearl earrings through her ears as she walked to get her coat.

In the car George used the wipers to clear off the windshield as the car heater blasted luke warm air though the vents. Althea could see her breath, and George looked at the frosty air spiraling out from his girlfriend's full, lipsticked lips and thought he was an especially lucky person. As they drove into the Eta Chi parking lot, George had to pull in between a number of cars to park. As Althea moved to open her door, George said, Wait a sec.

You didn't get me anything for Christmas, right? he asked. Althea said no, not yet. Then she looked at him suspiciously. Why?

There's some Christmas love for you in the glove box. Althea's eyes widened. She popped open the compartment, and the little gift-wrapped box fell on her lap. She looked at her boyfriend. Part of her was afraid to look in the box and she sat there looking at it for a moment. Then she unwrapped it slowly. George could smell her perfume in the warmth of the now-heated car.

Althea pried open the box while George watched her face. Then she smiled widely, and his center spun wildly as she looked at him and told him it was beautiful. Not as beautiful as you, he replied.

Althea pulled the ring from its indentation, and tried it on her middle finger. It slid around slightly, but it was close. George told her she could have it fitted where he had bought it downtown. Althea felt herself getting warm, and the slightest tear welled in her eye. She couldn't believe what this past two months had been, and she couldn't believe she deserved this. George was so romantic with her that it made her feel like she was a different person. Her mother was crazy – she loved this guy and it felt perfect.

George put his finger up to her eye and brushed away the tear he saw forming. He told her he hadn't expected to make her sad. She gasped, and put her head softly against his shoulder and told him to shut up. He put his arm around her and hugged her gently. She composed herself quickly and sat up and turned her body to look at him. She held her hand out and gazed at the ring, and then looked back up at him and shook her head back and forth. How am I not supposed to love you? she asked.

Don't ask me such complicated questions, George answered, smiling. The lights from another car pulling in the driveway illuminated Althea's face briefly, and George puzzled over her reaction. What did "not supposed" mean? Then Althea leaned over and kissed him, and life was good.

The Buck Trellins Jazz Standard was playing *I'll be home for Christmas* as George and Althea walked in from outside. Well, actually only five of the sixteen band members were playing. The rest sat around waiting for the real music to get going after dinner. Althea walked off to find Holly, and George went to the bar to get them both a drink. Stoobie and Mitsy were surveying the scene from the bar and smiled broadly as people approached. The smooth wail of a trumpet gave the scene a traditional luster.

Fritz and Jane walked in as George was leaving with drinks in his hand, and he greeted Jane warmly. Fritz looked uncomfortable but Stoobie and Mitsy acted like parents welcoming the two into their home. Mitsy already had her flower pinned to her dress, and Jane told her how pretty it was. Fritz pulled his mouth up in a straight line and raised his eyebrows at Stoobie. The band started playing *Deck The Halls*.

Dinner was rock Cornish game hens with sweet potatoes and green beans. Andy's signature banana crème pie followed, and the boys stood ceremoniously at their chairs as they sang the Darling Song to Holly. Althea watched George smile as he sang. She wiggled her hand with the ring on it to distract him. George concentrated on hitting the notes, which he was beginning to be able to do.

Jane Quissling was so happy to be at the formal, her energy lifted the entire table where she sat with Fritz. He held her hand under the table during dinner, and when they looked at each other the anticipation of the evening made their eyes bright in a diffused way. Fritz couldn't believe he had almost blown this off. Then he felt Jane's hand resting lightly on his thigh, and put his arm around her chair and let his fingers touch the soft material of her dress.

Jane had decided she was going to sleep with Fritz tonight, and wanted the night to build for them both. She was a virgin, but she was extremely well read on the topic of sex, and had it pictured fully in her head. Once she locked her lips on Fritz later tonight, he didn't stand a chance.

Across the room, Mitsy Smith was letting herself have similar thoughts about Stoobie, although she certainly did not plan it out like Jane was doing. She only thought about kissing Stoobie with more abandon, and seeing where it might lead, once they were both losing their inhibitions. It was time, she thought, to see whether they were ready for a more serious commitment to one another, and the Christmas formal was a wonderful setting for it to happen.

Mitsy sat next to Janette Emilio who was thoroughly enjoying her banter with Danny Carvello. Danny was trouble, but he was charming and smart and enormously entertaining. He seemed more mature than so many of the other boys. Janette had resisted his advances so far, because she was not interested in joining the pile of girls on his scrap heap. But she continued to think that they were developing a nice relationship without the sex. The sex would come someday.

Martha Higgins had not dated much this fall. She had focused on her studies for a change, and avoided all the bar hopping of last spring. But when Harold Wise called her out of the blue to invite her to the Christmas formal, it was exactly the tonic she needed. She couldn't sit in her sorority forever, and Harold was fun to party with. Since the summer, she had not really allowed herself to think about having sex. It wasn't that she wouldn't in the right circumstances, and it wasn't that she would. She just ignored the issue in her mind. As she sat with Harold at dinner, and his arm rested comfortably along the back of her chair, she made no indication to him, or to herself, whether she appreciated his advance.

Charles Lord stood at the conclusion of the meal, and asked everyone to join him in thanking Andy for the delicious meal, and the servers for their kind efforts, and everyone cheered and applauded as Andy came out from the kitchen with his chef's hat on and waved to the crowd. The Buck Trellins Band started in earnest about two minutes later, and the horns blared out a fast, rollicking tune that beckoned the group into the great hall and onto the dance floor. The really fast music was not easy to dance to, and a number of people just hopped around loosely. But when the band offered up a more classic jazz beat, Stoobie and Mitsy danced the jitterbug and swing, and twirled through the room with élan. Mitsy looked beautiful, and felt the flush of her cheeks as the night wore on. Stoobie felt the old glamour of the house had returned a little, and was proud to be with his date in the midst of his brothers.

At the end of the night, following a raucous, improvisational, high-octane finish, the crowd applauded and dispersed slowly. Stoobie took Mitsy up to his room to unwind a bit. There were a number of boys and girls sitting all over the house. Some couples had headed out for one last drink at the Creeker, in their fancy dress and all. Mitsy reached up to Stoobie and wrapped her arms around his neck. She told him what a lovely night she was having. Stoobie's hands were on Mitsy's waist, and they kissed. They had kissed before, of course, and Stoobie had occasionally enjoyed the taste of her lips and the soft fabric of her dress, but he had never felt the stirrings that he so desperately hoped he could. It was like there was a cellophane barrier he could not breathe through, or a cardboard-like vagueness to the exchange that left him unmoved.

In the past, he had worked his way through their kisses, and they had shifted away to other conceits, but this time Mitsy's hands were more insistent on the back of his neck. Stoobie could sense her winding herself up. It was as if she were opening herself to him, as she parted her lips and pushed her tongue delicately into his mouth. He fought back the distaste in his mind, and then, for the first time in his life, imagined himself kissing a boy. The thought of it aroused him, and shamed him, and intrigued him. Mitsy sensed the difference in him and grew more excited herself.

She wanted whatever was happening to continue, and she moved her hands to different places on him, so he would know he was free to roam his hands across her. But Stoobie kept his hands on her waist, lost inside a rapid succession of conflicting emotions, and afraid to open his eyes and confront himself. Mitsy put her right hand on his left, and pulled it up toward her breast, and Stoobie willed himself to try and enjoy her invitation. He let his hand glide gently across her chest and felt the outline of her bosom, and heard Mitsy sigh slightly in the middle of their kiss. He momentarily felt himself grow hard, but it did not last, and when he thought of it, he was repulsed by himself, and his predicament.

Mitsy was on overload. She could not believe how daring she had been, or how moved she was by his touch. It was distinctly more intense than the scenes she had devoured in books, and she understood quickly how easily it would be to give way to the moment. She discerned her boyfriend's turn of emotion, crediting him with the integrity to pull himself back, lest they lose their self control, and relaxed in his arms as their lips pulled away from each other.

Mitsy, Stoobie began, but she shushed him and put her head sideways against his shoulder, and told him she knew. Stoobie looked at the painting on his wall, sure that she didn't have a clue. Then she told him how much they believed in the same things. Stoobie looked at her carefully, and said that he was lucky to have found her. To himself, he thought lucky was actually not far from the truth. But he had a new, private dilemma. He had admitted to himself that he really was attracted to boys *that way*. It made him want to puke.

Jim Steuben had done nothing to deserve this. He had been raised by loving parents, who had given him a normal childhood. His father, who had been raised with wealth, but was not very wealthy himself, had always been sure to give his son a keen sense of the world around him. He had taken him to ball games and museums, to debutante balls and soup kitchens. Stoobie's parents obviously had a strong marriage, and their love for each other pervaded their home. They had stopped after Jim, so he was an only child, but they had made play dates for him, and sent him to camps. He had not been lonely or neglected. But here he was, attracted to men. It didn't seem fair.

It would be a long, and eventually enjoyable road to acceptance, and Stoobie would one day look back to this night as the turning point in his life. But standing in his room at Eta Chi with Mitsy Smith, it looked like a disaster. He was surrounded by boys with testosterone levels north of the arctic sea, who would not appreciate learning that he was...different. He was in a burgeoning relationship with a wonderful girl who expected him to return her advances, and he was unable to bring himself to do so. And he was totally unequipped to know what this really meant for him. Or even if he really believed that this was to be his destiny. Maybe he was just confused.

⁓

At Mary Donnelly Hall, Jane Quissling took Fritz's hand and walked slightly in front of him as she led him to her dorm room. On the dance floor, they had touched each other in increasingly intimate ways, though Jane was careful to be discreet. It had been so crowded, she was certain nobody noticed them, and she was thrilled to control the tempo of their exchanges. They had been drinking the eggnog that Stoobie had been sure to serve for the Christmas theme, and then they had switched to beer. It had been a special night because Jane had literally forgotten about her hot spot for a while. She was just Jane Quissling, hot kisser in a cobalt blue dress, flirting with her new boyfriend. At one point she even smiled flirtatiously at the boy behind the bar who refilled their drinks.

When they got to her room, Jane had already removed her key, and pushed it into the lock, twisted it around, and then used the same hand to turn the door handle so she didn't have to drop Fritz's hand. Fritz followed her like a dutiful puppy. Inside, Jane removed the key as she closed the door and threw it on her desk. Before they left Eta Chi, Jane had refreshed her lipstick and put a new dab of perfume on her neck. She smelled great.

Fritz looked at his date expectantly. She had taken charge of things the whole night, and he waited for her to continue. Her hot spot poked toward him, but he didn't care. It was no longer an oddity or impediment. Jane Quissling was hot, and Fritz had high hopes.

Jane saw the delicious anticipation in his eyes, and understood that this was her night. She had not allowed herself to think about it, but the fantasy she had enjoyed for years began to surface in the back of her mind. It had taken root when she was fifteen, when the permanence and meaning of her hot spot had led her to see her distinct feature as a sort of super-characteristic. She imagined her hot spot as her unique erogenous zone – a secret source of pleasure for herself and her partner, once discovered and accepted. If only she could find the right boy!

Jane took Fritz's hand and led him to her bed, and they sat down next to each other at the same moment. Jane led her date on a slow exploration of their faces, using her trademark kisses to let their desire build, and then floated her hands across his body, accepting his in return. She was becoming preoccupied with leading him to her hot spot, but he did not go there willingly. She knew it had to be at just the right moment, and backed off for awhile. They focused on their bodies, and undressed clumsily, laughing at their own fumbling desire. Then they were naked and making love, and it was every bit as good as Jane had anticipated.

Fritz was breathing heavily, lost in his own sensations, and for a long time Jane joined him in the simple joy of it all. This was definitely something she was going to get a lot more of, now that it was real to her. Then her fantasy returned, and as their lovemaking heightened, Jane put her hands on the sides of Fritz's face, and maneuvered his head so that her hot spot was directly in front of his mouth. She was so close. Her brain was on fire.

Fritz's eyes were closed, and he felt her guiding him and kissed her face, and then felt the unusual protuberance brush against his lips. It was like a slap in the face as he realized where his lips were, but he was too far along in his own journey to stop. Jane's breath was ragged beneath him, and so he tenderly kissed the thing and made her moan. And when he realized what pleasure it brought her, he continued.

For the rest of her life, Jane Quissling's hot spot would be for her the ultimate gift to her lovers, something she withheld until she was prepared to give herself to her partner. Her fantasy, once realized, changed forever her perspective on her disfigurement. The low cards life had dealt her suddenly became wild in a game reserved for grownups. And Fritz found her the most extraordinary woman he had ever touched.

CHAPTER SEVENTEEN

O n New Year's eve, George Muirfield drove west on the Massachusetts Turnpike in his red Camaro, toward Althea's house in Vermont. Christmas break had taken him home to a tender and sad holiday without his father. Henry Muirfield had been a great source of energy at holidays, and it would never be the same without him, but George enjoyed the music and the feel of the decorated house. His mother sighed a lot, but smiled wanly when the children struggled to put up the tree in the living room, and recalled the oversized trees that their father had always insisted on.

Much to his mother's dismay, George had announced he would be leaving on New Year's Eve to visit his girlfriend's family in Vermont, and from there heading on to the fraternity for formal rush. Beth Muirfield wished her son would stay through the second holiday. His male voice and resemblance to her husband helped to remind her of when she had been happy. But George was unequivocal, and she knew that this sort of thing had to happen.

A light, powdery snow blew across the highway as George drove, and once he was past Worcester, the road opened up and allowed him to watch the dry snow swirl aimlessly before him. The car heater was on high, and the hot air felt good on his feet. A cassette tape of Ten Years After was playing. Althea had told him yesterday that she couldn't wait to see him, and he was excited to meet her family and see where she had grown up.

He reached the Berkshires and headed north as she had instructed him, on the open highway that runs straight north through the middle of the state. Althea's house was only an hour or so further, and he had only just begun to feel his car strain to climb the ascending hills when her exit appeared. George marveled at the austerity of the place. Tall evergreens blanked the landscape, and the roads were empty compared to home.

The cassette tape ended, but the tape player had an automatic reverse feature, so there was a clicking sound, and short whir, and then the music on side two started up. Something about the song made George think about the theater, and as he drove along a country road, he wondered about the choices he had made. He had been obsessed with the theater for almost two years, and then stopped cold. He had expected to feel remiss, and regret, but the year had picked him up like an enormous wave and flung him in a different direction.

There was Althea, of course, who filled his waking moments with an intensity of emotion and desire totally new to him. Every time she put her fists in front of her, and moved them like a locomotive, he experienced a joy that shamed him. Every time he saw her with another boy, his skin itched with the inflaming insecurity of jealousy. He was sure that he was being taken advantage of, that she was being tempted by another because the boy must be better than he. Then she would turn and wink at him, and he would ridicule himself for being foolish. It was a delicious, unregulated tide of passion, and it made him redouble his efforts to be worthy for her.

And there was the house, which had continued to wriggle itself under George's skin, like a fishhook. He found himself delighting in the camaraderie of his fraternity, in the sheer bombast of it all. There were many other boys with whom he socialized, but there seemed to be a special syncopation between himself and Harold, Danny, Fritz, Cullen, and Stoobie. They didn't spend all of their free time together, and in fact, led quite disparate schedules. But there was a sense of belonging, an unspoken bond amongst them, which carried with it obligations of brotherhood. It did not come free. So much happened week to week that constant communication and flexibility was needed to meet the unspoken obligations of the unit. And each of them consistently came through.

And there was his academic work, which he had thrown himself at with unabashed vigor. He liked his creative writing class, but even more his Early American Literature class. The professor was a lunatic, a mesmerizing, one-man scholarship show, who lectured in his stocking feet, with a pipe upside down in his mouth, facing the blackboard with his arms outstretched. George found him smarter and more insightful than anyone he had ever met.

And George had happened into new campus responsibilities because Charles Lord had asked him to cover a campus tour for him one day.

Just walk them wherever you feel like around the campus, he had instructed George, and tell them how wonderful the school is. George said Got it!, found the family in the Admissions office, and led them around the Arts Quad and to the Straight.

He regaled them with stories of theater and fraternities and Johnny's Hot truck, and immediately adopted the gait of the father who was striding with gusto as they toured. It had been fun, and George was quickly on the schedule giving tours, and being asked to speak to assembled groups about undergraduate life at Cornell. It was like improv, and he reveled at turning the somewhat stilted presentation into humorous stories and offhanded remarks that made the people laugh and connect with him. It was like an actor's high, without any risk.

His life had assumed a pace and a style that felt right. It was responsible, and made him feel so grown up. If there was a natural order to things, this call to service on behalf of his brothers and the campus was an expected progression toward a professional life. Still, he wondered about what was happening in the theater department. He had heard from his freshman roommate that Caitlin had done a wonderful turn as an old woman in Ibsen's *A Doll House*. Stephen had invited him to come to the show, but George ducked out of going to any productions. He doubted his ability to stay away from that world, and so avoided it totally. So why was he driving on a country road in Vermont, toying with the idea of trying out for a spring production? As he thought this, he saw the bright red mailbox Althea had told him to watch for.

Althea was standing in her driveway by the time George reached her house from the road below. He pulled his car off to one side of the enormous drive, and left the warmth of his car for her waiting arms. Althea smiled widely. She wore an oversized patchwork sweater over a white turtleneck, and blue jeans. She kissed him quickly, and he let the familiar pull of her eyes and the comfort of her touch invade his senses. She shut his car door and pulled him along behind her toward the house. He didn't know that there was no one home, but she led him quickly for some reason.

Althea walked him through the house directly to her bedroom, telling him this was probably the only time they would have alone, and they fell into her big bed together, laughing and saying how much they had missed each other. They touched each other through their clothes, and talked until they heard a car approach. Then Althea yanked him up off the bed, smoothed out the comforter, and ran toward the kitchen, urging him to follow her.

They sat at the kitchen table, and Althea jumped back up to pour them Cokes from the fridge and sat back down. The door opened and her parents pushed into the room carrying groceries. George stood up as Althea introduced him to her parents, and George offered to take the packages from Dottie, but she demurred, and carried them to the counter herself. Then she turned and shook his hand and looked objectively at the boy her daughter seemed so smitten with.

He had a good, strong handshake, which Dottie appreciated, and an openness to his gaze that led her to think he was intelligent. But he stood awfully casually, almost back on his heels, or tentative, which she thought might suggest a softness to him. She didn't think Althea needed too soft of a man. He was handsome, although he did not have the jocular sort of ruggedness her husband affected. She watched Alexander shake George's hand and welcome him. George became formal, and intent as he looked at her husband. Dottie wondered if he was play-acting. Althea had talked about how he had been in the theater. Her daughter stood next to him, watching her father, and Dottie smiled to herself. Althea was beaming.

Althea suggested that George get his bag from the car, and he walked outside with her, rummaged around in the car, and pulled a small duffle bag out from a pile of things he had shoved in the backseat of the car. Althea stood behind him, talking, and George could feel her anxiety as the cold air made his hands cold. His car already had that clanking brittleness from sitting out in freezing temperatures, and George blew his own warm breath into his fists, before he withdrew his parka from the passenger seat, and pushed the door closed with a metallic thud.

Dottie watched them from the kitchen window. She saw how they touched each other in the way that only lovers do, and mused about the two of them. She remembered how she and Alexander had been, although they certainly had not been lovers after only a few months. But she didn't object to the idea. In fact, she liked the fact that her daughter was experiencing life now. But it would clearly be a mistake for her daughter to latch onto this boy. Althea needed to play the field, and get a full picture of her options before she settled down. It did not occur to Dottie that her daughter would not necessarily settle down any time soon.

There were thirty people expected at the Redmonton's for New Year's – family and friends and neighbors – and it was Alexander's favorite party of the year. He loved New Year's because the rush of Christmas was past, and he had been off work for a number of days, and the only objective of the night was to get drunk and kiss as many women as you could at midnight. Dottie liked the party too. Ever since her husband's widowed partner had too much to drink and kissed her passionately in the kitchen when people shouted Happy New Year, she had looked forward to the holiday. It wasn't that she wanted anyone to kiss her (let alone the partner who had never been invited back); it was the sheer naughtiness of her memory that made her engine rev.

By six thirty at night, the first of several couples had arrived to help with the preparations. Dottie mixed sour cream and cream cheese and herbs and vegetables together for some sort of dip, and Althea and George helped her set up the bar on a table in the den. Neighbors arrived first, and Dottie listened to them exclaim as they saw Althea, and greet George. She heard George talk to her guests about Cornell, and the neighbors react with high voices. He seems to ingratiate himself quickly, Dottie noted to herself. Perhaps too quickly.

By eight, the house was abuzz with people laughing loudly and wandering about with drink glasses. The hors d'oeurvres piled high on numerous tables and the men hovered near the table with the hot appetizers, talking sports. Dottie watched George meander through the rooms, chatting in a clear, strong voice with all of the guests. She thought he should stay more with the men, but she liked the fact that he did not cling to Althea, who moved graciously among all of the guests as well. At least he was not a hoverer.

At a quarter to twelve, the group had already dispersed and then regrouped, and Althea and George helped Dottie pop the cork on the champagne bottles and pour the wine into the flutes on the serving trays. George said silly things as he poured the wine, making Althea laugh. Even Dottie found herself smiling.

Then the two kids served the wine to all of the guests, and someone turned the television volume up, and Dottie walked around handing out hats and noisemakers. She had carefully put a hat on her own head, to get people in the mood, and when the ball dropped the room cheered, and people reached to the people nearest them and kissed. Dottie ended up kissing her next door neighbor first and then looking for Alexander, who walked up behind her, and put his arms around her waist before he kissed her. Dottie was on the lookout for her daughter, and saw George and Althea quickly exchange a look and a kiss before they smiled largely at the people around them. Something about their kiss angered her. It was a little too intimate.

New Year's Day started late. By the time Dottie found her way into the kitchen, Alexander had already mixed Bloody Mary's and Althea was frying bacon in her bathrobe. George whisked eggs in a bowl. He was dressed, but his hair stuck straight up, so he had obviously not looked in a mirror yet. The television blared in the den, and snow fell lightly in the yard. Althea was talking about how one of the neighbors kept putting his arm around her last night, and how creepy it was.

George poured the beaten eggs into a frying pan coated with melted butter and tossed pieces of tomato, onion, and shredded cheese on top as the eggs began to set. Dottie watched him take just the edge of the omelet and turn it over, wait, and then fold that over again on itself, going in the same direction across the pan. When she observed that she had never seen an omelet prepared this way, George explained that this was how Andy in his fraternity did it. When it was cooked, the omelet was rectangular and layered. The cheese and vegetables slipped out of the ends a bit as George used two spatulas to lift the omelet onto a plate. George sliced the omelet into thirds, and then returned to whisking new eggs while fresh butter melted in the pan.

Althea leaned against the counter in her bathrobe, tousling her hair with her right hand. Dottie had poured herself a cup of coffee and sat at the kitchen table to watch. George finished a second omelet the same way, removed it from the pan, sliced it into thirds, and brought the plate to the table. He smiled at Dottie, and told her how much he appreciated the invitation to visit. Dottie nodded her head.

We've been looking forward to meeting you, Dottie said.

The slight gnaw in George's mind intensified. He had not felt comfortable here, and there was something disconcerting in Dottie's response – a reticence, perhaps, or disdain. Maybe he worried unnecessarily. But he was also having trouble connecting with Althea's father.

Alexander acted perfectly pleasant, but his look was as dissembling to George as Althea's was open. Alexander Redmonton had that stiff bearing of men who get what they want and don't think about what others want. George guessed that he was somehow disappointed by him. He was too young to understand that Alexander Redmonton was subconsciously competing with him. But what really threw him about Alexander Red-monton was how he resembled someone that he could not put his finger on. There was a look or a way about Althea's father that was weirdly familiar to George. And it was a look that George really disliked.

Althea told her boyfriend to tell the story about Brandy in the psych class. George was sitting opposite Dottie as Althea brought orange juice and bacon to the table, when he began the story. He looked directly into Dottie's eyes and used his arms and hands dramatically as he spoke.

First of all, he began, it's important to understand that Brandy is truly the BDOC!

Dottie smiled warmly and said, Big Dog On Campus?

Precisely! George replied. Brandy is the BDOC. Everybody knows him. All of the other dogs on campus move out of his way as he moves across the quad.

Dottie scooped a piece of the omelet on her plate, and took three slices of the bacon from the other plate. George couldn't tell if he should go on.

Anyway, George explained, my psychology 101 class is held in this enormous amphitheater. There must be five- or six- hundred kids in the class. So Brandy, who often accompanies my fraternity brothers to class, walks in mid-way through the lecture, and looks around.

That day we had a guest lecturer, a woman with a high, officious voice. George imitated her voice, and Dottie laughed. Althea looked oddly at her mother. George plowed on. Our normal professor would have known Brandy, of course, but this woman looked a little freaked out. So Brandy saunters in and slowly walks down the large steps through the rows of students, toward the center of the stage. George imitated the dog's pronounced girth and gait by thrusting one shoulder and then the other forward and back. Then he laughed and went on.

I was sitting in one of the aisle seats, but didn't say anything as he passed. Brandy walks straight toward the lecturer, who gets more and more agitated as Brandy gets close.

So the lecturer continues to speak, but she starts to move away from the podium, away from this big beast coming toward her. She ends up walking in a circle around the podium, because the microphone she's wearing is connected to the base of the podium. So good old Brandy keeps following her until she has wrapped the microphone wire so tightly around the podium she can't move.

George leaned back and spread his hands expressively. So here's a psychology professor, he said, fumbling with the microphone on the lapel of her dress with Brandy standing about a foot away from her, panting and drooling. The entire room is dead silent. I look over at some of my fraternity brothers across the hall, but none of us really wants to get involved, so we smile and shrug our shoulders.

The teacher is frozen in place when Brandy literally shrugs himself! George imitated the big dog shrugging. Then he turns and saunters back up the wide steps of the amphitheater and out the door. Dottie shook her head appreciatively.

You have a wonderfully dramatic way of telling the story, George. Dottie said. Are you going to be an actor?

George looked sincerely at his girlfriend's mother and responded instinctively. He had heard the accusation in her voice. It stabbed him deeply.

Actually, I gave up the theater, he replied.

Mr. Redmonton chose business school, Dottie said. Perhaps you should chat with him about his recommendations. George nodded, and thanked Dottie. He wished he was already back in his car, headed for school.

The same uneasy repartee between George and Althea's parents continued until George left their house early on the morning of January third. George worked hard to please them, but with little obvious success. He told Althea he thought her parents weren't so sure about him, but she just sighed and said they were always a pain.

Althea hugged her boyfriend hard in the cold morning air as his car tried to warm up. They were the only ones up in the house, and they had held hands at the kitchen table while they drank coffee. Althea wished she were driving up with him, but it didn't make any sense. George was going to be totally preoccupied with rush and no one else would be on campus until the day before classes started. So they sat quietly in the big kitchen, smiling at each other until George stood up and said he had to go.

Althea waved goodbye as George backed down the long driveway and sped off down the road. She had her parka on over her pajamas, and her feet were freezing in the half slippers she had put on to walk George outside. She hurried back in, and sat at the kitchen table to rub warmth back into her toes. Her mother shuffled in in her bathrobe and Althea looked at her mother accusingly.

What is it, dear? Dottie asked.

You know what it is, mother, she said as strongly as she could. When I asked you if George could come visit for a few days, I didn't think that you were going to spend the time undermining him and me.

Dottie looked at her daughter and shrugged. You're over tired, honey. Your boyfriend is nice. And he certainly seems taken with you.

Maybe she was just tired, as her mother had said. But her mother had clearly baited George, and her father had kept jutting his chin out and making stiff pronouncements about stupid things. Althea looked out the window at the wintry landscape and sighed. Her mother was her mother, and she really liked her dad. He had a brusque way of taking charge that made her feel safe.

In the afternoon, Althea wandered into the kitchen where her parents still sat around the big square table with newspapers spread open. Her father asked her what she had been doing, and Althea said, Reading. Dottie looked out the kitchen window from where she stood at the kitchen sink. She told her husband that Althea thought they had been unfair to her boyfriend. Alexander snorted and asked what that meant.

I'm not sure, Dottie replied. Althea, why don't you let us in on what you think?

Althea went to make herself some tea, and told her parents they knew the way they had acted. She doubted that they needed her to explain it to them. Of course, she wasn't sure she could explain it to them, if pressed, so she suggested that they tell her what they thought about George.

Nice enough fellow, her father responded blithely. He was polite, seemed smart enough. Alexander looked at his wife. Don't you think so, honey? Alexander rarely called Dottie honey.

Dottie dried her hands at the sink, and moved to the table. He's a very nice boy, she said in a firm tone of voice. I don't know why you think we were bad to him, Althea.

He seemed like he was having a nice time. Alexander raised his eyebrows slightly, and looked questioningly at his daughter.

So what if I told you that George and I were serious about each other? Althea asked in a small voice. She purposely looked down at the newspaper on the table as she said this, but focused intensely on her mother.

Dottie took a breath in, and then exhaled slowly. Then, I would say that the two of you should take your time to make sure that you are right for each other. There is certainly nothing gained by rushing in to anything. Dottie eyed her husband as she spoke, making him part of the conversation.

I agree with your mother, sweetie. George seems like a nice enough young man, but you shouldn't make big decisions so quickly. Her father's voice was flat as he said the words.

For once, Althea felt like she had achieved some leverage with her parents. They were uncomfortable because they did not control her relationship with George.

But at the end of the day, if George is the right one for me, you will support me, right?

Dottie smiled. Of course we will, she said brightly. We just want to be sure that you think hard about the person you end up choosing as your mate. Make sure that you know everything about George, and be critical in your assessment of him. Life can be tough, Althea, and you need to be sure that the boy you choose is tough enough to make it through at your side. Alexander nodded, but the look on his face was one of disinterest.

So you think George isn't tough?

I don't know if he is or isn't, dear. You have to make that decision. Dottie grinned at her daughter and patted her hand. Alexander said he was going to pack for his run into Manhattan in the morning. Althea felt completely disconnected from her parents, and wondered if they had always been so…remote. Their relationship, which she knew to be strong was so rigid that it seemed constructed out of steel beams. She and George had an almost opposite thing. Their passion was raw, mutual, and blindingly hot. It seemed true and righteous, by comparison.

⌘

George pulled into the Eta Chi parking lot at noon. He was early to the house. Whatever had riddled his thoughts about his visit to Althea's (God, how he loved her!), the prospect of formal rush brushed it away. He carried his things into the house, and yelled in its hollow mass for Edward Stamer. He got no answer, but Edward's car was in the driveway, so he knew he was about. It took him three trips to unpack his car, and then he went to find Edward. Edward was sitting in his room, hunched over his desk in front of lists of brothers.

George saluted him as he walked in. Edward smiled, and handed him some lists. Tell me what you think, he said. George threw himself on Edward's bed and the two of them sat quietly looking at lists for a bit. And then they started trading names, like they were forming teams in a draft. It was the beginning of an extraordinary five days of partnership between them.

Edward had asked George to be back early and help him with rush. George "got" rush, and Edward found him an incredible ally in the process. He thought differently from Edward, but between the two of them, they created very strong balance in all of the teams, and particularly the power teams. George, Danny Carvello, and Charles Lord would lead the first three power teams. And finally they settled on Mike O'Hare, who had been named consul for the spring semester, to lead the fourth team. Mike made an unusual choice for consul, but George pointed out that, in his own emotional way, he was a good choice to lead a power team. He would put his heart and soul into it, and the genuine character of his love for the house would not be lost on any freshmen. Edward grinned in response. Mike O'Hare was a wild man.

But both boys thought that the other teams were going to be the key to this rush. They thought that the power teams would deliver, but if they wanted to maintain the luster of past performance by getting every freshman offered a bid to accept, the entire house needed to be effective. And so they fretted over every team, picturing the dynamics of, say, David Dalrumple's joking demeanor with the solemn face of Cullen Hastings. Every team had to be just the right combination of talents and characters.

As they worked they could hear the brotherhood arriving, unpacking, yelling, playing music, laughing. Edward asked George to post the lists on the upstairs hallway while he went down to start the five p.m. meeting. So George sat in Edward's room until he heard the boys romping through the hallways on their way down to the great hall. Then he gathered up the papers and walked down to the second floor to the bulletin board and posted the lists. By the time he finished and walked downstairs, the group was hushed, listening to Edward recite the well-worn rules of Eta Chi rush.

By the last day of formal rush, Eta Chi had made twenty-six bids, and twenty-four had been accepted. The mood in the house was high. George was on tender hooks. The only two hold outs were both assigned to George's team, and he felt the pressure of the entire house on him. Each hold out was genuinely torn between Eta Chi and another house, and George spent every waking moment thinking about them. He liked both boys a lot.

Wendall Wellington was a sophomore – a transfer from California who was as unlikely a candidate for the traditional notion of a fraternity as George had been when he rushed. Wendall had toured the world with Up With People, was snide and sophisticated, and would go on to make movies in Hollywood. But for now, he was a college sophomore, hot for a social network at his new school, and a perfect addition to the characters in Eta Chi. He definitely made the lights go up when he entered the room. The only problem was getting him to see it that way. As of Saturday night, he appeared to be leaning toward a very small house with a substantial endowment. It attracted boys with sophisticated tastes and trust funds.

Since it was the last night of rush, George, Danny, Edward and Mike formed a special power team for their two remaining dorm visits. Mike O'Hare drove in his Chevy Nova. They walked into West Campus and went immediately to Wendall Wellington's dorm. They had agreed that Edward would actually start off the meeting by explaining that this was his first room visit – Wendall was that important to the house. Wendall greeted them jovially at his door.

He was small, about five-feet six, and slender, and dressed in expensive clothes. He had sharp, pointed features, and a huge head of brown curly hair. He was a social animal, and loved the spirited hellos and exchanges. Edward grew serious once in the room and the Eta Chis looked to him expectantly.

Edward stammered as he started. He was, after all, out of practice, but he quickly returned to his form and spoke well. George watched him intently, and occasionally glanced at Wendall to gauge his reaction. Wendall looked awfully comfortable, and George guessed that he had already made up his mind. So at the end of Edward's remarks, he broke in. He asked Wendall if he had reached a decision yet, and Wendall said he had not. But his eyes communicated something different as he looked at George, and George asked him how important passion was to him.

George's brothers looked oddly at George. His question was certainly a normal one for a formal rush room visit, but his tone surprised them. It was like he was taunting the boy. Wendall responded in a gush that it was critical to him. Why?

Because passion should be the key to your decision – and it's the key to Eta Chi. You may not have noticed it, but there's a buzz – an intensity – that seeps out of my brothers' pores. George looked at Mike O'Hare as he continued. It is one of the few common threads that run through the eclectic clan of my brothers, and it is something that pledges absolutely must have in order to make it in our house. Again, George's voice was taunting. Wendall looked like he was getting irritated.

Don't you agree, Mike? George asked.

Mike's face had reddened as he watched the exchange between George and Wendall. Given the chance, he unloaded on the poor bid candidate. He spoke in a jumble of words about his love for the house, about the passion and the privilege he felt every time he walked through the door to his house. Then he looked almost accusingly at Wendall and told him that his brothers were the most outstanding people on the entire campus, people that he would know and treasure for all time. If Wendall was not ready for this kind of passion, that was fine. But they were offering it to him, because they saw in him the capacity to belong.

In Mike's Boston accent, "treasure" had sounded like "trezsha." Wendall was transfixed. Danny Carvello asked Mike if he needed a glass of water. Everybody laughed. George, who had spent long conversations with Wendall, trading stories about the theater, turned and said, Don't you wish we could bottle up Mike's passion and then release it on stage?

Danny narrowed his eyebrows, and brought the meeting back into focus. The diversity you see in this room is only a glimpse of our house, he said quietly. We do not seek people who are athletes, or engineers, or sophisticates. We seek people for our house whom we believe can add to its luster, and make the rest of us stronger. It's not for everybody, Wendall, but we believe it's for you. Danny lifted his head and put his hands next to his face to suggest that now it was up to him.

George talked about the different ways to be a brother in Eta Chi. There's room in our house for you to be what you want to be, he said, and I'm a perfect example. I guess what we want you to do is challenge yourself to compare us to your other choice. Only you can really see where you belong. And we will completely respect your decision.

Wendall Wellington's eyes were moist. Something inside him welled up. The other fraternity had been so nonchalantly arrogant about how special they were. Wendall wiped his eyes with his hand. He favored Eta Chi, but the other house had seemed so much more logical. But his reservations were wiped away by their performance. I accept your bid, he said in a rush.

The four Eta Chis whooped in one rising chorus. They shook Wendall's hand excitedly, and patted each other on the back. After they had chatted with Wendall for another twenty minutes, they said they had one more stop they had to make, and had to get going. They invited him to come by the next day, and left the room with his signed pledge card. Once outside, they slapped each others' hands and laughed together. Edward wrapped his arm around George's shoulder and told him that had been brilliant. George responded that Mike O'Hare had brought Wendall home, and all three boys clapped Mike on the shoulder.

Their next stop was nowhere near as fun. They arduously answered the multitude of concerns that the last remaining candidate had about his choices. He was genuinely torn, and they left without an answer, but the next day the boy turned in his pledge card for Eta Chi. George slumped in his chair when he heard. It had been far closer than he had expected, but the house was 26 for 26. But only 25 boys actually became Eta Chis. The last boy transferred to another school mid way through the semester, and left a week before initiation.

Chapter Eighteen

By the time initiation rolled around, the winter of 1976 had heaved more snow on Ithaca than in the past two years combined. It had been unremittingly frosty and difficult to walk because the snow banks were so high. The walkways froze solid, and became slick as boots wore away the snow, leaving extended icy patches. March had shown not a single hint of spring, but April suddenly warmed up a few days in a row, and students threw snowballs at each other in shirtsleeves, from the diminishing mounds of snow.

Many of the boys at Eta Chi had responded to winter by spending their evenings studying in the dining room, instead of heading up to campus along the slippery walkways. George divided his time between Althea's apartment and the house. The radiators in Althea's apartment would hiss comfortably as they sat at the kitchen table studying together. Althea wore a hooded sweatshirt, sometimes over her pajamas, and George wore bulky sweaters. They almost always made love at the end of the night before George walked out in the snowy cold to dust off his windshield and huddle in the car as it tried to heat up and clear the fogged glass.

George had begun politicking for Althea to be named Darling for their senior year, and Cullen Hastings had been working it hard too. George thought she'd be the perfect Darling, and imagined her being the center of attention at date nights and formals when the boys sang to her as she sat next to him. He saw her candidacy in concert with his own, for he had begun to think he wanted to be consul of the house. Together they were a compelling couple, he thought.

George walked down the stairs to the foyer on the Thursday before initiation weekend, and made way for Cullen Hastings. Cullen asked excitedly if George was ready and George shrugged. They spoke for a bit about Althea and George scrutinized his brother carefully. Cullen was a true friend, and would never pimp George. But his fascination with Althea always reminded George of how appealing Althea was to others. And here he was, trapped in the house for the entire weekend when Althea was going out to party with Holly. George felt his stomach churn. Althea had teasingly said she and Holly were going out to chase boys. Sometimes he imagined Althea kissing other boys, and it made him unable to think clearly.

Could he trust her? They were glued to each other when they were together. George knew Caitlin would never have been unfaithful to him, but Althea was not Caitlin. He saw her flirt with boys and anguished inside over their visceral reactions to her attention. Even his fraternity brothers felt obliged to tell him how incredibly sexy Althea was.

As much as George appreciated Cullen's passionate homage for his girlfriend, he wondered about the source of it. Was it Althea who was creating his behaviors? George shook his head to clear it. Sometimes he amazed himself by his own insecurities.

Initiation began Friday night, and George participated passively. It was his first time on this side of Initiation, and his only recollection was that of his own, awkward experience. It did not take him long, however, to catch the groove to the event, and he found the weekend hilarious in spite of himself. His own remembered humiliation at not knowing the answers to the questions during the mock interrogation became something to laugh about as he watched the pledges stumbling through their own responses. Curiously, he found his brothers far more compassionate and loose than he ever would have recalled.

Of course, certain things were etched forever in his mind. He would never forget, for example, the naïve ridicule he experienced at not being able to answer the question posed to him about L.E.O. Pennington.

So, the interrogator had begun, we have seen that you have taken a particular liking to the brother who stands next to you. George looked to his side, where L.E.O. stood formally. Brother L.E.O., the interrogator went on, do you stand in support of this pledge's candidacy?

I do, L.E.O. responded curtly. Behind them boys snapped their fingers approvingly.

Pledge Muirfield, please identify the brother who stands in support of your candidacy. George answered that it was L.E.O. Pennington.

Then the boy asked George how well he felt he knew L.E.O. George answered that he thought he knew him pretty well. The brothers standing behind George, out of his sight, clicked their fingers appreciatively.

So, surely you can tell us what the initials in Brother Pennington's first name stand for, the boy suggested lightly to George. George had no idea, and he looked briefly to L.E.O. who looked straight ahead. He had always wondered, but never asked.

The boys behind George started to make sounds of disbelief and disgust in the silence that followed the question. Then the boy leading the inquiry raised his hands to quiet the room, and asked George whether or not he knew the answer. George shook his head negatively. He was so tired, had gone so long without sleep, he thought he could fall asleep as he stood there.

Perhaps those worthy of the brotherhood can inform the pledge? asked the leader. And with that, the entire body of brothers standing in the background had shouted at the top of their lungs, LEONARD EVANS

OSGOOD PENNINGTON!!!, and clapped their hands wildly. L.E.O. turned and smiled broadly to the crowd, and then George had been led away and told to contemplate the guiding light of Eta Chi.

As George watched the proceedings now, he enjoyed the inanity of it all. He had clearly been too exhausted to see the event objectively. Most of the boys going through initiation seemed to be having fun. On Saturday afternoon, Cullen Hastings pulled George aside and wanted to talk about the event coming up in the middle of the night. George told him he had never been through it, and Cullen looked horrified. George explained what had happened to him, how Scottie had let him sleep through it, and then how he had missed the entire weekend for his dad's funeral the next year.

Cullen put his arm around George's shoulder, and told him not to worry. It was the best part of the weekend, and Cullen was looking forward to seeing George experience it for the first time. At the last chapter meeting, George had watched the boys nominating each other for the lighting event. He had not understood fully what the event entailed, and had listened to some of the boys whisper about how wonderful it was.

It began in the wee of the night, about two in the morning, when the pledges were getting much needed sleep. The brothers gathered in the great hall in their monks' robes, which were garishly striped in the colors of the lighting ceremony – blue, red, yellow, green and purple. They looked silly with their hoods darkening their faces, and the striped robes swishing around the room self-importantly.

Then the Pledge Captain called them to order quietly, and the boys listened carefully to their instructions. The first wave of pledges needed to be led from their rooms to the great hall, separated by the brothers in their robes, and sent off in their search for the guiding light.

When the first pledge was led, still half asleep, to the great hall, it was entirely dark. There were a number of robed boys in the room, and a single candle flickered on a desk where the Pledge Captain sat in silence. The Pledge Captain looked up from his scrolls to confirm which pledge was standing wearily before him, and then ask the pledge if he knew the meaning of the guiding light.

The answer was invariably no. Then the Pledge Captain would intone that the pledge needed to search for the guiding light. It was within the pledge's grasp, if only he would search earnestly. Other boys surrounding the pledge would then begin to whisper to the pledge. Look for the light! Seek the true light! Where is the guiding light? Search Pledge!

And then lights would flash in different corners of the room – blue lights, red lights, projected through round, thick glass lens in front of bright light bulbs. The pledges always did the same thing. They wandered toward the colored lights, thinking they were supposed to be searching for something. Many were so tired that they yawned, or coughed, and moved slowly. Others moved quickly, thinking that they must be timed for the exercise. Then the brothers would urge the pledge through the different rooms, where he would find 100 candles lit in the library, and purple and yellow lighting in the dining room, and a strobe light flicking rapidly in the kitchen.

All the time the brothers would be helping the pledge to continue the odyssey, out into the yard, where boys were stationed everywhere. At appropriate moments, a huge spot light would shoot straight up into the April sky as the brothers surrounded the pledge called out, Is that the guiding light? Choose your light, pledge! Seek your guiding light!

George was outside with Cullen when the pledges began to come outside. It was their only time outside the entire weekend, and he watched some of them breathe the fresh spring air hungrily. Cullen and George guarded the south side of the property, to be sure that the pledges remained on the grounds. After a number of pledges had been taken through the outdoor section, one of the pledges came out looking bewildered. Cullen saw that he looked afraid, and started toward him to tell him to relax.

Other brothers surrounded him, urging him to find the guiding light. Then the boy began running around the yard, like a crazy person, and before anyone could corral him, he took off out the driveway, and started running fast toward campus.

Holy shit! Someone yelled, and began to chase him. Cullen and George took off after him, laughing uncontrollably. Come back, pledge! Come back! The guiding light is back here at the house! The boy ran about half a mile before he slowed and then stopped, out of breath. George and Cullen caught up to him, and he said, in total seriousness, I haven't found it yet.

Cullen took charge. Relax pledge, for in fact you have found the guiding light, it simply is not yet clear to you. The boy looked at Cullen dubiously. He could not see Cullen's face, and he was standing on a darkened sidewalk in the middle of Ithaca looking at two boys in wildly striped monks' robes. Unh-huh, said the pledge. George smiled and pulled back his hood so the pledge could see his face. Pledge, we need to return to the property now. Let's walk together as brothers. The pledge smiled. Is it over? he asked hopefully.

No, Cullen replied, but you will really enjoy what's left. The three boys walked quietly back to the house, and as they approached they saw another pledge searching the sky for the guiding light as the spotlight flashed up into the night. They escorted the pledge inside, and back to the Pledge Captain, at the table in the great hall.

The Pledge Captain looked up solemnly. Have you found the guiding light, pledge?

The pledge said he wasn't sure. Continue, said the Pledge Captain, and returned to examining his scrolls. The boys in the room immediately put a hood over the pledge's head, and led him carefully to the basement, into the huge recreation room beneath the dining room. There, they moved the pledge into a wooden cubicle with curtains on the front and back, removed the hood, and told the pledge to stand quietly and await.

It was obvious to the pledge that there were other pledges in the recreation room, but they could not see each other, as they were separated from each other by the thin wooden walls that made up the cubicles. There was occasional scraping of feet, and hushed instructions as more pledges were led into their cubicles, or so it seemed. It was hard to tell what was happening in the close darkness of the cubicle.

Then the curtains to the front were drawn up, and the pledges were instructed to stand still. In front of them stood five brothers, hands behind their backs, with only a hint of light illuminating their frames. The first brother on the left stepped forward, and a blue light suddenly glowed everywhere in the room. The light seemed to be everywhere, and made the pledges' skin glow.

I am the blue light of Eta Chi, the brother said into the hushed silence of the room, and I stand for Integrity. The boy then read from the Benjamin Trident on the meaning of Integrity: *Integrity is a foundation to the brotherhood. From the Latin **Integritas**, meaning purity and completeness, Integrity reflects the soundness and complete bond amongst and between the brotherhood.*

Then Fritz, who was the blue light for this initiation, drew in his breath and said, For me, the integrity of our fraternity is demonstrated by the complete trust I put in my brothers. I came to college unprepared for the meaning of this house. I am an only child, and never had brothers until I came to Eta Chi. I know that I can reach out to anyone in this house and they will respond, they will be there, they will reciprocate as a brother. And for me, that is a special bond that I will carry with me for the rest of my life. Fritz stepped back in line.

Quintin Wells stepped forward and the profuse blue light turned to a crimson red. I am the red light of Eta Chi, and I stand for Achievement. *Achievement is the accomplishment of a goal through perseverance and exertion. It is the individual and collective result of service by the brotherhood toward a greater good.*

Quintin paused, and then spoke quietly. He told the pledges standing in their makeshift cubicles about his own experience as an Eta Chi; how he had learned how to study from his big brother, how he had come to understand that there was a greater purpose to life through service to others. He told them that he was a different man today than he would have been because of achievements he reached through the support of his brothers.

Charles Lord stepped forward as Quintin moved back into line, and the light turned from red to yellow as he said, I am the yellow light of Eta Chi and I stand for Honor. *Honor is a foundation to our brotherhood in its many forms – as a token of respect for each other, as distinction by association with each other, and with the brotherhood as a whole, and as the esteem with which we hold one another for the credit of our good name and reputation.*

Charles stood still and looked at his feet in uncharacteristic humility. The pledges watched him and listened carefully. It has been my honor to associate with the men you will now join as brothers. I am humbled by their achievements, and by the challenge I have been given by each of them to surpass my own objectives in service toward ourselves and each other. Honor yourselves, and honor each other in your pursuits. The only standard by which we live is that of honor shared in the bonds of brotherhood.

The yellow light shifted to green and Charles withdrew as another boy stepped up and said, I am the green light of Eta Chi and I stand for Honesty. *Honesty in our brotherhood means simply that we speak sincerely and truthfully with one another. We respect our individuality, and demand respect, with honesty of thought and words.*

The boy lifted his head defiantly and stared at the pledges. He spoke in a clear voice, telling them of how he came to understand the strength of honesty in the house when he wanted to cheat on an examination because he thought he would fail the course. He confided to a brother that he was thinking of doing this, and the brother immediately gathered three other boys in the same class, and sat him down to study. They told him they would help him prepare so that he could take the test honestly and honorably. And he did, and he passed. This, he said in a flat voice, will never leave him, and will give him the strength to overcome adversity in the years ahead.

The boy stepped back and the light switched to purple as the last boy in line stepped up and said, I am the purple light of Eta Chi, and I stand for compassion. *Compassion is a key to our brotherhood because without it we would not share the suffering of each other's feelings, nor demonstrate the mercy needed for the complete interdependence of brothers in our pact*

The boy teared up as he spoke the words, and pulled himself together after a moment of silence and went on. I stand before you as a brother who suffered something personal. It was paralyzing me and I thought I would have to leave college. But my brothers gathered around me and went to the university to get me help without me even asking. No one asked for credit, and no one ever explained the effort that many of my brothers went to to help me through my crisis. They just did it. That's my bond with Eta Chi. The boy stepped back in line.

Mike O'Hare stepped from behind the pledges and stood in front of the line of brothers, to address the pledges. He carried a large, oval prism, which he held out in front of him as the purple light faded to black. Then a bright, white light from directly above the prism began to shine, and when it hit the prism, it refracted through the lens and spread a rainbow of colors across the floor beneath it.

This, Mike said, after a moment, is the guiding light of Eta Chi. Observe how the white light breaks into its component parts as its heat is processed through the prism. Through your initiation into our brotherhood, until you carry the weight of your actions elsewhere, you will experience each of these lights individually. If you are true brothers, you will also directly give others in the brotherhood the benefit of each of these lights. But do not forget that with your oath of brotherhood, you are guided by the supreme light, encompassing all virtues that make us Eta Chis. Honor, achievement, integrity, honesty, compassion. You will not hear such words in the day to day lives you lead as brothers, but I ask you to place this thought deep within yourselves. This group of men is nothing without your commitment and your pursuit of glory. Do not rest, do not falter, for this gift is as fleeting as it is timeless. And it is yours to give or to lose.

Mike raised his hands, and said, Step forward into the guiding light of Eta Chi. The pledges moved uncertainly out of their little cubicles, which had somehow become comfortably private during the ceremony. The single bright light above the consul was joined by blinding lights all across the ceiling, and the boys stood harshly illuminated, blinking their eyes. The lights dimmed to a normal range, and each pledge realized that his big brother had silently moved next to them, so that they were standing shoulder to shoulder.

Mike instructed the big brothers to teach the pledges the fraternity handshake and to give to their little brothers the symbol of the guiding light. The big brothers, smiling widely at their little brothers, laughed as they showed them how to perform the handshake, and then reached into their pocket and handed each pledge a small blue plastic box containing their fraternity pin. Some of the big brothers put their arms around their little brother's shoulders, while others shook hands formally and returned to facing forward.

Mike dismissed them, and told them to return to their rooms to reflect and rest, and the big brothers took their little brothers, unhooded, up the stairs to their rooms. There was a warmth and conviviality in the air that replaced the austere gravity earlier in the weekend. Then the brothers immediately began to prepare for the next group of pledges, since they had to do this ceremony in two waves because of space limitations.

George had sat in awe as he watched the lighting event. His eyes grew moist as he thought about what he had done with his fraternity pin, without the benefit of seeing what other initiates had experienced upon the receipt of their pin. He was ashamed to have missed this event when he was a freshman, or to have misconstrued the weekend of initiation. It seemed glorious, and empowering to him. Cullen who sat next to him, saw the visceral reaction on George's countenance, and smiled uncontrollably. He assumed that George was simply as enamored of the lighting event as he always was, and would never know what George really thought.

The special connection that the ceremony created in George for his father, and the melancholy the ceremony dredged up in him was a secret George would never share. It was a guilty pleasure that he allowed himself to hide from others, a secret communion with his dead father and his own inner core. He did not consciously understand its meaning, but it refreshed and rejuvenated him. Listening to the five boys speak of their lights was emotional fuel for his spirit. It was such a selfish revelation, it made him feel guilty.

George was not alone in his secret introspection. Fritz Hublein's own, hidden desire to speak at the ceremony had been driven not by the fact that he was an only child, but a fatherless one. Fritz had only been five-years old when his father died of cancer, and his father could not have died at a worse time. The illness had been brief; Fritz had not even adjusted to the gray coloring in his father's complexion when his mother found him on the floor of his room, building blocks into imaginary castles.

She sat quietly on the carpet that made it so hard for the blocks to stand up, wrapped her arm around her little boy, told him that Daddy had gone to Heaven. Fritz could no longer recall the smell of his mother's dress, or the way that he had bravely stood up and started to put all of his blocks into the wooden box at the foot of his bed. But the transformation that traced back to that moment would be with him forever.

At five, he was yet to reach the age of his reason, but Fritz was big enough to feel the full brunt of his own, inexplicable pain. Death was not nice, and apparently very powerful. It was an insidious, heartless assassin that forever changed his life and hurt his mother. Instinctively, from that day forward, Fritz grew a rubber-like second skin, to seal himself off from the malevolent turbulence surrounding him. If Death was irrepressible, he could at least anesthetize himself from future injury.

That layer of protection was double-sided, too. If he managed what emotions passed through in either direction, how much more damage could occur? And because this was not a conscious response, Fritz would not appreciate its existence, or see himself with great clarity until he was well into adulthood. It would hamper his ability over time to share himself completely with Jane Quissling or other women in his life. It would end up both protecting and desensitizing him. Until his own son entered the world and sent chills down his spine.

This second skin shielded him even more from the males in his life. Fritz enjoyed a normal childhood, laughing and teasing with his friends and as he moved through high school, playing sports at the junior varsity level. But he always maintained a personal distance, a watchful distrust.

Joining Eta Chi had been the first genuinely emotional commitment that Fritz had allowed himself to make with men since his father's death. And the joy he experienced in bonding with his fraternity brothers exhilarated and shamed him.

Of course, joining Eta Chi did not make a new man out of Fritz. The rubbery, protective layer that the boy wove around his persona as a little boy remained in tact. He wore his heart not on his sleeve, but in a remote chamber deep inside himself, where he only ventured occasionally. But the fraternity allowed him increasingly to go there.

And next to George, Cullen Hastings, whose eyes glistened in the pure reflection of the passage of Initiation, dreamed of being Pledge Captain, of leading these boys through the passionate indoctrination all clans require. It was, for him, the completion of a circle left incomplete by his own upbringing, a desire forged of distant and disinterested parents too old to have responded to their son's conception and birth. Through the familial trappings of Eta Chi, Cullen would find the solace that eluded him in the silent, empty house of his adolescence. To his wife, many years later, Cullen would confide that it was at Eta Chi where he found some evidence of the power of love.

Ironically, it was this same night when George, Fritz and Cullen were wrapped in their own thoughts of longing that Althea Redmonton found herself at a crossroads of her own making. With George tied up at the fraternity on Saturday night, she went with Holly and another Kappa Psi to a number of bars in succession. First the Nines, then the Chapter House, and finally the French Connection, with its ever-present scent of freshly popped popcorn. It was at the French Connection that Althea's eyes came to rest on a girl with black hair and a low-scooped blouse who was leaning up into Matthew Stollings' face with obvious intent.

Althea and her cohorts had been drinking, of course, but nothing prepared Althea for the immediate, physical sensation of jealousy that rippled across her forehead when she watched the girl try to pull Matthew under her sleazy spell. This girl was so calculating, and so available, that the more Matthew appeared vulnerable to her advances, the more Althea wanted to save him. Had only George slipped off to meet her, a different fate may have prevailed, but it was as if Althea had never even met George Muirfield.

Then Matthew looked over at Althea, and smiled, and she smiled back. She heard Holly say, Oh no, but all Althea could see was the cheap haircut of the girl with Matthew. Then George finally crept into her mind and she fretted, but told herself quickly that looking across a room wasn't cheating. She was simply saving Matthew from a girl who certainly was beneath him. When she looked up again, Matthew stood next to her saying hello in a way that let her know he was drunk.

I think you have a floozy across the room waiting for you, Althea said in a small, determined voice. The imperious look she could see on Holly's face only egged her on.

You look fantastic, Althea! Matthew said in a firm, boisterous voice. Then he turned to Holly and said hello, and asked how she was.

Holly smiled sardonically and said she had to go the bathroom.

I know what that means! Matthew said, beginning to laugh deeply. Althea went to the bathroom on me once!

Holly just walked toward the back of the bar. The beer buzz in Althea's head made the recollection hazy, but she knew she had it coming. She had flipped him off. The other Kappa introduced herself to Matthew, and Althea swayed a bit, and tried to collect herself. She looked over to see where the floozy was, but saw no one where she looked.

Matthew was drunk, obviously, but Althea liked the way he stood there, smiling. The fine edge to his jaw dipped low, and his sarcastic attitude emanated from the gleam in his eye. Althea could feel his temper brimming beneath his conviviality. It made her skin tingle.

Matthew said he had to be getting back to his floozy, and winked at Althea, and then leaned in and kissed her on the cheek. She caught his lips half on her own and kissed back, mischievously. Matthew pulled away and said maybe he should call her sometime. Althea said, Maybe you should. The words felt good in her throat. There was a familiar whirl in her abdomen.

Holly returned as Matthew walked away, and said, What was that all about!?

Althea shrugged. I like Matthew, Holly. Always have.

Are you bombed? Holly asked her friend. You must be drunk. Matthew Stollings is a shithead.

Althea smiled and said nothing. The other Kappa said she thought Matthew was nice looking. Althea giggled.

Monday night, Matthew Stollings called Althea and asked her if she wanted to go drinking. Althea paused. She was sitting in her apartment, and she knew George was studying at Eta Chi. She asked Matthew where he wanted to go. He suggested the French Connection, and she hesitated. What was the harm? It made her feel lightheaded, and dangerous. She said, One beer. Matthew said he would pick her up in twenty minutes.

Off the phone, Althea shook her head and went into her bathroom to look in her mirror. She knew what she was doing violated her relationship with George. She stared into her own eyes, and said aloud, What if you lose George over this?

The face in the mirror told her not to worry. George was fine. This was just a little fun.

Do you love George? she asked the mirror. She peered silently but her stomach hurt. Her eyes told her this was a stupid idea, but then some other part of her noted that it had been lodged in the back of her head since Saturday night. If it had been lodged there, didn't that mean she needed to explore it? How would she ever know if she really loved George or not, if she did not yield to this temptation? Besides, George was almost too nice, too trustworthy. She missed the hunger and sport of chasing incorrigible boys. Boys like Matthew were so...bold, or rough, or elusive. If only George was a little elusive!

When Matthew knocked on the door, she was still looking into the mirror, and was startled by the knock. She ran to the door, let him in, and told him she needed a few minutes. Matthew looked around the apartment with a familiar gaze and sat at the kitchen table to wait. Althea moved around the corner to her bedroom area, and pulled something to wear out of her closet. She stripped off her jeans, put on black slacks, and lifted the simple top she had been wearing scissor-like off her chest. She picked out a cream blouse and buttoned it down her front quickly. Then she walked quickly to the bathroom, and said she'd be one more sec.

Behind the door to the bathroom, she stopped, guiltily. She was acting identically to the way that she acted sometimes with George, and it made her feel shame. What would he say to her if he could see her? She looked in the mirror, and said, Too late now! She put lipstick to her lips and a bit of blush on her cheeks. She didn't have time to really do her eyes, but she flicked mascara on her eyelashes quickly.

Matthew was standing when she reappeared, and smiled crookedly when he saw her. He asked her is she was ready, and she said Yup, the same way George would have. Matthew saw something pass across Althea's face and began to remember what he found irritating about his old girlfriend. She looked great, though, and he wanted to conquer her again. And he could tell she wanted him to, which gave him deep satisfaction.

Later in the night, after they had gone to the bar and gotten drunk, they walked back to Althea's apartment, and through her door quietly. Matthew had been aggressive with her, touching her on her hip as he spoke to her in the bar, and leaning in and kissing her, just for old time's sake. Althea had not resisted, but had been coyly passive. Matthew took off his jacket, once in the door, and rubbed her shoulders. Her shoulders sprang up defensively, but she turned to him and they kissed softly.

They pawed each other for awhile, and Matthew pushed himself with determination on her. Althea felt his desire mounting, but found herself curiously ambivalent. She liked the rough play of his hands on her, and the insistence of his mouth. But there was something lacking in it all. She had the sudden image of herself standing at a deserted train station at night, looking down the empty tracks into nothing. Then Matthew's hand was between her legs, and her body responded to his immediacy.

Althea lay awake after Matthew had left. The sex had been crushing, rushed, impersonal. She kept thinking of the image at the train station, trying to recall whether it was a train station she knew, but nothing came to her. The look on Matthew's face had been gloating as he stood at her door. He told he wanted to see her again, and she had said nothing. Then he had walked back to her, and brushed her hair back tenderly, and said he would call her the next day. She knew he wouldn't. He never did. But he did call a few days later, and she saw him again, the following Monday. It was pretty much a repeat of their last time. Althea had been unsure before, but now she was certain.

For that one week, she lived the lie with George. But it ate at her, and she wanted it to stop. Matthew was taunting and fun, but she always felt empty afterwards. She had not fully appreciated the fullness that emotion and tenderness brought to sex until George Muirfield popped into her life. George was all emotion. So what did she want? She wanted to stick with George, but part of her wanted more room. It was just that the room no longer included Matthew Stollings.

For now, she needed to end it with Matthew. She was not going to risk losing George. Every time she thought of him, she could see the disappointment on his face, and she cringed. She guessed that there were many different kinds of love, and she felt more than one of them for her boyfriend. She had told herself for a long time that she wanted to be thirty when she got married, and she wished she had met George Muirfield about eight years from now. She could picture that clearly. It was just the intervening years that were out of focus.

Althea met Matthew for lunch. She kept control of their conversation. They sat in the University Deli, eating sandwiches and drinking orange sodas. Althea looked coolly at Matthew when he told her he wanted to date her again, and said she didn't think that made any sense. Matthew smirked. She saw the callow superiority in his look, and it made her mad, but she let it go. When he walked away from her outside the Deli, he called back to her that they'd be back together someday. Althea was glad to be free of him.

She would never know that it was Bob Woodbridge who saw them. On Mondays, Bob liked going alone to the French Connection where he'd sit in the corner drinking beer and munching on bowls of popcorn. Sometimes he buried his head in a book as he sat there, and sometimes he just munched, and thought about things. Lucy was happy to get him out of the apartment so she could spread her books all over the kitchen table and study. Sometimes when he got home, he'd find her asleep with her head on her books.

The first Monday that Althea went drinking with Matthew, Bob watched them from his corner musingly. He could see how strongly Matthew Stollings pushed himself on Althea, and this led him to conclude that it was new. Bob wondered about George, and if the two of them had broken up. They left the bar together before him, and he would have probably forgotten about it if he had not seen them again the following Monday.

The second time he saw them, Bob found it more than curious. Mondays were not a popular night for dates, and it struck him that they were in the same place again, on the same night. One of them was sneaking this, he concluded, though he couldn't guess which one of them. Maybe both, he mused. They appeared ritualistic. Matthew leaned into her the same way, and Althea resisted faintly. The next morning Bob ran into Danny Carvello at the Straight and he asked about George and Althea.

Hot and heavy, Danny replied. Why?

Bob told Danny what he had seen. The two of them looked at each other. Not only was Althea cheating on their brother, but they both knew that Althea was up for the Darling vote for next year. There was certainly no requirement that a Darling date only one Eta Chi. Many Darlings dated several boys in the house on a casual basis, and others, like Holly, was a serious girlfriend to Charles Lord. But her misleading George did not sit well with them.

Danny said, He's head over heels about her, you know. Bob said he had guessed that much.

We have to tell him, they both said at once. Danny offered to be the one, and they agreed that he could explain how Bob had seen them. If George wanted to know more, he could speak with Bob.

CHAPTER NINETEEN

The following date night was the first week in May and the air felt suddenly spring-like. The dining room windows at Eta Chi were all opened to let the inviting warm air loll through the room, and boys were in a gleeful mood. As the boys sang the Darling song between the main course and dessert, a long line of boys stood together, arm in arm, and rocked back and forth as they sang. Their voices were intentionally loud, and slightly mocking. Jack Ellis kept adding deep, raspy wails during breaks in the song, that sounded like "AAARGHHH."

Afterwards, the boys in the line broke immediately into a rendition of *Muddy Roads*. Stoobie was just walking from the kitchen back to his seat at a table, and as he passed the line of boys, Jack Ellis grabbed him to join them in line. Stoobie stood stiffly in line, and did not sway back and forth with the others. He mouthed the words half-heartedly. The girls who had clapped at the conclusion of the Darling Song, widened they eyes at the graphically homosexual lyrics. The boys in line laughed heartily at the end of the ditty and returned to their tables.

Danny had invited Janette Emilio, and led her to the table where George and Althea were sitting during dinner. Danny and George had stood at their chairs to sing the Darling song, and Danny scowled to George as they sat down and listened to the chain of boys sing Muddy Roads. Danny said, Pretty classy, eh? to their dates, and the girls said it was always a unique experience at Eta Chi. Danny watched George with his arm draped casually along the back of Althea's chair. It was going to hurt when he told him.

House elections for all offices and for next year's Darling were a week and a half away. Danny and George were both running for consul. There was never much in the way of campaigning for election within the house. It was understood that everybody lived together, and that it was too close of an environment to allow desire for an office to get out of hand. About the most that anyone ever did was softly ask their friends if they would support them. Having done this, George knew already that Danny would probably win. Boys told him that they were both qualified, and would both be great, but Danny had more experience.

As wary as Danny and George may have been with each other because of the coming elections, they were becoming close. It was because of this friendship that Danny had volunteered to tell George about Althea. But the elections complicated things, and Danny worried that George might think he was being spiteful. But if Janette Emilio was bopping someone else behind his back (which he doubted, since she was not even bopping him), he thought he would have wanted George to tell him about it.

Danny looked at Janette smiling at him. She had told him last week that if it was too much for him to bear, she would understand it if he had sex with other girls on the side. She just was not prepared to have sex with him yet. The "yet" had hung in the air between them like an apparition. For the first time in his life, Danny felt pains in his stomach. Janette looked more beautiful than ever to him as she said this. It was about the most clever thing a woman could have said to him. He had replied that he was thinking of joining the priesthood, so this was excellent practice. But he pointed out that being given a license to fool around was not something he took lightly. He asked her if there was anyone she might recommend, and she elbowed him hard in the side. Then he told her he thought her roommate was attractive. Janette just rolled her eyes.

On following day, as they finished dinner, Danny asked George to hang back for a minute. When the dining room had cleared Danny made small talk for a minute, joking with George about the lima beans served for dinner that night. Then there was a silence, and George looked at him carefully. So? he asked.

Danny told him to sit down. George told him he was under the impression he was already sitting down. Danny said he had something to tell George about Althea. George's gaze became guarded. He jumped to the conclusion it had something to do with her being up for Darling.

Danny told George how Bob had approached him. George listened silently as Danny told him the whole story. Danny could not tell what was going through George's mind. He finished by telling George he knew he would want to know himself. George leaned back in his chair and looked out the window, and then looked back and asked Danny if he was sure. Danny nodded.

I can't fucking believe this, George said to his lap. He stood up, thanked Danny, and said he was glad he told him. Then he walked up to his room, threw himself down on his bed, and held his stomach with both hands. He felt like he could vomit. He closed his eyes, but when he did he pictured Althea taking Matthew Stollings into her bed, so he opened them again and stood up. He wanted to hit something as much as he wanted to cry. He could not believe how humiliated he felt. She had defrauded him, and played with him. Panic replaced reason. He fretted out loud about how to get her back, how to convince her that only he was hers. He trembled, and called her a fucking whore. Then he prayed Danny was wrong. But Danny had been too factual to be wrong.

George pulled himself together and headed for the library. He was supposed to meet Althea there to study. As he walked up the hill toward the suspension bridge, he talked out loud to himself. You have to decide what you want to do, he said to the cool spring night. Maybe you should find out what she thinks. His mind did not think that was appropriate. Maybe you should coldly break it off right away and walk off with your dignity. He nodded his head in agreement, but knew he wouldn't do that.

The truth was that underneath the bravado and indignation and fury he was afraid to lose Althea. He had never been so consumed by another person, or so infatuated.

What he really wanted was for this to go away. And he knew he would somehow give it a chance to. He and Althea belonged together. He knew this passionately. And the fact that Althea had been in a bar on two occasions with her old boyfriend didn't mean that she was cheating on him. It required explanation, for sure, but it was not proof of anything. (*She was kissing him in the bar, George. Bob watched them both nights.* This was how Danny had said it. Like a voyeur.)

Althea was sitting in the main room of Uris Library with Holly and Charles Lord, and she smiled brightly and waved when she saw George. Her reaction was genuine – she had come to a new level of appreciation for her boyfriend in the past several days. The sight of her smiling and waving enraged George, but he waved back casually. Look at her sitting there, acting so innocent he told himself. She probably spent the afternoon in bed with that asshole. George stopped at a table to say hello to a girl he knew vaguely. He had no interest in talking to her, but he needed time to think. Althea watched him with her eyebrows raised. He asked the girl he was speaking with to write down the pages they were supposed to read for history class, and she wrote them down and tore off the little edge of her paper and handed it to him smiling. He smiled back and thanked her, stuck the paper in his breast pocket, and walked toward Althea who squinted at him.

If you're going to ask for her phone number, honey, don't do it in front of me! Althea whispered humorously. In fact, she was curious what George had taken from the girl. George smiled slightly, and told her that he would never cheat on her. His words slid across her face without a ripple. Althea said, I know, softly. Holly stared at her book but George could tell she was listening. Charles seemed genuinely preoccupied with his textbook.

When Althea said, "honey," George had sucked in his breath. How dare she screw with him this way? What terms of endearment did she use for Matthew Stollings? He pulled out his books and opened them half-heartedly. He was not going to be able to concentrate, but he had to make it look that way. Althea's leg moved between his, and he looked up to acknowledge her flirtation. She grinned, and wagged her head. He smiled and squeezed her leg lightly between his own, and she smiled approvingly.

The brush of her leg against his, and the devilish grin she gave him made him feel he was going insane. He wanted this to end, right now, with her in his arms, swearing her love for him. But that was not what had to happen, he thought. I have to lure her to the point of truth, or I will be racked with uncertainty, he said in his head. George looked levelly at Althea and she smiled warmly to him. She wanted to scoop him into her arms and hug him ferociously. And she wanted to see what that girl had written on the paper in his pocket.

At nine, George wrote on a piece of paper, Let's go get coffee, and slid it across the desk to his girlfriend. He watched her hands pick up the paper, and could feel her hands on him. He knew her hands, and how they roamed over him. His temples pulsed.

Althea stood up, leaned over to Holly and whispered something, and nodded to George. He rose, and they walked out holding hands. The night air had cooled, and Althea pulled herself against George as they made the short walk to the Straight. Neither of them said anything. Althea felt so natural on George's arm, he wavered in his mind. What did he really know?

They went through the abbreviated line for coffee and George picked up a big chocolate chip cookie and placed it on its cellophane sheet on their tray. Most of the full service cafeteria was closed for the night, and was dimly lit. They moved to the middle of the huge cafeteria and sat opposite each other in the middle of one of the long benches in the middle of the room. George faced away from the cafeteria area, toward the library.

Althea reached over and broke off a piece of the cookie between them, and dunked it into her coffee as she nibbled at it. She looked at George and asked him why he was so quiet. George looked at her, aching inside himself, and afraid of the conversation he was about to have. He wished he had never heard the story from Danny Carvello. But he knew he had to say something.

Althea stared hard at her boyfriend, with a sinking feeling in her stomach. He looked like he was about to either throw up or slap her. He must have found out about Matthew. She thought immediately of his line in the library ("I would never cheat on you."). It had made sense in the context of the conversation, but it smoldered in her mind. What should she do? How much did he know? Should she tell him everything, or was she imagining this?

I'm concerned, George said, looking off into space, about the French Connection between us. In his head, he liked the fact that he had made a pun out of it. It made him seem in control when he was not. Althea did a quick intake of her breath, and stopped moving. She waited for his eyes to come back to hers, and cringed inside. But before George looked back at her, he added a thought.

And, he said, the lovely walks back to your little apartment afterwards. It was his way of testing his theory. Maybe she hadn't taken Matthew Stollings back to her room – their sanctuary! – after going out with him. If she immediately protested and asked what the hell he was talking about, there was hope. She didn't.

You mean you are fucking following me now? was how Althea responded. George felt the full weight of his despair drop onto his frame.

His shoulders literally drooped, and then he pulled himself back up. Althea glared at George until he returned her gaze. The pain in his eyes, the acidic insecurity, made her even angrier. She told George to answer her, now.

Fucking following is an interesting way for you to put it Althea, but no, I didn't follow you. I was at Eta Chi studying, at least on the nights I know about. Glimmers of hope made him want to put parameters around Althea's indiscretion, to isolate and minimize it if he could. It wasn't working very well.

Althea lost a bit of her steam, and she looked down at her coffee, and said, Look...

George watched her, as if he was watching a slow motion movie. He felt like he might burst open.

Let me tell you exactly what happened. I bumped into Matthew when you were doing your initiation thing. We were both drunk. Old feelings surfaced, and I saw him a couple of times. But I broke it off with him for good after that. Althea looked searchingly at her boyfriend. I mean it George. I met him at the Uni Deli and told him we were done.

In her mind, Althea had come completely clean. She had purposely covered the lunch, since that was the only other time she and Matthew had gone out together. And she genuinely regretted the whole thing. She pictured Matthew with her in her apartment, his callous, physical approach to her, and wished she had never touched the idiot.

George picked at the cookie between them, but left the pieces on the cellophane. Part of him was ecstatic at her words. It was over. She was his again! Then the distrust roared back into his head, like nausea. He was being duped again. For all he knew, she was lying, or trying to cover up other things she had done.

How many other boys have you been with since we began? George asked her quietly. Althea burped, and then laughed. It was a ludicrous question, and he obviously didn't understand her. She reached over to take his hand, but his hand stayed limp on the table. It felt sweaty. Jesus, George, none. The answer is none. How could you even say that to me?

I didn't think I'd be saying anything to you, Althea. George stabbed her in her eyes with his own. And I am quite sure, that you were not about to bring it up to me. Instead, one of my fraternity brothers had to tell me because he was so concerned for me. The whole goddamn world had to know before I found out. George didn't realize it, but his fists were clenched.

Althea began to rock forward and backward, with her arms wrapped around her waist. She had not expected to feel so strongly about the boy in front of her. If you had asked her a week ago, she would have told you that she was done with Matthew, but uncertain about committing herself completely to George. But now the thought of losing him was making her tremble. You know, she said, I think I really do love you.

George winced at her words. What the hell did that mean? Althea stopped rocking, and sat in front of him, with her eyes open wide to his. The rabbit hole was beckoning desperately. But George was in a whole different place. He was far away from Althea's gaze, looking downward at the two of them. And he was panicking again. First he had had to absorb the confirmation that the girl he loved, needed, desired, adored, was fucking her old boyfriend (the image of it humiliated him). And then he had to hear her say *She thought* she loved him. A nanosecond ago, they had loved each other desperately.

I have to go, he announced.

Where are you going?

George didn't answer Althea. He just shook his head, and walked slowly away from her. Not looking back was the hardest thing he had done since he met Althea Redmonton. But whatever nerve had enabled him to walk away without looking back was replaced with searing doubt by the time he reached the library. What the hell was he doing? He wanted her, he had to find a way past his own fury, before he sent her running back into the arms of that asshole.

Holly looked up when he reached the table, and he leaned over to her and whispered, When you see Althea, tell her to think really hard.

Holly squinted her eyes, and said okay, curiously. She asked him where he was going as he gathered up his books. The French Connection, he answered. And that's exactly where he went. Somewhere in the back of his confused thoughts, he prayed that Althea would ask Holly what he had said, and follow him to the bar. There would be some amount of justice in that, perhaps.

When Althea arrived back at the library about twenty minutes later, she had walked the circumference of the Arts Quad twice. She took one look at Holly and burst into tears, grabbed her things and walked outside. Holly hurried after her, and they walked outside to the stone bench under the portico at the entrance. She told her friend bits and pieces, but was confused and ashamed and skipped around a lot. When Holly realized that this was about Matthew, she put her own disapproval to the side and tried to comfort Althea. She asked her to tell her slowly what had happened tonight. But first, Althea emphatically wanted Holly to know that she had only gone with Matthew two times and then broken it off. Then she repeated the conversation she had just had with George.

Oh my god, Holly said when Althea explained the French Connection reference, that's what George meant!

What?

He said he was leaving to go to the French Connection! Althea thought that was unbelievably cruel. Holly said she didn't think it was mean of him. Althea was the one who was the cause of all this, after all. After awhile, Althea said she was going home. Holly hugged her and went back into the library. She told her friend to give it time. Althea just shrugged. She was exhausted. Her route to her apartment took her within fifty feet of the French Connection, but she purposely avoided looking at its sign, as she turned up the road toward her apartment. It never occurred to her that George had actually *meant* that he was going there.

George was sitting at the bar, which by midnight had thinned out. He was drinking Jack Daniels on the rocks and inhaling popcorn. Every time his mouth felt like a cavern of salt, he took another gulp of the sweet whiskey. Then he put the drink down, and sucked the coating from the popcorn off of his fingers. Eventually he switched to beer. His head was spinning, and he knew he had to slow down. When he got up to go the bathroom, he had to steady himself at the stool before he lurched toward the back of the place.

The bartender told him they were closing up before George realized he was alone with the boy behind the bar. George thanked the boy, left him a five-dollar tip, and rolled out the front door. He went in a hurry, because he needed air suddenly, and then he felt his stomach turning over. There was a nauseating swirl in his head. He put his hand on the side of the building, and found his way to the back, near the trash cans. The stench of the trash cans was the last thing George noticed before he threw up. He went to his knees and threw up whiskey, beer and popcorn. It was a taste he would remember forever.

His walk to Eta Chi took an hour. Eventually, he reclaimed enough balance to walk steadily. When he reached the suspension bridge, he gripped the railing in the middle of the bridge and closed his eyes. Then he began to cry, and curse, and eventually all of this subsided and he resumed his trek back to the house.

From the time George awoke at eleven the next day until the following Wednesday, he snarled at his brothers and moped by himself around the house. He went to his English and history professors and got extensions on papers that were due, and smoked cigarettes in his room. Danny finally confronted him on Wednesday, and told him he was being a jerk, and to cut it out. George told him to get lost.

Listen, Danny told him, a lot of people who were probably voting for you for consul are asking each other what the hell has happened to you. Go take a shower, and get your ass back in the real world. I don't want to beat a retard in the stupid election. George stared insolently at Danny, but said okay and went to the showers. He knew his friend was right.

He had not called Althea. Althea had called twice and left messages to please call, but he ignored them. By the time Danny brought him up short, he had worked through Althea's cheating with Matthew Stollings. He hated it, but knew that he had no right to expect her to be faithful to him. The problem he now saw, was that his interest in a relationship with Althea was different from her own. It was not Matthew Stollings who got under his skin now. It was Althea with the future Matthew Stollings – the ones he didn't know yet – that frightened him. He was trying to see his way clear on that point before he talked with her. And every fiber of his being wanted to talk with her.

And he had the house election to think about. He probably did look like a retard. In the shower, he began to consider in earnest whether he wanted Althea to be elected Darling for next year. He knew instantly what he thought – he wanted her to be the Darling. It was a way of assuring himself that he would work it out with her somehow. If she was the Darling, she would pretty much have to come around, wouldn't she?

The next few days, he assumed his old persona, joking with his brothers, and trying to position himself for the election. On Saturday morning, he called Althea and when she answered the phone, he said Hi, and then nothing else. She said nothing for a minute and the two them sat listening to each other's silence across the telephone wires. Then she said Hi back, and he asked if they could talk. She said she would like that. He asked her if she had a date for tonight – he couldn't help himself – and she exploded into the phone. She told him she had been worried sick about him, but if he was going to pull that shit, he could go to hell.

George smiled to himself, and asked if he could still come over. She said Just a minute, I need to check to see if any of my other boyfriends are still here. Silence. Then Althea sighed. What do you want me to say? Please? George told her he'd be right over. There was a cadence to their speech that made both of them feel comfortable.

George got to his girlfriend's apartment and walked quickly up the little steps to the door. He didn't knock this time. He just quietly opened the door and looked at Althea who sat at her kitchen table, smoking a cigarette. She wore a Cornell T-shirt, and sweat shorts, but her hair was brushed and lipstick glistened on her lips. They said nothing, just looked at each other, and then embraced for a long time, hugging each other as hard as they could. George felt whole for the first time since Danny had told him. He kissed Althea and they moved each other around the corner to her bed, where they toppled together onto the comforter.

Their lovemaking was warm, intense and filled with emotion. Afterwards they stayed wrapped together on top of the covers, their lips close as they spoke softly of how badly they felt, how desperately they wanted to be with each other, how sorry they were. Until they pulled themselves apart, George was ecstatic, and rejuvenated. He was reunited with his Althea, and order returned to his world. Then he walked to the little bathroom to relieve himself, and looked at himself in the mirror as his water splashed in the bowl, and whispered, Nothing has changed. The truth of his whisper depressed him.

Nothing had changed. He could leave the bathroom and sink into Althea's arms, and all would be right with the world. But those future Matthew Stollings loomed unseen in their path, and George saw instinctively that regardless of what Althea might say to him today, they were there. He gazed at himself in the mirror for a bit, and then whispered, Maybe love includes doubt. He shrugged, and returned to his girl-friend's embrace. But this time he did not feel inseparable from her. He felt distinct.

The Eta Chi chapter meeting arrived, and there was high interest in the session because the brotherhood was divided about a number of the elections and issues to be resolved. Sixty-two boys crowded into the chap-ter room, which was filled with energy and chatter. Elections were held first, and George and Danny stepped outside the room as the vote was debated. They moved away from the door and leaned against the washer and dryer. George told Danny he would be a good lieutenant if Danny won, and Danny said that in his mind, they were going to run the house together, no matter which boy the brotherhood elected.

They walked back into the room when summoned, and Mike O'Hare announced that Danny had been elected consul for the fall semester. As he had for every chapter meeting, Mike was wearing a light green leisure suit with a cream colored shirt. He looked like he was ready to start danc-ing. The boys clapped and shook Danny's hand. Danny wiped his brow in mock anxiety, and put his arm around George. George was speaking with Edward Stamer, who was asking him what his decision was.

Edward had been pressing George to run for rush Chair for senior year, succeeding him. It had started days before, when Edward had cor-nered George in the library. Edward knew that George hoped to be consul, and had urged him to run for rush chair if that didn't work out.

Listen, George, Edward had said, leaning down so that their faces were close, I see why you want to be consul. But I know that where you can be the most important to the house is running rush. I can give a speech for you that will blow away everyone else. He paused for a mo-ment, and then continued. I know why you would run for pro consul if Danny gets to be consul. I know that being president of a fraternity means more on a resume that being rush chairman. But you and I both know which job is more important.

Edward's face was flushed by the end of his words. The bylaws of the house prohibited a boy from serving as rush chairman in the fall and con-sul in the spring semester, since the rush chairman's office did not technically conclude until after the start of the spring semester. So if George ran for rush chairman, he could not be considered for consul for the spring semester, because it was not permitted for a brother to hold two posts at once. The natural path to be elected consul in the spring was to be elected proconsul, or vice president, in the fall. That was what George had told Edward he intended to do, if Danny was named consul.

Because of the unusual overlap in positions, the vote for rush Chair was held second, before the vote for proconsul. So a boy could not try out for proconsul and still be able to run for rush Chair if he lost the proconsul's race. A clear choice had to be made. And, of course, there was no guarantee that a boy who aspired to both posts, but who opted not to run for rush Chair, would be successful in the bid for the proconsul's position. While the proconsul's job was a feeder position for consul, it also attracted more candidates, because it was viewed by some boys as a way for them to play an honorary role in the house. It was very possible that George could choose to wait to run for proconsul, and lose to Harold Wise, or other boys who had nominated themselves.

The nuances of the election procedures were clearly understood and often debated in the house. And Edward Stamer was particularly poignant in his argument that if George chose not to run for rush Chair, the leading candidate was Joshua Finch. Joshua Finch. They both viewed Finch as someone who did not perceive the meaning of being an Eta Chi in the same way as they did. He was heretical on most topics, and an outspoken advocate of eliminating the rules that had been rigidly enforced when Edward and George had rushed the house as freshmen. He typified what Edward dismissively called the New Guard.

As Edward looked at George, he knew that his cause was lost. George looked knowingly at him, and said, Here's what I think. You will still be here. I will be here, and I may or may not be consul, but we will be able to have a lot of influence over Joshua, if he's elected. And if I do get the consul job for the spring, I will be able to influence Joshua. George had the look of a politician, and Edward almost didn't bother to respond. But he straightened up and said, I know it's wrong, but I see your mind's made up. I hope you're right. Then he moved away.

When the vote was made for rush Chair, George and Edward both stood and spoke in favor of Hank Broussard, but the sophomores ardently supported Joshua Finch. They said he was the fairest and brightest brother they knew and should be given the post. The vote was thirty-three to twenty-nine with three abstentions, in favor of Finch. Edward shook his head dismayingly. George mouthed that it would be all right.

The next vote was for proconsul, and George walked out of the room with the three other boys who were running for the office. Danny winked at George as he left. He wanted George to be his sidekick, and made a compelling speech about how he wanted to work with him. That was really all the boys needed to hear, but the nomination speeches went on for some time. Then Mike O'Hare asked for the candidates to be brought back into the room, and announced that George was proconsul.

The remainder of the posts – pledge captain (Cullen Hastings), guardian of the door (Ronny Trillo), social chairs (Larry Dobrinski and Dexter Billings) and house manager (Jack Ellis) – were conducted and then the boys turned to the issue of Darling. Cullen Hastings nominated Althea Redmonton in a loud voice, and one of the sophomores proposed that Diane Southington, a sophomore's girlfriend, be elected. In accordance with tradition, boys associated with the girls nominated were required to step outside, so George and the sophomore nodded to each other and walked outside.

Once outside the room, George told the sophomore that he would be very happy if either girl were chosen, because Diane was a wonderful girl. The sophomore breathed a sigh of relief, and said he had hoped this wasn't out of line. George guffawed and assured him that it was more than fine. Of course, in his mind, he was certain that Althea would be elected as Diane would obviously have the chance in later years.

Inside the room, The boys engaged in serious debate over the election of Darling. Cullen Hastings had asked to be heard first, and waxed eloquently about how wonderful a person Althea Redmonton was, and how well she would get along with all of the brothers. She knew everyone, of course, and was very familiar with the traditions of the house. She had a pleasant personality, and was outgoing. He also thought she would do a great job of introducing other girls to the house system.

Others seconded Cullen's comments, and at least two boys also noted to some hoots that it didn't hurt that she was a knockout. Then a number of boys raised their hands to speak about Diane. A couple of the boys supporting Diane wondered if it was such a good idea for the house to name girls from the same sorority two years in a row.

Then Harold Wise stood up and said that he had been thinking hard about this. (In fact, Danny Carvello and he had been discussing this after dinner, and Harold had been heavily influenced by Danny's thinking.) He told the assembled boys that there was another dimension for them to consider. It was not easy for him to talk about, but it kept bothering him, so he decided he should say something. He knew that many of the boys had heard about how Althea Redmonton had pimped their brother behind his back. Everybody had noticed how George went native for almost a week because of how she treated him. And he wanted to know what the brotherhood thought about that.

There were a number of finger clicks scattered across the room. Mike O'Hare stood at the podium with his leisure suit gaping open, and recognized Tom Baker. Tom was a sophomore, and Joshua Finch's roommate. Tom snorted before he began to speak.

I don't know what the hell that is supposed to mean, but I can't imagine voting for or against a girl simply because she is or isn't dating one of us. We have no idea whether she should have been faithful, or if she was unfaithful, or whatever. What on earth are we doing here? This isn't a test of virginity or values, it's a glorified beauty contest, for chissake! So let's pick the girl we want, and forget about who she is or isn't cavorting with. A number of sophomores mumbled their agreement. Quite a number of seniors raised their hands to be heard.

Quintin Wells stood stiffly and spoke slowly about how much the house seemed to be changing. I see us turning away from the values that make us Eta Chis, he said solemnly. We must consider the values or the attitudes of the girls we are voting on. This is a girl whom you will look to and sing to every week. It isn't enough for her to be pretty, if she is going to cheapen the position of Darling by being sleazy.

More seniors rose to be heard, and Danny Carvello nodded in appreciation as they talked about the values and the meaning of the house. Two boys said they would not support naming someone a Darling that they wouldn't be willing to bid, if she were a boy. Then Stoobie rose and sniffed. The boys looked oddly at him. He was wearing a jacket and tie, as he usually did at chapter meetings, and he held himself tightly erect. This issue is a perfect example of the larger issue in our fraternity, he began, and some of the sophomores groaned. His look silenced them.

We are a fraternity based on certain principles, and with the highest expectations for each other. If we honor the rule that one brother does not pimp on another, why shouldn't that same rule apply to our Darling? He sat back down.

Because she wasn't with another brother, she was with some guy from another house! Joshua Finch replied garrulously. Jeeesus! How holy are we going to make ourselves out to be? I didn't join this house because I wanted to promote someone's idea of morality! What happens between Althea Redmonton and George Muirfield or any other brother is totally off limits for this vote, in my opinion. Heads bobbed across the room.

Bob Woodbridge had listened with fascination to the debate. He was thinking about how so many of the boys drooled over Lucy Fitzwaller when she flirted so brazenly with them. There was a fine line between the bond of brotherhood and the natural impulse of males, and he wanted to scribble notes to himself to use in one of his short stories someday. But the issue at hand needed to be addressed. He raised his hand, and Mike O'Hare recognized him. As Bob moved to the front of the room, he looked at the chest hair sticking out of the top of Mike's open shirt with its wide lapels.

Gentlemen, he began. The rich resonance of his voice brought the group to silence. We are social animals, and we are moral ones too. We cannot separate the rules we live by into only the categories we want. We are human, and we carry with us all of the baggage – good and bad – that being human entails. Bob paused and looked around the room for effect. I was the one who saw Althea Redmonton cheating on Brother George. A hum of breaths and clearings of throats traversed the room. Now here was something new and interesting!

And whatever the quondam relationship between those two may have been, it is obviously different now. But none of us have any real knowledge of what it means. And has Brother George asked any of us not to vote for his girlfriend? Bob looked around the room again. I thought not. He is leaving this to the wisdom of his brothers. So let's be wise. I per-

sonally believe that Brother Harold has raised an interesting issue, one
that has given me pause. And I have listened patiently to all of you speak.
I propose that we vote secretly on our choice between these two girls.
That way, we do not have to let the pressure of seeing who feels one way
or the other interfere with how we really want to vote.

Bob took his seat, and more boys rose and spoke, but added little new
to the debate. The air in the closed room had grown warm, and the boys
were intensely focused on each other. Mike O'Hare finally asked if anyone wanted to second Bob Woodbridge's proposal for a secret ballot, and
someone yelled out second. Mike handed out slips of paper and asked the
boys to write one name or another on the paper, fold it, and hand it back
to him. When he had collected all of the paper, he went back to the podium, and opened each paper and put them in one of two piles. The boys
watched with interest. The piles seemed pretty even at first, but then one
pile grew larger.

Diane Southington is our next Darling, Mike reported calmly. He
took the papers and pushed them in the pocket of his leisure suit.
There was scattered finger clicking, but the mood in the room was
wary. Cullen Hastings was humiliated about Althea, and couldn't believe what had happened. He couldn't bear to look at George when he
returned to the room! But he looked up and watched George smile
broadly at the news. If he was surprised, or hurt, there was not a hint
of it on his face.

The last proposal voted on that night was one to amend the dress
code, eliminating coats and ties except for date nights. Cullen fought hard
to keep the dress code, which he really liked, as did Stoobie and Harold
and a number of the seniors. But in the end, the measure passed by five
votes.

After the seniors had made their farewell speeches, which were alternatingly solemn and funny, Cullen caught up with George as the boys
filed out of the room. He told him he needed to talk to him, and began to
tell him about the vote for Darling. George watched Cullen's face redden
as he retold some of the salient points made by the boys during the debate, and George smiled serenely. Cullen, George said softly, I'm okay.
Maybe it's fate. I'm okay. He patted Cullen on the shoulder, and Cullen
immediately took the flat of his palm and patted George twice on his
chest emphatically. George smiled again. He knew it was Cullen's way of
saluting or expressing his joy.

The Girl Outside The Library didn't have her bicycle the next day
when George spotted her. She was looking at the ride board in the
Straight. The ride board was where kids looked for people driving places
as a way to get a ride. George walked right up next to her when he saw
her, and pretended to be looking at the board for a moment. He could feel

her next to him, absorbed in looking at the ride notices. She was wearing
blue shorts and a red Cornell T-shirt. Her backpack was at her feet. She
smelled like fresh air.

Where are you looking to go? He asked casually, as he scanned the
board. The Girl Outside The Library considered him for about one second, and then turned back to the board and said, "Chicago." George could
tell she didn't like him talking to her. He asked her if she remembered
him, and she said No, without looking back at him.

He nodded, and said, I didn't think so. We sat opposite each other
outside the library one day. You're hard to forget. George was wincing
inside as he said the words. They didn't come out sounding natural, because they were not words he would naturally say. He was trying to think
of words that Danny or Harold might use, because he was out of his
league and he knew it.

Sorry, I don't remember you. She walked quickly away, slinging her
backpack over one shoulder. George watched her disappear. Then he
whispered to the place she had been standing, See Althea, that's about as
far as I ever got cheating on you!

He had been on his way down to the cafeteria to wait for Althea when
he had made his play for the Girl Outside The Library. He went through
the line and got some lunch and went to the middle of the cafeteria, in the
middle of the immense room where they always sat. She'd find him easily. He ended up sitting in a spot where no one else was sitting, but was
joined almost immediately by a mother, father and their high school
daughter. George wondered who had given them the tour. He had slowly
become responsible for scheduling the tour guides, and had agreed to succeed Charles Lord as the chairman of the student organization for his
senior year.

Then the room went strangely silent, which was followed by hoots of
laughter, and before George could turn around to see what the commotion
was, the three faces of the parents and their daughter turned ashen. Then a
naked black boy with, George noted, an impressive physique, came
streaking slowly through the cafeteria. He was almost sauntering, he was
running so slowly.

About two tables beyond George and the visiting family, the boy
leaped up on one of the long, wooden tables, and raised his arms out and
stood there, swinging his manhood in a big arc and smiling wickedly. The
entire cafeteria cheered and clapped. Streaking had been immensely popular when George was a freshman, including organized mass streaks down
the hill from Uris Library to West Campus. But it had died out his
sophomore year. Now it was making a slight comeback, though most students thought it was yesterday's fashion.

George clapped wildly and laughed, and people whistled and girls
shouted "All right!" from one corner of the room. The streaker eventually

waved and took a bow, before he plopped down on the floor and ran just as slowly back through the room and out the door. George returned to eating his lunch and watched the parents whispering furiously to their daughter. She had a funny smile on her face, as if she knew she was never going to get the chance to attend this school.

Then Althea slid next to him and asked George why he had never done that kind of an exhibition for her. The parents heard her and looked mortified. Althea burst out laughing when she saw the parents gaping at her, and George just looked at them and shrugged. It happens every Thursday at Cornell, he told them in mock seriousness, and Althea elbowed him hard. And you being a tour guide and everything, she scolded him good-naturedly. The father stood up and told his wife and daughter they were leaving, and George and Althea broke into laughter all over again.

It was like this between them now, and George sometimes saw it and sometimes didn't. They would be jocular and boisterous with each other, as if the energy passing between them were a salve to their wounds. But this never made George feel any better. At the same time that Althea's elevated demeanor enticed and lured him, he sensed the struggle underneath, the slightly manic need to cover more ground between the past and the present. It highlighted what they were trying to whitewash. But Althea was working hard, and George saw the genuine need in her eyes to keep going.

After lunch, Althea left George at the entrance to the Straight, to go to her economics class. She kissed him quickly and raised her eyebrows and smiled, and George watched her sashay away from him. Morning clouds had partially cleared, and the sun was bending around the remaining white puffs to make the day bright and clean. Soon humidity would arrive, but only a hint of it was in the air. George walked over to one of the benches outside the Straight and leaned his head back to look at the sky.

He had told Althea over lunch that she was not elected Darling, and she had acted surprised that she was even considered for it, although she knew that it had been discussed. George had told her to stop pretending, and she had confessed to hoping it might happen, but she certainly understood. Their eyes exchanged the angst and folly and unspoken understanding that mark the gaze of all vested partners. It was sweet, and caring. They knew where not to go. Then they had switched topics and finished lunch, relieved and pleased with each other.

So Althea was not Darling (and think about why!) and George was not consul, but he was proconsul. He wished he could see this thing with Althea with more clarity, but it stuck in a blurred part of his sight. Like a shadow he could not chase away, in spite of his genuine effort. He rose and walked slowly toward the Arts Quad, until he was between the two libraries, and hesitated about what he wanted to do. He knew he should head in and study, but couldn't get his body to take him that way.

Then he saw Maria Kitsoujas approach and he smiled widely to greet her. He had not seen the former Darling in almost a year, and he liked her very much. Maria waved as she came close, and then kissed him on the cheek when she reached him. George asked how she was, told her how good it was to see her, and asked her where she had been. They spoke hurriedly, as people do to catch up. Maria told him she had taken a semester abroad in Greece, and then had really been absorbed in writing her psychology thesis. She told him she had barely socialized all spring.

They sat on the stone bench between the two buildings, and Maria asked George how his acting was going. She was surprised to hear that he had left the theater, and wanted to understand why, and eventually George told her about his father, and last spring, and his choice of a major, and Caitlin. He talked about Eta Chi, and his preliminary thinking about graduate school, and all the time Maria sat, nodding her head, listening intently.

Well, God, it all makes perfect sense, she said warmly. She smiled and shifted herself to face him more directly. George said he was glad someone could make sense of it.

George, think about it. You lost your dad. I'm so sorry about that. Really. But now it's time for the son to stop fooling around with the theater and follow his father's legacy. It's psychology 301. George felt his neck tighten.

That's really not it, Maria. I honestly didn't think that I had what it took to go the distance in theater. And all of the literature says if that's the case, get out now. And the funny thing is, I feel totally divorced from it, as if it never really existed. It's got nothing to do with my father.

Maria sat quietly for a moment. It's okay, she said. It's not a bad thing. But it's textbook, George. Listen. She took his hands in her own as she spoke, and the coolness of her skin surprised him. I'm not a psychologist yet, but think about it. Maybe theater was a rebellion for you. Maybe you just concluded that you weren't right for it. But at some point, children follow their parents. We all do, in one way or another. It's not something you can fight, or control. It's the order of nature.

The ire in George ran deep. How dare this girl analyze him in ten minutes! She had no clue and yet she was making pronouncements left and right. He told her he thought they should agree to disagree, and she shrugged and complied by asking him about Eta Chi. He told her stories and told her how much the brothers would love to see her. She smiled broadly, agreed to come by before school ended. They talked about Greece, and her graduate school plans, and more than an hour passed before they stood and said goodbye.

George watched her enter Olin Library where she said she worked religiously on the third floor in the stacks. When she walked she swayed her substantial hips in an accentuated arc. George fretted about what to do. He really didn't want to study now. Maria could not have been more wrong about him. He walked off across the Arts Quad, on a diagonal. He knew where he was going, but wouldn't admit it to himself.

He came to a stop in front of the Theater Arts building, and looked for a moment at its old, faded red door with the ornate trim, and then hauled it open and moved gingerly into the musty hallway. It was near the end of the semester, and the hallway was deserted, which pleased him. He didn't want to see anyone, just feel the place. Just prove to himself that he was right, that he had made the right decision, that it was for the right reasons. He wandered over to the callback board, and read the notices, mostly old, of one acts and voice recitals and classroom assignments for the spring term.

The air in the hallway was still and smelled just as he remembered – like a mixture of chalk and sweat and floor cleaner. He leaned against the opposite wall, facing the callback board, and closed his eyes and smelled the air. He was picturing the hallways filled with students running from one practice room to the next, dressed in sweatpants and tights. He heard the resonance to their voices, the open, nondescript sounds of voices trained to metamorphose and carry across great distances.

He smiled to himself, and with his eyes still closed, he began to do the mouth stretching exercises he had done daily for over a year. First you make your mouth into a square, then a circle, then a rectangle. Repetitions stretched the lips and the muscles and enabled you to loosen up and dramatically increase your ability to shape your face as well as articulate and imitate. His mouth was in the square position on the third repetition when Derek Steele walked past him without a word. George did not hear him because he was in his socks. But then Derek turned and spoke, and George leaped away from the wall out of his reverie.

Jesus Christ! All I said was Hi George! Derek fumed. He peered intently at the boy he had not seen in a year. George recovered and just laughed.

You look sort of preppy now, Derek offered. George said thanks.

You're welcome, I guess. What are you doing? Walking down memory lane?

And with that George followed Derek down the hall and into his office with the tall, half glass door.

CHAPTER TWENTY

In the summer of 1976, Nadia Comaneci, from Romania, took gold at the summer Olympics in Montreal. She was the first to ever score a perfect "10" in the gymnastics competition. She scored a perfect "10" seven times. She wore a memorably impertinent look on her face as she held her arms outstretched and flipped and twirled her way across the balance beam.

At about the same time as Nadia turned the Olympics on its ear, a new dance called the hustle became a sensation in the discotheques and dance halls on Long Island. Relatively simple to learn, starting with *And, One, Two, Three,* the hustle shook the dance floors of Long Island to the stomping, gleeful rhythms of disco, along with The Bump. And Harold Wise, senior at the Cornell hotel school and summer intern of The Golden Goddess club on Long Island, was there to catch it all.

The Golden Goddess was a warehouse that had been converted into a rollicking, full-service restaurant and disco. Spiral, wrought iron staircases had been installed all over the massive building, leading to tables which were suspended above dance areas. People could eat and drink while the dancers swirled below them across the open floors. The thump, thump, thump of the speaker system blasted out the likes of *Disco Inferno*, and *Play That Funky Music*. And in late August, while cruising across the floor as the music thumped out another tune, Harold met a girl.

Barbara Huston was tall, blond, and imperial. She had a long, narrow face with a full, strong smile, and a boatload of street sense. She took one look at Harold as he bopped across the floor in his self-important assistant supervisor role, and yanked hard on his tie to get his attention. Before he could recover, Barbara pulled him into an open space on the dance floor and swiveled her hips into his to dance the Bump. With one look at her flashing blond hair and the pink suit she wore, Harold didn't hesitate to bump back. And within minutes, Barbara had taught Harold more sensual ways to do the bump than he had ever imagined. Her perfume was everywhere.

So when Harold finished up at the Golden Goddess a couple of days later, he took two important things back to school with him – the *Happiness Is Being With The Spinners* LP, and Barbara Huston's phone number. Barbara was twenty-three, and worked as a receptionist in a Manhattan office. She wanted to know how soon Harold was coming back. She was, after all, a city girl who couldn't wait around for College Boy to come home for Thanksgiving. Harold said he'd be back in two weeks, and Barbara rewarded him with a long, involved hug and kiss, and ordered him to hurry back. Harold laughed and rubbed his belly.

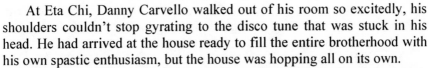

At Eta Chi, Danny Carvello walked out of his room so excitedly, his shoulders couldn't stop gyrating to the disco tune that was stuck in his head. He had arrived at the house ready to fill the entire brotherhood with his own spastic enthusiasm, but the house was hopping all on its own.

He could hear The Spinners playing on a stereo in the senior corridor, as he threw his things in his room. Although his election as consul gave him the most points in the house lottery system, Danny opted to keep his room from last year. It was tucked out of the way, near the stairway to the third floor. He liked it there because he could sneak off to bed early and get up at four thirty in the morning and do his work with no one the wiser.

At the far end of the senior corridor, the music poured out of Stoobie's room. When Danny walked in, Stoobie was standing on a chair, setting up a rotating light that splashed purple, yellow and green lights all across the walls of his room. Below him, Harold Wise demonstrated the hustle to George Muirfield.

What the hell are you guys doing?!? The boys greeted their new consul with whoops of laughter. Harold guffawed. Wait 'til you see this new dance! He beamed at Danny.

Some people, like Stoobie, glide smoothly and carefully when they dance. Harold's moves were all about athleticism and the beat. George always looked like he was performing some sort of interpretive dance. But Danny Carvello was a bundle of nervous energy that, when channeled into a rhythm, produced a hypnotic swirl of subtle, instinctive grace. He made people around him tap their feet and snap their fingers. He loved to dance, and it showed. So when Harold said he had something new to show him, Danny immediately started to snap his fingers and shake his shoulders as he joined Harold and George in their line. Come on, I'm ready, he said in an elevated voice. So Harold showed him the elementary steps of the hustle, laughing, and Danny caught the wave flawlessly.

Boys gathered at the door, and Wendall Wellington, who had spent the summer in New York, pushed his way through and yelled, The hustle! He fell into line next to Danny. Then Fritz Hublein came up the back stairs at the end of the corridor, and yelled, Room!

ROOM!! Harold bellowed in reply.

George Muirfield stopped mid-step and echoed Harold. ROOOMM!! Everybody laughed.

The Spinners started singing *The Rubberband Man*, and boys up and down the hall started yelling ROOM! at the top of their lungs as they picked up the simple steps of the new dance. Senior year had begun.

The second weekend back, Danny scheduled a chapter meeting for Sunday night, and sent word around the house that he had a special surprise for the brotherhood. Come prepared! he said whenever he walked past brothers. Danny opened the meeting at ten p.m. in a solemn voice. He stood at the podium in front of the consul's high-backed chair, with George Muirfield seated to the right and George's first little brother, Rick Frye, to the left. Rick was recording secretary.

My brothers, Danny began, welcome back to the greatest house on the hill. Fingers snapped across the room. Danny walked through the meeting regimen, conducting business efficiently. Then it came time for the boys to speak individually if they chose. It was a powerful segment of the chapter meeting, where boys aired grievances, or thanked brothers for their help on something. This being the first chapter meeting of a new school year, boys stood to speak about reflections they had over the summer, and their hopes for the coming year. One boy talked about the importance of tolerance and compassion for each other. Throughout the session, Danny kept nodding his head in support of what was said.

It was traditional for the proconsul and consul to speak last. When all comments were exhausted, George rose and talked about the incredible impression that had been left on him when he first attended a chapter meeting as a freshman, and the seniors had been giving their farewell speeches. He talked to the hushed room about the need for open and honest dialogue amongst all the boys. He also asked his brothers to be true to the ideals of their brotherhood, and thanked them for his chance to be a part of something so special. When he finished, Danny waited a moment, and then stood and told the brothers before him how special a moment in time this was.

We have a brief time together, and we have the unique opportunity to act as brothers – brothers united in the pursuit of each other's dreams. We also have the duty to fill these days and nights with the pursuit of women.

The boys looked uncertainly at their new consul.

So here's what we are going to do, Danny went on, nodding sagely. He looked at Dexter Billings, the new social chair, and asked him to bring in the goods. Dexter stood and motioned to the boy next to him, and they went into the back of the room, and carried cartons into the middle of the floor. They repeated this until ten cases were stacked together. The whole time, Danny nodded sternly.

He looked at his watch. It is now eleven twenty, he said. At eleven forty-five, we are assembling in the foyer and going up to Delta Gamma Nu. Brothers started asking questions, and were hushed quiet.

Now, this is the rule. When we get there, we assemble silently on the doorstep at the front of the sorority. When I give the signal, we will sing the Darling Song in the best harmony we can muster, until the girls are leaning out the windows. And then we explain that we have all of this champagne – Danny pointed to the cases in front of him – and need their help to drink it. The boys all hooted and clapped their hands. Danny held up his hands. This will only work if we all go together as brothers and sing the song to the best of our abilities!! Everybody cheered.

As the boys left the room, Danny talked to someone about getting the glassware into the car with the champagne, and bringing a boom box and disco music. He bopped around and jutted his chin in and out with exaggerated swagger. Twenty minutes later, the foyer was filled with brothers speaking excitedly. Some of them were yelling, Who's driving!?, and others reminded each other to be sure that they sneak up on the front lawn quietly. Then Danny led them out the door.

At Delta Gamma Nu, the moon shone brightly, and the girls' windows were open to the warm night air. The boys parked a block or more away from the house and walked silently to join each other at the front door. The evening was still and slumbering. Danny stood on the red brick stoop, and raised his hands like a maestro. As he did, he hummed off-key for a prolonged moment, causing many of the boys to giggle uncontrollably.

Then the brothers' voices lifted into the darkness. Tentative at first, but then buttressed by some of the boys with good voices, the song resonated nicely in the courtyard. They finished the song, expectantly. Nothing happened. Then one light came on, on the second floor of the sorority. Seeing no other signs of life, Danny instructed the boys to really sing, and their voices carried the song much more emphatically into the night air –

Come now, my darling, the Darling of Eta Chi
When the stars still shine but the morning is nigh
And dance with me one more time

Your dulcet lips and treasured eyes
Tell me all that I care to know
So lift me high to the ancient sky
Where guiding lights pierce the evening's glow

Your simple love is all I ask, its purity unmasked
For you alone and no one else could bring my heart to rest
The time we have will soon be passed
Please, please, my darling, so beautiful, so blessed

You say time passes, but I say love stays
The heavens might wait, the gods smile our way
If only to hear your sweet words of reply
Come my darling, My Darling of Eta Chi

As the boys finished their song, the door opened, and a girl in her nightgown and bathrobe (who was the sorority president and had agreed with Danny to keep this a total secret) said in a loud voice, What have we here!

Does anybody want to play house? Danny asked with a big smile. We have lots of cold champagne to convince you! And with that the girl held the door open, and the boys pranced in. Three girls came tentatively down the staircase as the boys filed into the living room. Someone plugged in the boom box and started playing Earth Wind & Fire. Within moments, the room filled with girls smiling (and protesting loudly) while boys popped the corks on champagne bottles and filled glasses that other brothers quickly set out on every table in the room.

Harold Wise asked Martha Higgins to dance, and as he began to bump his hips against hers with his hands clasped together, some of the sophomores started calling out, "All right, Harry-Harry!" Danny waited to dance until Janette Emilio entered the room, and then he twirled her around to teach her the hustle. Janette had taken the time to dress and put on lipstick, and Danny eyed her excitedly as he walked her through the steps.

Jim Dart, the hockey player from Canada, walked over to a heavy-set girl who stood off to one corner with her arms pulled close to her waist. Jim asked her to dance. She was not the sort of girl often asked to dance, but she grinned and said sure. The two of them bounced their way into the middle of the room to the music. This led a number of boys to ask girls they did not know to dance, and soon the room gyrated to the beat of the music. All around the room, girls and boys sipped champagne and laughed.

It was three thirty in the morning before one of the girls finally yelled, Enough! and turned the music off. By now couples were scattered across the room and a number of people were feeling the first slow signs of a headache. Danny sat with Janette, surveying the scene with a tired smile. He hadn't been up this late in years, but it had been worth it. He looked across the room at George Muirfield, who had a girl sitting on his knee. She was not really being cozy with him, just silly, as she told others around her some sort of a story. Danny winked at George, and George just shook his head.

The girl on his lap had her back to him and kept swiveling on his knees as she looked back and forth at the others. George increasingly felt the weight of her tiny legs and the soft plumpness of her petite bottom as she moved around on his knees. The casual intimacy of her motions sobered him up.

I think it's time for bed, someone volunteered, and a few people laughed suggestively. The room in general began to break up. Betsy, the girl on George's lap, turned to him, kissed him quickly and told him it had been a wonderful idea for a party. Then she stood up and stretched her arms and yawned. Her kiss surprised him, and he mumbled thanks and stood up himself to shake the stiffness out of his legs. Give me a call sometime she said simply, as she turned to head upstairs. She didn't wait for a reply. George watched her walk away, impressed with the matter-of-fact way that she seemed to dismiss him. It was beguiling.

Of course, George had no intention of calling her. But he had to admit to himself that this had been a pleasant reprieve from the roller coaster he still rode with Althea Redmonton. They had left last spring on uneasily shifting terms, and saw each other twice over the summer, in between numerous late night telephone calls on which they had sworn their mutual allegiance to each other. And when they had arrived back at school, Althea had rushed into his arms and kissed him passionately. But there was a place inside George that felt hollow and unfulfilled, like a distant drone in the evening that won't let the night be calm.

And over those summer months, George had flirted casually with girls at his summer job. He did not really understand himself. His blood would rise at the merest recollection of his Althea, of her voice and laugh and bedeviling eyes. Then he would call her and she would speak so softly and lovingly through the telephone to him, that he would reel inside and want desperately to be with her. But it was not as it once had been.

Althea, for her part, was pained by the slight ripple in George's voice, and the detached way in which he could go three or four days without speaking with her. They saw each other over the summer, but only twice, and she wondered what that meant. Each time he came to Vermont, they were ferociously attached to each other, and comfortably inseparable. Though she did not consciously see it, this new remoteness to George's demeanor made him more alluring. He became less attainable, or more enigmatic, somehow, and this put a small ache in her abdomen.

Then they were back together at school and George was alternatingly devouring and absent. They would spend hours and hours together and then he would remove himself to go do something at his fraternity, or that student organization he chaired. And he would remind her about the one-act play he was probably going to be in, forewarning her of coming absences as if he looked forward to them.

Althea did not know what to make of the one act play George kept mentioning. He told her that he had to go back and see his old professor, but he was pretty mysterious about the whole thing. He just kept suggesting to her that the theater was a different world, without elaborating. In fact, George didn't want to explain anything to his girlfriend until he was sure it was going to happen. He didn't know whether Derek would still want to do it.

When Derek Steele had sauntered into his dusty old office with George last May, he had only floated the idea to George, and said he wasn't sure himself. After Derek had found him leaning against the wall in the hallway of Ridley Hall, George had followed his professor into his office to reminisce. George had acted insecure and tentative, and for a minute Derek grew bored. He wished he hadn't bothered to say hello, but then George looked into his eyes, and spoke painfully about life, and Derek recalled the intensity with which George could emote. So many of the theater kids protected their own egos with acting technique.

So Derek had focused in and been a kind ear to the kid, offering him the best advice he could. He told George that he had made the right decision, that theater was really only for psychopaths and loners, or people like himself who didn't care about or even really understand money. But then something in him shifted as George's bright blue eyes searched his own, and he concluded by saying that George might be the sort who could find some happiness in dabbling in theater on the side.

It was after Derek said this to George that the idea came to him. He started shuffling through the pile of scripts and papers on his desk, looking for that manuscript. As he searched, he peered casually up at George and asked him how he got along with Caitlin these days.

George laughed. I don't get along with her, meaning that we don't have any contact with each other, he replied. Why?

Derek asked the boy if he thought he could get along with her, professionally. George looked curiously at him, and said he didn't know. It would probably be awkward, and would depend on her, he guessed.

Derek found the script he had been looking for, and handed it to George. It was an original, typed manuscript, not a photocopy of a published play. George looked at the cover, where the title was scrawled in large letters:

Big Kids

Or
The Peripeteia

An original play by Sturdevant Barrington.

What's this? George inquired of his old professor. Derek pushed at his bushy red moustache with his right hand, and looked at the script for a moment. Listen, he said, it's probably a stupid idea, and I don't even know if I want to do it. But Caitlin came to me in April and asked me if I would be willing to act in this play. It's a one act written by one of our new grad students. Caitlin needs to direct a one-act next year because she's taking Advanced Stage Direction. She wants me and one other person to take the two parts in the play and let her direct us.

Us? George asked incredulously.

No, not you specifically. Derek shook his head, irritated. Me and someone else I wanted to do it with. But I told her I couldn't think of any of the current students I wanted to do this with. And that wasn't my only reservation. The script is raw, and really out there, and I'd probably get in trouble with the Dean for agreeing to do it. But it's good.

The man and the boy looked at each other expectantly. So, Derek continued, I listened to myself telling you that you could dabble, which I don't really believe, but anyway, it occurred to me that you would be really good for the part, and maybe I'd be willing to consider doing it if you wanted to.

You want me to act with you in a play directed by Caitlin Fossburgher, George recapped, with his eyes wide. What is the play about?

Derek grinned slightly. It's about what all plays are about – the inability of people to talk to each other. He nodded his head for emphasis. It's about two men, one young and one old, who don't really know each other, but who are on this sort of parallel track. There's this beginning and ending like the womb and the grave, and in between they have these conversations about their lives and become scared of each other's revelations. The more they connect, the more they disconnect.

George laughed at Derek's description and said, Okayyyy.

It's like <u>Waiting For Godot</u> on acid, Derek said smiling. It's either brilliant or bullshit, but it sticks in your mind. George looked dubious.

Listen, take it home for the summer. I have another copy here somewhere. If you want to do it, and if I want to do it, which I'm not saying I do, then we can talk in the fall. There's no pressure. Think through the Caitlin thing too. She'd have to be the director.

George stood up and said he would come back to see him no matter what. Then he turned away, and turned right back with a big smile on his face. Even if this doesn't work out Derek, you really, really made a difference for me on a day when I needed one.

With that George stuck out his hand and made Derek shake it. Derek told him to stop being an idiot, but he liked it when he took George's hand. After George left, Derek mused for a bit about how much he would benefit from having someone like George to act with. Derek wasn't a particularly good actor, which is why he had ended up teaching and directing. But like all people in the theater, he thought he could be terrific if he could just find the right chemistry and vehicle. He bet he could work well with George.

George's initial excitement about returning to acting had quickly waned. Didn't he have the rest of his life to consider? He had no appetite for giving up Eta Chi, or the student organization. More importantly, he had to start thinking about what he was going to do after graduation. An image of his father obscured his thoughts.

Near the end of July, George finally picked up the play to read it. He looked at the title page and wondered if he could take direction with Derek from Caitlin. Of course, Caitlin might put the kibosh on the idea herself. He wondered what Althea would have to say about Caitlin.

Reading the play didn't help. It was opaque, and odd, and if he understood the liner notes correctly, there was nudity at the beginning and end. The middle of the play was quite interesting, though, and he readily pictured himself with Derek, and saw what Derek had seen. The play was filled with symbols and open questions, but the gist of it was that the younger man and the older man were coming at life, were in fact born into their lives from opposite directions, and were meeting in the middle, each on their way to the other side.

Neither one of them wanted to make the leap across. The younger man was afraid, and full of himself, and doubtful. The older man was sadly reminiscent and cynical of the younger man's conceits. There was, George thought, one gorgeous moment, where the two men had been conversing for quite a while, irritating and enthralling each other, when the older man suddenly poses a question.

I see where we are headed and where I have been. But where are we now?

The younger man says he doesn't know. The older man looks all around them, searching, and says,

We're in between! I see that now. We are In-Betweeners. On the Cusp-ers. On the razor edge between ageless and aged. At the juncture between destiny and fate. Don't you see? Look at me! Look at you! We won't remember this, ever. It's too painful.

George looked up from reading the play, lost in thought. The older man was so resigned, so jaundiced. But it could be a gorgeous theatrical moment. And then a couple of pages later, the younger man asks the older man if he ever had children. The older man gets teary as he replies:

Do you know what children of the universe means? Are you asking me if I ever sired offspring, or if I was once, myself, a child? I remember so much, as in a dream, so unreal. I think I am looking forward to my childhood. But yes, of course, I must have had children, because I certainly remember them. I watched them grow. First they grow up. Then they grow down. And then up again. Do you feel the flux? You must. I feel it. It's...now. We're those big kids we always looked up to. (Pause) *Once you break through, you look down on them, you know. You can't imagine it, but it's true. I see now why you have been afraid. I am afraid, standing here with you.*

George sat on his porch as he read the play, and the light summer air brushed softly against the screens. He pictured Derek making this speech, and smiled at the image. The play, and the world of the theater seemed so far away from him it was surreal. He finished reading the play. Derek was right. It stuck with you.

George put the play away and dismissed it from his thoughts. He would have told you that it left him untouched. But on a deeper level, the play, as well as the notion of acting, anchored in his psyche with new authority. The steel cable in his mind that linked responsibility with adulthood began to unravel. He just didn't realize it.

And now, here he was, at a quarter to four in the morning, on his way back to Eta Chi after a modern-day panty raid at Delta Gamma Nu, thinking about the play when he should have been thinking about sleep. When he got to his room, he searched through the boxes he had brought back to school until he found the play, and plopped it on the old desk that was wedged into one corner of his tiny, rectangular room. It was time to find out if this was going to happen or not.

At eight thirty a.m. the sunlight woke him, and George drearily pulled himself up and yawned. His head ached from lack of sleep, and the champagne had left a crimp in his temple, but he sensed eagerness underneath it all. A long shower and three Bayer aspirin made him better, and he dressed and walked up to campus. He would skip his first class, and then make his second class at eleven twenty, and still have time to swing by the theater department to look for Derek.

When George reached the building, he yawned again, considered that he needed coffee, but pulled himself erect and walked inside. It was dark in the hallway, and cool. He walked slowly down the hall to Derek's office and knocked. No answer. He tried the knob and the door swung open. He walked in, looked around, and sat at the desk to write the teacher a note. He didn't see Caitlin Fossburgher at the door until he lifted his head from finishing the note.

They looked at each other, silently. Caitlin's long, red hair wrapped both sides of her face. She looks like she has had plenty of sleep, George thought absent-mindedly.

You'll have to grow a moustache, she said finally. George said, Hi Caitlin.

Caitlin sat in the chair next to the desk, and asked how he was. He said, Fine. You?

I am great, thanks. Caitlin looked closely at her old boyfriend. You look like hell, George.

George grinned sheepishly. I know. No sleep.

Caitlin harrumphed. The sound out of her throat flooded George with memories of his old girlfriend's idiosyncrasies.

I have to admit, I was furious with Derek when he told me that he talked to you about my play. Caitlin began. But he's right. You would be a good choice. And I have gotten over my dread at even speaking to you again. So I hope the reason you are here is to say you are interested. Because so long as we are able to put the past behind us, I'm willing to do this. What do you say?

George stared at Caitlin, completely unsure of himself. He had expected to talk this over with Derek, but Caitlin was another story. And he was so tired. I don't know what to say, he answered. She looked at him critically. All right, he went on, look. Part of me misses this, but the bigger part of me is now elsewhere. And I don't know about you, but it feels really strange to be sitting here with you, talking about this.

Caitlin laughed, and agreed. George, she said, let me be clear. I am living with Derek. George dropped his jaw. Caitlin smiled. And I have

heard how you are with someone too, so this would be a professional relationship. It's an unbelievable chance for me, and Derek has said it's you
or nobody. I know I can do this, and I would be shocked if you said you
couldn't. And it's only a one-act. A month of rehearsals at the most. Can't
you picture what a great time the three of us could have?

George smiled tepidly. What the hell, he finally muttered. Caitlin
clapped her hands excitedly. This is going to be so cool. Wait until you
hear how I want to stage this. Her eyes sparkled. In the back of his mind,
George mused over whether Caitlin was still a virgin. When he realized
he didn't care, he gave in to his old girlfriend's enthusiasm. He told her
about the wonderful crux in the middle of the play. Caitlin curled her feet
up under her knees, and told him that he would have to take her seriously
as a director. The two of them laughed.

Later that afternoon, after classes, George walked across the Arts
Quad toward the library to meet Althea. The late afternoon sky was filled
with colors – reds, purples, blues – and George marveled at them as he
walked. He started to sing, and when he neared someone coming the other
way, he lowered his voice, but didn't stop. He had started to sing to himself the previous spring when he realized that he really couldn't hold a
tune. He knew he had a good ear, and that it was just a matter of teaching
his voice to modulate.

So whenever he walked in the late afternoon from campus to the fraternity, George sang to himself. Irish songs, the Darling Song, popular
tunes that he could remember some of the words to. Anything that he was
confident he knew the right notes to. And slowly, over time, his voice
began to respond to his ear, and he taught himself to carry notes and
switch from one to the other. He sang with abandon sometimes, and other
times under his breath. When people passing by looked oddly to him, he
would smile, raise his eyebrows the way that Fritz Hublein did, and trek
on. He didn't normally do this headed into the campus, but today the colors of the sky made him think of Tom rush, and he tried to imitate the
folksinger's gravelly voice on the way to the library.

Althea sat waiting for George when he reached their usual table,
and George smiled broadly and plopped down next to his girlfriend
and said, Hi.

What's got you so energized? Althea asked, buoyed by his spirit.

I'm gonna do that play I told you about! Let's go outside and talk!

The two walked out into the fresh air, and George began to tell Althea
about the play. He explained about Derek, and the graduate student who
wrote the play, and tried to describe what it was about. Althea listened
intently, saying Cool! and trying to picture George onstage. She couldn't.
Then George hesitated and said there was just one more detail she needed
to hear.

You remember Caitlin? Althea's stomach twisted slightly as she nodded her head.

She's going to be the director. George didn't wait for a reaction. Immediately after he said that, he told her that Caitlin was actually *living* with Derek, she knew about Althea, and they had agreed they could do this without any personal complications. George nodded his head to emphasize the point.

Althea looked levelly at her boyfriend and said, WHAT?

George answered What?

You barely see me all summer, you act like Jeckyl and Hyde around me and now all of a sudden you are going to go back into acting IN A PLAY DIRECTED BY THE SWAN? Althea was convinced that this had been coming for a long time and she hadn't seen it. The idiot wanted to go back to his old girlfriend! It was obvious from the look on his face! But then she looked hard into his eyes and saw none of the real kind of remorse or guilt she expected to find there. He actually looked scared.

Scared was an apt description. But it wasn't for the reason Althea guessed. Althea read the fear in his eyes as concern over losing her, and was immediately comforted. But George realized that he was afraid of losing the play – it was suddenly more important to him than Althea Redmonton. He wanted Althea, and would make her see that this was not some stupid ploy to get back with Caitlin, but if she couldn't get passed it, he knew what he was going to do. And that frightened him.

George Muirfield was not the only Eta Chi who was putting on a theatrical production in the fall of 1976. In fact, a total of fifteen brothers were drafted to take part in one of the hotel school's enduring traditions – the undergraduate theatrical spoof of the school by the senior class. The production was a major fundraising event that drew scores of alumni back for a weekend of reminiscence and opportunistic recruiting. For this year, Jim Steuben had been honored with the job of putting it together.

Stoobie immediately drafted a number of his brothers to help in the production, including seven boys who had nothing to do with the hotel school, but thought it sounded like fun. This project fit Stoobie perfectly for the person he was becoming. He had not really come to grips with his sexuality yet. But once he failed to fulfill his heterosexual relationship with Mitsy Smith, he had conceded the stirrings deep within himself. Over the summer he thought hard about who he was.

He had not been an honest broker for himself. The things that he really liked he had hidden from the world, out of insecurity. But if he couldn't quite get his arms around the sex thing, as he blithely referred to it in his mind, he sure as hell didn't see why he had to pretend about other things. So the hotel school annual spoof was a great way for him to introduce his real personality to his friends.

Stoobie had a wonderful sense of tradition and an old-school set of manners. But in his heart he didn't care for the sort of stern, masculine arrogance he assumed. What he really liked was the flamboyance and bouncy feel of musicals. What was more, his wry humor had too long masked a wicked satirical bent. The Hotel Spoof would be a flashy musical send up of the foibles of being a hotel student and hospitality professional. It would be his own coming out party. To start, though, he needed to recruit writers and set designers and costume makers, as well as the actors themselves. This was huge.

Mitsy Smith sat next to her boyfriend at Date Night in late September, listening to him describe to others at the table the glitzy show he imagined. Mitsy had met a boy at home over the summer who showed her a different kind of masculinity. She fell for him, but he went to Stanford, which meant that she was only going to get to see him at Christmas. So when she reconnected with Stoobie the night of the Eta Chi champagne party, she explained this to him immediately, so as not to mislead him. But Stoobie had seemed totally fine with the fact that she had a boyfriend at home. He told her he was happy for her, but hoped that they could still see each other once in a while. Mitsy thought Stoobie was a special boy indeed, and enjoyed still seeing him.

After the boys had sung the Darling Song following dinner, Stoobie asked Mitsy if she would care for some sherry up in his room. Mitsy smiled and said, Sure! On the way down the Senior hall, she asked Stoobie softly whether he liked the way that the boys stood in a line when they sang the Darling Song now. God, no! Stoobie snorted. You don't see me up there with them, do you? It's creeping DU-ism, if you ask me.

Mitsy inquired what that meant, and he told her the house was sliding down the short hill to mediocrity. Soon, he warned, we will be nothing more than Delta Upsilon! They waved hello to George Muirfield who sat in his room across the hall, and Stoobie punctuated his statement by pointing to George and saying, Present company excluded.

George asked what they were talking about, and Stoobie yelled, Creeping DU-ism! George walked to Stoobie's doorway and stood there chatting with the two. Creeping DUism had become a recurring theme amongst the seniors, many of whom found the sophomores' attitudes toward Eta Chi heretical. Stoobie flipped the little switch on his wall, and the tri-colored light splayed its colors around the walls. He poured sherry for Mitsy and George before he poured his own.

On one wall, Stoobie had hung elegant tapestries and glassware that looked like they should be adorning the burnished walls of some country club. On the opposite wall he had framed posters of old movies. A Top Hat hung on the poster to his bed. George asked Mitsy where she had found this character, and the three laughed as George headed back into his room, sipping sherry.

Next door to Stoobie, Harold Wise sat at his desk, silently staring at the picture on his desk. In the picture he stood with his mother and sister in the backyard of their house on Long Island. His mother had the exhausted look of a woman for whom life had become a burden. His sister just stared at the camera, vacantly, as if there were no interrelationship between her thoughts and those of her family. Harold is beaming at the camera. It is a good picture of him.

No one would have guessed his real reason for keeping this picture in his view, or that, for the longest time, he had to hold back his emotions whenever he looked at it. For it would be obvious only to Harold that the picture had been taken at Harold's insistence, about a year after his father's death, when his mother was selling the house. They were moving to a smaller place, to save money and escape from those memories. Harold had been frantic.

He had come to see himself as the source of optimism for his mother, and of wisdom for his little sister. It weighed heavily on his shoulders, and at age fifteen, he was ill prepared to understand his mother's rage and depression. So he urged them to smile into the camera, and forced himself to exude happiness and excitement to balance the lack of it in his mother and sister. His inability to make them happy – to fill them with the force and power of life – only escalated his anxiety and motivation to prevail.

So when Harold looked at the picture, he did not see himself beaming. He saw a frightened boy unable to overcome the scourge of death, and at the edge of his own sanity. It made him want to cry, which he sometimes did when he felt safe in the privacy of his room. He always told himself he wept for his mother, but in truth he cried for himself.

His mother was doing much better now, and had even started dating a man. His sister, who had opted to stay closer to home to be with her mother, was coming along too. It was Harold who had never really made more than a makeshift peace with his own grief. He understood that he was totally irrational about it. But the blame he assigned to his father for dying was wholly in line with the life view his father had imbued him with. As Harold grew up, he watched the people around him refuse to take responsibility for themselves. If a boy fell down on a playing field, it was because the grass was too slippery. If his mother yelled at his sister for spending too much time on the telephone, it wasn't her fault – her friends wouldn't let her off! As his father always drilled into him, "You make your own mistakes, and you make your own good fortune." Only weaklings and suckers don't take responsibility for themselves. He and his father said that to each other all the time.

Then his father died. It made no difference that it was an accident. His father had been on a business trip. But he always took business trips – he spent most of his life on the road. That didn't matter. His life had been in his hands, right? His father had let him down, and now Harold had to tackle life knowing that even his father had failed. It was a never-ending burden. It took Harold a long time to see any light at the end of the tunnel, but a solution formed in his psyche over time. There were only so many things any man could do to realize his pursuits, but there was a principle that Harold could control. He would redeem his father by committing himself to be there for *his* children. Wherever else his life led him, he would never leave their sides.

He needed to marry, of course, and have children. But it was easy to get that far. Once there, he would never do anything to compromise the visibility and constancy of his fatherhood. His family would be his first priority; everything else would come second. In his mind, he would not be there until he had children of his own.

As he looked upon his picture now, it was with more fondness than anguish. His resolve helped. And this past weekend he surprised himself when he opened up with Barbara Huston as they lay in her bed together on Long Island. It spilled out of him, and Barbara just hugged him harder the more he spoke.

Barbara Huston had really only expected a wild fling with the College Boy who had driven down to see her. They had gotten drunk, and danced until the perspiration dampened both their faces, and then she had taken Harold back to her tiny apartment. Barbara was as confident as she was demanding. She never could believe what sheep boys were. She just bossed her boyfriends around and they seemed to love it. She figured Harold to be an easy mark, and told him to go sit on her couch and wait there for her. But Harold had chuckled, rubbed his belly, told her a joke, and then pressed her up against the door.

He was not the slightest bit rough with her, and Barbara found herself enthralled. Their first kiss had been tender, soft, insistent. Then Harold had walked over to her record player, picked out Barry White, placed the disc on the spindle, and walked back to her as she stood against the door, watching him. He moved like a football player. Then Barry White and Harold started singing in unison. Barbara giggled softly. Harold picked her up in his arms and carried her to bed. They made love in a hurry. By Sunday morning, they felt like old friends.

On Saturday, they walked, and ended up at a Chinese restaurant for lunch where Harold made a spectacle out of sending the food back twice, much to Barbara's amusement. Then they returned to Barbara's apartment to make love again, showered, went dancing again Saturday night and then returned home and slept soundly with each other.

In the morning they lied in a tangle of sheets as the coffee percolated. Barbara finished telling Harold about her disastrous attempts to be a singer when she was in high school when he started talking. He told her about the crazy parties at college, and then about where he grew up, and about moving to a smaller house after his father died. She heard his voice thicken and hesitate, and looked at him carefully. It was the first time a boy had ever opened up to her, and she instinctively reached for him like a mother might, and told him to hush. It was the most romantic thing she had ever experienced.

And now he was back at Eta Chi, looking at his photograph, and trying to decide whether to keep the picture out when she came to visit this weekend. He didn't want to appear too maudlin. After all, he had already gotten teary-eyed in her arms like a wimp. She had been wonderful to him, but how much more could she take? He began to visualize Barbara's reactions to Eta Chi and smiled. There was a costume party planned for the weekend, and Barbara said she was going to come as Cleopatra. Harold chuckled to himself as he pictured the scene. Cleopatra!

In College Town, Althea Redmonton wasn't thinking about what to be for the party. She had just hung up with her mother, and was thinking hard about her boyfriend. She trusted George, and had come around to believing that he had no interest in Caitlin. But all the same, this meant that he was going to disappear for a month or more and be rehearsing with her all the time. Between that and everything else he was doing, they probably wouldn't see each other at all. Althea was not happy about pining away in her last year of college.

Her mother had listened and said she knew what she would do – play the field. If George wasn't around, what else did he expect Althea to do? Althea could see the look on George's face if she suggested that. She tried a couple of lines out in the silence of her apartment, but they all fell flat. Maybe she could wait and see. George said he didn't know when rehearsals would begin, probably not until October at least. But it was hanging over her too much. She had to resolve it with her boyfriend now.

When she met up with him at the library, she asked how dinner had been. They had agreed to skip date night this week because both of them had papers to finish. George said she didn't miss much, and began to settle down at the table with her when she asked him to go out in the hallway with her. They walked out where they could sit and talk, and Althea told him that she had been thinking a lot about their situation.

George eyed her cautiously. Okay, he replied.

What do you want George? Althea's eyes were already moist, and George quickly moved next to her and put his arm gently around her.

I mean, what should you and I do? I believe what you've told me about Caitlin. It's not that. But how are we even going to see each other?

George looked away to think. They had been headed here for a long time, and he had avoided it in his own mind out of fear. They both always froze up when they talked about what they might do after graduation. George had once raised the subject of marriage and Althea had panicked. She had told him in a sure voice that she wasn't getting married before she was thirty, so they could postpone that discussion for at least ten years. George had answered that he could picture the two of them married sometime in the future, but he was fine with waiting ten years. Inside himself, he had been aghast at Althea's vehemence. There was obviously something he didn't understand.

He brought himself back to the moment and told her that he saw the practical difficulties, but thought they could just work through them. As they sat there, Althea had come to a new realization herself. She was too dependent on George for her own good. As soon as she said it to herself, she felt better.

Okay, she said, I know. Listen, I love you. I do. But we are making a mistake...I take that back. I am making a mistake if I spend my senior year waiting for you to find the time to call me. I think we have to look each other in the eyes and see that. I want to continue to see you. Who knows, we may get married in ten years. But I think we should both feel free to date other people.

George started laughing. He laughed hard, almost crazily, and he felt his center spinning off kilter, as if he was tilting to one side. Saying the words made Althea nauseous. What she really wanted was for George to do something – to shake her out of her delusion and make sense of it for her. But that wasn't to be. She could see that from the manic way he was acting. George stopped laughing and apologized.

Althea, he said (her name came out of his mouth like a whimper), I can't do that. I cannot live with the thought of you with other people. It will drive me insane.

Althea asked George what he suggested.

I guess we're done, he whispered. George could not believe that he actually uttered those words. He was clenching and unclenching different groupings of muscles all over his body, and felt dizzy. He looked into his girlfriend's face and their eyes opened to each other as the regret and the pain and the honesty of their exchange sunk in. They both knew it. And they both hated it.

Well, George said in a shaky breath, now what do we do? Althea told him to take her home. They scooped up their books, and walked hand in hand to their apartment. When their lovemaking was over, they sat up cross-legged on the bed, naked, and talked for hours. Finally they nestled together for a few hours of sleep, wrapped tightly around each other. When George woke, his cheek was against the soft flesh of Althea's elbow, and he wanted to throw up. The familiar scent of her skin made him sigh. He couldn't fathom how they had gotten to this place, but he knew it was real.

Once dressed, George waited for Althea to come out of her bathroom, and pulled her to him and they hugged for minutes in the kitchen. George felt her sobbing into his shoulder, and waited until she had subsided. I'm still smoking for you, he said with a smile, and she burst into tears again, and told him to shut up. Althea, George said solemnly, forever is a long time, and this isn't forever. Okay? Althea said okay, and then told George to get going. She'd see him sometime. The sting of the word "sometime" would stay with him for three long days.

CHAPTER TWENTY-ONE

Janette Emilio decided to go to the Eta Chi costume party dressed as Pocahontas. She found an old tan leather outfit at a second hand clothing store downtown, with fringe on the top and bottom. It was perfect. She made a headdress out of silk and feathers. The outfit showed off her flat stomach and thin legs. She looked like something out of the 1920s. She loved it, and knew it would torment Danny. She was becoming serious about him and expected that they would be lovers soon. Maybe even this weekend, she mused. He had clearly shown his respect for her, and they had become so close. They had seen each other over the summer, and Danny seemed to grow increasingly romantic with her.

When he picked her up for the party, Danny wore a quilted, white mattress pad over casual clothes. It was one of those old pads with the little elastics on each corner of the pad to loop over the four corners of the bed. Danny had put his arms and legs though the four elastics so that the mattress pad extended the full length of his frame. He whistled when he saw Janette, and asked her if she wanted to smokem peace pipe.

What are you doing? Janette asked Danny as she shook her head in disbelief.

I'm a mattress! He exclaimed. Then he leaned in close to her and whispered, And I want to bed you!

Janette pushed him away from her hard, but was laughing hysterically. He was crazy, and always on the edge. She loved that about him. When they got to the house, Danny led her in the front door, whooping, and people moved through the house, speaking animatedly. A DJ was spinning disco music, and Danny dragged his date immediately into the great hall and began dancing with her. Harold was already dancing with a striking blond girl whose hair was done way up in the air and had layers of jewelry on her arms and neck. As Danny led her through the hustle, Janette watched Harold and the girl she didn't know do the Bump. Harold always kept his hands clasped together, but they managed to find countless ways to actually bump.

Harold would twirl, push his rear end out and swing his joined fists into the girl's swiveling hip, like he was doing a jack-knife dive. Then he would twirl back as she dropped low, and bump her shoulder against his knee. Every part of their bodies became the next touch point. Feet, hands, knees, hips, elbows, shoulders, fannies – in a dizzying but hilarious blur of rhythmic bumps and grinds. When the song ended they panted from exertion, and laughed heartily.

Janette and Danny hooted and Danny slapped Harold's hand. Harold introduced Barbara to Danny and Janette and the four of them headed to the bar for a drink. George Muirfield served them gin and tonics with lime. After breaking up with Althea, George had swapped off with someone to work the party. In fact he swapped off twice, to work the bar in the evening and clean up the next morning. He was filling his days to keep himself occupied. It was only partially working.

Janette asked why Althea wasn't here tonight, and Danny yelled Oops! good-naturedly. George smiled and said that there had been a change in plans, and Danny told Janette that George was an eligible bachelor again. Janette smiled at George and said, Ohhhhh. Then she asked him if that was a good thing or a bad thing. George told her it was a thing-thing. Janette perked up and said, Well, I know someone who may be interested in this news. I heard Betsy mention your name the other day! Harold chuckled, Oh – ho-ho-ho.

George grinned, and thanked Janette for thinking of him. He'd keep that in mind. He recalled Betsy sitting on his knees at the champagne party and perked up a little. He asked Danny what he was supposed to be, and Danny told him a mattress. Barbara roared laughing, as if she was already drunk.

Harold looked like he had dressed as a pimp. George told Harold he was afraid to ask, and Harold said he had come as Barry White. The five of them broke up laughing. In the back of his mind, George wondered if Holly Menard was already fixing up the woman he still loved with eligible bachelors. He took a long slug of the drink he had made for himself behind the bar before turning to his next customers.

As the night opened up, Danny Carvello danced across the great hall, being goofy and making up moves when he happened into a flutter step that reminded him of a baseball pitcher pitching. The room gyrated to the Doobie Brothers, and Danny began to develop the dance that had sprung into his brain. Hey! he yelled to the people around him, Watch this. He bopped to the beat of the music, and jerked his hands up and down, gradually ending up with his arms doing the wind up to a baseball pitch. He kept his body moving and twisted to the repetitive thump of the song, gyrating an imitation of an over-arm baseball pitch. At the end of the pitch, his arm extended all the way out, like a pitcher's, and he shook his hand as if letting go of the ball.

Somebody yelled out to ask him what he was doing, and Danny yelled back, the funky baseball!! A number of dancers started paying attention as Danny repeated the herky-jerky motions of a baseball pitch to the beat of the music, and people began to laugh and try it themselves. Janette stood in one place beside him, shaking her head to the music. Then one of the brothers called out, Hey, pitch it over here! Danny pitched an imaginary ball and the other boy danced sideways and jerked his hands together over his right shoulder as if he were preparing to swing a bat. He waited for Danny to deliver the exaggerated pitch, and the boy pulled his arms around in slow motion to the beat, to hit the imaginary ball. The funky baseball was born.

Boys all over the room began to imitate different baseball positions – outfielders, base runners, catchers – shaking and jerking their bodies to the beat. The uninitiated standing in the foyer would not recognize the motions. The boys looked like any other dancers at a rock party, jumping around the floor to the music. But in the middle of the dance floor, the dance connected the dancers to each other in a contagious wave of silliness that made even the shyest people laugh. Even Stoobie and Mitsy joined in.

The next morning, George dragged his weary body around the great hall, picking up glasses and setting them into the gray, plastic containers used to transport them back to the rental shop. Stoobie was with him, and Cullen Hastings, and they showed George the funky baseball as they cleaned. The house was quiet still, and the boys spoke in low, tired voices. Cullen asked George if the rumor about him and Althea was true, and George said, Yep. Cullen stopped what he was doing and walked up to George and put his arm around his shoulders. Then he rapped George's chest with the flat of his hand, and told him how sorry he was. It'll be all right. She'll be back! he assured his brother. Stoobie said he thought women were overrated, and the other two boys laughed.

Jimmy Dunbar walked into the room and began to pitch in by mopping the floor. You're late, Stoobie scolded him. Jimmy smiled and said, Beep! Then he began to move quickly as if he would make it up by working faster than the others. Jimmy, George asked, what are you going to do when you graduate? Jimmy shook his head as if he was trying to shake off the question, but the other three boys stood waiting for his answer.

Well, Jimmy began, I'm a physics major, so you might think I was going to be a physicist. Jimmy looked at the boys solemnly, then continued. But the problem, you see, is that all the outstanding physicists make their breakthroughs by the age of nineteen. I'm already twenty, and I don't have any breakthroughs. So I can't picture myself going into a profession where I know from the outset that I am doomed to mediocrity.

As he spoke, he helped the others unroll and push the enormous carpet out across the great room floor. The carpet had been rolled all to one end of the room for the dance. It took all four of them on their hands and knees, shoving and guiding to get it placed correctly. Just as Jimmy finished his answer, the boys flopped the last of the carpet down at the end of the room next to the foyer, and Ronny Trillo bounded down to the bottom of the stairs and grinned.

Nadia! Cullen yelled out froggily. Ronny had come to the costume party as Nadia Comaneci. He was small and compact, like Nadia, and had worn a black T-shirt and sweatpants. When someone at the party had asked him to perform her gymnastic routines, Ronny posed as if he was Nadia, extended his right arm out and let his hand droop at the end, as he eyed an imaginary floor mat. A few boys started to clap their hands, and yell, "Nadia! Nadia! Nadia!" Then Ronny twirled, kicked, and pranced into the middle of the dance floor, before he tumbled in a ball across the floor, ending up with his legs twisted like a pretzel above his little waist. The room roared its approval.

Now Ronny stood eyeing the carpet, and Cullen asked him to do his routine again. The boys were all lying on different parts of the big carpet. Ronny assumed the stance again, gave himself Nadia's impertinent look, and then spasmodically flipped around and across the carpet, until he fell, out of breath, amongst them all. The boys all laughed loudly. Stoobie shook his head, and said he lived in an insane asylum. Jimmy said Beep! Cullen said, I love this house. George propped his head on his hand as he lay on his side, and said nothing. The sun poured in through the windows, and the carpet felt hard underneath him. He was glad he wasn't a physics major.

⁓

By the time the next chapter meeting arrived, the boys had given up asking Danny Carvello if they were going on another sorority raid. He just told everybody to come prepared. As the elected guardian of the door, Ronny was responsible for guarding the door to the chapter room and admitting only true Eta Chis to the meeting. When the meeting started, he ceremoniously stood and puffed out his chest, turned and looked outside to see if anyone might be sneaking up, and then closed the door with a theatrical thud. Then he took his seat back and folded his arms in mock seriousness.

Danny was in the middle of inquiring about new business, when there was a knock on the door. Ronny leapt up as if he had received an electric jolt. He looked around the room, to quiet brothers who had started to laugh, and then strode self-importantly to the door and pounded on it three times. There was stunned silence, followed by an eruption of deep laughter everywhere in the room.

As guardian of the door, Ronny was, of course, supposed to rap on the inside of the door a number of times, and then the boy outside (if he was truly an Eta Chi) would respond by knocking the number of Ronny's raps *minus* three.

When the laughter deteriorated into giggles, the boy outside yelled, Come on Ronny!, and the room erupted in laughter again. Then Ronny opened the door a crack and told the boy to identify himself, and the room broke up again. Danny called the group back to order, but still laughed himself. He told the boys that they needed to get through with the meeting in time for a new adventure, and boys hooted as they began to refocus.

At eleven thirty, the meeting came to a natural close, and Danny announced that they were going to do something different with their champagne tonight. He said that they were going to repeat their singing performance, except at Delta Eta Phi! Danny did not have to wait long for a reaction. Three boys yelled What! Another said, We're going to go to Dogs, Elephants and Pigs!?!

Danny raised his hands to quiet the group. The fraternities had code names for most of the sororities, and Eta Chis mostly socialized with girls from three houses. But Danny had concluded that no one had any idea about what the rest of the sororities were really like, and their nicknames were based on idiotic legend. Listen, he said in a loud voice, there are seventeen sororities on campus, and we have been limiting ourselves foolishly to three. So we are going to take a walk on the wild side, and start visiting the ones we don't know. Does everybody know where DEP is? The boys all started talking and running up the stairs to get ready. This was something different!

DEP was located on a side street not far from the suspension bridge. The house was not in an area as well lit as Delta Gamma Nu. The property had more trees that rustled lightly as the boys gathered close to the front door. Danny hummed out of tune to lead the boys as they sang the Darling Song, and this time the boys sang deeply and joyously. Lights came on in the house, and three girls with startled looks on their faces opened the front door. They were in bathrobes, and one of them said, Oh my god! I've heard about this. You guys are Eta Chis, right?

Danny bowed dramatically, and asked if any of the DEPs drank champagne. The second girl guffawed. The third one took off upstairs yelling Pajama Party!!

The boys moved into the house uncertainly. They didn't know the layout of the house, and poked around the downstairs curiously. Stoobie instructed boys on how to open the bottles without shooting the corks at the ceiling, as he graciously handed a glass to each girl who came down the stairs. Somebody turned on some music finally, and Jim Dart immediately went up to the most unattractive girl he could find and asked her to dance. The girl's eyes grew wide, and she just stood there. Jim started snapping his fingers and smiling broadly at her. Come on, eh! Don't make me look so silly out here all by myself!

The girl joined him tentatively as other girls started to move a little to the music, and other brothers immediately stepped up to match their movements. Before long, the boys were showing the girls the Funky Baseball and Harry-Harry was instructing two girls on the art of the bump. George Muirfield went and found Danny and pulled him aside.

You're a genius!

Surely! Danny replied as he rolled his shoulders to the music. Danny had his eye on a girl who danced with Jimmy Schultz. She was thin, and blond with fine features. She swung her hips suggestively to the music. Danny headed over to dance close to her, and George smirked as he watched his brother.

By two in the morning over sixty bottles of champagne had been consumed, and the party had the inflated feel of a bash. George danced with
someone in the middle of the living room, between Harry-Harry and Wendall Wellington, his little brother. The three boys imitated each other to the
laughs of their partners, and the girl with George leaned in close to him and
asked what they were supposed to do about classes in the morning.

Go drunk! George answered loudly, and the girl giggled and shook
her head. The girl was flirting with him, and George debated what to do.
She was pretty, in fact George would say statuesque, but she struck him
as sort of dull. For a moment, he pictured himself with Althea, but just as
quickly put it out of his mind. He asked the girl where to find the bathroom. Hopefully she would be occupied with someone else by the time he
made it back.

Danny Carvello had been right on the money. There were girls the
brothers recognized from campus, and many new faces. And there were
just as many interesting and attractive girls here as at Delta Gamma Nu.
George pointed out to Stoobie that they seemed less pretentious than the
other sororities. The two boys were standing in the sorority's kitchen
when two girls wandered in and said Hi. One girl had a large face with a
huge smile and a gutsy laugh. The other girl was The Girl Outside The
Library. George gulped, and grinned too much.

Where's the champagne you guys brought? the girl with the big,
round face asked. The Girl Outside The Library cocked her head to one
side, and looked off as if she were too shy to look at them directly.
George couldn't take his eyes off her. She wore blue jeans and a pink,
round-necked T-shirt. George took her in with startling velocity. Stoobie
offered to show them into the dining room where the champagne was, and
George followed behind them, trying to think of some way to pierce the
veil of invisibility he apparently wore around himself.

After the two girls had taken glasses and stood there in a larger group
talking, George asked The Girl Outside The Library if she wanted to
dance. She told him she didn't think so - she was a terrible dancer. George
couldn't tell if this was a brush off, but he backed off, saying that he was
too. He looked at the Girl's hair, which she had pinned up on one side,
and the line of her cheek and the rosy softness of her skin. He had to do
something.

How long have you been a DEP? he asked her. The Girl Outside The
Library appraised George quickly. He felt the piercing blue of her eyes
take him in and roll him around quickly in her mind. Then she resumed
the noncommittal, offhanded style of someone not interested in the conversation, and told George she was not a DEP. She just rented a room at
the house.

George found that interesting. He did not realize houses would do that
sort of thing. She thought the topic unworthy of much dialogue. Then The
Girl Outside The Library told him she needed to get to bed for her classes,
and said it was nice to meet him.

Danny Carvello had entered the room and stood behind George's shoulder as she turned away and headed up the back stairs. God, you've got the touch! he whispered mischievously. George looked at Danny despairingly, and said, She's The One!

If you can't be with The One you love..., Danny offered, and then pointed with his head back into the living room. George was about to follow him when he saw Ronny standing alone off to one side of the dining room. He tugged on the sleeve of the girl with the big, round face and said, You know, that's Nadia Comaneci over there.

The girls looked oddly at him and said, What?

Trust me, George said, smiling. Go ask him if he's Nadia. It's a hoot.

The girl wandered over to Ronny as George left the room and told him that someone said he was Nadia Comaneci, whatever that means. A couple of the boys heard her, and immediately began calling out Nadia! Nadia! George smiled to himself as he listened to the din from the other room, preceding one of Ronny's clownish routines. He headed for the door, and thanked two girls who stood in the little front hallway to the house for their party. They thanked him back, and he took himself outside. It was four in the morning, and he could swear he saw the beginnings of daylight. Eta Chi was a short, pleasant walk away.

The next day George checked his mailbox and saw a phone message in his mailbox. Caitlin called. Rehearsal Room C, October 23. 7:30 p.m.. Pls call to confirm. As he walked out of the mailroom, Wendall Wellington walked by and asked George if he had gotten the phone message. George said he had. Wendall asked him if it was for the Hotel Spoof that he was working on with Stoobie, and George told him it was something else.

George had not told any of the Eta Chis he was going to be in a one act. Part of him wanted to keep it totally anonymous, a secret part of his life. And part of him was in denial. But he knew that was impractical, and Wendall would love to hear about it. So he told his little brother what he was doing. Wendall listened for awhile and said, Wow. I mean, it's great that you've decided to do it because I know you love the theater. But that's a wild story about your old girlfriend. I can't wait to see it!

Until his little brother said that, it had not really hit George that his brothers would expect to see the play. In his mind, he had pictured himself performing in an empty room. It gave him a funny feeling. Then he put it out of his mind and started to think about everything he had to get done before rehearsals started up. If he was going to apply to graduate schools, he better call and ask for admission packets to be mailed. The student organization he ran needed another meeting. And there was the matter of Hank Broussard's missing check.

It was George's first little brother, Rick Frye, who approached him about Hank's missing check. They had decided to speak to George because they thought he would know what to do. Hank always left his checkbook in the top drawer of his desk, and when he had received his last bank statement, there was a fifty-dollar withdrawal that Hank had not made. When he looked at the cancelled checks in the envelope, he found a check from his checkbook written in someone else's handwriting.

Hank had stared at the check for a long time, trying to fathom how it had been cashed. He checked to see if his checkbook was missing, but it was where it was supposed to be. Then he examined how the person had written his name, but the penmanship did not look familiar. It was not until his roommate looked at the check that they noticed that the number in the upper right hand corner was 349. Hank pulled out his checkbook and saw that he was only on check number 327. He flipped to the back of his checkbook, and found that two checks – numbers 348 and 349 - were missing. The two boys were horrified. Someone in the house had stolen Hank's checks.

It was Rick who decided they should go to George. George listened to their story, and was taken back by the thought that one of the brothers was stealing checks out of another brother's wallet. Rick wanted to immediately examine the handwriting of all the brothers. George said that was a good idea, but decided they needed to involve the police first.

The policeman who responded to the call was suspicious at first. It did not occur to the three boys that he might think they were trying to get away with something themselves. But their indignation at his questions convinced him that a crime had indeed been committed, and he told them that he would handle the matter. He asked to see any records the fraternity might have with boys' handwriting exemplars.

The boys said they would gather as many as possible, which they were in the middle of doing that week. For awhile they could not figure out how to get samples of every boy, but then Hank remembered that when they went through initiation, they all signed a book of some sort. So they went to Cullen Hastings who was the new Pledge Captain and asked him if he had the book. He did, and he made copies of the pages with signatures, and brought them to the police station himself. Now they were waiting to hear.

George felt the obligation of his office on his shoulders, and wanted to root out the thief. But he was also concerned about how boys would react to the news, and what the boys might decide to do if the thief was identified. After considerable discussion with Danny, they decided to announce to the house that there was an investigation underway, and that boys should examine their checkbooks to be sure they had not been robbed. When they made the announcement at dinner, the low, rumbling reactions of the forty boys in attendance was edgy. Some refused to believe it could be a brother, and immediately suggested that some visitor had committed the crime.

When others asked whose checks had been stolen, neither Danny nor George would tell them, and this raised, rather than abated, the boys' curiosity. When George explained that the police had actually been to the house, and that handwriting samples had been provided, a chorus of accusations and protests over the investigation rifled the air.

Aren't you glad we decided to tell them? Danny whispered to George, a bit peeved. He raised his voice, and told the group that they shouldn't speculate, and that there was nothing more to do at this time. He scanned the room, convinced in his own mind that he might be able to identify a guilt look on some boy's face, but that didn't work. Still, he had a sneaking suspicion.

Though George had hoped that the matter might be resolved quickly, the case of the forged check was to remain unsolved for a long time – long after George had gone to his first rehearsal with Caitlin and Derek in the theater arts building on the arts quad. He had read the script twice the weekend before the first rehearsal, and had begun to memorize his lines.

Some directors sat with a cast for at least the first five rehearsals, reviewing the scenes line by line, discussing subtext, and trying out different tonalities. Others wanted the language to unfold across the weeks of rehearsal more freely. But all directors assumed that lines would be memorized by the end of the first week. George was sure that would be the case with Caitlin, and the task was daunting. Both he and Derek had numerous, long paragraphs of speech which were hard to commit to memory as quickly as the give and take of simple dialogue. And the language of the play, while rich, was intricately interwoven between the two characters.

George walked with a bounce in his step as he entered the building and headed for the rehearsal room. Nobody was there yet when he arrived, so he kicked off his sneakers, and began to stretch. He sat with his legs crossed, and raised one hand at a time as far as he could in the air, letting the muscles along his sides and back crink and then stretch. He had just started to do the warm up exercises on his mouth when Caitlin bustled in, her smile wide and her eyes dancing around the room. She greeted George warmly, and pulled a large blue-covered notebook out of her bag while she complained about Derek being late. George just kept stretching, and tried to get the day out of his mind so he could concentrate. It was harder to do than he remembered.

Derek walked brusquely in fifteen minutes late, swept his red plaid lumber jacket off in a hurry and threw it toward the corner of the room. The jacket didn't make it very far, but Derek was already turned around and pacing in front of George. George sensed that he was nervous, and watched him quietly. Neither of them said hello.

Okay! Caitlin said in a voice that sounded a little too loud. Please stretch for a bit and when you are both comfortable, I want you to sit cross-legged facing each other with your knees almost touching. George immediately uncurled from his position and stretched his body out fully on the rubber floor mat. He closed his eyes and started breathing rhythmically. He had suddenly remembered how he could sometimes make himself feel like he was falling inward as he lay like that on the mat. He used to find it relaxing. But he couldn't replicate the sensation, and gave up. Derek bent and touched his toes, and then knelt on the mat and to go through tai chi exercises. Both actors avoided looking at each other. They didn't know what was coming, and a nervous tension was evident.

Caitlin had two envelopes in her hand and she kept checking the contents of each. When the two actors assumed the position asked of them, Caitlin sat down herself, with her knees not far from either of theirs. She told them that the first step in the rehearsal was for each of them to read the message in the envelopes she was about to hand them. At no time during rehearsals or the play itself, was either of them to reveal to the other the contents of their message. Caitlin went on to tell them that this exercise would take one hour, and so they should make themselves comfortable, because she wanted little if any movement.

They were not allowed to speak or break eye contact with each other. The two actors were already gazing at each other, smiling. Caitlin then explained that after the first thirty minutes, each of them was going to tell the other one thing about themselves. The more personal, and revealing the better. She asked them both to swear to each other that their confidence would not be broken, and they did.

Then she told them that they actually had a choice. If they wanted to, they could use the message in the envelope, as their secret. Of course, it might be a true statement about them, since she knew each of them so well. They couldn't be sure. Whatever they chose, she wanted them to exchange statements and then sit and look at each other in silence for the next thirty minutes. During the time of their exchange, she would leave the room, so only the two of them would hear each other, but otherwise she would be in the corner monitoring them.

She asked them if they understood, and they both shook their heads. Caitlin handed them their respective envelopes, and instructed them to open them, think about the message, and then begin the exercise. George watched Derek rip open his message and smile to himself as he read it. In Derek's envelope, Caitlin had written, "I love being a student but teaching is boring because students are sheep."

Something in George made him wait until Derek looked at him before he pulled his envelope slowly open and glanced at the words. George's message was: "You make me insecure and jealous." George remained impassive, but could not help but look at Caitlin for the slightest of moments. Then he returned Derek's gaze and the exercise began.

Their eyes were two to three feet apart, but it seemed closer, because their bodies touched at their knees. For the first several minutes, there was a playful nonchalance between them, but this gave way to a cautious exploration of each other. George's face acquired a serious cast as he puzzled over what he wanted to say. He didn't like what Caitlin had given him to say, but what else made sense to tell Derek Steele?

Derek found himself tiring and then re-energizing as the minutes passed. George's face and eyes were a virtual panoply of suggestion, and he felt himself beginning to trust the boy in front of him. It was like George pulled him closer, inviting him to some private place. His hands grew numb but he delayed shaking them, so as not to lose this momentum between them.

Caitlin rose and announced that 30 minutes had passed. She was leaving the room for five minutes, and would then return to complete the exercise. The door closed behind her tall frame, and Derek exhaled softly, and smiled. Neither of them said a word. Maybe, George said, she should have told us which of us is supposed to go first. Derek laughed, and said, Odds or Even?

George replied, Even! The two shook their fists three times and stuck out their fingers. Derek put out one and George three. Even it was. So George adjusted his shoulders, looked for a few moments at Derek, and said, I am afraid of what you mean to me.

The words had formed in his mind just before Caitlin had stood up, and while he didn't like them, they were true – down deep Derek frightened him – and he hated admitting it.

Derek's head cocked slightly in response. He wondered if Caitlin had given George those words. Probably, he concluded. Caitlin knew George well. But they were not what he expected. Interesting.

Derek had decided early in the process to use Caitlin's words, but now he hesitated. A minute passed. Finally he said, My problem is I was never afraid of the people I should have been.

George was chagrined at Derek's words. He had opened himself up a little, but Derek simply made a retort. He certainly hadn't learned anything particularly personal about him. He decided to say something.

Wow, Derek, how revealing.

Derek shrugged, then looked away, and then glowered at his young acting partner. Who the fuck did this kid think he was?

The door opened, and Caitlin's head appeared before the rest of her body slid through the closing door. Derek brought the sides of his mouth up as he looked to her, which made his moustache curve downward to frame his lips. Then he said, Wait. Caitlin stopped and focused on her teacher and companion.

Give us one more minute, he asked. Caitlin started to protest. This was, after all, her improvisational exercise. But she followed her instincts and removed herself from the room. Sixty seconds, she said as she left.

Derek turned back to George and they looked at each other carefully.

Fair enough, Derek said. My real name is David Stellingworth. *Nobody* knows that.

George took this information in, nodding. As Caitlin reentered the room, George whispered, Thank you. Derek looked sheepish.

Caitlin said, Okay, let's continue the exercise. Derek and George began to contemplate each other again in the prickly silence of the room. Even tiny brushes against the rubber mats magnified the vacuum of sound that enveloped them. Caitlin sat totally still in a corner, watching the two men who had played so prominently in her college life stare through each other. She was dying to know what had gone on between them, but knew she could not ask.

When the exercise was over, Caitlin said, Time. Neither Derek nor George moved at first. They explained to her later that it felt to each of them as if they were untangling themselves from each other's gaze. Derek reached over and hugged George briefly, and George smiled broadly, returning the man's affection. Whatever had passed between them had been honest and substantive. George knew Derek much better, and Derek liked George more.

For Caitlin, their reactions were perfect. The intent of the exercise was to make the two men bond in a secret way. It was a foundation for how she saw the play. She had hoped for the exercise to also create some competition or wariness between them, but their body language certainly suggested that this had not occurred. She reminded them that they were not to discuss what transpired between them until after the play, and were never to share it with anyone else. They both grinned and shook their heads affirmatively.

As the three sat together on the mat, Caitlin handed out the scripts she wanted them to use. She had broken the script down into parts as she had thought through the play and its blocking, and had decided to use her working version as the script. The three of them walked through the play conceptually. Caitlin explained how she saw the different pieces of the play, and described the effect she wanted to have on the audience.

I know that this is not necessarily the way that a director would work with actors, but I know how opinionated the two of you are. It's important to me that you understand that it is my vision we are going to bring to life. Her voice faltered slightly as she spoke.

George nodded as Caitlin spoke, and then broke in. Caitlin, this is your vision, but these are our characters. So how do you want us to do the character development piece?

Derek said nothing, and watched his current flame with a combination of pride and surprise. She had more focus and gumption that Catherine had ever shown, but on a personal level, Caitlin was confounding to live with. She made him melt, she showered him with affection and attention, and he desired her immensely. But she had also clearly drawn the boundaries. She played around, but was going to remain a virgin. In that regard, she was as screwed up as all the other actors. Just in a different way.

Caitlin answered George, and Derek watched her peer intently into George's eyes as she explained how she had worked up a series of exercises to help them build their characters, but the crux of this play was in the symbolic representations of the two people on the stage. She wanted the audience to feel like these two men were Everymen. She wanted the audience to feel they themselves were the characters in the play.

Derek tuned back in and said, Jesus, that's even more ambitious than I usually am.

George just smiled and rocked back and forth, thinking about her idea.

Caitlin moved to a chalkboard as she asked each of them what they thought the play was about.

Derek said he thought it was about growing old, about generational distance and the problems different generations have talking to each other.

George said, I don't really know what I am talking about, but it seems to me that the two men are somehow mirror images of each other. They hate each other, but love each other at the same time. There's something really cool about the middle of the play, which I assume is suggested by the title. Or subtitle, I guess.

Caitlin nodded. Beautiful, she said. Let's think about the play this way. Then she drew on the board –

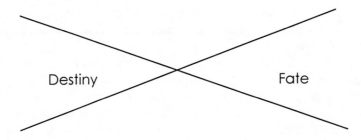

This is what the play is about, she offered. The middle of the play is a passage. For Younger Man it is a passage from Destiny to Fate, and for Older Man, it is the trip from Fate to Destiny.

The two men looked confused.

Look, she went on, turning away from the board, remember the liner notes in the beginning and end of the play? You're both naked. You get up and dress and head toward each other, right? Think of birth and death. Younger Man is moving forward from birth. Older Man is moving backwards from death. And they meet here, in the middle, between destiny and fate. Caitlin's finger was at the junction of her drawing.

So then what? George asked, perplexed. He had read the play and memorized many of his lines, but he had not visualized this at all.

Then, Caitlin said, pausing to beam an enormous smile at her men, you become each other. The three laughed in unison. And just remember, darling, Caitlin said to Derek. You wanted George to play the other part. It wasn't my idea. The three laughed heartily at her point.

Thus began an extraordinary collaboration between the three. Caitlin had intended to keep some distance from the two men, and to be what she thought a director should be. But she could not maintain that safe a distance. Both Derek and George were filled with ideas, and a progressive sense of what worked on a stage. She could not effectively ignore their enthusiasm to make the play better. And she found herself in an odd conundrum of feelings for each of them.

George had been her first major crush. She had loved him. It was impossible not to let some of those sensations creep back into the way that she touched him on the arm, or murmured something to him in an off moment. His eyes sparkled at her affection, and while he steered well clear of even the slightest compromise in their present relationship, she sensed an occasional conflict in his emotions.

Derek was either stoic or simply unaware of Caitlin's rekindled fondness for her old boyfriend. They argued once, at the beginning of the second week of rehearsals, as they stood in Derek's kitchen washing the breakfast dishes. But the squabble had been about Derek's willingness to take her direction. Caitlin told him he was unable to simply be the actor, and was trying to take control of the play. Derek thought she was being too sensitive, and immature.

But in the rehearsals that followed, Caitlin saw a new subservience in her mate. He listened more carefully to her instructions, and stopped answering her questions with another question. He actually seemed to enjoy himself more. And this new influence over Derek, despite the fact that it was contained within the four walls of the rehearsal rooms, improved Caitlin's perspective on both him and them as a couple. She saw more clearly the dominance Derek assumed with her. He was so used to having professorial authority over his students, he took his role for granted. George, Caitlin noted, had never, and would never have treated her so.

The play consumed all of them, but Caitlin thought of nothing else. When they stopped rehearsing, she would ride home with Derek, and then stay up after he had gone off to bed. She designed and printed up the simple programs to hand out to the audience. She coaxed the stage design majors into helping her set up special lighting and build simple wooden benches for opposing sides of the small stage area. By early December when the play opened for three nights, she wondered if she could ever direct a full-length play. This one act had exacted an enormous toll on her.

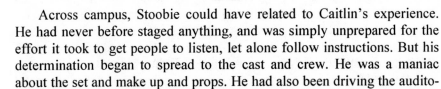

Across campus, Stoobie could have related to Caitlin's experience. He had never before staged anything, and was simply unprepared for the effort it took to get people to listen, let alone follow instructions. But his determination began to spread to the cast and crew. He was a maniac about the set and make up and props. He had also been driving the auditorium staff crazy with his persistent requests for special lighting. He knew what he wanted, but was totally in the dark about the technical jargon, and often confused the man who normally did the lighting.

At first, the cast had been skeptical of Stoobie's vision. When he had gathered everyone in the huge Statler auditorium and informed them that this was going to be a song and dance extravaganza, they raised their eyebrows and looked frightened. Most of the cast wanted to have some fun and make the audience laugh, but few of them wanted to devote so much energy to the show. This was supposed to be a way to network with alums and land job interviews.

In prior years, Stoobie intoned with importance, the senior spoof consisted of skits and sight gags. But this year, we are going to bring an entirely different level of performance to our alumni! The hospitality industry depends on entertainment, and we are going to bring the crowd to its feet!

One girl, a hotel school junior, had asked whether this meant she needed to know how to dance.

Of course not, Stoobie retorted in an irritated tone. This is, after all, a spoof! You will do fine, I promise you.

But Stoobie was not content to leave this show looking like a high school production. The next morning over breakfast, he asked Wendall Wellington to assume responsibility for directing the dance numbers.

You toured with Up With People, Wendall! You know enough of the basics to get people lined up and dancing, don't you?

Wendall could summon a withering gaze when he wanted, and he directed one then at Stoobie. But the idea quickly took root. He loved performance, and he thought he could have some fun. Besides, Stoobie promised he could direct the portion of the show devoted to the wines class. Wendall had a savage image in his head to do that topic justice.

The wines class was a three-credit, spring semester class about wine. Every Wednesday, students filed into Statler Auditorium and drank wine while they listened to the Wines professor describe its bouquet and origins. The class was so oversubscribed by students from other colleges within the university, that seniors were given first preference to enroll. Every Eta Chi senior in the past decade had enrolled in the class, and then rolled out of Wines and onto Date Night at the house. Brothers often found their dates for dinner at the class over a glass of Johannesburg Riesling.

But getting course credit for drinking was a side benefit to the class itself, run with thundering extravagance by the renowned Percival Lee. Professor Lee was the proud offspring of an enormous Japanese gourmand and a beautiful Sri Lankan model. Percival traveled the world with his parents, watching his mother model and his father eat. Once sent off to boarding school in Switzerland, Percival discovered his father's genetic appetite, and topped the scales at 310 pounds by graduation. He was, himself, six feet four inches tall, and he maneuvered his considerable girth with a pronounced swing as he walked.

It was largely rumored across campus that Percy, as the campus referred to him, was also a flaming homosexual. The prurient attention he paid to his teaching assistants was the grist of many whisper mills. Percy's sexual orientation may have been the source of much mirth, but his flamboyant love of the dramatic and the stirring tremble in his round, overstated voice made him a celebrity. Every time he opened his mouth on the stage of the auditorium to offer a pithy and disdainful review of the wine he had just sampled for the Wines class was another opportunity to laugh and catch his personal contagion. Percy loved his wines, and it showed.

Stoobie's send up would not be the first to caricaturize Percival Lee. But it was going to be memorable. And Stoobie also intended to poke some fun at the alumni who came to the show. He personally wrote a dance number called "The Hotel Alumni Rag" that included lyrics like–

By now everybody knows our alumni come to blows
Competing for those hot hotelie girls they want to hire
But balding, married workaholics wearing panty hose
Should get fired if they hire for desire

Wendall Wellington asked Stoobie if he had cleared all the lyrics with the Dean, and Stoobie said, Of course. Actually, he never actually got around to doing that. But in the end, it wasn't Stoobie's lyrics that got him into hot water. It was Wendall's song and dance number aimed at Percival Lee, headed up by none other than Harold Wise wearing a costume that made him look like a blimp.

As the hotel school Rollicking Revue neared, Stoobie began to fret over how to introduce the various acts and numbers. He was pleased with the show's progress, but as he watched the rehearsals, there was not enough segue between the bits. The show needed an Emcee, a master of ceremonies. Someone dramatic who could be the theatrical glue to the show, and throw out some funny one-liners. Someone, he decided, like himself.

This was, of course, a major step for Jim Steuben. In his own mind, it came dangerously close to coming out of the closet. Of course, it would never be viewed even remotely as connected to Stoobie's sexual preference, but such was the state of his confused mind. Identifying himself so dramatically with show tunes and the flamboyance of the Revue might give some of his classmates – or worse, his brothers at Eta Chi - some suspicion about him. He thought briefly of the sophomores singing *Muddy Roads* every time they saw him. Perhaps, he thought, he should ask Wendall to be the Emcee.

But in the end, Jim Steuben overcame his fears, and explained to the cast that he was going to guide the show as its Master of Ceremonies. The cast applauded. Stoobie blushed. The Eta Chis whom he had recruited to work in the show laughed amongst themselves, and loved how eclectic Stoobie was. They were proud of him, and told him so. Even Mitsy Smith told him she thought it would be wonderful.

Danny Carvello saw the play announcement for *Big Kids* on the Straight bulletin board. George had not volunteered much to his brothers, and Danny called him on it in the library before dinner one night.

When were you going to let us know about the play?

George looked at his friend for a moment before he answered. I'm not trying to hide anything, Danny, but it's pretty "out there." I'm not sure that many of the brothers would actually enjoy it, and I certainly don't want to make people feel like they are obligated to come.

Suuurrre! Of course, George. That makes perfect sense! Danny smirked. Actually what I think we should do is try to be sure that NOBODY AT ALL goes to the show. That way, it will be really out there!

The two boys laughed together. Okay, George said, I'm a space-shot.

Precisely what I have been thinking about! Danny said in an exaggerated way. Have I told you my plan to get us rich? George shook his head negatively.

All right. This is so simple, only geniuses like us could think of it. Who has too much money? George said, I give up.

The sheiks!

George looked askance. When Danny said "sheiks" it came out as "shakes." George had never heard that pronunciation before. Shakes? he asked.

OF COURSE! The sheiks have so much money from all the oil we buy from them, they want to spend it in a way that makes them special.

Oh, you mean the "sheeks" in Saudi Arabia!

The reason I want you in this, George, is that you are a quick learner. The two boys grinned at each other.

So, Danny continued, here's what we are going to do: Put a sheik on the moon!

George looked dubious.

Listen, Danny said, warming to the topic, All we have to do is find a sheik who wants to say he's been to the moon. Then he bankrolls us to get him there.

Do we know how to get him there?

Danny giggled uncontrollably. No, but that will be the fun part. We can do anything if we have the right funding. Are you in?

George assumed a solemn face and replied, Where do we find the sheik?

I was hoping, Danny said, that you could help me with that. The two boys nodded at each other as they squinted their eyes. Wendall Wellington came into the room, and they turned to greet him.

Wendall, George asked, do you know any sheiks?

What's a shake? Wendall asked.

We're going to put a sheik on the moon, Danny explained.

As soon as I finish my play and you guys are done with Stoobie's show! George added.

I can't wait to see my big bro in a performance, said Wendall. But what are you two talking about? Danny grinned profusely at George. George said he couldn't wait to see the two of them hoofing it on stage for Stoobie. Danny started to hum *Fly Me To The Moon* and dance.

Opening night of *Big Kids* perplexed the theater department. A line of people gathered outside the door at seven thirty, and the play did not start until eight. The theater majors and department professors who usually came to one acts never arrived early. And no one recognized the people standing in line.

The doors opened at seven forty-five, but when Caitlin looked out at the crowd, she told them the doors would not open for another five minutes, and closed the door behind her. She ran back into the little black box theater and yelled for George and Derek to take their places. There was already a crowd!

Derek and George hustled into place on stage. George lay down on the left bench, and Derek went to the right bench, and they each assumed their positions. Caitlin was running all around them, switching on the lighting and the music. She had not expected anyone so soon.

The black box theater seated 46 people in its normal configuration. Usually, the theater was about three-quarters full for the three performances of a one-act. It was an intimate setting for a performance, and Caitlin loved the feel of the place. It was a rectangular room with a square stage area in front of the rows of chairs. There was a small, windowed room behind the audience section where the technical staff could view the stage and control the lighting. Two black moveable walls created the only separations on the set, or provided a blind behind which actors could wait to enter a scene. Otherwise, actors watched through the half glass door that led to the basement corridor. They actually walked in through the door to walk on the set. The exterior walls were eighteen feet high, and painted black. Dust was everywhere.

Caitlin took a last look at the set, and went to open the doors to the outside where the people waited in line. She welcomed them as they filed into the theater, and thought she recognized some of the boys from Eta Chi. It made her smile. This would be interesting!

Danny Carvello, Wendall Wellington, Harold Wise, Fritz Hublein, Wally Stimpson, and Jimmy Dunbar were among the first in the door. They grabbed seats in the middle of the second row and began to take in the set around them.

The Doors were singing *Break On Through To The Other Side* through speakers hidden in the corners of the room. To the left of the stage, a large, round production lamp angled upwards from its iron stanchion and toward the middle of the seating area. A template cover masked the face of the lamp. Light shone through letters cut out across the template, spelling **BIRTH**. On the opposite side of the stage, another lamp faced diagonally across the stage. The template on the face of that lamp read, **DEATH**. The lamps were on a timer, which turned the lights on and off about every sixty seconds. The cycle of each light overlapped, so that for roughly half the time of each cycle, the audience read both words illuminated. Then one or the other lamp would cut off, and the audience would be left with the image of only one word.

Wendall leaned over to Danny and whispered, This is going to be wild! Danny was humming to the Doors, and nodded his head as he took in the room. Harold Wise asked Fritz, What the hell kind of a play is this? Jimmy Dunbar told Wally Stimpson this was bionic theater. Wally smiled broadly and asked, Is that George?

George lay flat on the bench to the left side of their view. The lamp blinked **BIRTH** next to him. His hands were folded across his chest, like a corpse, and he breathed deeply and slowly, to keep his body as motionless as possible. Across from him, Derek lay on the opposing bench, in the fetal position, underneath **DEATH**.

The Doors kept singing the same song in the background. Danny scanned the sheets that had been left on every seat. On one side, the cast and crew were named beneath the title of the play. George's name was opposite "Younger Man." Derek Steele was playing "Older Man." On the flip side, a large **X** centered the page –

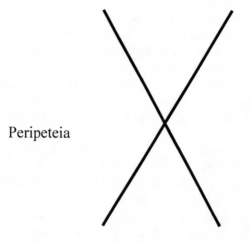

Peripeteia
n. An Abrupt or unexpected change in a course of events or situation. [Greek, from *peripiptein,* to change suddenly, "fall around": *peri-*, around + *piptein,* to fall]

At eight p.m., the lights dimmed partially, and people who had been standing took their seats. A number of faces looked in through the door from the basement hallway, scanning the audience and frowned. One young man entered through the door, looked around, and then shrugged as he slouched against the wall in the corner behind the audience.

Caitlin had taken a page from Derek's direction in Oedipus. She had instructed the two men to begin the play at their speed, when it felt right. To do so required that they be highly sensitive to each other, as they lay across the stage from each other. Their eyes were closed, and the quiet of the rehearsal room was replaced by the scraping of feet and coughs and laughter of a live audience. But through the exercises Caitlin had devised to bring the two together, the two men were now tied to the same umbilical cord.

That was the word she had used for the rubber tether that the two men had worn around their waists for the last week of rehearsals. Caitlin had worked furiously to block the play so that the men moved around the set in a complex unity. It was much more difficult than she had imagined, until she came up with the idea of tying them together. She had found a thirty-foot stretchy rubber hose and fastened them to each other.

As Derek moved away from George, George was pulled in the same direction unless he consciously strained the rubber umbilical cord to remain where he was. Caitlin was enthralled. There was a symbiotic tension between every movement on the stage. As George moved upstage, Derek naturally moved downstage to maintain the cord's balance. This gave the play an unnerving and unnatural balance. To her trained eye, it was a visual seesaw. To the audience, she hoped it gave a swirling, hypnotic reality.

Derek stirred first, at about five past eight. George felt the tug of his connection to his acting partner and pulled himself suddenly erect. The Doors stopped singing. The audience went dead silent. The lamps on either side were extinguished, and the center of the stage grew bright.

In the beginning of the play, the men are unaware of each other. Younger Man draws imaginary designs on the floor while Older Man sits tying his shoes as if he is exhausted. Then the two characters move from the sides of the set toward the middle and eye each other warily. They turn away, and then look back. Younger Man speaks first.

What do you want, Mister?

Older Man peers at the boy as if he has trouble seeing, and then says, I would say I want to be left alone, but I can see from the look on your face that's out of the question. Do you have a name?

Younger Man avoids giving the stranger his name, and asks him instead where he is headed. They talk of where they have been warily. Older Man looks out at the audience and flinches. He sees the audience, and takes a moment to examine a few of the faces in front of him. Younger Man, peering in the direction of the audience, asks the Older Man what he sees. Older Man guffaws, shrugs at the audience, and says, *Too much.*

The audience laughs uncomfortably. Older Man returns to looking at Younger Man, and speaks. *You don't need to fear me, my friend. I am too feeble to hurt you, and besides, you seem familiar to me. Come, shake my hand.*

Younger Man approaches to accept Older Man's hand, but before he can reach it, there is a loud clap from behind the audience that startles them, and makes the two characters face the audience with searching eyes. The two men begin walking in place, side by side, toward the audience. They are heading for the mysterious noise they have heard. The play continues this way with the two men walking along, swapping stories and guessing what they might find at the source of the mysterious noise.

One of the most difficult aspects of Caitlin's blocking was that neither actor could break the plane of the middle of the stage. At one moment, Younger Man stumbles into Older Man's side, and stops to stare at the audience. He runs back to his side of the stage, and looks toward the audience again. He waves to them, smiling. Danny and Harold waved back, giggling. From this moment on, Younger Man is more exuberant, and silly.

As the play nears its middle, Younger Man and Older Man have become closer. Their exchanges are longer, and more rambling. They stop heading anywhere as they stand closer and then further away from each other on a horizontal line that splits the set. Their language and their body movements grow personal, unguarded. Caitlin told them she wanted the sensation of turbulence, and Derek and George worked hours choreographing the tumultuous image. But the heart of the play was in its words, and Younger Man has grown impatient with Older Man's stories.

There is no sense, no reason, no purpose to your stories. You have nothing but excuses to teach me, and I will not listen anymore. For every complaint you harbor, I have a thousand solutions, but you do not care. We are polar opposites! You are an immovable object, and I am an irresistible force. Yet you see nothing. My heart soars with each coming day!

Older Man dismisses these words with a grunt. Then he laughs, and says,

You probably think you are free. You do, don't you? What a foolish conceit. Do you honestly know in your heart that you have arrived here before me as a consequence of your sacred free will? You dawdle, and diddle, you play with yourself and fancy yourself a titan. But you are adrift in an ocean you cannot even see. (He shakes his head.) *Man never hears the archangels fluttering above his head until the wind from their wings have blown him off his course.*

Younger Man has stopped listening, almost immediately. He is consumed by something he sees offstage, and then leaves and returns to Older Man carrying an apple.

What were you saying? I am so tired of your preaching. Here, look what I have found. It is a special fruit that grows only in this glen. Its sweetness will revive your spirit. Come, have some. Older Man replies: *You are mocking me, child. I see now that you are older than I guessed. But you are not yet what you will be. You're a kid. A big kid, but still a kid. I have nothing to fear. Give me your fruit.*

In dress rehearsal, the strobe light had sometimes not worked, and Caitlin crossed her fingers. It had been her idea to move the nudity from the beginning and end of the play to the middle. Derek and George thought it made much more sense.

When George handed Derek the apple, the strobe light started its disorienting stutter, and Derek and George began to disrobe and trade their clothes. At one moment, they are naked, staring at each other as the strobe light distorts the audience's view. Then as each man puts the other's clothes on, they change places. Caitlin choreographed the exchange so that it looked accidental and fleeting. Then the strobe stops flicking, and the room is momentarily dark. When the center lights come up, Derek is stage right, looking into the audience. George is sitting on the bench stage left.

Derek speaks first. As he speaks to the audience, he is giddy, childlike, and totally unaware of George.

I see you! I see myself! And my insides are a jumble of nerves! What was I thinking? You know, you know how the air comes through the morning window and you smell the hair of your lover? Honeysuckle and lemon

and oranges and spice! When I was twelve years old, I went to meet the girl in my class with the straight blond hair. We were meeting at the playground, and she was wearing a striped wool cap because it was winter. Ohhh, the ache in my abdomen was so intense. I took her little hand in mine, and she smiled and we walked for awhile. I could smell her hair, even in the cold winter wind. It was the beginning of what I knew would keep coming over me in endless waves. It's here again. The laughter, the pure delight...I am dreaming in vibrant colors! No one knows my secrets, my palpable longings for greatness. And Time! Time gets measured in purple dollops of hope, unspoiled by regimen. I, I, I.....

Derek is holding onto the handrail in front of the first row of seats, babbling to the girl in the first row and the people directly behind her. He is quivering with excitement. It is almost too much for him and he sputters into a long whoop of glee. The audience laughs. Danny Carvello, having struggled through the first half of the show is enthralled with Derek's transformation. He feels his skin tingling as Derek whoops.

George looks up at the sound of the whoop, amused. He rubs his knees and stands stiffly and saunters toward Derek, but frowns as he nears the center of the stage. What is it, Old Man? He asks.

Derek stands directly in front of George and dances a jig, pulls his cheeks apart with his index fingers, and turns around and moons him. George stares distrustfully in his direction, but does not really see him. The audience roars laughing, and George follows the stage direction in the script to look curiously out across the audience. Until that moment, George, Derek and Caitlin had not realized how humorous the stage direction was. It made George look foolish and the audience roared laughing again.

In the exchanges that follow, Derek shares his exuberance with George. George is energized and supportive, but he cannot sustain the momentum. He tells the audience to take the full measure of his friend. *Do not be sucked in easily*, he warns. *Separate the wheat from the chaff.*

Caitlin had insisted that Derek and George each stay in character after the switch. She thought the worst result would have the audience think that they had in fact switched personalities. So Derek's youthfulness was much more impertinent that George's, and George was much more optimistic in his adult view. And when they revisited the topic of freedom, it is George's character who stakes the high ground –

I no longer need a mirror, you see. Certitude and stamina have freed me of my insecurity. Those old, feckless reflections are now the exclusive province of daydreaming youngsters. I AM FREE!! Free to do so much more than any of you. Tell me what was so wonderful about the self? The consequence of self is the lack of sight, but vision merely anchors the self in the firmament of context. Of society. Of commonwealth. I see now the constraints of self. I see the blind subservience to passion and whim as shackles I am well rid of. Good riddance!

To which Derek's character responds –

When the curtain opens, is your heart free? Or does the convention of your life preordain the stage on which you move? The man has a bridle bit in his mouth, and doesn't have a clue. Soon he will be on all fours, on the floor of some miserable existence, with a child on his back as he crawls around, reenacting in his mind the elixir of fantasy he once claimed.

Listen to me. There is a moment, a place in time, when the angels glide restfully on the warm updrafts, and you are no longer buffeted on your way. It will happen, if it does at all, shortly after you have crossed over the divide. The sweet taste in your mouth curls to a subtle, new bitterness in the air. And then you drift backwards from whence you have come, regressing over territory you know by heart. Your heart races with the intimacy and the hilarity of everything you took to be important only moments before.

It is erotic, and mesmerizing to see clearly in youth, to arrive in a place where fantasy and reality do not collide. It is as fleeting as a snowfall on April lawns. But I tell you now, opportunity is there for those brave enough to dare. Dare to fly! Run across the dew-drenched grass of this dream and take flight until you can no more. For I have been there and back. I have seen the stream of light that streaks the divide. It is possible, yes, possible, for a few of you to find the continuum of flight across that light, hovering where the angels tread for sustenance, and joy.

The play ends with Derek lying down like a corpse and George like a baby, in each other's place. Before George assumes his position, he winks at the audience, smiling resignedly. The side lamps light, and the center stage dims. Softly, in the background, music starts up. But this time it is Jackson Browne's *I thought I was A Child.*

The audience erupted in applause. Caitlin blushed as she watched the room. There was so much in the play that was poorly wrought. She wondered what the crowd had really seen. She was sure that she had been wrong to direct Derek and George to speak directly to the audience. It had seemed so daring in rehearsal, but came across so forced in the performance. She saw one boy scribbling furiously on a pad of paper, and worried what he was doing. She looked up at the people walking out the doors, and watched George's fraternity brothers slapping each other on the back as they left.

Outside, Danny and Wendall agreed the play was fascinating. It was bold, and zany, and filled with import. Ahead of them, Harold Wise laughed at something Wally Stimpson said. The Eta Chis gathered as a group in front of the Architecture building, as Jimmy Dunbar said he thought Wally might be right.

It's us! Wally said garrulously. That play was talking right at us!

The boys laughed. Harold whistled, and asked Wally what the hell the play was about. He dared his brother to explain it. Wally told him to go see it again if he didn't understand it. Danny, unusually quiet, said he needed to see it again.

Back in the theater, Fred Wineberger continued scribbling his review in his Macroeconomics notebook. Just hours before, Fred had been walking through the Straight when he noticed the flyer for the play bearing George Muirfield's name. He chuckled to himself as he recalled the first boy he had met at college. He pictured George standing over him as he lay on that ridiculous bed in the university infirmary, bemoaning the fact that his parents had left him there. George had tried so hard to get him excited about college life. He had been so quick to see the positive, so sure of himself. On a whim, Fred had headed across the Arts Quad to check out what George Muirfield had done with himself, and got in line when he saw the crowd waiting to be admitted.

Fred thought the play was spectacular. To be fair, Fred was not a theater-goer. He had never written a play or movie review in his life. Although he was now the editor of the Cornell Daily Sun, he left the arts and entertainment sections to the associate editor who loved that stuff. Fred was strictly a politics and news journalist, just as he had intended to be.

So the forcefulness and symbolic heat of this production floored Fred, and as the play concluded, he decided to cover it himself. This was news! The next day Fred's review ran on page one, making it the first one-act play in the university's history to make the front page. The headline read, BIG KIDS IS HOT! In his opening paragraph, Fred described the play as "must see theater of the avant garde, with astounding performances by Cornell's two leading performance artists." He knew that sounded a bit extreme, but this show was special. The college community needed to know!

That night, the line outside the doors was double the size of opening night. Caitlin was agog with excitement. She convinced Derek and George that they needed to add three more shows. If exams had not been coming up, they might have added more. And so *Big Kids* ran for six nights, with a sold out house every night. A few people actually asked Caitlin, Derek and George to autograph the playbill. Even Derek blushed at that.

On the third night of performance, and again on the fourth, Danny Carvello went alone to see the play. He purposely sneaked away without telling anyone where he was going. The performance made his imagination soar, and his stomach churn; he did not consciously explore why.

Danny had just turned twenty-eight, and the conclusion to undergraduate life that rushed toward him made him blanche. Thus far, he had hidden from the larger truth that lay waiting for him on the other side of graduation, cleverly obscured by the frivolity he injected into his daily routine. But down deep, Danny's desperation grew exponentially. The magic of life – at its nadir, a positively manic freedom to choose – increasingly slipped away as senior year unfurled. His determined efforts to halt its ebb only exacerbated its progress.

And then George's play showed up and confronted him on the very issue he had so skillfully avoided for so long. There was much in the play that depressed him, and when he watched George age on stage, and crawl up under **DEATH** to end the play, the finality of the message corroded his spirit. But there were also those few words uttered by Older Man, so elusively embedded in his rambling speech, that hypnotized Danny into returning for more.

They were words of such hope, Danny clung to them the second night, and when he saw the performance a third time, the words blazed brightly in his imagination.

...It is possible, yes, possible, for a few of you to find the continuum of flight across that light...

When Danny fully digested their meaning the third night, he left the little theater in a rare state of bliss. If anyone could find the continuum, he could. Couldn't he? He walked back to Eta Chi so light on his feet, he swore he glided. The most inescapable human inquiry had been supplanted permanently in Danny's core. "When" was removed and "Why" took hold. There was no longer another shoe to drop, no eventuality to his existence. There was only promise.

He was on fire. He looked at the air around him as he neared the house, and could *see* it swirl. The arrival he had dreaded, the cursed fate, hung in ethereal suspension. Life need not be temporal. He would be true to the continuum of flight, and save himself. No, not just save. Stave!

When the last performance concluded, Caitlin chatted with people until the theater was empty, and ran upstairs to order pizza. When she returned, she was alone in the theater with Derek and George. As the three of them sat in the middle of the set waiting for the pizza to arrive, Caitlin leaned over and kissed George on the cheek, and then snuggled in Derek's arm.

George felt distracted by Caitlin's kiss, and wished he didn't. He smiled at Derek, who looked mischievously at him and asked him what was next. George just shook his head, and said he didn't want this night to end. Caitlin readily agreed. The pizza came and they ate ravenously. George had turned the **BIRTH** and **DEATH** lamps back on, and the lamps blinked on and off while they ate. It was Derek who eventually said, Let's break down the set and get on with life.

The next Saturday, the hotel school Rollicking Revue was performed at the Statler Auditorium. George invited Betsy from Delta Gamma Nu, and she told him it was about time. He walked to her sorority and they walked across campus toward the hotel school. As they passed over Triphammer Bridge, Betsy casually took George's hand in hers to help her look over the stone bridge, and never let go. George thought he liked the straight lines of her teeth and the tiny proportions of her figure.

As they entered the auditorium, Betsy asked what the show was about. She was in the School of Human Ecology, and knew nothing about this. George wasn't much help. He told her it was some sort of fun spoof directed by the fraternity brother who lived across the hall from him. Betsy smiled as if she were thinking about something else.

The long, tan curtains hung from the enormous rafters above the auditorium stage, revealing nothing of what was to come. There was a lively verve to the room, with alumni speaking loudly to each other across aisle ways, and undergraduates chatting energetically with their dates. George mused to himself how different theater was from day to day. Betsy leaned against his arm and asked George what he was thinking about.

George raised his eyebrows like Fritz Hublein, and folded his arm through hers. Then he pointed to their left, where the curtain captain was preparing to hoist the massive cloths, and said, I'm trying to make my heart free for when the curtain opens. Before she could respond, the lights dimmed, and the curtain swept majestically to the sides.

A spotlight was the sole light upon the stage, and it beamed down on Jim Steuben, who stood far upstage, in the center. He wore a tuxedo and top hat, and posed with his hands outstretched on the handle of an umbrella that angled sharply to the floor. A piano started playing and Stoobie waltzed half way downstage, and stopped again. The piano kept playing, but more lightly.

Good evening and welcome to the hotel school Rollicking Revue! Stoobie said in the best Cary Grant voice he could imitate. For your entertainment pleasure, we have dancing maidens and singing waiters, supporting the finest ensemble of talent ever to grace the doors of this hallowed institution. But don't take my word for it. Let the show begin!

George reflexively covered his mouth. This wasn't performance, it was circus entertainment! But he couldn't help but smile as thirty students then lined each side of the stage and kicked their legs Cabaret-style

to the pounding piano played by one of his brothers. When all thirty dancers started to sing a spoof on the University's cherished alma mater, the
room erupted in cheers.

Throughout the show, Stoobie waxed melodramatically, introducing
acts and skits with imitations of Ed Sullivan, Jackie Gleason, and Carol
Burnett. George thought his Carol Burnett was inspired. The crowd
around George, including Betsy, roared laughing.

As the crew cleared the stage for another number late in the production, Stoobie introduced the piano player, and the crowd applauded. The
piano player then imitated Donald and Daisy Duck singing a duet as he
played one of the popular Cornell Drinking Songs –

Give my regards to Davey, remember me to T. Phee Crane
Tell all the pikers on the hill that I'll be back again
Tell them of how I busted, lapping up those high-high balls
We'll all have drinks at Theodore Zinks when I get back next fall!

When he finished the duet (no small feat, since you could hear both
Donald's and Daisy's voices coming out of his mouth at the same time),
he invited the audience to join in, and the song thundered through the
enormous hall.

Then the moment came that George had been waiting for. Stoobie
quieted the audience down, and in a hushed voice, introduced the entire
ensemble in a new version of Swannee. The stage walls fell away, and a
group of performers lined each side of the stage, leaving the middle open.
Wendall Wellington and Danny Carvello anchored stage right, and Larry
Dobrinski and Dexter Billings were opposite.

George leaned over and explained to Betsy that this was actually an
Eta Chi production. She squinted toward him, and he told her that almost
everyone on the stage was an Eta Chi, and only about a third of them were
actually in the hotel school. They both giggled as the music started.

Following Wendall's cues, the dancers started gyrating their hips and
vigorously shaking their hands in front of their bodies as they sang –

Tits and Ass, Tits and Ass
Ohhh, don't you love me, don't you love me
Tits and Ass, Tits and Ass

It was then that Harold Wise pranced down the center of the stage,
looking like a sumo wrestler in drag. He had his hair slicked back the
same way that Percival Lee wore his hair, and balloons beneath his costume made him look like a bloated circus clown. He was singing the song
too, and pointed to the audience and nodded his head. In his other hand,
he carried a glass of wine.

The room erupted in cheers and laughter that drowned out the middle refrain of the song. Harold turned his back to the audience and shook his fake rear end at them as he held his arms outstretched. George laughed so hard the tears were rolling down his face. This may not have been his kind of theater, but its entertainment value was enormous.

Only Percival Lee, sitting quietly in the balcony with eight alumni as his guests was not amused. In fact, he was enraged. Being parodied was one thing. Being the brunt of jokes for his weight was nothing new, either. But Harold was also made up to look Japanese, with make-up reshaping the contours of his eyes. That made Professor Lee's head boil. Then Harold had added a swish with his limp hand at the end of the number. That was one detail that he had not reviewed with Stoobie in rehearsal.

The show ended with Stoobie reminding the audience that the show had been in fun, and he invited the crowd to sit in reflection as the Cornell Alma Mater was performed by a sophomore hotel student. A tall, shiny-faced co-ed with an enormous head of curls walked to center stage, and when the room had quieted, she sang the school song with reverence and polish as the lights dimmed to dark. The crowd erupted again as the auditorium lights went up.

Stoobie was ecstatic. He was mobbed by the cast and by well-wishers from around the auditorium. George and Betsy chuckled as they walked outside into the cold December darkness. The moon glowed faintly above them as they agreed to walk into College Town and meet up with the Eta Chi cast members for some beers. Betsy told him she couldn't imagine a bigger difference between the hotel show and Big Kids.

You saw the play? George asked, surprised. It had not come up in their conversation before. Betsy grinned, and said, Yup. George asked her if she liked it, and she told him she thought it was wild. But the hotel show was more what she was used to.

George nodded. He could not fathom how anyone could compare the two forms of performance, but he understood her point. Stoobie's show *had* been fun, even though he wouldn't call it theater arts.

At the bar, they caught up with Eta Chis and girls from Betsy's sorority, and drank beer and talked until their voices were hoarse. Across the bar, George glimpsed Althea Redmonton at one point standing with a gaggle of girls. He turned away to concentrate on Betsy, but struggled to keep his composure. When he finally gave in and look around, she had gone.

He walked his date across campus, to the door of her sorority, and she stood one step up on the stoop as they kissed goodnight. Betsy's little tongue darted in and out of his mouth, and George felt the familiar adrenaline rush in his abdomen. But when he said goodnight, and turned to walk back to Eta Chi, he was not consumed with the image of Betsy. He was not consumed with the thought of anyone. He felt comfortably alone.

The following night, George was elected consul of Eta Chi for the spring semester. He had been worried about his chances, since he had not been around much. Plus, he was running against Fritz Hublein, who was clearly popular in the house.

Numerous boys spoke in favor of the two candidates as they leaned against the washer and dryer outside the Chapter Room. In the end it was Danny Carvello's emotional pitch for George that carried the day. Danny and George had grown very fond of one another, and Danny had done such a great job as consul that the brotherhood willingly followed his passionate words.

Immediately following the chapter meeting, the Eta Chis headed for another unknown sorority, Delta Sigma Pi. By now, sororities were calling Eta Chi asking to be included in the monthly raids, and the brotherhood could not believe their good fortune. Danny had promised the president of DSP that they would come there in December, and when the brothers began to sing the Darling Song on the walkway outside DSP, the girls glided down the stairs wearing make-up and carefully-selected clothes. George didn't notice it until Danny pointed it out, but they both agreed that they preferred the sleepy, just-out-of-bed, rumpled look. It was so much sexier! They agreed to keep the sorority choices for the coming months a secret between the two of them.

At three in the morning, as Eta Chis and Deltas danced in the living room of DSP, there was another activity beginning across campus. The University Administrative offices in Day Hall were taken over in a protest by the residents of Ujaama. Ujaama was the all-black residential dormitory on North Campus where white students were persona non grata. Ujaama wanted to protest the possible closure of the Africana Center, and were worried about losing some scholarships for African-American applicants. So about one hundred and fifty black students sneaked into Day Hall in the middle of the night, to hold a sit-in.

The sit-in lasted two and a half days. It created serious problems for the university administrators who couldn't get access to their offices, and was widely covered by the Cornell Daily Sun. George recognized some of the protesters in the front-page stories as boys he had acted with in *Some Place To Be Nobody*. They wore colorful African clothing.

For the rest of campus, the Ujaama sit-in was a non-event. Classes went on as scheduled, and even when students walked past Day Hall, there wasn't much to see. All the action was inside, in the hallways. After numerous diplomatic efforts, the university reached an understanding with the Ujaama protesters, and before classes ended for the fall semester, the Cornell Daily Sun was back to covering national, local and college news.

On the last day of classes, George sat on the stone bench between Uris and Olin libraries, waiting to meet Betsy. They both had classes to get to, but had agreed to meet and decide where they would be going out later. He stared off in the direction of the Straight because Betsy had said she would be coming from a class on the engineering quad. He was so lost in thought that he didn't notice Brandy saunter up from the other direction. The dog stopped six inches away from George's face, and stood silently. George turned his head and jumped as his head almost collided with the massive jaw of the Saint Bernard.

Brandy! he cried affectionately. For the past two weeks Brandy had spent more and more time with George on the Arts Quad. George rubbed the St. Bernard's ears, and asked him if he wanted to come to class with him. Brandy wagged his tail and drooled. George looked one more time for Betsy, decided she wasn't coming, and headed off to his creative writing class.

Advanced Creative Writing was held on the third floor of Goldwyn Smith Hall, in one of George's favorite rooms. The ceilings were lower on the third floor, and the low windows framed the Arts Quad in tight little squares. An enormous oaken table dwarfed the room to the point that it was difficult to move behind the old wooden chairs without rubbing against the dusty old walls.

Each week, his writing professor selected prose from one of the students and read to the class. George's last short story had been well received, and the entire class enjoyed the guilty pleasure of sitting back to hear each other's work. It helped that the teacher read each work so gently and respectfully.

George was the first to arrive in the classroom, and Brandy followed him dutifully into the room. There was no room for the dog to follow George around the table without bumping into the chairs and the wall, so he wandered under the table. George heard Brandy slump to the floor to rest. Despite his size, no one else who entered the classroom could see Brandy under the twelve-foot wide table.

The class began, and the teacher read a selection from a boy who sat opposite George. It was a delicate story, and the class strained to hear its nuances in the understated way that the professor chose to read it. It wasn't until mid-way through the reading that Brandy started to snore.

The snore was soft and human in sound, and it came directly from the middle of the table. Students peered cautiously around the room, trying to see which of their classmates had fallen asleep. The author smiled and looked a little perturbed. But it was mysterious, and suspicious because everyone's eyes were open.

The teacher paused and looked up. The snoring stopped. George thought he was going to burst out laughing, but he looked incredulously around with everyone else. The teacher resumed reading, and for minutes, Brandy slept silently. Then he snored once more, but only for about twenty seconds, and then was silent for the rest of the reading.

Then students commented on the work. Some people smiled down into their laps. The author thanked everyone for their comments and the fifty-minute class came to a close. People stood up to leave, but George stayed still, pretending to make notations in his notebook. He prayed that Brandy, who was obviously awakened by the scraping of chairs and movement of people out of the room, would wait until he saw George's feet move.

He said goodbye to a few students who lingered briefly, and then waited a few more minutes until the hallway was silent. Then he stood, and heard Brandy stir beneath the table. He walked to the door, and turned and called the St. Bernard to him. Brandy lumbered out from under the table and looked up, panting. George told him he was the best and most brilliant dog in the entire world, and sat back down to rub the dog's head in his lap.

Brandy had made a perfect comment on the writing, as it lacked much. As he stood and left the room with Brandy in tow, the newly elected consul of Eta Chi fraternity was too excited to tell his brothers about what happened to notice the stupendous drool that Brandy had deposited on the crotch of his black, thin-wail corduroys.

CHAPTER TWENTY-TWO

Beverly Clifton didn't intend to go to formal rush with her son. She really didn't. It was just that she was so bored that when Will gave her the option, she thought it would be fun to see what her son was going through. Will spoke so glowingly about Eta Chi, describing the house and the brothers, that her curiosity simply got the better of her.

They drove up to Cornell from their home in Delaware the day before formal rush in January, 1977. Beverly reserved a room at the Statler so she could see her son off, get a good night's sleep and then drive home at her leisure the next day. She loved driving her son to college. They could have afforded him a car, of course, but her husband said he didn't have a car when he went to Cornell, and he wanted his son to have the same experience. Beverly didn't understand her husband's logic, but was glad he had insisted.

Beverly Clifton was forty years old, and her husband was fifty-five. They had a nice enough marriage, but part of her yearned for something more. Something exciting and fresh. So as she drove Will to school, she imagined she was heading back to school herself. She pictured herself at classes, flirting with boys, and laughing with girlfriends over coffee. Will made college sound so much more open and refreshing than when she had gone to school.

Will loved his mother. She was fun, warm, and sincere. She kept his secrets, and pushed him to experience life. She often told him she wanted him to wait until he was in his late twenties to get married, and that he should look for someone his own age. When he asked why that was so important, Beverly always told him that she and his father had been exceedingly lucky, because many couples who were far apart in age didn't end up making it. Whenever she said this, Will took his mother at face value. She always felt tinged with guilt.

It was in the car on their way through Pennsylvania that Will first suggested that he show his mother Eta Chi before she left to go home. The formal rush teas were held morning and afternoon, and Will was focusing almost all of his attention on Eta Chi. He was going there first thing, and he was sure the boys at the house would think it was neat for him to show her around. Beverly rejected her son's idea at first. She doubted there would be a place for mothers in a fraternity rush process. But by the time he raised the notion again over dinner in the Statler dining room, Beverly had decided that spending ten minutes at Eta Chi before she left for home would be a hoot. And besides, her husband had been an Eta Chi when he went to Cornell. He would get a kick out of her seeing where he lived!

As Beverly and Will were finishing their dinner, rush preparations were in full swing at Eta Chi. George Muirfield had just left Joshua Finch's room, worried. He had gone there to offer his assistance to the rush chairman in putting together the power rush teams. Joshua told the consul that he did not plan to make power rush teams. Joshua sat at his desk, and looked down and to his left as he spoke. It was a practiced mannerism that others found unsettling.

George stared at the boy, incredulously, and finally asked why.

Because, Joshua said, staring at his wastebasket, I don't believe in power teams.

George nodded thoughtfully. Okay, he finally said, what do you believe in?

Well, I think freshmen should get a full, undistorted picture of who we are as a house. I think it's misleading for only certain brothers to be the representatives of the house. And I also think it's demoralizing to the brotherhood to give certain brothers special rank.

George took in Joshua's theory slowly and rolled it around in his head. This had never occurred to him, and he knew instinctively it was a bad idea. But this was going to take some time to put right. He looked at the boy in front of him. Joshua looked like he wanted George to leave his room, but George threw himself on his bed, and suggested they talk about it.

Joshua sighed, and turned to face George, without looking at him directly. George noticed how Joshua's eyes looked slightly crossed at moments, and he wondered if it was a voluntary or involuntary affectation. Just then, Frank Shanahan knocked on the door and asked if he could speak with them for a sec. George invited the boy into the room and asked him what was up. Frank Shanahan was a chubby, round-faced junior who tended to trip over his own words, and it took him a moment to make his request clear. He wanted to be excused from rush so he could study.

Joshua Finch smiled in a distracted way, and said that rush was mandatory, but in any event, why on earth would Frank need to study before the semester even started?

Frank looked beseechingly at George as he explained that he had two incompletes from last semester. He had arranged with his professors to take one of the make-up finals this week and one next week. He acted sheepish.

George told the boy that of course his studies came first. He asked Frank to get to as much of rush as he could, but they would understand. Frank thanked George profusely as he sidled out the door.

Joshua told George that he was the rush chairman, and that even though George was consul, he didn't think he had the right to overrule him. George knew Joshua had returned to their real topic, and he heartily agreed.

But, George said, this is my house too. And I really think you are making a huge mistake. I honestly don't see what you are trying to do. Look, we have successfully run rush for long before you and I got here by creating power rush teams. Your job is to get the right freshmen to pledge this house. But it is also your job, and no one else's, to get *every* pledge we bid. And I am quite sure that that won't happen if we don't match people to freshmen who are on the fence.

Joshua told George he didn't think it was important to get every single pledge. That was when George realized that something different, something irreparable, was happening to Eta Chi. He couldn't articulate it, and he struggled with what to say to the boy in front of him. But he knew he couldn't let it go. Before he left the room, he told Joshua Finch that he thought he was trying to play god with something he shouldn't.

Listen, Josh, it seems like you are doing this on personal principle, which I respect. But promise me that you will at least consider this: the freshmen come here for seven hours every day, and they have full access to the entire brotherhood during the morning and afternoon teas. They have the chance to see everybody! But if you are really intent on sending random teams to talk to the freshmen we are competing the heaviest for, and you want the Frank Shanahans of this house to get the job done, you're dreaming. Your legacy, our legacy, will be the strength of the house we leave, not the one we joined.

George was pleased with his speech, and he could see Joshua thinking it over. Joshua nodded curtly, and acknowledged that George had a good point. Maybe, he said, depending on the circumstances, we might have to do a little of what you're talking about. But I do not want to do what we have done in the past. The two boys regarded each other carefully. George shrugged, and suggested they talk again later. When he left the rush chairman's room, George walked directly to Edward Stamer's room to tell him about this development, but Edward was not there.

Joshua Finch called the brotherhood together a few minutes before nine the next day, and told the assemblage to be themselves, enjoy the day, and think hard about the people they met. Beyond that, he gave no instructions. George raised his hand and reminded everyone that Eta Chis never criticize another house. Joshua nodded in agreement, but George wasn't sure that the sophomores would understand the point, so he explained it with an example. Across the room, Edward Stamer stared at Joshua Finch, and then looked at George questioningly.

At nine, Joshua assumed the greeting position at the front door, and within moments, the first freshmen arrived and the day began. At ten after nine, Will Clifton and his mother walked through the door and Will introduced Beverly to Joshua. Joshua's eyes widened, and a huge smile stretched across his face as he welcomed Mrs. Clifton to Eta Chi. Across the room, Harold Wise elbowed Fritz Hublein, and told him to get a load of this.

Beverly Clifton was five-feet, six-inches tall. She had an athletic, supple build, and nicely-tailored clothes that accentuated her figure. When she smiled, her whole face lit up, and the fashionable cut of her hair surrounded her face in a youthful way. Understandably, a number of brothers approached to welcome the newcomer. Danny Carvello got there first and offered to give Mrs. Clifton a tour of the house. When she protested, claiming that she should let the boys get on with their rush, Danny insisted. He told her that parents were an important part of the fraternity, and were always welcome.

As Danny led Mrs. Clifton away, Cullen Hastings approached her son and told him he still needed to meet a number of brothers. Will looked questioningly toward his mother, but Beverly told her son not to worry about her. She would take a peek at the house and then be on her way. So Will walked off with Cullen, and Danny escorted Beverly upstairs to show her the sleeping rooms.

Cullen Hastings had pictured Will in the pledge class since early in the year, and as the elected pledge captain, he was determined to get him bid early in formal rush. Will had come as close as a freshman could to receiving an oral bid from Eta Chi during the fall. He was an energetic and interesting conversationalist, and the brothers who knew him liked him. Every signal he had been given implied that he would soon become a pledge. But when Cullen made a concerted push to bid Will Clifton before Christmas, too many brothers said they didn't know him well enough. So Cullen was making it his personal mission to get Will around to meet people.

Danny Carvello was having fun telling Beverly Clifton stories about college as he led her through the different corridors upstairs. She acted more like a coed than a mother, and when she walked in front of him up to the third floor, Danny admired the woman's svelte figure. He had no idea how old she was, but she was not that old. And after all, he was twenty-eight, and he knew when someone was flirting. Mrs. Clifton was flirting.

Danny knew better than to push the issue so quickly, so when they had toured all the room accommodations, he took Beverly down to the Great Hall and introduced her to Fritz and Harold. At one point George approached and introduced himself too. But he was just trying to pull Harold away to meet a freshman. Harold complained good-naturedly, and told George he thought Will Clifton's mom was hot. George just shook his head.

When the morning tea ended, Beverly Clifton was still at the house. Will found her in the library talking with Stoobie and Dexter Billings, and said, Uhhmm, Mom? We, um, need to go now. Stoobie asked Beverly to come back in the afternoon, and she said she couldn't. Fritz appeared behind her and agreed that she *had* to come back. He raised his eyebrows repeatedly. Will looked confused. Beverly turned and looked at Fritz and smiled because he reminded her so much of her husband twenty years ago. She said she'd talk to Will, but she really should be heading home. In her head, she had already decided to stay over and go home in the morning.

Over lunch, she told her son that she was going to stay over and take her own tour of the campus. Then she would pick him up after rush and take him out to dinner. Will frowned and explained about the room visits and that he had to be in his dorm room by eight p.m. His mother was undeterred. It was fine with her to grab something quick. Will felt a little awkward about the whole thing, but he didn't know how to tell his mother that. Plus, he could see how happy she was, and Cullen Hastings had told him it was absolutely fine that his mother was hanging around.

Beverly dropped her son off at Eta Chi after lunch, and then drove up to campus and parked in the hotel parking lot. She walked through the Agricultural Quad, and then headed south to the campus store to buy her husband a sweatshirt. Then she started to walk across the Arts Quad but it was freezing and empty, so she hurried into the library to get warm. A handful of people sat in the main room, so she sat and read magazines for a few minutes. Fritz Hublein kept reentering her thoughts and this shamed and amused her. She kept picturing the roaring fire at Eta Chi and the boys chatting so energetically, and she gave in to herself. Ten minutes later, she walked in the front door and boys fell over themselves to make her comfortable.

The boys were hard at rush, and Beverly sat near the fireplace watching the scene. She loved the ambiance of the room and the melodious male colloquy surrounding her. When she saw Fritz Hublein he smiled and said, Hello Mrs. Clifton! Beverly told him to call her Beverly and asked if they had a ladies' room. Fritz escorted her into the mailroom and showed her the little bathroom off the back. He told her he would wait for her to be sure none of the boys ran in to use it. She touched him softly on the arm and told him he was a gentleman, and if she were younger, she knew who she would be chasing around campus.

Fritz stood next to the wall of mail cubicles, lost in the image of the woman using the bathroom. Did he dare try something? Part of him was repulsed by the idea. She was a mother, for heaven's sake! But Beverly Clifton didn't remind Fritz of any mother he knew. She was attractive, and she was certainly coming on to him. Wasn't she?

When she emerged from the bathroom, she told him he was sweet to wait, and he smiled politely. He asked what she would like to do next, and Beverly reached both of her hands up to his face and pinched his cheeks. She knew it was the wrong thing to do, but the slippery slope she had started down kept steepening, and the rush of dormant youth inside guided her actions. And besides, she was just being friendly to her sons' friends.

That's when Fritz leaned in and kissed her, and she pulled back abruptly. Fritz started to apologize, saying he misunderstood, but Beverly put her fingers to her mouth to hush him. Outside the little room, the boisterous voices of boys rose and fell as they walked past the room. Beverly pushed her hair off her face and told Fritz this was her fault. She was on the path to resurrecting herself when she impulsively leaned up and kissed him back. It had been his moustache, and the moment, and above all else, her desperate desire to remember how it felt. That was all. She certainly was not seducing him.

She suggested they better be getting back out there, and Fritz huskily agreed. Before long, the afternoon tea had ended, and Beverly reunited with her son in the Great Hall. They left to a chorus of goodbyes from the boys. Minutes later, the Eta Chis gathered in the Great Hall to review the day and consider bid prospects. Harold Wise was listening intently and chuckled as Fritz told him what had happened. Harold was jealous, titillated and appalled all at once. Room, you can't be serious, he said finally. She's a mother for chrissakes! And her husband's an Eta Chi! You've pimped on a brother!! Oh my god, oh my god, we may have to bring you up on charges in the chapter meeting!

Joshua Finch called the meeting to order and the brothers engaged each other energetically as they debated the merits of a number of prospects. When Will Clifton's name was put forth, a number of hands shot up. Patrick O'Hare was recognized first, and he started off by saying, I don't know about this guy. I'm just not sure about him...

The room broke up with laughter. Patrick O'Hare had not liked a single candidate during the entire rush season, and he started every objection the same way. He smiled at the room's reaction, and pressed on. No! I'm serious. What's so special about this guy? And if no one else is willing to say it, I will – what's the story with his mother? Doesn't everybody think that's sort of weird?

Fritz waved his hand dramatically and Joshua recognized him next.

I appreciate Brother Patrick's thoughts on this candidate, he began, and I, myself, don't know about Will, but I have already given Mrs. Clifton an oral bid in the mailroom!

The boys hooted and clapped and cheered. Of course, no one believed him; they thought it was a great joke. Fritz recalled the creamy texture of Beverly Clifton's lipstick and smiled.

What a body! Harold volunteered, and the boys laughed a second time. But Cullen Hastings was not amused.

Excuse me, he said in a stern voice, but this isn't funny. Will Clifton is a great guy, and I think it's awful for us to be speaking this way about his mother. I want Will Clifton to become one of our brothers. Let's get back to business here. I, for one, would like to propose that we talk about Will.

Danny Carvello raised his hand solemnly and said he agreed with Brother Cullen, but he would, nonetheless, ask to be assigned to the team that would visit Mrs. Clifton's hotel room tonight. The room cheered again.

Joshua Finch asked all those in favor of bidding Mrs. Clifton to raise their hands, and the boys started clicking their fingers and raising their hands jubilantly. Then he raised his hand authoritatively, and asked for more comments about Will and the meeting came back to order. But Will once again had not made enough of an impression to be considered ready for a bid.

Across town at L'Auberge du Cochon Rouge, Beverly and Will Clifton were having an early supper of the evening special - rabbit, served with parsleyed potatoes and snow peas. L'Auberge was an old inn located on a wooded hillside near Ithaca College. In the largest of its dining rooms, there was a roaring hearth where the proprietors burned apple wood. The window nearest the fireplace was always open a crack to let the cold fresh country air circulate with the apple scent. Beverly's cheeks flushed with warmth as she spoke with her son about Eta Chi. She agreed it seemed a wonderful fraternity, and she hoped he would get his bid tonight.

Privately, Beverly was not as supportive as she appeared. Her heart raced every time she recalled the way she had kissed that boy. What had she been thinking? Of course, she knew exactly what she had been thinking, and the moment had met every hidden desire in her body. But she didn't allow herself to accept that notion. She forced it out of her mind like a dream, and focused on her son. But the idea of Will joining Eta Chi after what she had done this afternoon was like a bad dream that she couldn't shake.

Will ordered an apple tart with crème fraiche for dessert, and Beverly admired the strong line to her son's jaw as she asked for a cup of hot tea. The fire crackled near her, and she turned to watch the glowing wood hiss for a moment. Will asked his mother if she would like to see Phi Delta as well, as long as she was still here. Beverly smiled and told him that she had intruded enough, and it was time for her to go. But, she rejoined, it's so cold, why don't I pick you up in the morning and drop you off wherever you are going, and then I'll head home. Will thought that would be great, and heaved a sigh of relief to himself. His mother was distracting him from formal rush.

The next morning, snow fell heavily when Beverly knocked on her son's dorm room on West Campus. Will popped out the door, and said Hi! in a big voice.

So? How did last night go? Beverly ventured, assuming her son had been offered a bid.

Oh, it went fine, Will answered. I didn't get a bid, but the Eta Chis were really optimistic, and told me that I was going to come up for a vote today for sure. They're great guys.

Beverly told her son she thought they seemed nice. Then she asked where she could drop him, and he said Eta Chi, please!

By the time they pulled into the Eta Chi driveway, two inches of snow had already fallen, and the roads were slick. Beverly drove a Volvo that was supposed to be good in the snow, but she didn't have much experience. The traction didn't seem all that great. Will got out of the car and asked his mother if she was going to be all right, and she said, Of course. Then she said she better come in to use the bathroom before she left, and left the car running as they both walked quickly to the front door. When Joshua Finch greeted Beverly more energetically than her son, Beverly immediately said she was on her way home. She just needed to use the little girls' room.

Joshua smiled and moved to greet some freshmen walking in behind her.

Beverly told her son to get going, and gave him a kiss on the cheek. Will headed off in the direction of the dining room saying, So long! and Beverly walked into the mailroom. When she emerged a minute later, she headed for the door, where Fritz Hublein stood with Joshua chatting with freshmen. Fritz looked happily surprised, and asked, Are you heading home so soon Beverly?

The two eyed each other mischievously, and she said she was. Harold Wise walked up, and announced that the snow was falling heavily, but it was supposed to stop by noon. You might want to wait until the roads have been cleared, he suggested. As he spoke, he winked at Fritz and rubbed his stomach lightly. When Beverly looked at him, Harold looked like a concerned father. She asked if he was serious, and he said, Absolutely! That's the smart thing to do. What do you think Fritz?

Fritz concurred. He told Beverly she could sit somewhere out of the way, if she felt like she was imposing. Beverly was sliding downhill again, and she knew it was too late. This was too damn much fun, and she might never get a chance like this again to feel so young. So she said if they didn't mind, she'd just sit somewhere inconspicuously until the snow stopped. Fritz suggested that she would be comfortable in the guest bedroom off the Darling room where it would be quiet. He led her there, and explained that it was possible people might poke their heads in as they toured the house, but not to worry. In the quiet of the bedroom, Beverly looked intently at Fritz and told him she was sorry about yesterday. She didn't know what had come over her. Really.

Fritz nodded. Then he reached one arm around her and gave her a light squeeze and said, Me too. He stayed like that for a prolonged moment, and Beverly stood totally still. Part of her wanted Fritz to take charge and kiss her. Part of her was horrified at herself. Finally, she wrapped her arms around his neck, and said, This is not going anywhere, Fritz. But you have given an old woman a big kick. Then she brushed her lips lightly against his cheek, and they stood there, embracing at first, and then kissing for several minutes.

Finally, Beverly pulled herself away. She had felt his arousal, and shame overcame her again. Go! She commanded. Do your rush thing, and stay away from me! Fritz grinned, and said she would always be welcome at Eta Chi. The two of them broke up laughing as he walked out of the room. Beverly smoothed her skirt, and looked out the window. The snow couldn't end soon enough. But she felt more alive than she had in years.

That night, the brotherhood of Eta Chi was even more divided over Will Clifton. His mother had left that afternoon, and was no longer the subject. Brothers had begun to find the boy too eager to please. When he was put up for a vote, he was turned down and Harold Wise moved that he be No-bid, and told this evening so he could consider other houses. Harold felt bad about Will's mother, and suggested that the brotherhood was now leading him on.

Cullen Hastings protested. He said that Will Clifton was already in at Phi Delta, so why not give him one more day to prove himself. In the end, the group didn't care enough one way of the other, and Will was brought back for the final day of rush. The next night, when his name came up, there was strong sentiment both ways. Some of the brothers thought the house owed it to Will because they had led him on all through rush. Others said he was a legacy, and if the house was on the fence about him, why not let him join?

David Dalrumple asked what the policy was about legacies. Joshua said he was unsure, and George stepped forward and explained that there was no requirement that the fraternity bid a boy simple because his father or brother was an Eta Chi. It was a factor, but not a controlling one. Vote your conscience, he advised. Some debate ensued on what significance should attach to the legacy factor. Then Joshua recognized Danny Carvello, who strode in mock seriousness to front of the room as boys laughed softly.

I finally have a point of view about young Will Clifton, he began. I don't know about the rest of you, but this kid has been wandering around our house like a lost puppy for months. None of us have really wanted to claim him, but no one wants to admit it. He may have a hot mother and his father may have been an Eta Chi, but I, for one, am already tired of the guy. Think about how tired we will be of him if he's here all the time! Let's unload him. The room clicked their fingers in support.

Joshua said, all in favor of bidding Will Clifton? Only Cullen Hastings and three other boys raised their hands.

All opposed?

The rest of the fifty-five boys raised their hands, except for George Muirfield. George was embarrassed, and had decided not to vote at all.

At the end of formal rush, Eta Chi had bid twenty-seven boys. Twenty-four accepted. One went to Phi Delta, one to Chi Psi, and one to Alpha Phi Omega. Of the three boys who declined, George had been in on the last room visits with Joshua, Danny and Edward Stamer, but there was not enough steam left to swing their decisions. When they walked out of the last boy's dorm room on the final night, George swung his fist hard against the dorm wall, and walked off without saying another word. To be sure Joshua Finch understood his displeasure, he didn't speak to him for a week. It didn't seem to faze Joshua.

CHAPTER TWENTY-THREE

January is a serious month. Winter makes heads bow to make headway through the frigid wind, and professors load up students with assignments to make headway through the curriculum. It is also the deadline for graduating seniors to file applications for graduate schools. The mood at Eta Chi was suitably workmanlike. There was not much on the social calendar until February, and boys spent more time at their desks. But Sunday dinners were still a time to relax before the week began, and since Andy the chef had Sunday nights off, that meant going out.

Danny Carvello had discovered that the Odyssey Steak House offered specials on Sunday evenings, so that became a popular destination. But on the third Sunday in January, a number of the boys decided to head over to McDonalds. McDonald's, a hamburger chain that was starting to open restaurants all over the country, was quickly becoming a landmark across upstate New York. But there was still only one McDonald's in Ithaca, built across the street from another relatively new phenomenon – an indoor mall.

It seemed crazy, but Ronny Trillo said that anyone who brought their food up to the McDonald's counter with a complaint received a fresh meal. So Ronny demonstrated this policy to the half dozen boys, eating two-thirds of his hamburger, and then bringing it to the counter to complain that his food was cold. He immediately returned with a fresh hamburger.

See, he said, this way you can get almost two hamburgers for the price of one. And there's really nothing wrong with this, because it's their policy! Across the hard plastic table from him, Gregory Smythe snickered in his high-pitched voice, and continued eating his dinner. Gregory Smythe had blond, wavy hair, and a face that would look youthful his entire life. His skin was fair and unblemished, with a shiny glow. Even his voice was higher than it should have been.

George Muirfield was down the table, watching Gregory curiously. Before the boy began eating, he had removed the bun from his hamburger, and centered the brown patty on the bottom bun. Then he held the sandwich in one hand as he methodically dipped a French fry in catsup and bit off about a third of it. George could not stop staring at the junior once he realized the boy ate in a pattern. One bite of his sandwich, one dip of the French fry in catsup, then another, then a third (until the fry was consumed) and then back to the beginning. After every third hamburger swallow, he took a measured sip of his drink. He did not vary once from this order through the meal. George was enthralled.

Gregory was enthralled, too, but not with his eating habits. He was thinking about the girl behind the counter who had served him his food. She had smiled so fetchingly at him as he took his tray away, he was sure it meant something. He was a mechanical engineering major, and prided himself on the clinical perspective he applied to his world. If she smiled that way, she must be attracted to him. If she was attracted to him, he should ask her out. So when dinner was over, he returned to the counter as the boys headed out to the cars, smiled, and asked Daisy Lavallee in a high-pitched, perfunctory voice if she wanted to go out sometime. A few people around Daisy laughed, but Daisy immediately wrote her number on a piece of paper, and stuffed it into Gregory's hand.

Great! Gregory exclaimed, as he examined her number. He loved it when things went logically. Later that night, Gregory called Daisy and invited her to the Eta Chi Valentine formal. Daisy almost fell off the chair in her parents' kitchen. This was something new!

The following Wednesday, at date night, the Cornell University president was a guest speaker. Eta Chi had pursued him for two years to come and speak at the house, and he had finally relented. President Wilson was a reserved and humble engineering academic who did not connect easily at such functions. But he knew it was an obligation of his office, and occasionally accepted invitations from different parts of the university. This was his first visit to a fraternity, and he was impressed.

Eta Chi had secured a podium for him to speak from, and had arranged rented metal chairs in the Great Hall in straight lines. Dinner was pleasant enough. He sat next to the house president and an attentive boy from the engineering school named Carvello. The fraternity Darling sat opposite him. After dinner, everyone filed into the Great Hall with a respectful silence. Wilson was impressed with the civilized decorum of the place. He liked the boys' jackets and ties, and the girls' pretty dresses.

The president's remarks concerned the challenges facing large academic institutions and touched lightly upon the Ujaama sit-in of last semester. He was so stilted and careful in his speech that George Muirfield was sleepy before he finished, but the room clapped loudly as he thanked them. The boys clapped more for the fact that they had managed to get the university president to come to their house, than out of appreciation for his comments. But the president dropped a bomb at the dinner table.

When Danny Carvello had inquired at dinner about the president's thoughts on the fraternity system, Wilson replied that the system served an important residential purpose at the school, but he worried about some of the antics. He described his professional chagrin and personal outrage when one of the agricultural school professors had his career's labors mocked by a fraternity in December. To the professors' shock, the fraternity's mantel was decorated for Christmas with cut evergreens. Unfortunately, the evergreens were instantly recognizable to the professor, who had spent his career growing a unique evergreen in the Ag School's botanical forest. It was the only known species of the tree in North America, and had been protected by a chain link fence from all of the surrounding trees so that the professor could study its development as he tried to grow new members of the species.

Apparently, President Wilson explained, the fraternity had gone off in search of a Christmas tree for their living room, and stumbled upon that part of the forest where the professor's prized tree was located. The boys first cut down a neighboring tree, but then decided the tree inside the fence had a better shape, so they climbed over and cut it down. The first tree could be cut up for other decorations. But when they had gotten the two trees home, they hacked up the professor's tree for the mantle, and stood the first tree in their living room.

You know, President Wilson admitted, it really didn't matter which tree they cut up – both trees were obviously doomed. But for the professor to see his life's work butchered on their mantle piece, was truly salt on his wound. The university leader shook his head slightly as he averted his tired eyes. This sort of destructive and uncaring attitude has no place in a school like Cornell.

After dinner, the president concluded his formal remarks and took respectful questions from those in attendance. Eta Chi presented him with a book on the history of engineering that one of the boys had thought he would like. The man seemed genuinely touched. As soon as he left the house, his dinner story became the topic for discussion. No one had listened much to his speech, but the Christmas tree story was riveting. Stoobie immediately said that it had to be DU, which revived the Creeping DUism discussion amongst many seniors.

All the fraternities went out into the woods and found a tree to cut for Christmas, but Eta Chi would never choose a tree that someone obviously was trying to protect! Cullen Hastings said he had no idea that the house did not pay for their Christmas tree. In a disgusted voice, he said this was no different from the water debate. George smiled benignly at his brother. He liked Cullen's virtuous principles, but he disagreed on this point. First of all, he reminded Cullen, the house had done the right thing about the water. And second, cutting down a tree in the middle of some forest was not really the same as stealing water from a municipality.

The water debate occurred every spring, when the brotherhood discussed how to fill the swimming pool with water. Inevitably, one of the brothers would propose bypassing the water meter to avoid surcharging everyone twelve dollars for the water. But the house always voted out of conscience to pay the extra money and avoid the criminal feel to the proposal. By comparison, the Christmas tree was obtained by a few brothers without any debate at the chapter meeting. It was an entirely different issue.

George was surprised by how easy being consul really was. The house ran pretty much on its own, with the different officers attending to their responsibilities. But George was aware that his office needed to be more than an honorary one. He had watched with a keen eye as Danny Carvello established a pulse to the fall semester through his zany leadership.

His first Aha! occurred when he sat and counted out the sororities that Eta Chi had not yet raided. There were not enough chapter meetings to possibly get to all of the sororities! George mused over this for a number of days. George thought that Sunday brunches might be a new avenue, so he and Harold discussed the idea, but they agreed that it was too complicated. Girls routinely stayed over at the house on Saturday nights now, and how would they manage that issue if a sorority was showing up on Sunday morning for a party? That's when it struck them. Why not bring brunch to the sorority! While each of the boys would claim ownership of the idea, it took Danny Carvello to refine it into its final form. The three boys put their heads together, and agreed to announce it at the next chapter meeting.

⁂

The Eta Chi Valentine formal woke the house from its January slumber with a bang. The organizing committee had created a new game for the event – pink, paper hearts that people could exchange in return for a promise of a dance. And the entertainment was divided into two parts. The Cayuga's Waiters, the all-male a cappella singing group, performed a short set during the first dinner course. A number of Eta Chis headlined the group, which delivered stirring renditions of Cornell songs and popular modern songs like Orleans' *Dance With Me.* They even finished with a hushed, serious version of the Eta Chi Darling Song, which brought down the house.

Dinner was prime rib au jus, with twice-baked potatoes and julienne vegetables. Dessert was Andy's Baked Alaska and coffee. Then the brotherhood sang the Darling Song. The seniors stood behind their chairs, but the majority of the boys joined the swaying line in front of the tables as they sang. Jack Ellis' signature AARRGGHH! at the end of the song perforated the air like a foghorn to the amusement of many.

George Muirfield had invited Betsy, who wore a red, long-sleeved dress and patent leather shoes. George, wore his father's old tuxedo. Throughout dinner, Betsy kept her left hand under the tablecloth on George's thigh. He was hot and cold about her, but he loved the way she did that.

Gregory Smythe had entered the dining room with Daisy Lavallee on his arm and a huge smile on his cherubic face. Daisy wore a ruffled, round-necked blouse that showed her neck and shoulders, and a cabled, knee-length black skirt. She was short, and a little stocky, and when she saw how the other girls were dressed, she wished her mother had never talked her into this outfit. But Gregory certainly didn't seem to mind. He was effusive as he introduced her to the president of the house. George Muirfield could not have been nicer. He told her that her haircut made him think of Betty Boop, and she beamed at him. It was true!

After dinner, everyone adjourned to the Great Hall, where a rock band with a horn section rocked the room with all the newest songs. For fun, Danny Carvello had invited Holly Menard when Janette Emilio had to be home for job interviews that weekend. Danny and Holly danced across the room, switching from the funky baseball to the hustle to the bump. Holly had not been back to Eta Chi since Charles Lord graduated last year, and she loved seeing everyone again. She had started dating one of the assistant football coaches, and was finishing her undergraduate experience in a different place, but she had not been able to resist when Danny had asked her to come back for old time's sake.

Not long after people started dancing, the room was called to attention and asked to gather for a photograph. Eta Chi always hired a photographer for big formals, and brothers and their dates crowded together in the Great Hall as the photographer snapped pictures with a large, square camera on a tripod in the foyer. When the photographer finished, the music started up again, and everyone returned to dancing. But Wally Stimpson chased after the photographer to ask him for a favor.

Moments later, Wally tapped the shoulders of George, Stoobie, Danny, Cullen, Ronny Trillo, Fritz Hublein, Nick Cohen and Harold Wise. He told them to go meet in the library without their dates, and each excused themselves. As they assembled, Wally said the photographer was taking another picture just of them, and they all posed seriously in front of the piano. When asked what this was for, Wally smiled and told everyone to trust him.

By the end of the night, after the band had finished, Holly taught everyone who was left a line dance. She danced in front of the line, facing away like an instructor, before she finally joined the first line at the end. The boys were hooting, and improvising, and the tempo of the night stayed elevated until two thirty a.m. George and Betsy slumped onto a couch at the end of the room, exhausted and elated. They had been building up to sleeping together, and they both knew it was going to happen tonight, although neither of them said a word about it. It just made sense. When they caught their breath, George suggested they sneak off somewhere, and Betsy smiled serenely as she took his hand.

The next morning they awoke in George's narrow little bed. It was eight a.m., and the only sound George could identify was the little buzz in his head from the beer. Betsy snuggled in against him and told him how good this felt. He stroked her hair absent-mindedly, and looked out his little window, above the steam radiator. Betsy was an enigma to George. He liked her a lot. They had great conversations, and liked to do so many of the same things. And she was attractive. Their lovemaking, an unknown until last night, had turned out to be wonderful, and she fit perfectly in the crook of his arm as they lay together in his bed.

But Betsy left George unfulfilled, and he didn't have a clue why. He assumed that he must leave her unfulfilled as well, even if she didn't realize it. Didn't it make sense that that sort of thing was always mutual? There was more logic and convenience between them than passion or lust. They made sense together – everyone could picture them together. So what was his issue? He felt her hand moving beneath the covers and stopped thinking. A moment later, Frank Sinatra started singing in Harold's room, and they broke up laughing.

Barbara Huston had moved on from disco. She was leading the renaissance of Frank Sinatra, and his new album, *Ol' Blue Eyes Is Back!* would play repeatedly from Harold's room throughout the spring. George and Betsy kissed in the privacy of his room as they heard Stoobie yelling to shut that music off please! Soon the distractions outside the room seemed to dissipate.

When they were finished, George left Betsy alone to dress while he headed down the hall to the bathroom, and shaved standing next to Danny Carvello. Danny pretended his razor was a spaceship landing on Planet Cheek. George watched Danny in the mirror, and then applied Noxzema shaving cream to his face. Hot, steamy water splashed noisily into the sinks at their waists.

When do you think it's necessary for us to wake up? George asked his friend sleepily.

There is no "When," there is only "Why," Danny replied.

George cupped water in his hands, splashed his face and halfheartedly wiped it off with his towel. Hunh! he finally said.

When George returned to his room, he escorted Betsy down to the bathroom that was unofficially designated as the girls' powder room on Sunday mornings. She pushed her way in the door, and asked him to wait for her in his room, so he walked back and put Tim Weisberg on his turntable. The senior hallway was coming to life, and a familial banter reverberated between the rooms.

Fritz and Jane Quissling laughed in his room, across from Gregory Smythe's room where Daisy Lavallee hid under the covers. This was all new to her, and she didn't feel comfortable yet. Stoobie was already dressed in black dress trousers and a cashmere sweater. He was getting ready to go pick up Mitsy Smith for brunch, and teased Harold and Barbara's musical preferences through the thin wall that separated them. When Betsy walked down the hall from the bathroom, she stopped and chatted at each room on her way. She had never felt so comfortable in the fours years she had been away at school.

The second chapter meeting of the spring semester was convened that evening, and George solemnly stood at the podium in the front of the room, dealing with new and old business. When they reached the social committee report, George excitedly explained a new addition to the Eta Chi arsenal of sorority raids. On the second Friday of each month, the brotherhood was going to awaken a sorority at five in the morning with intoxicating beverages and dancing. They would party until eight a.m. and then head off to classes with the girls! The brothers whistled and clicked their fingers. George took the time to help them imagine girls with tousled hair descending the stairs with that sleepy-eyed sexiness, and the room hooted appreciatively.

Their first Eta Chi Wake-Up party would take place on the coming Friday. All those wishing to participate should be in the Great Hall at five a.m. sharp! Would they be singing the Darling Song on the steps at that time of the morning? someone asked. Not exactly, George replied. We are going to try to get inside the house before we sing, but we will still start off the festivities with the song. What sort of beverages will people want to drink at five in the morning? another brother inquired hesitantly. George turned to Harold and Said Brother Wise, please explain! And Harold described the mimosas and milk punches they had chosen for the events.

At the end of the meeting, when the brothers rose and spoke about whatever was on their minds, the participation was strong, which George took as a sign of harmony in the house. He loved this portion of the meeting. Just before Fritz, who was the elected pro-consul, spoke at the conclusion of this segment, Bill Dunn rose to speak. George had fond memories of the esoteric boy whom he had first met in the dining room during his freshman rush. Bill Dunn may have been hard to follow in conversation, but he was nobody's fool. He just acted a little out to lunch.

Bill began in a hushed voice standing directly in front of George –

My brothers, I have never been more proud to be an Eta Chi. (Fingers snapped appreciatively across the room) *As many of you know, I left school for over a year and a half, and have just now re-enrolled in order to complete my degree. My time away from Cornell has given me a fresh perspective on life, on college and on the tradition of Eta Chi.*

George and Fritz exchanged looks and smiles. They could tell this was going to be a great speech.

I have the unique position of having seen our house in almost two different eras – the first one that I joined as a freshman in 1972, and the house I have just returned to now. I don't think I really understood the meaning of Eta Chi when I was a freshman or sophomore. But I can tell you now that it is not easy to recreate the atmosphere of this house outside these four walls. We have something precious here, something to be proud of and to care for. We have a brotherhood that gives each of us something different but all of us one bond, one enduring friendship. This I say to you now is the most special thing I can imagine.

The room snapped fingers again and Bill's eyes grew moist and he halted for a moment to regain his composure.

I do not want to go into why I left school, or why I came back, but I also want to share with you some additional thoughts that it seems necessary to say...There is something missing here. I see it when I walk into the dining room. I see it when I look into my mirror and then open up the medicine cabinet and examine the razor and the shaving cream and the other things that by themselves are so lifeless, but indicative of so much that is real about life.

George and Fritz exchanged alarmed looks for a moment. They could not see Bill Dunn's face, but they could feel the anguish in his voice, and they were completely lost by his words. George quickly inventoried the bathrooms and Bill Dunn's room in his mind. There were no medicine cabinets in the house. (Although his reference to shaving cream made George think of shaving with Danny in the bathroom.) What on earth was he talking about? He looked out beyond Bill to the faces of the brothers sitting around the room. They were transfixed on Bill, and hushed. George saw Joshua Finch move uncomfortably in his seat to fix his underwear.

So what am I trying to say? I want you all to know that this is your house. I see the low morale and the new, rude way that brothers treat each other. I hear the sarcastic barbs exchanged between brothers at the dinner table. There should be no room in this house for such actions. I never saw this when I joined this house. Don't others feel it? This is a great house. This is the finest group of people I will ever associate with. So thank you for accepting me back into the house. I am thrilled to be here, and prouder than ever to be an Eta Chi...

Bill Dunn returned to his seat, and no one moved. George finally started clicking his fingers and others followed his lead. George looked to Fritz, but Fritz shielded his eyes as he nodded negatively to indicate he did wish to speak. George knew he was trying not to laugh, and had to look away before he laughed himself. Then he stood and collected himself at the podium for a moment before he began. He had planned to give a funny and inspirational speech, but nothing seemed appropriate. So instead he told his brothers that they stood at the junction point between destiny and fate. The true magic of Eta Chi was the balance between individuality and brotherhood, and as Brother Carvello would say, the honorable pursuit of women! So let's get ready to party!

George didn't think what he said made any sense, but as he sat back down, a relieved brotherhood clapped their hands and immediately began to marshal the champagne and glassware needed for their next raid.

At four fifty-five the following Friday morning, George awoke to the sound of his alarm, and jumped out of bed, instantly awake. He dressed quickly and headed downstairs to the Great Hall. Already there was significant movement in the house. He could hear boys laughing in the bathrooms. Finally someone in the sophomore corridor yelled, Pajama Party! Chuckles could be heard up and down the rooms. George had told the sorority president to expect them at five thirty, but he hoped to get everyone there by five twenty to start the party. This would add at least a modicum of spontaneity if the girl he had spoken to had told the entire sorority they were coming.

The boys were ready to depart by twelve after five. George praised his brothers for their punctuality as they yawned and scratched their heads sleepily. Harold Wise came prancing down the stairs singing, "Boom-boom-boom-booooom" and wiggling his hips. Following right behind him, Danny Carvello was singing *Mighty, Mighty Love* as he snapped his fingers and gyrated his shoulders to the imaginary beat. Eta Chi was in the mood.

George tried the front door carefully when they arrived on the doorstep of Sigma Sigma Nu. The girl had told him she would leave it unlocked, but who knew if she remembered. The door swung open easily and George poked his head in smiling. There was no one to be seen. The living room was warm and open, and George shuddered as he felt the chill in the morning air seep into the front parlor. He motioned everyone inside quietly, and the boys grouped together in the open space of the living room. Danny hummed off-key, and the boys started to sing in loud, jubilant voices.

Upstairs the boys heard the thumping of feet down a hallway and a chorus of exclamations. One girl leaned her head around the banister of the main staircase, and said, Oh my god! The Eta Chis laughed and someone immediately turned on the stereo playing Fleetwood Mac. George saw the girl on the stairs was in her nightgown, and smiled happily. The sorority president must have kept her word, and not told her house what they were planning.

Moments later, girls walked down the stairs in bathrobes, giggling. Stoobie had already assumed his position at the base of the steps and handed out hastily-poured mimosas. The second girl down the steps said, Do you guys even know what time it is? Gregory Smythe looked at his watch and said, It is five twenty-eight, and all the boys laughed. Girls soon flooded the stairway, wearing jeans and sweaters, and smiled broadly at the boys greeting them. By five forty-five, The Spinners had replaced Fleetwood Mac and the milk punch flowed freely.

George and Danny invited two girls coming down the stairs to dance, and led them to the middle of the living room floor. The girl with Danny was tall and slender, with short, brown hair and a pointy chin. George's partner, who held a drink in her left hand as she wagged her head back and forth to the beat, had an enormous head of blond curls, and big, round lips. The black turtleneck she wore accented the soft plumpness of her frame. She had the rumpled, just-out-of-bed look.

By eight a.m., a number of people wanted to forgo classes and keep the party going, but George stood on a chair and announced that the party was suspended until Happy Hour. He invited everyone to meet at the Nines at four that afternoon, and hopped off the chair. Instinctively, George sensed that bringing the party to a close now so that people would go to class under the influence of milk punches and mimosas would establish the lore of the event. He was dead on.

Throughout the day, Eta Chis met up with Sigma Sigma Nu's on campus, high-fiving each other and swapping stories. By the time they were buying each other hair-of the-dog Bloody Mary's at the Nines, Eta Chis were being approached by Kappa's, complaining about being left out. Holly Menard cornered George at the bar and made him promise that Kappa would be next on Eta Chi's list. George said he wasn't sure that Kappa's wanted to get drunk before class, and Holly promised him a chugging contest when they came. They smiled at each other. Holly was thinking about how funny George had been as he sat next to her at class this morning, well-oiled from the party. George remembered the chugging contest when he had first flirted with Althea Redmonton. A pang of desire rifled through him.

George had not thought of Althea much in the past number of weeks, but the thought of her suddenly sloshed around in his head. He swore he could smell her perfume. Then he pictured himself with Betsy and smiled to himself. He would never be serious about Betsy, never imagine a future with her. But she was fun, and he needed to move forward. It was clear to him that Althea was not in his future. He went to the payphone in the bar and called Betsy's sorority and left a message.

Danny Carvello didn't go to Happy Hour. He went back to Eta Chi after classes and slept for awhile before he was ready to head out. A sophomore approached him as he walked down the hallway and wanted to know his secret with women. The boy in front of him needed lessons in personal grooming, but Danny didn't think he wanted to hear that.

You're known throughout the house as a lady killer, the boy explained. There has to be something you can share!

Danny told him he had never killed a lady in his life, but suggested that whatever he knew was best understood on the field of battle. So he asked the young lad if he wanted to accompany him to the Chapter House. The sophomore thanked Danny reverentially; Danny could barely contain his mirth.

The Chapter House was packed to capacity, and Danny encouraged the sophomore to drink up for his courage. He mused about what to do with his young protégé, and bantered mindlessly with him as he surveyed the room carefully. Finally, he turned to the sophomore, and told him that the real secret to getting girls was biting them on the ass.

Whaaatt!?! the sophomore replied. You can't be serious!

Danny nodded his head up and down very slowly, trying to convey how important a pointer he was giving. The sophomore said that he should have known this was going to be wild. He could not imagine biting a coed on the ass, but he wanted desperately to ally himself with the legendary senior. So he asked which kind of girl was the best target. Danny nodded quickly to acknowledge the question, and began to describe the different ways that girls around the room would likely react to such a meaningful act.

Do you see that girl over against the wall? Danny asked as he squinted knowingly at his companion. Well, she's the type that might take you right here on the floor, if you do it correctly. But that would not be in keeping with the Eta Chi standards. You need to do it to someone who will maintain an appropriate level of decorum. He scanned the room for other potential targets.

Across from the two boys, a girl with shiny, shoulder-length blond hair stood with her back to them. Her name was Mary Strusky, and Danny knew her, but it had been a while and he didn't recognize her from behind. In fact, Mary was one of his early conquests. She had been a naïve freshman when Danny took her out on a date, and when he pressed himself on her, she had told him she thought it was too soon. Danny asked her why.

We've just met! I don't even know if you'll call me again. I'm certainly not interested in a one-night fling!

That was all Danny had needed. Of course he was going to call her. He couldn't believe she would even think that way. The mere notion offended him. So after considerable repartee, they had slept together. Danny never called her.

That was almost two years ago, but Mary had never forgotten how stupid she had been. Danny had not given it a second thought, and moved restlessly on to other girls. Of course, he had no idea as he stood at the Chapter House with his sophomore trainee that it was Mary who stood with her back to them. He just saw a girl with pretty hair, and a nice figure in tight blue jeans. So he went for it.

You see the girl with her back to us? he asked his brother. She's perfect. And just look at that ass. Of course, you are really going to have to bite hard to make the right impression. Those jeans are pretty tight on her. But go ahead. There's no time like the present! When Danny said this, he put his palms to either side of his face as if to say, *Why not?*

The sophomore studied the back of the girl for a moment and began to get cold feet. Danny sensed the moment passing, and kicked into action.

Come on, he said, pushing the boy closer to her, don't lose the advantage of surprise. Girls love to be surprised when you bite them on the ass.

The sophomore swallowed the rest of his fourth beer, and looked briefly at his mentor. Promise me, you'll be right behind me!

Hell, Danny replied, I'd hold your hand, but that wouldn't look right. Let's go!

The sophomore went right up to the girl and got down on his haunches. Danny stood behind him, smiling. He didn't really think the boy would do it, but the fantasy of it was a hoot.

The sophomore shoved his face against the girl's rear end, and tried to bite her. The material of her jeans didn't allow him to really take hold of her at all, but he made a slight indentation.

Mary Strusky whipped around, shocked. The sophomore was still on his knees, but Danny was right there in front of her face, grinning wildly.

Hi Mary! He shouted as he recognized her.

It took Mary a moment to absorb what had happened. She assumed that it had been Danny who had....what? *Bitten her on her fanny?!* That's when the sophomore stood up in front of Mary, and said, Hi! I'm Steve....

She was speechless for an instant, but more than anything, the memory of her stupidity flooded her mind.

You never even had the decency to call me, she said condescendingly to Danny. As she spoke, she rubbed the place where the sophomore had pushed his mouth.

Actually, I've been looking for you all night! Danny replied.

That was when Mary Strusky swung her right hand with all her might from the back of her jeans across Danny's face. He toppled backwards, and over the sophomore who had bent back down to tie his shoe.

Danny sprang back up and said, Well, if you're going to get all huffy about it, we're leaving. He took the sophomore by the collar and rushed out of the bar. The sophomore couldn't stop laughing, and Danny finally joined him when his breath came back. They headed toward upper College Town, and the sophomore asked how he had done. Danny pulled himself erect, and said, Excellent job, my son! His cheek stung from Mary's slap, but the lesson he learned had been invaluable. Even he had not thought he could go this far!

CHAPTER TWENTY-FOUR

ebruary closed its doors with an enormous snow storm that deposited a foot and a half of hard-packed snow on Ithaca. Not to be outdone, March opened up like an enormous wind tunnel, blowing artic air across the piles and drifts of icy snow. When the Eta Chis walked to campus in the morning, boys pretended to be blown into each other by the relentless weather. A premature thaw arrived in the last two weeks, but in the meantime, the fires roared in the Great Hall fireplace and an ever-changing collection of boys sat staring into the flames.

It was on such an evening that George Muirfield found himself helping Cullen Hastings to get the fire blazing. They were alone at first, and as Cullen heaved the largest log around on top of the smaller ones trying to get it lit, he told George about the pledge class. He loved his position as pledge captain, and was proud of his pledges, but he was mad about the lack of interest the brothers took in the pledge process.

It's not the same house at all, George. There isn't the same interest, the same devotion to the house. And I don't know what to do about it.

George looked warmly at his brother and friend. He told Cullen that the house would rally around as initiation got closer. He would see.

But Cullen said it wasn't the pledging or the initiation per se, but a more general malaise in the house that worried him. We don't care about each other as much, he said forcefully. The fire got going and they curled their stockinged toes at the edge to feel the smoky heat. Soon others joined them, and over time as people came and left, a core group of boys stayed to talk. The fire cast its glow out into the room, and the boys lied on their stomachs with their hands holding their heads, facing each other in a circle.

Stoobie lay next to Harold, who was next to Fritz. Wendall Wellington decided it was too cold to go the stupid library, and settled in next to Fritz. Jimmy Dunbar lay quietly between Wendall and George, staring into the flames with his head resting on one hand. Wally Stimpson lay with his feet nearest the fire, next to George, and Danny Carvello squeezed in between Wally and Stoobie asking if they were going to have a circle jerk.

Harold immediately started talking about the elephant walk, and when Jimmy Dunbar glanced up and asked what that was, Harold chuckled deeply. Oh my god, you never heard about the elephant walk that used to be part of initiation!?! Ohhh, ho-ho-ho, you know what I'm talking about, right Fritz?

Wendall said he wasn't sure he wanted to know, but Harold was already on his game.

They used to line all the pledges up in the library and make them take all their clothes off! Then they made them stand in a line, holding a hot dog. And I don't have to tell you where the other end of that hot dog was, do I? Oh my god, it was scandalous! This was a house of sin! Harold laughed with a leering, flushed look on his face.

George told him he was full of shit.

No I'm not, Room! (Most of the boys down the senior corridor now called each other "Room.") I'm serious. My big brother was pissed off that they didn't do it our year! But you remember what we did, right?

Before Harold had the chance to go on, Wally said that when he was in high school, he belonged to a secret society that had an initiation ceremony that was even worse. The boys all turned to listen. Everybody had to roll around naked in baby oil, he said. Then we had to rub dirt and feathers all over our bodies while we danced in a circle and made sounds like a chicken! Everybody laughed. Wally's mouth was wide open in a big smile as he nodded emphatically.

Harold said he was worried that all the guys joining fraternities had to be queers if they liked doing that stuff.

That's disgusting, Stoobie said. He usually made negative comments whenever the conversation roamed near homosexuality.

Jimmy Dunbar said he thought that there were a lot more homosexuals these days.

Do you want to share something with us, Jimmy? Fritz asked coyly. All the boys laughed.

Cullen asked if anyone thought that there could be homosexual brothers in Eta Chi.

Oh, please! Stoobie said, grimacing. Inside, he felt his stomach roiling, but he also wanted to hear what people thought.

I know one thing, Harold offered. I am always careful when I take my showers. You know that old rule about standing against the wall to pick up your soap, right?

George said he had to admit that he didn't like showering in the main bathroom. He was referring to the locker-style shower room with eight shower heads on the second floor. George preferred the third floor bathroom, where there were two separate stall showers with curtains. The fire crackled loudly, and Wally sat up to throw another log on.

Fritz told Harold that he had it backwards. The rest of the house worried about him when they hit the showers.

Cullen suggested they go around and say what each really felt about the issue.

That's it! I'm leaving, said Harold. He got up and left the room as people laughed.

All right, I'll go first, George suggested. I have actually had to think about this because of a play I was in. This guy was supposed to be a homosexual and was trying to get me, so the director made up this exercise where I had this little ball in my hand while the other guy tried to pry it away. Anyway, it turned out the guy I was doing this with really was, you know, a homosexual. Anyway, I had to go through this thing, and at the end I knew I could never be one. Never.

Danny said, Ohh, come on! If you are honest about it, everyone has moments when some person of the same sex looks pretty attractive. It's just nature! He was lying with his hands in a fist, with his chin resting in the center of his hands. He looked pensively at the middle of the carpet between them as he spoke. Stoobie peered at Danny with his eyebrows raised.

George knew that Danny had never once had such an inkling, and pondered why his friend was saying this. It did not occur to him that Danny was impishly opening the door just to get others to put their foot in. Wendall said he thought people put too much stock in sexual identity. He could care less if some brothers didn't like girls. This evoked an immediate response.

Fritz said he would not want to be associated with a fraternity filled with flamers. Jimmy Dunbar thought he would struggle with it too. George looked at Cullen, thinking about their conversation a week before. Cullen and another brother had come to the consul to report that they believed another brother had actually "entertained" a boy in his room. What was he going to do about it?

George wasn't sure. He asked them why they thought this had occurred, and they gave him enough details that he believed them. The brother's guest had even spent the night and left in the morning. George had tried to make light of the issue, but was terrified that the news would somehow get out. Surely, the reputation of the house would immediately sink. He imagined the curled lips of the Phi Deltas whispering to freshmen about *that Eta Chi house.*

Wally Stimpson said that his high school had been filled with them, and he had to fight them off as he walked down the corridor. The boys let his comment pass.

Danny's revelation had cast a more intimate aura around the circle of boys, and they spoke cautiously but warmly about the topic. Even Stoobie felt less threatened, and said that the revulsion he had used to feel for homos had been replaced with a laissez faire attitude. That made Fritz shake his head in agreement. I don't really care either, he said. Whatever they do is their business.

So, Cullen asked, if I told you that five of the pledges were of that persuasion, you wouldn't care?

No, Cullen, Fritz answered. I am definitely not saying that.

Wendall, who dressed stylishly and walked in a slightly effeminate way, but who would not embrace his own homosexuality for another five years, suggested that people were people. He readily understood Danny's point about beauty. Bodies are beautiful, and we shouldn't be so afraid to think about it that way.

Stoobie wished to himself that it was that easy. If only he could find himself attracted to both sexes!

Danny nodded into his hands. Wally said he was getting aroused, and people laughed gently. Jimmy Dunbar said he didn't believe anyone in the house was a homosexual. Wouldn't they all know?

George said it wasn't necessarily obvious. He certainly had no clue about the boy he had acted with in the play. It was entirely possible, and even likely, that someone in the house was "that way," but just hid it well. George and Cullen exchanged looks. Cullen finally said, Well, I'm pretty sure that there somebody in the house must be. Stoobie stared at his hands, which were sweaty, but nobody noticed that. I just think, Cullen continued, that it doesn't matter so long as the brother doesn't tell anyone, or do something stupid to make it public.

Jim Steuben relaxed. He would never have brought a boy into Eta Chi, even if he had reached that point in his journey to sexual self-fulfillment. He loved this house too much, and would never have endangered its good name by doing something so foolish. Certainly his obligation to the heritage of Eta Chi outweighed his proclivities. He knew with certitude that all of his brothers shared this viewpoint. Ironically, Stoobie would graduate unaware that another brother had already done what he found unthinkable. And ten years later, when he died from complications due to acquired immune deficiency syndrome – a disease unknown as he lay on the rug with his brothers – he would still have been chagrined to learn this. For the moment, though, Stoobie simply basked in the comfort and rapport of his brotherhood, secure in the knowledge that his secret was obviously safe.

While many brothers tired of winter's long reach into March, few were as irritated as Danny Carvello. Motile by nature, Danny was obnoxiously restless for the passions of Spring. He had put up with enough of sitting indoors, and as he looked around his tiny room, even his belongings grated on his nerves. Everything looked old and dusty and worthless. He stared at the clutter of odds and ends on his desk, until he finally picked a few up, opened his window, and threw them as far as he could into the woods below. The fresh, cold air in his room and the cathartic sensation of throwing things combined to lift his spirits, and he began to look around for other things to throw out.

There was an old, beaten chair that he had lugged around with him for years, and it suddenly gave up its ghost to his petulant irritation. The only problem was that the chair was too large to fit through the window. Danny looked around the room for something else to launch out the window, but his glance returned to the chair. It was not enough to simply throw the ugly thing away. He wanted to launch it into the abyss of woods behind the house.

Danny walked over to the sophomore corridor where one of the rooms had a fire exit onto a small roof above the kitchen alcove. He smiled as he walked into the room and examined the roof. It was flat, and big enough to stand on and throw the chair. He propped open the door and walked back to his room whistling. The chair was easy enough to drag through the hall, but he would need someone to help him launch it, so he yelled down the sophomore corridor and found a few boys who came to help as gleeful puzzlement rushed across their faces.

Danny got three of the boys out on the roof with him and the chair, told them to each grab a corner, and count to three with him. The boys instinctively began to swing the old chair back and forth and they each rhythmically shouted out the numbers. The chair flew out of their hands as they shouted THREEE! and sailed about ten yards before it hurtled downward. Its initial landing disappointed Danny, but then it took a fortuitous bounce further down into the grove and disappeared behind an ancient oak. They all cheered.

Danny immediately asked them what else they wanted to launch. He told them this was an Eta Chi tradition to make the winter go away. Find stuff in your rooms, he urged, stuff nobody in their right mind would want, and let'er rip! The boys laughed, and ran back inside to look for things to launch. Soon boys were ceremoniously throwing old boxes and textbooks, broken clock radios and sneakers off into the woods. Danny chided them for their lack of imagination. You need to be more creative! He ordered. Then he walked off whistling, pleased with his assault on the freezing weather. Two days later the weather broke, and the sophomores shook their heads in amazement. The Eta Chi tradition worked!

The March thaw was not all that extreme – the sun shined brightly and the days warmed up into the forties, but the contrast made it seem like summer to the boys on Cayuga Heights Road. As the snow softened and melted, walks to campus became noisier and more relaxed in the crisp, fresh air. Midday, the Arts Quad filled with students between classes, lingering in the sunshine and chatting loudly as snowballs whizzed by.

George Muirfield and Danny Carvello met each other heading out the door for class. It was after nine in the morning as they walked to campus. The sun glinted off the thousands of clear sleeves of ice that wrapped tree branches in the deep glen to their right. They talked about the identity of Brother Thief, as they had come to call the brother they suspected of stealing Hank Broussard's checks.

At long last, the police had reported to George that their handwriting expert could not positively identify the writing on the cashed check with

the signatures the fraternity had provided them. There were three signatures that came close, said the tall, overweight officer who sat with the
consul in the fraternity library one morning. But we can't even be positive
that it was one of those three.

George looked intensely at the man, listening for some solution to the
problem. The policeman didn't have one. George noticed the perspiration
circles under the man's arms as they examined the scrolls of brothers'
signatures. He couldn't fathom why the policeman was nervous, but it
made him feel sorry for him. Maybe this whole handwriting thing was out
of his league. George asked how else they might prove who did this, and
the man shook his head. As his neck moved back and forth, George
watched the skin on his neck rub against his collar. His collar was too
tight.

Without additional evidence...you know, like an eyewitness or an
admission or something, I am afraid that there is nothing further we can
do. The policeman hunched his shoulders forward to put his clipboard on
the table next to the couch they sat on, and George saw the man's pants
pull tight against his thighs. His pants stayed tight when he sat back.
George told him they didn't have any eyewitnesses, and no one had come
forward. They nodded to each other.

You still think that it's the person we told you, right? George asked
knowingly. We just can't prove it.

The policeman nodded and shrugged. Be careful, he said. If you make
accusations you can't prove, some people will get mad enough to sue you.
And the police department can't help you out. Then it was George's turn
to shrug.

On their way up to campus, Danny was far less accommodating. In
fact, he was apoplectic. We know who did it, George!

George said he knew, but what were they supposed to do? The boy
they suspected was a senior, who had been identified by others as the
most probable source of petty theft from their rooms over the last couple
of years. A few dollars here, a few dollars there. Even a couple of record
albums. Nobody thought they could prove it, which is why they had never
come forward before. One boy had seen the senior in question wandering
out of someone's room during dinner, when he had no reason to be in
there, but there was no proof he had actually taken anything. His was one
of the three signatures the police had concluded could be a match, but that
was certainly not enough to make anything stick.

He's a scumbag! Danny said bitterly. George had never found the
senior to be all that likeable, though he certainly had friends in the house.
There was something insincere or callous about him. But George didn't
want to believe that any brother living amongst them would do what this
boy had done. Above all else, though, it was the smarmy way that he pro-
fessed his love for the house that got under George's skin.

He's a two-faced, lying pimp of a scumbag! George retorted.

There are some people, Danny said, so worthless and so disgustingly deceitful that it's hard to believe that they can get through their lives. Brother Thief is a perfect example of the shit heads we have to spend the rest of lives avoiding. The two boys shook their heads in agreement. Maybe, Danny said scornfully, we can convene a special meeting of the brotherhood and flog the son of a bitch.

They laughed together as they reached the suspension bridge and stopped for a moment to watch the water rushing far beneath them. Danny asked George what he was going to do after graduation. The slick, gray faces of the beveled, slate walls on either side of the gorge glistened with moisture in the bright sun. It's time to move on and do something, George said to the water. Then he looked at his friend. They had both applied to graduate schools. But both were a little ambivalent about going. It just seemed like the natural order of progression.

Danny clapped George on the shoulder, and they headed up the steep cement steps to the Arts Quad. You know what I dislike even more than homosexuals? Danny asked. George said he didn't have a clue.

Fat girls, Danny said emphatically. George protested. I can see why you may not like fat girls, but what is so particularly abhorrent about them?

There's no excuse for a girl being a beached whale, Danny said. I think homosexuals can't help themselves. George told his friend he was out of his mind. Of course I am, Danny answered, and I am in excellent company! By now the two boys walked diagonally across the quad toward Goldwynn Smith Hall. Look at them! Danny said excitedly as he left George at the door to the building. Beached whales all over the quad! I wish I had a harpoon! George told his friend he would see him at Wines, and headed inside.

George almost skipped the lecture at the Andrew Dixon White House in the afternoon. It was such a glorious day he wanted to just fool around until it was time for Wines, but his conscience made him go. His curiosity had been piqued by the occupation of the visiting lecturer. He was a former Minister of Disinformation in Yugoslavia. Whatever that was. He arrived at ten to three and walked up the middle of the aisle between large, comfortable chairs that were arranged for the lecture. The Andrew Dixon White House, which was reserved for the University President and visiting dignitaries, was suitably formal and lushly decorated. The house stood at the top of a bluff looking down over a corner of the Arts Quad in the center of campus.

George took an aisle seat to his right, and noticed a petite girl with black hair sitting opposite him on the left. She smiled at him as he took his coat off and hung it off the back of the large chair. George smiled back, and said hello. The chairs were upholstered in the university's trademark red, and had thick, sculpted dowels for side arms. The side arms were stained mahogany.

The lecturer was introduced, and George settled in to hear the man's story. He spoke emotionally about his role in the apparatchik of the Soviet Union. It was his job as the Minister of Disinformation for Yugoslavia, to take news sent to him from Moscow, and rewrite it consistent with the doctrinaire manner he had been taught, for release as news in his country. He had been proud of his important role in the fight against western imperialism until he discovered one day that the news items he received daily were already the product of "disinformation." He was creating disinformation from disinformation. He had been aghast at his discovery. Where, he asked the audience, did the lies end? What could he know to be real, when someone in his preferred status – a party insider and a loyal communist – was consistently being lied to by his superiors?

George was engrossed by the images depicted by the man as he struggled with his identity and his worries about his family, and his circuitous route to defection. He looked around the room to see if others were as intent as he was, and his eyes came to rest on the girl sitting opposite him. She looked at him out of the corner of her eyes, smiling. Her right hand was stroking the side arm of her chair in a rhythmic pattern. At first George thought that she was simply rubbing the arm mindlessly as she listened, but her look told him something else all together. He stopped listening to the lecturer, and began to keenly observe with subtle glances the girl's hand motion. There could be no mistaking what she was doing.

To convince himself that this was what he suspected, George casually rubbed the arm of his own chair up and down once. The girl across from him smiled more, and slightly increased her stroke. George looked straight ahead, thought about going to Wines later, and wondered if the girl was a senior. He had never seen her before, but that meant nothing. He tried casually to take in everything about her. She was extremely short, but of medium build. Medium length black hair was pushed back off her shoulders, revealing a pointy chin, and the sauciest grin he had ever seen.

The girl stopped stroking her chair arm and sat demurely listening to the lecturer conclude his remarks and answer questions. The room applauded, and as people rose to leave, George reached across and stuck out his hand. George Muirfield, he said pleasantly.

Gail Mahoney, the girl replied. There was a beguiling nonchalance to her manner, as if she really wasn't sure why he was introducing himself. You don't happen to be going to Wines, do you? George asked hopefully.

Gail Mahoney said she didn't know what he was talking about. George explained what he meant, and she said she was just a freshman. She knew nothing about that class. George nodded, and asked her if she liked wine. Gail said she did. Perhaps we could share a bottle sometime, George said. Gail smiled brightly. She thought that sounded like an outstanding idea. George looked at his watch, and said he needed to get going.

Gail said okay, but stood very still, gazing at him. George asked her if she might be free for dinner. He explained about date night at Eta Chi. I could meet you after wines, and we could pick up a bottle on the way, he offered. She said that sounded like fun. All he could picture in his mind was her hand on that chair. Gail grinned and asked where she should meet him, and he said he would meet her right here, outside, at five thirty.

George headed off quickly to the Statler building. He knew he had just put himself in a pickle, because Betsy and he sat together in Wines, and she usually went to date night with him afterwards. But the urge had been irresistible. It was the warmth and early beckoning of Spring in the air, and the outrageously provocative gestures that Gail Mahoney had made in the lecture. Whatever it was, he had gone with it. Everything would work itself out somehow.

In the Statler Auditorium, the five- to six- hundred students were particularly boisterous as they took their seats in preparation for class. Percival Lee was in rare form on the stage, his rotund girth assuming a larger than life presence as he barked instructions to his graduate students. This was Percival Lee's favorite moment of the week, when he could expound in his booming voice to hundreds of thirsty students on the character and origins and key details of wines from around the world.

Students were served the wines in plastic cups carried on large trays by teacher's assistants whom Percival always called "Sommeliers." When he called out to them to dispense the French cabernet, or the Australian Chirac, or the Italian Chianti, he would elongate the word as it rolled off his tongue. Sooohh – muuuh – yayssss! he would exclaim in his deepest baritone, Now the Chirac! The students would toast each other, and drink the wine in their cup quickly so that the sommeliers would finish off the bottles in their cups.

George sat next to Betsy, surrounded by Eta Chis and their girl friends. Holly Menard sat with them, as did Martha Higgins and Mitsy Smith. Danny and Janette Emilio and Fritz and Jane Quissling sat behind George, talking softly as Percival ranted about the proper way to decant, or the incorrect assumptions about how to read labels from Italy, or the like. Betsy leaned against him, and clinked her plastic cup against his and told George she wasn't coming to date night this evening. George looked neutrally at her, and said, Okay. She said she'd be in the library working on a paper if he wanted to swing by later. He said he might, but thought immediately of Gail Mahoney.

Wines ended and the Eta Chis insisted that all of the girls around them come to dinner with them. Betsy grimaced, and George could see her debating, but she held her ground and said she couldn't. The rest of the girls asked if there would be more wine, and the boys promised additional libations of all sorts. Betsy kissed George on the cheek and told him to be good, and picked up her books and left. Danny had his arm around Janette, and his eyes glowed with pride. The group headed off together, while George held back and then left through a different door. He waited to be sure they would not call after him, and then walked swiftly to the Andrew Dixon White House to look for Gail Mahoney.

Gail waited outside the building and George waved to her as he approached. She said she had been worried that he wouldn't show, and George smiled. She looked different and even shorter than he recalled. As they walked to the house, George told her that he might have to substitute vodka for wine, and Gail snorted. He asked her if she liked Black Russians, and she answered that she didn't know. Oh, then you do, he replied. Trust me.

The sweet, black cocktail had become a favorite between him and Betsy, and he knew he had the makings in his room. On their way, the two swapped stories about themselves, and when they looked at each other, George felt a rush of adrenaline every time she squinted her eyes toward him. It wasn't that George found Gail attractive. Her body was compact and solid, and her face was pleasant but not really distinctive. But she radiated a sexuality that George absorbed from her eyes and even the simple way the girl thrust her hips as she walked.

They reached Eta Chi and George escorted her up to his room, where he put music on and made them drinks. The senior hall was alive with boys and girls, and Fritz and Jane soon stood at George's door with glasses of wine in their hands. George introduced Gail and Stoobie appeared over Fritz's shoulder asking if anyone cared for a glass of sherry. Frank Sinatra started blaring from Harold's room. Dinner was in fifteen minutes, and George told his date they could come back up after dinner to have a second cocktail.

Down the hall, beyond the stairway to the first floor, Janette Emilio was lying on Danny Carvello's bed, kissing her boyfriend passionately. Danny was consumed by her, and they moved quickly to remove their clothes as the footfalls in the hallway announced that dinner was about to be served. They had finally made love for the first time the weekend before, and this was the first time they had reunited. Danny cracked jokes to his girlfriend as they huddled together under his sheets, and the hallways became quiet. Janette stared at Danny with an intense longing as his hands found their way across her slight frame. The wine in class had given them both a slight blush, and they looked openly at each other as their bodies warmed together in the cool room.

It had been such a long road to this point, filled with romance and Janette's testing of Danny's fidelity. Danny would tell her later, in the middle of the night as they lay awake and spoke softly that she was the first girl he ever loved. Janette pulled him against her fiercely, wrapping her arms around his head, trying to mesh her body into his. From the beginning, he had been so different than his reputation. So upright, so even, so genuine with her. The girls she told about their relationship didn't believe her, but no one disputed his devotion to her. And for every zany, irreverent stunt he pulled, there was a private, intensely serious facet to his character that she guessed she alone was privy to. She loved Danny Carvello, and she was scared to death about what would happen when they graduated. But now was not the time to tell him that. Now was the time to love him.

At dinner, George and Gail sat with Harold Wise and Martha Higgins, and some juniors and sophomores without dates. George had tried to avoid their table, but Harold beckoned him jovially, and it would have seemed out of place for them to sit elsewhere. Martha scrutinized Gail carefully, and George knew that she was absorbing every nuance between them to report back to Betsy at their sorority. Gail was funny and lively during dinner, asking Martha questions about Delta Gamma Nu, and smiling devilishly at Harold when he made the table laugh. George had to resist the impulse to put his arm on the back of his date's chair.

After dinner the upstairs hallway was even livelier than before dinner. The warm air had put everyone in a great mood, and the senior hallway was soon clogged with couples drinking Black Russians. Bottles of vodka appeared in boys' hands, while George supplied the Kahlua. By eight p.m., the laughter was loud and music blared from a number of rooms. George looked at Gail who sat on his bed, about three feet from him. She was having a good time, talking to Martha Higgins who was on her third cocktail. He wondered if they would ever get to be alone, but could not tell if she was thinking along the same lines. She had an impenetrable caste to her face, but her eyes sparkled when she glanced in his direction.

Martha asked if George could take her to the bathroom, and he rose to extend his arm to her in a formal way. She giggled and put her arm on his, and told Gail they'd be right back. Gail was already laughing with Jane Quissling and Fritz about the garish lights revolving in Stoobie's room, and barely looked up. In the hallway, George told Martha they should go up to the third floor bathroom, where she could have more privacy. They walked up the back stairwell between George's and Stoobie's room and down the hallway to the bathroom. Martha's arm was still on his and George realized she was drunker than he thought.

George opened the door and confirmed that the room was empty, and told Martha he would wait outside for her. She kissed his cheek sloppily. Her hair, heavily teased to the point it felt dry against his skin, tickled his ear. Martha was an imposing woman, and George mused about how boys were so attracted to her. She was at least five seven, with a full and substantial figure, and her huge hair swirled around a wide face with dramatic features. Everything about Martha Higgins seemed outsized, and she had a personality to match. He heard her flush the toilet and waited for awhile longer, but she did not emerge from the bathroom.

George knocked on the door, and he heard Martha say, Yeah? in a soft voice. He poked his head in a little, and asked if she was okay. He saw her standing with her hands on the sink, staring into the mirror. Mascara ran down her cheeks, and she dabbed at the black streaks with a wet, brown paper towel. George approached her, and put his hand on her shoulder, asking her if she was okay. Martha was not the sort of woman George could picture crying easily.

Martha rubbed the mascara off her face, and sobbed anew. She turned to George and put her arms around his head, crushing her head against his left shoulder. Her hair covered the bottom half of his face, up to his nose. He wrapped his arms around her and told her he was right there. What was upsetting her? She pulled herself away, and looked up into George's eyes, almost as if she was about to kiss him. But she didn't, and put her head back against his shoulder more gently, telling him he was a good person.

George stood quietly rubbing his hand up and down her back, trying to soothe the girl. He tried to picture himself with Martha, and couldn't. He felt slightly unsteady as she rocked a little against him, and he realized he was feeling the Black Russians too. First Gail, and now this. This day was clearly getting out of hand. George asked the woman leaning against him if she wanted to talk about it.

About what? Martha asked quickly. Her bloodshot eyes peered at him accusingly.

About whatever is making you cry, he said softly.

Martha patted George's shoulder. Find some place that's private and I will tell you. Martha said in a tiny voice.

George looked around the bathroom. This is as quiet a place as we are going to find, Martha. Here, sit in here with me. He led her to the shower stall and swept open the old yellow curtain, with a flourish. Martha laughed in spite of herself. You want me to sit in the shower with you? she asked incredulously. George said, Of course! He had no idea why this had occurred to him. Maybe he was drunker than he thought. He licked his lips and tasted the Kahlua as he plunked himself down on the shower floor. Look, he said, it's not even wet!

Martha sighed and slumped to the floor, against the wall opposite him. Her legs stuck out across his and he rested his hands on her legs and said, Spill.

Martha stared up at the light in the stall, and her eyes welled up again. You are a good person, George, she said.

George nodded. We've established that, he said lightly, so tell me what's awful enough in this world of ours to make you cry. Someone entered the bathroom, and George immediately put his finger to his mouth. Martha pursed her lips in a smile, and then put her hand on her mouth as they listened to a boy urinate in the toilet, flush and leave.

I wish we could stand while we pee, Martha said when he was gone.

Now I see what's got you so down! George offered teasingly.

Men will never understand, Martha replied. They don't have the equipment. Her face had darkened, and her tone of voice grew serious.

She stared at George for several moments, and George could feel the liquor running around in her brain. Finally she asked him if he could keep a secret. A really bad secret.

George said he was quite proficient at that.

I had to have an abortion, Martha said simply. She looked down at her lap as she said the words. Then she looked levelly at George. It sounds so simple, doesn't it? Well it isn't, George. It's a fucking nightmare that I can't get rid of. First to be so stupid as to get pregnant (the word struggled to come out of her mouth), and then to do that! I am a horrible person, George. And there is nothing I can do about it.

George tried to remember the name of the girl from freshman biology who had spent that afternoon in the Straight with him, telling him about her abortion. He asked Martha if this had just happened.

No! Why, George? Are you trying to figure out who the father is? What would make you ask that question?

George recoiled from the vehemence of her voice. He told her that he was simply trying to understand how new this was for her.

Martha shook her head rapidly, as if to shake the notion out of her mind. It happened about a year and a half ago, she said. She spit the words out of her mouth.

George paused, waiting for the emotion in her to subside a little. He wondered what it was about him that made girls want to confess their abortions to him. It wasn't just that girl at the Straight and Martha. Althea had told him about three friends of hers that had gotten abortions during college. He was beginning to think that most of the girls at college got one somewhere along the way.

Listen, he finally said, you are not a horrible person. Martha burst into tears. She rubbed her sweater against her nose, sniffling. In fact, George said, most of the girls I know have gotten abortions.

It wasn't true of course, but in his own inebriated state, it was the best shorthand he could devise to give her a balanced picture of her confession. Martha looked at him hesitatingly.

What do you mean? she asked. The red blush to her cheeks began to fade unevenly, making her skin blotchy.

I mean, George said, that many girls have told me that they have had abortions. I am sure that it was the right thing for you to do under whatever circumstances you found yourself in. You are not horrible because you got pregnant, and you are not horrible because you got yourself unpregnant.

God, that sounds stupid, Martha said. Don't you see that inside of me I had a person? You don't get it. Here, let me help you...I had another George Muirfield inside me. See what I mean? I made a decision that has *changed* me, that has changed my own fate, and the fate of another person. And you act like it's the same as falling off a bike and having to put a band aid on a cut. Martha's face was flushed. She looked spent.

Right then, Harold Wise entered the bathroom, saying HELLO! in a big voice. ANYBODY HOME?

George called out that they were in the shower stall.

WHHATTT? Harold boomed accusingly. Room? Are you decent?

Oh, for Chrissakes, Harold! George replied. He pushed open the curtain that he had closed to give Martha a feeling of privacy. Harold stood at the opening, nodding as he checked the two of them out. He rubbed his belly as he chuckled. What's going on? Are you two showering together?

Martha said it was obvious they were not showering together. Harold said, All right, all right. Hmmm. What am I supposed to tell your date, Room? She's downstairs wondering what the hell happened to you! The two boys grinned at each other.

George said they would be down in a minute, and Harold kept muttering Oh my god, Oh my god, as he left.

George turned back to Martha and assured her that her destiny drove her to do what she did. She was obviously not supposed to have a baby yet. Martha sniffed.

So you think what I did was meant to happen, or what? What are you saying? George's words didn't make sense to her. Unfortunately, they confused him, too. The Black Russians made the whole thing awfully hazy.

Martha struggled to her feet, and when George followed her, she wrapped her arms around him and gave him an enormous bear hug. Then she put her lips close to his, and told him he was a very good person. Their eyes were inches apart, and it was as if they were each resisting the impulse to kiss. George kissed her forehead, and said, You are a good person too, Martha. You going to be okay? She nodded and hugged him again.

George looked at the walls of the shower stall around him and squeezed her back. In the back of his mind, he linked this moment to a rapidly fleeting blur of images – his father's funeral, Caitlin's virginity, the moment in Big Kids when he and Derek stood opposite each other naked, his sister at the kitchen table saying, "Now it begins...," Danny Carvello's byzantine comment that there is no "When," only "Why." His mind played connect-the-dots with his psyche, but the image still didn't make sense.

So what's with this Gail person, Martha asked coyly. George refocused and said, I met her at a lecture today, and invited her to dinner because she'd never seen a fraternity.

I'll bet, Martha said. Come on, let's go downstairs before they think I've attacked you in the bathroom.

Too late for that, George replied, as he put his arm around her waist and guided her down the hall. But we'll have to make the best of it. The swirl in his head disappeared.

The party downstairs had broken up, and Gail Mahoney sat in Fritz's room with Fritz, Jane, Stoobie and Harold. George and Martha walked in, and Gail eyed him carefully. He didn't look guilty. And she hardly knew him. She didn't know what to think.

He really knows how to show a girl a good time, doesn't he? Harold asked her humorously. He and Stoobie now drank scotch on the rocks, and he clinked the ice cubes around in his glass as he chuckled. Martha looked at Gail, and said, I needed a friend. That was all. Gail nodded. George volunteered to drive Martha and Gail home, and the three of them stood to go. Martha insisted that she climb into the backseat, and thanked Gail again for letting her have George for a bit as they drove up to the sorority. Gail told her it was fine, really.

Gail got out of the car to let Martha out from the backseat, and Martha waved goodbye as she walked unsteadily up the front walk. George looked at his date when she was back in the car, and said he was sorry. This had not been what he expected. Gail asked him if he had dated her...or something. George smiled, and said, No. She got drunk and wanted somebody to talk to about something. I happened to be the lucky guy.

What was it about? Gail asked.

Choices we make, George replied. And the ones we think we make, but don't. He stared through the windshield, and was obviously not going to say anything more. Gail shrugged, and said she lived on West Campus. George put his car into gear and drove slowly across Triphammer Bridge to the light.

He pulled into the West Campus parking lot, and found an open space. They sat together, just as George had sat with Caitlin Fossburgher as freshmen, when he had driven them back from their first dinner at Eta Chi. He parked only a few spaces away from where they had sat. He looked at Gail and said he hoped that this hadn't ruined her evening, and Gail told him she actually had a good time. She just expected to spend more of it with him.

They laughed and as George asked how she liked the Black Russians, Gail leaned over and kissed him. Her kiss was insistent and her tongue salty. She pulled away and said she hoped he called her and hopped out of the car. He rolled down his window, and said he would need her phone number to call her, and she pranced back to his window, giggling. He handed her a pen and a scrap of paper, and she scribbled her number on it. Then she leaned back in the window and kissed him again. You taste good! she said impishly as she strutted away. George thought it a clever thing to say.

The next day, Betsy met up with George in the Straight cafeteria and raised her eyebrows in mock curiosity. Anything to tell me, honey? she asked. George said, I took an impressionable young freshman to date night and ended up in the shower stall with your sorority sister.

Betsy furled her brow. Obviously more had happened than she knew about. George invited her to sit. She sat across the lunch table from her boyfriend. She had been furious, but now felt on uncharted waters. George looked at her and extended his hand toward her. She opted not to take it in hers. Tell me first, she said.

George described meeting Gail Mahoney at the lecture. He left out the part about Gail rubbing the chair's arm. But the rest he told as best he could. He did not tell Betsy exactly how he had ended up in the shower with Martha, but he carefully described the nature of the incident, without going into any details about the topic.

Betsy shook her head. I don't care about Martha, you knucklehead. Martha said you were a gentleman and a wonderful friend. But you asked another girl to date night and you did it even before I told you I wasn't coming this week.

George acknowledged that was true.

And?

George looked carefully at his girlfriend. She looked great today, but he knew he had to be honest with her. Look, he said. It happened. I should have just told you when I saw you, but I didn't. I'm sorry. It was wrong.

Betsy was shaking. Fuck you, George. She stood up, and struggled to pull her legs out from the picnic-style seating. I can't believe you. She walked away.

George sat still, watching her disappear. He was supposed to drive her home to Connecticut this weekend, and he wondered if that was going to happen. He felt almost nothing inside. His honesty felt good on his lips, and he realized that this moment had been coming. Betsy was beginning to imagine them beyond college. He knew it even though they really didn't speak about it. It was just there in her face when she talked to him. But it wasn't in his, and now she knew that more clearly.

The warm snap, which George kept calling "Indian Spring" lasted five days. Then winter returned for another three weeks before it was banished to the past. George did not drive Betsy home that weekend. She called him up that night and said she was getting a ride from someone else. So George was actually sitting at his desk on Friday night when Wally Stimpson popped into his room with a big smile in the middle of his gaping mouth.

He handed his consul a brown manila envelope marked "Do Not Bend," saying that he had a present for him. George withdrew a black and white, eight and a half by eleven photograph of the seniors standing in the library. It was the picture that Wally had arranged on the night of the Valentine formal. The boys staring at the camera looked like something out of the forties. They were somber and stilted in their tuxedos, and even their smiles seemed constrained. Only Ronny Trillo, who had joined the picture at the last moment dressed in sweatpants and a Santa Claus hat looked lighthearted. The bottom of the picture bore the inscription, *"The Big Kids."*

George loved the picture. He slapped Wally on the shoulder and told him it was brilliant. Wally snorted happily, and said, I told you we were the Big Kids, didn't I? They laughed again. George didn't recall Wally ever saying that before, but it didn't matter. He hung the photograph on the wall above his desk, and the two boys pointed out minor details to each other. I knew you'd like it, Wally said again. George thanked him, and asked if he had handed the other copies out yet. Wally said he had handed out about half. Everyone thought it was cool.

In the last week before Spring arrived in earnest, graduate school notifications started to appear in the Eta Chi mailboxes. Danny was accepted to the Cornell Business School first. Fritz received his acceptance two days later. The first letter George received was thin, and he knew that meant bad news. Acceptances always came in large envelopes.

The following week, on the first day of spring warmth, George was admitted to the Fuqua School of business at Duke University. George loved the name of the place. He had applied to several schools, but not to Cornell. The need to go try something else was strong in him, and he found his brothers' interests in staying on at Cornell for another two years almost depressing. The next two envelopes he received in the mail were from law schools placing him on the waiting list. He had options!

The magic of Spring did not arrive all at once. First the sun and air softened and warmed the earth, tempting from slumber the seedlings and foliage. It took days before the moist, pungent smells of rebirth broke loose from the mud and brittle branches at the tops of the trees. It was always the smells that preceded anything green that caught George by surprise. It made the air fuller and sweeter and tangy. There was, at once, a heady perfumed scent and a musky, distasteful aroma in his nostrils.

The combination made George's heart soar as he walked to classes. His center spun faster, and on its edge, as he allowed his lungs to expand and fill with the limitless energy and promise of coming growth. Every early flowering tree made him dizzy as he passed by and breathed in its slight invitation to gaze at its fleeting colors. There was new urgency and joy in the gaits of students as they traversed the quads to classes. Peels of laughter rang out across the air like crashing cymbals from a distant marching band.

In the late afternoon, George walked from Goldwynn Smith to Uris Library when he ran into Harold Wise on his way back to the house. George asked his brother about that new girl he was dating, and Harold guffawed good-naturedly.

Remember a couple of days back when I went out for a jog? A girl from my advanced accounting class had leaned out the window of a house and waved hello. So I stopped and started talking to her. The next thing I know, she wants me to come upstairs.

Get out of here! George said.

I'm not kidding Room! Before I knew it, we were lying on her bed, and she's pulling my sweat suit off!

George shook his head in disbelief. It had been the perfect antidote for Harold who was suffering from his breakup with Barbara Huston. George asked Harold what her name was, and Harold said he didn't know. They roared laughing together. Then Harold said, No, I'm just kidding. Her name is Delores. Delores Tecklenberg. And she's a very nice girl. A *very* nice girl! The two laughed again.

Across the Arts Quad, they turned to hear two boys yelling something incomprehensible. It sounded like a long imitation of a trombone's wail. In the distance they could barely make out the boys making the sound, standing at the edge of the quad with their fists cupped against their mouths.

I think that's Danny Carvello! Harold exclaimed. What the hell is he doing?

George didn't have a clue. But after a minute, Danny approached, and Harold asked him what the hell he was yelling at the other end of the quad. Danny smiled to the sophomore with him, but turned serious and said that he was performing a public service for all Eta Chis on the Arts Quad. The sophomore broke into hysterics.

Whenever we see a beached whale, we sound the alarm, Danny explained, nodding his head. Then he broke up laughing. George asked him if he was just making a bizarre sound, and Danny frowned. No, I am yelling, "Beeeeeaaachhhhedwwwhhhallle!" Harold shook his head disapprovingly. He often thought Danny went too far. George told him he sounded like a humpback whale when he yelled like that. Perfect! Danny replied. I hope it's not a mating call!

Danny and the sophomore headed off toward College Town and Harold asked George about that new girl he had brought to date night recently. George shrugged. He had not called her, even though Betsy had broken up with him over the incident. He asked Harold if Marriott had told him yet where his first rotation was going to be. Harold had accepted an offer with Marriott to enter their management training program.

They told me it was probably New York City, which is fine with me. I'm excited to get going and start working. Did you hear about Stoobie? George had not heard.

He's going with Intercontinental to Khartoum, The Sudan!

You're kidding! Where the hell is that? Harold wasn't sure.

The two parted, and George walked into the library and headed for the stacks where he had studied lately. He loved how quiet they were, and how he could feel rather than hear the hum of activity in the main reading room below him. He opened his books and was soon lost in the research for his writing project. It was Friday, but George was intent on putting traction to his project before the end of the term got too near.

At ten p.m., he finally pushed back away from the desk, and rubbed his neck. The paper was starting to fall together in his head, and he was excited about his idea. He bet the professor would love it. He threw his books into his bag and uncrinked his neck as he walked slowly down the stairs and out into the night. He felt in his pants to see how much money he had, and counted fifteen dollars. More than enough to buy beers in College Town, and still have money left for the weekend. He flung his books on his back and strolled past the Straight, over the little gorge to the intersection where the lights of the Uni Deli shined through the plate glass windows.

He crossed the street to get to the side where the bars were, and tried to decide which one to enter. He was likely to find Eta Chis at just about any of the bars except The Palms. The French Connection's neon lights and half curtains turned him off for some reason, so he continued on to the Nines. He usually found the Nines too jocular, but the Spring air energized him. He wanted an onslaught of people and voices, and the Nines fit that bill. Once inside, he looked for Eta Chis and found a group standing in the rear.

The bartenders kept ringing the cowbell that hung from the top rail of the fire engine every time they got a decent tip, and people cheered for the hell of it when it rang. George bought himself a Rolling Rock and hung around with the Eta Chis for awhile, but they were already on their fourth or fifth beer, and content to just stand around, watching the room. The Spring's renewal fizzled inside of him like a toy sparkler, and he wanted something new and different to happen.

It took him several minutes to get through the line of people standing four deep, but he got lucky when a group in front of him decided to leave for the Chapter House. He asked for another Rolling Rock and then told the bartender to make it a boilermaker. People on either side of him unintentionally squeezed him in, so he kept his elbows close to his sides, and drank the shot of whiskey quickly when the bartender poured it. He turned sideways as he leisurely drank the beer, looking toward the front door to see who walked in. If he didn't find someone interesting by the end of his beer, he'd head out.

Cullen Hastings and a number of the pledges walked in the door and George waved to them. Behind Cullen, George saw Danny Carvello leaving with Janette Emilio, and he was sorry he had not seen them earlier. Two girls he remembered from Eta Chi's last sorority raid walked in next, but neither one of them was very interesting. He was so intent watching the door that he failed to notice that the people next to him at the bar, to his back, had changed over.

Gee, George, are you purposely ignoring us? George turned to look directly at Holly Menard who was crammed into the bar inches from him. He said Hello! in a big voice. Her boyfriend, the assistant coach, was at her side, and stuck out his hand to George. As George took his hand he saw Althea Redmonton behind Holly. Althea was in the process of turning around and saw him at the same moment. As she turned in the tight little space she occupied, she laughed gaily with her companion, a man who looked like he could bench press George with one arm. The man smiled pleasantly and nodded at George. George did the same. The pang in his stomach was instantaneous.

Holly asked Althea's companion something, and he turned to her to answer. George thought it was almost as if she wanted the two to have a moment to themselves. Althea and George just looked at each other, and for a fraction of an instant, their eyes collided and opened up and swallowed each other whole. George wished he were outside breathing the clean night air. He wished he had left before he had seen her. But his internal gyro splashed around, and he couldn't have moved if he wanted to.

So, do you two know each other? Althea's companion asked lightly. George turned to him and shook his hand as he introduced himself. Yes, we do. I'm George Muirfield. Althea's an old friend of mine.

Althea had been fine, if unprepared, to see George. She was even okay with the incredible rush she felt as they gazed into and through each other. She knew that was something that would never change between them. And they absolutely had done the right thing last fall. But when George described her as an old friend, she looked down at her shoes and did a quick intake of breath. She should have been pleased that George was carrying on so nicely with Dick, but instead it made her dizzy. And even worse, she knew instinctively that George experienced every nuance of emotion that ran through her. The conduit that seemed always suspended between them fed him every change in her pulse. And her, his. She felt him reeling inside. And she loved it.

She looked up, and George smiled at her in such a way that Dick would never suspect the electric rapids flowing back and forth between them. He turned away, and asked Holly softly if she was ready for the morning raid that Eta Chi had promised Kappa. It was coming next Friday, but she was not to tell anyone about it. Holly beamed at him, and said she'd be there. George nodded in approval, and turned to each of the men and told them it was nice to meet them. They shook hands, and George turned in Althea's direction to leave. He winked at her quickly and was gone.

Althea looked hopelessly to her friend, and Holly smiled. Dick wasn't really her type anyway. And even if he was, running into George on their first date was really bad karma. Timing, she noted to herself, really is everything. Holly asked Althea if she wanted to go to the bathroom, and the two girls walked off together. So? Holly asked. Althea said she wanted a cigarette, and the two of them burst out laughing. Althea hadn't smoked since the day she and George broke up. I think you should sleep over at the house next Thursday night, Holly said innocently. It's been awhile since you have.

Althea looked puzzled. Trust me, Althea. And bring your make up.

CHAPTER TWENTY-FIVE

The cool morning air slipped through the two-inch crack in his window, and George kept the edge of his bedcovers pulled tight around his neck. He left the window open since the warm weather had arrived, and loved waking to its chill under the warm covers. The morning light was up when his alarm switched on and he reached over to hit the snooze button. He turned on his side and closed his eyes, but then suddenly awoke and jumped up to get going. It was Friday morning, and the house was raiding Kappa in twenty minutes.

This was Eta Chi's third early morning raid and the first two had been highlights of the semester so far. George walked quickly to the bathroom, where a number of boys were already shaving. They greeted him pleasantly, and he threw his shaving kit on the edge of the only open sink and started lathering his face. The linoleum was cold on his feet, but the warm moisture emanating from the locker shower gave the room an artificial sense of warmth.

He hustled back to his room, threw on corduroys and a plaid shirt, and half-heartedly pushed a brush across his hair. He knew the girls at Kappa, and wasn't really enthusiastic about any he could think of. His chance encounter with Althea the prior weekend had only made him more sure of himself. He was glad to be free of Betsy. Somewhere there were other Altheas in the world, but he couldn't think of any at Kappa.

The boys standing in the foyer were eager to get going. Eta Chi had always had a great time socializing with Kappa, and this was their first real social event with them since the beginning of the year. It was time.

At five fifteen, the boys headed out to their cars with hoots and hollers, and drove convoy-style up the short distance to the sorority. They parked all along Thurston Avenue, careful not to park directly in front of the house, and walked swiftly to the driveway on the side of the house. George had told them they were going in the back way. He did not tell them that he wanted to reenact the way that he had sneaked into the sorority as a freshman, but he knew the memory of it would excite the boys who had been with him that night.

The same window was unlocked, and George made one of the juniors step into his cupped hands as he hoisted him through to unlock the door to the kitchen. The boys filed in through the kitchen. Harold was chuckling loudly about the last time they had done this, and he high-fived George in the pantry. Then Danny waved them quietly into the living room, hummed for a prolonged time off-key, and signaled for them to start the Darling Song.

Upstairs, there was a rush of feet, and laughter, and as the boys finished the song, girls were already coming down the stairs. The first four girls looked like they were ready to go out on a date, and George whispered, "Surprise, surprise" to Danny. Danny said, Be still my freaking heart! and waltzed up to the first girl and bowed ceremoniously. The Spinners started singing *Mighty, Mighty Love* on the boom box and the party was underway. Harold graciously served milk punches from an enormous punch bowl, promising the girls that it was only lightly spiked. Stoobie poured champagne into wineglasses filled halfway with orange juice.

George helped two boys carry additional cases of glassware from their cars into the dining room where the social chairs had set up a serving space. So he didn't see Holly and Althea walk expectantly down the stairs. Holly was in her bathrobe, but her hair was pulled back and freshly brushed. Althea wore blue jeans and a white, cabled sweater. She was shoeless, and bright red socks poked out from the cuff of her jeans. Fritz Hublein moved immediately up to the two girls and welcomed them to the morning bash. He asked Holly for a dance, and she smiled at Althea as she moved off into the middle of the floor where the room swayed.

Althea kept to the perimeter of the room, and wandered into the dining room, where she saw George with his back to her. He was taking glasses out of the gray plastic cases and setting them up on the long dining room table. As he worked, he talked to Cullen and a junior who worked alongside him. Then Cullen saw Althea and his face lit up. Heyyy! he boomed.

George turned to see who Cullen was speaking to, and froze in place. The first thing Althea saw was his hair sticking out off one side of his head, and she giggled. Her shoulders were moving forward and back rapidly and her lips were pursed in a joyous grin that made George melt. Someone had switched the music to Orleans' *Dance With Me* which drowned out Althea's voice as she said, Hi George!

George recovered, smiled, and took her hand to pull her out in the middle of the living room to dance. Cullen beamed as he watched them together. He couldn't think of a better way to start off initiation weekend than to have this party in the morning and see George reunite with his favorite coed. The floor was crowded as George and Althea swirled and bumped to the music. People laughed and bopped around them with drinks in their hands, and Holly and Fritz did the hustle right next to them.

Good morning George! Holly yelled. She smiled widely, and winked at Althea as Fritz moved her around. A buzzing lightness fluttered through George's body, and every time he exchanged looks with Althea they drank each other in with an uncontrolled ferocity. But they barely touched and did not really speak until they had danced to four songs. The fourth song was slow, and they held each other tightly as they moved imperceptibly to the music.

Hi, George finally said to her when they stopped for a milk punch. You can't believe how much I have missed you. His words were soft, and Althea immediately pulled herself up to his face, and kissed him lightly. George heard the words, Me too, as the sensation of her lips brought sunken recollections surging to the front of his brain. They both took gulps of their punch, and laughed as they realized they had done the same thing.

What are you doing today? George asked her. Althea just smiled and shrugged, and the two of them took more gulps of the sweetly potent drink. Danny bopped up next to them, and smiled brightly when he saw the two of them together. He's been miserable without you, Althea! Don't let him tell you otherwise, Danny instructed. Althea said she didn't believe that. George told Danny to go pick on someone his own size. Danny's feet had never stopped tapping to the music, and he strutted off shaking his shoulders.

At eight, Stoobie clanged a fork on a wineglass and announced that the party was suspended until happy hour. He stood on the third step of the main staircase, in a black turtleneck and gray slacks. He acted more like an English butler than a drunken fraternity brother, and when he heard grumbling he raised his voice, and yelled, Onward to Classes!

George didn't think he had had all that much to drink, but he felt inebriated. After the brothers had cleaned up and packed the party equipment, they headed out with Kappa's to class. George and Althea strolled toward campus. The sun peeked through the clouds, promising a warmer afternoon, but for now the air was still in the high thirties. They stopped and looked over the Triphammer Bridge at the water rushing down the gorge. Althea spread her hands over the stone side to lean over for a better look. George watched her feet lift slightly off the ground, took in her white sweater pressed against the wall, and then followed her example. Neither of them was quite sure what to do, but they knew that they were going to spend the day together.

How about a picnic? he finally asked. Althea frowned.

Really? she asked. She didn't know what to expect, but this hadn't been one of her alternatives. She took his hand and they kept walking onto campus, walking slowly between the theater arts building and the school of architecture.

Are we back together? she asked softly. His offer of a picnic had made her stomach turn. Maybe he wanted to politely tell her this wasn't a good idea.

He stopped and turned to her. How could we not be? he replied. I haven't had so many butterflies since the first day I met you.

Althea snuggled against him, and they walked down the side of the quad clinging to each other. A picnic, she said, is a splendid idea.

George steered them around and pulled Althea in the direction of the suspension bridge. He realized suddenly that he had never kissed a girl there. He asked Althea if she had ever been kissed on the suspension bridge. As soon as the words came out, he thought he had made a mistake, but she smiled and said she had never kissed anybody on the suspension bridge.

The two held hands as they climbed down the concrete steps, and stopped midway on the bridge. George pointed to the grassy knoll on the far side where he had first seen Matthew Stolling kissing another girl, and told Althea the story of how he went right back to the house in pursuit of her. Althea told him the story about standing in line with the Swan at the Uni Deli, and the two laughed until their eyes teared. Then they pulled each other close and kissed for a long time in the still morning.

George finally said, Come on, and they walked to Eta Chi and piled into his car. He drove them to a supermarket where they lingered over what to buy for the picnic. They settled on thick cheese and tomato sandwiches on sesame baguettes with a hot, grainy mustard in a bottle shaped like a heart. Then they picked out apples and thin chocolate wafers in a brightly colored tin. George chose a white Bordeaux he recalled from class, and Althea insisted on buying a red-checkered cloth for them to sit on.

They drove to a state park that George had seen once when he got lost, and walked for quite a while from the parking lot until they were near a small pond bordered by trees that had yet to unfurl any greenery. It had warmed up considerably, and the wine tasted wonderful in their mouths as they worked together to make the lunch. It was only eleven a.m., but they were both famished from the morning's festivities.

When they finished lunch, they lay facing each other on their sides, with their heads propped on their hands. They talked in intimate detail about who they were when they were together, and what had happened to each of them since they broke off. There was not a nuance of thought that went unnoticed or uninvestigated by the other, until they realized that the day was beginning to cool and looked at their watches. It was close to four in the afternoon. George needed to be at the house for initiation at five.

My god, Althea kidded. We're back together for a few hours and already you're leaving me.

Listen, he proposed after they had packed up and were driving back to Althea's apartment. Aside from this weekend, when I will be needed at the house most, *but not all*, of the time, I want us to spend every moment we can together. He paused. He started to ask her if that was okay, but stopped. She was turned in her seat, watching him think as he steered the car. For the first time in her life, Althea was ready to give herself wholly to someone. It was a moment she would recall at many future events in her life, when she wanted or expected to feel the same way and couldn't.

The actualization of this desire in Althea, which she knew to be in her grasp as she gazed at George struggling to find his own words to express what they both wanted, was tinged with a new, unacknowledged urgency. Each intuitively sensed the aposiopetic quality of this moment, as they swore – to themselves and each other – the complete surrender of their beings. It made almost every sentence between them poignant and charming and awkward. It was easier for them to rely upon the wordless visual conduit between their eyes.

Initiation came and went. Cullen Hastings had worked tirelessly to stage every ceremony with such passion that even the most sardonic sophomores were roused to dramatic participation and recommitment to the stated values and tenets of the brotherhood. George was able to disappear twice during the weekend, each time driving with childlike anticipation to Althea's apartment where they consummated their reunion with lighthearted joy and passion.

For the lighting ceremony, George was surprised to learn that there was really no script for him to give at the end. Each consul read over the speeches of consuls who had come before and revised the words to fit their views and circumstances. George wrote much of his own speech, with the words of his predecessors ringing in his head. When his turn came, after Danny had spoken for Achievement, Harold for Honesty, Cullen for Compassion, Rick Frye for Integrity, and Jim Steuben for Honor, George stood silently waiting for the bright beam of light to hit the prism he held before him and break into all the colors of the guiding light.

My brothers, he began as the light grew strong, *for that is what you are becoming as I speak, the guiding light that spreads from my hands is a symbol. A symbol of promise. A symbol of pride. A symbol of commitment. So much of life cannot be captured in words that we seek symbols as a way to convey key truths. We seek your commitment to this brotherhood as a gift we earn mutually between us. We value you as an individual more than as a brother. But we value our commitment to each other above all else. Consequently, you must see your commitment to the symbol of this light in the same mutual and selfless way.*

Generations of men have passed through this house, and their collective words have echoed tonight in the words and phrases of people whom I have had the privilege to know and love. Have the courage to embrace these lights, and make your experience a shining example for those who follow you. Trust what you have heard here on faith, as a gift of strength, and pride and honor which will return tenfold what you bring to it.

Step forward and bathe in the guiding light of Eta Chi...

On Sunday morning, over brunch, Harold sat quietly next to George as he spoke sincerely with new brothers about their coming contributions to the honor of the house. The pledges left, and the two seniors stayed behind for more coffee.

I'm going to New York for a few days, Harold said simply. George looked at his friend with eyebrows raised. Don't let anyone borrow my Frank Sinatra records while I'm gone. George grinned and said, Ohhhhkay. Did she call you or did you call her? It could only be Barbara Huston. Anything else he would have been more forthcoming about. Harold smiled, but was deep in thought. Both, he finally replied.

Harold returned Friday, whistling *I Did It My Way* as he jingled his car keys in one hand and carried a large suitcase that belonged to Barbara Huston in his other hand. Barbara carried a garment bag and walked in front of him. A huge smile creased her long face. They proceeded to his room, where Barbara immediately hung her garment bag and began to unpack her suitcase. Harold cleared out three drawers for her use, putting his own things on the shelf in his closet. They laughed and spoke loudly as they worked.

Fritz had been sitting at his desk when they passed his room, and walked out his door to welcome Harold back. But first, he looked both ways up and down the hallway, and sneaked into Gregory Smythe's room and shuffled the pencils that were lined up on his desk. Two of the pencils he put diagonally across a notepad that was centered on the desk, and another one he put on the floor, next to the desk, as if it had rolled off. Then he went to Harold's door.

Welcome back you two! he said in a large voice. Barbara rushed to him and kissed him on the cheek. Harold watched the two of them, smiling. ROOOMMM! He boomed. Anything happen while we were gone?

Fritz told him about the wild date night they had following Wines. Cognac had been the subject of the class, and everybody continued to sample cognac afterwards. He and George had suffered the next day for it. Barbara asked Fritz how Jane was, and Fritz said, Jane's terrific, Barb. Thanks for asking. She'll be thrilled to see you're back.

Barbara smiled and told him his "Room" could be very convincing. Fred watched them putting away her things, and said, It looks like you'll be here for some time! They all laughed. Harold said that Barb was coming up for the next three weekends so that they didn't miss a thing leading up to graduation. Barb chimed in that she made Harold promise to give her three drawers so she didn't have to pack every time.

George and Althea walked past the room and everyone said hello. George carried a garment bag and a small valise of Althea's, and went to put them away in his room as Althea kissed Barbara on the cheek and asked her how she was. Barb scolded Harold for not telling her that Althea and George were back together. Harold said you never knew how long things were going to last around here, and Althea hit him hard on the arm. Fritz suggested that, once Jane arrived, they could all run down to the Creeker and play *Here's to Eta Chi for the First Time*. George groaned, but everyone else said that was a perfect idea for the evening.

The next morning, George woke with Althea's head in his elbow, and her legs crossed over his in his narrow bed. His head ached from too much beer, and he lay still, hoping the ache would subside as he watched his girlfriend sleep. He loved the round fullness of her cheeks and strong, straight nose. Her hair smelled like cigarettes, but that only made him smile. They had managed to avoid smoking together for the whole first week, but the drinking games at the Creeker did them both in. He wondered if his headache was really due to the cigarettes, and decided he had to get some aspirin now.

He slid himself carefully out of bed, thinking he had managed to not disturb her, but as he began to leave Althea asked where he was going. She kept her eyes closed, as she turned on her side. I need aspirin, he whispered. Me too, she said, and smiled. Will you bring me some? George smiled at the image of his girlfriend curled up in bed, and said he'd be back in a minute.

When he returned with two tall glasses of water, Althea sat up and pulled the covers around her. They each popped three aspirin in their mouths, and George said Here's to Eta Chi for the first time of the morning as he handed her her glass. They both drank the water thirstily. My god, she said, what did you do to me last night?

The drinking game they had played at the Creeker involved correctly sequencing the tapping of various numbers of fingers, feet, glasses, and fannies with certain phrases in order to avoid chugging the beer in front of you. People almost always made a mistake, especially the later it went and drunker they got. Last night had been no exception.

Althea put her fingers to her temples and asked George again why they had to spend the weekend at Eta Chi. She desperately wished she could wander in the privacy of her apartment when she felt like this. But she already knew the answer. He was consul. It was important for him to be at the house, and they were going to be there most of the weekend anyway.

George avoided the question and asked if she wanted to shower. Althea yawned, and said she'd rather shower in the afternoon before the formal, and snuggled back into bed. George joined her and they fell back asleep until ten thirty. When they awoke they could hear jazz music coming through the door from Stoobie's room. They made love to the muffled pulse of Dave Brubeck's *Take Five* before they dressed and went down for lunch.

It was three p.m. before they found their way back upstairs. They followed Gregory Smythe up the stairs and stopped at his door to say hello for a minute. George asked Gregory if Daisy Lavallee was coming to the Darling formal, and Gregory smiled, and said "YUP!" in his high-pitched voice. As he answered, he rearranged the pencils on his desk so that they were ramrod straight, in line, with the tips sharpened to the same fine point. He looked around for a moment, and then picked the last pencil off the floor and added it to his line. The pencils were identical in length. He clucked absentmindedly and said his pencils had a mind of their own.

George and Althea headed off, and when they were out of earshot, George explained how they all took turns rearranging his pencils. Althea sighed and shook her head. George told her she should see him eat a hamburger, but didn't elaborate. Althea was already disrobing, and putting on a bathrobe. They had agreed that they would go up to the third floor showers before others started to get ready for the party.

George suggested they shower together...for her protection. Althea closed her eyes with feigned exasperation and told him to hurry up. So George pranced around the room, picking up two towels and his shaving kit with a big grin on his face. They walked up the back staircase, and down the deserted hallway to the bath. The entire third floor seemed deserted, which suited Althea perfectly. Inside the bathroom, Althea pulled the yellow shower curtain to the side, and said she was pleasantly surprised at how clean it was. George turned the water on, and stood in front of Althea so she could hide behind him to get naked and jump in the shower. Then he removed his clothes, hung them on a peg on the wall, and pushed his way through the curtain.

Their laughter echoed off the tiled walls in the steamy stall as they took turns wetting their heads under the stream of water. Someone rapped loudly on the bathroom door, and George poked his head out through the curtain to let whoever it was know that the facilities were temporarily off limits. He saw Harold's face in the doorway, and said Hey Room! We're taking a shower for a few minutes. Harold laughed. Well, would you mind if Barb and I did the same thing across from you? She's in a hurry to get showered before it becomes crazy. George's eyes widened, and Harold grinned. Sure, George said, the more the merrier.

He drew his head back in and looked at Althea, who shook her head in disbelief. But George told her this would be something to remember. As Harold and Barbara came in, George pressed the edge of the shower curtain along both sides of the opening for privacy. They heard the couple outside giggling as the shower started in the opposite stall and Harold said, Okay, honey, let's get inside before anything wild happens.

About thirty seconds later, Harold started singing Al Green at the top of his lungs – *Let's get it on, Let's get it on, baby...* The four of them roared laughing. George was soaping Althea's back and he joined in with Harold, which brought fresh peels of laughter.

Then Harold switched to Frank Sinatra.

Fly me to the moon and let me play among the stars
Let me see what spring is like on Jupiter and Mars
In other words, hold my hand!
In other words, darling kiss me!

Barbara yelled, Stop that Harold! which made George and Althea laugh. Then they heard Barbara say, No, not your singing, what you were doing...which made everyone, but especially Harold explode with laughter. Then George, who had heard the song so much from Harold's room that he knew it by heart, continued the song from their shower –

Fill my heart with song. And let me sing for evermore
You are all I long for, all I worship and adore
In other words, please be true!
In other words, I love you!

As he sang, George extended his left hand to Althea, put his right hand on her back, and then pressed her against him as he led her in a circular dance under the cascading water. Althea smiled and looked at her boyfriend and kissed him as he finished *I love you.* Harold and Barbara applauded, and when Harold started up again, George joined him with gusto.

Fill my heart with song. And let me sing for evermore
You are all I long for, all I worship and adore
In other words, please be true!
In other words, In other words
I love...you!

Barbara and Althea both cheered gleefully, and Harold's deep chuckle resonated throughout the room. There was a moment of silence with the water splashing on the shower floors and the steam billowing everywhere. Then Harold said, Hey Room, give me a little Barry...

George started to ask what the hell that meant, and then laughed. Okay, wait a minute, I have to get Frank out of my head. Althea looked at him curiously. She had just put shampoo on her hair, and George reached up and began to build it into a lather on the top of her head. She rubbed her hands over his chest and smiled naughtily. Then he closed his eyes and hummed to himself for a moment, and yelled to Harold that he had it.

He sang, Ba,ba,ba bummm, in rising notes, paused, and then Bum, bum, ba, ba, bum stepping down the scale. Then he started to repeat it slowly, rhythmically, over and over. Catching the rhythm, Harold started speaking in the lowest voice he could muster –

Feels so good, you standing here next to me
You have no idea how it feels
I love you baby, ohh, I love you, I love you, I love you
Just want to hold you, rub my fingers through your hair
Ohh baby, Ohhh baby

Barbara had wrapped her hands around her boyfriend's neck and was already swaying to the coming song. Harold put his arms on Barbara's hips and pulled her close against him as he started to sing,

Give it up! Ain't no use
I can't help myself if I wanted to
I'm hung up, No doubt
I'm so in love with you
For me there's no way out, because

George had continued his steady background rhythm, but when the song reached its natural crescendo, he stopped and joined Harold as they sang –

Deeper and deeper in love with you I'm falling
Sweeter and sweeter your tender words of love keep calling
Eager and eager, yeah, to feel your lips upon my face
Please her and please her, Anytime or anyplace

I'm gonna love you, love you, love you
Just a little more, baby
I'm gonna need ya, need ya, need ya
Ev-er-y day
I'm gonna want you, want you, want you
In every way

As they belted out Barry White, Althea took George in her hand and he stiffened instantly. He could barely contain himself as they finished the song. Barbara cheered again and Althea yelled, I want more! But she never let go of her boyfriend, and George said that he and Harold didn't want to get the girls too excited. Harold and Barbara laughed, and a moment later announced they were getting out. George and Althea didn't finish for a while longer.

At dinner, George escorted Althea to a table in the corner of the dining room, where they were joined by Danny and Janette Emilio, Wendall Wellington and Martha Higgins, and Rick Frye and his date for the night. The boys all wore tuxedos. Althea wore a black cocktail dress with a wide diagonal white stripe that went from her shoulder across her front. She looked radiant. After George recited the fraternity grace and they sat down, Martha Higgins was not bashful about telling Althea what a great guy she had. She said that George had helped her with something recently. George grinned. The image of sitting with her in the shower stall talking about abortion mingled in his head with this afternoon's episode. Thank god Althea was on the pill.

Everyone danced long into the night, except for Danny and Janette who disappeared upstairs at eleven. Harold, Barbara, George and Althea were all drinking scotch, and by two in the morning, Harold really wanted to go out for breakfast. So they piled into Barbara's car and drove downtown to the State Street Diner. They sat in a booth with stainless steel trim running around the perimeter of the table and ordered huge breakfasts from a tired looking man in a dirty apron. The lights in the diner were bright, and the place was three-quarters full. George dipped a piece of toast into the bright, yellow, runny yolk of his eggs and said, This....is living. Harold said, Amen. The girls smiled at each other.

When they arrived back at the house it was twenty to four. Barbara said they had a pressing matter to attend to upstairs, and they all laughed quietly in the still of the softly-lit foyer. George looked at his girlfriend and said, Let's stay up for the sunrise. He told her to wait here, and ran up to his room. When he returned he had the blanket off his bed, two Black Russians, and cigarettes. Althea asked where they were going, and George took her hand and walked her outside. They headed north, away from campus, along Cayuga Heights Road to a little strip of land looking out toward Cayuga Lake called Sunset Park.

They sat bundled together in the warmth of the blanket with their drinks sticking out through little scooped folds. When the morning light finally crept up behind them, they had smoked three cigarettes and spilled the last half of their drinks onto the grass at their feet. Althea had taken her shoes off and tucked her toes under her boyfriend's thighs. She looked at him staring out at the lake and asked him what they were going to do.

He looked at her slowly, and smiled. We are going to run as fast as we can right up to the brink, and let life figure the rest out for us. So, she said, leaning her face against his shoulder, you think this is up to fate? Like the man believed in that play you were in?

George pulled away, surprised. You came to it? Althea nodded. Why didn't you tell me? he asked. She told George she had waited for the right moment. You were really, really good George. I never would have understood if I didn't go. So I sneaked in and sat in an exit row near the back, and left as soon as it was over.

George studied his girlfriend's face for a moment. She was right about what he had said. Had he really crossed over the line already? It made him sick to think it. Althea watched him now, seeing the whirl in his head. She murmured, What?

He had no answer for her. He refused to believe that he was not in command of his destiny. In fact, he knew he was. Wasn't he? But he could not see clearly beyond the next few weeks, even when it came to Althea Redmonton. He couldn't explain it. Finally he said, All I know is, we are going to see this through. Because nothing makes any sense without you.

Althea kissed him lightly on the lips and said, Let's go get some sleep.

⤛⤜

The first week of May rushed mercilessly into the weekend, and Eta Chi's final social event of the Spring. Girls from Wells College were coming for a late afternoon barbecue and early evening dance. Harold, Danny, Fritz and George all invited their respective girlfriends for the weekend anyway. Harold said, This isn't a fraternity. It's a Holiday Inn!

They also noted, with some mirth, that Gregory Smythe had said that Daisy was coming to spend Saturday night with him too. Harold asked him why he wasn't going to play the field a little more, and Gregory smirked and said that Daisy didn't like that idea. Then Fritz asked him if his bed was ready, and everybody laughed.

Last weekend, on Sunday morning after the Darling formal, the entire senior corridor had yelled when they heard someone hammering something loudly at about half past nine. Gregory had yelled "SORRY!" and the hammering had stopped. But in the afternoon, when the hallway was awake and Frank Sinatra sang in Harold's room, the hammering resumed. The boys gathered around his door to watch Gregory nailing his wooden bed frame back together.

What happened here, Greg? Harold asked with his lips pursed.

Just putting my bed back together. It broke, the junior explained in a matter of fact voice.

How'd it break, Greg? Fritz asked, laughing. You and Daisy do something strange last night? The boys in the hallway slapped each other's hands. Gregory was unperturbed. The frame came apart, he explained. And now Daisy was returning for a repeat performance.

George and Althea had agreed to go to the library for the day on Saturday, and then go back and hang around the house. Part of her was curious to see what these girls from Wells College looked like. But then the four couples decided to go to the Odyssey Steak House for dinner, rather than watch what Harold referred to as "the meat market" at the barbecue. Danny called and made a reservation. When the hostess walked into the bar calling out Dr. Benjamin Trident, party of eight, the girls didn't react, but Danny stood up and said, That's us! The boys all chuckled. Benjamin Trident was the name of the Eta Chi fraternity manual and they all used that name to make reservations. It was a practice all of them would continue for years afterwards.

After dinner, they went back to the house and danced for a while with the rest of the party-ers. George grinned as he watched Althea size the girls up and down. After a bit, they said good night and headed upstairs. The dance was ending soon anyway.

About an hour later, a knock came at George's door. He and Althea were lying on top of the bed, and George yelled, Come in. Cullen held the door knob in his hand as he leaned in and said he needed to see George right away about something. George told Cullen to come in, but Cullen said he needed to speak to George alone. He looked alarmed. George stood up and told Althea he'd be back.

Outside his room, after George had pulled the door closed, Cullen said he was really concerned about what was going on up on the third floor. George squinted at him, not understanding. They have a girl up there, George. They say it's a train.

What the hell is a train? George asked, yawning.

Cullen told his consul that there was a long line of boys waiting to have sex with a girl in the Bordello Room. George chuckled. You mean to tell me there's a girl who wants to service the entire house up there?

Cullen frowned. That's the point, George. I don't know whether she wants to or not. George's jaw dropped. He leaned in through his door and told Althea there was something he had to go do. Stay here, okay? he closed the door behind him and bolted up the back staircase and down the hall, past the bathroom, toward the Bordello Room.

Starting at the front staircase, there was a line of boys along the wall leading to the room. They were talking and laughing. George walked to the middle of the line, and asked them what the hell they were doing. One of the boys, a sophomore, said they were pulling a train. Another boy said, "Choooo-chooooo" in a loud voice. A third boy asked what the problem was.

George looked at the boy silently, and said nothing. The boy reddened, and shuffled his feet. George walked to the front of the line and asked the boy standing first who was in the room now.

Brother Stoobie! the boy replied, grinning.

George pulled his face back in surprise, and knocked on the door. Someone yelled, Hey, no cutting! and some others chortled. George entered the room and pulled the door shut behind him. The room was dark, except for some light spilling in from the front window.

Stoobie? George called out in a whisper.

In here, Stoobie answered. George walked in the dark down the little corridor and turned into the main section of the room. His eyes started to adjust to the darkness. Stoobie was sitting at the end of the bed which lined the interior wall George had just walked along. His hand rested on the leg of a girl who lay on the bed, passed out. George could see that the girl was still dressed.

What's going on in here, Stoobie?

This girl got so drunk that she needed to lie down, and now she is very soundly asleep. His voice sounded sad. He patted her leg gently. She needs someone to take care of her.

Has anybody else been in here? George asked. Stoobie said that he had insisted on going first. They think I'm in here with her, don't they?

She has all her clothes on, right Jim?

Yes, she does, he answered. All I could do when I got in here was protect her, he added.

George put his hand on Stoobie's shoulder, and told him he had done the right thing. He was proud of him. He asked Stoobie to stay with her to be sure that she was safe. Stoobie said, Okay. George noticed a tear that fell from Stoobie's eye as he left the room, and was struck by how compassionate the boy was about the girl's predicament. Then he looked down the line of boys who looked expectantly in his direction.

The party's over, gentlemen. Some of the boys groaned and complained. One of them said, She wants this!

George looked carefully at the boy who said that, and told him the girl had passed out. And no one is going to be allowed near this room until the girl awakes tomorrow morning as a guest of Eta Chi and is driven back to Wells.

The line started to fall apart. Some of the boys accused others of misrepresenting the girl's predisposition, and others said, Oh shut up. I didn't know anything either. George waited until the boys had headed down the stairs, and then returned to the room. Cullen had watched him from the stairway, and followed George into the room. George flipped the light switch, and Stoobie covered his eyes from the glare. Cullen looked at the girl; she slept peacefully. He said he bet she'd be hung over in the morning.

George asked if one of them would be willing to sleep on the other bed until the morning. Cullen said he was a really light sleeper, and would take the job. George told Stoobie to lift the girl's legs as he pulled the covers up. The girl didn't even stir as Stoobie hoisted her up and George yanked the bedspread down and then back up over her. As he did, he confirmed that she was fully clothed. He looked at his two brothers before he left, and said he didn't know what to say. Then he left the room and walked slowly down the back staircase to his room. All he could picture in his head was Althea passed out like that. He wanted to throw up.

Althea looked at him sleepily when he came in and asked what the matter was. Some of the brothers got a little too rambunctious, he told her. It's over. I'll tell you about it someday.

On Date Night the following Wednesday, George and Althea walked back to the house from Wines with Fritz and Jane Quissling. Since he and Althea had reunited, George had insisted that Althea come with him to Wines. Jane was in a great mood. She had never developed much of a tolerance for alcohol, and drinking made her lively and talkative. She was telling Althea about the graduate program she was going to enter at the University of Michigan. Fritz said something about Cornell having a good program too, and Jane hugged him hard. She turned to Althea and told her that Fritz wanted her to stay at Cornell with him, but she was going to Michigan. He was welcome to join her there!

Fritz glanced at George and raised his eyebrows a couple of times. It had always been hard to tell what Fritz thought, but George guessed that Fritz was really taken with Jane Quissling. George wondered if Fritz ever let himself get carried away with Jane. He always acted so even, so steady, so...unemotional. Maybe, George thought, Fritz was really struggling with what to do about Jane Quissling.

Althea said that graduation was hard. She took George's hand as she said it, but didn't look his way. George focused on Jane. She was wearing a wildly striped skirt and a white blouse that showed off her nice figure. George liked how she always dressed a little over the top. He had come to find her an astute and bold thinker. He thought she was smarter than Fritz. Hell, she was smarter than him too. Except for the singular disfigurement on her forehead, Jane Quissling was quite a package.

They arrived at the house, and went straight into the library. Fritz excused himself to go to the bathroom, and the three of them sat casually on one of the couches. Danny Carvello danced into the room with Janette in his arms, which he ended dramatically by dipping her in front of the couch. Althea asked Janette how she managed to keep up with him, and Janette shook her head despairingly. George and Danny walked off for a minute and the three girls spoke alone. After dinner, Althea told George that Jane was going to break up with Fritz this weekend.

George said, Uhh-ohh.

Althea asked if Fritz had a clue. George shook his head negatively. Why this weekend? he asked. His girlfriend told him that Jane wanted to get it over with. There were only a couple of weeks left, and she couldn't bear to let it get to the point of waiting until she was driving away for the summer. George sighed. What a shame, he finally said.

Jane ended up not telling Fritz that weekend. The weather had grown prematurely hot, and the Eta Chis staged an impromptu pool party. It was simply too much fun, and Jane had started to have second thoughts. She knew she was heading to Michigan. She knew she didn't want to have a long distance relationship with Fritz, and the two had never really talked seriously about marriage or a long-term commitment. But Fritz Hublein had swept in and given her great years at college. He had made her see herself completely differently. And while she didn't owe him anything, her feelings for him ran deep. Too deep to let go so easily. And she had come to love the house too. Eta Chi had accepted her completely, and she would hold the house near to her heart for the rest of her life.

The next week went by in a blur. Danny Carvello came to find George one night at dinner. He was breathless, and insisted that he come with him to the movies. George said, Okay, and as they headed out, Danny grabbed Joey Padillo and told him he had to come too. Danny drove them to the Triphammer Mall and kept telling them to hurry. He had seen the afternoon show, and didn't want to be late for the seven p.m. show. They bought their tickets and popcorn, and sat in a half empty movie theater to watch *Star Wars*. Danny was even more excited after the show than he had been before. It was extraordinary. It was revolutionary. It was magic. George and Joey agreed that the special effects had been incredible. George thought it was the worst acting he had seen in years, but one of the best movies he had ever seen. They argued about the acting in the car on the way back to the house.

On campus, as Eta Chis walked across the Arts Quad, the long, unintelligible wail of "Beeeachhhedwwwhhhaaallle" would erupt from any number of brothers with their hands cupped to their mouths. Back at the house, Danny Carvello finally convinced Wally Stimpson to perform the ultimate launch. For weeks, he had badgered the senior about the decrepit, worthless, piece of transistorized junk that Wally called his stereo. At first Wally had defended his stereo, but Danny flipped its switches and showed him how they didn't even work. He pointed out the crack in the woofer in one of the speakers. He told him that Wally was an Ivy Leaguer graduating and taking an important sales management position at General Electric. Surely he, of all people, should recognize the importance of keeping up appearances.

Wally remained steadfast until Danny offered the ultimate temptation. The launch didn't have to be off the kitchen roof. In fact, that was not impressive enough for such an important launching. Wally should be the only Eta Chi to launch his belongings into the Gorge! Wally's eyes lit up. Now Danny was talking.

They walked ceremoniously out the front door of the fraternity with a half dozen boys and down Cayuga Heights Road to the lower car bridge. Danny walked behind with George, as Wally led the way for Rick Frye, Ronny Trillo and Edward Stamer. Danny asked George if he realized that Wally was a topper.

George asked what that was.

A topper. You know, Danny said, grinning. Somebody who always has to top whatever he hears. Watch this. Hey Wally!

Wally looked back as he carried his stereo toward the bridge and said, Yeah?

Did I ever tell you about the time that I had to do an experiment in engineering class on the destructive force of weight? We dropped a hundred pounds of bricks ten feet to demonstrate how much weight it took to crush a single brick.

Wally thought that was interesting. He said that he had done something like this in high school, when they rolled a four hundred pound container on wheels down a hill into a brick wall.

Danny said that was really interesting with a straight face. George burst out laughing. Wally looked at George quizzically. Under his breath, Danny whispered, Told you so!

When they reached the bridge, the boys gathered at the metal rail, and stood for a moment staring at the water rushing beneath them. I love to launch things, Danny said seriously. Then Wally said, Gentlemen, the first ever Eta Chi Launch into the gorge! He dropped the entire stereo with the speakers sitting on top of the receiver down into the rushing water. The boys cheered. The stereo disappeared without a sound.

Final exams were scheduled for the following week, and most everyone wanted to spend the weekend studying. George and Althea spent most of their time at the kitchen table in her apartment, smoking cigarettes, and rubbing each other's necks when they got sore. It was hot, and they sweated even though they sat in shorts with the door and windows open. George took a break on Saturday afternoon and drove to Eta Chi. He found Harold and Fritz alone in Harold's room. Barbara was in the shower and Jane was at the library studying for finals. Harold didn't have much in the way of finals, and Fritz liked to study in his room. When George walked in they both said, ROOM! Harold bellowed it. Fritz said it under his breath. Gentlemen! George replied. How goes the war?

The three friends sat down. Harold sat at his desk. George sat on the bed, and Fritz crossed his legs on the floor. Harold was somber, and he asked them if they wanted a short scotch. George really did not want to start drinking, but he couldn't say no. Fritz said he was hoping Harold would ask. Harold poured three short drinks and handed them out. He stared at them until George said, What?

You know why we are different, don't you? he asked in a quiet voice. Hunh? You two must see it like I do. We see things different than the rest of the house. I know we do.

Fritz asked him what the hell he was talking about.

Listen, Fritz, look around at the rest of this house. There's a real difference between the way we see things and the way they do. We look at things more deeply. We know what we have to do.

We do? George asked. Harold looked at him quietly.

Yes, he said. You may not want to admit it, but the rest of our brothers are like little kids, by comparison.

Right! Fritz agreed. We're Big Kids! Harold shook his head dismissively.

I don't know whether you call it maturity or wisdom or something else. But I see it in the three of us, and nobody else.

Fritz and George looked on silently.

And I know why, he went on. It's because the three of us lost our fathers. We had to grow up. It's obvious to me. Tell me you don't see the same thing.

In all the time George had known Fritz, he had never once spoken of his father. But it was Fritz who spoke first.

I think you're right, Room. It does make a difference, and it is probably the reason the three of us are a little tighter, a little more...I don't know....

George said he understood completely what Harold was saying. But he had to admit it had not really crossed his mind before. Harold looked at the picture on his desk of himself with his mother and his sister, and slurped his drink. Well, he said, I won't ever forget either of you. You helped me make it through, even if you don't know it.

Fritz and George looked at each other. Fritz raised his eyebrows, and pulled his mouth up in a line to make his moustache straight. The invisible rubber layer that Fritz had grown to protect himself when he was five-years old was no more than a thin, translucent membrane. George raised his right eyebrow and told Harold he would never forget him either.

Jesus! Harold snorted. Then Barbara walked in with a towel wrapped tightly around her, and looked at the three boys holding their scotches with serious casts to their faces. She asked who had died.

Harold pulled his shoulders up, and said, Exactly!

CHAPTER TWENTY-SIX

The final chapter meeting of the year was conducted that Sunday. The house had agreed to hold the meeting at six p.m. so that boys could get back to studying. They were holding elections for fall offices, so the turnout would be high. On Sunday, George kept thinking about the meeting as he sat at the table in Althea's kitchen, watching his girlfriend inhale and exhale smoke from the cigarette she held distractedly in the air as she crammed for exams. He needed to say something to the brotherhood, and he wondered what the other seniors would think to say.

He convened the meeting promptly at six. It was hot in the Chapter Room, and George was instantly dismayed by the turnout of seniors. Only Fritz, who as the proconsul had to be there, and Danny Carvello came. George walked through the agenda, explaining that all business would be conducted before the elections were held. He didn't tell them why, but he sequenced the meeting to be sure people didn't just vote and leave.

Significant new business included proposals to eliminate the dress code and the prohibition against smoking in the dining room. The only dress code left by this point was coats and ties for date night. The proposal put forth by Joshua Finch was to make ties optional for date night, and eliminate the prohibition against athletic clothes on the remaining nights. George looked around the room and doubted that there were enough votes without the seniors to reject the proposals, but he asked for commentary nonetheless.

Some sophomores stood against the relaxation of the code, complaining that they didn't want to sit next to sweaty guys in shorts while they ate. When it was put that way, the room turned against the idea, and the brothers voted to eliminate the need for ties at date night, but rejected all other changes.

The smoking vote was more controversial. Boys argued that smoking was disgusting, and it made some boys sick to their stomach. Plus, it was probably bad for your health to have to eat while people smoked around you. Wendall Wellington, who smoked, whispered to Joey Padillo that looking at Frank Shanahan made him sick to his stomach, but he still had to put with him. So, what exactly was the difference? Joey burst out laughing, and then apologized to his brothers for his outburst. The smoking measure was defeated.

Joshua Finch proposed that at the conclusion of the meeting the votes for office be held upstairs where it was cooler, and George quickly agreed. He also thought it was clever of Joshua, who was running for consul and instantly appeared as a leader.

George brought the meeting to the final phase, asking for comments. As the first boy stood and started to speak, George reached over and asked Fritz if he was prepared to speak. Fritz whispered back that he wasn't planning to speak today. George frowned and looked out at the room. He pictured seniors from years past standing and speaking at some length about the meaning of Eta Chi in their lives. When all the comments appeared done, he nodded to Danny, who rose and thanked the brotherhood for an incredible run. He told them how much he had learned from his time at Eta Chi, and the life-long friendships he would carry with him. The brothers snapped their fingers appreciatively as he sat down.

George looked at Fritz, who shook his head negatively. George rose and walked in front of the podium, and paced back and forth for a moment, collecting his thoughts.

My brothers, he began, *it would be easy for me to simply reiterate to you what Danny Carvello just said. And, in fact, this has been an extraordinary time in the life of the entire senior class, me included. I just wish that they were here to share more of their thoughts with you.*

So I find myself in a funny position, because I feel I have to say something to you that I know reflects the thoughts of some of the missing seniors...

When I was a freshman, the first chapter meeting I went to was the final chapter meeting of the year. The seniors all stood up and spoke at length, and pretty emotionally, about what the house had meant to them. One of those seniors made a controversial argument about something he called Creeping DUism...

He said that Eta Chi was beginning to slide downhill, that it was the obligation of the classes that followed his to ensure that this house continue to stand for something. If we didn't, we would find ourselves no different from DU, which, in his view, had descended into disarray.

This is no longer my house. I am leaving, and the house now belongs to you. I have a different point of view about the dress code, but I said nothing this evening, because it won't affect me. You need to decide how you will govern yourselves. But I believe that you must stand for something. The people that came before you handed you something that they valued. It is yours to change and pass on. So pass on something that you can hold up to the world as having the same or greater value...I'm proud to be an Eta Chi.

The room clicked their fingers, but George sat down deflated. He had wanted to say so much more. He couldn't believe that the rest of the seniors had not even shown up.

He adjourned the meeting and told everyone to gather upstairs for the voting. The boys went to the Great Hall and voted on the offices. It was the responsibility of the consul and the recording secretary to count the votes, so when the boys had all cast their written ballots in the big pot that someone had grabbed from the kitchen, George asked Rick to carry the pot into the library. They needed space to put the ballots in piles, and the table in the library was closest. Rick started opening the papers and piling them on the table. He asked his big brother how he was doing. George replied that he was worried Joshua Finch might win.

Rick stared into his big brother's eyes and said he hated that thought. He also told him how much he agreed with what he said downstairs. This place is going to hell in a hand basket, he complained.

They counted more ballots and Joshua's pile got bigger. You know, Rick said, we are the official counters...our determination of the winner is final, according the rules.

George looked at his little brother cautiously. Then he said, You know, Rick, it might be for the good of the brotherhood.

Rick said he knew.

George said he couldn't believe they were even thinking about it.

Rick said he knew, again.

Let's count first. We don't have an ethical issue until we see what the outcome actually is, George finally said. They counted out the remaining ballots, and the bottom of the pile was heavily in favor of James Desmond. Joshua Finch lost by thirteen votes.

George looked at his little brother and said, Thank God.

Rick said, Right.

George walked back into the great Hall where the brothers milled about and announced that James Desmond was their new consul. The room clapped, and slapped James on the back.

Althea asked George how it had gone when he got back to her apartment. He told her that James Desmond was the new consul, and Althea said she liked him. She was glad. Bonnie Raitt came on the little radio playing in the kitchen, and George asked her to dance with him. Althea smiled, stood up and took his hand as they smiled at each other and danced through the apartment.

On Wednesday George dropped Althea off at the Arts Quad so she could take her history of art final. He drove to Eta Chi to study in his room for the afternoon, before they met at the library. They needed a break from the apartment. The house was quiet with boys studying on the lawn, in the dining room, and upstairs in their rooms. George threw his books on his desk, and wandered around to see what was going on. Cullen saw him and ran up to pat him on the chest with the palm of his hand. He told George a bunch of guys were about to walk down to Sunset Park for a break. Did he want to come? George did.

They walked downstairs and the rest of the boys had already started walking, so Cullen put his arm around George's shoulder as they walked behind and told him how much he was going to miss him. George asked him if he was going to live in the house next year, and Cullen said that he had decided against it. He was taking a fifth year to finish up his architecture degree, and as much as he loved the house, it was time to try something new. It wouldn't be the same, anyway.

At Sunset Park, some boys threw a Frisbee and leapt with exaggeration to catch it so they could fall down and roll around on the grass. Danny, Harold, and Fritz sat on one of the benches. Everyone was tired and stressed from studying.

Cullen asked George how Althea was, and George smiled and said she was fine. Harold said he couldn't wait for finals to be over. He was going to the city for the weekend with Barbara before coming back for graduation. Fritz asked Harold if he thought he was going to get serious with Barb. Harold chuckled and said he wasn't sure.

Cullen said they made a great couple. George asked Cullen if he had met anyone yet he could picture marrying. Cullen said that was why he was taking a fifth year – he hadn't found her yet. Unlike George…

The boys all laughed smugly. George looked at them with his eyebrows raised. Fritz said he was actually beginning to think more seriously about Jane. The boys looked at each other, but no one said anything. They all knew that Jane planned to break it off with him. What were they supposed to say?

Cullen asked Danny if Janette was someone he could marry. Danny looked with total serious at Cullen and told him he was going to marry her twin sister.

She has a twin sister?! Cullen said.

No, Danny replied. But if she did, that's who I would marry.

Harold said he didn't think he would ever get that serious with Barbara. But he planned on having a lot of fun with her in New York when he started work there in a few weeks.

George said he didn't think that he and Althea were going to get to that point. The boys all mocked him. George smiled. In his innermost core, he already knew that it wasn't to be. He didn't know why, and he didn't know when, but he knew that the winds were going to blow them in their own directions. Their reality was too bound in time and circumstance, a predestined impermanence that would, thankfully, give them each the courage and conviction to never settle for less.

Cullen finally challenged his brother to look him in the eye and tell him that he had yet to meet his future bride. Because, we will remind you of it when we are at your wedding!

George looked at Cullen, and thought for a moment. Then he said it was possible he had met his bride. There was a girl he met once outside the library he could imagine marrying. Harold asked what her name was. George said he didn't know. They all laughed. Only Danny Carvello realized George was serious.

Finals were over Thursday, and the house emptied out of underclassmen anxious to get home after the grueling week. There would be parties and celebrations all through the weekend, and families would start to arrive for the graduation ceremony at Schoelkopf Field. George and Althea drove over to the house on Friday afternoon, in the gloriously sunny weather of late May. The fraternity parking lot was two-thirds empty, and there was a sense of disarray to the house as a result of the mass exodus the day before. Jane Quissling and Janette Emilio grabbed Althea and told her to hurry and change into her bathing suit. The pool was fantastic!

George held back to talk for a minute with Wendall Wellington and Danny Carvello who were standing just outside the front door, in the cooling shadow of the house.

Brother George, Danny said impishly. We were just talking about you. George thought Danny Carvello had the extraordinary ability to be totally serious and totally silly at the same time. Wendall grinned, and said, Hi Big Bro. He always called George that.

What are you two cooking up now? George asked. Danny and Wendall had grown close over the Spring.

We have a business proposition for you. Danny said. George just looked at him.

Wendall and I have reached the startling conclusion that this is all a bunch of unmitigated bullshit.

What is? George asked. Danny raised his hands, pointing all around him.

All this schooling and final exam bullshit, he answered. So we have put our considerable intellects together and concluded that we need to accelerate life.

Ohhkayyyy, George said.

We are going to skip right to the sweet spot. We both know that what we want to do is get into entertainment, right? So Wendall and I are moving to Hollywood, because that's where entertainment is.

Danny waited a moment for this to sink in.

So, George summarized, you are not going to B School, and Wendall is going to forget about graduating, and the two of you are going to go terrorize Hollywood?

By Jove, Wendall, I think he's got it! Danny said. But that's not all. We don't think we can do it without you.

George stared at Danny and then turned to take the measure of Wendall's face. He knew Wendall was bored by school, and he knew Danny really wanted to make movies. Especially since *Star Wars*. And although it frightened him, he knew he didn't need to ask if the two boys were serious. Danny's most remarkable quality was his unswerving conviction to follow his own inclinations. He rejoiced in it. George said he didn't know what the hell they needed him for.

Danny made his lips thin and nodded thoughtfully. That's true, he replied. We don't know precisely because we aren't there yet. But we do know that you've got more brains and more creativity than the idiots we are going to be competing with, so we can't lose.

Wendall said, He's right, Big Bro. We'd make an incredible team out there.

George wondered why he thought his life was somehow already laid out. He didn't consciously plot out his own future, but it sure seemed like he followed a predetermined path. He thought about Althea, who was going to be in graduate school in New York City. He thought of his mother coming up to watch him graduate and welcome him home for the summer before graduate school. He guessed he had about three hundred dollars to his name. He looked up at the house they stood under. He thought of Derek Steele asking the audience, *When the curtain rises, is your heart free?*

Danny knew better than to press his brother too hard. He could see George's mind racing through the insanity of it all. He waited patiently. Wendall lit a cigarette.

George said he had two questions. First, would what they do out there be meaningful? Would the three of them commit to that? Danny looked at Wendall and the two of them said yes at the same time. They had not really talked about why George seemed so important to their idea. Now Danny saw why.

Second, did they believe they could actually do it?

Danny said he wouldn't be ready to do it otherwise. Wendall just smiled and said, God, yes!

George shook his head. Every inch of him screamed for him to say he couldn't. But he heard himself say, Then what are we waiting for?

Janette and Althea walked up wet from the pool, with towels wrapped around them. They wanted to know whether they had to find new boys to entertain them. Danny winked at George, and asked if the girls liked southern California. Janette looked into her boyfriend's eyes and said, Oh no.

Althea smiled at George and said she'd never been.

George looked from Althea to Danny, to Wendall, and back to Althea.

Well, he said, that is certainly something we can change!

Printed in the United States
105653LV00001B/2/A

9 781595 261243